The WESTWARD
Christmas
BRIDES
COLLECTION

9 Historical Romances
Answer the Call of the American West

The WESTWARD

Christmas

BRIDES

COLLECTION

Wanda E. Brunstetter

Susan Page Davis, Melanie Dobson, Cathy Liggett, Vickie McDonough,
Olivia Newport, Janet Spaeth, Jennifer Rogers Spinola, and MaryLu Tyndall

BARBOUR
PUBLISHING

Published by Barbour Books, an imprint of Barbour Publishing, Inc., P.O. Box 719, Uhrichsville, Ohio 44683, www.barbourbooks.com

Our mission is to publish and distribute inspirational products offering exceptional value and biblical encouragement to the masses.

 Member of the
Evangelical Christian
Publishers Association

Printed in Canada.

CONTENTS

A Christmas Prayer

by Wanda E. Brunstetter

Continue in prayer, and watch in the same with thanksgiving.
Colossians 4:2

Prologue

Independence, Missouri
April 15, 1850

Dear Diary,

Tomorrow Mama and I begin our journey by covered wagon to California—the land of opportunity. We are traveling with Walter Prentice, the man I've agreed to marry. There's gold in California, and Walter plans to open several businesses when we get there. Walter wanted us to be married before we left New York, but I said I would rather wait until we get settled in California. After all, the dirty, dusty trail is hardly a place for a honeymoon.

When we arrived in Independence four days ago, Walter spent over $1000 for our supplies, plus the covered wagon and three oxen we will need for our nearly 2,000-mile journey west. Our prairie schooner is filled with 200 pounds of flour, 150 pounds of bacon, 10 pounds of coffee, 20 pounds of sugar, and 10 pounds of salt. We also have our basic kitchenware, which consists of a cooking kettle, frying pan, coffeepot, tin plates, cups, knives, and forks. That's in addition to our trunks of clothes and personal items, a few small pieces of furniture, and our bedrolls, tools, and several other things we'll need to survive on this trip. I'm glad Walter did a little research before traveling. He said it's advised that our supplies should be kept below 2,000 pounds of total weight for the wagon so as not to tire the draft animals.

It will take us anywhere from five to six months to reach our destination, and we'll be traveling with two other wagons, as the larger wagon train we were supposed to join left a week ago, due to the fact that we were all late getting here. Walter says it's nothing to worry about. We'll follow the other wagon train's trail and should be able to catch up with them if nothing goes wrong. I shall pray every day for traveling mercies and look forward to spending this Christmas in a new land.

I'm looking forward to getting to know the people in the two wagons we'll be with. I haven't met any of them yet, but Walter has. He said a widowed man with two small children owns one of the wagons, and the other wagon is owned by a young single man and his sister. The men will get together in the morning to decide whose wagon will lead and which of them will be in charge of our small group and act as the scout.

Cynthia Cooper stopped writing and sighed. Knowing Walter, he'd probably insist that he be in charge. But then, what did he really know about wilderness travel? While Walter owned two stores in New York City and had a good head when it came to business ventures, as far as Cynthia was aware, he knew nothing about leading a wagon train, even a small one such as theirs.

9

As she pushed a wayward curl under her nightcap, a vision of Walter came to mind. At thirty-five, Walter had small ears compared to most men, and his nose was thin and kind of birdlike. Many men his age sported a beard, or at least a moustache, but he chose to be clean shaven. His light brown hair had already begun to recede, although his sideburns were thick. Walter's most outstanding feature was his closely set brown eyes. Sometimes when he looked at Cynthia in a certain way, she felt as if he could see right into her soul and know what she was thinking. When Walter studied Cynthia in that manner, she shivered, and not in a good way.

Cynthia didn't think Walter was ugly. He just wasn't the handsome man she'd dreamed of marrying; not to mention that he was fifteen years older than her. Walter seemed more like an uncle or big brother, if she had one, that is. Unfortunately, Cynthia was an only child.

Cynthia hadn't agreed to become Walter's wife because she loved him. She would become Mrs. Walter Prentice so she and Mama would be taken care of financially. Truthfully, she was doing it mostly for Mama's sake. When Papa died from an unexpected illness six months ago, they'd been left almost penniless. Unbeknownst to Cynthia and her mother, Papa had taken part in a business venture that went sour, and he'd used up all their savings. In hindsight, they realized the stress from all that may have been what killed him, but it was one of those things they'd never know for sure.

Since Papa's death, poor Mama had been forced to take in boarders in order to put food on their table. Struggling for six months might not seem very long, but it was difficult for a woman who'd been used to the finer things in life. Walter, whom they'd met at a social function before Papa's untimely death, had saved the day when he'd asked Cynthia to marry him.

Pulling her gaze back to the journal, Cynthia finished her entry:

I'm looking forward to our trip to California for the adventure of going someplace I haven't been before. It will be exciting to see new things along the way, and good to start over. It was always Papa's dream to see the West, so I'm sure he would be happy to know Mama and I have the opportunity to make this trek. My only regret is that Papa isn't going with us.

Cynthia set her pen and paper aside and placed one hand against her chest. *Oh, Papa, I miss you so much. No matter where I go, you'll always be here in my heart.*

Chapter 1

Three days out of Independence

P apa, I'm tired."

Jack Simpson glanced at his four-year-old son, Alan, slumped on the wagon seat beside his sister. Amelia, who was six, stared straight ahead, seemingly unmindful of her brother. Of course, Jack's daughter had been unresponsive to most things since she'd witnessed her mother's tragic death six months ago. Jack's precious wife, Mary, had been crossing the street in their hometown of Cedar Rapids, Iowa, and was struck down by a team of runaway horses pulling a supply wagon. Clem Jones, owner of the wagon, hadn't tied the horses securely enough. Poor little Amelia, waiting across the street with her grandma, had watched in horror as her mother was knocked to the ground and trampled to death. Since that time, the child had not uttered a word.

Jack, struggling with his own grief plus trying to keep some sense of normalcy in his children's life, could only hope this trip west might be the turning point for Amelia. There was no doubt that Alan was excited about the trip and a new place to live. The boy had been bursting at the seams waiting to head west ever since Jack first mentioned the trip to his children. Truth was, Jack needed the change, too, and looked forward to joining his brother, Dan, already in California, where he'd established a cattle ranch.

Being a hog farmer, Jack knew a thing or two about pigs, but not much concerning the business of raising cattle. He was eager to learn, though, and would do his best to help Dan make a go of things. Jack just needed to get his little family and all their belongings safely to their destination.

"Papa, I'm tired," Alan repeated, bumping Jack's arm as he guided their team of oxen down the trail. "Can't them ox move faster?"

"Why don't ya crawl in the back and lie down?" Jack suggested. "Amelia, you can go, too, if you're tired. It shouldn't be much longer before we stop to make camp."

Alan scrambled over the seat and into the back of their wagon, but Amelia, her long auburn locks moving slightly as she shook her head, remained seated.

Will my little girl ever speak to me again? Jack wondered as he held on to the reins, bringing up the rear of their three-wagon train. He drew in a deep breath, trying to focus on the wagon ahead, driven by a stuffy city slicker from New York who thought he knew a lot about everything but probably knew very little about roughing it. The man's name was Walter Prentice, and his traveling companions were a woman named Mable and her daughter, Cynthia, who was Walter's fiancée. Jack had only spoken to Cynthia briefly, but she seemed nice enough. She was pretty, too, and from the way she talked, Jack figured she didn't know much about roughing it either. It would be a miracle if this refined group ahead of him made it to California at all. Thank goodness, back in Independence when the men drew names to see who would lead out, the man in the first wagon got the luck of the draw. Jack was pretty sure Cole Edwards knew a lot more about driving a team of oxen than Walter Prentice did.

≈

Cole had never been one to take the easy way out, and he knew heading to California in search of gold wasn't going to be easy. But he was tired of the long hours he put in at his blacksmith's shop in Kutztown, Pennsylvania, and the money he hoped to make in the gold mines near Sutter's Mill would make the trip worth every mile and inconvenience. If he didn't make his fortune in gold, he could always fall back on his blacksmith's trade. He just hoped his sister was up for this trip.

Sitting astride his sturdy quarter horse, Blaze, Cole glanced back at Virginia, whom he'd nicknamed Ginny when they were children. She sat on the seat of their covered wagon, looking this way and that, as though trying to take in everything on all sides of the trail. Skillfully, she guided their oxen as if she'd been doing it all her life. While Cole's twenty-six-year-old sister wasn't as adventuresome as him, she'd been willing to make this trip, despite negative protests from their parents. Virginia had been teaching school for the past six years and hoped to teach when they got to California. Having been jilted by Clay Summers, the man she'd planned to marry, Virginia told Cole she was ready for a change. In fact, she desperately needed it.

At the age of twenty-four, Cole had courted a few young women but none who'd held his interest or captured his heart. Most women he knew wanted to settle in to a nice little house with a white picket fence. They weren't seeking adventure the way Cole was, and he wasn't ready to settle in and accept the mediocre comforts in life. He wanted more and aimed to get it.

"You doin' okay, Ginny?" he called. "Do ya need me to take over awhile? I can tie my horse to the back of the wagon."

Smiling, she shook her head. "Thanks, Cole, but I'm fine."

Cole smiled in response. His sister had a determined spirit. She would do fine out West. He wasn't so sure about the two refined ladies in the wagon behind him though. Three days out and they looked exhausted. They obviously weren't used to sitting on a hard bench or walking long hours every day. The fancy fellow accompanying them didn't look much better, although he was trying to put on a brave front and acted like quite the know-it-all. Cole wondered if the high-and-mighty Mr. Prentice would be so confident after they had several weeks of traveling under their belts. It was a good thing Walter wasn't trying to lead the way. He'd probably have them lost already.

Glancing upward, Cole noticed dark clouds. No doubt a storm was coming, and he wanted to be sure they were safely camped before it hit. "Ginny, I'm goin' out ahead and find a good spot for the night," he called. Then Cole turned his horse around and went back to tell those in the other wagons.

≈

"Are you okay, Mama?" Cynthia asked, concerned when she noticed lines of fatigue on her mother's face. "You look awfully tired."

"Mable is fine, and so am I." Walter spoke up before Cynthia's mother had a chance to respond. "We have a long journey ahead of us, and we need to toughen up. Otherwise, we won't make it to California. We haven't been on the trail a week yet and have hundreds of miles ahead of us."

"That may be true, but I believe my mother can speak for herself." Cynthia patted her mother's hand affectionately.

"I'm fine, dear," Mama replied, reaching up to touch the bun at the back of her head. "No need to worry about me. It takes some time getting used to sitting on this hard bench, and walking is just as uncomfortable. But I'll make it—we all will."

Cynthia smiled. Her mother might be slender and petite, but she had a determined spirit. Mama's brown hair and eyes were accentuated by her oval face, thick dark eyebrows, and thin lips. Except for their slender build, Cynthia and Mama looked nothing alike. Cynthia had inherited her father's curly auburn hair and green eyes. Even the two dimples in her right cheek came from Papa.

Looking back at Mama, Cynthia noted that even at the age of forty-five, her mother was still an attractive woman. It was unlikely she would ever marry again. Mama had been deeply in love with Papa and said that no one could take his place. That's what Cynthia had always wished for, too, but it seemed she'd never know the kind of love her mother and father had.

It doesn't matter whether Mama remarries or not, Cynthia thought. *Once Walter and I are married, Mama won't have to worry about anything, for she'll be well taken care of.*

Cynthia glanced at Walter wiping some dust from his eyes with his clean, crisp, monogrammed handkerchief. His expression was one of determination. She knew with a certainty that his desperation to get to California was about the money he planned to make. She guessed she couldn't blame him for that. After all, everyone needed money these days—some just wanted it more than others. Walter was one of those who measured people by their wealth and social standing.

Cole Edwards, the man who was leading their little group, was also after money; only his would be earned by the sweat of his brow as he searched for gold. That wasn't to say Walter was lazy; he just didn't work as hard physically as some men she knew. Walter had a good head for business though.

Just then, Cole pulled his horse alongside their flat-bedded wagon made of hardwood and covered with canvas like the others. "Just wanted to let you folks know that I'm ridin' up ahead to find a good place to take shelter for the night. It'll be dark soon, and there's a storm brewin'."

"It doesn't look as if a storm is coming," Walter said.

"Take a closer look. See those clouds?" Cole looked at Walter with piercing blue eyes, as if daring him to question his decision. "If we get caught out here in the pouring rain, the trail will be muddy, and it'll bog us down. It doesn't take much for these wagon wheels to get stuck in the mud. Best to stop for the night and hope the rain lets up."

"What are we supposed to do while you're looking for a good place to stop?" Walter questioned.

"Keep moving—following the ruts in the trail made by wagons that have gone before us." Cole glanced at Cynthia and gave a nod. "You and your mother doin' okay?"

"They're fine," Walter answered before Cynthia could open her mouth. "Even if they weren't, it's my business, not yours."

"Walter, I'm sure Mr. Edwards is concerned for the welfare of everyone," Mama intervened.

Cole gave a nod, reaching under his hat and pulling his fingers through the ends of his coal-black hair. He really was a good-looking young man. But then, so was Jack.

Walter said nothing, just gripped the reins a little tighter, making the veins on his hands stick out.

"I'll tell Jack Simpson where I'm goin', and then I'm off," Cole said. He tipped his hat and rode quickly away.

They rode in silence for a while, until raindrops began to fall. Mama looked over at Walter and said, "I guess Mr. Edwards was right."

Walter grunted.

Cynthia hid a smile behind her hand. For some reason, she was glad Cole had been right about the weather. No man should think he was always right. *And Mama, she sure isn't afraid to stand up to Walter. Maybe I ought to take a lesson from her.*

Chapter 2

South fork of the Platte River

Dear Diary,

We've been on the trail a week already, but it feels more like a month to me. The rain we had awhile back caused our wagons to bog down in the mud. I feel like I'll never be clean again, not to mention my poor dresses with mud-stained hems. What I wouldn't give right now for a warm tub to soak in.

No sign of the bigger wagon train yet. I hope we're not going the wrong way and will miss them. But Cole insists we're on the right trail, so we have to trust him.

We take turns walking when we're tired of sitting, and riding in the bumpy wagon when we're tired of walking.

I feel sorry for Jack Simpson. His children are too young to drive the wagon and too little to walk very far without their legs giving out. Mama and I have begun taking turns riding in Jack's wagon with the children, driving his team of oxen so Jack can walk awhile each day and stretch his legs. Little brown-haired Alan looks a lot like his father, and he certainly is a chatterbox. But Amelia doesn't speak at all. Jack explained that she's been like that since she witnessed her mother's death. Poor little thing. I wonder if she'll ever get her voice back. I've begun praying for her.

Cynthia stopped writing and looked up as Cole hollered that it was time to go. With regret, she put her journal away and joined her mother on the seat of their wagon. Every day on the trail seemed like the one before. They got up before daybreak, and while the men rounded up the livestock, the women cooked breakfast over an open fire. After the meal, it was time to head down the trail.

Some days they stopped to rest for an hour or two; then they'd continue on their journey until early evening. At night they pulled the wagons close together for protection. The men took care of the livestock, while the women cooked the evening meal. After they ate, they'd often gather around the fire to sing songs and tell stories. This helped pass the time and gave them a chance to get better acquainted. The women and children slept inside the wagons, but Cole, Jack, and Walter slept under the wagon or in a makeshift tent, depending on the weather. It made Cynthia feel safer, knowing they were out there where they could be alerted to danger.

Cynthia shivered. At least they hadn't seen any Indians yet. If and when they did, she hoped they would be friendly natives and there'd be no trouble. From what Walter had been told, fewer people died from Indian attacks than from mishaps or illness along the way.

"What do you write in that book of yours?" Walter asked as he took up the reins.

"Oh, just the things we see and do on our daily journey," Cynthia replied. "I've been journaling since I was fifteen."

Walter shrugged. "If it makes you happy, it's a good thing. Maybe someday you can read me what you've written about our trip."

Cynthia cringed. Since she'd written about her lack of interest in Walter, she wasn't about to let him know what was in her diary.

He leaned closer to Cynthia—so close she could feel his warm breath blowing gently on her cheek. "You look lovely this morning, my dear," he whispered.

Her face heated. "I thank you for the compliment, but I certainly don't feel lovely," she said. "I feel dirty from all the trail dust, and even though I wash every evening and morning, I feel unkempt."

"You'll feel better once we get to California," he said, letting go of the reins with one hand and clasping her hand. "After I get my new businesses going, you'll be the finest dressed woman in all of California."

Cynthia forced a smile. She didn't care about being the finest-dressed woman. All she wanted was to be happily married and see that her mother's needs were met. Cynthia wasn't sure if she would be happy married to Walter, but at least Mama would be taken care of.

✧

"Papa, I'm hungry," Alan complained, squirming on the wooden seat beside his father.

Jack relaxed his hold on the reins, reached into his shirt pocket, and pulled out a piece of peppermint candy. "We won't be stoppin' to eat for a good while yet, so you can suck on this for now." He handed it to Alan. "Just be careful to suck it slowly, and whatever ya do, don't swallow the candy."

Alan popped the candy in his mouth and grinned up at his dad. "Yum."

Jack smiled and took another piece from his pocket. It was all he had left from what he'd purchased before they'd departed Independence. There was no doubt about it—his son had a sweet tooth. "You want this?" he asked, holding out the last piece of candy to Amelia.

She shook her head.

Jack couldn't believe Amelia didn't want a piece of candy. Was there nothing that could get through to his daughter? He wouldn't force her to take the treat. He just needed to be patient and keep trying to get her to talk.

"Can I have the candy?" Alan asked, tugging on his father's arm.

"Thought maybe I'd eat it," Jack replied with a grin.

Alan's bottom lip protruded. "Please, Papa. I'll save it for later."

Jack looked at Amelia again. "Are ya sure you don't want the peppermint drop?"

She shook her head again.

"Is it okay if I give it to Alan?"

Amelia gave a slow nod.

Jack handed the candy to Alan.

"Can I drive the wagon?" Alan asked, looking up at Jack with expectancy.

Jack shook his head. "You're not old enough for that yet, Son. But someday, when you're a mite bigger, you'll be helpin' me and your uncle Dan on the cattle ranch."

Alan's eyes twinkled. "Can I ride a big horse and chase after cows?"

Jack chuckled. "I don't know how big the horse will be, but yeah, you'll be ridin'."

Seemingly satisfied with that answer, Alan leaned his head against Jack's arm and fell silent.

❦

That evening, as everyone sat around the campfire after supper, Cole couldn't help but notice the look of fatigue on the women's faces. Particularly Cynthia's and Mable's. They'd walked a good deal of the day, while that high-and-mighty gentleman they were traveling with remained in the wagon.

"I don't know about anyone else, but after that bland supper we just ate, I could use something sweet," Walter spoke up. "Think I'll head over to my wagon and get my jar of candy."

"There was nothing wrong with the rabbit stew my sister fixed," Cole was quick to say. "Maybe it didn't measure up to the standards you're used to, but it filled our bellies, and I thought it was right tasty."

"I agree," Jack spoke up. "And since I'm not much of a cook, I appreciate everything the ladies make for us."

Cole looked at Walter, wondering if he would apologize, but the snobbish man just rose to his feet and reached for Cynthia's hand. "Come, take a walk with me. It's a pleasant evening with a star-studded sky, and we shouldn't waste it."

Like an obedient child, Cynthia went with Walter. As they strolled, arm-in-arm, Cole couldn't help but frown. *Sure can't see what that pretty woman sees in such a stuffy man.*

❦

Cynthia and Walter walked for a bit, making small talk, but as they headed toward Walter's wagon, he stopped, pulled out his gold pocket watch, and checked the time. Just as he was putting the watch back in his pocket, Cynthia caught sight of little Alan peeking into the back of the wagon. Walter must have seen him, too, for his face turned red as he shouted, "What do you think you're doing, boy?"

Alan jumped. "N—nothin'. Just wanted to see what ya got there."

"Nothing that pertains to you." Walter gave the boy a little push. "Now go on. . .scat!"

Alan glanced up at Cynthia with a pathetic expression then darted off toward the others still gathered around the campfire.

"That wasn't a nice way to speak to the boy," Cynthia said, looking at Walter. "I'm sure you hurt his feelings."

"Well, he shouldn't have been snooping around my wagon. The boy's father ought to keep a closer eye on him."

Cynthia watched as Walter peered into the back of the wagon, presumably making sure nothing was missing. She sighed. "I'm sure Alan meant no harm. He was no doubt curious about your load of supplies. Little boys are like that, you know. Surely you can remember those days when you were an inquisitive child."

Walter folded his arms and huffed, "More to the point, he was probably looking to steal something from me."

"I doubt that. I mean, what do you have that a little boy would want to take?"

Walter shrugged, pulling on the lapels of his jacket. He took out his pocket watch once more to check the time. "It could be anything. A child like that with no mother to teach him right from wrong could take things just for the fun of stealing.

But everything seems to be in place. That rascal is lucky this time."

Cynthia didn't argue with Walter. It was obvious that he had made up his mind. She did wonder, though, what kind of father he would make. Would he be so strict with their children that they wouldn't have any fun? Worse yet, would his harsh tone and expectations cause them to be afraid? Was Walter Prentice the kind of man she should marry? She'd noticed that he did do some peculiar things, like just now, checking the time, when he'd looked at it only moments ago. Perhaps it was something he did without thinking.

Cynthia glanced back at the campfire, where Mama sat with the others. *I have to marry Walter,* she told herself. *If I don't, Mama will be disappointed. And what would become of us when we reached California? With no money of our own, we'd be on the streets, begging for food.* She looked up at Walter and forced a smile. *Does he love me, or does he want to marry me for some other reason?*

Chapter 3

Dear Diary,

Three more weeks have passed, and so far we haven't incurred any serious problems along the way. We saw a band of Indians the other day. Fortunately, they followed us for only a few miles, watching from a ridge a good distance away, but they made no move to bother us, which was an answer to prayer.

Cole told us a few stories as we sat around the campfire last night, about things he'd heard that a few of the Indian tribes had done to some of the earlier pioneers. Horses and food had been stolen. Some people had been killed trying to protect their belongings. I pray every day that God will send His guardian angels to watch over us and take us safely to our destination.

There is still no sign of the wagon train that went ahead of us, and I'm worried. After this much time, we should have caught up to them. Of course, we have been moving rather slowly. Can our three bumpy wagons make it to California with Cole, an inexperienced guide, leading the way?

When Cole rode up to their wagon and said it was time to get the wagons moving, Cynthia stopped writing and slipped her journal into her reticule. "You holdin' up okay?" he asked.

She smiled. "I'm doing fine."

"What about you?" Cole asked, looking at Cynthia's mother, sitting beside Cynthia on the wagon bench.

Mama sighed while fanning her face with her hand. "If it weren't so hot, I'd be doing a lot better."

Cole lifted the brim of his hat and wiped his wet forehead. "You're right. It is kinda warm, but it's bound to get hotter in the days to come. Just be sure to keep that sunbonnet on your head."

Mama folded her arms and scowled at Cole. "Of course I'll wear my bonnet. I'm not addle-brained, you know."

"Never said you were," Cole shot back as he got down from his horse. "Noticed the lid on your water barrel is about ready to fall off." After adjusting the lid and making sure the water keg was tied securely to their wagon, he climbed back on the horse. "Water is precious out here on the trail, so make sure someone in your party checks it before we head out each morning."

"Thank you for letting us know." Cynthia smiled when Cole tipped his hat before riding away.

"That man thinks he knows everything," Mama complained. "It's not like he's a real wagon train leader, after all."

Sometimes Mama speaks her mind a little too much, Cynthia thought. *And I wish she could be a little nicer about it.* She decided to let the matter go. The last thing she needed was an argument with Mama today. Truth was, Cynthia's mother had always been quite outspoken, but since Papa died, Mama could be a bit too vocal at times. Maybe she was angry with Papa for leaving them virtually penniless and struggling to pay the bills on the meager amount she made with a few boarders. Cynthia couldn't blame her for that but felt certain Papa hadn't made poor business decisions on purpose.

"What was Cole complaining about now?" Walter asked, coming from inside the wagon and taking a seat on the bench.

"He said we'd better make sure the water barrel is secure and the lid's on tight before we head out each morning," Cynthia answered.

Walter grunted. "That man sure likes to bark out orders."

"My sentiments exactly," Cynthia's mother agreed.

Cynthia rolled her eyes. It seemed that Walter just liked to complain, and Mama said whatever she thought he wanted to hear. *Is she worried that if she doesn't agree with Walter on every little thing, he might not marry me?*

"Are you two ladies ready for another boring, tiring day?" Walter asked, taking up the reins.

Cynthia nodded. "Every day sort of blends into the next, doesn't it?"

Walter reached over and gently patted her hand. "It will be worth it when we reach the Promised Land, my dear."

Promised Land? Cynthia mentally questioned. *The Bible says the Israelites were headed to the Promised Land, but it took them years and years to get there. I hope our journey takes only months, not years. At the rate we're going, we'll never make it there before Christmas.*

⌒⌒

Around noon that day, their travels were halted when a wheel came off Jack's wagon. "Oh, great," Jack mumbled. "One more thing to slow us down." He took the children down from the wagon and told them to stay close while he fixed the wheel. He felt bad about holding the other wagons up, but there was no other choice.

"I'll give you a hand with that," Cole said, stepping up to Jack after securing his horse.

"Thanks, I could use another set of hands."

Cole looked over at Walter, standing beside his wagon, checking his watch. "Guess we won't be getting any help from him today," he said with a grunt.

"That's okay," Jack responded. "I'm sure we can manage without his help. From what I've seen of Walter so far, he'd probably tell us we were doing it wrong, and that his way was better. Not that he would know much about putting a wagon wheel on."

"Ya got that right. Mr. Fancy Pants would probably just get in the way." Cole motioned to Cynthia, walking beside Virginia, with little Amelia between them. "I'll bet either one of those ladies would be more help fixing your wheel than Walter."

Jack smiled. Cole's sister might try to tackle something like that, but he couldn't picture the pretty little gal from New York lying on the ground, attempting to get the wheel put back in place. Cynthia had other qualities, though—besides her beauty. Since the women took turns fixing their meals, Jack had quickly discovered that

Cynthia was quite a good cook. She was also good with his children. Amelia, although she still hadn't spoken to anyone, seemed to light up whenever Cynthia talked to her, and that gave Jack some hope.

"Do you need any tools?" Cole asked.

"Nope. Think I have everything I need," Jack responded, going to the box where he had them stored.

Before turning his attention back to the task at hand, Jack glanced around for his son. He figured the boy would be near his sister, but Alan was nowhere to be seen.

"Have you seen my son?" Jack called to the women.

"Not since you lifted him down from the wagon," Virginia responded.

With deep concern, Jack cupped his hands around his mouth and called, "Alan! Alan!"

No response.

A sense of panic welled in Jack's chest. If Alan had wandered away from camp, he could become lost or get hurt.

"If ya want to go look for your boy, I'll take care of the wheel," Cole offered.

Jack gave a nod. "Think I'd better check in all the wagons first. If Alan's not there, then I'll be heading into the woods to look for him."

Chapter 4

Jack called Alan's name again and again.

Still no response.

Jack looked in the back of his own wagon first, but there was no sign of Alan. Next he checked Cole's wagon. The boy wasn't there either. Just one more wagon to look in, and Jack would have no choice but to head for the woods.

Please let me find him, Lord, Jack prayed as he hurried to Walter's wagon.

"Is there a problem?" Walter asked when Jack approached.

"I'm lookin' for my boy. Thought maybe he might have wandered over here and climbed inside your wagon."

Walter's forehead creased. "He'd better not be in there, or I'll tan the little runt's hide."

Jack's eyes narrowed as he glared at Walter. "Let's get one thing clear, Mr. Prentice. You are never to lay a hand on my son. Is that understood?"

"Then keep him away from my wagon!"

"I don't even know if he's here." Jack pulled the flap of the wagon open and blinked when he saw Alan crouched in one corner, holding a jar of candy. "What do you think you're doing?" he shouted, feeling anger and relief as he fought for control.

Alan hung his head and moved toward the open flap. "I wanted candy, Papa."

Before Jack could respond, Walter reached inside and snatched the jar from Alan. "Why, you little thief!" Red-faced, he turned to Jack. "What are you going to do about this?"

Jack lifted his son into his arms and set him on the ground. "It was wrong to get into Mr. Prentice's wagon and take his jar of candy. Now tell the man you're sorry and that you'll never do anything like that again."

"I—I'm sorry, Mister." Alan's chin quivered.

Walter folded his arms and glared at the boy. "Well, you should be. If I was your father, I'd teach you a good lesson and you'd never steal from anyone again."

"He didn't exactly steal the jar of candy," Jack defended.

"He would have, if we hadn't caught him in the act." Walter held the jar of candy close to his chest. "If anything like this ever happens again—"

"It won't. And don't worry. I'll make sure my boy stays clear of your wagon and your precious jar of candy." Hoisting Alan onto his shoulders, Jack headed back to his own wagon, where he found Cole had finished putting the wheel back on.

"Glad to see you found your boy." Cole motioned to the wheel. "It's fixed, and we're set to roll. I saw you brought some grease along, too, so I lubed it up for you."

"Thanks. Guess I should do that more often," Jack said. "I'll be ready in a minute. Just need to have a little talk with Alan."

As Cole headed for his horse, Jack set Alan on the wagon bench and took a seat beside him. "Now listen to me, Son, and listen good. What you did was wrong, and you need to be punished."

Tears welled in Alan's eyes. "Are ya gonna whip me, Papa?"

"No," Jack said, shaking his head. "But if the women fix dessert this evening, you won't be getting any. And you'll be goin' to bed as soon as we're done eating."

"Ya mean before Amelia?"

"Yes, your sister will get to stay up longer than you tonight."

"I'll be scared in that ole' wagon by myself," Alan whined.

"I'm sorry about that, but maybe some time alone in the dark will give you a chance to think about what you did today."

"Said I was sorry."

"Sorry is good, but God's Word tells us that it's wrong to steal, and I want you to realize that and make sure it never happens again."

"It won't, Papa."

Jack raised his eyebrows and patted Alan's knee. "I'm glad to hear it. Now sit real still while I get your sister, because it's time to get the wagons moving again."

༄

As they continued their trek along the rutted trail, Cynthia sensed irritation in Walter. She'd never met a man as moody as him. His eyebrows always seemed to be furrowed, and for the last hour he hadn't said more than a few words to her or Mama. Did she dare ask what was wrong, or would it be best to say nothing and hope he became more agreeable as the day wore on?

Deciding on the latter, Cynthia turned to Mama and said, "The next time we stop for a break, I'm going to get down from the wagon and walk. Sitting on this unyielding bench is hard on my back, and it'll feel good to stretch my legs."

"Walking's not easy either," Mama complained. "It won't be long and the soles of our boots will have holes in them."

"It's a good thing we had the presence of mind to bring along more than one pair of boots," Cynthia said.

"Yes," Mama agreed, "but unless we walk less and ride more, two pair may not last till we get to California."

"You women are worried about nothing," Walter chimed in. "When we were back in Independence, I bought you both an extra pair of boots, as well as a few new dresses. They're in the trunk with the other clothes."

Cynthia smiled, appreciative that he'd been so considerate. Perhaps Walter had more good qualities than she realized. He really did seem to care about their welfare. Mama must have thought so, too, for she looked at Walter and smiled.

༄

"Did ya get it?" Cole yelled in the direction of the gunfire. When they'd stopped for the night, Cole had left Walter with the women and children while he and Jack went hunting for fresh game.

"Yep. The feathers are still flying, but I got that big bird!" Jack hollered back.

"Hot diggity!" Cole let out a whoop as he approached Jack on the other side of a small ridge. "That's a nice one."

"You bet." Jack grinned, obviously proud of the wild turkey he'd shot. "Everyone's bellies will be full tonight. I can taste this bird already."

Cole gave Jack a slap on the back. "Just look at the size of him. Why, I'll bet that turkey weighs at least twenty pounds."

"He's a big one—that's for sure."

"Guess we'd better get back to the wagons so we can get it cleaned and roasting over the campfire," Cole suggested after he'd offered to carry Jack's gun. "I'll let you carry your prize."

"Can't wait to see the look on everyone's face when we walk into camp with this," Jack said.

Jack was about to pick up the bird when Cole heard a low growl. He stopped abruptly. Jack did the same. The men looked at each other, but neither moved any farther.

"Here, take your gun." Cole handed Jack the gun he'd shot the turkey with. "Now, we're gonna turn around real slow."

They both turned in unison to face the growling menace. Standing on a rock a few feet away was a large gray wolf, with head lowered and teeth barred. Off to the right, stood another one, and to the left a third wolf.

"Looks as if they want our supper," Jack whispered as the other two wolves started growling.

"They haven't come any closer. Maybe they're testing us," Cole said, hoping he was right. One thing for sure, he figured they were hungry and waiting to steal Jack's catch. Cole wasn't about to let that happen. "I hate to waste ammo on those varmints, so let's make a lot of noise and see if that spooks 'em off."

"Sounds good to me," Jack agreed, and he and Cole started yelling and waving their arms.

Without breaking eye contact, Cole leaned down, picked up a hefty rock, and threw it at the biggest wolf. It must have been enough, because all three wolves ran into the woods.

"Come on, let's get outta here and head back to camp," Cole said as Jack picked up the turkey and slung it over his shoulder.

Jack led the way while Cole practically walked backward, making sure the wolves didn't return and chase after them. "We're gonna have to keep a watch for those wolves," he panted. "We only saw three, and hopefully, there's no more of 'em."

⟋⟍

That evening, as they sat around the campfire, everyone seemed content after eating the meal they'd recently finished. Cynthia had to admit, eating turkey basted over an open fire was just as good, if not better, than the oven-roasted turkeys they'd had back home. It wasn't like the lavish meals they used to have, but cooked potatoes along with the succulent, tender turkey meat sure tasted good.

When Virginia brought out a pan of bread and some jam for dessert, Jack looked over at his boy and said, "None for you, Son. Remember what I said today?"

Alan hung his head.

"And it's time for you to go to bed."

"Amelia, too?" Alan questioned.

"No, she gets to stay up awhile, remember?" Jack picked up his son and headed toward their wagon. While he put Alan to bed, Cynthia moved over to sit beside Amelia. She was such a pretty child and so well behaved. What a shame Amelia wouldn't talk. Cynthia was sure there was a lot to say locked inside the little girl. If there was just some way to get her to open up. Amelia did flash Virginia a small grin when she handed her some bread slathered with jam. Cynthia thought that was progress.

A short time later, Jack returned, and Virginia handed him a slice of bread with jelly.

"Thanks," he said, offering her a weary smile. It was clearly hard for him to make this trip with two small children and no wife. Cynthia admired his determination to make a better life for Alan and Amelia in California. She hoped he did well as a cattle rancher.

Hearing a noise, Cynthia glanced to her left and was surprised to see Alan running away from Walter's wagon. Walter must have seen him at that moment, for he leapt up from the log where he sat and hollered, "Were you in my wagon again?"

With eyes wide and head hung low, Alan made a beeline for his father's wagon.

Cynthia held her breath, waiting to see what Jack would do, but before he made a move, the boy began to choke.

Cole, sitting the closest to Alan, jumped up, grabbed the child, and turned him upside-down. Then he gave Alan's back a good whack, and out popped a lemon drop. Everyone gasped, and Alan started to howl. Whether it was from the trauma of choking or from fear of being found out, Cynthia didn't know.

Walter's face turned red, and he scowled at Jack. "I can't believe that boy stole from me! I thought you had talked to him about this."

"Walter, it was only a piece of candy," Cynthia put in, hoping to diffuse Walter's temper.

"No one asked you," he said sharply. "As I said earlier, that child needs to be taught a good lesson!"

"I did punish him," Jack said defensively. "And he will be punished again."

"Maybe you should remove the temptation," Virginia interjected, looking at Walter.

He frowned. "What's that supposed to mean?"

"Perhaps you should throw out the candy," she said. "Lemon drops can be dangerous, especially for a child."

"Which is exactly why the little thief shouldn't be eating my candy!" Walter faced Jack with an angry expression. "You'd better take care of that boy of yours, because I'm not getting rid of my jar of candy!" With that, Walter stalked off toward his wagon like a stuck-up little rich boy instead of a grown man.

Cynthia cringed. She couldn't believe how stubborn and selfish Walter was being. Alan was only a child, and the temptation of Walter's candy was hard to pass up. Surely those lemon drops couldn't be that important to the man. Why couldn't he be kinder and have more patience, like Jack?

"Well," Cole said, "I think it's best if we all head for bed. Mornin' comes quick, and since we're already behind in our travels, we need to get an early start tomorrow. So make sure you're up bright and early."

Everyone headed to their wagons, and when Cynthia and her mother crawled into the back of Walter's wagon, Cynthia expressed her thoughts about Walter. Unfortunately, Mama didn't agree.

"Personally, I think Walter was right," Mama said. "I also believe that as his betrothed, you should support him on this matter, not take sides with a man like Jack."

"A man like Jack? What's that supposed to mean?" Cynthia questioned.

"He's clearly not a good father. What those children need is a mother to keep them in line."

Like you've always kept me in line? Cynthia thought. Ever since she was a child, she'd done whatever Mama said. *I wish I felt free to break my engagement to Walter and find something new and adventuresome to do. I fear that my life as Mrs. Walter Prentice will not be easy.*

Chapter 5

Dear Diary,

Cole says we're over halfway to California now, and even though we're all quite weary, everyone shares a sense of excitement.

We've had some setbacks along the way—repairs to the wagons, rain and mud bogging us down, and trouble crossing some of the rivers, but nothing we weren't able to handle. Things are going along fairly well now, albeit slow, as some days we only make five miles or so. Other days we're able to travel ten to fifteen miles. We have given up catching the larger wagon train that went before us, but Cole thinks we're managing fine on our own. I pray he's right about that.

We must be on the right trail, at least. We've passed several places along the way where things had been discarded, probably to lighten their load. Some of the pieces of furniture we saw had no doubt been beautiful once. I can't imagine how the people felt leaving behind belongings—perhaps family heirlooms—to rot away in this untamed wilderness.

Even sadder than seeing personal items cast along the trail was looking at the occasional mounds of dirt with a wooden cross that had someone's name carved on it. I can't help wondering what took those people's lives. Was it smallpox, cholera, or some other disease? Or perhaps their deaths had been caused by something else. Thankfully, no one from our three wagons has gotten sick, so that's something to be grateful for.

Some time ago, I volunteered to take turns with Cole's sister to look after Jack's children during the day. They ride in Cole's wagon with Virginia during the morning hours and with me in their father's wagon throughout the afternoon. That has kept mischievous Alan out of trouble, and there's been no more of him sneaking into Walter's wagon in search of candy. The boy really isn't a bad child. He's just curious and eager, like most boys his age. Alan's sister, Amelia, still hasn't spoken, but she's an agreeable child and does whatever she's told. In the evenings when we've stopped for the night, the children hover close to their father, especially when those terrible wolves start to howl. I don't think I'll ever get used to that eerie noise. It frightened me when Cole told how he and Jack had encountered some wolves, and I've been wary ever since. I try not to think about it, but sometimes it sounds as if the wolves are right outside our camp, and I'm afraid they might be following us.

Virginia and I are well acquainted by now, and I find her to be quite pleasant. She talks a lot about Cole's dream of finding gold and also how eager she is to teach school once they're settled in California. I wish I could say that I was as eager to get there as Virginia is, but maybe I'll feel differently once we arrive.

Cynthia sighed and lifted her pen as her thoughts turned back to Alan and Amelia. Spending time with Jack's children made her wish she was a mother. Maybe she would be someday, but it still concerned her as to what kind of father Walter would make. No matter how hard she tried to fight it, Cynthia was nowhere near ready to become Walter's wife. He could be so stuffy at times when she herself was so full of life. Sometimes it felt as if she were bursting at the seams.

But what other choice do I have? she thought, glancing at Walter as he took his seat on the bench and gathered up the reins. *I accepted his proposal and gave Mama my word that I'd marry Walter, so I can't back out of it now. Besides, Mama and I would have no way to support ourselves once we get to California, so I need to get the crazy notion out of my head that there is someone better for me than Walter.*

Mable watched her daughter out of the corner of her eye, wondering what she was thinking. She hoped it wasn't about Jack or Cole.

These days Cynthia said very little to Walter, and that concerned Mable. What worried her even more was how attached Cynthia had become to Jack's children, acting as if she were their mother. As she rode in Jack's wagon with Alan and Amelia, no doubt making conversation with their father, Mable had seen the way Jack looked at Cynthia—like she was something special. Cole looked at her that way as well and often made snide remarks about Walter whenever Cynthia was around. Was he trying to poison her against the man she was engaged to marry? Did Cole think he was better than Walter because he had more knowledge about wilderness survival and could do many things with his hands? Walter could do things, too—things neither Cole nor Jack were capable of. Walter was a smart man when it came to business dealings, and in Mable's book, that meant a lot.

I need to keep an eye on things, she told herself, swatting at a pesky fly buzzing around her head. *My top priority is making sure Cynthia doesn't get any ideas about Jack or Cole and goes through with the wedding once we get to California. After all, Walter's a much better catch for my daughter than either of those men. He's a lot wealthier, too.*

"When we gonna get to Californy?" Alan asked, tugging on the sleeve of Virginia's dress.

"It's California," she patiently replied. "And we'll get there when we get there."

"Papa says 'fore Christmas."

Virginia nodded. "I'm sure we'll be there in plenty of time for Christmas."

"Does Santy Claus know the way to Californy?" the boy questioned.

She let go of the reins with one hand and gave the boy's knee a quick pat. "I'm sure he will be able to find it."

"That's good, 'cause I wouldn't wanna live there if Santa couldn't come."

Virginia smiled, remembering how when she and Cole were children, they used to sneak downstairs on Christmas Eve after everyone was in bed, planning to wait up for Santa. They'd never gotten a glimpse of him and had always fallen asleep. She could see little Alan doing something like that. With his determined spirit, he'd probably stay awake all night in the hopes of getting a look at Santa Claus as he put presents under the tree.

"What about you, Amelia?" Virginia asked. "Are you looking forward to spending Christmas in your new home?"

The girl gave no reply, not even a nod or shake of her head. Instead, she stared at her hands, clasped tightly in her lap.

I wish I knew what she was thinking, Virginia thought. *If only I could think of something to say or do that would pull the sweet little girl out of her world of silence.*

Being a schoolteacher, Virginia had dealt with children who had all sorts of problems, but none were locked in a world of silence like Amelia. She wondered if the child would always be like this or if there was a possibility of her speaking again.

As Cole urged his horse forward, ever mindful of what was ahead, he couldn't help but worry. Days on the trail had turned into weeks, and weeks into months. They'd gone over South Pass, and their last stop for supplies and fresh animals to pull the wagons had been at Fort Hall. Now they were following the Humboldt River in the direction of the Sierra Nevada.

They were behind where they should be by this time, but from what they'd seen left from previous wagon trains, they must be on the right trail. But Cole had other matters to be uneasy about. He was anxious not only about another incident with wolves or some other wild animal, but about the possibility of encountering bad weather—particularly snow—before they reached California. Warm days were being replaced with chilly mornings, and at some point they were bound to hit snow. He hoped it wouldn't amount to much and that they could make it to their destination before any bad weather set in. It wouldn't be good for them to get trapped in the mountains due to foul weather. He hadn't shared his concerns with the others, not even Ginny. For now, it was best to keep those thoughts to himself.

Thanks to the wind that had recently whipped up, they were moving slowly again—too slow to suit Cole. The trees seemed to groan as they swayed from the force of the wind, and a light drizzle had begun to fall. Even the oxen seemed miserable, plodding along at a slower pace.

So far, they hadn't run out of food. Between the supplies that were packed in their three wagons and the game that had been available whenever he and Jack hunted, none of them went to bed hungry. Cole had to admit he couldn't wait for a good home-cooked meal that Ginny would make once they got settled in California. For now, rabbits and the occasional sage hen would have to do, along with the never-ending beans that seemed to accompany most evening meals.

He glanced behind at the wagons and tipped his hat when Ginny waved at him. She had Jack's children riding with her, and the smile on her face said it all. His sister had a fondness for children, and it showed. She was a good schoolteacher, and he was equally sure she'd be a good mother someday. Unfortunately, his sister had never had a steady beau other than that creep Clay Summers. After Clay jilted Ginny, she never got interested in anyone else. Maybe it was because she'd been too busy teaching, but more than likely it had to do with her shyness around men. From what Cole had been told, California was home to a lot of men, so if Ginny came out of her shell, she was bound to find a husband. She certainly enjoyed fussing over Jack's kids. Each morning she fixed Amelia's hair and made sure both children washed up. Cole felt sorry for Jack.

It couldn't be easy losing a wife and trying to raise two youngsters by himself.

Cole wanted to get married someday and settle down. But first he needed to find gold. He knew it was a risky way to make money, but he had to give it a chance. Yet in the back of his mind was one nagging thought: *What if I spend all my money on supplies, only to come up empty-handed and never get rich?*

Chapter 6

Dear Diary,

We've come to the foot of the Sierra Nevada and started up the Truckee River. Unfortunately, things haven't gone well. One of our oxen has died, and to make things worse, yesterday it began to snow. It's very rocky here, and since we've had to work our way around the rocks, we've only made it a short distance in two days.

This morning it's still snowing, and I'm worried. What will we do if it gets worse?

I must close now, as Cole just rode up to our wagon and said it was time to move out. I didn't like the concern I saw on his face, and when I asked if he thought we were going to be okay, he just gave a quick nod and rode away. His silence spoke volumes.

"I don't like this. I don't like it one bit," Walter complained as he got their wagon moving. "If this weather gets any worse, we could be stuck out here in the wilderness with no protection from the elements except our wagons. My hands are frozen, and my gloves aren't helping anymore."

Mama's face blanched. "Oh, dear, haven't we been through enough already? Do you really think we might get stranded in the snow?"

Walter shrugged, blowing into his gloves for more warmth. "Guess it all depends on how bad it gets."

Cynthia reached over and gently patted Mama's arm. Even though she felt concern about the snow, she didn't want her mother to worry. "Try not to fret. I'm sure we'll be fine. We need to pray and ask God to take care of us."

Mama nodded slowly, but Walter just grunted.

After all, Cynthia reasoned, *it does no good to dwell on something that's out of our control.* She watched as Walter pulled his hat down tighter on his head. *Poor Walter. I don't think he could be any more miserable. This kind of existence is definitely not for a man like him. Of course, it's not exactly my cup of tea either. I'd rather be home in New York than here on the trail, bouncing around on a hard seat in terrible weather. Somehow, the adventure of going to California has worn off.*

Cynthia thought about Cole's wagon ahead of them and wondered how Jack's children were doing as they sat up front with Virginia. Amelia and Alan would be riding with Virginia all day, since Jack needed to stay in his own wagon. Cynthia wanted to ride in Jack's wagon with the children but figured with the way Walter had been acting lately, he'd probably have something negative to say about it. He'd become quite protective of her lately, acting as if they were already married. Just the other day when Jack was talking to her about the children, Walter stepped up to him and said,

"I hope you don't get used to Cynthia taking care of your children, because as soon as we reach Sutter's Fort, we'll be going our separate ways."

How embarrassing, Cynthia thought, pulling the brim of her bonnet down in an effort to shield her face from the blinding snow. *I'm sure Jack realizes I won't always be there to help with Amelia and Alan. I should have spoken up when Walter told Jack that, instead of turning away with regret. Is it always going to be this way—Walter treating me like a piece of property and acting like he owns me?*

Another time when Cole was talking to them, Walter had told Cole in no uncertain terms to stop gawking at Cynthia. Cole had looked at Walter like he was loco, and Cynthia had fumed at the mere suggestion, although she'd said nothing to Walter. Obviously he disliked Cole, and she didn't want to say or do anything to make it worse. Cole had every right to respond negatively toward Walter, but Cynthia admired how he had simply turned and walked away.

⟋〇⟍

When the wagons stopped for the night, Cole waited until Jack's children were in bed then gathered the adults together. "With the way the snow's been comin' down all day," he said, "I'm afraid we may have to hunker down somewhere for a few days and give our oxen time to rest."

"Are you crazy? And just where might that 'somewhere' be?" Walter shouted, spreading his arms out and looking around. "If we sit here with our wagons, we're likely to freeze to death. Besides, we've little protection from the elements, so I say we keep moving."

"If we had a better place to get out of the weather, it would be good if we stopped traveling for a few days," Jack put in.

The women all nodded in agreement.

"Well, we don't have a better place," Cole said. "So we have two choices: we can either stay put with our wagons for a day or two, or we can keep moving and hope the oxen don't give out. With the snow bogging us down, it's putting an extra strain on what little strength those poor animals have left. If we don't stay put, we'll have to start lessening the load in our wagons to make it easier for the oxen. We've already lost one, and I don't want to lose more."

Cole watched as Cynthia's mother bit her lip, no doubt thinking about his words.

"Let's take a vote," Walter said. "How many are in favor of us moving up the trail come morning?"

Jack, Mable, Cynthia, and Walter raised their hands. "That's a majority, so it's settled. We head out in the morning."

"Wait a minute, now," Cole said, glaring at Walter. "I thought I was the one in charge here."

"You were supposed to be leading us up the trail," Walter reminded, "but that doesn't mean we have to agree with or do everything you say."

Cole grimaced. It seemed to him that the irritating man hadn't agreed with anything he'd done so far, but against his better judgment, he'd go along with everyone's wishes and leave in the morning. It didn't mean it was a good idea though. All he could do was try to get a decent night's sleep and see how things shaped up in the morning. Maybe they'd get lucky and it would quit snowing.

By the next evening, the snow that had begun falling earlier had turned into a blizzard. The blinding snow came down sideways, making it hard to see anything at all. There was no doubt about it: they were definitely lost. If that wasn't bad enough, Cole had no idea what to do for the people in his charge. Unless the weather improved, they'd be trapped here in the Sierra Nevada. If only they could find some better shelter. Their covered wagons didn't offer enough protection from a storm such as this. Even if they survived the storm, what was going to happen when they ran out of food? Would they end up like the Donner party who had gotten trapped at Truckee Lake a few years ago? Many had died during the tragic ordeal, and worse, some of the dead had become food for those who still lived.

Cole gulped and looked heavenward. *Dear Lord, please don't let a terrible thing like that happen to us. Give me the wisdom to know what to do, or provide us with a miracle so no one will perish.*

Chapter 7

Dear Diary,

We're in the worst possible situation. Not only are we in the middle of a terrible snowstorm, but Cole says we're stranded and he can't find the trail. Once again, Cole has left Walter and Jack here with the women and children, while he goes hunting for fresh meat.

Are we stuck here until spring? Could we even survive that long? Have we come this far, only to have it end in tragedy? I'm really getting concerned. It's so cold and hard to function. I'm colder than I've ever been before. My teeth chatter so hard I'm afraid they might break. All any of us can do at this point is pray that God will spare us.

Tears splashed on the paper, smearing the last few words of Cynthia's journal entry. She sniffed and wiped her nose. "Oh, Mama, I'm so scared. I wish we'd stayed in New York instead of letting Walter talk us into making this trek through the wilderness, which can only end in our demise."

"Don't let Walter hear you talking like that," Mama warned, glancing toward the lean-to Walter was trying to set up with Jack's help. "He thought he was doing the right thing, and it's not his fault the weather's turned bad or that we've had so many delays. If things had gone as they should, we'd be in California by now." Mama's lips pursed. "I blame Cole for that, too."

"It's not his fault we ran into snow," Cynthia said in Cole's defense. Briskly, she rubbed her arms, hoping to stimulate warmth in her limbs.

"That's true," Mama agreed, "but he should have kept the wagons moving faster."

"Mama, he did the best he could, and he's not to blame for any of the setbacks we had."

Mama sighed. "I can't believe he left us here in the middle of this storm to go hunting. He's likely to get lost out there in the snow. Then what'll we do?"

"We need fresh meat," Cynthia said, although she was equally anxious. What if Cole got lost in the woods and they never saw him again? "Don't worry, Mama. He'll be back soon." Cynthia's gaze went to where she'd last seen Cole walking in the deep snow with his gun, hoping against hope for his safe return.

❧

Cole yanked the brim of his hat down, as he trudged through the forest on makeshift snowshoes, looking for wild game. So far he'd seen nothing, not even a rabbit. *Guess the animals are bedded down or burrowed in till after the storm,* he thought. With the snow swirling around him, he didn't dare venture too far, because the last thing he needed was to get lost and be unable to find his way back to camp.

Moving a little farther, he was taken by surprise when he spotted a small cabin. No smoke rose from the chimney, and he couldn't see any livestock or other sign of life outside the cabin. Cautiously, Cole approached and knocked on the door.

No response. The only sounds to be heard were the wind blowing through the pines and the snow filtering down as it blew off the branches.

Opening the door and peering guardedly inside, Cole called, "Anybody here?"

No response.

He waited a few minutes then lit a match. Seeing a lantern on a small wooden table, he lit that, and instantly, the cabin became illuminated. After a quick scan of the two small rooms, Cole knew with certainty that the cabin had been abandoned.

Cole pulled his coat collar tighter around his neck. It was cold inside the cabin, and while there didn't appear to be any food on the shelves, this would be a place for them to get in out of the weather and hunker down until spring if necessary. There was a fireplace, and a small stack of firewood outside the cabin would get them started until they found more. The biggest problem would be keeping them in food. Cole thought between the supplies they still had, plus any game he or Jack might bag, they could survive. At least he hoped that would be the case.

Closing the cabin door behind him, Cole started back for the wagons, thankful for the tracks his snowshoes had left in the snow. He figured everyone would be glad with the news he was about to bring them. Staying in this cabin would be better than trying to survive in their wagons, which he doubted they'd be able to do much longer.

༄

"I found an abandoned cabin in the woods, where we can take refuge," Cole announced when he entered the camp and found everyone gathered under the lean-to Jack and Walter had constructed. He bent over, trying to catch his breath after trudging back through the heavy snow. Sweat that had been worked up during the vigorous return was replaced with chills seeping right through his skin.

"What about our wagons? Can we get them and the livestock through the woods?" Jack questioned.

"I think so," Cole answered, rubbing his hands as he held them over the fire. "It might take us awhile in this snow, but we need to try."

"Is there food in the cabin or any other supplies?" Walter asked.

Cole shook his head. "No food, but there's a fireplace, a table, and a few chairs. I think with what we have in our wagons, if we ration the food we should be okay."

"What about fresh meat?" This question came from Cynthia's mother. "Were you able to shoot anything while you were in the woods?"

"I didn't see any game, but after I found the cabin, I quit lookin'." Cole motioned to the wagons. "Right now I think we need to head for that cabin. Once we get there, we can discuss sleeping arrangements and how we're gonna survive till the weather improves."

Walter sneered at Cole. "Don't you mean, *if* it improves? We could be stuck here until spring—if we live that long."

Alan started to cry, and he looked up at his dad. "Are we gonna die, Papa?"

"No, Son," Jack assured the boy, before giving Walter an icy stare. "Not if I can help it."

Amelia's chin quivered, but she said nothing. It was obvious that both of Jack's children were afraid.

Feeling the need to calm everyone's fears, Cole said, "I think we can find plenty of fresh game. We'll have a sturdy roof over our heads and be warmer. There's a fireplace for warmth and to melt snow for water. We have plenty of beans left, so if nothing else, we can survive on bean soup."

Walter wrinkled his nose. "Oh good, I can hardly wait for that."

"What about Christmas, Cole?" Virginia spoke up. "I'd hoped we'd be in California to celebrate the holiday."

"We'll just have to wait and see how it goes," Cole replied. No way could he make them any promises.

Surprisingly, Walter was the first to start for his wagon. Everyone else did the same, and Cole mounted his horse. They'd soon be headed to the safety of the cabin, and maybe come morning things would look better.

⁂

Cynthia was anxious to go, but before getting into Walter's wagon, she paused to thank the Lord for leading Cole to the cabin and for keeping him safe. She was about to add more to her words of thanks, when Walter, helping her into the wagon, said, "Well, isn't that just wonderful? Who knows how long we'll have to stay cooped up with everyone in that cabin before we can head out again?"

Cynthia sighed with exasperation. "You should be glad God has gotten us this far and that He led Cole to the cabin. What's more, we ought to be thankful nothing happened to Cole while he was out there looking for fresh game."

"Oh, is that how you see it?" Walter shot back. "Well, maybe you should ask yourself why, if Cole is so perfect as you seem to believe, aren't we in California by now, like we are supposed to be?"

"Nobody can predict the unknown, Walter." With her arms crossed, Cynthia held her ground. "I think Cole's done a great job so far. Which is more than I can say for you," she quickly added, surprised at her ability to speak up to Walter like this. Maybe Mama's outspokenness was beginning to rub off on her.

Walter's face flamed as his eyes narrowed into tiny slits. "What exactly is that supposed to mean?"

"You haven't gone hunting, not even once, and you don't—"

"Now hold on a minute, missy. I may not be good at firing a gun or gutting a deer, but I have managed to drive the oxen pulling our wagon, and that ought to count for something." Walter's finger shook as he pointed at Cynthia. "And don't forget that you have agreed to become my wife, so your loyalty should be to me, not some fellow who thinks he knows everything."

"This isn't about loyalty," she argued. "I just think you should realize that Cole has done his best by us and try to be more grateful."

Walter's face hardened, and his gaze bored into her. Just as quickly, his expression softened. "My dear, we are all quite tired. So let's stop quarreling and go see what this cabin is like. I suppose it'll be better than me sleeping in a tent, or you and Mable taking refuge in the cold wagon."

Cynthia relaxed some, and when the wagons headed out, she was almost glad for all the obstacles that had slowed their travels these last couple of months. Maybe there was a reason for the delays, giving her time to rethink things. Right now, she wasn't sure she was ready to become Mrs. Walter Prentice. But did she have the nerve to tell him that? If she could choose another man, who would it be?

Chapter 8

Dear Diary,

I can't believe we've been cooped up in this cabin together for eight long weeks with no letup in the weather. If anything, the snow and frigid temperatures have gotten worse. There's so much snow piled on the cabin's roof, I'm afraid it might cave in.

Wild animals are scarce, and fishing is almost impossible due to the frozen river. We're running dangerously low on food, and if the men aren't able to find fresh game soon, they'll be forced to slaughter our oxen. It's hard to find wood for the fire as well, and everyone is sick of eating beans.

Tempers are flaring and sharp words have been exchanged, especially between Walter and Cole. Last night Walter accused Cole of trying to kiss me, which is ridiculous, since we are never alone. I think the stress of what we are going through has caused Walter to have irrational thoughts. I have to admit, though, Cole looks at me strangely sometimes. Is it a look of desire I see on his handsome face, or does he feel sorry for me, being engaged to a man like Walter?

Jack's children grow restless, and little Alan whines much of the time, which I'm sure gets on everyone's nerves. Virginia and I take turns trying to occupy the children, but there's only so much we can do with them.

Remembering the words of Colossians 4:2, I pray every day that God will bring us out of this travesty, even though, at this point, it seems futile. Short of a miracle, we could very well die in this tiny cabin.

"I hate being cooped up like this," Cynthia's mother complained. She wrapped her shawl tightly around her shoulders and moved closer to the fireplace, where Cynthia, Virginia, and the children were huddled.

"I know it's hard, Mama," Cynthia said, setting her journal aside. "At least we have a place to keep dry and somewhat warm, and it's a lot better than the protection we would get from trying to live in our covered wagons."

"You're right about that," Virginia agreed. "I'm thankful my brother found this abandoned cabin when he did, or we'd have frozen to death by now."

Cynthia looked around their simple dwelling. Since arriving, the womenfolk had cleaned the cabin the best they could, using a broom Virginia had in her and Cole's wagon. Each of the women had brought in a few other things as well, to give the cabin a homey feel. A red checkered cloth covered the table, and they'd used a piece of material from Mama's trunk to drape over the window. It wasn't the frilly curtains that had adorned the windows in their home back East, but it added some color to the once-drab room. Jack had used the wheel grease to plug a few drafty holes they'd found in the cabin walls, and it was definitely warmer in the tiny abode than what they'd been used to in their drafty wagons.

"We'll be out of wood soon, and then what will we do for heat?" Mama asked, frowning. "Nothing we experienced on the trail before the blizzard hit was as bad as this—not the broken wagon parts, seeing those Indians, ferocious thunderstorms, deep rivers to cross, steep mountain trails, hordes of mosquitoes, or frightening wolves." Her voice trembled, and Cynthia knew her mother was close to tears. Cynthia felt that she must try to put on a brave front in order to offer courage and hope to her mother. The trouble was, she didn't feel courageous or hopeful at the moment. In fact, she'd never been more scared or discouraged. If worse came to worst, would they have to start using things they'd brought along to burn in place of real firewood? And when they ran out of food, how long would it be before they starved to death?

Of course Jack, in his gentle, positive way, kept telling his children that everything would be okay. When little Alan mentioned Christmas and asked if Santa Claus would find them, Jack had patted his son's head and said he was sure Santa would come and that they'd have a Christmas no matter what.

But what kind of Christmas can we have here, with no tree to decorate, no gifts to give, and so little food to go around? Cynthia asked herself. *There is certainly nothing festive or tasty about bean soup or chewy venison jerky. I hope Cole and Jack have success wherever they are hunting right now.* She glanced toward the back room, where Walter had gone to rest on a cot. He'd complained of a headache earlier and said he needed to lie down. Mama had gone in to check on him awhile ago and returned to the main room, saying he'd fallen asleep.

I wonder if he faked a headache to avoid going outside in the cold and helping Jack and Cole look for a deer or some other wild game. He certainly doesn't carry his weight around here like the other men do. The only thing Walter's really good at is complaining and telling others what he thinks they should do. I'm beginning to believe he must have been quite spoiled when he was growing up, used to getting his own way and pouting when he didn't.

"Let's try to make the best of things, Mable, and trust the Lord to see us through," Virginia said, smiling and pushing Cynthia's thoughts aside. Cynthia could see, though, that Virginia's smile was forced. Truth be told, she was probably frightened, but for the children's sake, sweet Virginia was trying not to let on.

"Let's read some verses of scripture," Virginia suggested. "Hearing God's Word always makes me feel better."

"That's a good idea," Cynthia agreed. "It'll help pass the time while Jack and Cole are out hunting."

Virginia went to get the Bible from her reticule, and the women took seats at the table while the children reclined on a blanket near the fire. Opening the Bible, Virginia said, "Here's a verse from 1 Peter 5 that offers hope when we feel depressed: 'Casting all your care upon him; for he careth for you.' " She turned to another passage. "Psalm 31:24 says, 'Be of good courage, and he shall strengthen your heart, all ye that hope in the Lord.' "

Mama sighed and clasped her hands. "It's hard to be strong and wait for the Lord when we're not sure if He will rescue us from this seemingly hopeless situation."

"That's why we must continue to pray and trust Him to answer our petitions," Virginia said.

"I believe what you're saying is true," Cynthia interjected, "but my faith has weakened. Things really do look hopeless," she whispered, in case Alan and Amelia were still awake.

"When our hope is lost, that's when we need to rely fully on Him, for with God, all things are possible." Virginia clasped the other women's hands. "Shall we pray?"

Both women nodded.

"Heavenly Father," Virginia quietly prayed. "Calm our fears and give us hope. Help us to trust You, even when things seem hopeless. Protect the men as they search for food, and we ask You to provide for all of our needs. Amen."

When Cynthia opened her eyes, she saw Amelia staring up at her with an angelic expression. It tugged on Cynthia's heart. She didn't know how, but she was determined to see that Jack's precious children had a merry Christmas.

⁓

"If we don't bag a deer or even a rabbit today, we'll need to come up with something else to feed our group," Cole said to Jack as they traipsed through the woods on the snowshoes they'd made.

"We're not quite out of beans yet," Jack reminded.

Cole rolled his eyes and groaned. "I've never cared for beans that much, but I can honestly say that if I never saw another bean again, it would be fine with me."

Jack smiled. "I agree. That's why we need to bag a deer."

"Let's hope that won't take too long, 'cause if we don't find food, we may not have long to live."

Jack's smile turned upside down. "I wish you wouldn't talk like that."

"Just statin' facts as I see 'em." Cole stopped walking and looked up. The snow had stopped, but it was still extremely cold, and he seriously doubted that the snow already on the ground would melt before spring. "I've been wondering about something, Jack."

"What's that?"

"Do you think Cynthia's in love with Walter?"

Jack shrugged his shoulders. "I don't know, but they're planning to get married, so I guess she must love him."

Cole huffed, "I don't see how any woman could love a crotchety, stuffy man like that, much less a lady as sweet and pretty as Cynthia."

Jack's eyebrows lifted as he stared at Cole. "Are you interested in Cynthia? Is that why you're wondering if she's in love with Walter?"

Cole rubbed his chin as he thought about the best way to answer Jack's question. The truth was, if Cynthia wasn't engaged to be married, he'd have already made his intentions known. But it didn't seem right to move in on another man's territory, even if that man was an irritating fellow like "Mr. Fancy Pants."

"Cole, did ya hear what I said?" Jack asked, bumping Cole's arm.

"Yeah, I heard. Just wasn't sure how to answer." Cole paused and rubbed his chin. "Uh, you're not interested in Cynthia, are ya, Jack?"

"Well, um. . . You're right. She is pretty, and my kids like her, too." Jack's gaze dropped to the snow-covered ground. "Truth is, I. . ."

Hearing a sudden noise, Cole turned in time to see a nice-sized buck step out of the bushes a few yards away. Immediately, he took aim and fired. The buck dropped to the ground, and Cole breathed a sigh of relief. They wouldn't go hungry tonight, at least. For that matter, the venison they'd get from this big fellow should last a good many days. Maybe, as Virginia often said, God was truly watching out for them. If that was the case, Cole hoped God's mercy would continue until the spring thaw.

Chapter 9

Dear Diary,

Tonight is Christmas Eve. Mama, Virginia, and I have been busy all day preparing for tomorrow, hoping to make it special for Jack's children. The men brought in a small pine tree with soft needles. We've decorated it the best we can with pinecones, paper snowflakes, and pieces of colorful yarn we tied into bows on the tips of each bough.

Earlier in the week, Cole brought in some freshly broken pine branches that worked perfectly for making garland. We women were able to bind enough together to hang over the cabin's one window and doorway. Now, with both the tree and garland, it even smells like Christmas here in the cabin. Virginia cut out a star and Jack put it on top of the tree.

I went outside to get a few more pinecones this afternoon, and Walter followed. I thought at first he'd come to help, but then he pulled me into his arms and tried to kiss me. When I turned my face away and said I was saving my kisses until our wedding night, he said I was acting like an immature child and that he had every right to kiss me. I was relieved when Jack walked past, interrupting us, but Walter looked none too happy about it. I quickly returned to the cabin to help Virginia and Mama wrap a few gifts for the children in pieces of cloth and place them under the tree. We each found some things in our wagons we thought Alan and Amelia might like. I'm giving Amelia the china-head doll Papa gave me when I was a child. I probably shouldn't have brought it along, but I just couldn't part with it. Now it seems more important to give it to Amelia than to hang on to it for sentimental reasons. For Alan, I have a set of dominoes. I think he'll have fun playing with them.

Virginia plans to give both children a small blackboard with eraser and chalk. They should enjoy that as well. My prayer is that the children will have a special Christmas and we'll all make it safely to California in the spring.

Since our food supply has dwindled to almost nothing, there will be no fancy Christmas meal tomorrow. Instead, we'll each have a bowl of venison stew, for which I know I should feel appreciation, but I'd really hoped for a turkey. I guess I ought to be grateful that we haven't starved to death. Prayers and faith to believe that God is still with us are what's keeping me from giving in to despair.

Cynthia looked around at the dwelling that had been their home for a good many weeks. When they'd first settled in, they had plenty of arguments from being cooped up in such cramped quarters, but after a while, the nitpicking stopped, and they realized what had to be done. Knowing their survival depended on it, the weary pioneers settled into a routine and worked together.

Cole and Jack searched for firewood and went hunting, occasionally coming back with small game. Thankfully, the little rabbits and squirrels provided meat and also helped to make their dwindling food supplies last a bit longer.

The women took turns bringing in buckets of snow to melt in the pot they used for cooking. Between them, they were able to prepare simple dishes, adding to what the hunters had been able to provide.

Walter was another story. He kept busy doing mediocre tasks, but mostly sat at the table, pen and tablet at hand, figuring out details concerning the businesses he planned to open once they got to California, and checking his watch for the time. Sometimes he would surprise everyone and bring in some firewood while Jack and Cole were out hunting. But if the other men were there, Walter let them do most of the work. Cynthia was surprised there weren't more arguments, especially where Walter was concerned. But everyone seemed tolerant. What was the point in arguing with him when he was so set in his ways?

Cynthia couldn't help being a little excited though. She'd always loved the Christmas holiday, and with the special touches they'd managed inside the humble abode, it actually felt like Christmas. The little pine tree, with its few decorations, almost seemed prettier than the Christmas trees Cynthia remembered from the past. While there weren't any store-bought ornaments or fancy garland, this tree, in all its simplicity, was like no other. It was amazing how a little tree could do so much to lift one's spirits, and in their precarious situation, it was certainly needed.

✐

"Sure wish I could give my kids a better Christmas," Jack said as he and Cole began cutting up a tree that had recently fallen. Just as they'd been about to run out of the fallen deadwood they'd been able to gather in the area, a huge dead white fir tree, not far from the cabin, had toppled over, unable to bear the weight of the snow. It was a miracle from heaven that would provide them warmth for a while longer. Despite their situation, it seemed that God was intervening, giving hope each time they felt defeated.

"Kids are kids. I'm sure they'll be happy with the few gifts Virginia and Cynthia are planning to give 'em," Cole said.

"That may be, but I do have a gift for each of them," Jack responded. "I have a small wooden horse that I carved for Alan, and I'm givin' Amelia her mother's locket."

"I'll bet they'll like those things." Cole bent down and picked up an armload of wood. "Guess I'd better take this to the cabin. Then I think one or both of us oughta go hunting. We haven't had any fresh meat since I shot that deer a few weeks ago, and the women will be cooking what little we have left for our Christmas dinner."

"You're right," Jack agreed. "If we don't find some game soon, we'll once again be in jeopardy of starving."

"Didn't want to say anything in front of the kids, but I saw wolf tracks beyond those trees yesterday mornin'. We'll have to be careful when we go hunting and make sure we stay close together from here on out."

"Good idea. I haven't forgotten what happened before. Why don't we go out on Christmas morning and see what we can find? It's a cinch that Walter won't make an effort to help us find any game. He sits around with the women all day, checkin' the time, counting his money, and making plans for those businesses he wants to open if we ever make it to California."

Jack grimaced. "You mean, *when* we get to California, don't ya?"

"Yeah, that's what I meant," Cole corrected. Truth was, at this point, he wasn't sure they'd ever make it out of these mountains.

∽

That evening after everyone had eaten their venison stew, Cynthia suggested they sing some Christmas carols.

"That's a good idea," Virginia agreed. "But before we sing, maybe one of the men would like to read the Christmas story from the Bible."

"I'd be glad to do that," Jack said, smiling at Virginia. "It wouldn't seem like Christmas without reading how God sent His Son to earth as a baby."

"Is Santa comin' tonight after we go to bed?" Alan asked, looking hopefully at his father.

Jack gave the boy's back a light thump. "There'll be a few Christmas presents for you and your sister in the morning; don't ya worry about that."

Apparently satisfied with his father's reply, Alan climbed onto Virginia's lap, while Amelia rested comfortably on Cynthia's lap, and they listened to Jack start the story.

Cynthia looked at her mother and wondered if she was remembering past Christmases. Oh, how she missed Papa reading them the same story. She closed her eyes and could almost hear her father's deep voice repeating the words Jack now read.

After the story was over, with Jack accompanying them on his mouth harp, they sang some favorite carols, bringing merriment to the cabin. Cole sang the loudest, and Cynthia suppressed a giggle. No doubt, the songs held precious memories for him, too. Even Walter joined in, but Cynthia wondered if it was because he wanted to outdo Cole. *Forgive me, Lord. I shouldn't think such thoughts. I'm glad if Walter's feeling the Christmas spirit.*

As they sang "O Come, All Ye Faithful," Cynthia felt a sense of peace. Tonight this quaint little cabin was full of good cheer, something each of them needed.

They'd just started the second stanza of "Joy to the World" when the cabin door flew open. A gray-haired man with a matching beard, wearing a buffalo robe and carrying a pack over his shoulder, stepped into the cabin, bringing snowflakes and cold air with him. Blinking his eyes several times, he stared at them with a look of astonishment.

Before any of the adults could utter a word, Amelia pointed to the man and exclaimed, "Santa Claus!"

Chapter 10

Cynthia didn't know what had surprised her most: seeing the big, bearded man who'd entered the cabin unannounced or hearing Amelia speak. Probably the latter, she decided, for it wasn't just astonishing; it was downright miraculous—especially on this very special night.

"Oh, Amelia, my sweet girl," Jack cried, scooping his daughter into his arms. "It's so good to hear you talking again."

"Santa Claus came to see us, Papa," she said, smiling widely as she stared at the stranger who'd entered the cabin.

Was Amelia suddenly released from the emotional trap that had held her captive all this time? Cynthia wondered.

Eyes sparkling brightly, showing life from within, Jack's daughter giggled, as any child would, seeing the whiskered Santa. The little girl couldn't take her eyes off the man, and neither could Alan.

"I ain't Santa Claus, and I'd like to know what you all are doin' in my cabin," the man said gruffly, his gaze traveling from person to person. Then he quickly shut the door.

"We're a small wagon train heading to California," Cole spoke up. "When the weather turned bad and we couldn't go any farther, we took refuge here, thinking the place was abandoned."

"Well, it ain't. My name's Abe Jones, and this here cabin you've taken over is mine." The man's tone softened as he looked at Amelia and Alan staring up at him with wide-eyed expressions. "Sorry to disappoint ya 'bout Santa Claus." He gave his beard a quick pull. "Guess I do kinda look like him."

"If this is your cabin, then why was there no sign of life when we got here several weeks ago, and where have you been all this time?" Walter questioned.

"I was visiting my wife's tribe, like I've done every year since Two Moons died ten years ago," Abe explained.

Walter's eyebrows lifted high on his forehead. "You were married to an Indian?"

Abe gave a nod. "You got somethin' to say about that?" His steely blue eyes narrowed as he glared at Walter, challenging him to say more.

Oh please, Walter, don't make any trouble, Cynthia thought. *If you offend this man further, he's likely to throw us out in the cold.*

"I'm sure Mr. Prentice didn't mean anything by his question," Cole was quick to say. "We're sorry for intruding, but we needed shelter. Guess we're just surprised to learn that someone owns this cabin."

"Yep," Abe said, tossing his pack on the floor and going to stand in front of the fireplace. "Built it with my own two hands after Two Moons and I were married." He

45

paused and rubbed his hands briskly together. "As I said before, I've been holed up with Two Moon's Shoshone kin, so that's why the cabin looked empty."

"If you were living with your wife's family, then why'd you come back here in the dead of winter?" This question came from Jack, who had taken a seat at the table and lifted Amelia onto his lap.

"Always come back on Christmas Eve," Abe replied, glancing into the fireplace. "That's when Two Moons died givin' birth to our baby, so I come to the place where I last saw her purty face. Helps me remember how things were before she died."

"I'm sorry for your loss," Cynthia said sincerely.

Abe looked at her and gave a quick nod. All was quiet while Abe stoked the fire, watching as sparks went up the chimney.

"What about the baby?" Cynthia's mother asked, breaking the silence. "Did he or she survive?"

Abe shook his head. "It grieves me to say it, but both mother and son died on that Christmas Eve night."

"I, too, am sorry for your loss," Virginia said with feeling.

Abe nodded to the womenfolk. "It's bittersweet, but the good times Two Moons and I had together is what I hold on to."

"Whatcha got in there, Mister?" Alan asked, pointing to the pack Abe had tossed on the floor.

Without saying a word, Abe picked up the pack, opened it, and pulled out a small object with a point on one end. "How'd ya like to have this?" He handed it to Alan.

"What is it?" Alan asked, turning the item over in his hand.

"It's an arrowhead," Abe replied. "The Injuns make 'em to put on their spears for hunting, spear fishing, and as a weapon to protect themselves."

Cynthia smiled as she watched Alan rub the arrowhead as though it were a piece of precious gold.

"Wow! Thanks!" Alan quickly put the carved stone in his pocket.

Abe reached into his pack and withdrew a string of colored beads. "Here's a purty necklace for ya," he said, slipping the beads over Amelia's head.

Amelia's eyes glistened as she looked up at Abe. "Thank you, Santa Claus."

Abe didn't argue with her this time—just smiled and patted her head. "I hafta say, the place hasn't felt this homey since my wife died," he said, gazing around the decorated room. "It needed a woman's touch." Abe grew quiet, looking toward the fire as though lost in memories from long ago. He looked back at them and said, "Guess I should be thankin' you folks for makin' this Christmas a little less lonely for me."

Cynthia felt that Abe showing up when he did was a miracle of sorts. Seeing him and believing he was Santa Claus was just what Amelia needed to get her speaking again. And the fact that Abe carried in his pack two items any child would be intrigued with made Cynthia think God must have planned it all to give Jack's children a special Christmas Eve. She just hoped Abe would allow them to continue staying in his cabin, for they'd never survive the harsh winter in their wagons.

Chapter 11

Dear Diary,

    Today, as we celebrate Christmas, everyone is relieved that Abe has allowed us to stay here in his cabin. Not only did he give Alan and Amelia those items from his wife's tribe, but he brought food with him—enough to get us by until he or one of the other men is able to get fresh meat again.

    Abe seemed upset that we were here at first, but his attitude softened and he's agreed to let us stay until we're able to travel again. How I thank God for that. I think all of us being here, especially over Christmas, has helped Abe, too, and that warms my heart.

    This morning Virginia and I gave the children the gifts we had for them. Alan and Amelia were excited and were also pleased with their father's gifts. Jack said the best Christmas present he could have received was to have his daughter laughing and talking again. Being trapped in the mountains has been frightening, but finding this cabin and experiencing Abe's generosity are truly answers to prayer. I'm confident that once the weather improves God will take us safely to California.

    The only part I am dreading is becoming Walter's wife. How can I live the rest of my life with a man I don't love? If only there was a way Mama and I could make it on our own without relying on Walter to provide for our needs. I know I should be grateful and quit wishing for the impossible, but my selfish desires seem to keep creeping in. I pray every night that God will help me accept my plight and be a good wife.

    I must close and help Mama and Virginia prepare our Christmas dinner. Thanks to Abe's hunting skills, a wild turkey is roasting in the fireplace. My mouth is already watering as the delicious aroma wafts through the cabin. Virginia used the last of her flour to bake two pies with some dried huckleberries Abe brought back to the cabin, so we're in for a special treat.

"Looks like you're workin' up a pretty good sweat," Jack said as Cole chopped some firewood from the big tree that fell. "Don't cha think we have enough already?"

"We can always use more." Cole paused a moment to wipe his wet forehead and started chopping again, as vigorously as before. "Who knows what the weather will bring in the next few days? It's best to get the rest of this tree cut and stacked close to the cabin where we can get our firewood easily."

"That makes sense, but you're not upset about anything are you?" Jack asked.

"What makes ya think I'm upset?"

"You've been sorta moody this morning, and you're attacking that wood like there's no tomorrow."

Cole set the ax aside and drew in a couple of deep breaths. He glanced toward the cabin before he answered. "To tell ya the truth, I am kinda upset."

"About what?"

"Cynthia."

Jack quirked an eyebrow. "Did she say or do something you didn't like?"

Cole shook his head. "It's not that. It's just. . ." He stopped talking and motioned toward Walter, who had come outside and was heading toward his wagon. "That guy really bothers me, and I don't understand what she sees in him."

"I don't either, but then it's not my place to be sayin' anything about who Cynthia marries."

Cole gritted his teeth. "She's too sweet for an old sourpuss like Walter, not to mention that she's a lot younger than him. I think he's using her, but I'm not sure for what."

"That may be true, but it's her decision, and I don't think she'd have agreed to marry him if she didn't want to."

"You're probably right. I just wish. . ." Cole's voice trailed off. He'd most likely said more than he should.

Jack moved closer to Cole. "You're in love with her, aren't you? Don't deny it either. I can see it written all over your face."

Cole shrugged his shoulders. "Don't matter what I feel one way or the other. She's gonna marry Walter, and that's all there is to it."

∽

Cynthia was about to help Virginia set the table when Walter reentered the cabin. He was really getting on her nerves, especially today, watching him sit around most of the morning while the rest of them hustled about making preparations for a nice Christmas Day. She'd been glad when he'd finally gone outside, but frowned seeing him back inside already.

Walter paused near the door, watching Cynthia a few minutes. Then he stepped up to her and said, "I need to speak to you about something. Will you take a walk with me outside?"

"Now?" she asked. *This makes no sense. Walter was just outside. Why didn't he ask me to go out with him then?* "Can't it wait until after we eat? I'm busy right now, helping to get things ready."

"I won't take but a few minutes," he said. "I need to talk to you alone."

"It's all right," Cynthia's mother interjected, shooing Cynthia away after glancing briefly at Walter. "I'll finish setting the table for you."

Cynthia couldn't imagine what was so important that it couldn't wait until they'd eaten their Christmas dinner, but wanting to avoid an argument, she slipped her bonnet on her head and wrapped a heavy woolen shawl around her shoulders then followed Walter out the door.

I hope this doesn't take too long, she thought. She didn't want anything to spoil the day—something she knew Walter was capable of doing in just a matter of seconds.

Once outside, he took her arm and they walked toward his wagon. Pausing near the back of the wagon, he cleared his throat and said, "Your mother and I will be getting married when we reach California."

"What was that?" Cynthia asked, thinking she must have misunderstood.

"I am sure this must come as a shock to you, but Mable has agreed to become my wife."

Cynthia's mouth dropped open.

"Over the past few weeks, I have come to realize that Mable would be a better choice for me." A muscle on the side of Walter's cheek twitched. "The truth is, Cynthia, you're simply too immature for me."

Her forehead creased. "You really think that?"

"Yes, I do."

"Then why did you try to kiss me recently?"

"It was a test. To see if my feelings for you were stronger than I'd thought."

Cynthia's jaw clenched. The idea that Walter would need to test his feelings for her by a mere kiss made her angry. And the fact that he saw her as immature only added to her irritation. And while she was relieved he no longer wanted to marry her, she couldn't believe Walter had asked Mama to marry him. It made no sense at all.

"What does my mother have to say about this?" Cynthia asked, challenging Walter with her eyes.

"She's agreeable to it."

Cynthia stared at Walter in disbelief. Never had she expected such a turn of events. "I—I don't believe you. What would make Mama agree to this?"

"I think it would be best if you asked her that yourself." He leaned against the wagon with a smug expression.

"Yes, I certainly will." Cynthia pulled her shawl tighter and turned to leave, but he stopped her by placing his hand on her shoulder.

"There's one more thing," Walter said.

She turned back around. "What's that?"

"I want you to know that as my future stepdaughter, I will provide for your needs."

"There's no reason for that," Cynthia said with a huff. "I can make my own way." She pivoted around and hurried toward the cabin, anxious to speak to her mother and get this resolved. *The nerve of that man, trying to keep a hold on me! And now as his stepdaughter—no!*

Chapter 12

Cynthia rushed into the cabin but realized right away that this wasn't a good time to talk with her mother, as dinner was ready to serve. Their talk would have to wait.

Soon everyone gathered around the table, and after Jack offered a blessing, they ate and visited. The whole time, Cynthia kept glancing at Walter and Mama to see if they might say something about their future plans, but neither said a word.

Maybe Walter made the whole thing up, she told herself. After all, she'd never seen much interaction between her mother and Walter except the usual conversation. *Of course, I have no idea what Walter may have said to Mama when I was out walking or spending time with Jack's children. When we reach California, he might be planning to discard me and Mama like pieces of unusable luggage. Maybe after traveling all this way with two women in his wagon, Walter's decided he doesn't need a wife telling him what to do. But what if Walter was telling the truth when he said Mama had agreed to marry him? Where will that leave me when we reach our destination? I wouldn't feel right about taking any charity from him.*

"You're awfully quiet, Cynthia," Mama said, pulling Cynthia out of her musings. "Don't you care for the delicious turkey that has miraculously graced our table today?"

Cynthia blinked several times. "Uh, yes, it's delicious. I was just thinking."

"About what?" Cole asked, looking at Cynthia strangely.

She smiled and said, "Oh, how grateful I am for this good meal and being able to spend Christmas in the warmth of this cabin with the friends I've made on our journey."

"We've all become friends," Virginia said, reaching over and giving Cynthia's arm a gentle squeeze. "When we first began this journey, we were strangers, but working together and helping each other through each trial that's come our way has strengthened us as people and given us a better understanding of each other."

All heads bobbed, except for Walter's. He sat quietly eating the food set before him.

Maybe he doesn't see any of us as friends, Cynthia thought. *He probably thinks we're all beneath him.* She was glad Walter was no longer interested in marrying her, but if he had somehow talked Mama into becoming his wife, he would be her stepfather. *I will not have that man thinking he can tell me what to do.*

Her appetite gone and her head pounding, Cynthia pushed her chair away from the table and stood.

"Where are you going?" Mama called as Cynthia grabbed her shawl and headed for the door.

"I—I need a bit of fresh air."

Cynthia had no more than gone out the door when it opened again, and Mama stepped out behind her. "Are you all right?" she asked. "You're not feeling ill, I hope."

Cynthia shook her head. "I'm upset about something Walter told me earlier."

Mama stepped forward and placed her hand on Cynthia's arm. "Was it about me agreeing to marry him?"

Cynthia swallowed hard. "Is it true, Mama? Did you tell Walter you would become his wife?"

Mama nodded.

"When did this happen?"

"During the time you've spent with Jack's children, Walter and I have done a lot of talking. And since being here at the cabin, we've reached an agreement." Mama rubbed her hands briskly over her arms, obviously trying to warm them against the cold. "When Walter informed me that he didn't think you were the right woman for him, I nearly panicked, knowing how much we needed him. But then Walter surprised me by saying that he thought he and I should be married, and that I would make him a better wife. So after talking about it some more, I agreed to marry him."

"I never saw this coming, and I surely can't let you make that sacrifice," Cynthia said, shaking her head. "I don't believe you love Walter any more than I do."

"It's not about love," Mama said. "It's about financial security and companionship, and Walter can offer me both."

"But he's several years younger than you, Mama, and he's not a very nice man."

"I'll admit, he does have some irritating ways, but he's smart and rich, and. . ."

"Did you make this decision for your sake or mine?" Cynthia asked.

"Both. I knew you didn't love Walter, but we still need his financial support, so I figured it would be better if I married him, leaving you free to marry the man of your choice. Besides, I think Walter and I will get along quite well together. We both know what it takes to run a business, although my boarding home was small by comparison. Still, Walter and I have a lot of other things in common that involve the finer things in life."

Cynthia couldn't argue with that. Ever since she was a girl, she'd known that her mother fit better with high society ladies than some of the more down-to-earth, common women who'd attended their church in New York. "Are you absolutely sure that marrying Walter is the right thing to do?" she questioned.

"Yes," Mama replied.

Cynthia gave her mother a hug. "If that's what you want, then I wish you and Walter well. But I want you to know that when we get to California I plan to look for a job. There is no way I will let Walter provide for me as his stepdaughter."

Mama patted Cynthia's arm. "Let's not talk about that right now. I think we should get back inside where it's warm and finish that good meal we took all morning to prepare." She giggled. "The way Abe was eating, there may not be much left."

"You go ahead," Cynthia said. "I want to stay out here awhile longer."

"But it's cold, and looks like it might start snowing again," Mama argued.

"I'll be fine. If I get chilled, I will come back inside. Right now I don't feel like eating."

Mama hesitated, but then she turned and headed back to the cabin.

Cynthia released a deep sigh. If Mama was determined to marry Walter, there wasn't much she could do about it. She needed to pray about her own situation and give it time to sink in.

～

Cole waited until everyone was finished eating; then he mentioned that they needed more firewood and would head outside to get it.

"I'll get it!" Jack jumped up, put on his jacket, and hurried out the door before Cole could say another word.

So much for getting a chance to speak with Cynthia alone, Cole thought. She'd acted strangely during dinner, and he wanted to find out if something was wrong. If he worked up the nerve, he might have a talk with her about Walter—see if he could persuade Cynthia to break her engagement to Mr. Fancy Pants and agree to marry him. Of course that was probably a dumb idea, because a refined lady like her probably wouldn't want to be married to a blacksmith who was going on a quest for gold. But if he didn't ask, he'd never know whether he had even the slightest chance with Cynthia, the first woman to capture his heart.

Cole gulped down the cup of coffee his sister offered him. Then, using the excuse that someone should help Jack get more firewood, he put on his jacket and went out the door.

When Cole stepped into the snow-covered yard, he was surprised to see Jack standing beside his wagon next to Cynthia. What surprised Cole even more was seeing them embracing. "That's just great," he mumbled, kicking a hunk of ice under his boot. *Shoulda known if she was gonna pick anyone it would have to be Jack. Guess he's better suited to her than me, and I know she really likes his kids. May as well take it like a man and give 'em my best wishes.*

As Cole approached Jack's wagon, the couple broke their embrace and whirled around to look at Cole with surprised expressions.

"Oh, Cole, you startled me," Cynthia said.

Jack nodded. "Same here. Didn't hear ya come out, I guess."

"No, don't suppose you did." Cole's irritation mounted. "Looked to me like you two were pretty busy when I came outside." He looked Jack in the eyes. "Thought ya said you had no romantic interest in Cynthia, and that you believed I oughta keep my feelings for her quiet 'cause she was promised to Walter."

"Never said that exactly," Jack replied. "Just said—"

"I'm not going to marry Walter," Cynthia spoke up.

"Y–you're not?" Cole stammered. If he weren't so upset with seeing Jack and Cynthia together, he'd have leapt for joy.

She shook her head. "Walter thinks I'm too immature for him, and he's decided to marry my mother instead."

Cole bit his lip to keep from laughing out loud. He couldn't imagine Mr. Fancy Pants married to Mable Cooper any more than he could her daughter. "Your mother agreed to this?" he asked, looking at Cynthia with raised brows.

She nodded. "And for your information, Jack was only hugging me because I gave him some advice."

Cole's eyes narrowed. "What kind of advice?"

"She was advising me to admit to your sister that I've come to care for her," Jack said.

52

Cole blinked a couple of times. "You're in love with Ginny?"

"That's right. I just haven't worked up the nerve to tell her yet." Jack raked his fingers through the ends of his thick hair. "I'm afraid she might not return my feelings."

Cole thumped Jack's back. "If I know Ginny like I think I do, I've got a hunch she's smitten with you, too."

"Do ya think so?" A wide smiled stretched across Jack's face. "Think I'll go inside and see if Virginia would like to take a walk with me."

Cole grinned. "That's the best idea you've had all day."

As Jack headed for the cabin, Cole drew in a deep breath then cleared his throat. If he was going to talk to Cynthia, it had to be now, because with them all being cooped up in the cabin like they were, he may not have another chance to tell her the way he felt. "Umm. . .Cynthia, there's somethin' I'd like to say."

"What's that?" she asked, smiling up at him.

"It's not snowing right now," he said, feeling suddenly tongue-tied.

She gave a slow nod, looking across the land. "I've noticed."

Cole jammed his hands in his pockets and rocked back and forth on his heels.

"Is something troubling you?" Cynthia inquired.

"Yes. No. Well, you see. . . The thing is. . .I'm in love with you, Cynthia, but I've kept my feelings hidden 'cause I knew you were promised to Walter, and I didn't know if you felt anything for me."

Cynthia tilted her head back and gazed at Cole in such a way that it made his toes curl inside his cold boots. "I do care for you, Cole. Very much, in fact. But until a few hours ago, when Walter revealed his plans to marry Mama, I wasn't free to even dream of a relationship with another man, let alone express the way I feel."

As the snow began to fall, Cole lifted Cynthia's chin and kissed her gently on the lips. "I don't have much to offer, and there's no guarantee that I'll make it rich searching for gold, but when we get to California, would you do me the honor of becoming my wife?"

She nodded slowly, tears welling in her pretty eyes. "I'd like that very much." Cynthia sighed and leaned her head against his chest. "What a wonderful day this has been. My Christmas prayer was answered in more ways than one."

Epilogue

One year later

Dear Diary,

Cole and I found out that we're expecting a baby. What a joyous way to celebrate Christmas, knowing that next year at this time we'll have the laughter of a child filling our humble home here in Northern California.

Cole's plan of getting rich in the gold fields didn't pan out as he'd planned, but he made enough money to open a blacksmith's shop and build us a small home. The spirit of adventure we both felt when we first came here is still with us, only our focus is not on making money, but enjoying one another, helping others, and worshiping God, who has blessed us immeasurably.

I saw Mama the other day, and she seems happy being married to Walter. It didn't take him long to get a general store going, and more recently he's opened a hotel with a restaurant. Mama stays busy helping Walter at the hotel and hosting various social events.

Last week I received a letter from Virginia. Jack is busy helping his brother with the cattle ranch, and Virginia's time is taken up caring for Amelia and Alan. She said Alan can't wait until he's bigger and can go on cattle drives with his dad and uncle Dan. Virginia's also teaching at the one-room schoolhouse not far from their home. She sounds happy and has settled into her life as a cattle rancher's wife.

The mountain man Abe, whose cabin we stayed in last year, came to see us this fall. We invited him to stay, but he said his place is with his wife's Shoshone tribe, and that he won't be going back to his cabin to live again. He will check it from time to time and leave the place stocked with supplies that might be helpful to any other pioneers who may need a shelter during a storm.

Cynthia stopped writing and placed her hand against her stomach. She felt such peace. It was hard to believe that just a year ago things were so uncertain.

Thank You, Lord, for answering my prayers—not just at Christmas, but every day of the year.

Another Christmas Story

by Susan Page Davis

Chapter 1

Nebraska Territory in what is now Wyoming
1856

Dust hovered in the air as the wagons lumbered along, and Beryl Jenner coughed. Her shoulders ached from holding the reins all day. Usually her father drove the team of six mules, but he'd ridden off that morning with four other men to hunt. Fresh meat would be welcome, but her father's presence would be even better.

"Sam, do you see them yet?" she called over her shoulder.

Her little brother had been playing in the back of the wagon and keeping her posted whenever he saw anything interesting outside the canvas cover.

"Not yet," came his muffled voice, still babyish though he was four years old, going on five.

Beryl heard him scrambling over the crates and sacks in the wagon bed.

"Can I get down for a while?" Sam asked, squeezing out between her arm and the front curved wagon bow.

Beryl wished she could climb down from the wagon seat and stretch her legs, too. Normally, she and Sam walked most of the day and chatted with the other women and children on the train, but their father's absence kept them both cooped up today.

"Not unless you find someone you can walk with. Do you see Mrs. Markham?"

"No." Sam steadied himself with a hand on her shoulder and stood on the seat beside her, squinting as he studied the scene around them. Straight ahead of their mule team, another wagon rolled along the rutted trail. Leaning to the side, Beryl could see trees and bluffs ahead, which probably meant they would be crossing the river again. Pa would find them at the encampment if the men came in late from the hunt. But she had no confidence in her own ability to get the wagon across the river without his expertise.

Sam sighed and crouched down. "All I see is Danny Bowden and his brother."

"Well, those boys aren't big enough to watch you."

Sam climbed over the seat back, into the wagon bed. Beryl could hear him working his way to the rear. She arched her back in an effort to ease the strain on her muscles. She hoped they would make camp soon—on this side of the river. Then she could leave this hard, unyielding board seat. Of course, she would have to unhitch the team if Pa hadn't returned, and care for them before making a fire and getting supper.

"There they are," Sam yelled.

Beryl tried to see around the wagon cover, but it was hopeless. She turned back to her driving, though the mules plodded along with little guidance so long as the wagon ahead kept on at a steady pace.

To her right, two horses loped past. One rider had a gutted antelope slung behind his saddle. Beryl smiled. Her father was on his way. Several people called out to the men, but they didn't stop. Instead, they rode on toward the head of the column. Beryl felt a twinge of unease. One of the hunters was Mr. Arnold, and she knew his wagon was two behind the Jenners'.

She turned her head and called, "Sam! Do you see Pa yet?"

"Nope."

Beryl pushed the brim of her bonnet back and wiped her brow with a grimy handkerchief. She hoped they would stop long enough to do laundry soon.

A few minutes later, the wagon master, Mr. Etherton, rode back along the train, calling out to the drivers, "We'll make camp a half mile on, near the water."

It wasn't until she had driven her team into position in the wagon circle and begun to unhitch the mules that Mr. Etherton approached her, accompanied by Mr. Arnold.

"Miss Jenner?"

"Yes?" She turned toward them with a tight smile, still fumbling with the straps on one of the leaders' bridles.

"I'm afraid I have some bad news," Mr. Etherton said.

Beryl's heart seemed to melt. "My father?"

"I'm afraid so."

She glanced about for Sam and remembered she had sent him with Mr. Bowden and Danny to fetch water.

"Tell me."

"Perhaps you should sit down," Mr. Etherton said, taking her arm.

At the side of the wagon, she let down the shelf they called the "lazy board" and sat on it. She looked up at the wagon master. The hunter hung back, as if reluctant to take part in the conversation.

"Now tell me," she said. "Is he dead?"

"No, but gravely injured. There was an accident."

"A hunting accident?" So many things could happen on an emigrant train. In the last two months, she had seen men thrown from their horses, a boy gored by an ox, a woman who drowned, and a man who fell from a cliff.

"Yes."

She hauled in a deep breath. "What happened?"

"A horse spooked when your father fired at a pronghorn. The rider fell, and apparently in doing so, he discharged his rifle. The bullet hit your father from the side, just above the waist. I'm sorry, Miss Jenner. They say it looks bad."

Beryl jumped up. "Where is he?"

"They're bringing him in slowly."

Beryl rose and walked to the gap between her wagon and the one behind and stared out at their back trail. The wagon master went with her. The dust was still thick in the air.

"What shall I do?" Beryl asked.

Mr. Etherton pushed his hat back, frowning. "I'll ask Mrs. Bond to be ready to help you with him."

Beryl took small comfort from that. Mrs. Bond was the closest they had to a doctor among the thirty-seven wagons. She was good at birthing and tending the sick, but a critical wound?

"We're only ten miles from Chiswell Rock. There may be someone there with more skill. We'll reach the trading post by noon tomorrow."

"Will you send a rider ahead tonight?" Beryl asked. "If they have a doctor. . ."

"There's no settlement," Mr. Etherton said. "But there might be other trains that have stopped there. You never know. I'll send the scout now." He strode away. Mr. Arnold had already faded into the dusk, no doubt to help his wife unhitch and tell her what had happened.

Sam! Beryl hurried out between the wagons. She lifted her skirt and ran toward the river path, where her brother and the Bowdens had gone. She had to tell Sam before he heard it from someone else.

◔℈

James Lassen watched his mother climb into an emigrant wagon. He pitied the family inside. The train's scout had ridden in the previous evening, his horse in a lather, desperate for a doctor. James's father, Wolf Lassen, had the unpleasant task of telling him no medical help was available.

This morning the train had crawled into sight and circled for nooning in the field set aside for the purpose across the trail. The injured man's wagon had driven right up to the door of the trading post.

His mother poked her head out the back and called to him.

"James, come and take the boy."

Curious, James hurried across the yard. Inside the covered wagon, his mother was holding the hand of a youngster of about four. Tears and dirt streaked the child's face as he tugged against her grip.

"I wanna stay with Pa."

"I'm sorry, Samuel," James's mother said gently. "It's best if you let me and your sister tend to him for a while. My boy James will take you inside and give you a peppermint stick." She looked down at James. "Just lift him down, please. His name is Samuel Jenner. His father's in a bad way."

James raised his arms to the little boy, who eyed him distrustfully.

From farther back in the wagon, a hushed, musical voice said, "It's all right, Sam. You can go with Mr. Lassen. He'll mind you well for a little while, and then I'll come and get you."

Sam looked back at her and whimpered. "Beryl. . ."

James arched his eyebrows at his mother. "Barrel?"

"His sister's name is Beryl," she whispered. "It's a gem."

"Oh." James tucked that away to think about later. "So, Sam, let's go, pard. I'll get you that candy, and you can help me and my pa in the store."

The little boy leaned toward him, and James lifted him over the wagon's tailboard and set him on the ground. Sam swiped at his dirty face with a sleeve.

James pulled out his folded bandana, shook it, and held it out to Sam. "Here you go."

Sam looked at it for a moment then took it and wiped his eyes and the rest of his face. The tear streaks were gone now, but his cheeks were smeared with dirt, and his eyelids remained puffy.

By this time, other people from the wagon train were making their way on foot

59

from the encampment to the trading post.

"Come on," James said. They always had an hour or two of confusion and bustle when a train first arrived and the people wanted to replenish their supplies.

His father and the scout were chatting near the counter when James took the boy inside. The room was dim compared to the searing sunlight outside. He let Sam stand still for a moment to blink and let his eyes adjust.

"Well, now, what have you got there?" his father boomed.

"The hurt man's little boy." James looked down at Sam and realized he was shaking. James put a hand on his shoulder. "Sam, this is my pa."

"Howdy, young feller." Pa clomped across the floor and bent over, sticking out one of his huge hands. Sam crowded against James's leg and looked up at him with terror in his eyes.

"It's all right," James said, crouching beside Sam. "My pa's a big man, and his name is Wolf, but he doesn't bite. Once you get to know him, you'll like him."

Sam put out a trembling little hand, and Pa shook it solemnly and released it.

"Glad to meet you," Pa said. "And I'm sorry about your pappy."

The door opened behind them.

"Take him out back and clean him up," Pa said. "Then I'll need you in here."

James hustled Sam through the door behind the counter, leading through the storage room and into the family's living quarters. He set a basin of water on the seat of a chair so Sam could reach it.

"Here's soap. Go ahead and wash your hands. I'll get a cloth for your face."

A few minutes later, he took a pink-faced Sam back through the storeroom toward the front part of the trading post. As they walked, Sam's eyes grew wide. Even though this was the end of the season and the stock of goods was getting low, the array of merchandise must seem vast to the boy. Crates and barrels lined the walls on each side, and harnesses, tools, lanterns, and kettles hung from the rafters.

"We keep everything back here. When people tell us what they want out front, we come and get it for them," James told Sam. "Would you like to help me fetch stuff for them?"

Sam nodded, eyeing a pair of snowshoes hanging on the wall.

James led him into the trading room. People from the wagon train crowded the open space before the counter. When he came to the Nebraska Territory to open his business, Wolf Lassen had learned that it was best to keep the merchandise where the customers couldn't handle it. Some of the settlers passing through were so worn down and desperate that they weren't above pilfering, and the Indians—well, James knew his pa liked to trade with the tribes, because it meant they were friendly to the trader and his family, and they'd see no trouble for the most part. Pa got along fine with them. Even so, one of the first things James had learned in the business was to lock everything up at night and not turn your back when you had merchandise laid out on the counter.

"What do you need me to do, Pa?"

His father was opening a crate of tinned beans with a crowbar, and he looked up at James. "About time. Bring out a ten-pound sack of sugar and a set of tug lines."

For the next twenty minutes, James and Sam were kept busy, fetching items from out back and taking them to Pa, who amassed each customer's pile of goods and figured how much was owed.

Every time they went into the storeroom, James let Sam get the items low enough for him to reach and light enough for him to carry. James collected the hanging things and heavy items. The boy seemed happy to be helping, but after a while, his steps began to flag.

"Tired, Sam?" James asked.

Sam shook his head, clutching a cone of twine and a can of cinnamon to his chest. James smiled and hefted a sack of cornmeal. "Come on, pard. I know a place you can rest your legs a bit."

Behind the counter, they kept a tall stool so that Ma could sit down when she totaled up the bills. After depositing his load, James pulled it forward and lifted Sam, sitting him squarely on top, close behind the counter.

"Now I'll get you that peppermint stick we talked about."

James brought it from the crock out back and placed it in Sam's hand. The boy's eyes widened.

"Thank you, Mr. Lassen."

"Call me James. My pa is Mr. Lassen." James continued to dash back and forth to fill orders. Most of the travelers bought only a few necessities—a strap to replace a broken piece of harness, or a small amount of flour or cornmeal. Prices were high at the trading post, and most of the emigrants had bought as much food as they thought they would need back East. Even so, they always ran out of something.

A middle-aged couple stepped up to the counter.

"What'll it be?" Pa said in his naturally loud voice.

The woman flinched, but her husband said, "Half a pound of tea and a pot of axle grease."

"We're out of tea," Pa said. "Sorry. End of the season, you know. I have some coffee left."

Of course, he didn't mention the tea he had put away for the family's use over the winter. All of the Lassens understood that their personal supplies were never on sale. When he brought the freight wagons full of goods in the spring, Pa had measured out their own stockpile and stored it in the lean-to behind the kitchen. That way no one would ever mix up their food with the supplies in the storeroom.

The woman's face fell. "We've got coffee. I was hankering for a cup of tea. Oh well."

"I'll get you the grease," James said.

When he emerged from the storeroom with the tin in his hand, his mother was coming through the trading post door. Her apron was bloodstained and her face gray. She beckoned to him. James set the grease pot on the counter and joined her near the door, behind the travelers still waiting for service.

"What is it?"

"Can you get me more gauze?"

James nodded. "He's bad, isn't he?"

"Very. I'm afraid he won't make it, but the girl, Beryl, won't give up hope. How's the little boy doing?"

"Fine." James looked toward the counter. Sam still sat on the stool behind it. "He sure is enjoying that candy."

"Probably the first he's had in some time," Ma said. "The train's moving out in the morning."

James frowned. "What about Mr. Jenner?"

Ma shook her head. "He can't travel. Beryl begged the wagon master, but he says they're late as it is. If they stay here even a few days, they might not get over the mountains before snow sets in."

"He's right." James shrugged. Every year the trains passed through all summer long and then dwindled to a few last stragglers. Wagons that hadn't made it this far by now surely risked not making either California or Oregon by the time the passes were filled and crossing was impossible. "Will they stay here? She can't be over at the encampment all alone."

"There's that spot near the pasture where people have camped before," his mother said, "but it's going to be hard for her, tending to her pa and having her little brother to mind."

"Aren't there any brothers and sisters between them?" James asked.

"No. Beryl's nineteen and Samuel's four. Beryl said there were two girls who died of fever when their mother went, and a brother who lived to eight years old died of smallpox some time ago."

"What a shame," James said. "I'll get the gauze. Anything else?"

"She'll need laudanum."

James nodded. "Mr. Etherton bought some to replenish his supply for the train."

"Well, Beryl will need her own. Take the things out to the wagon. I'm going to get her a plate of leftovers from our dinner. Poor child hasn't had a bite all day."

When James had retrieved a length of rolled gauze and taken a small bottle of laudanum from the locked cupboard in the back room, he went to the stool where Samuel was still sucking his peppermint stick. Pa was waiting on the last customer.

"Sam, did you have any dinner?" James asked.

Samuel shook his head.

"Well, you wait here with Pa."

The boy looked up at Pa with wide eyes, but his fear seemed to have dissipated.

"I have to go outside for a minute. When I come back, we'll get something to eat." James considered asking Sam to give up the candy stick until after he'd had dinner but changed his mind. With that in hand, Sam seemed content to stay in the trading post.

He went out and hurried to the back of the Jenner wagon. The wind blew strong off the prairie, keeping the heat down.

"Ma?" he said.

No answer.

"Ma, I've got the things you needed."

Rustling sounded inside the wagon, and the floorboards creaked.

"Mrs. Lassen went inside."

He looked up in surprise at the young woman who peered down at him. Somehow, he'd got it into his head that a girl whose name sounded like "barrel" would be plump and round. She was just the opposite—slender, though not to say spindly. And her hair! Even though she probably hadn't washed it for weeks, the braid hanging over her shoulder and the wings that swept back at her temples shone a rich brown, with a glint of red in them. James sucked in a breath and made himself look away.

"Here. Ma said you need these."

"Thank you." She bent to take the bottle and the roll of gauze. "Is my brother all right?"

"Sam? He's doing fine. If you don't mind, I'm going to feed him."

"That would be very kind of you."

James stole another glance at her face. Her eyes were brown, or golden, or maybe hazel. When she tilted her head, the color seemed to change.

"Uh, you're welcome."

From within the wagon came a low moan. Beryl nodded and turned away from the opening, and James stepped back.

He saw lots of ladies from the wagon trains, but they only stayed a few minutes in the trading post, and he usually never saw them again. Was this beauty really going to camp in their dooryard for days on end?

Chapter 2

Beryl watched the wagons roll out of their encampment one by one. Her family's wagon sat behind her, in front of the trading post. The mules grazed in a pasture with Mr. Lassen's livestock, and her father lay in a laudanum-induced sleep under the canvas cover.

As she watched the train pull away, Beryl tried to still her heart, but the fearsome future yawned before her. A woman walking beside the last wagon waved. Beryl recognized the faded green calico dress of Mrs. Markham, who had befriended her family over the past two months. Numbly, Beryl lifted a hand in farewell. She would never again see the people in those thirty-six wagons.

Wolf Lassen came from the barn and ambled toward her.

"I'm sorry your friends are leaving you behind, Miss Jenner, but your pa surely couldn't stand to travel any farther."

Beryl blinked back the tears that sprang to her eyes. "I hoped they'd stay a day or two, but Mr. Etherton said they can't."

"Well, the scout said there's another train behind you, and they'll be here soon." Wolf ran a hand over his luxuriant beard. "I think your pa would be more comfortable if we got him out of that wagon and into a proper bed."

"Thank you, sir, but I can't impose on you."

The big man shrugged. "No imposition. There's a little cabin beyond the barn, where I lived the first year I came here. The crew I hired stayed in it while they built the post and the barn."

"You did a good job," Beryl said.

"It kept me busy between emigrant trains. I'd brought three wagons full of goods that first year. Sold nearly all of it and went back for my family that fall. Clara and James and I came out in the spring, and we've been here ever since. They stay winters, and I go to St. Louis for the next season's goods. Anyway, the cabin's empty. You might as well use it."

"I hope Pa will get better and we can go on." Beryl hated the quiver that crept into her voice.

"I hope so, too, miss." His sober eyes told her he knew that Pa wasn't going to get better.

"I. . .couldn't move him by myself."

"James and I will do that. It'll be better for you—it's getting chilly at night now, and you'll have a little stove in there to cook on. Be better for the boy, too."

Beryl knew the truth of that. Samuel had come to the wagon last night, his eyes full of fear, and asked her where he was to sleep. She had reached for his bedroll.

"Curl up under the wagon, Sam. I'll have to sit with Pa again tonight."

"Mrs. Lassen says I can sleep in the trading post if you don't care."

Beryl had hesitated, but she let him go in the end. The wagon that held their father smelled of blood and worse things, and she knew it frightened Sam to see Pa's drawn, white face. She hoped he had slept well—was still sleeping now, carefree and unaware of Pa's pain.

At dusk two days later, the sounds of a large wagon train reached James as he tended to the stock in their corrals—the creak of wheels and harness, the occasional lowing of oxen, and the shouts of the teamsters. A large cloud of dust drifted over the trail and the encampment spot. They'd had no rain for nearly a week, and the travelers would find only a little dry grass for their livestock.

He walked past the barn to the little cabin where they'd settled Mr. Jenner. At his knock, Beryl opened the door and gave him a tired smile.

"I thought I heard the train coming in."

"You did," James said. "I'll give them an hour to get situated and let the dust settle, and then I'll go over and ask if they have any medical help."

"Thank you."

"How is he?"

Beryl glanced over her shoulder. "He's failing."

"I'm sorry. I pray they have someone who can help."

James walked to the camp without much hope. He recognized the scout, Frank Collier, from his previous visits to the trading post. Every year he accompanied a train to Oregon. He had staked out his paint gelding on the edge of the campground nearest the post and was arranging his bedroll.

"Mr. Collier, good to see you," James called out.

The scout lifted his head. "Hello, James. Has your pa got anything left in his storehouse?"

"A few things. We're cleaned out of some though. No sugar or molasses or tea left."

"Well, I reckon we're the last train through," Collier said.

"Do you have a doctor with you? We've got a man here who needs one bad."

"Doc Burgess." Collier eyed him keenly. "Not your pa, I hope?"

"No, it's a feller off the last train. Hunting accident. I'm afraid he's done for, but his daughter is nursing him and hoping."

Ten minutes later, James carried the doctor's satchel as they walked past the trading post to the little cabin beyond the barn. Beryl, when she opened the door, looked so desperate, James almost thought she would seize the doctor by the hand and drag him into the room.

Tears glistened in her soft brown eyes. "Thank you so much for coming, Doctor. I've prayed a man of your skill would be on that train."

Burgess, who was a man of about fifty and graying at the temples, cleared his throat. "Where's the patient?" He gazed about the one dim room of the cabin.

Beryl led him toward the narrow bunk on the east wall.

To James's surprise, his mother stood up from the bedside chair.

"Welcome, Doctor," she said. "I'm Mrs. Lassen. I came over to see how Beryl was doing and to offer to take Samuel to the post while you examine his father."

James saw Sam then, huddled at the foot of the bed, clutching a little wooden animal to his chest and gazing anxiously at the newcomer. He walked over and put a hand on the boy's shoulder.

"Come over to the post with Ma and me, Sam."

"Did you eat yet?" Ma asked Beryl.

"No," Beryl said as Sam climbed down from the bunk, "but you mustn't feel you have to—"

"Nonsense." Ma reached for Sam's hand. "We're neighbors now, if only for a short time. James can bring him back in a half hour, and I'll send a plate over for you."

Beryl's tears spilled over. "Thank you. You've been very kind."

James forced a smile when he gazed down at Sam. "What's that critter you've got?"

"J'raff," Sam said.

"Oh, a giraffe."

"Pa made it," Sam whispered.

"Ah. Very nicely made, too."

The doctor had already moved to the bedside and opened his bag.

"All the folks from the new wagon train will be coming in to trade tomorrow," James said. "You can help me and my pa." He steered Sam toward the door as the doctor turned back the bedclothes.

❧

"Mrs. Lassen sent me," Beryl said with a weary smile.

James and his father were seated at the kitchen table, enjoying their pie and coffee. Perched between them on a stool, Sam also had dessert before him, and half a glass of milk.

"Welcome," Mr. Lassen boomed. "Roast pork today, and plenty of it. I finally butchered a hog."

"How is your father?" James asked.

Beryl had come to dread the question. "He's weaker."

"I'm sorry."

"I could only get him to take a few spoonfuls of broth today." She sighed, not happy with her bleak prospects. "I hoped, after the doctor dressed his wound and left more medicine, that he was doing better, but I fear it's only a matter of time."

Dr. Burgess had told her a week ago not to hope, but on days when her father seemed to rally, Beryl couldn't help thinking the best. In spite of the encouraging signs, her father had had too much damage to his organs, the doctor had said.

Mr. Lassen pushed back his chair. "I'm sorry. Now, young Samuel, are you going to help me load my pack?"

"Yes, sir." Sam scrambled down from the stool.

"You're leaving us soon, then?" Beryl asked.

"In the morning." Mr. Lassen glanced at his son. "I was saying to James I wish I could wait and take you and the boy with me, but I'm usually gone by now. I need to get as far as Independence before a heavy freeze."

"I understand," Beryl said. She had refused to make the final decision of whether she would go on to Oregon, as her father had planned, or back East. Nothing waited for her and Sam back there. Their grandparents were dead. One uncle had been killed in the War between the States, and their two surviving aunts had families of their own to worry about and hadn't stayed in close contact with the Jenners. Returning seemed pointless. But they couldn't continue westward until the spring, when the trains started coming through again. And what would they do once they arrived in Oregon? She had no home, no relatives, no job awaiting her.

She had to think of Sam now. What would be best for him?

When Sam had left the room with Mr. Lassen, Beryl sat down beside James. "I don't know how we'll ever repay your family. It seems certain we must stay the winter."

"Yes, we figured that," he said, brushing his light brown bangs away from his eyes. "But you're not to worry."

"We must pay you something. You're feeding us half our meals, and the firewood alone. . ."

"You'll need your money when you leave here," James said.

"Pa wouldn't want us to be beholden."

James's expression tightened, and his blue eyes flashed. She knew he wouldn't relent. His parents wouldn't either. She had tried with his mother, and Wolf Lassen, though he was a shrewd businessman, seemed to have a tender soul when it came to women and children in distress.

"Perhaps later on you can help Ma with the housework."

He meant after her father died, but neither of them would say that.

"Eat up now." He passed her the platter of sliced pork.

The smell of it alone made her mouth water. "What is all the hammering I've been hearing?" she asked.

"I'm building a new storeroom on the back. Pa hopes to bring back even more supplies than usual this year. There's talk of regular stagecoaches coming through. With more commerce back and forth, he thinks we should increase our inventory."

"I'll do whatever I can to help, once. . ."

James nodded and drained his coffee mug.

"Does anyone come by in winter?" Beryl asked.

"There always seem to be a few military detachments on the move, and in a bad winter the Indians will stop by for a trade. We'll get a few hunters and trappers. And the Mormons go through with their mail. They try to keep it running all winter, and we've had a couple of their men bunk here during snowy times."

"It sounds as though Chiswell Rock is a social beehive."

James laughed. "Not quite. You know it's been a week since we've seen a soul pass by. And by mid-December it's pretty quiet. If the snow is too deep for wagons, we may not see anyone for three months or more. But as soon as the thaw begins, watch out. It starts all over again."

"Do you and your mother feel secure here with your father gone?" This was a fear that Beryl had not allowed herself to examine too closely.

"Now and again we have some trouble, but it gets less every year. More civilized. Pa hopes that someday there'll be a town here." James gazed at her while she took a few bites of the delicious food. "I've wondered about your family."

"Have you?" Beryl asked.

"Ma said your mother passed away. I'm sorry about that."

"Yes, last year. We had a bout of fever back home. I. . .had two sisters, as well. Pa thought that with just the three of us left, we needed a new beginning. He hoped to get a homestead and farm." The memory of her father's excitement while he planned this trip made her falter. All her anticipation was gone now. Would she be able to work past her grief, as Pa had, and plan for a new start?

"I'm sorry." James rose and took his dishes to the worktable. "When Sam is done helping my pa, do you mind if he comes out back with me? He likes to hand me nails and fetch things for me."

"I don't mind. Thank you."

"He might make a carpenter one day." James's smile glinted. For a moment, Beryl's heart stirred, and she envisioned happier times.

"Yes, he might. Pa loved to work with wood. He carved a menagerie for Sam."

James's smile broadened. "I saw the giraffe."

"He has an elephant and a water buffalo, as well. He used to carve by the campfire in the evening." A wave of sadness overtook Beryl. "He'd started a lion, but"—she looked up at him—"I don't suppose he'll ever finish it."

James nodded soberly. "I know this is difficult for you. I wish I could do more."

"You and your parents are a tremendous help. Just keeping Sam occupied lifts such a burden from me. I wouldn't want him in the cabin all the time when I'm tending to Pa. It's good for Sam to get away from it. And I think he's learning from you as well. He's small, but he soaks up all that he sees and hears. I was going to teach him how to read and write when we got to Oregon."

"There will be time for that," James said.

"Yes." Too much time, Beryl thought as she looked down the lonely months and years to come.

Chapter 3

Before mounting his horse to head eastward, James's father took him aside. "The ground's freezing up, boy," Pa said. "Best dig a grave now and be prepared."

James nodded. "I will, Pa."

"I'd stay and help you, but I need to get moving."

"I know. It's all right."

He would do the job tomorrow, without telling Beryl. His mother could keep Samuel occupied at the house while he was gone. James hated to do it. It seemed too much like prophesying Mr. Jenner's death. But Pa was right. The man had no chance, and Beryl would be upset if they had to keep his body until spring for burial.

Pa clapped him on the shoulder. "I'll be back when the snow's off." He strode to the doorstep, where Ma and Sam stood. He kissed Ma and shook hands with Sam. "Take care of your sister, young man."

"Yes, sir," Sam said.

James stood with the boy and Ma and watched Pa ride away. He always hated the day Pa left—but this year was different. He looked down at Sam. "Ready to get to work, pard?"

Sam nodded eagerly.

⁂

Sam entered the cabin quietly, shutting the door behind him, and tiptoed over to Beryl's chair beside Pa's bed.

She smiled at him. "Did you get a lot done today?"

"Uh-huh. We finished the roof."

"The roof? Goodness! You weren't up there, were you?"

"Some."

Beryl stared at him. It hadn't occurred to her to tell James not to let her little brother climb on the trading post roof. "But it's done now?"

Sam nodded, setting his mop of chestnut hair bouncing. If she didn't give him a haircut soon, he'd look like one of the shaggy mountain men who stopped occasionally at the trading post.

"I'm not sure you should be climbing ladders," she said.

Sam made a face. "I was careful. Besides, when I was up there with James, he tied a rope around my middle, just in case."

"Aha." So James wasn't as imprudent as she had first imagined.

Sam gazed at their father. "Is he any better?"

"I'm afraid not."

A month had dragged by, and still Pa lingered, his breathing shallow. His white face barely stirred, but he accepted liquids by the spoonful. Not once since the day he'd been shot had he opened his eyes and looked at Beryl. She wished he would speak to her, just once more, even if only to say good-bye.

"Everyone said he would die," Sam whispered.

The ever-near tears threatened to overwhelm Beryl in her state of fatigue. "He will," she said softly. "It can't be much longer."

"How do you know?"

"He doesn't drink enough to keep him going."

"Are you sure he's alive?"

Sam's voice trembled, and Beryl put her arm around him and pulled him close. "Yes, dearest."

Over the weeks, a subtle change had come into her feelings and her prayers. At first she would have done anything to keep her father alive. Now she knew it was time to let go. It would be best for Pa, and for them, too, if he went peacefully and soon. "When he goes, he'll be at rest." Her voice cracked, and Sam looked at her anxiously.

"Isn't he resting now?"

"Yes, but. . ." She didn't know what else to say, so she hugged him tighter.

Sam put his arms around her neck and squeezed. "What will happen to us?"

"I don't know, but God will provide for us." Beryl had nothing more to offer.

❧

James went to the cabin just after sunset. Beryl's eyes were shadowed with weariness.

"Any change?" he asked.

Beryl shook her head.

"I could sit with him for a while if you'd like to go over and have a cup of tea with Ma."

"I. . .I feel as though I shouldn't leave him." Beryl glanced over her shoulder toward the bed.

"Thought you might need a respite. Besides, Ma's a bit lonesome."

Still she hesitated. She leaned closer and whispered. "I know I said no change, but I don't think he can hold on much longer, James."

"I understand. Let me take Sam for a while?"

"You've had him all day."

"I know. But I could tell him a story."

"He'd like that."

Sam rose from the bench by the stove. James had made sure Beryl had plenty of fuel and water each day. She used to let his mother spell her in her bedside vigil, and occasionally James himself. But for the past week, she had hardly left the cabin.

Sam pulled on his short wool jacket and tugged a knit hat down over his ears.

"I'll bring him back in an hour or so," James promised.

"What will the story be?" Sam asked as they crossed the yard to the house door at the side of the trading post.

"Have you heard the one about Jim Bridger and the grizzly bear?"

"No. Tell that!"

James grinned and pulled the boy into the kitchen. Ma was just taking the stew kettle off the stove.

"I couldn't persuade Beryl to come over, but I expect this little fellow could use a bowl of stew," James said.

Ma smiled and reached for her ladle. "Take your coat off."

"Don't forget about the story," Sam said anxiously to James.

"I won't, and when that's done, maybe Ma will read to us from the Bible."

"I surely will." She ladled out portions for the three of them and put the kettle back on the stove.

An hour later, James sat in Pa's comfortable oak chair by the stove, with Sam sprawled on his lap. Ma sat opposite them in her rocking chair, softly reading about the battle of Jericho. When she finished, she looked over at her son and Sam.

"I'd have thought that exciting tale would keep a little one awake, but he seems to be asleep."

"I'll take him home," James said. "If he doesn't wake up, maybe Beryl will slip away for a few minutes."

"Go," Ma said. "There's still plenty of stew, and hot water for tea."

Samuel roused a bit when James eased his arms into his coat, but he lolled against James's shoulder and allowed himself to be carried to the door. James pulled his mother's shawl around the boy and stepped outside. The cold air didn't wake Sam, and James walked swiftly to the cabin. A few snowflakes drifted down in the moonlight. He tapped gently and opened the cabin door.

Beryl came to meet him with tears streaming down her cheeks.

"The lad's asleep," James said. "Are you all right?"

Beryl put a hand to her throat. "It's Pa. I think he's gone."

James caught his breath. "I'm sorry." He laid Sam on his bunk and stepped to Beryl's side. "May I?"

She nodded, and James pulled off his glove and touched Mr. Jenner's brow then moved his hand to his neck to feel for a pulse. The man lay utterly still, not breathing. After a moment James stepped back.

"I'm so sorry."

Beryl sniffed and then let out a sob.

James fumbled in his pocket for a handkerchief and handed it to her. Beryl snatched it and wiped her face. She started to crumple, and James feared she would hit the floor in a heap. He reached to steady her and found himself holding her in his arms while she cried. Although her weeping distressed him, it was not an unpleasant experience.

He wondered what the etiquette was in a situation like this. If Ma were here, she would cosset the girl and offer words of comfort. He couldn't think of anything to say that he hadn't already said, so he stood awkwardly holding her while she sobbed against the front of his coat. After a minute, she still wept, and he dared to pat her shoulder gently.

Beryl pulled away and looked up at him through her tears. He feared he had offended her, but she grabbed a fistful of his lapel and clung to it, almost desperately.

"James! What will become of us now? I must do for Sam, but I've no idea where to turn. East or west? Throw myself on the mercy of relatives, or forge on into the unknown?"

James gazed down at her, his heart racing. She was beautiful in the dim lamplight, though her eyelids were swollen and her cheeks glistened.

"You needn't worry about that now," he said. "You can't go east or west for several months. There's time to think and to plan, and to wait on God to show you what is best."

She let out a long breath, and her shoulders slumped. "You're right of course. Thank you. I had a moment of panic, and I'm sorry."

"No need to apologize," James said. "I'll send Ma over to help you, but I'd be happy to talk anytime you want. Maybe in a few days, things will look clearer." He wouldn't mind lending a shoulder again either, but he didn't say that. The very thought made him blush.

~

"If you won't move into the house with us, you and young Samuel can at least take your meals there," Clara urged.

"Oh, you mustn't—" Beryl began.

"Nonsense! No use both of us cooking. It's too late for you to move on, so I'm afraid you're stuck with James and me. We can combine our efforts to get the meals. And it will be much easier for you, rather than trying to cook and wash dishes over here."

"All right." Beryl was still numb from her father's death.

Yesterday they'd laid him in the ground wrapped in a blanket, and she had folded his clothing and taken his things out to the wagon. James had rolled the wagon into the barn to protect it from the winter weather. The rest of the Jenner family's supplies were still in boxes and barrels in the wagon, along with all their household goods and Pa's tools. She could take some of their foodstuffs in to share with the Lassens— although, if they ate all their stores this winter, what would they take when they left in the spring? She wasn't sure the money left in Pa's cache would buy enough new supplies to get them either to Oregon or back to New York.

The icy wind snaked about the cabin that night. The firewood James had brought them was consumed before dawn, and Beryl shivered as she dressed and hurried out to the woodpile to get more. Despite her woolen stockings, coat, and muffler, her hands ached when she got back inside, and tiny icicles had formed on her lashes.

When she and Sam arrived at the Lassens' kitchen door for breakfast an hour later, Clara opened it and pulled them inside.

"Quick! Come in and get warm. Why, Sam, your lips are blue!"

"I hadn't planned to come over until noon," Beryl said, "but it was so cold, even though I kept the stove roaring. I was afraid Sam would take ill."

"You were right to come." Clara bustled them toward the warm stove. The big kitchen range radiated warmth, and steam puffed cheerfully from the teakettle's spout. "Sit down. I'll bring you both some tea with plenty of sugar."

Beryl peeled off her gloves and helped Sam unrig. She was determined to do everything in her power to make things easier for Mrs. Lassen. She and Sam would not be a burden.

On a frigid morning four days later, Beryl dashed back toward the cabin to retrieve her workbag and slipped on the slick surface in the barnyard. Her bruises weren't serious, but they made her think. She could as easily have broken her leg.

She could see the sense of moving into the trading post. The Lassens were burning coal now, as wood was scarce on the plains. They would burn less fuel if she and Sam moved into the post. They would be safer, especially if the brutal cold lasted.

When she finally relented, James set up two army cots in the trading room. The small stove in the middle of the room put out enough heat to take the chill off, but they wouldn't keep this room as warm as the kitchen. He had hung a blanket so that at night they could curtain off two-thirds of the room—everything but the counter and doors to the storeroom and family quarters.

"I was thinking, you could take my room over the kitchen," James said, eyeing her cautiously.

"Absolutely not," Beryl said. "I'll stay out here with Sam. It's bad enough you're saddled with us for the winter. I won't turn you out of your room."

"All right then."

She was glad he hadn't argued. The situation was awkward enough as it was.

"I'm very grateful for your kindness," she said in a gentler tone.

James smiled. "We don't mind."

His mother appeared in the doorway. "Did you bring everything you'll need?"

"The necessities," Beryl said. "When it gets warmer, I'll go back for the rest of our things and the extra food supplies that are in the wagon."

Mrs. Lassen nodded. "No doubt this cold snap will lift soon. For now, just make yourselves comfortable." She smiled at Beryl. "I hope you'll spend a great deal of your time with us. It's a treat to have another woman here in December."

"Thank you," Beryl said.

"And we've got plenty of blankets and such. Anything that will make you more comfortable in here, just speak up."

Mrs. Lassen's generosity surprised Beryl. The entire family seemed to be kind-hearted and selfless, though practical. Before the wagons had reached Chiswell Rock, she had been told that Mr. Lassen was a sharp bargainer and prices would be high. But that also made sense, since he went to such trouble and expense to stock his post. He held back what his family needed, and he drove a hard bargain with his customers, yet he hadn't complained when his wife and son opened their doors to her and Sam.

"Where do I sleep?" Sam asked, eyeing the two beds.

"You can pick," Beryl replied.

"Where's the mattress?"

She chuckled. "You lie on the canvas without any mattress. If you don't like it, we can fetch your little featherbed when the weather's not so bad." Beryl glanced at James and his mother. They were both smiling. Maybe this arrangement would be good for all of them and they would enjoy having a child in the house.

☙

During the summer and fall, Wolf had accepted several mules and ox teams in trade from emigrants and hoped to sell them next summer at a profit. James often took Sam with him to the barn and the corrals to care for them. The four-year-old asked questions that kept James thinking while he worked, but more than that, Sam made him laugh.

They spent the greater part of the long, cold days inside with James's mother and Beryl in the close confinement of the family's kitchen-sitting room and the storage and trading rooms. James got to know Beryl more slowly than Sam, but he liked what he found in her.

Before Christmas, he and Sam came in from their morning chores to find the two women hard at work in the storage room. His mother counted items in the stockpiled merchandise, and Beryl wrote down her totals.

"Taking inventory without me?" James asked, stooping to undo Sam's coat buttons for him.

"I thought I might as well start," Ma said. "Beryl offered to help, and I couldn't say no."

"My hands prickle," Sam said.

Beryl turned to him with a frown. "You'll be all right in a few minutes, but it may hurt for a while. That happens when you get very cold."

"I'll help him." James led Sam into the kitchen and sat him down on a low stool just out of reach of the ticking stove.

"Ma's got hot water in the kettle. Would you like some tea and sugar?"

Sam nodded eagerly. James warmed his own hands for a minute and then set about preparing a pot of hot tea. He wished they had milk to put in it for the boy, but their only milk cow had gone dry a week earlier, and she wouldn't produce again until she calved in the spring. But Sam seemed healthy enough, and he stayed active as much as possible under the circumstances.

James set Sam's tin cup before him. "Easy now. That's pretty hot." He slid his own mug before his chair and sat down.

"Will your ma read to us tonight?" Sam asked, gazing at him wistfully over the rim of his steaming cup.

"Probably. One of us usually reads from the Bible in the evening."

"My ma used to read to us, too."

"You remember that?" James asked. He had thought the boy was too young to have much memory of his mother.

Sam nodded soberly. "And Ruby and Pearl."

"Who are they?"

"My sisters." Sam's features drooped.

"I'm sorry," James said. "Beryl told me you had sisters who died."

Sam's eyes were filled with tears.

"Aw, Sammy, I didn't mean to make you sad."

"It's not your fault," Beryl said from the doorway. She walked over and placed her hand lovingly on Sam's shoulder. "I'm afraid we both get mournful when we think about Ma and the girls, and now Pa."

"That's understandable," James said.

His mother came in behind Beryl, carrying the inventory list and smiling. "Well, there. We've done all along the west wall. It's a good start."

"Would you like some tea?" James asked, rising. "I made a whole pot, and Sam and I haven't drunk half of it."

The ladies sat down, and James brought cups for them.

"Such whimsical names," his mother said. "Ruby, Pearl, and Beryl."

"Our mother's name was Coral," Beryl said with a chuckle. "Pa used to tease her and say that if Sam had been a girl, she'd have named him Emerald."

Sam made a face. "I'm sure glad I'm not a jewel."

They all laughed.

"Sam has requested that we read tonight," James said.

His mother smiled at the boy. "A fitting occupation on a winter's evening. And James, with Christmas so close, perhaps after our scripture reading, you might get out the Dickens?"

Sam's eyes widened, and James chuckled.

"She's talking about a writer, Sam. Charles Dickens. Ever hear of him?"

Sam shook his head.

"He's an English gent, and he wrote a very nice Christmas story a few years back."

His mother turned to Beryl. "Are you familiar with the story?"

"I've heard of it, but I've never had the pleasure of reading it."

"It's a moral tale, but it does have ghosts in it. Of course, they could be dreams. But it's all very uplifting. I don't think it would be too scary for Samuel."

Beryl hesitated then said, "I'll leave it to your judgment, since you know the tale."

That evening they all settled by the open hearth for their time of devotion. Afterward Ma sat at her quilting frame, and Beryl took the chair on the other side to help her.

"This is a lovely pattern." Beryl gazed at the multicolored pieces of calico that formed an intricate geometric design. "I've never started a project so ambitious, but maybe once we're settled. . .somewhere."

"I started this last winter," Ma said. "I appreciate you helping me get it done. I'll be glad when it's finished, and I expect James will be happy not to have to walk around the frame for a while."

"I don't mind," James said. He lifted the slender volume by Dickens from the shelf of three dozen books his parents had collected.

"We haven't many books, but you're welcome to borrow any you please," he said to Beryl.

"Thank you! The only one we brought with us is the Bible. Pa said books were too heavy to haul over the mountains."

"Most of ours came from settlers looking to lighten their loads," Ma said.

James sat down on the settee with Sam, and the boy crowded close, looking on eagerly as James opened the book. He turned to the first page and began to read as the women continued their stitching.

Sam's interest was immediately caught by the tale. James wondered if he understood it all, but he didn't pause to make explanations. After a few minutes, Sam leaned against his arm. James wondered if he'd fallen asleep, but when he paused a few minutes later, the boy said softly, "Don't stop."

James realized he was far from asleep. However, the story was a long one, and he wondered if he could get through it all in one sitting.

A half hour later, he stopped reading at the end of a section and looked down at Sam. The boy was still wide awake.

"I was thinking we ought to continue this tomorrow evening," James said. "I'm going hoarse."

"Oh, please," Sam cried. "I need to know what happens to Tiny Tim."

Beryl smiled. "I could take over the reading if you don't mind, James. I'm afraid I wouldn't sleep either, not knowing the outcome."

James turned the book over to her and let Sam curl up in the curve of his arm. The boy was yawning and his eyes drooping when Beryl at last finished the story.

"It's very late," Ma said gently, sliding her needle into the fabric where she could leave it safely for the night. "This was a wonderful evening, but I fear we'll all sleep late in the morning."

"Does it matter?" James asked.

Ma chuckled. "I suppose not. Last time I looked outside, it was snowing. I don't think we'll have any early callers."

Chapter 4

Beryl still felt a bit awkward in the household, as though she and Samuel had forced themselves on the Lassens, but Mrs. Lassen and James made an effort to bring them into the family circle. In return, Beryl helped with the meals, cleaning, and finishing the inventory of supplies. In the evenings, they continued to quilt.

James kept working on the added storeroom, and Samuel spent many hours helping him. A week before Christmas, the room was closed in, and James was finishing the inside. Beryl appreciated the patience he showed her brother as he assigned him small tasks and showed him how to use tools correctly.

At supper one evening, Beryl watched Sam for signs of fatigue. He had helped James for several hours, including an expedition to the barn and corrals. Although the temperatures were slightly milder now, the boy looked worn-out.

"I think it's early to bed with you tonight, Sam," she said as she helped Mrs. Lassen clear the table.

"No, I want to read to you," Sam said.

Beryl eyed him closely. While she had taught Sam his letters and some rudimentary arithmetic on their journey over the summer, she knew that he couldn't read. What was he thinking?

"What are you going to read?" James asked.

A Christmas Carol.

"I see." James looked at Beryl, his light brown eyebrows arched. "Well, let's get the dishes done, and we'll hear you."

"I'll help your mother," Beryl said. "You two go on. We'll only be a few minutes."

When she and Clara had put away the last plate, James and Sam were seated on the settee with the book resting on Sam's lap. Beryl and Clara sat down in their chairs. The quilt was finished, and they each took handwork from their workbags.

Sam said solemnly, "Are you ready?"

"I am," Clara said.

"Oh yes," Beryl replied.

James nodded. "And I can hardly wait."

Sam carefully turned the pages to the opening of the story.

" 'Marley was dead, to begin with,' " he said gravely in his sweet, childish tones. " 'There was no doubt about that. The register of his burial was signed by the clergyman, the undertaker, and the chief mourner. Scrooge signed it, and Scrooge's name was good for anything he put his hand to. Old Marley was dead as a doornail.' "

"Why, that's amazing," Mrs. Lassen said. "Samuel, I had no idea you could read so well."

"Me either," James said. "He did miss a few words, but still. . ."

"Such advanced material for one so young," his mother added.

Beryl smiled. "'Fess up, Sammy." She had noted that Sam did keep his eyes on the words, and he had indeed skipped over a couple of bits.

Sam's impish mouth quirked upward. "I did good though, didn't I?"

"You did very well." Beryl looked at James and his mother. "Sam has an extraordinary memory. I've no doubt he could recite the whole thing, though he might miss some details here and there. Why don't you 'read' a bit more, Sam?"

He grinned and continued with the story. When he had recited a few paragraphs, James nudged him.

"Turn the page now."

Sam carefully turned one leaf in the book without stopping his recitation. When he reached the end of another paragraph, James touched his shoulder, and the boy paused.

"It's like with the tools," James said slowly. "He never forgot any instructions I gave him. And I only needed to show him once where to fetch an item for the customers, and he would always go right to it after that."

Beryl nodded. "Yes, it's remarkable. Pa said it was a gift from God. But he's not truly reading."

"Any boy with a memory like that could learn to read in no time," Mrs. Lassen said, pausing in her knitting and eyeing Sam with wonder.

"You're right," Beryl said. "This winter may be the perfect time to attend to Sam's lessons. He can already recite the alphabet."

James shook his head. "I still can't believe it. He heard the story only once, yet he sounds as smooth as any adult reading it."

Beryl chuckled. "It may interest you to know that over the past few weeks, Sam has related several stories to me—ones you told him."

"Really?" James shot the boy a glance and turned back to her.

"Oh yes," Beryl said. "There were several about King Arthur and his knights, and a couple of fairy tales, and one about your grandfather the sea captain that I particularly liked."

James smiled in delight. "He told you all that?"

"Yes. When we were staying in the cabin and I tended Pa all day, Sam would come back from working with you and tell me everything he'd done that day, and probably every word you spoke to him."

"That's disconcerting," James said. "I shall have to be careful what I say."

Beryl laughed and said to his mother, "I can attest to the fact that your son has never said a cross word to Sam or let any unsavory word fall from his lips in Sam's hearing."

"That's a comfort for any mother to hear," Mrs. Lassen said.

"It was a comfort to me, too," Beryl said. "All those long, anxious days, sitting with Pa and waiting for the inevitable, Sam's stories—your stories, James—gave me something new to think about. Stories I can carry with me for the rest of my life and think of again. I thank you for that."

James nodded and looked away, his cheeks flushing slightly. "I've enjoyed telling them and having Sam with me."

Beryl decided to drop the subject. She hadn't intended to embarrass him. She suspected the young man felt a bit of reserve that he apparently dropped when with Sam. That was another gift they had received here—friendship.

"So now what?" James asked. "Shall we continue with the tale?"

"I really think Sam ought to retire," Beryl said. "He was up late last night, and he worked hard with you today." She caught Sam in the act of yawning as she spoke, and she rose. "Come, Sam. Say good night."

Without hesitation, Sam reached up to hug James, who caught the book that slid precariously off the boy's lap. James returned the squeeze and set Sam on the floor.

"There you go, pard. Say good night to Ma now."

Sam toddled over to Mrs. Lassen's chair. "Good night, ma'am."

She leaned over and kissed his cheek. "Good night, Sam. Thank you for the story."

Sam beamed and took Beryl's hand.

✍

The next evening, James didn't read to them but immersed himself in his father's business ledgers. Each winter, after the inventory was taken, he totaled the year's accounts and wrote a report for his father so that Wolf could see at a glance on his return how the trading post was doing.

Beryl and his mother sat once more doing their needlework by lamplight, while Sam played on the rag rug with the small wooden figures his father had carved.

"When we lived in St. Louis, we made more of Christmas," Ma said.

Beryl looked up from her mending. "We always had a tree."

"I should have asked James to get one."

"It would take quite an effort to get one in this spot, wouldn't it?" Beryl had seen few trees during her final weeks on the wagon train, and most of those had been willows or cottonwoods. She couldn't remember when she had last seen an evergreen.

James's pencil was getting dull, and he took his penknife from his pocket to sharpen it. Sam came over and stood at his knee, watching. James proceeded, being careful not to cut toward Sam. When the pencil had a sufficiently sharp point, he put the knife away and looked over at the ladies.

"It's a bit late now—tomorrow is Christmas Day. I wish we'd thought of it earlier."

"It was so cold," his mother said.

"Yes, and I doubt Sam even remembers the tree," Beryl added. "We didn't have one last year, after Ma and the girls had died. We weren't feeling much like celebrating.

James reflected that Sam would have been two and a half the Christmas before that.

"How about it, Sam?" he asked. "Do you recall having a Christmas tree at your house?"

Sam nodded slowly. "There were snowflakes Mama made."

"Snowflakes?" James glanced at Beryl.

She smiled and her eyes misted. "That's right. My mother crocheted them from twine. I packed them in a box, since they didn't take much space. Thirty of them, I counted. Sam, when we get to Oregon—or back to New York—we'll get them out again."

"Aren't we going to Oregon?" Sam trotted to his sister's side and stared at her earnestly. "Pa said we were going to Oregon."

"I know." Beryl put her arm around his shoulders. "That was our plan, but we had Pa with us then, and he would have built us a house in Oregon or found one to buy. I'm not sure what we'll do now."

The little boy gazed at her for a long moment. "Does God know?"

Beryl smiled. "Of course He does. God knows everything, including where we will spend Christmas next year. Every day I ask Him to make me wise and show me what we should do."

"I'll pray, too."

"Thank you, Sam."

He seemed satisfied and went back to his toy animals. James watched him for a moment. If only he could accept hard things in life as easily as Sam did. Was it only his youth? The boy was so innocent he couldn't understand the agony of the decision for Beryl. Yet James felt it was more than that.

He turned back to the ledger and sat for a moment, staring at, but not seeing, the neat columns of figures.

Father in heaven, he prayed silently, *give me the trust that Sam has.* In that moment, he realized something else. Every year, he and Ma had to trust God to bring his father safely back to them. That was an understood part of his life. But Sam and Beryl's future was a new concern. How he would miss them when they left! Sam, his faithful little helper, the winsome boy with the uncanny memory. . .

He gazed across the room at Beryl. Patiently she wove her needle in and out as she mended the heel of a small sock. She was lovely, but he had learned that she was also beautiful inside. He had observed her gentleness, her loyalty, and her diligence. James was beginning to think of her presence in his home as right and normal. Come spring, whether she headed east or west, he would be bereft.

Chapter 5

On Christmas Day, Beryl rose long before Sam awoke and went to the kitchen. James's mother was building up the fire in the range.

"Merry Christmas, Mrs. Lassen."

She turned and smiled at Beryl. "Merry Christmas to you, dear. But won't you call me Clara?"

"Thank you, I will." Beryl's gaze landed on a large ham resting on the worktable. "Oh my! We are in for a feast."

"Yes, my husband always butchers a hog before he leaves. I fix one ham at Christmas, though with only James and me here most years, it seems a bit pretentious."

"When do you cook the second one?"

"The day after Mr. Lassen gets home. That is always a time for celebration."

"Yes," Beryl said, tying on her apron. "Now, what shall I do for you?

"While the oven heats, you can peel the vegetables, and I'll set the bread dough. And then, once the ham's in the oven, we can work on pies."

The festive dinner tasted wonderful but was made even better by their camaraderie. Afterward, Clara suggested they all sit down.

"It's time to present the Christmas gifts," she said.

An uneasiness crept over Beryl. She had nothing to give her generous hosts. Would they do even more for her and Sam that she could not repay?

James brought a wooden box from his bedroom and set it down next to his mother's rocking chair. Out of it he pulled a book.

"This is my gift to you, Ma."

She took the book from him. "*Poems of Lord Byron.* Thank you, James. So very thoughtful, and we can enjoy it together in the evenings."

James smiled. "I thought you'd like it. The rest of these things are from Pa. He brought them last spring and asked me to stash them away for you."

"What? All this?" Clara peered into the box. "Besides the things he gave me when he came home?"

James looked so happy in that moment that Beryl wished every day was Christmas. He seemed most joyful when he was able to do something for someone else.

Clara took the items from the box one by one and showed them to Sam and Beryl. A new teakettle, shining bright; a dress length of wine-colored checked silk; four skeins of soft, pearl-hued wool; a set of bone knitting needles; and a cookbook.

"New recipes!" Clara glanced inside the book and then set it aside. "I can't believe you've hid all this since May."

"You never look under my bunk," James said.

"That's true. You're a tidy young man, and I never see the need of cleaning your chamber." Clara looked over the bounty of her gifts and sighed. "Your father is a kind and generous man."

"He is," James agreed.

"Well, here is my gift to you. I wrapped it in brown paper so you wouldn't see it."

James took the package and untied the string. Inside were a new shirt and a set of leather reins.

"Your father said you needed new reins," Clara said.

James nodded in satisfaction. "He's right. These will last a good, long time." He folded the paper carefully so they could use it again in the trading post.

Clara stood. "And now, Beryl, my dear, James and I would like to give you this."

She walked to the far end of the room where the quilt they had worked on for the last few weeks lay folded on a bench. As Clara gathered it into her arms, Beryl gasped. Surely she didn't mean to give away the quilt she had worked on so long.

A smile wreathed the hostess's face as she carried the quilt to Beryl. "With love, my dear."

Beryl rose and laid a hand on the bright patchwork. "You can't! Surely you don't mean it."

"I do."

"But. . ." Beryl glanced at James, but he was grinning, too. "Sam and I have nothing to give you, and you've put so much work into this." Tears welled in her eyes.

"My dear," Clara said, "you have no idea how lonely I've been the past three winters while Wolf went away for supplies. And poor James, without a soul to speak to but me and the livestock for nearly half the year. While we love each other, your presence has been a gift. Although you've had sadness here, I hope you'll remember us with warmth."

"Oh, I will," Beryl said earnestly.

"Just talking to you is satisfying," Clara went on, "but watching young Sam learn new things has been pure joy. The past few weeks have flown, and I hope the rest of the winter will be as enjoyable."

Beryl threw her arms around Clara. "Thank you so much." Through her tears, she looked at James and nodded to him, hoping he knew he was included, as she didn't think she could say another word.

She took the quilt from Clara and sat down with it on her lap. Sam came over and ran a finger over a line where a blue strip met a yellow block. Beryl cleared her throat. "Isn't it lovely, Sam? This will be so nice and warm." She glanced anxiously at Clara. "But don't you need it?"

Clara shook her head. "I quilt in the winter to keep busy and to save any scraps from going to waste. In the storeroom, we have more blankets than we'll ever use, and this is my fifth scrap quilt since we've been here. I'll be pleased if you can use it."

"I'll treasure it always," Beryl said.

"And Samuel, this is my gift to you." James walked over to the boy, carrying a ledger, and placed it in Sam's hands. He knelt down so they were eye to eye. "It's full of stories. I wrote down every one I could remember—the ones I've told you and a few you've never heard. This way you can read them after you leave here, as a remembrance of your time with us."

"Lovely," Beryl said.

Instead of voicing his thanks, Sam tumbled into James's arms, with the precious book between them. "It's the nicest present I ever got," Sam said. "I want to learn to read it for myself."

"I shall teach you," Beryl said.

Sam turned to look into James's eyes again. "Thank you."

James drew him close for another squeeze and then let him go. "You're very welcome. Now I'd better bring in some more coal."

A week later as James and Sam prepared to go out and tend the stock, Beryl reached for her cloak. "May I go with you to the barn?"

"Of course." James was always glad for Beryl's company. "Do you want to see the animals?"

"I'd like that," she said, "but I also thought it might be a good day to get some things from our wagon. I want to start Sam's lessons, so we'll need the slate and a few other things."

James nodded. "If you're lacking anything we can supply, let me know."

James had shoveled a path through the snow to the barn, and the banks on each side were nearly to Sam's chin. The boy ran ahead, and Beryl followed with James. The cattle and horses had trampled and dirtied the snow in the corrals, but on the other side of the path, the sun glittered off the unbroken expanse of white.

"I haven't played in the snow in years," Beryl said, "but this scene makes me want to."

James laughed. "I have a sled I haul wood on. Perhaps we can take Sam over to the hill beyond the encampment this afternoon."

"I'd like that, and Sam would adore it." Beryl gazed off toward the deserted camp and sobered. "He's such a pensive child. I know Pa's death has hit him hard, and I'd like to give him any scrap of pleasure I can."

James glanced up at the sun. "It's a fine day. Let's do it."

In the barn, he led her to where the Jenner wagon was parked.

"You've got to work around this all winter," she noted.

"It's all right. Pa made this place big enough so a freight wagon could be driven inside if need be. Indians, you know, or severe weather." James held out a hand. Beryl put her gloved hand in his and climbed to the wagon seat. "I'll light a lantern for you," he said. "Sam, go ahead and feed the horses and Daisy."

They kept the saddle horses and the milk cow inside during the winter, but the draft animals had to make do in the pasture or corrals except for during the most extreme weather. If a blizzard was coming or if the temperature dropped to bitter cold, James would drive them all inside to shuffle about in the barn throughout the night. He hated to do that, however, because as they tried to get at the feed, they knocked down things that hung on the walls and left a mess on the floor.

When he took the lantern to the wagon, Beryl was rummaging inside a large wooden box.

"Oh, thank you. You're right—I could barely see a thing in here." She reached for the lantern and hung it on a hook on one of the bows. "James, I don't want to embarrass you, but I've been thinking about Pa's clothes. It will do me no good to take them with me. Could you possibly use them? I don't think he was as tall as you, so his trousers mightn't fit. . ."

He gazed into her eyes. "I. . .I can take a look. And anything I can't use, we could put in the trading post for you. Sometimes people who come through need new clothing or boots or a coat."

"That makes sense. I'll set them aside, and whatever you can't wear can go in your inventory. I'd suggest your father could use some of it, but he's such a huge man. . ."

James laughed. "Yes, he always has trouble finding boots large enough."

"James," Sam called from near the horse stalls, "I've fed them all. Are we giving the mules some hay today?"

"I'll be right there," James replied. He smiled at Beryl. "We'll be a few minutes."

"I'll be fine."

Her cheeks were touched with rose in spite of the chill in the barn. With her reddish-brown hair spilling out of her hood and her eyes gleaming with reflected lantern light, James thought she was the most beautiful woman who had ever passed through Chiswell Rock. He realized he was staring and cleared his throat.

"Right. See you soon."

Chapter 6

B eryl made Sam's schooling her biggest project for the winter, and Clara joined in, listening to Sam recite and setting him small problems in arithmetic while she cooked or sat with her stitching. Even James took a hand, though he wouldn't have called it teaching. Every time he and Sam were in the storeroom or the new addition, James answered Sam's many questions and asked a few of his own.

"Look, Sam," Beryl heard him say one day, "I'm making these bins for the hardware, and I want twenty. I've got twelve so far. How many more do we need?"

After a moment's silence, Beryl thought Sam was stumped. She peeked around the door frame. Sam was contemplating the wooden bins. He walked in front of them, silently touching each one. At the end of the workbench he stopped and turned, frowning.

"Eight?"

James grinned. "I believe you're right. Eight more it is."

By mid-February, Sam was reading well from the primer Beryl had packed, as well as from some passages of scripture and the Lassens' books. He could write all his letters on the slate and was learning to spell out words.

"I fear his coordination is lacking," Beryl told Clara one morning as she swept the floor and Clara kneaded the week's bread dough.

"Ah, that's a boy for you. Great at running and throwing and chasing, but not so good at fine work. James was that way, too. Give him time."

"I expect you're right." Beryl stood the broom in the corner and untied her apron. "He can write his name legibly, and that's something for just-turned-five."

"It is indeed. James turned out all right. He keeps neat ledgers now."

Beryl smiled. "Sam's begun puzzling out the stories James wrote for him. I offered to read one to him yesterday, but he turned me down. He says he wants to read them for himself."

"Good for him," Clara said. "If he wants to read badly enough, that will spur him on in his studies."

Four cavalry troopers stopped by that afternoon on their way from Fort Laramie to Fort Hall. James invited them to have coffee in the warm kitchen while his mother and Beryl prepared a hot meal for them. Noontime was long past, but Clara didn't seem to mind the extra work.

"We like to have their presence known," she told Beryl as she fried some potatoes and bacon. Beryl mixed a double batch of biscuits. When they were in the oven, she helped Clara throw together a dried apple cobbler.

"The first year we came, we had renegade Indians stealing our stock. They took supplies and tools from the barn. That's why we lock everything up at night, even the barn. Back then we had to keep the animals inside or the corral would be empty in the morning."

"How did you stand it?" Beryl asked.

"It wasn't pleasant, though I must say the Indians never harmed us. I was more afraid of the trappers who would come in and demand liquor. Of course we don't stock it, but they could make quite a ruckus anyway when they were disappointed."

A few minutes later, they carried plates in to the soldiers. Sam was watching them carefully from his corner by the wood box, while James sat with the visitors to get the latest news.

"Ma," James said eagerly, "the sergeant brought along an Independence newspaper. He's letting us keep it until he passes back through."

"How kind of you." Clara eyed the folded newspaper in James's hand with anticipation. Beryl wondered at her restraint. Even she had the urge to snatch it from James's grasp and read every word.

"Seeing much traffic over the road?" the sergeant asked James.

"Hardly any the past two months," James said. "The snow kept most folks away, I'm sure."

"It were bad this year," said one of the troopers. "We kept close to quarters last month."

"But it looks like we're in for a thaw at last," the sergeant said. He took a big bite of a biscuit. "Mmm! Ma'am, these are right tasty."

"Why thank you," Clara said, "but Miss Jenner prepared those."

Beryl smiled. "I only assisted Mrs. Lassen. She's the real cook."

Clara took their praise with good nature and kept the coffee flowing. When she brought out dishes of apple cobbler a few minutes later, the compliments multiplied.

At last the sergeant wiped his lips with his kerchief and sighed. "We ought to move along or we won't reach our next stop before dark. Mrs. Lassen, Miss Jenner, this was a real treat. And James, thank you for your hospitality."

"Anytime," James said.

The troopers retrieved their mounts from the corral and departed with a flurry of hoofbeats and creaking leather.

"I hope he's right and we'll have spring soon," Clara said as they stood waving to the soldiers. The air outside was well above freezing, and the icicles on the trading post's eaves dripped steadily.

"I expect we'll see a few trappers soon, bringing their furs in to sell," James said.

His mother smiled. "If spring comes early, maybe your father will return early."

Sam went into the curtained-off sleeping area. A moment later, he emerged with his storybook ledger in his arms.

"Going to read some more?" Beryl asked. Sam was beginning to puzzle out James's handwriting, but occasionally he asked her to help him.

He nodded gravely. "I'm going to make it last. When I finish the first story, I won't read any more until Sunday. If I read one story a week, how long will it last?"

"Let's see." Beryl took the book from him and paged through it. "There are twelve stories. Twelve weeks is about three months. It should last you until May, I think."

"May. That's summer." Sam's eyes opened wide.

"It's late spring. May is when we left Missouri last year. What's the first story about?"

"It's a boy named Bob who is a working on a ship. He's the cabin boy. The ship's mast broke, and they're hoping someone will come and help them."

"That sounds exciting."

"He's climbing up to the crow's nest to see if he can wave a signal flag at another ship."

Beryl ruffled his hair and let him go to the kitchen. She hoped that by the time Sam finished reading all the stories, they would be on their way to a new home.

◌∾

The weather broke the last week in February, and by the middle of March a trickle of riders came over the trail. They all stopped at Chiswell Rock, and short letters from Wolf began to arrive, updating them on his progress in outfitting his freight wagons and securing merchandise.

On March 12, a detachment of soldiers came through from Fort Laramie and brought news written on February 16. Wolf planned to leave St. Louis by the end of the next week, barring heavy rains. Too much water would make the roads impassable for his heavily loaded wagons. James and his mother prayed for dry weather.

Coming with five big freight wagons full of goods for the trading post, Wolf would probably need at least eight weeks to get to Chiswell Rock. He would push his teams hard, but he always started out with stout, fit animals and would travel farther each day than the typical emigrant train did.

At the end of March, James began riding east each morning to a high outcropping of rock. From there he could see several miles along the trail. Often he met scouts and trappers along the way. Occasional mail riders came through, either troopers for the army or a small group of Mormon men carrying news to their settlement in Deseret.

Parts of the trail were still too muddy for wagons. The new grass began to come in, and the prairie greened up. Wolf would need grazing for his mule teams—ten pair to pull each wagon—as he couldn't carry enough feed to sustain them the entire way. Once they arrived at Chiswell Rock, Wolf would begin fattening them up to be sold to travelers who needed replacement animals.

On April 2, James got the first word of his father's outfit on the road. A scout riding through to the Columbia River had passed him a week earlier.

As he sat on his horse looking eastward one morning three weeks later, James counted the days in his mind. It was really too early to look for Pa yet, but he couldn't stop himself from going each day. His father should be nearly across Nebraska by now. But there were still many miles of rough trail between him and home. He turned and walked his horse carefully down off the bluff then let the gelding lope toward home.

Beryl was out in the side yard hanging wet clothing on the line, with Samuel beside her, handing her clothespins.

"See anything?" Beryl called as James dismounted.

"A couple of riders heading this way, but nothing substantial enough for Pa's outfit."

"He'll be here soon."

James shrugged. "I hope so. But one year it was the end of May before he got through."

"That must have been a late spring," Beryl said. "It's warm now. He'll come."

"I expect you're right." James led his horse toward the barn.

Sam trotted after him. "James! Can I help with the saddle?"

"Sure." James smiled. Sam wouldn't be big enough to saddle a horse by himself for quite some time, but with some assistance, he could feel he was doing nearly a man's job.

He wondered if Beryl was any closer to settling her burning question—east or west? Could she make a life for herself and Sam in Oregon? Or should they join someone going back East? People headed that way would soon be coming through, James had assured her. Would she have a better chance in New York, relying on the goodwill and contacts her distant relatives could share?

⁊

James rode off again the next morning, and Beryl wished she could go with him. Perhaps tomorrow she would ask him if he could saddle one of the mules for her. Though the air was cold again this morning, that wouldn't last long. Spring was here, and she longed for the freedom of the trail and the expanse of the prairie around her. Not that she didn't appreciate the snug home inside the trading post. Indeed, Clara's warm kitchen had become her favorite refuge.

Beryl hauled in a deep breath. She wished she didn't have to make the decision that would determine her future and Sam's. In her daydreams, a little town sprang up around the trading post at Chiswell Rock, and she was able to eke out sustenance for herself and Sam as a seamstress. Her stitching was more than adequate, and they wouldn't need much.

She sighed and turned to fill the dishpan. That would never happen.

After the breakfast dishes were done, she sat down with Sam at the table to give him his lessons. Clara settled in her rocker to crochet an edge on a red wool blanket and listen.

Not ten minutes into their arithmetic lesson, the door on the front of the trading post opened, and heavy, booted feet clumped across the board floor. Beryl's heart jerked, and Sam whirled around to stare at her in question.

"Hey! Lassen, you here?" called a deep voice.

Clara gasped and jumped out of her chair. "Stay here, Beryl. It's one of those trappers, I'm sure. I'll tell him he'll have to wait until James can help him."

Beryl laid a hand on Sam's sleeve and said, "Shh." She listened to Clara's muffled voice as she greeted her visitor.

"We h'ain't got time to wait," the booming man declared.

"Yeah," said another man, "we got to get on the trail."

Beryl stood and tiptoed to the kitchen door.

"Well, bring in your furs," Clara said. "James will likely be home by the time you unload your packs."

"How about getting us a bottle first?" the deep voice said. Beryl peeked out into the trading room. The bearded man was almost as big as Wolf Lassen. His long hair and steely eyes made her shudder.

Sam had left his seat and was halfway across the room.

"What's going on?" he whispered.

"There are two men, and we need James. I don't suppose he's on his way back yet."

Sam crept toward her, but Beryl held out her arm, stiff as a broom handle. "Stay back. I don't want them to see you."

Sam's mouth closed in a scowl too grim for his childish features.

"You must have a bottle or two stashed away," one of the men declared.

"No, we don't," Clara said.

"Your man must like a nip now and then."

"Don't make us go all the way to Fort Laramie for a taste of liquor," the second man snarled.

The voices grew louder as they moved closer. The two trappers had advanced into the storage room. The big man shoved Clara before him as she cried, "We have none, I tell you."

"Well, you must have some foodstuffs in the house. Come on now. We're hungry."

"We haven't had a woman-cooked meal in months," the second man said. "What do you got?"

Clara stumbled toward her, and Beryl caught her in her arms. She frowned at the burly men.

"What is the meaning of this? You mustn't treat Mrs. Lassen so."

"Oho!" The big man looked Beryl up and down and grinned at his friend. "We got a bonus, Burke!"

"Looky there." The second man ogled Beryl.

She wanted to flee, but she had nowhere to hide. She backed into the kitchen, pulling Clara with her. A quick glance behind her to locate Sam gave her no assurance. He was out of sight, but where? She wanted to know he was safely out of harm's way. Probably he had scooted under the table into the shadows. She avoided looking toward the most likely hiding place.

Clara turned toward the men and pulled herself to her full height. "You rascals calm down! We have some corn bread left from breakfast and a bit of venison stew."

"Venison?" The one called Burke curled his lip. "We been eatin' venison all winter."

"Ah, but did your stew have carrots and turnips and onions in it?" Clara asked in an almost cordial tone.

"Well, no," Burke admitted.

"I've got canned peaches, too." Though a bruise was forming on her cheek, Clara stayed amazingly calm.

"Bring it on!" The big man strode toward the kitchen range. He held his hands toward it.

"I'll have to heat up the stew," Clara said. She nodded at Beryl. "Can you get it from the cold cupboard?"

Beryl nodded and opened the door to the woodshed at the back of the kitchen. She scurried out and shut the door behind her so they wouldn't lose heat from inside. Clara used a plain wooden cupboard in the woodshed during cool weather. It kept the vermin out, and any food she put there stayed cold.

As Beryl hurried toward the cupboard, a blast of cold air hit her. The back door, leading outside, was open a few inches. She quickly pulled it shut. Had Sam sneaked out the back way? She hoped he was hiding in the barn and would keep safe from these rowdy men. No telling what they would do. Her best hope, as well as Clara's, was to feed them well and keep them occupied with food until James returned.

A sudden thought flitted through her mind. What if Sam got one of the mules and rode out in search of James? But no, Sam was far too small to saddle or bridle one of the animals, let alone climb onto its back. She hoped he wouldn't try and get hurt. Maybe he had run off down the trail in hopes of meeting James. But his woolen coat was still in their sleeping quarters. She hoped he wasn't outside in just his shirtsleeves.

A voice rose in the kitchen. She grabbed the icy kettle from the cupboard and determined not to worry about Samuel. *He's in Your hands, Lord,* she prayed silently.

Clara had brought out the pan of leftover corn bread and the last jug of molasses. Beryl set the stew kettle on the stove.

"Could I pour you gentlemen some coffee?" She hated the quaver in her voice.

"That's a good idea," Clara said in an overbright tone. "A cup of hot coffee will do you fellers good. Warm your insides while you wait for the stew to heat."

Burke grunted, but the big man looked toward her and nodded. "Bring it here, gal. I'm startin' to thaw."

Beryl poured a mug full of coffee and walked over to him warily. She stopped at arm's length and held it out toward him.

"Come closer, sweetheart."

"This is fine," Beryl said.

He took it from her with one hand but grabbed her wrist with the other. As he set the coffee on the table, his grip tightened like a bulldog's jaws.

"Let go of me," Beryl said. Her cheeks heated, and she was sure her face had gone scarlet.

"In a bit." The man drew her closer, and Beryl could smell his unwashed body and rancid buckskins.

"Take your hands off her!" Clara sprang toward them with her cast-iron skillet raised.

Chapter 7

Burke stepped between the two women, pulling out a knife. The blade gleamed as he held it close to his waist, pointed at Clara.

"I'd think twice if I were you, ma'am." He glanced at his friend. "Joe, you're likely to spoil our dinner."

The big man threw back his head and laughed. "You're right. We oughta eat first."

He shoved Beryl away, letting loose her wrist. She collided with Clara, who dropped her skillet and pulled Beryl into her arms, backing away from the men. Beryl clung to her, staring at Burke's knife. How long would James be gone? Shouldn't he be back by now?

Joe picked up his coffee mug. "Get the food on the table. We'll worry about pleasantries after."

Clara's eyes narrowed. "Our men will whip you."

Burke laughed. "What men?"

"We didn't see no men when we rode in," Joe said. "You said your son would be back any minute, but I reckon we can handle him. Now, let's have some of that stew and cornpone, and while we's eatin', you can go put some gunpowder and lead balls on the counter, and some whiskey. Don't say you've got none. Everybody keeps a bottle for medicinal purposes, if nothing else."

Beryl moved toward the stove, pulling Clara with her. She reached for a wooden spoon and began to stir the stew. It wasn't anywhere near warm yet. How long would these men wait?

"Where's Sam?" Clara whispered.

"Don't know. Cut them some corn bread. Maybe that will hold them while this heats."

Somehow they managed to set the table. The stew was still only lukewarm, but Beryl half-filled two bowls.

"Well, now, that looks right edible."

Beryl jumped at the nearness of the man's oily voice. She turned to find Joe only a pace behind her. She forced a smile. "Sit right down and enjoy, gentlemen."

"Got more coffee?" Burke asked, plopping into Wolf's usual chair at the head of the table.

"Certainly." Beryl moved for the coffeepot, though she hated to get close enough to them to refill their cups.

When she approached Joe, hoping to quickly fill his mug and get away from him, he laid a hand on her sleeve. Beryl flinched and nearly dropped the coffeepot. She clutched the handle, knowing that if she spilled it on him, nothing could shield her from his wrath.

"You and your ma get our supplies ready. And don't get any ideas about hiding on me. We got business to settle."

"Mrs. Lassen will take your payment," Beryl managed to say, though her voice was not as steady as she would have liked.

Joe laughed. "Hear that, Burke?"

"Oh, yeah." Burke smiled around a mouthful of stew. "We'll pay up all right. No worry about that, missy."

Beryl shuddered, but Joe released her. The coffeepot's weight made her arm tremble as she filled his mug.

Clara had stepped toward the storeroom door. She lifted her chin slightly. Beryl set the coffeepot down on the range top. Both men were engaged in eating, their slurps and smacks giving testimony to their pleasure. She edged toward Clara and the door. Slowly, Clara drew her through the doorway. In silence they tiptoed out to the trading area.

"Did James take his rifle?" Beryl whispered.

"He always does in case he sees some game."

"He ought to come back soon."

Clara shrugged. "If he meets someone on the trail, he'll stop for the news, and if he shoots some meat, he'll dress it out."

"I'm worried about Sam," Beryl said. "I think he may have gone up the trail to find James."

"Pray he does." Clara jerked her face upward, staring at the rafters above them. "What's that?"

Beryl heard it too, a soft *thud, thud* on the roof.

"Not Indians," Clara said.

"Listen." Beryl's keen ears had picked up the drumming sound of hoofbeats—a rapid, galloping gait.

Clara's face brightened, but before she could speak, the *clomp* of footsteps sounded in the storeroom.

"You got our supplies ready?" Burke asked from behind the counter.

"Uh. . .almost," Beryl said. "Did you say you needed bacon?"

"Yeah, gimme some of that and some hardtack, if you've got it."

"I'm afraid we don't," Clara said. "The last of that went out of here on one of the last emigrant trains."

As Joe loomed in the doorway behind Burke, Beryl wondered that the two of them hadn't heard the hoofbeats, but the sounds had stopped. Had she imagined them?

"You get our lead and powder first," Joe said. "What have you been doing, anyhow?"

"Just discussing what we had to fill your list of supplies," Clara said, her face whitening as the huge man strode toward her.

Instead of menacing Clara, Joe grabbed Beryl's wrist and jerked her toward him. He twisted her arm behind her and held her so tightly that Beryl gritted her teeth.

Joe glared at Clara. "You get them things together fast while I keep company with the missy."

Beryl sucked in a breath, but before Clara could take a step toward the counter, the front door, behind Joe, flew open. James stood in the frame, his rifle raised. He quickly sized up the situation and pointed the muzzle toward Burke, who stood clear of the others and made a fine target.

"Let the girl loose," James said tightly, his blue eyes burning, "or your friend's a dead man."

☙

James kept his sights on the man near the counter, but the larger man worried him more. Would he risk disobeying?

Suddenly the big trapper laughed and let go of Beryl. She dashed to Clara and fell into her arms.

"Take your furs and get out of here," James said.

The big man stirred, and James turned to aim the rifle at him.

"We only wanted to trade with you," the trapper said.

"You're not trading here. Go somewhere else."

The second man took a step toward him. "Man, don't make us go all the way to Fort Laramie."

"Yeah," said the bigger man. "At least give us some hard money for our catch. We can get our supplies down the line, but we don't want to take our pelts any farther. We had to run off a band of Arapahoe last night."

"They likely wanted your horses," James said. "Now get moving. You've got most of the day left and a lot of miles to cover."

The smaller man eyed his friend uneasily. "All right, if that's the way your feel. We was told you gave a fair trade on furs."

"Generally we do, but not to men who harass our women."

"Aw we wasn't—" the big man started with a smile, but he broke off and sobered when James raised the rifle a hair.

"I heard what I heard," James said. "Now go."

He stepped back and stood just outside while the trappers strode out, reloaded their furs, and mounted their saddle horses. They rode away, and Ma and Beryl stepped out onto the doorstep.

"Oh, James," his mother said, shaking her head. "If you'd been much longer. . ."

"That's what I figured."

"Where's Sam?" Beryl asked, eyeing James's panting horse. "Did you meet him on the road?"

James grinned then and looked up at the roof. The women followed his gaze, and Beryl gasped.

"Sam!"

The boy perched on the slant roof of the trading post with a red blanket wrapped around him.

"Land sakes," Ma said. "What are you doing up there, Samuel?"

"He signaled to me with that red flag he's wearing," James said. "He stood on top of the roof, flapping it. I could see it all the way from the bluff yonder."

"That's more'n a mile," Ma said.

"Yup." James walked over to stand beneath Sam. "Well, come on down, pard."

Sam beamed at him and shoved off from the eaves, the blanket flying out behind him like a scarlet cape. James caught him and set him on the ground.

"You did fine, boy." He tousled Sam's hair.

"I guess you did," Beryl said. "How did you think of it?"

"I remembered the story James wrote about the boy who signaled the clipper ship. So I grabbed the blanket and climbed up to our crow's nest."

"You did just right," James said.

They put the kitchen and the trading post to rights, and his mother once again sat down to finish edging the blanket while Beryl quizzed Sam on his numbers. James had time to think at last. He whittled away while he thought, and the piece of pine began to take the shape of a horse. Sam would like that, he thought. The boy could add it to his menagerie.

If the Jenners hadn't stopped here for the winter, Ma would have been alone when the trappers came. He'd been foolish to leave her alone repeatedly, even for an hour.

He looked at Samuel, whose head was bent over the slate. What would he have done if he'd come home and found those ruffians had harmed little Sam? Or Beryl? Gazing at her, James realized how much she meant to him. He didn't want her to leave. Yet he'd seen the fear in her eyes when he burst into the trading post and found the trapper menacing her.

Was there any chance he could convince her to stay? James scraped away at the wooden horse's mane, making little ridges in it to fashion realistic strands of hair. How could he ask Beryl to live here in the wilderness? He was barely able to protect her today. Any number of things could happen to her, or to Sam, the same as they could to Ma, and he would not always be able to prevent them.

He sighed, and Ma looked over at him.

"Anything wrong?" she asked softly.

"No. Yes." James gave her a rueful smile. "I don't know."

"It hits you afterward," Ma murmured.

"Yeah." James gazed at Beryl again. He had put the shutters down, and the sun streamed in through the window by the table, burnishing her hair. "It sure does."

Chapter 8

James rode to the top of the bluff but didn't go as far as he used to away from the trading post. He sat his horse for ten minutes, trying to decide if the haze beyond the hills blocking his view was dust or fog off the river.

He turned in the saddle to look back. At this distance, the roof of the trading post stood in faint contrast to the blue sky. He should go back soon. Since the trappers' visit ten days ago, he never stayed away long.

When he looked back up the trail, his heart leapt. A team of mules appeared around the base of a distant hill. One pair, two, three, four. . . He waited until ten spans of mules rounded the bend and the billowing top of a massive freight wagon came into sight. That was all he needed. He pivoted his horse and galloped for home.

"He's coming!" James leapt from the saddle and ran inside. "Ma, he's coming! I saw the first wagon. It's got to be him."

"I had a feeling." Ma smiled as she pulled an oatmeal cake from the oven and plunked the pan on her worktable. "Let me get my apron off. You didn't ride out to meet him?"

"No, I didn't want to leave you."

"Well go, Son! We'll be fine."

Sam hopped off his stool and ran to James. "Can I go?"

"Sure." James hurried him outside. He lifted Sam onto the saddle and swung up behind him. "Hold on now." His horse sprang eagerly toward the trail.

Both women waited outside the trading post, shading their eyes against the sun. Clara looked beautiful in her eagerness to see her husband, despite the lines etched into her face.

At last the five big wagons rolled into view, and James rode back toward them, the sun making his light brown hair look almost blond. Sam sat in front of him, clutching the saddle horn.

Something wasn't right. James's mouth was a grim line, and he didn't race up to them. He trotted his horse into the yard and dismounted slowly, as though he were bone tired. He reached up and pulled Sam down. Up close, James's face frightened Beryl.

"What's wrong?" Clara asked. "That's not your father?"

"It's his wagons," James said, "but Pa's not with them."

"Why not?" Clara reached a hand toward him.

"He's dead, Ma."

"No!"

James put an arm around her to steady her. "He paid the men in advance to bring the wagons out, but he died in St. Louis."

"How. . . ?" Clara shook her head, her eyes blank.

"There's a letter from the doctor who attended him." James reached inside his shirt and drew it out. "Let's go inside and sit down while I read it to you."

"The teamsters. . ." Clara looked vaguely toward the trail.

"Don't worry about them," James said. "They'll unhitch the teams and tend to them. I told them they can sleep in the cabin tonight. Pa promised them each one of the mules to ride back and one pack mule among them."

Clara nodded, still with an absent air. "They'll want to eat."

"I'll take care of it," Beryl said. "Sam, come with me. You can help me get dinner ready for the men."

"They'll want lots of coffee," Clara said.

Beryl nodded and pulled Sam inside with her.

In the kitchen, Sam tugged at her skirt. She crouched down to his eye level. "What is it, Sam?"

"Is Mr. Wolf dead?"

"Yes, I'm afraid so."

"Like Pa?"

Beryl nodded.

Tears filled Sam's eyes. "Poor James and Mrs. Lassen."

"Yes. We must do all we can to help them now. Can you fill the wood box?"

Sam pulled in a deep breath and squared his shoulders. "I can do whatever you need, Beryl."

She hugged him for a moment. "Good boy. Thank you."

"What do I tell James?" Sam's watery gaze brought a new ache to Beryl's heart.

"Later on, when it's quiet, just tell him how sorry you are about his pa. That's what he needs now—friends who understand."

"We understand," Sam said.

Beryl nodded. "We surely do."

☙

That evening, James took Sam to the barn with him to tend the livestock. The teamsters were having a lively card game, but their laughter broke off when James and the boy entered.

"Don't stop on my account," James said. "Sam and I have only come to milk the cow and feed the horses."

"We're sorry about Mr. Lassen," the lead teamster, Dunbar, said.

"Thank you." James managed a smile and guided Sam toward the feed bin.

"James, are you going to leave here?" Sam asked as James dipped out oats for the saddle horses.

"No, this is our home. Ma and I will get by, even without Pa, I expect."

"Who will go to St. Louis next winter for the stuff you'll need?"

"That's some mighty far-reaching thoughts for a boy your age," James said. "I plan to talk to Mr. Dunbar before they leave. He might be willing to let me send him my order next fall and bring the supplies out in the spring. He seems a trustworthy man."

"Was your pa sick a long time like mine was?" Sam asked, his eyes clouded with sorrow.

"Not so long," James said. "The doctor says his heart failed, but he had time to dictate his last words to Ma and me and to give Mr. Dunbar instructions for the wagons. He lived two days after his heart trouble began."

"What made his heart bad?"

James shook his head. "Nobody knows. It just happens sometimes."

Sam looked up at him for a long moment. His bottom lip trembled. "Will you die?"

James set down the bucket he'd been holding and swept Sam into a warm hug. "No, Sam. I'm planning to be here a long time. But you know, accidents and things do happen. We have to trust God to keep us safe."

Sam clung to him for a moment. "I don't want to go away from you, James."

James's throat tightened. The first of the season's emigrant trains would come through soon, and more freighters and soldiers. Would the travelers who brought his family sustenance take Sam and Beryl away from him?

"Have you read all the stories in your book yet?" he whispered in Sam's ear.

Sam shook his head. "There's one left for this Sunday."

"Read it tonight." As soon as the words left his lips, James wondered if he had been wise. If Sam knew his thoughts, and his dream failed to materialize, would that totally break the boy's spirit? Still, he couldn't help feeling that his story would encourage Sam. Knowing they had the same dream would strengthen James, too, when he made his hopes known.

∽

The next two days kept everyone busy. The teamsters unloaded the wagons while the mules grazed in the pasture on the new grass. Beryl helped tick off the merchandise on the bills of lading as the men carried the crates and barrels into the storeroom and the new addition. James arranged the new stock in the back rooms, while Clara replenished the display shelves behind the counter in the trading room. Sam's lessons were neglected as he scurried about, helping James.

"Your brother's good with the animals for one so wee," one of the teamsters remarked to Beryl on the second day.

"I think when he's big enough to control them, he'll make a good driver, or maybe a post rider," she said with a chuckle. "He loves to ride about with James on his horse."

"So, are you and James. . ." The teamster eyed her speculatively. He was the youngest of the lot, not five-and-twenty, Beryl guessed, and when he'd shaved off his trail beard, she realized he was good-looking, with thoughtful gray eyes and reddish hair that curled slightly over his brow.

She felt her cheeks flush and looked away. "No. We were on a wagon train. My father died last fall, and Sam and I stopped here for the winter."

"I see. Are you wanting to go back East? We'll be heading out for St. Louis in a couple of days. James wants us to take the freight wagons back. You could put your things in one of them."

Beryl's heart pounded. She couldn't consider traveling all that way with a crew of teamsters and no other women. Besides, the thought of leaving Chiswell Rock brought with it a dismay that startled her. For six months and more, she had known she would leave in the spring, but now that the time was here, it terrified her. She couldn't leave Clara, who had become like a second mother to her. And James! Could she leave him and not leave a piece of her heart?

"I'm not sure what my plans are yet. I. . .I'm still considering taking my brother to Oregon."

The teamster nodded. "Let me know if you change your mind. We'd be delighted to have your company, and you'd be safe with us, Miss Jenner."

"Thank you." She believed for a moment that he would keep her safe, or at least do all he could to that end. But it still wouldn't be proper. And it would take her away from James.

Why should she think that would matter? Perhaps James would be glad to be free of the responsibility of looking after her and Sam. But it would matter to her.

⁂

"Beryl," Sam said that evening when she tucked him into his cot, "I read my last story."

"Oh? It's only Friday."

"I know. I read ahead."

She smiled. "It's all right. Was it a good story?"

He nodded soberly. "It's another Christmas story. Like *A Christmas Carol*, only here instead of in London."

"That sounds interesting." She sat down on the edge of the cot. "Can you tell me about it?"

"It's about a man who runs a trading post with his wife and little boy."

For a moment, Beryl wondered if James had written about Wolf and Clara and himself, but she knew they hadn't been here that long. Then Sam said, "The grandparents live with them, too."

"Oh." An imaginary family. Beryl settled her mind to focus on the tale.

"It's called 'A Frontier Christmas Tale.' One snowy Christmas, they see strange lights in the hills," Sam said. "They take a sleigh and drive out there. They find four families from one of the last wagon trains of the year. Sickness had run through their train, and they're the only ones who didn't die from it."

"How sad," Beryl murmured.

"Yeah. They tried to get back to a town, but their oxen were too weak and couldn't make it. They didn't know how close they were to the trading post. So the family brings them in and arranges for them to stay nearby until help comes in the spring."

She smiled. "That sounds familiar."

"Uh-huh. The man and his wife were happy to help those people, and the wagon train folks said they were like angels coming to rescue them on Christmas Day."

"That's a nice story," Beryl said.

"The little boy in the story was named Samuel. Like me."

"Oh!" Beryl eyed him cautiously. Again she thought of the Lassen family—but with Wolf still alive and herself added as a wife for James, and with Sam as his son. Was it possible James had flirted with the thought way back at Christmastime when he'd written the story? Or was she reading too much into it? Unexpected tears burned her eyes. Whether he consciously framed the story to fit their situation or not, James was too dear to leave. Though she couldn't say so, she longed to be the wife in Sam's Christmas story, to be here at Chiswell Rock when the next Christmas came.

"Time for your prayers," she whispered.

A few minutes later, she left Sam and went into the kitchen. Clara pored over her lists at the table, but she looked up and smiled. She had donned a black dress that morning, and her eyes were red-rimmed, but those were the only concessions to her bereavement that she let others see.

"James is in the storeroom, sorting hardware. I couldn't get him to quit, and I suppose it's distracting him from thoughts of his father."

"It will take some getting used to," Beryl said. "You do plan to stay and run the post, then?"

"Yes. We've talked it over, and we can't see a better course of action. James will do fine. We may have to hire an extra person to help us though. There's talk of a regular stagecoach line going through, and James hopes he can get a contract for a way station."

"That would mean more work."

"Yes, but it would mean a steadier flow of income as well."

"I'll do all I can while I'm here," Beryl said.

Clara nodded. "I know you will, dear. You're a tremendous help. Perhaps you'd take James a cup of coffee? If he's going to keep working all evening, he could probably use it."

Beryl poured coffee into the mug James liked. The cow had freshened a fortnight ago, and she added a generous dollop of cream, as she'd seen James do at the breakfast table. A little voice inside her head seemed to scold her. *You know him so well! You care for him, and he cares for you. How can you think of leaving now?*

He looked up as Beryl entered the storage room.

"Hello. Oh, just what I need." He reached for the steaming mug, smiling.

"How are you doing?" she asked.

"All right." He took a sip of the coffee. "Mmm. Thank you. That new coffee is so good, especially with the fresh cream in it."

"It's wonderful to have new supplies, isn't it?" She looked around at the chaotic piles of crates and barrels. "Can I do anything to help you?"

"I'm just puttering." He took another drink and set the mug on a pile of boxes. "Pa seems to have sent us a lot of canned goods this time—more than we had last year. Maybe we won't run out before all the trains have gone through this time around."

"Good. I hope he sent extra sugar, too. You had already run out for the customers when I got here."

James smiled ruefully. "Yes, Ma had a time reserving what she thought we would need for the winter, and after you and Samuel arrived, she wished she'd saved more."

"She's fed us very well, I must say." Beryl sat down on a keg of nails. "James, Sam has finished reading his storybook."

"I hope he enjoyed it."

"He did. Tremendously."

"Perhaps I can think up a few more."

"I know he'd like that." She hesitated, and for some reason her pulse seemed to quicken and her corset felt tighter than usual. "He was especially taken with the last one."

"I'm glad." James didn't meet her gaze. He reached for the pry bar he used to open crates. "I have to admit, I made that one up."

"I thought perhaps. . ."

"What?" He glanced her way, and Beryl thought his cheeks held a little extra color.

"That you'd based it on your own family."

"I did. Of course, I thought Pa would come back."

She frowned, thinking about the family in the story. "You weren't the little boy, were you? Sam said he was named Samuel. I think he may have thought—"

"I couldn't imagine you and Sam not being here with us another Christmas," James said in a rush.

Beryl caught her breath. She forced herself to fold her hands and give at least a picture of serenity, though her heart now thundered.

"It's hard for me to imagine, too." She dared to glance up at him.

James stood with the bar in his hand and his head cocked to one side, studying her. "Do you think you could live happily in this isolated spot?"

Beryl chuckled. "It's only isolated five or six months of the year. In summer, you tell me it's hectic, and the rest of the time it's just. . .cozy."

"Yes." James laid down the pry bar. "Beryl, if I thought. . ."

"What, James?" She gazed up at him, hardly daring to hope.

"Would you. . .would you consider marriage? To me, I mean. We could have that family here at the post. I love you, Beryl. You could make me so happy." He reached for her hands.

"I believe you could make me happy, too." She let him draw her to her feet.

"Do you mean it?" His eyes sparkled in the lamplight. "I don't know when there'll be a preacher through here, but there's bound to be one on one of the wagon trains. Or perhaps an army chaplain will ride by."

"Yes." She reached up and touched his cheek. "Either of those would be fine."

James bent down to kiss her, and after the first jolt of joy, Beryl slid her hands around his neck.

"I love you," she whispered.

"We'll ask the first one who comes along, then." James pulled her close and kissed her again.

The Reluctant Runaway

by Melanie Dobson

Chapter 1

Omaha, Nebraska
December 1889

Lavinia Starr twisted her embroidered kid gloves in her lap as she waited for the morning train to depart Union Station. Once Patrick discovered her missing, he would search all over Omaha for her. She'd never be able to hide from her stepbrother in this city, but she could hide in New York.

Even though it was still two hours before daylight, the platform was crowded with travelers. A pine tree glowed with white candles inside the depot, and below her windowed seat, she watched a small family hurry through the crowd toward the back of the train. A familiar ache tugged at her heart. Every Christmas she longed for her mother and her father.

Years ago, when she was a girl, she remembered holding the hand of her father when they'd boarded a train for New York City, but she hadn't been away from Omaha since she was eleven, and she'd certainly never traveled on her own.

Her fingers brushed over the emerald and diamonds adorning her right hand. Her father had given her the ring more than two years ago, for her sixteenth birthday. She never could have imagined what the months after her birthday would hold for their little family.

In the aisle across from her sat a portly middle-aged man who'd already introduced himself as Mr. Barkley, the proprietor of Barkley's Billiards in the Sporting District. She hadn't told the man her name nor did she plan to. Eventually, her stepbrother would offer a reward for her return, and a gambling man wouldn't hesitate to wire a telegram back to Omaha to receive it.

Mr. Barkley leaned toward her, eyeing her ring. She slipped her fingers back into her leather gloves.

Then he pointed toward a rack. "Would you like me to hang your coat?"

"No, but thank you," she said, smoothing out the fur collar that tickled her neck.

"It really is no trouble—"

"I would like to keep it." She would not part with her winter coat until the wheels on the train began turning, and perhaps not even then.

Surely the train would leave soon.

"But you will be warm," Mr. Barkley pressed.

Sighing, she inched closer to the window. Closed her eyes. Why did the men in her life never listen to her? All of them refused to accept that she was capable of making decisions on her own—like whom she would marry and where she would live and whether she wanted to keep her coat.

Eddie, the Starr family's elderly groomsman, was the only exception. He was the one man who respected that she had ideas of her own, and he was her co-conspirator in her escape. He'd secured her trunk in a wagon last night before Patrick came home, and then he was waiting at five this morning when she emerged from the Starr family mansion on Davenport Street.

"All aboard," the conductor yelled from the platform.

Lavinia's heart raced as she scanned the crowd one last time, and when the two doors of the carriage closed, she took a deep breath, waiting for the train to begin its journey. Finally, she would be leaving behind a future as bleak as winters in this town. In New York she would find freedom from Patrick and the man he demanded she marry.

But then, just as quickly as the doors closed, they opened again. She glanced at the door behind her seat and then strained her neck, searching the front of the car. A man stepped up into the train and took off his hat, his black hair gleaming in the gas lamplight. She gasped.

Patrick had found her.

She started to duck, but her stepbrother rapidly scanned the heads of the passengers until he found her face. Then a smirk crossed his lips.

Mr. Barkley turned toward her. "What's the matter?"

"That man—" she began, but didn't finish. Instead, she reached for the satchel stored at her feet and leapt up, racing toward the back door. She couldn't run fast or far in her wool coat, but she wasn't going to give up now. If she didn't hide, he would destroy her.

As she hopped down to the platform, she heard Mr. Barkley's voice again. "Mr. Dittmar," he said. "It is a pleasure, sir."

She hoped Mr. Barkley would step into the aisle and profusely shake Patrick's hand. It didn't matter one whit whether he detained Patrick for selfish reasons or to protect her. All she needed was enough time to lose herself in the crowd.

She elbowed her way across the platform, people pressing against both sides of her.

"Lavinia!" The shout came from her right, but it wasn't Patrick who called her name. It was Charles Mahler. The man she was supposed to marry.

When Charles shouted again, she froze. If Charles or Patrick caught her, they would never give her an opportunity to escape again. They would probably place a guard outside her chamber if they must, and the guard wouldn't be a friend like Eddie.

The cold wind stung her cheeks. Her wool coat felt like an anchor chained around her traveling gown. But she couldn't surrender to these men or the life they'd mapped out for her.

Determination sparked inside her, and she forced her feet to move left, away from Charles. On the other side of the platform was a second passenger train, but even if she ducked inside it, Patrick and Charles would search it until they found her.

Glancing around the platform, she looked for another place to hide. On the other side of the waiting passenger train, she saw a blur of movement, and then in the dim light, she watched the slow revolution of steel wheels, heard the rattle of freight cars preparing to leave the station.

"Lavinia," Charles shouted again. "Wait!"

She didn't stop to think. Lifting the hem of her coat and dress, she stepped off the platform, down into the rocky bed of the train yard, and over the tracks before crossing around the engine of the passenger train.

The freight train was three tracks away, the wheels circling faster. All the doors of the cars were closed. Except one.

Near the end of the train, one door remained partially open, a small portal just for her.

Bolting toward the door, she hobbled alongside the car, lifting her skirt to her knees before she tossed her satchel inside. Then she jumped through the narrow opening and hit the hard floor with a thud, her long coat cushioning her fall.

For a moment, she lay stunned on the steel floor. If her father were still alive, he would never believe it. She—Lavinia Kathryn Starr—had hopped onto a moving train.

She brushed off her sleeves, and when she righted herself, she glanced back outside and saw two shadows running across the yard toward her. Jumping up, she tried to yank the door closed, but it wouldn't budge. At this pace, it would take only seconds for Patrick and Charles to catch her.

"Help me," she prayed, the same prayer she'd uttered for eight years even though her plea always seemed to bounce back to her.

She watched in horror as the men drew closer, close enough for her to see Patrick's sneer. When she'd threatened a trip to New York, he'd sworn that he would never let her leave, and now—

Suddenly the men stopped.

Confused, she glanced forward and then ducked back into the freight car as it passed by another train, still asleep on the tracks.

The men couldn't chase her any farther. The train beside her blocked their path.

Lavinia slipped down onto the cold, straw-covered floor, her hands trembling. Then she began to laugh, relief pouring out with her laughter as she hugged her knees close to her chest.

She didn't know which direction this train was headed, and she didn't particularly care. Her two trunks may be on the way to New York, but she and her satchel would travel as far as this freight train would take them.

Neither Patrick nor Charles would be able to find her now.

Chapter 2

Aspen, Colorado

Rocky peaks towered like sentinels on both sides of the train tracks. Powdery snow clung to the peaks along the narrow valley and carpeted the banks of the Roaring Fork River below the tracks. Before Isaac traveled to Denver, there had been almost two feet of snow outside the entrance of his mine. With last night's storm, it had probably grown to a good three feet or more.

Isaac buttoned his leather overcoat as the train began to slow and then reached for the suitcase above his seat. A freight train arrived in Aspen almost every weekday, delivering provisions to the town and hundreds of copies of the *Rocky Mountain News*. Until the snowy valley became impassable, the Denver and Rio Grande also delivered the few travelers who dared travel to the heart of Colorado's mining country during winter. This train didn't linger in Aspen. It quickly loaded the passengers ready to escape along with the mounds of silver from the mines and then returned north to Glenwood Springs and back to civilization in Denver.

Isaac had spent almost a week in Denver, assuring Marcus McCann, his brother-in-law, and other nervous investors that his men were about to uncover another silver vein at the Coronado Mine. Then he visited his brother-in-law and sister at their home. His sister had begged him to stay two more days and spend Christmas with the niece and two nephews he adored, but he had to return to his mine right away. Isaac and his men needed at least three months to unearth the silver vein, but the investors had given him just one more month. Thirty days to do the impossible.

The depot appeared ahead in the narrow valley, and he tapped his foot near the door as he waited for the train to stop. His desk would be piled with reports from his superintendent, but he would have to neglect those, for a day or two at least, in order to plan the excavation of a new tunnel. If they didn't find this vein, Marcus would lose his investment—and Isaac would lose his savings as well as his home and property outside Aspen—but right now he was more concerned about what would happen to the forty-five miners he employed.

The engineer blew the whistle as the metal wheels screeched on the tracks. Then a cloud of coal dust blackened the windows. He reached for his suitcase and stepped down onto the platform with a handful of men, most of them probably new miners hired to replace those who'd tired of the harsh conditions.

In spite of the cold, men—most of them employees of competing silver mines around Aspen—lounged on the bench outside the depot, waiting to return to families for Christmas or leaving the snowy wilderness until spring. They acknowledged him with a slight nod before he stepped into the depot.

The cramped room was blistering hot from the fire in the woodstove, and it reeked of steaming leather and sweat. He eyed the exit on the other side of the room.

He would go directly from here to the Coronado Mine.

But before he reached the exit, the daughter of his mining supervisor moved toward him. Her raven-black hair was swept back at the nape of her neck, her long coat folded over the pale blue sleeve of her calico dress.

"Hello, Mr. Loritz," she said quietly.

Isaac took off his hat and tucked it at his side. Most people in Aspen called him Mr. Loritz, but the formality still sounded strange to him. "Good afternoon, Miss Tucker."

She blushed. "Please, call me Daisy."

"Daisy," he said awkwardly. Most of the women in Aspen were married, and they never asked him to call them by their first name. "You're not planning to leave Aspen, are you?"

She shifted her coat to her other arm. "Just until spring," she said. "My father says no lady should live out here between December and March."

Isaac didn't know much about the business of the ladies in Aspen, but he knew the majority of women who remained in town all year either ran a business or worked at Madame Dumont's place. His best friend, Dr. Josiah Kemper, married a decade ago, and his wife and two children also stayed here during the winter, but they hibernated in their fancy Victorian house on the West End until the snow began to melt.

He stuffed his gloves into his pockets. "Are you headed to Denver?"

"To my cousin's house outside the city, in the town of Highlands." Her smile grew bigger. "Are you going to Denver?"

He pointed back toward the train. "I just returned from a trip to visit my sister."

"The next time you come"—she blushed again—"perhaps you could pay a visit—to my cousin."

He forced a smile. "I don't believe I know your cousin."

"Well, you should—" She stumbled over her words before her smile began to grow again. "I would love to meet your sister."

He backed away, worried about the direction of this conversation. Daisy was barely sixteen, and Ned Tucker just might shoot him if Isaac hinted at any interest in his daughter without following through. And he had no intention of proposing to her or any other woman right now.

"I hope you have a splendid time with your family," Isaac said with a slight bow of his head. Then he backed toward the main doors.

If his sister found out about the invitation, she would insist that he visit Daisy Tucker and her family when he returned to Denver. He was living in the shadow of his thirtieth birthday, and his sister thought it a travesty that he had not yet found a wife. Neither of them ever discussed the woman he almost married back in Philadelphia.

When he married, if he ever married, the thought of shipping his wife off to Denver for four months out of the year sounded miserable to him.

Daisy lifted her hand to wave at him before she moved to the platform. He almost turned back toward the exit when he saw another young lady on the platform. A stunning woman with a cream-colored winter cloak and strands of honey-brown hair escaping from her fur hat. As she strolled across the platform, she looked dazed, as if she weren't sure which direction to turn.

Had she come from Denver as well?

He sighed. She was probably one of the new recruits at Madame Dumont's brothel, and he hated the thought of this beautiful woman, just a few years younger than his sister, selling herself—

But perhaps he was wrong. Perhaps she'd come to Aspen for another reason. She could even be here to visit her husband for Christmas.

She walked into the depot, and when she looked up at him, he was struck by the color of her eyes—a crystal green that reminded him of a mountain creek in the spring, flowing from the runoff of melted snow. In her gaze, he saw a mixture of desperation and determination.

He stepped up to her. "Can I—" He started and then felt foolish. Surely she would have someone here waiting for her arrival. "Do you need assistance?"

She shook her head.

"How about your luggage?"

She didn't smile nor did she flirt like Daisy. "I need to find a hotel."

"Of course," he said, relieved that she hadn't asked for the brothel. He pointed toward the main street of Aspen. "We only have one here. It's two blocks that way."

She picked up her satchel. "Thank you."

He stuck his hands into his pockets. "Are you coming from Denver?"

Fear flashed through her eyes, and he felt stupid. He never should have intruded on her personal affairs.

"I was there last night," she said, her gaze locked on the exit.

Two men at the depot began unloading the passengers' trunks and crates of supplies. "I can help you with your luggage," he said.

"No—"

"It's no trouble."

She arched her shoulders, her eyes narrowing with frustration. "I don't need help."

He glanced back at the train, confused, but when she stepped toward the doors of the depot, he didn't offer to assist her again. She reminded him of the wounded mountain lion he'd come upon last spring. The cat had been trapped in the rusted barbs of an old fence, but when Isaac drew close, it snarled at him, threatening with its claws. The cat had been determined to free itself without any help from him.

Isaac could do nothing to help this woman either if she didn't want his assistance, but still he trailed behind her about a block to make sure she arrived safely at the hotel before darkness set in. He watched until she stepped up onto the portico of the Hotel Jerome, and then he walked along the shoveled path to his office, a half mile out of town.

The woman would be safe in the hotel for as long as she stayed in Aspen. He must focus on his work tonight—if they couldn't find the new silver vein in thirty days, the Coronado would close its doors for good.

He would do everything in his power to keep the mine from failing.

Chapter 3

Lavinia shivered as she stood on the portico of the elegant hotel, looking into the picture window at the colorful glass bulbs and ribboned wreaths. The cold mountain air revived her, but it also frightened her. She'd spent most of her money on the ticket to New York and then spilled her remaining coins onto the ticket counter at the station in Denver to buy a ticket on a passenger train headed as far away from Omaha as possible.

The coins bought her a ticket deep into the Rocky Mountains, and she'd been elated, knowing that Patrick would never find her hidden in this mountain town. In New York she'd been planning to stay with a childhood friend of her mother's, but she didn't have any friends in Colorado. With the little money left in her money purse, she couldn't afford even one night at the Hotel Jerome.

Where was she supposed to sleep?

Before her mother died, she'd never thought much about money. Her father—Albert Starr—had always taken good care of his only daughter, providing well for her and sheltering her from everything ugly in this world. Unfortunately, he married again eight years ago, bringing the very trouble he'd tried to protect her from right into the heart of their home. After his death, Lavinia's stepmother made certain that Lavinia was keenly aware of how much it cost to provide for her. In the eyes of Omaha's society, Eloise had cared well for her since Father's death, but her stepmother didn't have a choice—Albert Starr's will stipulated that Lavinia receive food and shelter.

Now that Eloise had passed on as well, Lavinia didn't have anyone left to care for her, and she wasn't quite sure how to care for herself. She glanced up the empty street again. The ticket agent in Denver said Aspen was a mining town. Perhaps she could find work at one of the boardinghouses for the miners. She could learn how to wash clothes or clean or even help in the kitchen in return for food and a warm place to sleep.

No matter what happened, she wouldn't return to Omaha.

She stepped onto the wooden sidewalk and wandered past a barbershop, a saloon, a blacksmith. On the other side of the street was the Maroon Bells Mercantile and an assay office with a half dozen men crowded around a desk inside. The mountains that surrounded the village were majestic, but the white-laced peaks to the west were luring the sun quickly away from town. It wouldn't be long, she feared, before the mountains swallowed up all of the sunlight. With her trunks on their way to New York, it was much too late to change her attire, but she wished she'd selected a warmer traveling gown and carried a muff in her satchel.

She passed by a dilapidated two-story house with a hand-painted sign hanging crooked in the window: ROOMS AVAILABLE.

Her heart racing, she knocked tentatively.

The proprietor was a weathered woman who silently surveyed the ruffles of Lavinia's tailored mantle and the glass beads and silver motif embroidered in her lavender skirt and bodice. Lavinia inquired about work, but the woman said a lady in the house would be a distraction for the miners who boarded with her. Then she said Lavinia looked like she would be more burden than help anyway.

Shivering, Lavinia rushed from the house. She could not be deterred from finding a warm place to sleep and a meal for the night.

A block away was a second house—Cora's Boarding. Taking a deep breath, Lavinia knocked again. A younger woman answered this door, her hair tucked back under a faded red bandana. Cora, she presumed.

The woman's eyes narrowed when she saw Lavinia. "What do you want?"

"I need work," Lavinia begged. "I can wash or clean or—"

Cora's eyes softened a bit. "I can't afford an employee."

"I have a little money," she offered. "Could I spend one night here?"

"I've got no place for you to sleep, but there's a hotel in town." Cora pointed back toward the Hotel Jerome.

Lavinia began to back down the steps. She didn't want to tell the woman she couldn't afford the hotel.

Cora eyed the ornate gold-and-pearl button on Lavinia's mantle. "Where'd you say you came from?"

Lavinia turned away. Gossip, she imagined, would balloon quickly in this town. She'd hoped she could enter quietly and stay for a few days until she was able to contact her father's solicitor. She couldn't afford to make a spectacle. People would start to ask questions—

"Wait a moment," Cora called to her. "I have something for you."

Lavinia contemplated hurrying away, but she was curious as to what Cora might have. The woman returned minutes later with a small parcel wrapped in brown paper. "It's a little food. . .just in case."

Lavinia stared at the parcel for a moment. When she was young, she and her mother had taken food to people in need, but she never imagined that she would be the recipient of anyone's charity. Still, with the exception of the potato soup and bread she'd had on the train, she hadn't eaten anything of substance in the past two days. And she needed to reserve her last remaining coins for a telegram.

"Thank you," she whispered, tucking the package quickly in her satchel.

Cora pointed to their left. "At the edge of town is a fancy green house," she said. "Dr. Kemper and his wife might let you stay the night."

Lavinia nodded.

"And down at the courthouse there's a man—" Cora hesitated as if she didn't want to insult the woman before her. "He can give you a free train ticket back to wherever it is you've come from."

Lavinia hurried away, stopping only to eye the painted porch on the doctor's house and the fire blazing inside the bay window. Then she kept walking.

She didn't stop again until she was a good half mile outside of town.

Smoke snaked up through the moonlight hovering over the trees on Isaac's property. With his lantern swinging at his side, he hurried down the side of the mountain from the Coronado Mine and rushed past his house. The smoke was coming from the abandoned barn, about a quarter mile away from his house. There was no time to gather men from town, but if the fire was still small, he might be able to stamp it out on his own.

As he drew closer to the trees, he realized the barn wasn't on fire. The smoke was rising from the iron chimney in the center of the roof—a chimney that hadn't been used, to his knowledge, for at least five years. An old miner, he'd been told, put in a woodstove while he squatted on the land.

Isaac slowed his pace, his lungs stinging from the frigid air, his pants caked with snow. He'd only been gone a week, but it was long enough for a drifter to claim this place for a temporary home. If only he'd stopped to retrieve his rifle at the house—

He had no intention of shooting a trespasser, but in his years in Colorado, he'd learned much about the desperation of man and a desperate man might kill another, especially on a cold winter night like this. As long as the man inside wasn't a threat, he could stay until the morning, and then Isaac would direct him to the courthouse in Aspen for help.

He pushed back the barn door, and his lantern light flooded the room. Quickly he scanned the room, searching for the man who was trespassing on his property, but instead of a man, he saw a woman. Asleep on the hay.

He held up his lantern and crept closer to the hay. Was it possible?

As he stood over the woman, he recognized her honey-brown hair and the fancy winter coat, partially covered by a yellow afghan draped over her. It was the woman he'd seen at the train station. The woman who was supposed to be spending the night in Aspen, at the hotel.

He lowered the lantern to his side. Even with his light and the night air pouring in through the door, she didn't wake.

What was he supposed to do now?

Chapter 4

As morning light seeped into the room, Lavinia turned away from it and yanked her blankets up to her neck. Why was her room so cold? Her bed so. . .prickly? She bolted up.

There was no lace canopy above her, no mound of goose-down pillows under her head. No servant tending to her fire or pouring water into her basin. Last night she'd found a path outside the town, under a long strip of mines, and she'd rushed through the valley until she'd found an abandoned barn to shelter in for the night—at least she hoped no one was using this old place as their home.

She rubbed her arms as she surveyed her surroundings. The roof sagged over her head and daylight slipped through the cracks in the walls. Even with her wool coat over her gown, she was cold. All she'd had for the fire last night were three logs she'd found by the stove, but at least she had shelter. Cora had said she could obtain a free ticket back home, but she'd much rather wake up in a cold barn in Colorado than her warm bedroom in Omaha.

Near the door were two blankets sitting on a mound of hay. Funny, she hadn't seen the blankets last night. The light had almost faded when she found the barn, but still she should have seen the blankets—and the tiny pile of wood beside it. She was certain only two pieces of wood had been beside the stove last night, and she had used both of those to make her fire.

Her exhaustion must have blinded her more than she'd realized.

She brushed the hay off her skirt and carefully folded the small yellow quilt her mother made for her in the weeks after she was born, grateful that she'd stashed this treasure in her satchel. It was one of the few gifts that remained from her mother.

What would Mother think of her, running away from home like this? Her heart would probably break at the cruelty of Patrick and his mother, at the way they scorned and ridiculed her even before her father died.

After he married Eloise, her father spent longer hours at his office, leaving Lavinia to what he deemed the safety of their home. She clung to her belief that he didn't know what went on during his hours away from home, but whenever she tried to tell him the truth, he'd sided with her stepmother.

But she was free now—from Patrick and his mother, Eloise. From the man Patrick had chosen for her to marry. She may not be as worldly-wise as some, but she knew well that neither man intended to look after her well-being.

Patrick told her that he was the sole benefactor of the Starr family fortune, but if she could locate Mr. Tipton, her father's solicitor, he would surely tell her the truth about her inheritance. She didn't particularly care if her stepbrother got some or even most of her father's money. She just couldn't allow herself to believe that Father would leave her penniless. In his own way, he had tried to care for her, and the thought that he'd stopped caring. . .

It was too much to bear.

Using the edge of a blanket, she opened the door to the stove. Embers glowed in their bed, but the fire had faded away in the night. She placed another log inside and then tucked a handful of hay under it before stirring the embers with her breath. In seconds they leapt back into a blaze.

She sat on a barrel, watching the flames flicker inside the stove.

When she was a child, her father used to entertain her with what he called magic. On their back lawn, he would rub a piece of iron against a flint rock until it sparked. Then he would gently blow the sliver of fire onto a tiny bed of dried grass. She'd been so fascinated by his magic that he'd given her a small pouch with her own steel and flint rock when she turned ten.

Tears welled in her eyes at the sweet memory. When she left Omaha, she had taken the quilt to remind her of her mother and the steel and flint to remember her father.

Even now, on the brink of her nineteenth birthday, she still believed in a bit of her father's magic—a miracle, really, of the spark between hardened steel and rock, a spark that spread into a lovely, warm fire. She may not know how to obtain food, but at least she had a place to sleep and the ability to make it warm.

"You'll never make it on your own."

Patrick's angry declaration rushed back to her. Words he'd spoken after Eloise's death when Lavinia had said she wanted to visit her mother's friend in New York. Patrick planted the doubt in her heart and mind, and it had taken weeks for her to conquer those doubts. But when he and Charles chose a date for the wedding, desperation fueled her to run.

She closed her eyes and leaned back against the wooden planks on the wall.

Today was Thursday—Christmas Eve. She was supposed to marry Charles tonight. What were he and Patrick doing now?

Charles was much too docile to search for her, but Patrick would probably scour the plains of Nebraska today, stopping at every train depot to ask if anyone had seen his lost sister. She could hope he'd give up the search, but she'd learned years ago that Patrick refused to give up until he got his way, and for some reason, he was determined that she marry Charles.

Her stomach rumbled, and she reached for her satchel, but before she retrieved the food Cora had given her, something shuffled outside the door.

At first she thought it was the wind rattling the wood, but the door began to slide open and she jumped to her feet, clutching her fists to her sides. She'd read about wild animals in Colorado—the bears, wolves, cougars, and buffalo—but she thought she would be safe inside.

Winter air poured into the barn, and her heart pounded as she scanned the opening. Then a tall man stepped into her space.

He was dressed in a leather overcoat and his dark brown hair curled under his cap. Stubble peppered his jawline and chin, and his green eyes were clouded with questions. Even though he looked to be only about thirty, he had the aura of a seasoned mountain man.

When he took off his hat, she realized he was the same man who'd offered to help with her luggage at the train station yesterday. The man who'd refused to listen when she'd said she didn't need assistance.

Had he followed her?

She crossed her arms, her hands still balled into fists. "What do you want?"

"I thought"—he shifted his gloves between his hands—"I saw smoke in the chimney."

"I was cold."

"I wouldn't expect—" His smile was tentative. "Where did you learn to start a fire?"

"My father taught me."

"You have a wise father."

She tightened her arms around her chest. "How did you know I was here?"

"I didn't know. I thought the barn was on fire." He cocked his head slightly, and she slowly began to release her arms. Perhaps he needed a warm place to stay, too.

"How did you find this place?" he asked.

"I—" She couldn't tell him that she couldn't afford to stay at the hotel he'd recommended. "I couldn't find anywhere to sleep in Aspen, and I thought perhaps I could find someplace right outside town."

"You could have gotten lost in the dark," he said, his smile gone. "People freeze to death out here."

She couldn't allow herself to consider that possibility. "But I didn't freeze."

"You have to be more careful—"

She interrupted him. "Are you hungry?"

He pointed toward the door. "I actually brought—"

She reached for her satchel. "Because I have a little extra food."

Her offer seemed to set him off guard for a moment, but he reached for an empty barrel to sit beside her. Quickly she unfolded one of the blankets and spread it out on the floor between them. Then she unwrapped Cora's bounty—two pieces of salt-cured pork, a small mound of dates, a baked roll made of bread crumbs and cheese—and placed the food on the blanket.

Before they ate, the man bowed his head and thanked God for their food, for shelter, and for someone with whom to share a meal. Lavinia bowed her head, but she didn't close her eyes. Instead, she watched the stranger closely, wondering again why he was here.

ༀ

Isaac felt lousy for eating half of the little food this woman had, but he didn't want to insult her by refusing her gift or by offering her charity. He ate quickly and thanked her for the breakfast. When he finished, he stood and pointed toward the door. "There's something I wanted to contribute to our meal."

She shook her head. "There's no need."

In spite of her protest, he stepped outside. He'd been up for hours last night, long past when the clock in the hallway struck the hour of two. A late night wasn't unusual for him, but usually he lost sleep worrying about the mine. Last night he was worried about this woman instead.

He'd contemplated hiking back to the barn in the middle of the night and waking her up, but he hadn't wanted to frighten her. Nor did he feel in the least bit comfortable asking a woman he didn't know to stay in his house. Gideon, his manservant, lived in a room on the first floor, but still this woman's reputation—and his—would suffer with such an impropriety.

But then again, she didn't seem to be the least bit concerned with her impropriety or reputation.

Why had she come to Aspen? No one in their right mind came here this time of year without a purpose and a place to stay.

On a log outside the door was a picnic basket filled with biscuits and jam and the bacon Gideon had fried and wrapped for their guest. She may not want his charity, but how could she argue with something hot to drink?

Opening the basket, he dug out the tin kettle he used when he went trekking through the mountains, two enamel cups, and the small burlap bag that contained coffee grounds. Then he filled the kettle with fresh snow before returning to the barn.

He held out the tin pot. "You like coffee?"

Her gaze wavered between irritation and appreciation. "With sugar and cream."

He wasn't certain if she was joking or not, but still he laughed. "I'm afraid black will have to do."

He dumped the grounds into the melting snow and placed the kettle on the stove before he sat beside her again. Her long hair tumbled softly over her shoulders, a few stray pins clinging to the strands. Her skin was unscathed by the sun, but one of her cheeks was streaked with grime. Several pieces of hay hung on her lavender gown and the hem of her dress was caked with dirt. None of it deterred from her beauty though.

He looked back down at his calloused hands. "I suppose we should introduce ourselves."

"It's not necessary—"

But it felt necessary to him. "I'm Isaac," he said, deliberately sidestepping the more proper Mr. Loritz. There was no place for formalities when they were sharing breakfast together in his barn.

When he glanced up, the woman nodded but didn't volunteer her name.

He didn't give up. "What should I call you?"

She contemplated his question for a moment before she answered. "Kathryn."

"Kathryn," he repeated. "Are you planning to spend another night here?"

Her eyes widened. "Is this your home?"

"No, I—" He owned this barn, but his house had been built three years ago, away from the trees. "I live nearby."

The kettle began to rumble on the stove, and he hopped up, relieved for the interruption. He lifted the handle with his gloves and set it on the wood floor, waiting for the grounds to settle before he poured it.

She accepted a cup of coffee without complaint, and steam billowed around her face as she sniffed it. Then she took a sip. "Thank you," she whispered as if unaccustomed to receiving even the smallest of gifts.

They drank their coffee in silence while the wind banged the door against the barn. When she finished, she set her cup on the floor beside his.

"Where is the telegraph office?" she asked.

"Next to the assayer. I can send a telegram for you—" He stopped himself. She might need his help, but clearly she did not want it.

"Or you can send it." He stood up and pointed toward the door. "I must get up to the Coronado."

She cocked her head. "What is the Coronado?"

"It's the silver mine up on the hill, between here and Aspen."

She scooped up the cups. "Do you work there?"

He nodded.

She offered him the cups, but instead of taking them, he stepped toward the door. "I'll return for them tonight."

She didn't seem at all pleased by the news.

Chapter 5

Five Liberty dimes, six pennies, and one quarter lay forlornly in Lavinia's beaded coin purse. She spread them out on the dusty barrel and counted them twice as if she could somehow work her father's magic and make them multiply. But after the purchase of her ticket to Aspen and dinner on the train, this was all that remained to send her telegram to Mr. Tipton.

How much did it cost to wire someone in Arkansas? She'd almost asked Isaac this morning how to send a telegram, but she didn't want him to know how desperate she was. Or how naive.

She had little experience in conversing with men. She had adored her father, despised her stepbrother and his friends, and loved Mr. Tipton and Eddie, who were both like uncles to her. Most of her schooling had taken place at home under a governess, so except her Sundays in church, she hadn't been around many boys, and Father had turned away any men who had wanted to court her, saying he wouldn't even talk about it until she reached the matronly age of twenty-one.

Lavinia carefully returned her change to her purse and secured it back in her satchel.

Even though Isaac's company unnerved her, his bitter coffee along with Cora's food had revived her. She dumped out the used grounds from the kettle and melted more snow to wash herself. With the corner of a blanket as her washcloth and the kettle as her basin, she bathed in the warm water and dried herself with the other side of the blanket.

If only she could take a long, hot soak in a real bathtub—

As she hung the blanket back up on a hook, she laughed at herself, standing among the caked dirt and hay in a dreadful state of undress. The orphaned daughter of one of the wealthiest men in Nebraska.

If Patrick and Charles had caught her at the train station, she would be in her room right now, freshly bathed and preparing for her wedding. There had been no time to order a wedding dress from Paris, but Patrick had commissioned a fashionable gown from the finest seamstress in Omaha, a lovely affair of white satin and old point lace to celebrate the Christmas season along with the marriage. But there had been no celebration in her heart.

Lavinia dressed and buttoned her warm coat, her stomach pacified and her heart grateful. God had answered her prayer on that freight train three days past. He had given her that window in time to escape from those who wanted to dominate her. Here in Colorado she could celebrate her life and this season of rebirth.

The sharp wind pricked her skin when she opened the door. She may have little money now, but as she stepped through the snow, her confidence emboldened, she prayed that He would continue to provide. In time, she hoped, all things would be made new.

Wooden buildings lined the rocky cliffs to the right of the valley and columns of smoke spattered the crisp blue sky with gray. A pounding sound echoed through the valley as she walked back toward town.

Was this the Coronado Mine where Isaac worked? She'd been relieved to discover he was a miner and probably lived in one of the boardinghouses in town. At least she wouldn't be competing with him to sleep in the barn.

The Western Union was located beside the assay office, just as Isaac directed. She tried to take better care not to draw attention to herself as she walked toward the office. The less conspicuous she was, the better—at least until Mr. Tipton helped her navigate between the truth and Patrick's lies.

When she stepped inside the Western Union, the operator scanned her tailored cloak before he met her gaze. She moved up to the wooden counter, trying to muster her confidence. He didn't need to know that she'd never sent a telegram before.

She retrieved her coin purse and set it on the counter. "I would like to wire a friend in Little Rock."

"Then you've come to the correct place." He slipped a pencil out from behind his ear and tapped on the paper in front of him. "What do you want to say?"

She clicked open her purse as she tried to organize the words in her mind. She must communicate her whereabouts clearly, but she didn't want to alert the operator or the recipient of the message to her name or the specifics of her predicament. Also, she wasn't certain how many words she could afford to send.

Mr. Tipton was spending December with his eldest son in Little Rock, so she gave the operator the information to address it. Then she began to dictate her short message. "Visiting Aspen in Colorado. Please wire immediately."

When she paused, he looked up again. "Is that everything?"

"Do I need to write more?".

"No, but—whom should I say it's from?"

She couldn't include her name, but perhaps there was another way. "*L.S.* will suffice," she finally said.

He raised his eyebrows. "An initial is the same price as an entire word."

"Just the same," she said. "I want to use initials."

"It's your money." He scribbled down the remainder of the message and picked up the paper. "That will be seventy-five cents."

Her fingers trembled as she pulled out her quarter. She'd wanted to keep a little money for food just in case she didn't find work.

"I don't know if I have that much—"

He began to crumple the paper. "Well, you'll have to come back when you do."

Tears began to swim in her eyes, but she blinked them back. She would not give up now. "What if I sent less words?"

"Sorry." He shrugged. "It's the same price for ten words or less."

She slowly placed the quarter on the counter and then her five dimes. She'd hated her stepbrother's gambling, and now it felt as if she were gambling as well in her attempt to find Mr. Tipton. But without Mr. Tipton's help, she would never be able to return home.

The operator took her money, and as he tapped her message, she slowly recounted her pennies. There were still six of them left, huddling together in her purse as if they were afraid she might pluck them out, too.

The operator stepped back out to the counter. "I wouldn't expect a reply until after Christmas."

She tried to stop the trembling in her lower lip, but it wouldn't cooperate. "Of course."

"Where should I deliver your reply?" he asked.

She clasped the purse shut. "I'll return for it."

Her heart cried out for her father as she stepped back into the street. He may have been distant during those last years of his life, but he would never let her go hungry. Even his marriage to Eloise had been to help provide for her.

But neither her father nor his money could help now. Somehow she must stretch these pennies until she found work. Or until Mr. Tipton found her.

⟡

The steady rhythm from the stamp mill pulsed through Isaac's office. The hammering was a welcome sound in all the buildings that surrounded the mine. Enormous stamps were crushing the ore, separating the metal from tons of rock—the valuable pieces of silver from the waste.

Outside the window was a covered portal that led down into the Coronado Mine alongside a snow-covered mound of tailings that had been stripped from the tunnel. He and Ned Tucker had spent much of the day working on the plans to build another shaft so they could uncover the new vein of silver. The miners at the Coronado made a good hourly wage, so few would complain about the increase in work, and they were all keenly aware that their jobs were in jeopardy if they failed. Most of his miners were good, hard-working men, and he didn't want to lose a single one of them to a mine closure or a cutback.

Tomorrow he would close the mine—the only day of the year the company did so. He'd have a strike on his hands if he asked his men to work on Christmas Day.

Harvey, the superintendent of the mill, stepped into his office. "Here's the paper for you," he announced as he slid the *Rocky Mountain News* across Isaac's desk.

Isaac glanced up at the clock, surprised to see it was already past four. As he and Ned hovered over their plans, scratching notes and diagrams for the new shaft, they'd lost track of the hours. It was nearly supper time and his noon meal still sat untouched in the pail on his shelf.

Harvey leaned back against the doorpost. "Are you two going to the service tonight?"

Ned erased a line before looking up. "I'll be there."

Isaac smoothed the wrinkles from the newspaper and set it beside his and Ned's drawings. "What service?" he asked.

Harvey sighed. "The Christmas Eve service."

Isaac looked back out the window at the sun dipping behind the mountains. "Perhaps."

A wisp of smoke hovered over the trees near his house, and his mind wandered back to the lovely woman who'd slept inside his barn. Was she still there, or had she left after sending her telegram? She'd hesitated when he had asked her name, and it made him wonder even more at her story and the reason such a beautiful woman, clearly accustomed to wealth, would find shelter in his barn.

What would she do if he invited her to the service with him? He smiled at the thought. The town would be shocked if he escorted a woman to church. It might be amusing to make his friends and even his employees wonder, but he guessed Kathryn wouldn't want the attention. It was probably better that he not be seen with her in public, but that didn't mean he couldn't celebrate the birth of Christ with her in the barn.

Harvey eyed the pencil drawings. "When do we start the new shaft?"

"In a week," Isaac said.

"We'll need at least three months to finish it," Harvey said. "Maybe four."

Isaac collected the diagrams into a pile. "We only have one month."

Harvey's eyes grew wide. "And then what?"

"Let's discuss that after Christmas."

Harvey opened his mouth as if to ask another question, but the whistle blew outside the office, and the miners began their short walk down to the boardinghouses in town. Harvey bid his good night, as did Ned Tucker.

Unless Isaac lit the kerosene lamp beside his desk, it would be too dark for him to work much later, but he had time to glance at the headlines of the newspapers before he began his trek down the mountain.

He perused the headlines about the silver mining boom in Colorado and the story about Nellie Bly's attempt to travel around the world, but when he turned the page, he dropped the newspaper back on his desk, shocked by the picture on page three. On the first column was an illustration of a woman who looked remarkably like the woman who'd spent the night in his barn. Except this woman's name wasn't Kathryn—at least not her first name. It was Starr—Lavinia Kathryn Starr.

Missing from Omaha.

He read the headline twice and then scanned the story. According to the article, Lavinia Starr, the daughter of the multimillionaire Albert Starr, had gone missing from her family's mansion in Omaha on Sunday. Her stepbrother, Patrick Dittmar, and her fiancé Charles Mahler were greatly distraught. Mr. Dittmar, the article said, was a successful businessman in Omaha and Lavinia's guardian. He believed his beloved sister to be near Denver and was so concerned about her mental state and whereabouts that he was offering a ten-thousand-dollar reward for information that helped him find her.

Isaac pressed his fist against his forehead, the number tumbling around in his mind. Ten thousand dollars would buy him the three months he needed to save the Coronado and begin making a profit again. And if Lavinia, in some sort of distressed state, had gotten lost, he would be helping by returning her to a safe place and to the care of her stepbrother and fiancé.

He slowly read through the article one more time. It was odd that the writer didn't mention the possibility that someone might have kidnapped her for ransom, and it was also strange that there was no report of this fiancé pleading for her return.

Mr. Dittmar said he was scared for his sister, but what if his sister had decided to leave on her own?

A snowflake whisked past his window, and as he stood, he folded the newspaper and tucked it into the pocket of his overcoat. The illustration of her features was almost as precise as a photograph. Plenty of other people in Aspen received the *Rocky Mountain News*, and if they recognized her, they would surely contact Mr. Dittmar to claim his reward.

He should probably wire Mr. Dittmar straightaway, but something seemed off about the entire prospect. Before he contacted this man, he wanted to give Lavinia the opportunity to tell her story.

Perhaps she had a perfectly good reason as to why she preferred sleeping in a drafty barn on a pile of hay to a mansion in Omaha. Or a marriage to Charles Mahler.

Chapter 6

The sandstone chapel was located near the edge of town, and the stained glass windows glowed from the light inside, a beacon on this cold winter night. Lavinia didn't dare go inside the church, but she stood nearby under a pine tree and listened. Beautiful music teemed from the pipes of an organ, flowing out into the churchyard, and she softly sang the lyrics with the congregation.

> *"Silent night, holy night,*
> *Shepherds quake at the sight;*
> *Glories stream from heaven afar,*
> *Heavenly hosts sing Alleluia!"*

In the starlight, she could almost see the heavenly hosts strewn over the mountains, rejoicing at the birth of the Savior. Perhaps it was a night much like this one when Christ was born, cold and clear as the men trembled at the sight of scores of angels spanning—illuminating—the sky.

The music faded into the night, and she closed her eyes and imagined the families standing together inside the church, fingers circled around a candle. How she longed to be among them, holding a candle and the hand of someone she loved. Just as she had done years ago with her mother and father.

Loneliness burrowed into her skin like the cold. Instead of idyllic Christmases past, painful memories flooded back to her.

Nine years ago, the Christmas before consumption stole her mother's life, her father had given his wife the most exquisite necklace with tiny oval-shaped rubies and a stunning diamond. When Father remarried, her stepmother confiscated all of the jewelry for her personal use. Eloise liked to flaunt the ruby necklace every Christmas, almost as if she enjoyed the pain it inflicted on her stepdaughter.

Patrick had been much more exacting in his cruelty. He was seven years older than Lavinia, and when she was younger, Father sent Patrick to attend a university on the East Coast. Each summer and Christmas he returned, and he seemed to thrive on tormenting her while Father was at the office and his mother looked the other way. Why he hated her so, she never understood, but his hatred ran as deep as her wounds.

One Christmas, when she was eleven, Patrick found the beautiful letters her mother had written to her before her death, the letters she treasured more than anything else, and he burned them. He locked the front door of their house so she couldn't save them, but through the living room window she watched him burn her prized letters over a candle, one at a time. A rock broke the glass, but it was too late to stop him. Patrick collected the ashes of her letters into his palm and brushed them into her bloodied hand.

She cringed at the memory, wishing she could erase it from her mind on this Christmas Eve. Patrick had threatened to hurt her dog if she tattled. She hadn't believed him and told her father what Patrick had done, but both her stepmother and stepbrother accused her of lying.

Eloise ranted for hours about her husband's spoiled child who broke windows. Lavinia had been confined to her bedchamber for a week, and she quickly discovered that she preferred the solitude of her room to the company of her stepbrother. She didn't come out again until he returned to school.

Two summers later, her dog disappeared. Patrick never confessed, but she suspected he knew exactly where Rose went. He had been angry with Lavinia that week for telling Father that he'd been frequenting a gambling hall. Even though Patrick hated her, he had a healthy respect for her father and what would happen to his future if he angered Albert Starr.

After Father lectured him, Patrick promised to stop, but Lavinia didn't believe for a moment that he quit. He may have respected Father, but Patrick hated the power he had over him. He gambled in secret, and his cruelty toward her became more covert until she wondered if her stepbrother was at fault for her persistent forgetfulness and clumsiness or if she was losing her mind. Whenever Patrick left for school, order was restored in her mind and their house.

After Father's death, Patrick began to pay her back in the open for the anger he'd pent up for so long, and now that his mother was gone, there was no reason for him to restrain himself. The marriage to Charles, she had no doubt, was quite calculated though she didn't know what the two men had conspired for her future.

In the months before he died, Father had promised he would provide well for her when he was gone, almost as if he knew his life was nearing the end. A carriage accident swept him away suddenly and there was no time for making new plans or even saying good-bye. Still he had promised—

Tears came again.

At Eloise's funeral, Patrick informed Lavinia that his mother left the Starr fortune and estate in his care. There was no provision left for her. Her only choice, Patrick had said, was to marry Charles. He insisted she do so right away before Charles changed his mind. Patrick's urgency frightened her almost as much as the thought of spending the rest of her life with a man notorious for his philandering.

Mr. Tipton would tell her the truth about her inheritance—if she had any inheritance. When she'd tried to send him a telegram from Omaha, Patrick had stopped her. She wouldn't stop fighting for the answers now. Somehow she would sift and separate the truth from the lies.

When the church doors opened, Lavinia rushed away from the building before anyone saw her. The host of stars led her through the valley and back to the old barn for the night. The embers glowed red from the fire she'd started before the service, and she added a log and stoked it until it turned back into a blaze.

As she sat back on the hay, she wondered again about the first Christmas almost two thousand years ago. What did Mary feel like the night before Jesus was born? She had Joseph beside her, but on the cusp of childbirth, she must have felt a twinge of longing for her mother. And she must have had some questions and even doubt perhaps in God's promise to her.

Lavinia glanced around at the worn walls and the rotting floor.

How could the Son of God be born in a cold, damp barn?

She reached into her pocket and took out one of the two penny candies she'd purchased at the general store—an almond with a candy shell. It was hardly a Christmas Eve banquet, but as she slowly ate, it pacified the aching in her stomach. She shouldn't have eaten all the salted pork and dates this morning or offered it to a miner who'd probably had a full meal for his breakfast. But she'd been so hungry and thought he was hungry as well—

Her eyes felt heavy, and with the clean blankets and fire warming her, she drifted off to sleep on her bed of hay. Hours seemed to pass before she woke, and when she did, she heard the deep breathing of someone asleep on the other side of the room. She looked over in the firelight and saw Isaac resting on the floor near the stove.

Her heart began to race at the impropriety of spending the night across the room from a strange man. But Isaac was beginning to feel less like a stranger. Not only had he brought her coffee, but she suspected that he'd delivered the blankets and wood as well.

She didn't want his help—and she could pretend she didn't need it—but the truth was that his provisions sustained her on this winter night. She was grateful for the food and warmth. And that she wouldn't have to spend her entire Christmas Day alone.

༄

Isaac's back ached when he woke beside the stove. The fire had subsided, but the room was still warm. It seemed ridiculous to sleep on this hard floor when he had a perfectly good bed at home, but he couldn't let Kathryn—Lavinia—stay in the barn alone.

Last night as he'd walked back from the nativity pageant, he decided to invite her to sleep in his guest room, but he didn't have the opportunity to ask. She had been asleep when he arrived, and he'd decided not to wake her.

He, on the other hand, didn't sleep much. The promise of the reward money taunted him, and if he was honest with himself, his motivation to help her was convoluted. But when he saw her asleep on the hay, alone, he hadn't been thinking about the money at all. His only thought was that he must keep this woman safe.

It made no sense to him why a woman would leave her fiancé and fortune to sleep in a barn. . .unless she was desperate. What happened to make Lavinia run?

Before he wired this Patrick Dittmar, he would find out why Lavinia was hiding out. If she was mentally unstable, as her stepbrother implied, he would contact Patrick or her fiancé right away.

But then again, why would this Charles Mahler want to marry a woman who was mentally unfit?

Isaac stood carefully so he wouldn't wake her and backed toward the door. Outside, a glimmer of sunlight illuminated the fresh snow covering the ground and coating the branches of the aspen trees.

The Kempers were expecting him at eleven for a Christmas brunch, and he was never late for his time with the Kemper family. But if they knew about his guest, they would excuse him for his tardiness.

What would they do if he brought a woman with him? He smiled at the thought. Maria Kemper would probably faint.

Until he had answers, he would guard Lavinia's secret. Then, perhaps, he could bring her to visit his friends.

Chapter 7

Lavinia had thought for certain that Isaac had been in the barn last night, but when she woke up, there was no one in the room but her. As she stood beside the fire, disappointment plagued her. Loneliness. She wasn't certain that Isaac was a friend, but he had been kind to her. Still she shouldn't have hoped that he might spend part of his Christmas with her.

She filled the kettle with snow and poured the remaining coffee grounds into it. As the water warmed over the fire, she tried to focus on the happy Christmases she'd had with her family. Before Mother passed away, the Starrs had celebrated Christmas as a family around an evergreen tree decorated with bright ribbons and candles and lace. They'd eaten roast duck and sipped eggnog, and her parents had listened as she played the piano.

How she missed those happier times.

The barn door began to creak open, but this time she didn't jump at the interruption. Instead, her heart filled with hope again. When Isaac walked back through the door, relief surged through her. Perhaps she wouldn't have to spend her Christmas alone after all.

He set a large picnic hamper on the hay and tipped his hat. "Merry Christmas."

"Merry Christmas to you." She pointed toward the kettle. "There's hot coffee if you'd like some."

"I would indeed." He opened up his hamper. "And I thought you might want something a little different than salted pork for your Christmas breakfast."

"Salted pork is fine—" Any food would be fine right now.

"Wait until you see what I have."

Then he spread the contents on a blanket. She sniffed the freshly baked biscuits and butter and blackberry jam and took a small bite.

Bliss.

She didn't want to devour his food, but she hadn't realized how hungry she really was until she tasted the sweet jam. While she ate, he slipped back outside, and when he returned, he was carrying a small pine tree with him. Lavinia hopped up to help him prop it in a bucket beside the wall. The poor thing was a paltry affair—most of the needles had fallen off and it bowed slightly to the left. She stepped back, examining it. "It looks so sad," she said.

Isaac dug a small burlap bag out of his pocket, and when he untied it, she saw yellow kernels inside. He smiled at her. "We'll have to cheer it up."

Curious, she watched him pour the corn into a cast-iron pan. He placed the lid on top and set it on the stove. Minutes later, one of the kernels popped and she jumped.

Isaac laughed. "Haven't you popped corn before?"

She hesitated, not wanting to tell him that she'd rarely gone inside the kitchen in their house and wouldn't be allowed to help the cook even if she asked.

Isaac's laughter faded, replaced with a smile. "Surely you've *eaten* popped corn before."

"Of course."

Another kernel popped, and she jumped again. This time Isaac withheld his laughter, but she could tell he was fighting it. "You can laugh if you want."

He cleared his throat. "Perhaps I can teach you how to do it."

Before she protested, he took her hand and placed it over the thick mitt that covered the iron handle. She followed his lead, moving the pan slowly back and forth over the heat. The steady rhythm soothed her like watching the dancing flames of the fire.

When the popping stopped, Isaac pulled the pan off the stove and opened the lid. Steam curled up around his face, and she fought back a smile. "I suppose you haven't ever strung popped corn either," he said.

She stood up straighter. "I have—when I was about six."

"So not very long ago—"

She raised her eyebrows in exasperation. "I'm almost nineteen."

His sigh was long, but she knew he was teasing by the glint in his eyes. "I suppose I'll have to reteach you."

She crossed her arms. "I can string the corn on my own."

His gaze settled over her, and she shivered. "I'm sure you can, Kathryn, but there is nothing wrong with asking for help."

He didn't understand. Her entire life, she had been reliant on someone else to provide even the most basic of her needs. For once, she wanted to be able to do something on her own, even if it was as simple as stringing popped corn.

He removed two needles, some fishing line, and another sack from the hamper—this one containing dried cranberries. He handed her one of the needles and then a piece of the line, but instead of saying a word to instruct her, he began to whistle.

She watched closely as he threaded three pieces of the popped corn and one of the cranberries. Then she lifted a small cloth out of the hamper and placed it on her lap before piling popped corn onto it. Following Isaac's lead, she began to thread the corn until the repetition of her task began to soothe her mind. Her fingers moved steadily. Three pieces of popped corn. One cranberry. Three pieces of popped corn. One cranberry.

Her mind flashed back to the winter evenings at her home, embroidering a pillow or another piece alongside her mother and a blazing fire. The memories along with the simple motion brought peace to her heart.

"You're smiling," he said, and she realized that he'd stopped working and was watching her instead.

She plucked another cranberry from the pile. "I do that on occasion."

He didn't look away. "It's nice when you smile."

She blushed, not sure what to do with his compliment.

Finally, he glanced back down at his growing strand and added another piece of popped corn. "Do you have family in Colorado?"

"I—" She stumbled over her words. Isaac may be close in age to Patrick, but she wasn't afraid of him. Perhaps it was her naïveté, but she wanted to tell him everything—how her father had died and left her in the care of a woman who didn't want her, how her family's fortune was going to a man who hated her, how her stepbrother had insisted she marry Charles. Part of her didn't want to burden him with her story and another part was afraid he would contact Patrick if he discovered the truth.

Still she could tell him part of her story.

"My mother died when I was a child and my father died two years ago." She paused, the wave of sorrow still fresh.

He put down the strand. "I'm sorry."

She piled more corn onto the cloth in her lap. "My father was a good man, but he lost his enthusiasm for life when he lost his first wife—my mother."

"It's hard to lose someone you love."

Her eyes widened as she looked back up at him. "Did you lose your parents?"

He shook his head. "Most of my family lives in Philadelphia, but I lost—" He poked his finger with the needle and stopped to wipe the blood off on his handkerchief. "A few years back I was engaged, but the woman I planned to marry decided to spend the rest of her life with my oldest brother instead of me."

Her stomach twisted. "Now it's my turn to be sorry."

"I used to be sorry, but I've realized Rebecca would have been miserable, and eventually I would have been, too." He glanced back over at her. "And I never would have come to Colorado if we'd married."

She pushed the needle through another piece of corn. "So you moved here to escape?"

"Partially. It was uncomfortable at home—" He paused. "My younger sister married a man who had invested in mines across Colorado. He'd been asking me to partner with him, but Rebecca didn't want to leave Philadelphia. After we ended our engagement, I decided to join Marcus and supervise the Coronado."

She stopped threading the popped corn. "I thought you were a miner."

He laughed. "Marcus says I'm much too impatient to be a miner."

She smiled back at him. "Are you impatient?"

"I suppose, though I'm trying to cure it. Impatience is never a good combination with mining, but sometimes it's good to act quickly." He put down the strand on his lap. "Like with you—"

Her shield of defense flung up before her, her back straightening as if she were prepared to fight. The shield might be invisible, but he seemed to recognize it. He paused before he spoke again. "You can't continue sleeping in this barn."

"Why not?"

He sighed. "Is there no place else for you to go?"

"There will be soon." She swallowed hard, trying to instill her words with conviction. "I'm waiting for a—for a friend to contact me."

Instead of responding, he stood and began draping the long strand of popped corn and cranberries around the tree's sparse branches. The trimming injected a bit of life in the paltry branches, and joy spilled into her heart. It was nothing like the grandly decorated trees that once graced her home, but it was a lovely reminder of the simple blessings of this day.

Perhaps Christmas wasn't relegated to the celebration in her childhood home. The wonder of the day, the miracle of the Son of God coming into the world, could be celebrated anyplace. Even in a barn.

Or, perhaps, especially in a barn.

She preferred remembering the humble birth of Christ here this year than in her family's mansion on Davenport.

"Kathryn?"

She glanced up, wondering at first how he knew her mother's name. And her middle name. Then she remembered she'd introduced herself as Kathryn.

He held out his hand. "Might I?"

She tied a knot at the end of her fishing line, and when she handed him her strand, he added it to their tree. With the humble trimmings, the tree almost looked happy to spend Christmas in the barn with them. When she looked up at Isaac's kind smile, her heart began to settle into something like contentment.

Isaac stepped back to stir the fire, silently chiding himself. He'd almost called her Lavinia, and he was fairly certain a slip like that would set a fire to her heels again. If she ran from here, he might never be able find her.

The *Rocky Mountain News* article seemed to burn in his pocket, yet he didn't feel right about confronting Lavinia with the story yet. The little she'd told him lined up with what he'd read, except he didn't know what frightened her. Was it her stepbrother or her fiancé or someone else who kept her from returning home?

He sat beside her in front of their little tree, sipping his coffee, before he pulled out his pocket watch. He needed to leave soon—the Kempers had expected him to arrive a half hour ago to celebrate with their family. If Lavinia wouldn't come with him, he could make sure she had plenty of food and more wood so she'd be warm. None of the miners knew she was here, and as long as she didn't leave this shelter, she would be safe until he returned. Then he would find another place for her to spend the night.

But he didn't want to leave her. He wanted to spend Christmas with her, even if it meant staying in this barn all day.

Usually he tried to avoid Christmas festivities. Most of his family would be gathering at the Loritz home in Philadelphia today, and his mother would dote on Sam and Rebecca and their three children. Isaac continually tried to force himself to be happy for his brother, yet the image of Sam and Rebecca together, laughing and loving each other, still burned him. Sometimes he missed his family in Philadelphia, his uncles and two sisters he'd left behind, but on Christmas Day, he was thrilled to be in Colorado.

He hadn't planned to tell Lavinia about Rebecca. For the past seven years, Josiah and Maria and their two children had distracted him from his final Christmas in Philadelphia, when he'd caught his brother staring at Rebecca in a way that wasn't at all brotherly. And his fiancée had smiled back.

He'd confronted his brother first and discovered that they had been meeting for months in private. Both Rebecca and Sam begged for his forgiveness, saying they hadn't wanted to deceive him, but at the time, he had been hurt and angry. He shuddered to think what might have happened if he had married Rebecca while she was in love with Samuel.

He may not have intended to tell Lavinia what happened, but he didn't want to conceal the truth with her, not when he wanted her to be honest with him.

He leaned forward, breaking the silence. "What was Christmas like when your mother was alive?"

She contemplated his words for a moment. "It was magical," she finally said. "She would decorate our home with ribbons and all sorts of greenery, and I remember her humming carols as she worked. When the snow piled high outside, she would turn off most of the lights inside and the house would glow with the candles and fire."

"It sounds beautiful."

"My mother loved beauty."

"Did your father continue to celebrate Christmas after your mother's death?"

Wind gusted through the cracks in the siding, rustling the pieces of hay before she replied. "Father married Eloise seven months after my mother died. She decorated the house even more extravagantly than my mother, but the warmth in our home was gone."

She stopped talking, and he knew he should say something comforting, something to reassure her, but he could think of no words to help heal such a loss.

Outside the barn someone shouted his name, and he recognized Josiah Kemper's voice. For a moment, he wished he could burrow himself under the hay before his friend found them. Lavinia stood and scanned the room as if searching for a place to hide as well. "Who is it?" she whispered.

"A friend," he said simply.

A friend who would have a whole lot of questions as to why he was hiding out in a barn with a woman he hardly knew.

Chapter 8

Isaac leapt to his feet when Josiah opened the door. "I'm sorry I'm late—"
Josiah froze in the open doorway, staring at Lavinia first, and then his gaze
ricocheted back and forth between the two occupants in the barn before it landed
on Isaac. "Maria and I were worried about you, but other matters seem to be occupying
your time."

"This is—" Isaac started to introduce her, but then he stopped. He didn't want to
deceive his friend by calling her the wrong name.

She stepped forward. "I'm Kathryn."

"Well, Miss Kathryn," Josiah said, his eyebrows raised, "I must admit that I'm
surprised to meet you."

"I've been—" She took a deep breath. "I'm new to Aspen and decided to spend the
night here."

Josiah's eyes narrowed. "In Isaac's barn?"

Lavinia turned to Isaac. "You didn't tell me this was your barn."

He shrugged. "You never asked who owned it."

Josiah took off his hat, and his reddish-brown hair fell over his collar. Isaac knew
for a fact that Maria had been trying to convince him to cut it for months, but Josiah
felt more at home among the men he doctored if he didn't take on supposed airs.

"Perhaps you two could sort this out later," Josiah said. "Maria's been cooking all
morning, and I'm supposed to retrieve Isaac before our meal is burnt."

"It's my fault he's late," Lavinia said.

Isaac shook his head. "We were visiting, and I lost track of time."

Josiah eyed Lavinia again. "Are you from around here?"

"She's not—" Isaac started, but she interrupted him.

"I'm only here for a few days."

Josiah crossed his arms over his chest, his gaze taking in the cranberries and corn
strung on the tree and the mound of hay. "Well, neither of you should spend Christmas
in this place."

Lavinia nudged Isaac toward the door. "You must go celebrate with your friends."

"I'm not going without you." The words slid out of his mouth quickly, surprising
him. And the words seemed to surprise Lavinia as well.

"I can't impose," she replied, her eyes wide.

Isaac petitioned his friend. "Tell her she's not imposing, Josiah."

Josiah glanced back and forth between them one more time before replying. "We
have a goose warming in the oven and more food than we could possibly eat on our
own." He stuck his hands in his pockets. "And my wife can help attend to any of your
needs."

"I still don't think. . ." She hesitated, and Isaac could tell she was wavering.

"Maria would appreciate the company of another woman," Josiah said as he opened the door. "She misses her friends this time of year."

Josiah stepped outside to let her and Isaac talk, and after he left, Lavinia slowly ran her fingers over the needles on the tree. "People will wonder who I am."

"It's nobody's business," Isaac said.

"Some people might make it their business."

"You can trust the Kemper family," he said slowly. "And you can trust me."

"I wish you would have told me you owned the barn."

He pulled his gloves over his hands. "I didn't want you to feel obligated."

Her eyes studied his face for several moments as if she could determine whether she trusted him enough to leave the security of this place. The reality was that he could make her leave his barn, but he didn't want to force her to go. He would simply stay here with her.

But she reached for her coat.

As Isaac extinguished the fire, Lavinia tied the hood of her coat over her head, and together they began to follow Josiah back to town.

The reward money would probably save the mine—and it would certainly help pay his miners until winter passed—but he wouldn't contact Patrick Dittmar. Nor would he mention the article for now.

It was odd that Lavinia hadn't mentioned her fiancé when he'd talked about his broken engagement. Perhaps she didn't want to marry this Charles Mahler after all.

And if he was honest with himself, he wasn't very fond of the thought of her marrying Charles Mahler either.

⁓

Maria Kemper was a feisty woman in her midthirties. She was dressed in a lovely white gown with dark red ribbons, and the smile that lit her brown eyes reminded Lavinia of her mother.

When she walked into the parlor of the Kemper's two-story home, Maria glanced down at Lavinia's torn travel gown and mud-soaked hem. In spite of her attempts to pin back her hair, Lavinia knew it must be a disaster. She hadn't looked into a glass for days. The same mud that flecked her dress was probably smeared across her face as well.

She thought she might see ridicule in Maria's eyes like she had seen in the eyes of her stepmother, but instead she saw compassion.

Her two children, Maria said, were playing upstairs with their new toys. She shooed her husband and Isaac out to the covered porch and waved Lavinia back toward the kitchen. Through an open doorway on the left, Lavinia saw a physician's office with an exam table and a black bag on top of a desk. To the right was a closed door.

Maria reached for the doorknob. "My husband said you spent the night in Isaac's old barn."

"I didn't know it was his." Lavinia prayed this woman didn't think she was trying to proposition Isaac.

Maria tsked, shaking her head. "That man has no sense when it comes to women.

He should have brought you here instead."

"It wasn't his fault," Lavinia said. "I insisted on staying in the barn."

Maria shook her head again as she opened the door. "I don't want to insult you either, but you shouldn't be sleeping in a barn any time of the year, especially not during the winter."

Before she could respond, Lavinia's mouth fell open. On the other side of the door she saw one of the loveliest sights she'd seen since she left Omaha—a wood-encased metal tub, a toilet, and a bureau with a mirror. Maria turned on both faucets, and the steamy hot water mixed with the cold. As she added bath salts to the hot water, Lavinia basked in the floral-scented cloud that billowed up around her.

Maria opened a drawer in the bureau and retrieved a clean towel and washcloth. Then her gaze wandered back down Lavinia's torn clothing. "Would you like to borrow one of my dresses?"

Lavinia shook her head. "No, thank you."

Maria stepped toward the door, and Lavinia waited for her to insist that she wear a clean dress, but she didn't. Instead, Maria said, "I'll be right outside if you need anything else."

Lavinia eyed the closed door and then looked down at her gown, at the lavender skirt streaked with coal dust and wet snow clinging in patches along the muddy hem. What was wrong with her? The woman was graciously offering to help her and she was too proud to take her assistance. She would like to wear a clean dress. Very much.

Why did she insist on being so stubborn?

Lavinia reached for the knob and opened up the door to find Maria nearby in the kitchen. "If it's all right with you, I think I would like to borrow your dress, just for today."

Minutes later, Maria returned with a lovely green wool dress, a matching jacket with black trim and lace collar, and clean underclothes. Lavinia hung the clothes beside the bureau, and then she unbuttoned her travel-worn gown and let it drop to the floor. She removed her underthings and left them in a pile on the floor before slipping into the bubbly water.

She wouldn't put it past Patrick to spend his Christmas tromping up and down the Rocky Mountains searching for her, but he had no idea where she went, and the world west of Omaha was immense. All she had to do was stay hidden long enough for Mr. Tipton to contact her. Somehow she would manage until then.

The hot bath invigorated her, filling her again with strength. She was grateful for Maria's offer to let her bathe and borrow her dress. And for Isaac's help in bringing her food and allowing her to stay in his barn. Until she could repay them, she must humble herself and accept their help. And pray that Patrick wouldn't be able to find her.

She sank deeper into the warm water.

No one in Aspen knew who she was. For now, she had nothing to fear.

Chapter 9

Josiah took a draw from his pipe, and the smoke wafted above the two wooden chairs on the covered porch. "I read a curious article in the *News* this morning."

Isaac buttoned his coat to ward off the cold and then leaned back and propped up his boots on the white railing that circled the porch. "There are always curious articles in the *News*."

"I haven't read many articles about women missing from Omaha."

Isaac stiffened. "I read the story."

"And saw her picture?"

Isaac crossed his arms over his chest. "Of course."

Josiah hiked his boots up onto the railing beside Isaac's and tapped his pipe on the arm of his chair. "We have to contact her brother to let him know she's safe."

Isaac turned and glanced into the picture window behind them. "We can't contact anyone until we know the reason she left."

"Her brother is concerned about her—"

"Her stepbrother," Isaac said, stopping him. "And we don't know that he's concerned."

Josiah pondered his words for a moment. "What if she is unstable?"

Isaac pushed his heels against the banister, rocking back his chair. "She seems to be thinking quite clearly to me."

Josiah's eyebrows climbed. "I'm not sure how clear you're thinking."

Maria opened the front door. "You gentlemen can come inside now."

Isaac stalled for a moment as he tried to sort out the confusing thoughts that collided in his mind. What if Josiah was right? What if Lavinia's beauty mixed with her plight had clouded his judgment? Her stepbrother could be wracked with worry.

The aromas of sage and plum pudding flooded onto the porch, and he stepped toward the door.

"Uncle Isaac!" Josiah's four-year-old son raced across the floor and leapt up into Isaac's arms. Isaac spun Ezra around once and set him back on the rug.

Ezra's sister, Elizabeth, was eight and much too mature to jump, so he extended his hand to her. "Good afternoon, Miss Elizabeth."

She shook it quickly, and then she gave him a hug.

Ezra nodded toward the kitchen. "We have a woman visitor."

"I know."

Ezra lowered his voice. "Mama says we mustn't ask too many questions."

"Your mother wants to respect her privacy."

"What's privacy?" Elizabeth asked.

Maria stepped out of the kitchen, her hands on her hips. "Something no one in this family respects."

The door squeaked behind her, and then Lavinia stepped into the room.

Isaac's mouth fell open. He'd thought Lavinia pretty the first time he saw her, but dressed in the fitted jacket and skirt, her damp hair pinned back, her green eyes glowing in the firelight, she looked stunning.

Josiah elbowed him. "You're staring," he mumbled.

Isaac cleared his throat and turned back to the children.

"It's time to eat," Maria announced with a clap of her hands.

The children rushed toward the dining room, the adults trailing closely behind. Isaac stopped at the doorway and forced himself to look at the table instead of the woman now standing next to him.

Colorful ribbons, pinecones and glass balls paraded down a silk runner in the middle of the table, and the centerpiece was a golden-brown goose on a silver platter, garnished with sprigs of pine and berries. There were crystal goblets, polished silver, and a feast of Christmas pudding, roasted potatoes, and mince pie.

Josiah pulled his wife close to his side. "You've outdone yourself."

Maria blushed and gave a small shrug. "It is Christmas, after all."

Elizabeth tugged on Josiah's coat. "I helped, Papa."

As Josiah enveloped both children in his arms, Isaac glanced over at Lavinia and saw the flash of envy in her eyes. Again he thought it odd that she hadn't mentioned her fiancé when he'd shared his story about Rebecca this morning. Perhaps she still longed to be loved, like Josiah loved Maria.

Isaac pulled out the chairs for Lavinia and Elizabeth, and then Josiah blessed their meal and began carving the goose.

"Thank you for letting me spend Christmas here," Lavinia said as she lifted her plate for a serving of the mince pie.

Maria smiled at her. "It is our pleasure to have you."

Ezra reached for a roll and began spreading huckleberry jam on it. "Where do you come from?" he asked, but Maria hushed him before Lavinia replied.

Elizabeth scooted closer to Lavinia and attempted to whisper, though everyone at the table heard her words. "Are you an angel?"

Lavinia smiled. "I am not."

"She looks like an angel," Elizabeth said as she turned to Isaac. "Don't you think she looks like one?"

He started to cough.

Maria passed the bowl of pudding to her daughter. "Let's not pester our guests."

Josiah lifted his drink. "Merry Christmas."

"Merry Christmas," Maria repeated.

Isaac lifted his glass with them, and when he glanced back toward Lavinia, she smiled at him. If he hadn't read the newspaper story, he would have thought she was an angel as well.

∽

An oil lamp flickered outside Lavinia's bedroom window on the second floor of the Kempers' house. When Maria asked her to stay the night, she didn't resist. Even though she didn't want to return to Omaha, she didn't want to spend another night in Isaac's barn either. Some might think it strange, but tonight as she basked under the warmth of a fur blanket and clean lilac-scented sheets, in the pillows and soft mattress, her heart was content.

She prayed as she watched the light. She had no money to leave Aspen or wire Mr. Tipton again, but if God was powerful enough to send His Son to the world, surely He could continue to guide her. First thing in the morning, she would visit the telegraph office to see if Mr. Tipton had sent a return reply. Then she would decide what to do next.

The Kempers had been incredibly kind to her, and Isaac—

The family had sung Christmas songs tonight around the fire, Maria accompanying them on the piano. While the others were watching the fire, she caught Isaac watching her, and the warmth in his gaze startled her. Usually when men looked at her, she saw greed, or in Patrick's case, hatred. But not Isaac.

Patrick had said no one else except Charles would want to marry her unless a fortune was attached to their future. And she'd believed him. When men back in Omaha thought she would inherit the Starr estate, they'd promised her all sorts of outlandish things if she would marry them, but she'd refused each proposal, knowing she would only be trading one prison for another.

Not that she was considering marriage now—

She yanked the covers up to her chin, glad no one else was privy to her silly thoughts.

She'd heard Isaac and Josiah whispering about the Coronado, and Isaac said the mine would be shut down the first of February if he didn't find a vein of silver. . .or another investor. If Patrick offered a reward for her return—and Isaac found out about it—everything would change between them.

The Kemper children adored Isaac, and she understood why. Even though he held an important position at the mine, he cared for those around him. He treated these children with kindness and brought food to a stranger who'd hidden herself away in his barn. Isaac felt sorry for her, that was all, and she was grateful for his concern. She may enjoy his company, but he didn't feel anything except perhaps pity for her.

As her eyes grew heavy, the image of Josiah and Maria flashed through her mind. The admiration that flowed easily between the two of them was like the sweet love she'd seen between her parents when she was a girl. Charles never looked at her like that, nor would he. He didn't seem to see her at all.

She glanced back out the window one more time at the snow falling softly outside the glass. What would it feel like to have Isaac slip his arm around her shoulders and tenderly kiss her cheek or even her lips?

She shivered again, but this time it wasn't from the cold.

Chapter 10

Lavinia stood paralyzed on the sidewalk in Aspen, her heart thundering under her heavy coat. Her eyes were fixed on the man inside the telegraph office and his crested gold ring that flashed in the light.

How had Patrick found her?

She had been in Aspen for almost a week now, hiding out in the Kempers' home, and she'd begun to think Patrick would never locate her. Had the Kempers wired her stepbrother? But how would they have known—

The oiled curl of Patrick's mustache rose and fell quickly as he talked in earnest with the operator at the counter. Then her stepbrother stepped back toward the window, and she swiveled before he turned around, picking up the skirt of her borrowed dress to rush toward the courthouse.

Would the government officials in Aspen really give her a ticket back home? If so, she would get on the next train. Patrick could search every mountain in Colorado for her, and she—

She didn't know where she would hide when Patrick returned to Nebraska, but she would sort that out later.

"Kathryn!" a man shouted behind her.

She didn't realize at first that he was calling for her, but when Isaac said her name again, she stopped.

He hurried to her side. "Maria said you had gone out—"

She glanced over his shoulder. The door of the telegraph office was beginning to open. "I can't stay here."

Isaac looked back at the telegraph office as Patrick stepped onto the street.

Her hands trembling, Lavinia lifted her skirts again and whirled toward the courthouse, but she'd only taken a step when Isaac put his arm around her waist. She jumped, startled by his touch.

"Walk slowly," he whispered as he guided her away from the telegraph office. "Is it Patrick?"

She stared up at him, questions tearing through her. "How—how do you know about him?"

"We will talk later." He slowed her pace by the weight of his hand. "If we rush, he will surely guess."

Even though everything within her screamed to flee, she and Isaac stopped in front of the hat shop, and he pointed at the window.

"We're going to stroll down this street like an old married couple," he said calmly as if they were discussing the purchase of a new hat. "And we are not going to look back."

Her voice shook. "What if he stops us?"

He stepped toward the next window. "Why are you afraid of this man?"

Answers spun in her head. She feared Patrick's anger, the power he had over her, the hatred that festered inside him. "I'm afraid he will hurt me," she finally said.

When he looked down at her, she saw the tenderness in his gaze again, but this time it was infused with strength. "I won't let him."

Would Isaac really be able to protect her from Patrick? When her gaze locked in his, she nodded slowly, and a ray of hope flickered inside her. Most men crumbled in a confrontation with Patrick, but it seemed he had no power over Isaac. Perhaps she and Isaac could withstand her stepbrother together.

But then again, what if Patrick offered Isaac money to look the other way? Few men in Omaha would turn down Patrick's offer, and she couldn't blame Isaac if he took money as well for himself or for his mine.

But she wanted Isaac to be different from other men. She wanted him to care more about her than about what he could get from Patrick.

Isaac turned away from the store window, but she hesitated. She could walk slowly by herself, all the way to the courthouse, but Isaac was here, willing to help her. She didn't have to do this alone.

She reached for his arm and followed his lead down the snowy sidewalk, willing her feet to stroll alongside his. When they reached the Jerome Hotel, Isaac held open the door and she stepped inside. They climbed the staircase to a sitting area on the third floor, and Isaac glanced out the window. "He's going into Cora's Boarding."

"She'll tell him that I'm in Aspen—"

"I believe he already knows."

Of course he did, but the thought still made her heart race again. "I have to get on the next train."

He held her again in his gaze. "I don't want you to run again, Lavinia."

The racing inside her chest stopped as her given name reverberated in her head. She lifted her hand from his arm and let it drop to her side. "How do you know my name?"

He reached into his pocket and unfolded a piece of newspaper. Then he smoothed it across a polished sideboard. "The same way Patrick probably found you."

She glanced down at the paper and saw a sketch of her face. And the offer of a reward for her return.

"It was in the newspaper before Christmas," he said. "Someone in town must have wired your brother."

Nausea swept over her, and she collapsed into a chair beside the bureau. Why couldn't Patrick let her go? He didn't need her. He had her family's money and their home and all of her mother's possessions as well. What else could he possibly want?

The reason didn't matter, she supposed. Patrick was determined to win.

Isaac sat in the chair next to hers, but she had nothing to say to him. Resignation washed over her. And rejection.

She covered her face with her hands.

She'd fooled herself into thinking Isaac might care for her, but all along he'd known exactly who she was. And he'd known about her family's money. No wonder he had taken such good care of her. He was a smart businessman. This morning he was probably trying to get her to a private location so he wouldn't have to share the reward.

Those times he'd been watching her, those moments on Christmas Day and the days after that warmed her heart. . . Had he been seeing the reward instead? She'd begun to trust him, but he had been deceiving her.

No matter where she ran, her stepbrother would find her.

She looked over at Isaac, straightening her posture. "You may as well take me to Patrick."

Isaac leaned toward her, and she hid her hands in the folds of Maria's gown so he wouldn't take one of them. "I thought you didn't want to go home with him."

"It doesn't matter what I want." She swallowed hard. "Patrick won't stop until he finds me."

Isaac focused on the window that overlooked the city street and then glanced back down at the article. "According to this, you are supposed to marry a man named Charles Mahler."

"My stepmother died the first of December, and Patrick won't provide for me any longer," she said. "Charles doesn't love me, but he and Patrick seem to have made some sort of deal so he will at least feed and clothe me."

She could see the compassion in his eyes. "I'm sorry," he said.

But she didn't want him to feel sorry for her anymore. She wanted—

She wrapped her arms across her chest. It didn't matter what she wanted. "I thought I could take care of myself, but I can't—"

He stopped her. "We all need other people."

"You don't need anyone."

"That's not true. My brother-in-law and sister gave me the opportunity to leave Philadelphia. My investors in Denver support the mine, and the men up at the Coronado partner with me to make it a success." He inched the chair closer to her. "Somehow you have managed to travel all the way here by yourself and obtain enough food to sustain yourself and a place to sleep."

"Because you helped me."

"There is nothing wrong with getting help when we need it."

But there was. For the past two years, she had been indebted to Patrick and his mother for almost everything.

She swallowed. "Did you wire Patrick?"

He shook his head.

Her heart began to soften. "But you could have contacted Patrick and got the money for your mine."

"I could have."

She studied his face. "Why didn't you?"

He shrugged. "I wanted you to tell me the truth first, and I—I wanted to find out if you wanted to return home."

"I don't want to go back," she whispered.

He reached for her hand again, and this time she allowed him to take it. A spark of hope reignited inside her. He cleared his throat. "Has anyone else in Omaha asked you to marry them?"

"Plenty of men have asked—"

"Do you want to marry any of them?"

She shook her head.

"Then perhaps I can protect you from your stepbrother—"

"You don't know what Patrick can do." Tears burned her eyes, but she didn't want him to see her cry.

"Marry me," he whispered.

Her eyes grew wide.

"Patrick can't hurt you if we marry," he said.

She pulled her hand away from his. "There is no money."

He lurched back as if she'd slapped him. "What are you talking about?"

"Patrick inherited the entire estate."

"I don't know what this has to do with—"

She sat taller even as her insides crumbled. "You won't get a penny if you marry me."

His mouth gaped open slightly as he studied her face. "I want to help you, Lavinia."

She didn't want his pity. She wanted his love.

Her heart began to harden again. "Then get me a train ticket home."

He opened his mouth again as if there was something else he wanted to say, but he promptly closed it. "I'll be back in an hour."

Chapter 11

Isaac stomped out of the hotel, his pulse pounding. Lavinia's stepbrother was no longer on the street, and it was probably a good thing. If he saw the man, he might pummel him for stealing Lavinia's ability to trust, replacing it with fear.

After everything, how could she think he wanted to marry her for money? She was right—he didn't know what Patrick was capable of—but he'd thought if she would marry him, he could protect her.

But maybe she didn't want to marry him. Perhaps she saw in him what Rebecca did—a man who would make a much better brother than a husband.

The train station was to the left, but instead of going there, he walked in the opposite direction, toward the Kempers' house. He wouldn't force Lavinia to stay in Aspen if she wanted to leave, but he needed a bit more time. He might not be able to save the mine, but perhaps it wasn't too late for him to help Lavinia without sending her back to Omaha. Or handing her over to a man she despised.

Patrick emerged from the boardinghouse, and Isaac watched him scrutinize the street as if he were hunting a fox for sport. Then the steely resolve in Patrick's eyes honed in on him.

Isaac stopped walking.

"Hello there," Patrick said, offering Isaac his gloved hand as he introduced himself. Isaac kept his hands in his pockets, both clenched into fists. Patrick quickly retracted his arm.

Instead of shaking Isaac's hand, Patrick removed a photograph of Lavinia from his satchel and held it out. "Have you seen this woman?"

Isaac studied her lovely but stern face, wishing he could make her smile. "Perhaps."

Patrick slowly lowered the photograph. "Where is she now?"

Instead of answering, Isaac asked, "Why do you want to find her?"

"I fear for her life," Patrick said as he put Lavinia's picture back into his case.

Isaac felt the muscles in his shoulders clench up like his fists. "And why is that?"

"She is slow in the mind," Patrick explained as if Isaac were slow as well. "She won't be able to survive without my help."

Isaac forced his voice to level. "Then I'm sure she will be very excited to see you."

He started to walk away, but Patrick reached out and clamped his hand over Isaac's shoulder. "I'm offering a substantial reward for her return," he said, his voice lowered as if he were conspiring with a friend. "I'll give you twenty thousand dollars if you take me to her."

Twenty thousand dollars?

Isaac could almost hear Harvey and Ned and even Marcus in Denver shouting from the sidelines, urging him to take this enormous sum of money. It would buy them

141

at least six more months to turn the mine around. . . . Or he could simply pocket the cash and start over.

But even if Lavinia didn't want to marry him, even if the money would save all that he had worked for, he'd never offer her up to this snake.

Isaac shrugged off Patrick's hand. "You're hiding something, Mr. Dittmar."

Patrick's eyes narrowed. "What do you mean?"

"I think there's another reason you want Lavinia to return, and it has nothing to do with her well-being."

Patrick swore. "What has she told you?"

"The truth."

Or at least part of it.

Patrick didn't say anything else, and it was just as well. No matter what the man said or how much money he offered, Isaac would never tell him where Lavinia was hiding.

⟋⟋⟍

From the third floor of the hotel, Lavinia watched Isaac and Patrick on the street below, their heads huddled together as they collaborated. She had dared to let herself believe that Isaac might be different, and her heart ached as she tried to make sense of this shift in a man she'd hoped would be solid.

Instead of obtaining a train ticket for her, Isaac had gone to solicit her stepbrother. Were he and Patrick negotiating the reward right now? She'd told Isaac that she feared Patrick would hurt her, and yet it seemed he was conspiring with her stepbrother on a way to imprison her. Had he been blinded by the Starr fortune as well?

She reached for her coat, her heart in tatters.

Perhaps the people at the courthouse would give her a ticket down to Little Rock instead of Omaha. She could find Mr. Tipton and then decide about her future. If her father's entire estate had really gone to Patrick, perhaps her father's solicitor would help her find work in Arkansas. She would never have to return to Omaha.

She stepped back toward the staircase.

She was tired of hiding from Patrick. Not just in Aspen, but for the past eight years of her life.

It may be a risk, but she wouldn't hide anymore.

Chapter 12

Isaac ducked into the blacksmith shop, tipped his hat to the two smiths working over the fire, and darted out the back door. Then he sped through two alleyways before he reached the Kemper home and swung open the door to Josiah's office.

Josiah hung his stethoscope on a ring by the empty exam table and slipped on his black suit coat before he turned toward Isaac. "Why aren't you at the Coronado?"

Isaac took off his hat. "I came down to check on Lavinia."

Josiah nodded toward the open door that connected his office to the kitchen. "She already went out this morning."

"I know," he said, his heart pounding. "Her stepbrother has come for her, but I won't let her leave with him."

Josiah sat on a wooden stool. "Why don't you want her to go home?"

"I want her to be safe."

"We all want her to be safe," Josiah said, tapping on his desk. "Perhaps we could find another place for her to stay."

Isaac paced across the floor and then stopped. "I offered to marry her."

Josiah leaned forward. "Are you crazy?"

"Apparently so. She turned me down."

"You just met her," Josiah said.

The floor creaked, and Maria stepped through the doorway, her arms folded over the top of her apron. "What did you say to her?"

"I—"

"Now, Maria. . ." Josiah interrupted him.

"It's important," she said, her brown eyes still focused on Isaac. "What did you tell Lavinia?"

He tugged at the hat in his hands. "I told her that I could protect her from her stepbrother."

"And—" Maria prompted.

"And what?"

She huffed. "You didn't say anything else?"

"Nothing of consequence."

Maria groaned. "You are such a fool."

Josiah stood up. "This isn't helpful."

Isaac didn't look at Josiah. Instead, his gaze was intent on Maria. "What did I do wrong?"

Maria put her hands on her hips. "Did you tell Lavinia that you love her?"

Love her?

He hadn't thought much about loving another woman after Rebecca. Lavinia was beautiful, and he admired her determination and faith, but he'd proposed marriage to rescue her from Patrick and a marriage she feared.

Was it possible that he did love her as well?

"No woman wants to marry a man who doesn't love her," Maria said before she moved back into the kitchen.

A memory from Christmas night flooded back to him, the way Lavinia had watched Josiah embrace his wife. And the way she'd blushed when she realized Isaac was watching her. He didn't want the Starr money, and if he was honest, he wanted much more than to keep Lavinia safe or keep her in Aspen. He wanted to marry her because he loved her. And he didn't want to spend another moment of his life without her.

The whistle of the arriving train pierced the silence.

He put his hat back on his head. "I must get back to her."

"Don't be rash," Josiah warned.

"I won't," he said. For the first time in weeks, he felt as if he was finally thinking quite clearly.

He ran down the street, not caring if Patrick Dittmar or anyone else saw him. If love made one foolish, then he was the biggest fool of all.

❦

Lavinia stepped onto the platform beside the depot, her fingers clutching a railway ticket for Little Rock as the train chugged into the station. She should be relieved that Patrick hadn't found her, but all she felt was sadness—sadness to leave this town. And Isaac.

The agent inside the train station said it wouldn't take long to unload the supplies and reload the cars with ore and a handful of passengers. She should be on her way back to Denver within the half hour and on to Little Rock in the morning.

Black smoke settled over the station, and the doors of the arriving train opened.

"Hello, Lavinia."

She froze for a moment and then slowly turned around. Her stepbrother stood in the doorway of the depot, a cigar cradled in his lips.

She scanned the platform to his right, but this time there was no other train headed out of town. No place for her to run.

This time she would have to stand instead.

She folded her arms over her chest. "How did you find me?"

"An old woman from one of the boardinghouses wired."

"But how did you find me here?" she insisted.

He sneered down at her. "I saw you leave the hotel."

"But you were talking to—" She swallowed, her mind spinning. "I saw you talking to a man on the main street."

"He wouldn't tell me a blasted thing." Anger flashed through his eyes. "And he won't get a single penny now."

His words soothed her at first and then they stung. Perhaps Isaac did care about her and not her money. Perhaps she should have trusted him to return. She'd been so unkind to him, and now—

Now she had left the hotel, and there was no one to help her.

144

She watched as Patrick lowered his cigar and tapped it against a bench, the ashes raining down on the wood. He thought he could control her, no matter where they were, but not anymore. She rolled her shoulders back. She may be alone, but he had no power over her in Colorado.

"What do you want from me?" she demanded.

"I want you to come home," he replied as he stepped toward her. "Charles misses you."

She buttoned the top of her coat. "I'm sure Charles has found someone else to entertain him."

Patrick lifted two tickets out of his pocket. "We will go home together."

She shook her head. Patrick could ride all the way to Arkansas with her if he wanted. He wouldn't deter her from finding Mr. Tipton and the truth about her father's will. "I'm not going back to Omaha."

He stood over her now. "Yes, Lavinia, you are."

She stared up at the man who despised her, but instead of determination in his gaze, she saw desperation. "I don't understand," she said slowly. "You've hated me since our parents married, and now that they are gone, you won't let me go."

When he didn't respond, she studied him for a moment. Fear seemed to harden his callous face, and when she glimpsed the anxiety in his eyes, her own fears began to dissolve. For so long she had been afraid of him, but even though she didn't understand it, she held some sort of power over him as well.

She tilted her head. "Why do you want me in Omaha?"

"I—" He didn't finish. Over his shoulder, Lavinia watched as one of the passengers on the incoming train disembarked. He tapped his walking stick as he stepped onto the platform, his fancy top hat slightly askew. Under the hat was a tuft of gray hair.

She stepped to the side. "Mr. Tipton?"

The man turned quickly, and when he saw her, he waved with his stick. She rushed around Patrick, and the older man greeted her with a kiss on the cheek. Then he clung to her hand, examining her face as if he wasn't certain whether she was real or a mirage.

She clutched his hand, breathless. "You received my telegram."

He nodded. "I was so worried—"

Patrick interrupted him. "There was no reason for you to worry," he said. "I was searching for her."

Patrick's arrival had terrified her, but his presence didn't seem to bother Mr. Tipton one bit.

"Oh good," Mr. Tipton said as he looked between them. "I'm glad you are both here. We must discuss the matters at hand."

Patrick checked the timepiece in his pocket. "The train leaves in fifteen minutes."

"We mustn't let a train deter us," Mr. Tipton replied as he looked at the row of shops beyond the platform. "Where can we find a spot of tea?"

Patrick stepped closer to the elderly man, looming over him. "There is no time for tea."

"There's always time for tea." Mr. Tipton nudged Patrick's arm with his walking stick. "You may choose whether or not you would like to join us."

Lavinia linked her arm through Mr. Tipton's, a lightness empowering her with the solicitor's indifference to her stepbrother. Mr. Tipton picked up his briefcase, and they moved across the platform toward the coffee and tea shop on the other side.

She assumed Patrick was trailing behind them, but when Mr. Tipton opened the door to the shop, she realized her stepbrother was gone.

She glanced back at the depot. "Where is Patrick?"

"Probably on the train," he replied. "I assume Eloise made him aware of the terms in your father's will."

She looked back over at the solicitor. "What terms?"

He smiled at her.

Chapter 13

M r. Tipton sipped his steaming Earl Grey with cream as she told her story. "Patrick demanded I marry Charles before you returned from your trip."

He set his cup on the saucer. "Mr. Dittmar had no right to place that demand on you."

"He said I had no other options, but I didn't want to believe him." She tugged on the paper ticket still in her hands. "Do I have options?"

"Oh, Lavinia." He sighed, and for a moment, she feared his answer. He, too, pitied her like Isaac and Cora and the others who had helped her.

He unlocked his briefcase on the chair beside him. "You have a thousand options if you care to take them."

"What—" She started, her mind spinning. "What do you mean?"

"With Eloise's passing, Mr. Dittmar will receive a generous monthly allowance from your inheritance, but it is not enough to support his—" Mr. Tipton hesitated as he seemed to search for the right word. "His business endeavors."

She assessed each of his words. "My inheritance?"

"Of course," Mr. Tipton said before taking another sip of his tea. "Your stepmother managed the estate after your father's death, but if she hadn't died, the estate would have become yours when you turned twenty-one."

He placed the will on the table, and as she read through it, her heart leapt. The house was hers now along with her father's business and a substantial portfolio of stocks and bonds. Her father hadn't neglected her after all.

"Patrick knew about this," she said, her gaze on the papers.

"Eloise probably told him before she passed."

Strength swelled within her again as the anger toward her father subsided. "Then he made some sort of deal with Charles."

"I assume so," Mr. Tipton replied. "There are plenty of rumors about Charles's gambling debts as well."

"They were bartering with me." She looked up at her father's friend and solicitor. "Charles would use part of my inheritance to pay back whatever he owes Patrick. Then he could be rid of me."

"That is precisely what your father was trying to avoid," he said. "In his will, your father states that if you disappear or lose your life before your stepbrother, all the money in your inheritance—including Patrick's allowance—will be donated to charity."

No wonder Patrick didn't want her to leave Omaha. And why he'd followed her all the way to Aspen.

The whistle of the train blew again as it prepared to leave the station. She quietly tore up her ticket, the pieces falling into her lap, and then reached for her purse at her side. Inside were four pennies, her mother's ring, and her rock and flint.

Thanks to her father, she had the ability to make fire and now the income to care for herself. But she didn't want to be alone anymore.

Outside the window, she watched as the train wheels began turning north. She was so grateful that she hadn't gotten on the train, with or without Patrick.

She would have Mr. Tipton sell the mansion in Omaha and send for Eddie and two other house servants who'd cared well for her. But then she would have to decide where they would live. She couldn't stay in Aspen if Isaac didn't love her as she did him.

The table rattled as the train passed them, and then to her left, a man ran across the platform after it, his arms waving as if he could stop the train. *Isaac?*

Her heart somersaulted, and then it felt as if it might break open.

Mr. Tipton shook his head as Isaac ran past the window. "Looks like that poor fellow missed his train."

Lavinia's eyes filled with tears.

Mr. Tipton glanced back at her, studying her face for a moment before he looked back out the window. "Or perhaps, he thinks he might have lost someone."

ॐ

Isaac didn't go back to the mine. Nor did he go home or return to the Kempers' house. Instead, he wandered the streets of Aspen for an hour, a giant hole seared through his chest.

Had Lavinia left on the train with Patrick? Or had she run away from him like she had Patrick and Charles? He'd wanted to ask her one more time to marry him. Wanted to tell her that he loved her as a man loves his bride. He'd tried to stop her from leaving, but Lavinia was gone.

Maria was right. He'd been an idiot. He should have told Lavinia this morning that he loved her.

After his long walk, Isaac knew he couldn't stay in Aspen. He ended up back at the train station to purchase a ticket to Little Rock, and it took ten dollars to convince the telegraph operator to give him the address where Lavinia had sent her telegram. In the morning, he would travel to Arkansas and propose the right way.

If she still refused, he would throw himself back into his work at the Coronado. And as soon as possible, he'd tear that old barn down.

He finally returned home after the sun set. Gideon, his manservant, met him at the door, and as Isaac hung his hat on the rack, he asked Gideon to pack a suitcase for him. But instead of inquiring about the contents of Isaac's suitcase, Gideon pointed back out the door. "There's smoke coming from the barn."

His chest lurched. "What?"

Gideon lifted Isaac's hat back off the rack. "Someone must be trespassing again."

He hadn't dared to look toward the barn when he walked home, but even if he had, clouds covered the stars tonight. He wouldn't have been able to see smoke.

"Are you certain?" he asked Gideon.

The man nodded. "It started about an hour ago."

His pulse began to race. Was it possible?

He reached for his hat and tugged it back over his ears. Perhaps it was a vagrant who'd discovered his barn, but perhaps—

"Be careful, sir," Gideon said as Isaac hurried back out the door.

He rushed across the field of dried grass and stone to the edge of the trees. The smell of wood smoke filtered through the air and light flickered through the cracks in the barn wall.

He took a deep breath and knocked on the door. "Lavinia?"

"Come in," she said with a soft laugh. "It's your barn."

He stepped inside, and there she was, standing before the stove dressed in a pale gray dress with pink ribbons and a strand of pearls around her neck. The woman who'd stayed in his barn had been determined but afraid. There was no fear in the woman before him. All he saw was confidence and beauty and a woman who deserved so much more than a marriage to him.

He placed his hand on the doorpost. "I was—" Words eluded him.

She pointed at a pot on the stove. "I thought you might be hungry."

His eyes focused again, and he glanced around the room. The dust and pieces of hay had been swept from the floor. Their paltry little tree leaned against the wall, and the room smelled like cranberries and seasoning from the stew.

"What are you doing here?" he finally asked.

She shrugged. "I didn't think anyone was living in the barn."

"No, of course not, but—"

She laughed again. "I wasn't sure you would come."

"I thought you were on that train. To Little Rock."

"Patrick was on the train." She crinkled her nose. "I wasn't going to travel with him."

He watched her in wonder. "What happened?"

She stood beside him, and he smelled the kiss of rosewater on her skin. He wanted to take her into his arms and never let go again. He wanted to—

"You asked me a question in the hotel," she whispered.

"Indeed." He reached out and took her hands. "But I did it all wrong."

She smiled. "I thought you might want to try it again."

He pulled her closer to him and looked into the depths of her eyes. "I love you, Lavinia. I don't care about money or a reward or—"

She put her fingertip on his lips to silence him. "I know."

He enclosed his hand over her finger and bent down to whisper in her ear. "But I do care very much about marrying you."

When he kissed her, the warmth from the fire engulfed them both.

Epilogue

Five Months Later

Outside the barn, a meadowlark's song joined the melody in Lavinia's heart. Today she would finally become Isaac's wife.

After she accepted his proposal, she'd spent another month in Aspen with the Kemper family and then returned to Omaha for the remainder of the winter to put her father's business and affairs in order. Mr. Tipton would manage most of the estate now, and if she must return to Omaha in the future, she would do so with her husband.

Isaac wouldn't take any of her inheritance to save the Coronado, but neither he nor his brother-in-law could argue with an official investment. As it turned out, her investment had been a wise decision. The miners found the new vein in three months, and silver seemed to pour out of the Coronado all spring. Isaac and his men had already begun blasting for a new shaft to the south.

"You look beautiful," Maria said as she straightened the satin in Lavinia's veil. It was the same veil Lavinia's mother had worn when she'd married Albert Starr.

Bells chimed outside the barn, and Maria urged her toward the door. She and Isaac had wanted to marry inside the barn, but there wasn't nearly enough room for the Coronado miners, Isaac's family, and all those who had traveled from Omaha to attend their wedding.

Maria opened the door, but before Lavinia left the barn, she fingered the strand around her neck one more time. Her mother's diamond and ruby necklace. For a moment, she imagined both her parents waiting for her outside, her mother smiling with pride and her father with tears in his eyes. If they were still alive, she was certain both her father and mother would be celebrating this morning.

Instead of her parents, Eddie waited for her in the sunshine, dressed in a formal black coat with tails. Taking a deep breath, she reached for Eddie's arm, and he escorted her along the path, through the trees.

In the meadow on the other side of the forest, at the base of the snow-laced peaks, hundreds of people waited to celebrate with her and Isaac. When she and Eddie arrived, the crowd forded a narrow path, but in the sea of faces, she saw only one. Isaac was smiling at her from the front, his hand outstretched as if he was afraid she might run away.

When she reached Isaac, she took his hand and gazed up at the fire in his eyes, a steady blaze that held two promises—first to protect the woman who'd once been afraid, and second to love the woman she'd become.

He squeezed her hand gently, and she smiled back at the man she loved with all her heart.

Never again would she run.

A Stagecoach Christmas

by Cathy Liggett

In all thy ways acknowledge him, and he shall direct thy paths.

PROVERBS 3:6

Chapter 1

Molly O'Brien gripped the edge of the seat, digging her ragged fingernails into the hardened leather upholstery. Even so, she could barely keep her balance as the stagecoach jerked and jostled mercilessly through the deep grooves of rain-drenched earth.

Surely even the three wise men hadn't had such a rough ride that first Christmas!

And they certainly hadn't had to travel in such cramped quarters.

Not that the other passengers were a problem. Charlotte Crandall, accompanied by her lively, gray-haired mother, Miss Vivian, were both nice enough. The retired barrister Mr. Benjamin Cottingham and his six-year-old granddaughter, Melissa, who hugged her doll, Josephine, tightly, were also an amiable pair.

But after hours packed inside the coach together, the air and the surroundings had grown stale. Especially with the endless rain and the thick leather curtains closed over the windows. The curtains may have kept out some of the cold, but they kept the air from stirring, too.

As it was, Molly already felt like she'd been holding her breath forever. Or at least ever since her granny had drawn her last one, leaving her all alone, not knowing where to go or what to do.

Oh, how she missed her granny, the only person who'd truly loved her unconditionally, the best friend she'd ever had. She hated thinking about Christmas without the sweet woman.

But you'd be proud of me, Gran. I'm headed to Huxley for Christmas. I'm starting a new life, like I promised you I would.

That is, if the stagecoach ever got there.

From inside the coach, the steady pace of the horses no longer felt stable or quick like it had when they'd first left St. Claire. Instead, the team seemed as clumsy and labored as a bunch of overworked plow horses. She had no idea what she'd do if their driver, Mr. Daniel Becker, failed to reach their destination. But she couldn't think like that. She mustn't!

Loosening her hands from the seat, she reached into the cloth bag on her lap, feeling for the packet of letters bundled together with a piece of twine. She'd been carrying the letters as close to her heart as she could for the past several months. She just had to feel them to calm herself. To be assured that all of her imaginings of the future were real—more than some make-believe conjuring.

As soon as her fingers touched the cool papers, her heart warmed, recalling a handwritten word or two. Instantly, everything inside relaxed. Until Miss Vivian spoke up.

"Why, Molly, what do you have in that bag of yours?" Miss Vivian's voice crackled. "It has to be something from a fella, the way you blush every time you touch whatever is hiding in there." Her eyes teased in a friendly way, but Molly looped her arm through the bag's handle, drawing it closer.

"Mother. . ." Charlotte clucked. "Just because you're an incurable romantic doesn't mean everyone is."

"I beg to differ with you, Daughter. Good or bad, there's a man in all of our lives somewhere along the way." Miss Vivian turned her twinkling eyes back to Molly. "Are you holding on to a locket from a fella? Or maybe a love letter from a man who is longing to see that pretty red hair of yours, and—"

Molly's heart lurched. At first she thought it was from Miss Vivian's revealing words. But it wasn't only that. Suddenly the stagecoach swayed violently, tossing all of them to and fro as easily as if they were a basket full of rag dolls.

Cloth bag still looped to her arm, Molly grabbed for the leather strap to the right of her head. At the same time, she instinctively flung her left arm across Melissa's body, fearing the child's grandfather wouldn't be strong enough to keep the small girl from being catapulted off the seat.

Trying to control her flailing feet, she attempted to dig her heels into the flooring and steady herself against the wild motion, but then just as unexpectedly as the horrific flinging and tumbling began, it all stopped. The stagecoach halted. The abrupt jerk hurled each of their bodies up in the air and then sorely back down again. Stricken with shock, they sat catching their breaths, staring at each other in stunned silence.

Molly couldn't help but think they looked like statues frozen in poses. She was still holding the strap. Mr. Cottingham and Melissa gripped their seats. And the two women embraced each other. All holding on for dear life in case the ruckus started up again. Eerie quiet pricked at her cheeks and the air. They sat listening and waiting for the horses to start up again. But time passed, and only one sound remained: the pummeling of raindrops beating on the roof above their heads.

The air in the stagecoach seemed to diminish as they waited for whatever was wrong outside the coach to be right again. Finally, Molly couldn't wait any longer. Leaning forward, she steeled herself and grasped the handle of the stagecoach door.

"Miss Molly!" Charlotte gasped. "What are you doing?"

"You'll get soaked to the bone, young woman," Miss Vivian warned.

"Surely Mr. Becker has everything under control." Mr. Cottingham tapped his walking cane authoritatively.

"He very well may," Molly agreed.

But despite their protests, she pushed at the door, forcing it open against the barreling rain. Icy raindrops smacked at her face, the wind blowing her hair from every which way. She tried to tuck her locks into her gray knit hood, at least enough so she could see. She had to know what was happening. Why, her dream was hitched to the stagecoach just like the team of horses was.

Yet as she peered through the raindrops, she wasn't prepared for the sight that met her eyes.

A man on horseback, only a few yards away, stared back at her.

Though the rain obscured the details of his clothes and horse, one thing stood out plainly. His eyes. Protected by the rim of his dark hat, his eyes shone clearly as he directly met her gaze.

Uneasy, her limbs trembled.

Was he a robber? A thief? Were there more of them out there like him? Her heart pounded wildly at her own frightening thoughts.

"Miss Molly, it's cold," Melissa suddenly cried. "Josephine is cold, too!" The girl hugged her doll.

Moved by more than the cold, Molly slammed the stagecoach door shut with a bang. Wide-eyed, she turned to the others.

Chapter 2

Samuel Harden had expected to encounter a whole host of things when he packed up a few belongings, saddled his horse, Tack, and turned his back on his life and ranch.

Things like inclement, unpredictable weather, for example. That sure didn't come as a surprise. After all, it was Missouri and late December. Bad weather was part of the journey. Something he would manage to overcome on his way west to sunnier and drier places where nothing around him would resemble what he'd left behind.

But coming around the bend in the trail, what he hadn't expected to come across was a stagecoach. Sitting eerily stopped in the pouring rain.

And what he most especially hadn't expected was to lay his eyes on her. The woman.

Flinging open the stagecoach door, she'd poked her head out, catching him totally unaware. Locks of her red hair tossed and flashed in the wind, flickering in a sea of grayness like a darting redbird blown off course. And even though he sat a few yards away on Tack's soaked backside, and even though rain pummeled down in steady streams, causing rivulets of water to spill over the rim of his hat, no way could it blur his vision of her.

Or hers of him evidently.

Her eyes went wide at the sight of him, looking more frightened than surprised. And very well she should be frightened—and all the other passengers onboard the stagecoach right along with her.

As far as he could tell, there was no driver manning the reins. Not a driver to be seen anywhere. And the wagon wheels were sinking deeper into the gullies of rainwater with each passing minute.

True, the temperature was dropping and tiny flecks of ice were replacing some of the raindrops. If the people aboard the coach were lucky, the sinking temperatures might cause the earth to harden some before the wheels sank to hazardous depths.

Only time and temperature could tell.

Luckily it wasn't any of his concern. Not the abandoned stagecoach. And not the red-haired woman.

When she'd slammed the stagecoach door shut, it hadn't hurt his feelings one bit. He was relieved. He didn't want to be her savior or anyone else's. He'd tried on the role for size once in his life—and had lost the battle when his young wife, Theresa, died in his arms. Certainly nothing a man his age wanted to experience again. He needed to be done with what was. He was ready to move on to whatever could be.

His sole traveling companion seemed to agree. Tack shifted impatiently beneath him. "I hear you, buddy," he muttered to the four-legged creature.

Turning up the collar of his wool-lined slicker, Samuel tightened his gloved hands on the reins. He'd had a heavy heart for too long. He was bent on traveling light for the rest of his livelong days.

"C'mon, Tack," he clicked, "we're outta here."

He turned the horse's head toward the far side of the trail. In a matter of minutes, he and Tack would be out of sight, enveloped in the rain-bent, shadowy limbs of the pines and all the grayness of the day. The stagecoach would be long out of his sight, too. Then surely that feeling tugging on him, trying to make him look back—that would be gone, as well.

⁂

"There's a man out there!" Molly exclaimed.

"A man?" Miss Vivian frowned.

"It has to be our driver, Mr. Becker." Charlotte shrugged as if Molly were too blind to see.

"I know our driver, Charlotte. Believe me, it wasn't him."

The man she'd spied was younger, around her own age. And his eyes didn't appear friendly, narrowing on her as if he was daring her to look at him. She shivered just remembering.

"Only one man?" Mr. Cottingham asked. "Was he talking to Becker?"

"I—I didn't hear any voices." Only the teeming rain. That's all she'd heard. Even now, she tried to listen for sounds of voices, movement, anything beyond the cabin of the coach. But all was spookily still outside—and inside the stagecoach, as well.

As they sat staring at anything but each other, the silence made Molly all too aware of the thumping in her chest and the jittery sensations in her limbs. She couldn't stay still. She forced herself to reach for the door handle once more.

"What are you doing?" Charlotte's saccharin voice came out in a hiss. "Let Mr. Becker take care of the stranger."

"I have to see!" Bracing herself, Molly turned the handle, opening the door ever so slightly, barely an inch or two. Bits of iced dotted her lashes as she peered out onto the muddy trail. But fortunately, no eyes stared back at her.

"I think he's gone." She shut the door. "The man's gone," she repeated, mostly to assure herself.

Mr. Cottingham strained to lift the leather curtain on the opposite side of the coach. "Don't see anyone out this way either."

"Well, good then." Miss Vivian smoothed out her coat and righted her hat. "That means we'll be moving along any second."

But minutes later when they still hadn't moved, Molly felt far too antsy to remain passive.

"Do you mind, Mr. Cottingham?" She reached across Melissa, placing a hand on the older gentleman's cane balanced against the seat. Crafted from solid hickory, a sculpted sphere decorated the top. He might've needed it to get around, but Molly decided it'd also make for a good weapon. Or at least the best one available. "In case I need it for protection?" she asked.

"You're going out there?" Charlotte squawked.

"Well, I can't just sit here." If she did, her dreams would sit idle, too. She'd miss any chance to possibly marry, to have a home to call her own. "Please, Mr. Cottingham?" She appealed again.

"I just don't want you to come to harm." He frowned.

She could tell from his eyes he was sorry he wasn't physically able to protect the women around him. "I'll be fine," she assured him, "and better with the cane than without it."

"It's yours then." He placed the smooth length of wood in her hands. "Be safe, girl."

"Oh, if only I had my rifle with me, I'd give it to you, Molly girl." Miss Vivian's eyes sparked to life. "And you tell that Mr. Becker, our friends in Huxley are expecting us on time for Christmas. Goodness, here we are already traveling without a guard and now delayed, too."

"I'll let him know," Molly replied.

Cane in hand, she stepped out of the stagecoach, closing the door on her only shelter in the storm. Instantly, her shoes sank in the mud, throwing her off balance, making her heart sink, too. No, it hadn't been wise to wear her very nicest shoes, but she had wanted to look her best when her letter-writing companion, Clement, was there to greet her at the station. Now she'd look a wet, muddy mess, not that this was any time to be lamenting about that.

It was hard enough just keeping her footing as she sloshed over the soaked ground, making her way up to the front wheel of the stagecoach. Standing there, the team of horses snorted, sending bursts of white clouds into the air. But Mr. Becker was nowhere to be seen.

She looked left and right and back again, scoping out the trail. Finally, she spotted movement on the other side of the barricade of horses. She let go of a giant sigh of relief.

Mr. Becker! At last! Surely he was attending to whatever was wrong and they'd be on their way again soon!

Her legs couldn't carry her fast enough as she battled the wind and icy rain, holding tightly on to the cane with one hand and on to her hood with the other. Slogging through the clumps of soggy earth to get to their driver, she made a generous arc around the front of the horses, got over to the other side, and then—

Oh please, God, no! Mr. Becker!

All the breath went out of her at the sight of their driver's limp body sprawled on the rain-soaked ground. But even more chilling and horrific was the sight of *him*—the man she'd seen taunting her in the rain—hovering over Mr. Becker's body.

Fear clutched at her throat, and she froze. Should she run? And if she did, would the man only catch her? And hurt her the same way he'd hurt Mr. Becker?

She had only one choice. One hope. Her heart beat wildly as she grabbed on to the cane with both hands. She'd never hit anything in her life, but then her life had never been threatened before. Eyeing the exposed skin on the back of the stranger's neck, she raised the cane in the air and took aim, ready to heave it as hard as she could. She'd only have one chance to get it right. One chance to save herself and the other passengers. To save her future as Mrs. Clement Jones.

Chapter 3

What in tarnation?"

Samuel jumped up from the ground and swung around just in time to deflect the wooden club aimed for his head.

As he groped forcibly for control of the cane, it took only a second to recognize the fiery redhead on the other end of the stick as the woman who had poked her head out of the stagecoach. And he needed about another ten seconds of struggling to wrench the cane from her grasp.

Not that she hadn't put up a good fight.

"What're you trying to do?" he shouted, unable to contain his anger. "Kill me?"

"Ye–s–s." Her lips appeared to tremble more with fright than with cold as she faced up to him, which didn't make him feel one bit good. Still, she stood her ground, causing him to soften some, which wasn't a good thing either. "Yes," she repeated, raising her chin this time. "Kill you, just like you tried to kill our driver."

"What? You think I—"

That accusation riled him all over again. He clenched his teeth, staring at her. But he wasn't as mad at her as he was at himself. He should've kept riding on like he'd planned. He didn't need this aggravation. Nor did he need to get maimed by some agitated woman. Not when he had to stay physically intact for all the other perils that might besiege him on his journey to a new life.

Why, it was just plain lucky the redhead hadn't clobbered him. If it hadn't been for Tack's neighing warning him, he would've been out cold the same as the stagecoach driver.

"For your information, lady, your stagecoach was already sinking in this river of mud when I got here. And if I had to guess, I'd say your driver has been lying here for more than a minute or two."

He followed her eyes as she looked toward the driver again. Dark spots of blood stained the rock beneath his head. She swallowed hard, bravely raising her face to him.

"If you didn't hurt him, then how did this happen?"

"How? You're asking me?"

"Yes."

"Well. . .I don't know." He shrugged. "Can't say for sure anyway." Although he had his hunches and suddenly found himself sharing them with her. "If I had to guess, I'd say your driver might've been trying to help the horses through this mess. He could've lost his footing and hit his head on the rock."

The woman took her time, trying on his conjecture for size. She glanced from the horses to the driver, and to the driver's cowboy hat lying some feet from his head. Again, if he had to guess, it must've gone flying when the driver hit the ground. The hat hadn't been any protection for the man's skull whatsoever.

"Look, it's not a good situation, and I'm sorry for you," Samuel told her sincerely. "But honestly, there's not much I can do about it. Besides, I, uh, I gotta keep going."

"Then why didn't you?" She turned her eyes on him, staring so hard her brows furrowed, drawing her face up like a pretty little bow.

"Well, I—" Despite the rain, he could tell her eyes were the clearest, truest blue he'd ever seen. Mesmerizing and intimidating. If he looked too closely, she'd have him babbling about things he wasn't sure of himself. Like the strong feeling he'd had when he had tried to ride away. How it tugged on him, urging him to turn around.

It'd felt as convincing as a gun being aimed at his back, forcing him to react. The dear woman who raised him would've called it his conscience speaking to him. Some days he loathed that the Lord created such a thing—at least within him. Regardless, he wasn't beholden to this strange woman in any way. There was no reason he needed to be standing in the rain explaining things to her.

"Look, I thought I could help. But I can't." He handed over the cane to her. "Like I said, I've gotta be on my way." He glanced away from her eyes to the already darkening, early afternoon skies. "When I get to the next stop, I'll tell the stationmaster to send a driver back for you."

"Well, we can't just sit here till then," she shouted defiantly over the rain. "You said yourself, the wagon's sinking. And Mr. Becker needs to be taken care of."

Laying the cane on the ground, she crouched down next to the driver. She placed two fingers at the driver's throat and then again at his wrist, as if she was accustomed to doing such a thing. "He's breathing, but his pulse is weak. I need to get him inside the stagecoach. You need to help me. I can't do it by myself."

She was a demanding little thing, all five feet of her. And before he could get beyond her boldness and answer her, she was back at it again.

"You did say you were meaning to help. Right?" She looked up, the directness in her gaze convicting him.

Of course he wasn't about to leave the poor man lying out in the rain. He might be in a hurry, but he wasn't inhumane.

"Yeah, I did," he conceded. "Why don't you go get whichever passenger you think can help me best, and we'll get him out of this cold."

But the woman didn't move.

"Well, are you going to get someone or not?"

"That someone would be me."

He looked down at her slight frame and her fancy, mud-caked shoes, not very solid or stable for the worsening icy conditions. Or for helping him move an unconscious man twice her weight. "You really think you can help me lift him?"

"Yes." She didn't hesitate.

Although he'd only known her for all of ten minutes, he hadn't really expected any other answer. Even if she couldn't be a significant help, no doubt she was one lady who would be determined to try.

Grasping the driver under his arms, he directed her to take a hold of Becker's legs. Between struggling with the driver's dead weight and the slippery earth, the best they could do was inch their way to the coach. By the time they finally reached the stagecoach door, lines of sweat were coursing down Samuel's back under the layers of his clothing.

Without a doubt, the other passengers were just as shocked to see him as they were their injured driver. But there was no time for introductions or inquiries, only action. Molly hopped into the coach as everyone worked together, shifting and lifting, making space for Becker's body. Removing some of the driver's wet garments, she wrapped him in warm blankets from under the seat.

For all of the other passengers' concern, Samuel could see that the redhead had been right. She was the most fit and able of the group, and from what he could discern, she was also the fifth wheel. The realization disarmed him, making him feel an instant concern and fondness for her. Not to mention a reluctance to say good-bye—even though he'd done what she'd asked and it was time to go.

Still, he gazed inside the crowded coach where she was crouched between the seats, straightening her hat and hugging her purse. "You just carve out a comfortable spot where you can sit tight till I get you a driver," he said, which seemed to make her smile.

"I don't need to sit tight," she said.

Before he knew it, she hopped down from the stagecoach and closed the door behind her.

He looked at her quizzically as she squared her shoulders and raised her chin to him. Then she gazed at him so evenly that he shouldn't have been surprised by what she said next.

"I'm taking over the reins."

Chapter 4

Y ou're going to do what?" Just one minute earlier Samuel had been staring at the
redhead, appreciating her spunky spirit. But now she'd gone too far. He could
hardly hide the irritation in his voice.

"I said I'm taking the reins."

"Lady"—his teeth clenched around the word—"that's one. . .bad. . .idea." He
spoke each word deliberately, slowly, thinking somehow that might impress the grave-
ness of the situation on her. Not only that, but he was trying to stay calm when what
he really wanted to do was spout off about how illogical she was being.

"Look," he said, with all the patience he could muster, "the rain is turning to sleet.
With the weather moving this way, the trail's not going to be passable for much longer.
Beyond all that, I'd venture to guess you don't know the first thing about leading a
team of horses."

"You guessed right. I don't. So I'm supposing I'm going to have to learn real fast,
won't I?" She placed her shoulder bag over her head and across her body then spun
around, leaving him dumbfounded in her wake. She'd almost made her way to the
front of the stagecoach when she stopped and turned to him. "I never did catch your
name."

"Samuel. Samuel Harden."

"I'm Molly O'Brien," she said. Then surprising him, she retraced her imprints in
the mud until she was standing close to him again. "Thank you very much for your
help with our driver, Mr. Harden. It was most kind of you."

She spoke to him all proper like. Taken back, he paused before he remembered his
manners, removed his glove politely, and extended his hand. She reached out in kind,
and he took her bare, cold hand into his. "Pleased to meet you, Molly," he said. "And
don't worry about the help. It was nothing."

"Oh, that's not so. It was something for sure."

He shook his head. "Only the right thing to do."

"And that's a lot of something, isn't it?"

The way she looked up into his eyes, as if she was sizing him up as a man, caught
him off guard. Suddenly they were acting like a man and a woman meeting properly
at church or a barn raising, when just minutes before they'd been two rain-soaked
travelers accidentally crossing paths.

Feeling slightly off-kilter, he sloughed off her compliment with a shrug. But
before he could say anything, she gave him a tight smile. "Well, I should probably go
now," she said. "I need to get to the next station before dark. Like you said, the weather
is worsening something fast."

He tightened his grasp on her hand and held it, as if by doing so he could also hold her back, make her change her stubborn mind for her own good. "You don't need to be going anywhere. I told you, I'll ride to the next station and send a driver back for you. An experienced driver."

"And I surely do appreciate that, Samuel," she said sweetly, all the while delicately wriggling her hand from his grasp. "I sincerely do," she added, clasping her hands together. "But the weather might get too bad for someone to come back for us. Meanwhile, we could freeze to death. Or be attacked by any number of things. And I don't plan to just sit. . .sit tight, as you said, and wait for who knows what to happen."

She tightened her wet hat under her chin then turned again to go. Watching her walk away, he ground his teeth so hard he came close to chipping a cusp.

Why on earth had he ever stopped and gotten involved? Gotten tangled up with this situation? This woman? He glanced up toward the heavens, as if his answer might be found there. But all was bleary and cloudy above as pellets of ice spit at his face. So instead, he asked for patience and understanding—heaps of it where this woman was concerned. This Molly who was. . .crazy, or at least crazily willful. Too much so for her own good.

Why, she didn't even have a decent pair of gloves to warm her hands. And her ridiculous shoes had to be soaked through. Still, she was so headstrong and full of gumption he wanted to take her in his arms and—well, settle her down long enough so he could talk sense into her so she didn't go bringing harm to herself or anyone else.

"You really are bent on going? On driving this thing?"

It was a ridiculous question. She was already in motion, hoisting herself up into the front of the stagecoach, only stopping long enough to wave good-bye as if she hadn't heard him ask a thing. "Thank you again, Samuel."

That was his dismissal, his cue to be on his way. Yet he stood clenching his fists, his conscience struggling with the same tugging feelings all over again.

It was one thing for him and his sure-footed Tack to take off, bear up under the awful weather, and possibly have a chance to make it to the next station. But a slow moving stagecoach? In this weather? Even if she could handle the team of horses, which remained to be seen, she couldn't possibly get them headed anywhere fast. It was a ridiculous notion. And that's all it was: a notion. Of course if she was going to be that obstinate, well, maybe he should just let her do whatever she cared to and be on his way, all free and clear like he'd planned.

But still. . .the eternal nagging inside him wouldn't let up. And whatever he decided, he was going to hate himself. It was just a matter of which decision—to help out or ride on—would have him hating himself more.

Heaving a sigh, he finally made his choice, reluctance weighing heavy in his bones. Looking up at her, he spoke the words his own ears didn't want to hear, "You're not going alone, lady. . .Molly. I'm going with you."

 ❦

While Samuel hitched his horse to the back of the stagecoach, Molly sat up in the driver's seat, gathering her bearings. The bench was somewhat higher than she'd imagined it would be, and looking down on a team of horses to command was downright intimidating. But she couldn't let any of that unnerve her. Not if there was a hope of ever getting to her new home—or at least headed in that direction.

Flecks of ice stinging her cheeks, she took up the reins in her stiff, cold hands. The bundle of leather strips stretched in varying lengths across the horses' backsides. She was trying to make sense of them when Samuel appeared, climbing up over the right side of the coach, carrying a red blanket in his arms. He appeared happy to offer it to her.

"This was stowed inside the saddlebags and is somewhat dry," he said. Without asking permission, he flicked the blanket into the air, settling the wool over her shoulders in one fluid motion. "Tuck the edges around you. It should help you stay warmer. Being high up like this makes a person vulnerable to the elements."

It was another show of kindness from him, yet moments later she had to wonder if he'd meant it more as a distraction. Because while she was looking at him, ready to express her thanks, he nabbed the reins from her hands—again, all in one motion.

"You'll be wanting to watch me so you can get the hang of this," was his only explanation.

"Watch you?"

Exasperated, she eyed him with resentment. The way he had so deftly and deceptively snatched the reins from her hands—and made his bold assumption—was beyond annoying. Annoying, too, was the way he wouldn't look at her or answer her. So much so, she reached out, trying to seize the leather straps from his grip. But he thrust his left elbow into the air, blocking her grasp, distancing her from him.

Feeling the fool, she could do little but fume. "And what makes you a seasoned stagecoach driver, Mr. Harden?"

"Not much," he answered. "Only some experience with plow horses."

"And now you're a master at this?"

"No, again. Just more experienced than you. And I'll be real happy to share the benefits of my experience." He kept his eyes fixed on the horses, not even glancing her way. "But it's far easier to show you how it's done than to tell you."

Her face burned from the truth of his words and from the simple fact that in a panic to take control of her destiny, she'd possibly overreacted. Actually, overreacted quite a bit. Instead of harping at him further, she studied the way he manned the reins. He was right. Getting the horses going again was going to be no easy task.

The once muddy gullies entrenching the horses' hooves had begun to ice over. Not only that, but the animals appeared weary and spooked. She watched Samuel patiently tug and release the reins over and over again, until one by one, he urged each horse to break free from its sunken spot.

The stagecoach rocked and jolted as the horses inched forward. Molly grabbed on to the underside of the bench for support, knowing the worst wasn't over yet. If Samuel didn't get the horses to react with just the right amount of pull, at exactly the same time, the stagecoach could slide back, becoming further immersed in the sunken wheel ruts—stuck there for good.

She prayed silently for all to be right as Samuel snapped the reins with incredible force, all the while shouting commands to the team. Thrust into action by the commotion, the horses lunged with awesome power, their massive bodies pulling and heaving, literally lifting the stagecoach out from the deeply rutted earth.

Finally, they were moving. Heading westward once more to Huxley. The horses whinnied, sounding triumphant to Molly's way of thinking. She couldn't help but shout for joy, too.

"You did it, Samuel! I could've never done it. But you did."

Still concentrating on the team of horses, Samuel didn't reply, which was more than fine by her. She was simply glad they were on their way again. At least they seemed to be, until she noticed him tighten his grip and pull back on the reins.

"Samuel, why are you stopping?"

It only took a moment to realize he wasn't stopping at all. It was worse than that. He was changing directions, turning the horses around. Heading back again toward St. Claire, back to where she'd come from.

"Samuel!" she yelled. "You've got to turn this stagecoach around. Right this minute!" she demanded. She sprung toward him, grabbing for the reins.

"Careful, woman! Do you want to fall off this thing like Becker did?"

With the strength of one hand, he pulled her back down onto the seat, closer to him than she had been before, as if he could control her better from there.

"Please. . .there's no reason to go back there," she pleaded, which for her was so very true.

When she'd first come to St. Claire after her mother had died, making a home there with her granny felt absolutely right. It was such a pretty place to be on God's green earth that she thought it would be her home for a long while. But a couple of quick years after her arrival, her granny had taken ill and then died, too. Without someone to share life with, the town didn't feel much like home anymore. Not when she was all alone. But then Clement's letters accidentally fell into her hands all the way from Huxley, feeling like a gift from heaven. She didn't know much about the town. But to her way of thinking, having someone to share a place with was more important than the place itself.

Yet Huxley and Clement both felt far away now. Her insides twisted in desperation. "Why are you taking us back? What are you thinking?"

"I'm thinking of you." He glanced at her. "And of the other passengers."

"But they want to get to Huxley just as bad as I do. Why, Charlotte and Miss Vivian—they're supposed to be celebrating Christmas with some folks they know there. And Mr. Cottingham and his granddaughter are celebrating with his sister. And I—" She stopped, not really wanting to share the details of her plans with him. "We all have our hearts set on making it to Huxley."

"I'm sure you do. But that's hardly going to happen tonight. It doesn't make sense."

"And neither does heading back to St. Claire. Not when it's no closer than the station in Huxley."

"You're right. That's why I'm not suggesting we do that."

"Well, excuse me, but so far I haven't heard you suggest anything."

"I know of a place—a farm on the outskirts of town. Not too far from where we are now."

"And you're thinking the owners are going to be letting all seven of us strangers stay there?"

"There's no one in the house right now."

"I don't understand."

"The property has been boarded up. We can stay there the night, and when the weather is better tomorrow, we can all start out again in broad daylight. Mr. Becker may even be up to driving again by then."

Molly considered his proposal, weighing his logic. "And what if the weather doesn't get better?"

She saw him take a deep breath and let out an equally long sigh before he answered. "It has to," he said quietly, almost to himself.

The way he answered made her realize she wasn't the only one who had an agenda. Evidently he must have important plans, too. She'd been so selfish, so driven to get to her new life, that she'd only been thinking of herself—which normally wasn't like her. Even though he hadn't said anything to make her feel embarrassed, she was.

"I'm sorry," she apologized.

He looked over and frowned, not seeming to understand. "Nothing to be sorry about."

"Yes, there is. I've been behaving sorely. Like a spoiled child. It's just—well, I'm so anxious to get to Huxley. Is that where you're headed?" she asked. "To celebrate Christmas?"

"Ha." He flashed a sardonic grin. "Not hardly."

"To where, then?" She couldn't help from prodding.

He shrugged slightly. "I was just going. . .west."

"West?" she asked.

"Uh-huh. West."

"Oh."

She looked at him, at his eyes so kind yet so set and unyielding. Looked at him and wondered if he really didn't have any more plans than just to ride westward—or if there was a whole lot more he wasn't sharing. He must've felt her gaze, because suddenly he glanced her way.

"Your hands warm enough?" he asked.

"The blanket helps a lot."

"You can reach into my pocket." He nodded downward, to the left side of his coat. "There's another pair of gloves in there. Hopefully they're still dry."

"Thank you." She looked up at him. "But. . .I'm all right. Besides, you'll be needing them."

"Not like I can wear two pairs at once. " He gave her a crooked smile. "Don't worry. I won't go biting you or nothing."

"I wasn't thinking you would." She returned his smile then dug eagerly into his pocket, pulling out a pair of leather gloves. They were too large for her hands, of course, but still felt wonderful against her freezing skin.

"Better?"

"Yes, thanks. My hands are much warmer now." And her cheeks were, too, just thinking of what a good, kind man Samuel Harden seemed to be. In her experience, those types were hard to come by.

Looking up at him, suddenly wondering about this stranger in her life, she couldn't help but notice ice accumulating on the shoulders of his coat and sticking to the rim of his hat.

"You must be freezing. There's ice building up on your hat."

"I'll bet there is." He let out a laugh, looking at her. "There's ice on your hat, too."

She reached up and even through the gloves could feel the crunchy hardness of ice. "Well, so there is." She laughed back. "Guess you're right about us heading to that abandoned house after all. We better get there quickly so we can get thawed out by morning."

He laughed again, the sound of it making her feel appreciated. So much so, before she realized what she was doing, she spread open the blanket, stretching the right side across his back so it draped over his right shoulder. She knew it was mighty bold of her, but lately it seemed life's circumstances kept making her grow that way. And after all, it was only right to share with Samuel what was really his.

"We'll stay warmer close together," she reasoned when he gave her a surprised look.

"You don't have to share."

"I know," she said. "Neither did you."

Giving her an appreciative grin, he flicked the reins slightly, trying to get a bit more speed from the horses. As the stagecoach rolled bumpily over the hardened, icy path, she thought about all the strangers she could've met along the way and felt fortunate to have met such a man as Samuel Harden.

For sure, she would tell Clement all about him. About how Samuel rode up from out of nowhere and how she almost maimed him. About how Samuel stole away the reins from her, but only because he was determined to get them all to safety.

But of course, she wouldn't dare say to Clement how close she and Samuel sat, huddled beneath the red blanket in the dire cold. Or how they'd shared moments of laughter—despite the unbearable conditions surrounding them. She surely wouldn't mention the way Samuel smiled at her, and how when he did, she tried to ignore the stirrings she felt inside.

Chapter 5

By the time Samuel had the boarded-up house in his sights, hours had passed along the trail and evening had set in. The temperature had changed, too, turning the sleet to snow. He would've preferred the precipitation to stop altogether. But after forging the treacherous trail under the harshness of icy rain, the snow was a soothing respite, almost comforting in comparison—a beautiful, soulful thing, illuminating the sky with a whitish-blue haze, outlining the evergreens and the house in a picture-perfect way.

Of course, it wasn't just the tranquility of the snow that had him suppressing his ill feelings about returning to the area. Deep down he realized it had something to do with Molly, too. An hour earlier, she'd nodded off to sleep, most likely exhausted from the day's events. In her sleepiness, her head found its way to his shoulder and stayed nestled there for the duration. Her closeness, the gentle weight of her cozied up to him—these were things he hadn't felt in a long while. Not in the years since Theresa had died. Somehow the mystifying feeling subdued his frustration about his sudden change in plans, at least for the moment.

Pulling up to the house, he halted the plodding horses with a slight tug of the reins. Instantly, Molly raised her sleepy head, looking confused.

"Samuel?" she asked, as if first making sure she had his name right.

He nodded. "We're here."

"Here where?" She rubbed her eyes.

"At the house I told you about."

Watching her glance left to right, he noticed her eyes widen. "It's big. Real nice looking, too. But are you sure it's all right for us to—"

A cacophony of voices rose from the side of the stagecoach.

"It's Charlotte and Miss Vivian," she said, letting go of the blanket. "I'd better go see how they're doing. I'm sure they don't know what to think."

Without a moment's hesitation, she stood up, causing him to do the same. He descended the coach first then helped her to solid ground. Legs and back stiff from the cold, he took a minute to stretch before following her. But he was in time to witness the younger woman rush up to Molly and hug her tight, all the while scowling at him over Molly's shoulder.

"Molly! You're all right!"

"Of course I'm all right, Charlotte." Molly broke free from the grasp. "Why wouldn't I be?"

"Well goodness, everything happened so fast." Charlotte clutched at her coat, shivering as she spoke. "One minute you were helping with Mr. Becker. And then you were gone with. . .with him, the stranger." Her teeth chattered. "The stagecoach started moving, and we thought that you. . .that we. . .had been—"

"Kidnapped!" The older woman, whom Samuel assumed to be Miss Vivian, moved in front of Charlotte, her eyes wide and bright despite her age and the weariness of the trip. "Have we been kidnapped?" she asked excitedly, as if hopeful he'd answer in the affirmative.

"No, ma'am." Samuel stepped forward, almost hating to disappoint her. "Not at all."

"Are you sure?" she prodded, some of the light retreating from her eyes. "Because this certainly isn't the Huxley station. Why, we're at a deserted house in the middle of—"

"In the middle of where?" An older gentleman, close to Miss Vivian's age, made a laborious descent from the coach. "Where are we? I demand to know."

"We're at a farm," Samuel told him. "On the outskirts of St. Claire," he added, bracing himself for the group's reaction.

"St. Claire?" The women's voices rose up in unison. "But we just came from there."

"And just who do you think you are, mister, to be making decisions for us like you have?" the man griped.

"His name is Samuel Harden," Molly said before he could speak for himself. "And Mr. Cottingham, I know you're just cold and tired, and your bones damp and aching; otherwise you wouldn't be talking in such an awful way to the man who saved our lives."

"And you, miss." Cottingham pointed an accusing finger at Molly. "You're not upset this man has gone taking us backward?"

"No need to go jumping on her, sir," Samuel said sternly. He didn't mind being the butt of the group's complaints, but there was no way he was going to let anyone scold Molly. Not when she'd been the only one who'd had the nerve to step out of the stagecoach, assess their situation, and get help for their driver.

"Of course I was upset, Mr. Cottingham," Molly admitted. "Why, we all have people we want to be meeting up with for Christmas—and we still can. We can start out fresh tomorrow. But tonight the weather was just plain ugly and dangerous. That's why I gladly turned over the reins to Samuel."

Samuel reacted quickly, coughing back a chuckle. That wasn't quite the way he'd remembered things going. Molly raised her brows, as if imploring him not to say so.

"We could've frozen to death out there. But he saved us. I could never have done what he did. I'm so grateful, Samuel." She turned to him.

Molly's words came totally unexpectedly and had him shifting on his feet uncomfortably. Her ardent explanation seemed to have affected Mr. Cottingham, too, who rubbed his face and murmured an apology to Samuel.

"I, for one, don't care where we are," Miss Vivian piped up. "I'm just glad to be out of that bucket on wheels."

"Can we build a fire inside?" Charlotte asked, her teeth still chattering.

"I'm sure that can be arranged." Samuel nodded.

While the group continued chatting among themselves, Samuel fetched his rifle from where it was holstered on Tack's backside. Using the butt of it, he wrenched away the wooden boards crisscrossed over the front door and windows. The next order of business was for them all to assist in getting Mr. Becker inside. The driver was woozy and weak, but the hours of rest must have helped, because he could at least limp some on his own. He was also coherent enough to ask them all to call him Daniel, feeling there was no need to be formal with people who had saved his life.

"Why, this house doesn't look abandoned one bit, Samuel." Molly eyed him quizzically after they'd situated Daniel onto a bed in one of the rooms. "There's furniture in every room."

"And it's not even dusty!" Charlotte chimed in. "How wonderful!"

"Yes, well, I'll start getting the trunks inside," he answered.

It took some time for Samuel to unload the trunks from the stagecoach. Molly and Charlotte helped bring them indoors. Meanwhile, Mr. Cottingham and Miss Vivian stayed in with Melissa and built a fire using dry logs stacked next to the hearth.

With the piles of trunks stacked all around, the fire blazing, Mr. Cottingham settled into a chair, and the women and little Melissa milling through the closets for supplies, the quiet, empty house suddenly felt overwhelmingly full to Samuel. And odd.

Lucky for him, the horses needed to be tended to. He closed the front door behind him, glad to escape.

ço

Molly looked at the table, set with steaming bowls of oats she and Charlotte had managed to locate in the cabinets and prepare over the fire. True, it wasn't much of an evening meal, but as hungry as everyone was, no one seemed to mind. For herself, she couldn't remember one time in her life when she'd sat down to eat with so many people. Even so, it didn't feel all the way right. Something—someone—was missing.

"Has anyone seen Samuel?" She glanced around the table.

"He slipped out the door awhile ago," Mr. Cottingham told her.

For a moment, she hesitated then excused herself. Grabbing up her coat from where it lay next to the hearth drying out, she bundled up and headed outdoors.

She had taken several steps through the mounting snow when she noticed a strip of light coming from the partially open barn door. She followed the light and slipped into the outbuilding.

Standing in the shadows of the lantern-lit barn, she watched Samuel tend to the horses, talking to each of them soothingly while offering buckets of feed. She told herself she didn't want to interrupt his work and that was the reason for being so quiet. But honestly she was glad for the chance to have a better look at him without his knowing.

At first glance, he was rough looking. No wonder she'd been so frightened when she'd initially opened the stagecoach door. But after spending so many hours on the road with him, she marveled at how her opinion had changed. Now the days' old beard didn't look unkempt; rather, it nicely outlined the strong set of his jawline. His hair was long, hanging unevenly from his hat, but it only added to his masculine appeal. His eyes weren't actually squinty, portraying an evil soul as she'd first imagined. They narrowed in the most caring way as she'd come to find out—even now, tenderly eyeing the weary creatures in front of him.

No, he was nothing like the man she first perceived him to be, and she would've been happy just to watch him longer. But a calico cat came up, curling around her feet, mewing loudly. Samuel immediately glanced over at the sound.

She straightened, pretending she'd just come in. "There you are!" she said. "I've been looking for you."

"Something wrong?"

She could hear his concern. "No, not at all. We made some oats. I thought you might be hungry. Hungry like the horses." She smiled.

He bent over a large barrel, refilling the bucket in his hand. "Thanks for telling me. I'll be there in a bit."

"All right," she said, but still she stood there, thinking about the house, the barn, that land. "This is all so hard to understand, don't you think?"

"What is?"

"Why someone would leave a place like this? Just board up things and go? The house is so welcoming, perfect for a family. Even the barn looks pretty nearly brand-new."

He looked at her and opened his mouth as if he was about to say something. Then he turned his attention to Tack and shrugged. "I assume the people must have had their reasons. You don't need to go worrying about it."

"I'm not worried, just wondering. But I suppose you're right." She sighed, thinking about how much she missed her granny. There wouldn't have been any reason for her to journey to Huxley if her granny had still been alive. And she'd almost lost her own life trying to get there. Maybe she would have if it hadn't been for Samuel.

"I meant what I said earlier today, Samuel," she said quietly.

"What you said?"

"About. . .about being thankful to you. You were—you are—a godsend, Samuel. I don't know what would've happened to us if you hadn't come along, befriending us like you did. You were right to bring us here. I can't thank you enough."

She'd blurted out far too much and was sure she'd embarrassed him with her emotional outpouring. Why, she was embarrassed by it, too, especially when tears of gratitude brimmed in her eyes without warning. And especially when he kept focused on his horse and wouldn't look at her, not acknowledging her thank-you one little bit.

"Your oats are probably getting cold," he murmured, a kind way of urging her to go. "I'll come in soon enough," he promised, and then he turned back to the creatures who had delivered them all to safety.

Chapter 6

"Eee! Eee!"

Samuel bolted upright out of a dead sleep, startled awake by the sound of a child's squeals. Sitting on his makeshift bed—a blanket thrown onto the floor—he squinted into the morning light seeping in the window, struggling to get his bearings.

Murmurings of voices drifted up the steps, quickly reminding him of where he was and who was there with him. More than likely, the screech had come from little Melissa. Thankfully she sounded happy—and not in harm's way as he'd first feared.

Listening to the movement below, he felt slightly guilty he'd still been sleeping. Hurriedly, he grabbed his vest and boots from the floor, throwing them on over the clothes and socks he'd slept in. If everyone was to be on their way again this morning, there were things to get done.

But his sense of urgency didn't last long. Coming down the stairs, he was stopped in his tracks by Molly. She stood at the bottom of the steps, a kitchen cloth in her hand, a smile on her lips.

"I'm sorry if we woke you up with our chattering," she whispered. "And with Melissa's chirping, too," she added with a playful wink.

Her greeting gave him pause, leaving him almost tongue-tied for a moment. What a rare thing it was, starting his day hailed with a smile that way.

"I needed to get up." He rubbed his whiskered chin sheepishly. "Can't believe I slept so late."

"I'm sure you were worn-out, taking care of us the way you did yesterday."

Her face looked just as lovely as he remembered from the day before—the same pretty face that had kept him restless and stirring for half the night. Not that it was her fault. Clearly it was his for not owning up to the truth.

He should've spoken up and told her right then and there in the barn the night before that the house and property belonged to him. But he'd hesitated, not sure if he wanted to share. Then stopped himself completely, already knowing so well that curious Molly would be full of questions and not too shy about asking a one of them. Understandably, she'd want to know the reason he'd closed up his house, turned his back on it, and all before another Christmas arrived.

But why try to explain? Why talk about how his wife of two years had passed away in his arms at just this time of year three years ago? Why talk about how he'd closed up his heart? Why go through such an explanation when he could see Daniel was getting better and when he knew Molly would be exiting his life as quickly as she'd come into it? What was the point when they'd never see each other again?

"It was a long day for sure. But I'm fine," he said to Molly, right as Melissa came

172

up, skipping around them with Josephine.

"Guess what, Mr. Samuel?" Her young eyes glimmered with excitement. "We're snowed in."

He looked to Molly for affirmation. "That true?"

"I'm afraid so," she said, but her eyes were also shining. She didn't look displeased at all.

"Isn't it pretty?" The little girl danced in circles.

He'd been so wrapped up thinking about last night's conversation with Molly that he hadn't even bothered to glance outside. But someone had opened the shutters, and he could see the snowdrifts. They made a pretty sight, but the new layers of snow meant no one would be going anywhere today. Not his guests. Not him.

Although no one seemed to mind.

Molly had rejoined the other women in the kitchen area where they were happily chatting and busying themselves. Remnants of flour, cornmeal, and whatever else dusted both ends of the table, making him glad he'd bolted impulsively from his homestead the day before. He hadn't taken time to discard one lick of his food supply. He'd only boarded up the front door and windows in his rush to be gone.

Meanwhile, a rested-looking Daniel and a subdued Mr. Cottingham sat near the window, bent over the crude checkerboard Samuel had crafted years earlier. Many a night he'd sat in one of the same chairs, playing against himself, hoping to ease the loneliness that so often descended on him.

He'd assumed after being on the receiving end of the group's ire when the weather had delayed their trip to Huxley the day before that his guests would be even grumpier with another setback today. But surprisingly, they all appeared just as content as Melissa. In fact, he felt as if he'd gone to sleep and woken up to an entirely different crew of people.

Eyeing the domestic scenes surrounding him, he suddenly felt uncomfortable in his own home. He needed something to do. A chore to set him right. He grabbed his coat off the hook.

"Samuel, wouldn't you like a little something to eat this morning?" Miss Vivian called out to him.

"She made some fine vittles out of little to nothing. Quite the cook." Mr. Cottingham grinned as he complimented Miss Vivian. Samuel could've sworn he detected a twinkling of eyes between the pair.

"Thank you, Miss Vivian. I'll eat after I fetch more firewood," he answered, glad that he'd thought to move the wood inside the barn the night before to keep it dry.

"Oh!" Molly set down her bowl. "I'll help." She wiped her hands on a cloth.

"Can I come, too?" Melissa pleaded with big dark eyes.

He hadn't meant for a trip to the barn to turn into a group project. Even so, he waited patiently while the girls gathered their coats and hats, and Molly, the oversized pair of gloves he'd given her.

It took a mighty push and some digging to open the front door far enough for them to slip out. The snow was up to Melissa's knees, and she couldn't stop giggling as she tried to forge her way through it.

"Look how happy she is!" Molly's rosy cheeks rounded with her smile.

"You look happy yourself," he blurted.

Molly sighed. "I feel that way."

"Here I thought you'd be upset. About not leaving for Huxley."

"I thought so, too." Her brows creased as if she couldn't believe her reaction either. "But when I woke up this morning and saw the snow, something came over me." She shrugged. "I can't explain it. Instead of feeling upset, I felt better than I have in a long while. At peace—and as free as a young girl." She smiled at Melissa, reveling in the snow. "Why, just look at all of this." She nodded toward the fields, blanketed in serene whiteness. "I feel so blessed to be here and have this beautiful day, Samuel. I truly do."

Samuel didn't reply. He couldn't. He'd made his place a prison. Now her joy of it nearly felt contagious. He could barely tear his eyes away from her dazzling smile and clear, shining eyes.

She looked at him curiously. "Did I say something wrong?"

"Wrong? No." He shook his head. "It's just. . ." He paused, embarrassed he'd been caught staring. And disconcerted by the thoughts in his head.

She leaned forward, brows piqued, waiting for his reply. His inane reply. "It's. . . your eyes," he told her.

"My eyes?" Her hands flew to her cheeks.

"They're. . .so blue," he replied with uneasy honesty, and couldn't have been more relieved when Melissa called out to him.

"Mr. Samuel! Catch!"

Out of the corner of his eye, he'd seen Melissa forming a snowball. As she threw one his way, he ducked. The snowball skimmed his hat, causing Melissa to laugh delightedly.

That started an all-out ruckus between the two of them, tossing snowballs back and forth, while Molly moved out of the way and looked on, laughing.

"I think Miss Molly needs a turn, don't you?" He winked at Melissa and tossed a snowball straight at Molly. She retaliated with a rather large snowball aimed at him. But as she threw it into the air, one of his oversized gloves went flying off her hand, hitting him smack in the face.

"That wasn't very nice," he teased. "Hitting me with my own glove!"

"I'm so sorry!" Molly apologized between fits of laughter. "Goodness, I couldn't do that again in a hundred years."

"Well, I hope not!" Samuel rubbed his face, pretending to be hurt, which only made Molly laugh more till she lost her footing, falling back into the deep snow.

He and Melissa stood looking at one another, waiting for Molly to reappear. But there was no movement.

"Mr. Samuel?" Melissa's eyes were wide, the gaiety instantly gone.

"She's all right," he assured the young'un, knowing Molly was capable of getting herself out of most any situation. Still, he clomped over to help just as Molly was clambering to stand up.

"Are you okay?" he asked.

"Yes, I'm perfectly fiii. . ." She wobbled to the left then swayed to the right, all before falling back into the snow again, which brought on more giggles. "I've never had so much fun since forever," she exclaimed, looking up from her bed of snow.

Despite all the silliness of the situation, she didn't look foolish to Samuel at all. Unquestionably, she was a pretty sight to behold. Laughter glinted in her blue eyes, and the ends of her reddish hair strayed from her hat, lying against the pure white snow.

"I'm glad for you." Samuel leaned in, holding out his hand. "But you're gonna be feeling wet soon."

He was almost surprised when she didn't balk at his help, when instead she reached back, letting him pull her up and hold on to her until she was steady on her feet.

"Oh, Samuel! It seems you're always rescuing me." She tilted her head, a sweetness all her own filling her smile.

As his gaze met hers, he didn't know if she was teasing or serious. All he knew was that rescuing Molly was beginning to make him feel as if somehow he was being rescued, too. Even if he didn't want to be. Even if he hadn't planned it that way.

All of Molly's possessions in the world fit into the one medium-sized trunk sitting in the corner of the bedroom she was sharing with Charlotte and Miss Vivian. Certainly none of her belongings could've been described as fine by anyone's standards.

But she did have one item special to her heart: a tortoise-shell brush and hand-mirror set that had belonged to her granny. Though it wasn't worth much, it was the only thing she had left of the only family she'd ever known. She treasured the pieces beyond words and kept them close by her always in her shoulder bag.

Taking the brush and small mirror from her bag to comb out her hair, damp from her rollick in the snow with Samuel and Melissa, she remembered something else in her satchel she'd been treasuring as well. Letters. From Clement. . .whom she hadn't thought about all morning.

A twinge of guilt tightened her stomach. It grew worse when she realized she'd also forgotten to ask God to bless him as she always did in her prayers the night before. How could that be?

Ever since her granny had died, she'd felt that possibly God had brought Clement into her life, from that first letter that had been mistakenly handed to her at the general store. Even when she tried to clear up the mistake, when she'd hastily written to Clement and told him no one in town knew of a Millie O'Bryan, his reply had been unexpected. Instead of never hearing from him again, he'd asked if he could correspond with her.

She sat down on the bed and set the brush and mirror aside. Retrieving Clement's packet of letters from her handbag, she stared at them. They weren't anything impressive to see. Less than a half dozen notes tied together with a piece of twine. Yet twenty-four hours earlier, those letters had been her whole world. Just yesterday she'd been prepared to travel through a horrendous ice storm, ready to risk her life for a future with Clement Jones.

And so. . .she sat with the letters in her lap and waited. Waited to feel the same hope in her heart she always did when she held them in her hands. She closed her eyes, recalled the words Clement had written to her, and waited for the feeling of security they used to give her. Strangely, she felt nothing. Nothing at all.

Except for her growing feelings for—

Samuel! The realization hit her with a mighty force. She dropped the letters onto the bed and hugged her arms around her chest, feeling happily awed yet woefully confused.

She'd never known there existed the kind of warmth from a man like what she felt when she was with Samuel. If she had, she would've realized so quickly that kind of emotion and caring was missing in Clement's words to her. When Clement asked questions about her, his inquiries read more like an interview for a housekeeper, wanting to know how well she cooked. . .and sewed. . .and gardened. She hadn't known at the time that the man she was going to make a life with should want to know other things about her. Things such as the way of her heart, the texture of her hair, and the color of her eyes.

"Your eyes. They're so blue!"

Her pulse quickened as Samuel's words came back to her. So did the feeling of tender yearning she'd felt when he looked at her. She'd made light of the moment but only because she didn't know what else to do with him gazing at her that way. Her insides had felt like they were melting, and she could feel her cheeks flushing crimson.

Now that she'd felt all of that, what was she to do? It seemed just as the snow had come and changed the landscape of the land, Samuel had come into her life. . .and changed the landscape of her heart.

Oh, dearest Lord, how can I be feeling this way? What would You have me do?

Chapter 7

Samuel couldn't remember the last time he'd sat down to dinner with a group of people in his home. He should've appreciated how the ladies had set the table, the plain white plates shimmering like fine china. He should've felt soothed by the way the candles bathed the setting with a golden glow.

But mostly he felt awkward—and guilty.

Ever since Molly had bowed her head to say grace, it was hard for him not to notice the way the gleaming light brought out sparkling highlights in her hair. It was hard for him not to feel drawn to look at her. Even as she prayed, her voice sounded markedly sweet to his ears.

"Dear Lord, thank You for this meal we are about to eat," she prayed. "Thank You for this warm place You provided for us on these snowy days. Thanks most of all for these people to share it with. They are the nicest I've ever met, Lord," she said, so void of inhibition that he felt a slight pang in his heart. "It sure is a lot to be grateful for, Lord," she added, "as we celebrate the birth of Your Son, our Savior. Amen."

A chorus of *amens* rose up, but even after that everyone sat still for a moment. Like him, Samuel was sure they were all touched by Molly's sincerity, maybe even surprised to be the focus of her prayer.

Her deep appreciation for their company, the day, the moment, brought a fresh wave of remorse over him. Reminding him that he hadn't been thankful in all circumstances in quite a long time.

It wasn't easy feeling guilty ten different ways in a span of five minutes. He was glad when Charlotte served little Melissa then passed the cornmeal pie across the end of the table to Daniel, who broke the silence—and his thoughts.

"Looks like the snow ain't meltin' fast," the stagecoach driver said, slipping a generous wedge of pie onto his plate, making Samuel think Daniel was feeling every bit as much better as he'd been saying. "Don't look like we're going anywhere, at least not tomorrow."

"I agree, Daniel," Mr. Cottingham said, taking the pie plate from him. "I do believe we may be staying put for Christmas," he added, though Samuel noted the older gentleman didn't seem to be upset by that. Neither did Miss Vivian, who gave Mr. Cottingham a warm smile.

"Being Christmas Eve is tomorrow," she said, "you could be right, Benjamin."

"I say we make the most of it." Mr. Cottingham surprised Samuel again.

"Indeed." Miss Vivian nodded across the table. "We should."

"We can make decorations," Molly offered. "Unless. . .Samuel, do you think the people you know will be coming back this way for Christmas?"

"The people I know?" he asked, confused and somewhat taken back by the conversation flying around him.

177

"The ones who live in this house."

"Oh, those people. . ." Taking the warm dish from Mr. Cottingham, he acted as if he was concentrating on which piece of pie to select. In reality, his conscience tormented him all over again.

Earlier in the day, he'd been quick to justify why he'd fibbed about the house's owners and not disclosed the truth. He'd told himself it hadn't made sense to share his life story, knowing they'd all be parting ways soon. But now, even though a part of him was warring to 'fess up, he found just the opposite rationale as a reason for being close-mouthed. He didn't want to share his past because they'd all be staying together for a while yet. That was a side of the coin he'd experienced, too.

After Theresa passed away, his neighbors went through thoughtful rituals, bringing food and checking on him the first weeks—even the first months. But after that, they mostly never acted the same way around him again—not even the ones who'd helped him build his house and whom he'd helped, too. They shied away from him. It felt as if a mile-high fence had been raised up around his property, just like the one around his heart.

He sure wasn't going to spend the next days with this group of people tiptoeing around him, acting all awkward and uncomfortable. Especially not in his own house. He'd rather keep with his false tale than have that happen.

"Do as you please," he told Molly, handing her the cornmeal pie. "I'm sure they won't be back. At least not anytime soon."

At that bit of news, the women could barely settle down to eat. They talked of nothing but the decorating and cooking to start the next day.

The more they talked, the more Samuel poked at his dinner, which didn't seem as tasty as it had at first. All the gabbing about Christmas and decorating was distressing. It was everything he'd been running away from. Now there was nowhere to go—and no way to escape it.

⁂

After dinner, Molly shooed Charlotte and Miss Vivian out of the kitchen area. She took over dishwashing duty since they'd already been on their feet for hours preparing the meal. Besides, she noticed Mr. Cottingham appeared bent on spending some one-on-one time with Miss Vivian. And Melissa was tugging on Charlotte to play a guessing game. Meanwhile, Daniel seemed pleased to be in the midst of it all, intermittently nodding off in his chair, obviously still recuperating from his fall.

"Is the water warm enough?"

Molly figured Samuel would make himself scarce as well once he'd heated a tub of water over the fire and set it on the kitchen table. Instead, he surprised her when he picked up a cloth and stood next to her, ready to dry.

"It's a perfect temperature, but you should go sit," she insisted.

"Not much good at sitting and don't need to feed the horses for a while."

"Maybe you want to rest before you tend to them." She didn't know why she was turning down his help instead of being glad for the time to spend with him. Except for the fact that she suddenly felt shy around him. And confused. Not about her feelings—but his.

She thought she'd felt his gaze on her when they'd first sat down to dinner. Just the same as she had earlier in the day outside. But later in the meal, he seemed distant. Had she misinterpreted his attention? Maybe mistaken his gazing for something more than it was?

"I can manage on my own," she said, dipping her hands into the water.

He chuckled at that. "I have no doubt about that."

She bit her lip, wanting to ask what he meant but then not wanting to know at all. When he held out his hand for the plate she'd scrubbed, he must've seen the puzzled look on her face.

"It's not a bad thing, Molly." He took the dripping dish from her. "Being able to take care of yourself is. . .well, it's admirable really."

She kept her head down, not wanting him to see the flush of pink his words of approval brought to her cheeks. "It's what it must be." She shrugged.

"Yeah?" He swiped at the plate. "How do you mean?"

She slipped a few more dirty dishes into the tub and sighed. "Well, if you truly care to know," she paused to look at him, "I haven't had a choice. I mean, I'm not feeling sorry for myself or anything, but I never knew a daddy. And I took care of my sick mama for years and years till she finally died. Then I drifted some here and there till I found my granny and came to live with her in St. Claire."

"Your grandmother lives in St. Claire?"

"She did. And I had a couple of really good years with her. And then she. . ." She turned back to the washtub, meaning to continue scrubbing, but an unexpected feeling of sadness overwhelmed her. Her hands stilled in the warm water. Her shoulders collapsed in on themselves. A painful lump rose up at the back of her throat, so large she could scarcely speak. "And then she. . ." She could barely utter the words, but she didn't have to. Samuel knew.

"I'm sorry, Molly," he said softly.

She was grateful for his caring hand on her shoulder. His touch steadied her, giving her the wherewithal to get ahold of herself and continue.

"I guess I never took much time to cry about her passing. I just had to move on. Keep going. But it's hard." She sniffed. "Granny was a sweet woman. As sweet as they come. She was the only person I ever loved who truly loved me back. Even my mama. . ." She shook her head. "She never did love me the way Granny did."

She could feel him shifting on his feet next to her. She was probably making him feel uneasy. Again. Just like in the barn the evening before. She worked to clear her throat. "I'm sorry." She blinked back tears. "I didn't mean to burden you like that, Samuel."

"No need to apologize," he assured her, but his forehead creased in thought. "That's why you were heading to Huxley for Christmas?"

"Yes, for Christmas and—" She didn't want to begin to tell him about the letters. Or Clement. Or about her hopes of finding a place to call home and a person to love and share it with. What on earth would he think of her then? "I've gone on too much about myself. What about you, Samuel?"

"Me? I—there's nothing much to tell." He shrugged off her question.

But there was always something to be told. Yet maybe one story was enough for the evening. She wouldn't prod. They settled into a comfortable silence, working together side by side. Everything feeling easy and familiar, as if they'd done the same thing hundreds of times before.

"I'm so excited to decorate tomorrow. We'll get this nice house all spruced up, and—" She suddenly realized she was chatting uncontrollably again. "I suppose women are apt to get more excited about such a thing than men."

"True." He smiled affably as he dried the last plate, stacking it on top of the others.

"So." He peered into the tub. "That's all of them? We're finished?"

"Seems so."

"Guess I'll just be dumping out this water then," he said.

"I'm much obliged for your help, Samuel."

"Glad to do it." He nodded, handing her his damp cloth. And she knew she wasn't imagining it when his fingers touched hers. Warmed her skin. And lingered there for just a moment. A special kind of moment.

"I should get started," he murmured. Then he picked up the tub and was almost to the coat hooks by the front door when he turned and came back to her. "You can help if you want. With the horses."

"One good turn deserves another," she said as lightly as she could manage. Though as she stored the plates back on the shelf and went for her coat, her heart was racing in her chest.

*

"Oh, my goodness!"

He'd kept a pace ahead of Molly, lighting the way to the barn with a lantern even though the fallen snow on the ground and the streaks of white clouds overhead were more than enough to light the winter night. At the sound of her voice, he turned quickly.

"Are you all right?"

"Oh yes, I am! It sure is a sight, isn't it?"

She stood with her coat wrapped around her, the collar up to her cheeks, staring up at the sky in wonderment, looking like something pretty enough to be painted in a picture. He followed her gaze to the inkling of a moon peeking out from the strips of clouds and the crystal dots of stars to see just what she meant.

"Why, every time I come outside, there's one thing prettier than the next around here," she exclaimed. "I don't know how I could've lived so close in St. Claire and never seen all of this."

From the first moment Molly arrived at his house, he'd noticed a sparkle in her eyes. She'd developed a quick love for the land—the same as he'd had when he first laid claim to it. Unfortunately, it'd been a joy Theresa wasn't always able to share with him because of her illness. He'd worked so hard for months on end, building the house, making it just right for her arrival from the East. So eager for them to start their lives together as husband and wife. But she'd caught an infection soon after she got there. Even though the doctor declared her cured, she never completely healed. She never stopped hurting. . .until she'd finally slipped away.

"Maybe you never got outdoors much where you lived before," he suggested, swiping moisture from his eyes.

"You're probably right." She directed a smile his way. The feel of it warmed him, easing the ache in his chest.

As they set out for the barn again, he knew he could tell himself that the reason he'd invited Molly to help was because he felt sympathetic about her granny. He could tell himself it was because he thought she could use a friend. But the real truth was, he enjoyed her company. It was as simple as that. Which was complicated and too bad, since they'd be parting ways so soon.

Chapter 8

Molly was blushing again. She couldn't help it. As she stood stirring sugar and flour, the only thing she could think about was Samuel. . .and the way he'd held her hand on the way back from the barn the night before. Of course, he was truly a gentleman and may have only been concerned about her falling in the snow, but still. . .

Her cheeks heated, remembering the caring feel of his grasp.

"I think you've about stirred those ingredients to death, Molly girl." Miss Vivian chuckled as she rolled out a sheet of dough. "Did you find any nutmeg to add in?"

"Oh. . .I nearly forgot." Shaking her head at her absentmindedness, Molly hugged the bowl to her chest, reaching for the spice tin from an overhead shelf. As she did, a sudden burst of cold air swept through the kitchen area, rippling the hem of her calico dress, causing her cheeks to burn even more. All because Samuel had just come through the front door.

"I brought in sprigs of evergreen for you ladies," he said, branches of green rustling in his arms. "Thought you could use some for decorating."

Miss Vivian and Charlotte squealed delightedly. Daniel and Mr. Cottingham looked up from their checkers, curious to see what their fussing was about. Meanwhile, Molly hugged the bowl more tightly as if it were a protective shield, willing herself not to blush or flush or anything else at the sight of Samuel. But it was mighty hard.

Why, his shoulders looked so broad in his rawhide coat. And though his cowboy hat was pulled down tight to keep from blowing off, it still added to his height. His presence saturated the area just the same way the scent of pine permeated the air. Despite her resolve, her stomach twittered unnaturally. She could barely seem to take a deep breath.

"How considerate of you, Samuel," Charlotte said as Molly tried to gather her wits.

"It's going to be a wonderful Christmas Eve." Miss Vivian nodded agreeably. "We'll decorate the mantel."

"Maybe even the banister," Molly added, finally finding her voice. "I mean, if there's extra."

"I can always get you more. It's no trouble."

He looked at her, his eyes appearing anxious to please. Warming her all over again.

"Oh, I wouldn't want you to go to any more trouble."

"Walking outside and gathering up more branches is the kind of trouble I don't mind."

He smiled amiably, and she worked to draw her gaze away, back to focusing on the job at hand. But she couldn't help but notice how even his boots had a distinctive sound to her ears as he crossed the hardwood floor and unloaded the sprigs near the side of the stairs.

"Melissa." She addressed the young girl sitting at the table in an effort to distract her wayward thoughts. "How about we go outside in a bit and try to find some pine-cones in the snow?"

"Ah, thank you for reminding me," Samuel said from across the room. He began to empty his pockets, laying pinecones on top of the boughs on the floor. "I brought some of those in for you, too."

"You've certainly thought of everything." Molly smiled. "I can't believe you found so many."

"I found something, too!" Melissa said to Samuel.

"You did?" Samuel walked over to the kitchen area, and Molly watched as his eyes settled kindly on the young girl.

"Uh-huh. Josephine and I both did."

"What might that be?" he asked.

But all at once Melissa hugged Josephine and hopped from the chair, suddenly more interested in the men's checker game than the ladies' food preparations. Molly could tell by his baffled smile that he was puzzled.

"Did I say something wrong?"

"No. Melissa received a mild scolding and is embarrassed is all," she assured him. "We thought she was upstairs playing, but low and behold she was going through the owner's trunk up there."

"She did what?"

Samuel had started to reach for a mug for coffee, yet with that bit of news, Molly noticed he stopped. Straightened. All hints of a smile retreated from his eyes and lips.

"Don't worry. She didn't break anything. All of your friends' items are safe."

"Yes, yes. All is fine." Miss Vivian stepped up between them, not seeming to notice Samuel's change in expression. Leading Molly to wonder if perhaps she was being overly sensitive. "But Melissa did find something special that might help with our decorating. Why don't you take Samuel upstairs for him to see, Molly?"

Before either of them could react, Miss Vivian snatched the bowl from Molly's grasp. "Go now." She pushed them toward the stairs. "You don't seem to have much of a mind for kitchen duties this morning anyway, Molly girl," she tittered.

Molly knew the older woman was teasing kindly rather than criticizing. Either way, Miss Vivian wasn't saying anything out of turn. All morning she'd been day-dreaming about Samuel. Now here he was, standing right in front of her. She may as well make the most of the moment. Besides, if he was concerned about his friends' belongings, she could show him all was well.

"Would you like to come see what Melissa found?" she asked him. "Do you mind?"

☙

Samuel followed Molly up the steps, paused on the pine flooring at the top, and then took a left into the room he'd been taking turns sleeping in with the other two men. All the while, his emotions warred, his mind clouded with deception. Undoubtedly, whatever Molly was about to show him was something he'd already seen. Yet he stood by, pretending to be clueless, not reacting or saying a thing. Not even when she opened

183

the grand trunk sitting there and took out the ornately carved box that had belonged to Theresa's grandmother.

"I've never seen such a beautiful box, have you?" Molly ran a hand over the unique surface. "Just look, each flower is different. No two are alike. And wait till you see what's inside."

He noticed how reverently she held the box, as earnestly as he imagined the magi might have guarded their gifts to the world's Savior. Clutching it tightly, she took her time to sit down on the cold pine floor ceremoniously. What could he do but follow her lead? He bent down on one knee to face her.

With deliberate slowness, she opened the box, as if hurrying might somehow diminish the preciousness of the contents. Then layer by layer, she peeled back the cloth kerchief protecting the contents. Admittedly, her respectful handling of his wife's heirloom gratified his heart in a way that surprised him.

"Aren't they precious?" She held out the box for him to see, and he had to feign surprise over the pair of angels inside. Just as he recalled, one angel held a harp in its arms; the other had a trumpet perched at its lips. Each wore a holly wreath halo. Both were made of delicate porcelain that seemed to have become more fragile with age.

"I've never seen anything so pretty," she said. "Just look at the eyelashes painted on this one," Molly said with breathless appreciation. "Oh, and Samuel, did you see this?" She held up the angel holding the harp. "Why, you can see each little fingernail on her hands."

"They're certainly detailed," he agreed. "If angels are real, well then, they sure look real as can be."

Molly's eyes immediately flashed from the angels to him. "Well, of course angels are real." She gave him a crimped smile as if he was just being plain silly. But suddenly her expression turned serious. "You do believe in angels, don't you, Samuel?"

If truth be told, he would say how he hadn't believed in anything in a long while. Yet somehow in just the past few days, the world around him was softening. Somehow he was softening. Was it just because the focus of his thoughts had turned from himself to someone else—to Molly?

Initially he'd only been concerned about her safety and how to alleviate his guilty conscience. But after spending time with her, somehow ensuring her happiness had begun to concern him, too. After hearing about her granny, he'd woken up thinking how much she deserved a nice Christmas. More than anything, that made him put his ill feelings about the holiday aside. That's what had him traipsing through the snow, cutting down pine boughs, and filling his pockets with pinecones.

But when she'd mentioned the trunk upstairs and the decorations Melissa had found, he was startled. He'd already guessed it was the angels—Theresa's angels—that the young girl had discovered. He'd packed up the pair of seraphs long ago. They'd been too much of a symbol of the dreams he and Theresa had shared. Even right up till the last Christmas, the two of them were still hoping and praying that all would miraculously be well and that God would give them a future with children to pass the angels down to. When that didn't happen, he had no plans to set eyes on the angels again.

He figured opening that box would be like opening a wound that could never heal.

Yet when Molly opened the carved box, he'd been surprised again. With her sitting near, with her close, he didn't feel that way at all. It wasn't like he forgot the past or Theresa. It was just that the aching emptiness of the loss didn't completely devastate him as it always had.

"Samuel." Her soft voice interrupted his thoughts. "You do believe in angels, don't you?" she asked again, her beguiling eyes searching his.

With her face poised toward the diffused morning light coming through the window, she appeared radiant. . .much like an angel herself. One who was slowly restoring his soul.

"Yes," he said, barely audibly. Then more strongly, "Yes. Suppose I do."

"Well, good then!" She sighed, apparently relieved. Then she picked up one of the kerchiefs and began to wrap the harp-playing angel. "You know, the more I think about it, I don't believe we should use your friends' angels. I'm thinking we should leave them be."

He knew she wasn't posturing or being long-suffering. She was simply being sincere. That's why he blurted, "No. I think you should set them out. Use them to decorate."

"You think that would be all right with your friends?"

"Yes, I do."

"Well then. . .we can put them on the mantel where they'll be out of everyone's way."

"That's a fine idea." He nodded.

"You're sure now? Be honest with me."

She looked into his eyes, and he recalled the first day they'd met. How even then her kind gaze somehow made him feel as though he wanted to share what was true. Though he knew she was referring to his honest feelings about the angels, all he could think about was how he hadn't been forthcoming with her at all. It was time to tell her the truth.

"Molly, I—"

"Molly!" Charlotte's voice rang up the stairs. "Have you seen the nutmeg?"

"The nutmeg? No, I don't think—"

Gently, she handed the box to him. He watched as she felt at her pockets. "Oh, silly me! I accidentally put the tin in my pocket." She shook her head at herself. "I have it," she called out to Charlotte. "I'll be right down!"

"You go ahead," he said. "I'll get the angels downstairs safely."

"Thank you." She stood up and smoothed her skirts. "I promise I'll be more careful with the angels than the tin of nutmeg."

"I'm sure you will."

She gave him the sweetest smile and started to go then turned at the doorway.

"Oh, Samuel, was there something you started to say?"

"I, uh. . .no." He shook his head.

But of course, that wasn't the truth either.

Chapter 9

It had been a long day of cooking and decorating. By the time Molly climbed the stairs to get dressed for the evening's festivities, the late afternoon sun was casting shadows about the bedroom.

She was far too excited to be tired from the day's activities. Instead, she lit a kerosene lamp then knelt down in front of her trunk and opened the latch. She rooted through her meager parcel of belongings until she located the special something she was looking for. The Christmas dress her granny had made for her when she'd first come to St. Claire.

Made from sumptuous green velvet, her fingers could've easily detected the dress's soft lushness with no light at all. She'd never known where on earth her granny had gotten the luxurious material. It was a secret Granny never divulged, only remarking it was from an "earlier time."

Molly's heart ached as she took the gown from the trunk, remembering the woman who had stitched it so lovingly and had hummed joyfully all the while she sewed. Pressing its softness to her cheek, how she wished she would've worn the dress more than once in her granny's presence. What had she been thinking when she put it away, setting it aside for some unforeseen special occasion? As if wearing it for the woman who had meant everything to her wasn't special enough?

Then just days ago, she'd packed the festive dress in her trunk, believing the special occasion she'd been saving it for was close at hand. She thought for certain she'd be wearing the emerald frock on Christmas Eve upon meeting Clement Jones.

Yet all along, God knew that wouldn't come to be. Clement was still just as far away tonight as when she'd first placed the dress in her traveling case. Perhaps, even further—as far as her heart was concerned.

Now, to her surprise, she'd be wearing the dress this Christmas Eve with people she never knew she'd meet, or become so close to. The dear Miss Vivian and Charlotte. Mr. Cottingham. Melissa. Daniel. And. . .Samuel.

He'd been so helpful all day long. Helping to hang things in high places. Lifting things, large and small. He and Daniel had even sneaked into the smokehouse, thinking Samuel's friends wouldn't mind if they helped themselves to a bit of meat for the Christmas stew.

She had to admit she liked the feeling of having Samuel nearby. And though their time together wasn't yet up, she found she was already missing him.

Sighing, she looked up and gazed out the window. With all her heart, she wished the weather would never improve. Then nothing would change. They'd all stay in this house, and Samuel would never have the chance to head west again.

It wasn't realistic, she knew. But still, she wished it. Because now her dreams of

Clement felt more uncertain than ever. Huxley suddenly sounded foreign, while everything around her was beginning to feel more like home than it had in a long time.

Clutching the dress, she felt torn in ways she hadn't for a while. She'd been quick to leave St. Claire when there was nothing and no one to stay for. But now there was.

Or was there? Her brow creased, wondering if she was being unrealistic in that respect, too.

After all, when Christmas was over—when the snow melted—how would things be then? Should she stay in St. Claire and hope her new acquaintances would become even better friends? Wait there in hopes that when Samuel left, he'd come back again soon? Or should she plan to set out, too?

Anxiety threatened to overwhelm her. Thankfully, in the midst of it, her granny's words came to her, clear as anything: *"When times come that you want to throw your hands in the air, best you get down on your knees and pray."*

Molly was already kneeling. So she closed her eyes and let her words and feelings pour from her heart.

∽

"Gotta admit, Tack, this situation's got me stumped."

Clean shaven. Hair combed. Dressed in his Sunday best for the Christmas Eve celebration. Samuel felt out of place in his own barn. But he was glad for the excuse to go out and feed the horses before dinner. It gave him time to mull things over with the closest thing he had to a best friend: Tack.

Taking his familiar seat on a nearby bench, he leaned back, spewing out his thoughts while the horses crunched and slurped.

"I look at that muddy old stagecoach outside"—he pointed toward the barn door—"and remember how I felt the first time I laid eyes on it. I was downright mad, remember? I grabbed your reins, ready to go. Then got angry when my conscience glued me to the spot. I was still peeved when I was driving the thing all the way back here." He shook his head at the memory. "Now, I gotta tell ya, I look at that stagecoach, and it's a different kind of feeling I get. Like I'm going to be sorry to see it go."

Of course, it wasn't the stagecoach he'd miss. Obviously, it was Molly. But that didn't help his consternation. It only added to it. He wasn't quite sure how he felt about that either.

"You haven't been around her much. But if you were, you'd take a liking to her, Tack." A smile crimped his lips. "Remember Daisy? That strong-willed filly we used to have? Molly's feisty like that, but with a good heart. Like Daisy, she's not afraid of anything."

As soon as the words left his mouth, he caught himself. Theresa had always said the same of him—that he was fearless. But that just wasn't so. The truth was he'd put on a good act for her. In reality, being helpless to find a cure to save her had frightened him like nothing else ever had. Losing her had torn him up in ways he never knew possible.

"I don't know, Tack. Just don't know if I ever want to go through that again— caring for someone. . .loving them."

And losing them.

He didn't say the words out loud, but instinctively Tack seemed to know just what he meant. Lifting his head from the feed, he gave Samuel a sympathetic look.

"I appreciate your concern," he said, "but I shouldn't be talking all serious like this, should I? Not tonight."

It was supposed to be an evening of celebration, after all. The ladies had worked hard preparing for a merry Christmas Eve. He reminded himself of that as he got the horses back to their stalls and covered Tack with a blanket for good measure.

"Thanks for listening, pal." He ran a hand down Tack's mane before gathering extra firewood and exiting the barn.

With arms full, he made his way around the stagecoach parked outside, trying not to notice it. But it loomed beside the barn door like a monster he hadn't been able to face. A constant reminder that change was on its way again.

There was no denying that the temperature was slowly rising—and had been all day. With the weather improving, his company would be going soon, and of course he'd be clear to go his way, too.

If he chose to.

His mind bantered, weighing his options as he strode across the yard to the house. He stopped in his tracks.

The house looked just the way Theresa had always loved it. *"So cozy,"* she would say. A thinning layer of snow edged the rooftop. White spirals of smoke swirled from the chimney, stretching into curlicues in the ebony sky. And each window shone with a friendly amber light, promising enough warmth to shake off the cold. As he stood and stared, he recalled that even in her pain such sights had always brought a pleased smile to her face.

Taking up his steps again, he was reminded of something else. Of how they'd stood outside, staring at their snow-covered house one night, and she wouldn't go in. Not until he promised—crossed his heart—that after she died he wouldn't live his days there alone. "It's people who make a house a home, Samuel," she'd said.

As if he hadn't already known that. As if he didn't know that now.

In the past days, the people he'd rescued had lifted the veil of gloom from his house. And Molly, she'd come into his life quickly like the whirlwind she was, stirring feelings that had been lost to him for years.

The only problem was, once again, he really wasn't as brave as he pretended to be. And even though Molly brought a brightness to his life that had long gone missing, he wasn't sure if he was willing or ready to accept it.

Did he really want to take the chance of losing someone again? Enough to be free to love again?

∽

Molly stood in front of the fireplace and let the first of Clement's letters slip from her hands into the blaze. The others she tossed more purposefully into the fiery pit. She watched the flames devour the coarse paper, instantly turning the creamy sheets into curly brown remnants and finally into puffs of dusty ashes.

She felt curiously relieved.

She didn't know what was going to happen to her next. Yet after praying, she felt that if she stayed true to her feelings and stepped out in faith, God would be there for her. Every step of the way. Vague as that immediate path seemed, letting go of

Clement's letters still felt more right than anything she'd done in a while.

When the front door opened and Samuel walked in, she'd been so lost in thought, she gasped.

"No need for alarm. It's just me." He grinned. "I figured we'd need some extra firewood this evening."

Her green velvet skirt swayed as she moved, and suddenly with Samuel close by depositing the logs, she felt so self-conscious in the elegant dress that she couldn't stop from fidgeting. She smoothed the lace edging around the waistband. Felt for each tiny covered button at her wrist. Anything to keep her fingers busy.

Meanwhile, he crossed the room to hang up his hat and coat at the door. When he turned, she startled at the sound of her name.

"Molly?"

Her hands immediately stilled. Looking his way, she felt as surprised as he sounded. His hair was raked back from his forehead. And his whiskers had definitely seen the sharp edge of a straight razor. Both made it easier than ever to see the inherent strength in his face. The square of his jaw. Each of his classically handsome features.

She knew she was staring. But fortunately, he appeared to be staring at her, too. He hesitated then walked toward her slowly as if scrutinizing each step.

"You look. . ." He paused, as if he didn't know the right word to say. "You look pretty, Molly. Beautiful."

Her cheeks lit on fire at his words. "Thank you, Samuel."

"And your hair. It's different, isn't it?"

"My hair? Why, yes." She touched the bow at the back of her head. "I thought I'd try it pulled back from my face," she added shyly, wondering if his noticing meant he liked it.

"It looks good. And the green is good, too. That dress is perfect—a perfect color for you, I mean."

"My granny made it," she said proudly.

"She did a fine job. Really fine."

"And look at you in your friend's clothes." She nodded at the outfit he wore, the black pants, white shirt, and the buttoned wool vest that noticeably outlined the contour of his chest. "Did you have any idea they'd fit you so nicely?"

"I, uh, well," he stammered. "I figured I needed to spruce up if I wanted to fit in around here. You ladies made everything look cheery."

"No denying you were a big help. Together we made it look very festive, didn't we?" She tore her gaze from his long enough to look all around them. To the windows framed in evergreens. To the banisters wrapped with greenery. To the mantel, where more sprigs laden with pinecones made a bed for the porcelain angels. "Though I truly never thought I'd be spending Christmas this way."

"You thought you'd be in Huxley."

"Yes, I did. But—"

"But neither of us ended up where we thought we might."

"True, we didn't. And we've nearly forced you into celebrating here in your friends' home, whether you wanted to or not. I'm sorry for that."

"You don't need to be." He shrugged. "It's not been a bad thing."

She laughed at his phrasing. "Does that mean it's been a good thing?"

He smiled. "I suppose things have a way of working out, though sometimes it can be puzzling how they do."

"Actually," she ventured, "I was just thinking that, too."

Or at least hoping it was true. There was so much more to say. So much more she wanted to explain and to ask Samuel about, if she dared to. But Daniel and Mr. Cottingham had already started down the stairs, disrupting the moment of privacy.

"Ah, that stew smells delicious," Mr. Cottingham commented. "And Vivian makes the very best biscuits. Molly, maybe you should tell the womenfolk to hurry and dress so we can eat."

"No need to rush us. We're already here." Miss Vivian chuckled as she and Charlotte followed behind with Melissa in tow.

As everyone gathered around the table, Molly felt pleased when Samuel sat beside her. And in that moment she realized she hadn't needed a special occasion to wear the beautiful dress her granny had made for her at all. Not as much as she'd needed a special person to wear it for. Someone who made her feel appreciated and special, too. Someone who looked at her just the way Samuel had.

Chapter 10

"And then there was the Christmas Eve my younger sister decided her favorite piglet should come to family dinner," Samuel told Molly as she handed him a dripping dish to dry.

As soon as Christmas Eve dinner was over, everyone had fallen into their places, much the same as the evening before. While the others had retreated to the sitting room, he and Molly had offered to do dishes. He rolled up his cuffs, and she pushed back her sleeves and donned an apron over her elegant dress. And once again, he found that he didn't mind the chore at all. Especially when Molly had asked him about some of his family's past Christmases.

"Oh, goodness!" Molly bent over the tub, laughing. "How old was she at the time?"

"My sister or the piglet?" he teased.

"Your sister, silly."

"Maybe four or so? Too young for my mother to paddle her when the piglet tore through the house, knocking over all the decorations. Luckily, Mother had made Sis a doll for Christmas, hoping she'd choose that over her pet porker."

"Did it work?" Molly's hands paused in the water.

"For a while. Until spring, when Sis brought the piglet inside for Easter dinner."

"Oh no, Samuel!" Molly giggled. "Surely that didn't happen."

"Oh, but it did." He grinned. "And mind you the creature wasn't as young and small as it had been months before. Neither was my sister. She did get into trouble that time."

Molly laughed out loud as she handed him another scrubbed cup. "Your poor sister! And mother! How funny!"

"It was quite a funny time," he said, taking the cup from her hands. There had been many an amusing time back then. Many good memories that he'd stored so deeply behind more painful ones that they never surfaced. Not until Molly. Strangely, being around her made it easier to recall happier days. . .better times.

Chuckling to himself, he was just about to tell her about another Harden Christmas when Charlotte called to them.

"Are you two almost finished? We don't want to start singing Christmas songs without you."

He looked to Molly for an answer.

"We're getting very close," she told Charlotte. "It'll take just a few minutes more."

Admittedly he felt disappointed when five minutes later their time alone was up.

"All done," Molly said and blew at a wisp of hair that had fallen onto her forehead.

Without thinking, he reached out to put the tendril back into place. It would've been the simplest of gestures. If only he hadn't looked into her eyes.

191

But he did. And for the second time that night, he felt stunned. Caught off guard. The same way he felt when he first saw her by the hearth, looking so pretty in her green dress. There was no denying the wonder he felt. Unable to fathom why such a special woman would be giving him the time of day. And though he kept trying to fight it, there was also no denying the pleasure he felt when she did.

"Hurry, you two!" Charlotte shouted, impatience tingeing her voice.

"We're coming!" Molly called back. "Goodness, that girl needs to hold her horses!" she whispered, making him grin.

"I'll empty the tub."

"I'll put the dishes away." She smiled.

It was starting to sprinkle when he stepped outside to empty the tub of water over the porch railing. Despite the chill in the air, as he turned to walk back inside, he stopped. And listened. Not to a howling animal. Or barking dog. Or gusty wind. But to himself. Whistling happily.

It might not have come as such a shock to him, but he'd never been a whistler. Yet there he was, Samuel Harden, warbling a Christmas tune from his childhood. On Christmas Eve. The day he'd dreaded. The day he'd been running from. And now the day he'd been able to find joy in again.

It felt like nothing short of a miracle.

Gladness welled inside him, and the gratitude he felt to God and to his first love, Theresa, was overwhelming. He'd always dwelled on how he'd loved Theresa. Until that moment, he hadn't appreciated the gift of love she'd given him. She'd told him he was fearless, so he wouldn't be afraid to love again. She'd encouraged him not to be alone. She'd said everything to help him before she'd died, and afterward he'd done everything to keep the hurt from healing.

But now Molly had stumbled into his life. No, God had brought her into his life. And despite everything he'd been thinking, running away didn't seem much of an option anymore.

He could feel it as clearly as he could see her through the window. Looking like someone he wanted to come home to. Someone to give his heart a home.

By the time he came back in the house, Samuel felt lighter. A crushing load had been lifted from his shoulders.

Settling into the empty chair next to Mr. Cottingham, he smiled at Molly sitting across the room. Daniel began plucking Christmas tunes on his banjo. They all sang timidly at first, but by the time they'd gotten through their third song, Samuel thought they sounded fairly good together.

Miss Vivian must have agreed. She clapped delightedly and flopped back in her chair with a sigh. "Thank you for playing for us, Daniel. Here I thought I'd miss having Christmas in Huxley with our friends," she confessed. "But they're truly a boring bunch compared to all of you."

"I'm glad you're not in Huxley either, Vivian," Mr. Cottingham said. "And Samuel, thank you again." He turned to him. "I would've never had this time to spend to get to know Viv—well, everyone—if you hadn't come along."

Samuel glanced at Molly and couldn't deny any longer that he felt exactly the same way. He hoped she'd stay in St. Claire. And he was ready to, as well. When the evening's festivities died down, he planned to ask her out to the porch and tell her everything about his past—and his thoughts for the future.

"I think all of us feel similarly, sir," he told Mr. Cottingham, glancing Molly's way.

She met his gaze shyly, gifting him with one of her sweet smiles. With her cheeks turning fiery as her hair, she seemed to be trying to turn the attention away from herself. "We have pudding for dessert," she announced. "If anyone would like some, I'll be happy to get it."

"Before you do, Molly"—Charlotte rose from her seat—"at the mention of Huxley, I just remembered. I have something from there that belongs to you."

"You what?" Molly's eyes grew wide.

"Oh, Molly, don't be coy," Charlotte said playfully. "Surely you know what I mean. I found this on the floor of the bedroom." Facing Molly, Charlotte drew a paper from her dress pocket. "I didn't mean to read it. But it fell open, and I just couldn't help it. It's a letter from your beau in Huxley."

A letter from whom? Her beau? At first Samuel didn't think he'd heard right. But then Molly stuttered, "Cle–Clement's letter?"

"It sounds as if you're betrothed. And you're going to live in Huxley?" Charlotte asked excitedly, while Samuel's stomach twisted violently. "When are you to marry?"

"Didn't I guess that, Charlotte? Remember?" Miss Vivian cut in. "When our dear Molly was clutching something so tightly on the stagecoach? I knew it had to be from a beau."

Samuel couldn't believe what he was hearing. Apparently Mr. Cottingham was surprised, too. "News to me. I didn't know she had a beau in Huxley." Mr. Cottingham leaned over to him. "Did you, Samuel?"

"No." His jaw clenched till he thought his teeth might fracture. "No. I surely did not know that." Jealous anger welled up in him quickly, mixing with confusion and hurt, turning his insides out. It was all he could do to sit still and not bolt from his chair.

Unfortunately, Melissa bolted from hers. "Molly has a beau-oh. Molly has a beau-oh," she sang, dancing around the room, flinging her doll in the air.

"Child, be careful," Mr. Cottingham warned. "You're going to hit someone in the face with your doll!"

But Melissa didn't stop. Samuel watched as the young girl turned one circle after another, singing about Molly's beau all the while. Until finally, she got so dizzy she started to stumble. Her arms flung upward, and Josephine went flying outward. The doll swiped a sprig of evergreen overhanging the mantel, and that's when the rippling started. The boughs of evergreen wavered. The pinecones bounced. And the angels— Theresa's angels—toppled from their nests and crashed onto the hardwood floor.

He couldn't believe his eyes. Pieces of porcelain, looking like bits of nothing, scattered everywhere. Shattered. Like his plans. Not an hour earlier, he'd given up and given in to his feelings. He'd set all judgment aside and was ready to take a chance, hoping Molly would, too. Thinking God had really meant for them to be together. But what a fool he'd been! A ridiculous fool!

"Now look what you've done!" he shouted, jumping from his chair. "What you've all done," he yelled like a crazy man. "I've had enough! Enough!" he fumed. Then he barged from the room and out of the house, slamming the front door behind him.

✂

"He's been out there forever." Molly sighed.

She peered out the window in the direction of the barn, hugging her arms around her waist. She could hear the tapping of the trickling rain far better than she could see it in the darkness. "It's been nearly an hour."

"And that's how long you've been standing at the window, too, dear." With Melissa cozied in her lap, Miss Vivian spoke more softly than usual. The young girl had felt so badly about the broken angels, she'd worn herself out crying. "Why don't you come and sit?" Miss Vivian urged.

"I'm fine. Really I am," Molly said.

She knew standing there, wishing for Samuel to come back inside so they all could set things right wouldn't make him come through the front door. But she couldn't stop hovering by the window anyway. She felt so badly for the way everything had happened.

"Molly, I really am sorry," Charlotte said from a rocker across the room. "I should've never read your letter."

Molly wished she hadn't read it either. But she had, and there was nothing to be gained from making Charlotte feel worse than she already did.

"Oh, Charlotte, please don't feel you have to keep apologizing." Molly turned from her watching—just for a moment—to reassure her. "Like I told you, I thought I'd thrown all of the letters into the fire. I had no idea one had dropped on the floor. Please don't worry yourself."

"Well, my poking in your business seemed to set off a chain reaction of ill events this evening." Charlotte sighed.

"It'll all be well," Molly said, turning back to the window. *It has to be,* she thought. "I just wonder if he's cold." She placed a hand on the pane to test the temperature. "Or wet. Maybe I should take him some hot tea—or his coat," she added, more to herself than anyone else.

Mr. Cottingham answered. "Give the man the time he needs," he said. "Give him space to think."

Over the past days, she'd come to admire Mr. Cottingham and to trust him, too. The man was a complete surprise, gentler and more compassionate than his sometimes gruff exterior let on. If he believed Samuel needed more time, she'd rely on his advice.

But it was hard to be patient. Every minute felt like forever. Wondering what on earth Samuel was thinking. . .and feeling. He'd said earlier that things had a way of working out. But she knew from past experience that didn't mean things always worked out exactly in the way she wanted them to. Not even if she hoped and prayed with all her might. Even so, as she stared out the window, hoping and praying was what she aimed to keep doing. She bowed her head, ready to start again. But Mr. Cottingham's voice stopped her.

"I've decided I won't stay silent any longer," he said. "There's something I believe you all should know."

"Goodness, Benjamin, what is it?" Miss Vivian straightened, and Molly did, too.

"It's something about Samuel."

Chapter 11

Samuel was angry. But mostly with himself.

He'd overreacted where Melissa and the broken angels were concerned, scaring the young girl terribly. She had burst into sobs as he stomped out the door. The sound crushed him so much he almost turned around and walked back in.

And where Molly was concerned, he'd underplayed things. He hadn't been at all honest with her about his past or his feelings. Maybe if he hadn't hidden the truth, she might've had the chance to be more honest with him. Not that any of it mattered now. She was involved with another man. And as much as he wanted to fight for her, why put her through that? Evidently he'd misread the situation between them. But to know he could have feelings for someone again—at least God had shown him that much.

Overall, he'd walked out on a roomful of people who had to be shocked at his behavior—not understanding it one bit. And why would they? The entire time the group was at his house, he'd acted nonchalant and unconcerned, suppressing the truth. Then right in the middle of the nicest Christmas Eve he'd had in a long, long time, he blew up like a crazy man. He hated any of them thinking of him that way. Molly most of all.

"So, Tack, looks like I have a choice to make." He crossed his arms over his chest. "I can either sit here in the barn all night trying to figure the right words to say to everyone. . ." He paused, not so fond of what he was about to say next. "Or I can get off this bench, go inside, and say whatever words come out."

Tack grunted once. Then twice, as if opting for Samuel's second idea. Either that or Samuel figured he was simply tired of listening to him talk and trying to be rid of him.

"Yep. Guess it's what I need to do." He drew in a deep breath, hoisting himself up. "Well, here goes nothin', boy."

Taking long, purposeful strides across the yard, he was barely cognizant of the splatters of rain coming down. It wasn't until he reached the porch that he noticed how wet he was. Pausing outside the door, he swiped the water from his clothes conscientiously, feeling like an unwanted visitor rather than the owner of the house.

He could hear one of the women on the other side of the door warning he was back. He heard some scuffling, too, and assumed everyone was getting in position for his entrance.

He rolled his neck and drew back his shoulders before he opened the door and let himself in.

He'd expected some sort of reaction. But everyone appeared as if nothing was the matter. Daniel was strumming his banjo lightly. Little Melissa was cuddled in Miss Vivian's lap. Mr. Cottingham was reading a book. And Charlotte and Molly were engaged in a quiet conversation with each other. The broken angel pieces had already been swept up, but he was certain, after the way he'd lost control, they wouldn't soon be forgotten.

He realized everyone was being kind, acting normal as could be. It would've been nice if he could've done the same. But his poor behavior weighed too heavily on him. He stood, dripping water on the hardwood floor he'd put down with his own hands. "I'm sorry," he said simply.

Everyone looked up at the sound of his voice as if they'd just noticed he was there. He strained to keep from looking at Molly, not wanting to see what he imagined would be disapproval in her eyes.

"I especially want to say I'm sorry to you, Melissa." It was difficult to look at the sweet little thing cuddled in Miss Vivian's lap, but he did. "Accidents happen. And I shouldn't have acted the way I did. You're far more important than those angels, and I hurt your feelings. I scared you, which wasn't right. I'm sorry I lost my temper like that."

"That's all right," she said sleepily. "Josephine and I were dancing too hard. Granddad told me to stop, and I didn't."

"Well," Samuel said, "dancing on Christmas Eve should be allowed, I think. After all, it's a night worth celebrating—and here I ruined it for everyone. It's just a lot of things built up. . .and well, I hope everyone can accept my apology." He hung his head.

Mr. Cottingham closed the book he was reading and set it aside. "There's no need to hang your head like that, Samuel. None at all. You saved our lives. You brought us to the safety of this house."

"But there's no accounting for the way I behaved tonight."

"I don't believe that's entirely true." Mr. Cottingham said matter-of-factly.

That wasn't the response Samuel expected. He frowned at the older gentlemen. "What did you say?"

"I said, I believe there's good reason why you behaved the way you did. After all, you brought us back to *your* house, to the very house I assume you were running away from. You fed us. Kept us warm. And I suspect we broke something precious to you. Actually, I suspect your anger stemmed from more than that, but we won't get into that part of it now."

"You know?" He gaped at Mr. Cottingham. "But how?"

"I've known since the first night we arrived. My bones were aching and I couldn't sleep well, and—"

"That was before I started making him a cup of ginger tea at night." Miss Vivian smiled.

"It definitely was, Viv." Mr. Cottingham returned her smile before turning to Samuel again. "Anyway, I thought reading Psalms would help me relax, so I slipped down here, remembering that I'd seen the Bible on the table there." He nodded across the room.

Samuel shook his head in disbelief. "And you saw the inscription. You saw that my parents had given the Bible to Theresa and me on our wedding day."

"I did read that." Mr. Cottingham nodded solemnly. "And sadly, I also saw on the family register page that your wife wasn't on this earth any longer."

"Yes, we, uh. . ." Samuel paused, cleared his throat. "We'd only been married two years before she died. It was three years ago on this very day," he said quietly. There, he'd said it. And wondered why he'd made so many excuses about sharing the truth before this. "Why didn't you say anything before now?"

"I figured it was your business, Samuel. Something to be told when you were ready."

"He only told us a few minutes ago," Molly said softly. "And only because he wanted us to understand why you were so upset about the angels. Oh, Samuel, I wish you'd said something. I'm guessing they were your wife's?"

"They belonged to Theresa's grandmother. We used to get them out every year on Christmas Eve."

"I'm so sorry." She looked down at her lap. "Very sorry."

"No one could've known. It was my fault. I should've told the truth."

"Samuel," Miss Vivian spoke up, "when we were still strangers, you offered us your hospitality. You shared everything you had with us. You didn't owe us an explanation, too. But young man," she said, sternly but lovingly, "we're not strangers any longer."

"That's right." Mr. Cottingham got up, cane in hand, and strode toward him. Samuel felt the well-meaning clasp of friendship when the man touched his shoulder. "And since that's true, I feel like I can tell you this. Son, there's no easy way around loss. It takes time. Faith. And believing that God knows you're hurting and believing that He'll see you through."

"Actually, this Christmas I've. . .I'm starting to believe that again," he admitted.

"Well, good." Mr. Cottingham patted his shoulder. "And Vivian is right. You've been more than generous, sharing all you have with us. But since the weather has warmed up, maybe it's best for us to be on our way in the morning."

Well, of course. Why would they care to stay? They probably felt like they had to tiptoe around him now. Afraid he'd lose his temper again.

"I think that makes sense," he agreed regretfully.

He gave Molly one more glance, trying to memorize the face of the woman who had opened up his closed-off heart. He'd never laugh with her again. Or be captivated by her again. She belonged to another man. Everything in him felt heavy with the realization, but he cared for her too much not to respect that.

"I need to get dry things from upstairs," he told everyone. "Then I'll be sleeping in the barn tonight."

"Oh, Samuel, that's not necessary," Miss Vivian said.

"It'd be better if I do. I'll feed the horses before you all leave in the morning."

ᖆᖆ

Even though it wasn't her turn, Molly offered to take the pallet on the bedroom floor and let Miss Vivian and Charlotte share the bed for the night. After all that had happened that evening, she knew she wouldn't be sleeping anyway.

Hour after hour, she lay in the dim room, her heart aching beyond belief. Though Samuel wasn't so far away—only across the yard in the barn—it felt as if each passing minute expanded the distance between them. She had wanted to explain everything to him, but he seemed to want to be as far from her as he could. He probably thought she was a liar. Or that she didn't know her own feelings. But oh, she did! She had ever since she met him.

She stared at her velvet dress hanging in the corner, hoping it would quell her sadness. Just looking at it helped to bring Samuel close again.

She hadn't imagined it, had she? The way he'd looked at her in the dress? And told her she was beautiful?

She hadn't imagined it later, when he touched her hair? As if it was the most natural thing to do? As if the two of them were simply meant to be?

The thought jolted her. She sat up, her heart beating wildly. It was true. They were meant to be. They'd both lost the person they'd been closest to. They'd each decided to run from the hurt and the past. But along their paths, they'd found each other. She couldn't just let him go.

Jumping up from the mat, she shook Miss Vivian's shoulder. "Please wake up. I have an idea," she said excitedly. "Will you help me?"

Chapter 12

The first hints of dawn were coming to light as Molly set out across Samuel's lawn with everyone else in tow. Leading the caravan, she felt a smile as wide as the Missouri sky settle on her face, although inside she couldn't have felt more nervous. She was aiming to make this Christmas one Samuel would never forget. And if her wish came true, she hoped it would be just the start of more Christmases together.

As each of them tiptoed into the barn, she spied Samuel across the way. He was still asleep, curled up on a bed of hay he'd made outside of Tack's stall. The red blanket they'd shared on the stagecoach covered him, along with several other warm layers.

Her heart beat erratically as she shuffled through the straw until she was bending down, staring at his handsome profile. "Samuel," she whispered.

He didn't respond.

"Samuel," she said a bit louder.

His eyelids slowly opened, and he looked at her. "Molly?"

She was thankful when his lips immediately spread into a fond, loving smile. It was all the proof she needed that she'd been right to do this. To come to him.

"Merry Christmas," she said.

He sat up and rubbed his face. But then as if remembering a bad dream, his expression clouded. "It's Christmas morning?" He got to his feet. "You're leaving?"

"Actually, we came bearing gifts. Everyone wants to thank you for your hospitality."

In the center of the barn, Charlotte and Miss Vivian had laid out a blanket where everyone was starting to sit down. Molly stepped to his side and let them explain on their own.

"We brought you fresh biscuits and marmalade," Charlotte told him.

"And your coffee just the way you like it with a sprinkle of cinnamon." Miss Vivian smiled.

"I have a book I'd like to give you, Samuel," Mr. Cottingham said. "I hope you'll accept it with my gratitude."

"And I'm offering the gift of my banjo playing this Christmas morning," Daniel said, placing the instrument on his knees. "I'm open to requests." He grinned.

Molly watched Samuel's expression change with each person's gift, his features going from troubled to touched.

"Melissa has something for you, too," she told him. "Melissa?"

The little girl bounced up and handed Samuel a piece of paper. "This way they can always be with you," she said.

Molly knew sure as anything Samuel would be incredibly moved by Melissa's gift. "A picture of two angels," he said, his voice hoarse with emotion. "This is the best gift,

Melissa." He kissed the top of her head. "I'll keep this always."

Giving him a moment to collect himself, Molly spoke up, hoping her voice wouldn't betray her extreme nervousness. "And now it's my turn."

"Your turn?" He shook his head. "Molly, you've already given me more than you know. I don't need a present from you."

"That's good, because I don't exactly have one." She looked into his eyes. "Except for me. I only have myself to give."

"Only. . .what? Yourself?" Puzzled, his brows furrowed inward. "I don't understand. You're not going to Huxley?"

"She's going to be staying with us in St. Claire," Miss Vivian spoke up. "We can use her help at my sister's eatery."

"Is that true?" He turned back to her.

She nodded. "Being around you. . . Samuel, now I know the difference between real love and empty paper promises."

"And the other man?"

"There's only you, Samuel," she said in a rush then bit her lip. "That is, if you'll have me."

Oh, she felt so bold! But once again it seemed life's circumstances had her acting that way. No doubt, her feelings for Samuel were worth risking all of her pride for. But even for all of her audacity, she couldn't breathe. It was as if everything inside her had stopped working while she waited for his answer.

Finally, he spoke. "Molly, it took me awhile to admit it to myself, but the minute I met you I couldn't say no to you. And I don't want to ever say no to you—not for the rest of my life."

"Isn't it amazing how you don't have to travel far to find your heart a home?" Miss Vivian said gleefully.

"Yes, Viv." Mr. Cottingham chuckled, patting her hand. "Amazing how sometimes God's leading takes us right back to where we started."

Molly had been so fixed on Samuel, she'd nearly the forgotten the others were sitting there, waiting for them. Apparently Samuel had, too.

"Would you excuse us for a moment, please?" he said.

With everyone's blessing, he led her over to a corner of the barn. The morning sun was streaming through the slats of wood, allowing her to see every sparkle of longing in his eyes. "What is it, Samuel?" she asked breathlessly.

"This. . ."

With his tender touch, he lifted her chin and brushed his cheek against hers. Then slowly, gently, his lips found hers. A delightful shiver ran through her as she drank in the sweetness of his kiss. It was like nothing she'd ever felt or ever known, bringing tears of happiness to her eyes. He seemed to know just what she was feeling as he pulled back from her and wiped a droplet from her cheek.

"Merry first Christmas, my Molly," he whispered.

She looked up at him, her heart so full she couldn't speak. She could only give thanks that her wishes and prayers had been answered at last.

Forging a Family

by Vickie McDonough

Chapter 1

Advent, Texas
1890

Rain pelted the windows of the tiny depot packed full of grumbling passengers who had disembarked the train when it made its unscheduled stop in Advent. Beth shivered and hugged four-year-old Lizzie against her cloak. The weather felt more like what she'd experienced growing up in New York than what she expected to find in Texas. She jumped as an angry slash of lightning skittered across the sky, casting its ethereal glow over the crowded room.

Poppa was out there. She prayed he found them accommodations for tonight—somewhere warm with a place to bathe.

"Miss Ruskin, I'm hungry." Lizzie pushed her spectacles up her nose and gazed at her with tired blue eyes.

She smiled down at her ward. "There's still a biscuit and a piece of cheese in my basket. Would you like that?"

Lizzie nodded and yawned.

The confined space of the tiny depot made Beth feel like a sardine in a can her father once purchased. After he'd rolled off the tin top with an odd key, she discovered the little fish lined up side-by-side. She squirmed sideways and lifted her basket, pressing it against the wall to hold it in place. She felt around inside and managed to locate the biscuit. As she handed it to Lizzie, the door opened and several men dressed in dripping wet dusters stepped in. A cold chill rushed in with them.

"There's a boardinghouse," one man said as he searched the crowd.

"Over here, Henry." His wife waved at him from near the back. "Excuse me. Please let me pass. That's my husband." She squeezed her way through, followed by a pair of children.

Two other women, one with a toddler, joined their spouses, and they all left. The crowd shifted, and Beth breathed deeply for the first time in a long while. She wished her father would hurry. It was way past Lizzie's bedtime.

"Your daughter is precious," the woman beside her said. "She must take after her father."

Beth smiled. "Actually, I'm an agent with the Children's Aid Society."

"Oh, forgive me for being presumptuous. I've heard of the Orphan Train."

Beth nodded and glanced back at the windows, still battered by the rain. "I have appointments to meet several families in the next town, and I fear if this storm continues, it will delay us so long that we'll miss them." She brushed her hand over Lizzie's blond head, and the blue-eyed girl glanced up and smiled. She'd been unable to place the sweet child simply because she wore spectacles, but Beth had hopes that just the right family would be found.

"Maybe the storm will pass overnight and we'll be able to get out by morning."

"That would be nice."

The door flew open, and a man rushed in. Water ran in a rivulet down the brim of his hat and sloshed onto the floor. The nearest woman gasped and jumped back.

Beth nearly giggled. Considering the downpour outside, they'd all be drenched before they made it a few feet.

"I've found three families willing to take in one person for the night, so if you're traveling alone, please step forward."

"Oh! Excuse me." The woman she'd chatted with pressed forward, followed by a thin man in a brown tweed frock coat and another in a black duster.

The trio left with the tall man.

"When are we leaving?" Lizzie asked.

Beth bent and wiped the crumbs off her mouth. "Soon, sweetie."

"Advent is a small town," a portly woman to her left said. "They aren't likely to find room for all of us."

Beth fished out the piece of cheese, unwrapped it, and gave it to Lizzie, wishing she had a bowl of hot soup to warm them both. The depot—probably no larger than ten feet square—didn't even have a stove.

Grumbles echoed around the room, making her uncomfortable. She tried never to complain. Having a father who was a doctor meant interruptions any time day or night. She'd gotten used to being flexible, and when she found herself lonely with him gone so much, she'd started working part-time at the orphanage near their home.

Ten minutes passed, and a woman sitting on one of the few benches caught her eye and waved. "Why don't you and your daughter come and sit for a while? She looks ready to drop."

"Are you sure?"

The pretty brunette nodded. "We've been sitting all day. I don't mind standing for a while." The woman rose.

Beth guided Lizzie to the bench and dropped onto it then lifted the child onto her lap. Lizzie cuddled against her, relaxed immediately, and closed her eyes. Beth glanced up and smiled at the kind woman. "Thank you."

Beth rested her head against Lizzie's and had almost fallen asleep herself when the door rattled open again and her soaking wet father stepped in and searched for her.

"Over here, Poppa."

He hurried to her side, looking worried. He lifted Lizzie into his arms and gazed around at the remaining people. "I'm sorry to tell you, but the boardinghouse is full. I don't believe there are any more people willing to share their homes either. Unfortunately, this is quite a small town. I've procured use of an empty building for the night, and the mercantile owner has been kind enough to open up should any of you wish to purchase food, blankets, or other supplies. I suggest you follow me unless you prefer to spend the night here."

More grumbling ensued as nearly a dozen passengers left the small building with them. Beth covered her head with her hood, thankful that the rain had slowed, but there was still the mud to deal with. By the time they'd reached their location several blocks from the depot, her legs ached and her skirt and cloak were soaked.

Her father set Lizzie on the boardwalk and pushed open the door to an empty building, which was illuminated only by a pair of lanterns hanging on wall hooks. Her heart plummeted. There'd be no bath tonight—and no bed either. There was nothing but a couple of blankets and a small crate near the stove, but at least the room was warmer than the depot.

Her poppa made a beeline for the back wall. "I've already purchased some things at the store, Beth, and claimed a spot near the stove so you and the girl should be warm."

She was grateful for his efforts, but she wished he'd quit referring to Lizzie as "the girl." She was a sweet child who deserved a good home, but Beth's father had not been happy when she requested that their trip west to settle in the Arizona Territory include a number of stops to take orphans to new families. She knew he was anxious to arrive in their new home, but she still wished he had more patience with little ones.

With Lizzie asleep and wrapped in her blanket, Beth and several other women took turns changing into dry clothing behind a blanket they held up in one of the back corners of the room. She finally settled onto the hard floor and looked around then ate the remaining peaches in a can shared with Poppa. Families and individuals had spread out and claimed their own places for the night. Lightning flashed, drawing her gaze to the big windows at the front of the building. She prayed the rain would end and they could leave tomorrow. Prayed that God would direct her to just the right family for Lizzie.

Closing her eyes, she tried to relax on the hard floor. At least the room wasn't moving as the train had been for the past three days. Her thoughts drifted to Arizona and what life there would be like. She hadn't wanted to leave New York permanently, but Poppa had made up his mind, and she had little choice. He was her only living relative, and she couldn't bear being so far away from him. She wouldn't miss the cold Northeastern winters, but how would she adapt to the hot weather? The rugged lifestyle of a territory? She was used to living in a large home in the city. She yawned and felt herself drifting off.

Beth jerked awake. She'd been dreaming of the train ride—of the constant movement. She sat up, suddenly aware that it wasn't the train but the floor that was vibrating. What in the world!

A man near the door surged to his feet and rushed to the window. People all over the room stood. The man opened the door and stepped out. Beth rose, her heart ricocheting in her chest. What was happening? Were they experiencing an earthquake?

Lizzie and her father slept on, but Beth walked toward the door. The man hurried back inside, and Beth heard a loud explosion.

"A rider just told me the river's flooded. That sound is the bridge washing away. Looks like we're stuck here, folks."

⁂

Cade Maddox pumped the bellows, heating the fire at his forge. "The repairs on your wheel should be done soon, but I don't think you should try gettin' home tonight. You aren't likely to get far with all the mud out there."

Jasper Everly stood just inside the door of Cade's blacksmith shop, staring out at the drizzle. "Maybe so, but there ain't a dry spot left in town, what with all them train folks stayin' over tonight."

"What about your daughter's house?"

Jasper shook his head. "They don't have no room there, not with all of her young'uns."

"You're welcome to stay here. Your wife and daughter can have my bed, and we can sleep in the barn. I've got a big pile of fresh hay on the other side of my—" The ground beneath Cade's feet shook, and his gaze collided with Jasper's. Cade rushed to the door and stared down the street.

"Sounds like a flash flood," Jasper said.

A loud crack rent the air, followed by the splintering of wood. "There goes the bridge."

Jasper's wife, Charlotte, rushed through the grassy area between Cade's shop and the small house next door. "What was that?"

"We think a flood took out the bridge." Jasper scrubbed his hand across his chin.

No thinking about it. Cade knew that sound. It had happened before. "I've got to go see if anyone needs help."

"Go." Mrs. Everly swatted her hand in the air. "I'll stay with Annie."

Already untying his apron, Cade nodded his thanks and took off at a run toward the river. Jasper limped along behind him.

At least the town, which had been built on a hill, was safe. No danger of it flooding. The train passengers Jasper had mentioned weren't getting across the river anytime soon with the bridge washed out. Sure was a good thing they had stopped in Advent and hadn't tried to cross, or the whole kit and caboodle of 'em might have been washed downstream. He jogged past the few small shops, drawing closer to the roaring water.

"Help! Over here."

Cade raced to the river's edge, pausing to catch his breath. As his gaze adjusted to the darkness, he searched the area. Lightning flashed. The bridge was gone, washed downstream. Jasper lumbered up behind Cade, breathing hard. Lightning flashed again, and he spotted a man holding on to a long tree root and struggling to climb up the side of the slick bank. The roaring water threatened to snatch him away any second.

"Jasper, if I lower you down, can you get ahold of the man?"

"Yep. Just don't let go."

"Hurry! I'm slipping," the stranger yelled over the roar of the water.

Cade wrapped his meaty hand around a cottonwood and locked wrists with Jasper. Lightning zigzagged across the dark sky, and Cade's heart dropped. A hundred feet upstream, a downed tree headed in their direction. "Make it fast, Jasper. Trouble's coming."

His friend stretched out his arm, just brushing the stranger's fingers. He tried again, reaching farther. Cade felt as if he were harnessed to two horses, each one pulling him in a different direction. He gritted his teeth and held on, stretching as far as he could. Lighting lit up the sky again. The tree had closed its distance by half and was racing toward them.

Jasper grunted. "Got him."

Cade pulled with all his might, straining against the weight of the two men.

Muscles coiled, he yanked hard, and all three men fell into a pile on the shore as the tree splashed past them. Relief made Cade weak. They'd saved the man's life.

He worked himself out from under Jasper and stood. "Are you two all right?"

"I'm fine." Jasper pushed himself up and swiped his muddy hands on his dirty pants.

The stranger groaned and grabbed his leg. "I—I think it's broke."

"I heard there was a doctor among them train folk." Jasper scratched his beard. "Want me to go see? They's held up in the old hat shop."

Cade nodded. "Go ahead. I'll bring the man."

"My name's Jack Garner," the man said, holding on to his leg.

"What were you doing in the river?" Cade leaned over to examine the man's leg, hoping for another flash of light.

"I was crossin' upstream, headed home from a day of huntin'. Didn't hear the water until it was too late—" Mr. Garner's voice cracked. "Lost my horse—best mount I've ever had—and my mule, which was carryin' the deer I'd downed. My wife's gonna be frantic."

"Sorry." Cade exhaled a loud breath, pained over the man's loss, but for the moment, he had to remain focused on helping the man. "This is gonna hurt."

Mr. Garner nodded. "Go on."

Cade lifted the man into his arms, ignoring his groans while absorbing his weight and pain. He muttered a prayer. Mr. Garner had lost a lot today. He just hoped his leg wasn't too bad off and that he didn't lose his life, as well.

Chapter 2

Beth had just sat back down, hoping to fall asleep quickly, when the door rattled open and a muddy man rushed in. A lady on the right side of the room groaned at the disturbance.

"There a doctor in here?"

"Over here." Her father pushed up from his pallet and stood. He pulled his spectacles from his vest pocket and plunked them on his nose. "I'm a doctor."

"Gotta injured man comin' in who got caught in the flash flood."

Her poppa grabbed his medical bag. "Beth, bring my blanket and come assist."

"Yes, Poppa." She tucked Lizzie's blanket around the girl's neck and rose, her whole body aching. She longed for sleep, but someone was hurt, and tending him was more important than rest.

A tall, thin man who'd been sleeping right below the lantern on the left stood and turned up the flame, casting flickering light across a third of the room. "I'll move so you can have the light to see by."

Beth smiled and nodded, but a commotion at the door drew her gaze. Her heart thudded at the sight of a huge man carrying another man as if he were nothing but a five-pound bag of sugar.

"Bring him over here." Her father looked at her and frowned. "Beth, the blanket."

She jumped into action, chastising herself for gawking. It was just that the man filled the whole doorway. She flipped the blanket across the floor and stepped back.

The large man laid the injured one down as gently as if he'd been carrying a child. As he stood, his gaze locked onto Beth's. Her heart thumped again as she stared into his black eyes. She couldn't look away as he straightened to his full height. Thick, black hair had fallen onto his forehead, and dark stubble framed his chin. The man was all muscle and brawn. He winked and then grinned.

Beth's eyes widened, and she forced her gaze back to the injured man. *Of all the nerve.*

Mr. Brown—at least she thought that was his name—set down a bucket of water. "Thought you might have need of this."

As her father cut away the groaning man's pant leg, she found two clean cloths in his medical bag, wetted them, and handed them to her father. She was well aware of the big man behind her. Why did he affect her so? Did his sheer size intimidate her? Or was it his handsome, dark looks?

It made no sense, because the man was covered in mud and smelled like he'd worked all day in a barn. Yet he had helped a man in need. Or maybe he'd also been caught in the flood.

The stove door creaked open, and Beth glanced over to see the big man feeding wood into it then shutting the door. He rummaged through the pile of wood, collecting several long sticks.

A man on this side of the stove mumbled something about all the ruckus and pulled his blanket over his head.

"I'll need you men to hold the patient down while I set his leg."

"Nooo," the wounded man moaned.

"Has to be done if you want to walk again." Poppa stood and moved around to the man's feet, while the two men who'd brought in the patient held down his shoulders.

She realized that the injured man had lost one of his boots. He was soaked to the bone. Once his leg was set, they would need to move him closer to the stove.

A loud cry arose, followed by a pop, and the deed was done. Poppa sorted through the sticks the brawny man had collected and kept two, placing them on either side of the patient's leg. Beth handed Poppa a roll of bandages, and he began wrapping the leg while the brawny man held the sticks in place.

It touched her heart that he'd had the foresight to know they'd be needed and had found them without being asked. The man was smart as well as caring enough to help another man in need. She looked down and swallowed hard as her gaze collided with his. What was it about this man that drew her? Why. . .she didn't even know his name.

༄

Cade stared into the flame of his forge, the fire reminding him of the beautiful copper-haired woman assisting the doctor. No, not copper exactly. Maybe cinnamon. It had been hard to tell in the dim lighting of the empty store.

Who was she? The doctor's wife? Daughter—sister?

Why couldn't he shake her image from his mind?

"Want out, Pa."

The tiny voice from across his blacksmith shop drew his gaze. He smiled at his daughter, who stood inside the fenced-in play area he'd made to keep her safe. "Pa has to work, sweet thang."

Annie's lower lip stuck out in a charming pout, and she plopped down on her blanket, hugging her rag doll. Cade blew out a sigh. He didn't like keeping his daughter in the small pen, but she liked to wander and got into things. His greatest fear was that she'd get burnt. A blacksmith's shop was no place for a little girl. If only Mrs. Gardner hadn't moved away. If only Nellie hadn't died and left him with a three-year-old to care for alone.

"You still got that young'un in that cage?" Fred Simons grinned as he entered the smithy.

Annie hopped up and reached out her arms to his friend. "Out. Pease."

Fred chuckled. "Ain't that the cutest thang—how she says *please*. Care if I pick her up for a bit?"

Cade shook his head, relieved to have someone give Annie some attention. He pulled the molten horseshoe from the fire, set it on his anvil, and slammed his hammer down, making a familiar clang.

Fred tossed Annie into the air, and she squealed her delight. He settled her in his right arm and leaned against one of the beams that supported the roof. "Did you hear there's an agent with the Children's Aid Society in town?"

The hammer froze in midair. Cade looked up, his heart pounding. How many times since Nellie's death had he considered giving Annie back to the Children's Aid Society? He placed the hammer down and dropped the horseshoe into the bucket of water near his feet. A loud hiss filled the room as steam rose.

"What're you gonna do?" Fred pulled Annie's hand away from his spectacles. "Don't you have somebody to bury—or some teeth to pull?"

His friend chuckled. "Nope. You saved that man last night, and I heard tell he's most likely gonna make it. Good thing there was a doctor in town. Now, don't distract me." He tickled Annie's belly, and she laughed. "How can you even consider doing what you're thinkin'?"

"How do you know what I'm thinking?" Cade crossed his big arms and glared at the nosy dentist/undertaker.

"Because you've only mentioned it a dozen times or so. Don't see how you could give up this darlin' little thang."

"I don't want to see her get hurt. And with Mrs. Gardner gone, I don't have anyone to watch her."

"Maybe I could help. Business is pretty slow these days."

While Fred had good intentions, the man was given to drink at times. Cade couldn't risk Annie being in his care if that happened. "Thanks, but I'd rather find a woman to do that task."

Fred snorted and rubbed his hand over his balding head. "Good luck with that. I'd like to find a woman to marry up with, but there just ain't none 'round here." He set Annie back in her pen then straightened, his eyes gleaming. "Did you see that doctor's pretty daughter? Woo-wee! She's a beaut'."

Cade didn't like Fred admiring the woman, and it irritated Cade that it bothered him. She was nothing to him—and she'd be leaving as soon as the tracks were repaired and the train could be backed out of town. There'd be no going forward for a long while. Not until the bridge was replaced.

He glanced down at Annie. How many times had he contemplated returning her to an Orphan Train agent? Nellie would turn over in her grave if she knew, but she didn't—and she didn't have to eke out a living while caring for an active youngster. It would break his heart to give her up, but he had to consider what was best for Annie. She needed a mother, not a father who worked constantly to forget the hurt of losing his beloved wife.

Fred stretched. "Guess I'll mosey along and see if I can catch me a glimpse of the red-haired gal."

Cade followed him to the open door and watched the man saunter down the street. Fred was probably a good twenty years older than the doctor's daughter, so there was little chance she'd fall for him. He kicked the door frame, frustrated that it mattered to him. Sure, the woman was pretty. And she'd been so calm and capable helping out last night with the wounded man. But she surely had loftier dreams than settling in a tiny town like Advent.

It would be nice to have a doctor though.

A shrill scream behind him nearly made his heart jump clean from his chest. He spun, his eyes aiming for the pen. Annie wasn't there.

Her loud screams filled the smithy. He raced around his workstation. She was lying in the dirt—right beside an ax he was going to repair. Blood covered her lower left arm.

Cade snatched her up and ran to the house. He grabbed a towel off the table and wrapped the wound, all the time murmuring to Annie. "Shh. . .baby, it will be all right."

She threw back her head and screamed as he held the cloth tight against the wound. She tried to pull away and pushed at his arm with her free hand. He was afraid to remove the cloth to look at the wound.

"God, show me what to do."

The doctor!

He bolted out the door and ran down the street. People rushed out the doors of the nearest shops.

"What happened?" Arnold Peavy, owner of the small mercantile, hollered.

"Annie's hurt." In less than a minute, he reached the building he'd taken the wounded man to last night and charged inside. His gaze searched the room until he found the doctor's daughter. "Where's your father?"

She rushed forward, concern etching her face. "He rode out to a farm to check on a man whose wife was sick."

The sight of blood had never bothered him, but seeing his daughter's blood dripping on the floor and hearing her pain-filled wails nearly did him in.

The woman latched onto his arm and tugged him outside. "Sit down before you fall. I'll get some supplies and clean the wound."

Cade cuddled Annie while carefully holding her injured arm. "It's all right, baby. Don't cry."

He wasn't cut out for this. He could feed and clothe the girl, but he wasn't father material. This proved it.

⁀

Beth rushed across the room to the stock of supplies her father had purchased and stared at them. She wasn't a nurse, but she had assisted her father on a number of occasions. What would he do? She rummaged through the supplies and pulled out a roll of bandages, a bottle of carbolic acid, and some salve.

"Who's that crying?" Lizzie stood, holding her dolly under one arm.

"A little girl got hurt. I'm going to help her." Beth smiled, hoping to reassure her ward.

"Is there something I can do to help?" Mrs. Buchanan, one of the train passengers offered.

"I'll need water, preferably boiled if you can locate some."

The woman nodded. "We'll scour the town for it." She pivoted, a woman on a mission. "Harold! Aaron! Let's go find water."

The rush of feet sounded behind Beth. She stood, trying to still her trembling hands. From the looks of all the blood, the girl's arm would need suturing—something she'd never done. *Please, Lord, send Poppa back—fast.*

The big man who'd brought in the injured man last night sat on the bench in front of the shop, hugging his wailing daughter. He looked so distraught. Beth was surprised at her desire to comfort him, but his daughter was her focus. She returned to his side, set her supplies down, and brushed her hand across the girl's head. Lizzie walked around Beth and leaned against the porch railing, watching. Beth wanted to shoo her away but didn't want to scare either child.

"What's her name?" She gazed up at the man, her heart leaping when his dark eyes connected with hers.

"Annie. And I'm Cade Maddox, the town blacksmith."

No wonder his shoulders were half a mile wide. "I'm Beth Ruskin." She smiled at Annie. "Could I take a look at your arm, sweetie?"

Annie shied away, leaning against her father's chest, and shook her head. Lizzie moved closer and held out her doll. "You want to hold my dolly?"

Annie's eyes lit up, and she quieted. After a moment, she pushed up and reached out with her uninjured arm, accepting the doll. Blinking the tears in her eyes, she offered a tiny smile.

"That was kind of you, Lizzie." Beth was more than relieved that her ward's action had helped Annie to stop crying. Mr. Maddox caught her eye and gently peeled back a portion of the towel, revealing the girl's long gash. Her heart jolted. She needed suturing for sure. Beth laid the towel back over the wound. "Keep a tight hold on that. It will help slow the bleeding."

"Will she need. . .sewin' up?" Mr. Maddox swallowed, his eyes filled with concern.

Beth nodded. "Yes." She looked at the wagon driving by and then back at him. "But I've never done that before."

He held her gaze for a long moment. "When will your father return?"

Shaking her head, Beth whispered, "I don't know."

His lips pursed, and determination replaced the concern. "Then you'll have to do it."

She gasped. "I'm not a doctor."

Mr. Maddox took a firm hold on her arm. "You have to do it." He covered the girl's ears and lowered his voice. "I'm not going to let her bleed to death because you're afraid."

Beth winced, angered by the man's impudence.

He blew out a loud sigh. "I'm sorry. I'm just—" He brushed his hand through his thick hair. "Scared—to be honest."

Beth softened. "I understand. I'll have to put her to sleep to suture her arm."

Mr. Maddox nodded. "That's probably for the best."

Beth stood and glanced at the building. Everyone still inside stood watching at the door or out the window. She didn't want an audience—and she needed a cleaner place. "Could we do the procedure at your house? There are too many people here."

His eyes widened, but he nodded. "Sure."

"Let me gather a few more things." She rushed back inside, the people moving apart to let her pass.

Mrs. Parker followed her. "I'd be happy to keep an eye on Lizzie while you tend the injured child."

"Oh, thank you." Beth smiled, more than a little relieved. Maybe the woman would see what a sweet child Lizzie was and want to adopt her. She quickly located a package of suturing needles, thread, and a bottle of nitrous oxide for putting the girl to sleep. She rose, trembling. *I don't want to do this, Lord, but I know I must. Please help me.*

Chapter 3

Cade held Annie against his chest, wincing at her whimpers as they hurried back to his house. He knew she was in pain, and it was his fault. If only he'd watched her better—but she'd been in her pen, and she had never climbed out before. How could he have known she would today?

Still, he was responsible for her, and he should have kept her safe. But he'd failed. Some father he was.

A woman with two sons rushed toward them, the boys holding a pail of water. "We found some."

"Wonderful." Miss Ruskin said, taking two steps to each of his one.

Cade slowed his pace, even though he wanted to get Annie tended to as soon as possible. If they didn't, she might bleed to death—and he couldn't bear that.

The women followed him into his modest home, and he glanced around, wishing he'd cleaned the place up earlier.

"We'll need to boil the needle. My poppa always does that. It's his firm belief it helps prevent infection."

"It will take too long to heat the stove. If you'll take Annie, I'll fire up my forge. The pail should hold up to the heat, and the water will boil quicker."

She nodded as she placed her supplies on a corner of his table. "We'll need whatever lamps you have and a place to perform the procedure."

Cade took the lantern from the kitchen wall and carried it into his room. He tossed the quilt over his mattress and replaced his pillow then hurried back to get one of the parlor lanterns. Annie's whimpers grew with his constant movement. He paused in front of Miss Ruskin. "You'll need to hold her while I tend the fire."

Miss Ruskin nodded and crossed the room to the other woman. "Mrs. Buchanan, would you mind staying? I may need you to assist me."

"Of course." The woman turned to her sons. "You two run along. Your pa may be wondering what happened to all of us."

"Yes, ma'am," the boys said in unison.

Miss Ruskin reached out to the nearest boy, taking hold of his sleeve. "Oh! If you see my father, would you please send him down here right away?"

The boy nodded, his ears turning red. "Yes, ma'am. I'd be happy to." He scurried after his brother.

"Mr. Maddox, I think it will work best for Mrs. Buchanan to hold Annie so I can administer the nitric oxide. Shall we go in your room?" Her cheeks turned a rosy red, and she looked away.

He knew how improper it was for her to be in his bedroom, but it was better than putting Annie on the hard table. Annie would probably pitch a fit when he gave her to the woman, but there was nothing to be done about it.

With Mrs. Buchanan seated on the bed, he passed Annie to her.

The girl squealed. "Papa. Hold you."

Miss Ruskin was prepared and placed a cloth over Annie's mouth and nose. In a few short moments, his daughter went limp. Cade blew out a loud sigh, spun, and hurried to his smithy. He got the fire going and set the pail in the center of the flames, wishing there was more he could do.

"Excuse me, but is my daughter here?"

Cade glanced up, more than a little relieved to see Dr. Ruskin. "Yes, sir. She was just gettin' ready to stitch up my daughter's arm."

The man frowned. "Was she now?"

The doctor's expression and tone made him wonder if he had been wrong to insist that Miss Ruskin treat Annie, but desperate times called for desperate measures. If it came down to it, he would have stitched up Annie's arm himself.

Dr. Ruskin cleared his throat.

"Uh. . .this way, sir."

Miss Ruskin looked up as they squeezed into the small room. "Poppa! I'm so glad you're here." She stood, and Cade nearly passed out at the sight of the cut on Annie's arm. "I've just started cleansing the wound."

"Good. Proceed while I wash my hands."

Cade couldn't miss the relief in Miss Ruskin's pretty features at the presence of her father. He had pushed her to do something she wasn't comfortable with, and she hadn't balked. He admired her willingness to face a scary task for the sake of saving his daughter, even though she'd been uncomfortable with the thought of sewing up Annie's arm.

"Once I finish cleaning Annie's wound, I can take over for you if you'd like to go on, Mrs. Buchanan."

The woman nodded, her face pale. "That would probably be a good thing. I'm feeling a touch queasy."

Miss Ruskin looked over her shoulder at Cade. "Is the needle ready?"

"No, but the water should be boiling by now."

"You might show Poppa where it is. He can prepare the needle and any other instruments he will need."

Cade nodded and fled the room. An hour later, the task was done, and Annie was just starting to rouse. He turned to the doctor, who was rolling down his sleeves. "I can't thank you enough."

"No need to thank me. It's my job."

Miss Ruskin grimaced. "I'm just glad we were here in town when Annie got hurt."

"A blacksmith shop is not a safe place for a child."

The doctor's comment heaped guilt onto Cade's shoulders, making him feel worse than he already did. "I know that, but my wife died, and then the woman who watched Annie while I worked left town recently, and I don't have anyone else."

Dr. Ruskin donned his jacket. "Maybe you should consider remarrying."

"Poppa, please. We shouldn't meddle." Miss Ruskin sent Cade an apologetic glance.

Her father's mouth quirked, but he didn't apologize. He pulled a packet from his medical bag. "If the girl seems to be in pain, mix a teaspoon of this powder into a small cup of water. I'm not sure how long we'll be in town, but I want to check her arm in a day or two. If you see any signs of redness or her pain seems extreme, bring her to me."

Cade nodded. "How much do I owe you?"

"A dollar."

Cade fished a coin from his pocket and paid the man. While Miss Ruskin was kind and friendly, her father was gruff to the point of being rude. The daughter must take after her mother.

Miss Ruskin gathered up the last of the supplies then looked at Annie again. "She's a sweet girl. Take good care of her."

Too late for that.

*

Cade stretched and yawned. His back ached from sitting in the straight chair all night, but he'd been too afraid to lie down for fear of not waking if Annie needed him. There was little need for concern about sleeping since Annie had woken up at least a half dozen times last night. The powder let her sleep for a time, but whenever she moved her arm, she'd cry out. He hadn't gotten a wink of sleep—and he had a full day's work that needed doing.

Next door, someone pounded on the front of the smithy. He glanced at Annie, sleeping for the moment, and hurried outside. He looked at the sun, surprised to see it so high in the sky. He must have dozed a little. "I'm not open yet."

A stranger walked toward him, grinning. "Have a late night at the saloon?"

Cade frowned. "Advent doesn't have a saloon, and I don't drink."

"Oh. Sorry." He glanced back at a man who sat on the bench of the wagon parked in front of the smithy. "We're from the railroad. Got some tools that need to be repaired. We're trying to get the tracks fixed that the heavy rains washed out so we can get the stranded passengers on their way."

The railroad paid well, and Cade could use the money, but what about Annie?

He caught a glimpse of Miss Ruskin sashaying toward him with the little girl in tow. His heart tripped but started back on its normal path again. She smiled and waved. The railroad agent looked in her direction and let out a whistle. Cade wanted to grab the man by the neck and shake him but had second thoughts. Not good to anger a customer.

"Good morning, Mr. Maddox. How did Annie fare the night?"

Lizzie waved at Cade, and he smiled at her and waved back.

The agent yanked his hat off. "We ain't got time for socializin'. You gonna be able to take on our work? The boss said to wait in town until you was finished."

Miss Ruskin cleared her throat. "I'm not doing anything. I can watch Annie for you so you can tend to whatever you need."

He lifted a brow, surprised she'd offered to stay in his home. "What about your father?"

And your reputation? he wanted to ask but didn't.

"He knows I came here to check on Annie. I doubt he'll miss us for a long while. He gets rather caught up in his medical books. Lizzie will be a good distraction for your Annie if she feels like playing at all."

She had a point. With the other girl around, Annie probably wouldn't mind his being gone—and he could get work done a lot faster without having to worry about her. Still, having Miss Ruskin in his home made him as uncomfortable as if he'd bathed in itching powder. But he saw no other option. "If you're certain you don't mind."

She cocked her head in a charming manner. "If I minded, I wouldn't have offered, and since you'll be in your smithy, no one will have reason to talk."

There was little doubt people were already talking about the doctor's pretty daughter. He wondered if any of the lonely males in town had asked her to marry him yet. They would if she stayed around for long. He blew out a sigh and nodded. "All right, then. Thank you."

She smiled, nearly stealing his breath away. It wouldn't do for him to make a fool over her with the railroad men looking on. He turned back to the man. "I'll open the smithy, and you and your friend can unload the tools. Let me take another peek at my daughter and get Miss Ruskin settled."

The man gave him an audacious wink and moseyed away. Cade fisted his hand, not liking what he assumed the stranger was thinking. He glanced at Miss Ruskin. "If you'll wait here a moment, I'll be right back."

She nodded, and he jogged to the smithy doors and unlocked them. What had prompted her to come visit today? Had she known he'd need her? Or had God answered his prayers for help by sending her? Either way, he was grateful and trotted back to her side like a faithful dog.

"It's a lovely day. Perhaps if Annie is feeling up to it later, I might bring her out to sit on a blanket and enjoy the day."

"I don't know. She was mighty fussy last night." He yawned and quickly turned his head.

"I suppose she kept you up?"

"Some, but I'll survive." He entered the house, once again wishing he'd taken time to straighten things up. What must she think? But then he was just a blacksmith—a man used to dirt and grime, although he didn't care for it in his home. The place needed a woman's touch, but that wasn't likely to happen anytime soon.

As he peeked at Annie, he thought about what the doctor said about him needing a wife. Needing and wanting weren't the same things. Reaching down, he lightly brushed Annie's blond hair from her face. The girl needed a mother, but he didn't know if he could bear to love another woman and lose her, and besides, the only woman to spark his interest since Nellie died was Miss Ruskin. But she would be leaving soon.

He kissed Annie and returned to the kitchen where Miss Ruskin waited. "Make yourself at home."

"You have a lovely house. I've always liked the charm of clapboard homes with big front porches. Our house was brick—and so close to our neighbors' that you could hear their conversations if we both had our windows open."

"Where is home?" He knew by the quick clip of her refined dialogue that she'd lived up north.

"New York."

"And may I ask where you're headed? Visiting a relative maybe?"

The smile on her face slipped. "Um. . .no. I'm afraid not. Poppa has it in his head to go to the Arizona Territory and set up shop. He heard they needed doctors out there."

"We need a doctor here. Maybe you could talk him into staying put."

She cocked a brow, as if reading more into his comment than he meant.

"I. . .uh. . .need to get to work." He tucked tail and nearly ran to the safety of his shop.

Chapter 4

Beth settled Lizzie at the kitchen table with a pencil and sketch pad and went to check on Annie. For the moment, the little cherub slept peacefully. How many times had she awakened her father during the night? He certainly looked like he hadn't slept much, with his ruffled black hair and red eyes. It must truly be difficult for him to take care of Annie and run his business.

Several pairs of overalls lay on the arm of a side chair that sat in one corner of the room. Even though Mr. Maddox had obviously worn them to work—more than once, Beth hung them up on one of the pegs on the wall. She crossed to the window, marveling that it was open in mid-December. Though the early mornings had been cool, the sun quickly warmed her to the point she didn't even need her cloak. One thing was for certain: she wouldn't miss New York's chilly temperatures.

On the chest of drawers sat a picture of a pretty woman. Beth walked over and examined it. Annie had her mother's blond hair and fair skin. The girl looked nothing like her father. Had her mother already had the girl when she and Mr. Maddox married? She sighed. It was none of her business. After another peek at Annie, she fled the room to check on Lizzie, but when she walked into the kitchen, the girl was nowhere to be seen.

Beth rushed from room to room, even checking the two empty ones upstairs. Where could she be? She hurried to the window and searched the town, hoping to catch a glimpse of the girl. Had she gone back to the store where they were staying for some reason?

Downstairs, she checked on Annie again then hurried outside onto the porch. "Lizzie? Where are you?"

Loud clanging rang out from the smithy. She hated disturbing Mr. Maddox, but she had to find Lizzie, and he needed to know she was going to search for her. She jogged down the stairs and across the dried yellow grass intermixed with green weeds. She could hardly imagine anything being green in December.

As she neared the smithy, she skidded to a halt. Lizzie stood at the doors, peering in. Beth hoped Mr. Maddox hadn't discovered her yet. In fact, she was sure he would have returned the girl if he had. "Lizzie," she called in a loud whisper.

The girl looked over her shoulder, her eyes growing wide. She took another look in the blacksmith shop then backed away. "I just wondered what he was doing to make all the noise."

"You shouldn't have left without me. I had to leave Annie alone to come find you." She took the girl's hand. "Let's hurry back to the house."

"Why is he making all that noise?"

"He repairs tools and make things out of iron. Sometimes he has to pound on them to get them to form the shape they need to be."

"Can I do it?"

"No, sweetie. It takes a big, strong man like Mr. Maddox to wield those heavy tools. And the fire and shop can be dangerous." Had Annie gotten hurt in there? Mr. Maddox hadn't mentioned how his daughter had cut her arm, even though he'd been quite distressed about it.

"He's awful big."

And tall. And handsome. Beth blinked. Was she actually attracted to the black-smith? She couldn't argue that his black eyes and tanned complexion intrigued her, and he was far manlier than the pale men dressed in their fancy clothing she'd known in New York. None of them had ever intrigued her enough to take a second glance, but she could barely keep her eyes off Cade Maddox. Even his name sounded masculine. "Ugh! Stop thinking about him."

"Who?" Lizzie looked up at her.

Beth shook her head and blew out a loud breath. "Nobody, sweetie. Let's check on Annie."

As they stepped into the room, Annie yawned and opened her eyes. She blinked several times, frantically searched the room, and then puckered up. "Pa. Want Pa."

Beth smiled and sat in the bedside chair she suspected Mr. Maddox had spent the night in. "Your papa is working in his blacksmith shop. Listen, and you can hear him banging his hammer."

Annie cocked her head then nodded.

"Lizzie and I came to take care of you until he comes home." She reached behind her and tugged Lizzie forward.

Annie stared at the girl for a long moment then smiled. She looked to one side and the other and pointed at Lizzie's doll. "Baby."

Beth reached across the bed and retrieved the toy and handed it to Annie. She glanced at Lizzie to see if she was upset that the younger girl hugged her doll, but she didn't seem to be, and Annie hadn't cried for her father again. Beth wasn't quite ready to relax yet. "Lizzie, would you please fetch my basket. I imagine Annie must be hungry."

"Me firsty." Annie used her wounded arm to try to push up and cried out.

"Shh. . . It's all right, sweetie. I know it hurts." Beth cupped Annie's cheek. She needed to get some food and drink down her and then more of the pain meds. The best thing Annie could do was sleep for the next few days. Her hopes of taking her outside were obviously premature.

An hour later, Annie was fed and back asleep. Beth had stared at the mess in the kitchen as long as she could. "Lizzie, why don't we bless Mr. Maddox and do the dishes?"

Lizzie wrinkled her nose. "I'm drawing a picture for Annie right now."

Beth turned away lest the girl see her smiling. She set a fire in the stove and filled the reservoir with water as well as another pot, which she set on a burner. She unwrapped the piece of meat she'd purchased at the mercantile and put it on to boil so they could have stew for lunch.

She scraped as much of the dried grime as she could into the slop bucket then washed the dishes. When she finished, she wiped down the table, chairs, and counters. Standing back, she admired how the kitchen gleamed, from its bright gingham yellow curtains to the oak table and chairs to the fine black stove with the gold crescent symbol on the oven door. The quality of the house and furniture had been a surprise. Mrs. Maddox must have had good taste.

Footsteps sounded on the porch, and Mr. Maddox walked in. He crossed through the parlor, and when he stepped into the kitchen, his eyebrows rose. "You cleaned up. Wow. Thank you."

The warm smile he sent her was all the reward Beth needed. He looked so much handsomer when he smiled and his eyes twinkled.

He sniffed the air. "What's that delicious smell?"

"Just a piece of beef boiling. I'm making stew."

He rubbed the back of his neck. "I didn't mean for you to do all of this."

"I know, but I couldn't just sit here and do nothing while Annie slept. Oh, by the way, I got her to eat a few bites of a muffin I brought, and she drank some water. Then I gave her more of the powder. She's sleeping again."

He nodded. "Good." He shuffled his feet, looking uncomfortable, then spun around. "Gotta get back to work."

Beth walked to the door and watched him rush back to his smithy. Did she make him nervous? Or had she upset him because she'd cleaned his kitchen? Or did smelling the cooking food bring back memories of times he'd shared with his wife?

She wished he would have stayed a bit longer, because she'd like to get to know him better. But then, she was here so he could work. She sighed. There was no sense in allowing herself to be attracted to Cade Maddox. Soon she'd be on a train, leaving Advent behind.

Besides, her father would never approve of her having a relationship with a blacksmith.

⌒⌒⌒

Cade pounded his hammer, finding some relief from his stress in the loud clang. The sight of Miss Ruskin in his clean kitchen, along with the homey aroma of food sent his mind wandering in a direction it shouldn't go. He slammed down the hammer again, focusing on the task of making a new spade to replace the one that had split. The handle was strong and could be reused, and with the spade he made, it would be good as new. He glanced at the railroad man who'd remained behind while the other walked over to the mercantile. "How long before the train will be able to back out of town?"

The man, sitting on Cade's chopping block, shrugged and stretched. "Another day or two if we don't get no more rain."

One day—maybe two—before he had to make his decision.

He stared into the flames, remembering the big open gash on Annie's soft skin. It was his fault she'd bear that scar the rest of her life. His fault that she was frightened and in such horrible pain. He wasn't cut out to be a father. Yes, he loved the girl as much as if she'd been born to him and Nellie, but he wouldn't risk her life for his happiness. She deserved a mother as much as a father, and he wasn't likely to find another woman who would see something in him worth loving like Nellie had. The thought of living out his days alone didn't sit well, but not many women wanted a bear of a blacksmith to cuddle.

He fought the sting in his eyes and raised his hammer again. He didn't normally dwell in self-pity, but he'd lost the woman he dearly loved, and if he followed through with his plan, he'd lose Annie, too.

By noon he'd finished repairs on the train tools and sent the men on their way. He paced to the back of his shop and then to the front again. He wasn't one to put off making a decision, and the sooner he made this one, the better it would be for everyone. He scrubbed his hand across his nape, hating what he knew he had to do. But it would be better for Annie. The girl needed more than a father who worked so much. She needed a mother—and he couldn't give her that. As much as it pained him, he had to let her go.

Cade hurried to the table where he kept track of the jobs that came in and pulled a piece of paper off a shelf. He quickly penned a note: TEMPORARILY CLOSED. Then he shut the doors of the smithy, locked it, and tacked up the note. He strode to the back entrance, placed a large iron top over the orange embers in his forge, and locked the rear entrance.

He glanced at his house as he made a beeline for the barn that sat behind the smithy, trying not to think of the domestic scene inside. Maybe if Miss Ruskin wasn't leaving, he might see if there was a chance he could gain her interest, but her father was going to the Arizona Territory, and no doubt she'd go with him. Too bad. She was the only woman to have caught his eye since Nellie.

Cade groomed Hercules and saddled the big horse then led him around to the front of the house and tied him to the porch railing. After washing up, he stopped in front of the door, steeling himself. "God, help me. You know it's best for Annie to have both a ma and pa. Help me to let her go."

As he opened the door, he squeezed away the burning in his eyes. Other than burying his wife, he'd never done anything so difficult. He needed to do it fast before he changed his mind.

Cade stepped into the kitchen, and Miss Ruskin turned from the stove, carrying a bowl of stew.

She smiled. "Perfect timing. Annie is still awake, I believe. She ate some stew and is ready for another nap. Why don't you go see her before you eat?"

Cade swallowed the lump in his throat. He'd thought to take the coward's way and not see Annie again, but he couldn't.

Lizzie slid out of her chair, rushed around the table, and took hold of two of his fingers. "C'mon, Mr. Max. Let's go see Annie."

He smiled at the girl's mispronunciation of his last name. "All right. You lead the way."

"Lizzie, you need to come and eat. Let Mr. Maddox and Annie have some time alone together."

The girl glanced up at him and frowned. She pushed her glasses up her nose then released his hand. "Aww. . .all right." She climbed back into her chair. As Cade entered the bedroom, he heard Lizzie say, "If they're together, how can they be alone?"

How ironic. Cade gazed down on Annie, feeling more alone than he had in years.

She yawned then opened her eyes and smiled. She lifted her uninjured arm up. "Pa! Hold you."

He picked up the little girl and cuddled her against him, rocking her as he had done the first days she'd come to live with him when she'd been scared and everything had been new to her. She was a year and a half older now. Would the transition to another home be easier? *Please, Lord, make it so.*

Annie grew heavy, and he realized she'd fallen asleep. He kissed her forehead gently and laid her in his bed. He brushed the wispy blond hair from her face and stared down, memorizing it. If he didn't love her so much, he'd never let her go. But it was better this way.

He turned away from the bed, taking a moment to compose himself, then walked back into the kitchen, ready to explain to Miss Ruskin that he was leaving. The delicious aroma of the stew made his stomach growl.

Lizzie pounded on the table. "Mr. Max! Sit by me. Right here."

Cade stared down at the place Miss Ruskin must have set for him. Steam rose from the bowl of vegetables and beef, tantalizing him. He didn't know when he'd eat again, and even though he had no appetite, the food enticed him as much as the little girl's invitation. He drew out the chair, waited until Miss Ruskin set down a bowl of biscuits and was seated, and then he took his seat.

Miss Ruskin caught his eye. "I had expected Poppa to join us, but he must have been called away. Would you mind blessing the food, Mr. Maddox?"

Cade nodded, staring at his bowl of stew. He could be thankful for the food, but the situation was breaking his heart. He mumbled a quick prayer for the food and the hands that prepared it then wolfed down his serving along with three biscuits. His left leg jiggled, shaking the whole table. He forced it to stop, only to find it doing the same thing a minute later. He swiped his sweaty palm on his pant leg.

"Annie's getting better." Lizzie gazed up at him, biting into her biscuit.

"It seems so." He smiled and nodded. In another year, would Annie be talking as well as Lizzie?

He looked at Miss Ruskin. There was one thing he had to be certain of before he left. "Is it true that you work for the Children's Aid Society?"

She nodded. "Yes, it is. I got lonely with Poppa being gone so much and started volunteering there. It was hard to leave last time I was there, knowing I'd never be back."

"That's a nice thing you did—working with orphans. I reckon you don't know that my Nellie and I got Annie from one of those Orphan Train agents."

"You did!" She sat back in her chair. "No wonder she doesn't look like you. I just figured she resembled her mother."

"Nellie had blond hair, and I think that's one reason she was partial to Annie— that and her being so young."

"How old was she?"

"Just shy of two."

"Lizzie is the youngest of the children I brought west."

"I'm four," Lizzie piped up.

"My, you're a big girl." Cade smiled at Lizzie then shifted his gaze back to Miss

Ruskin. "Have you done that before—taken children to families?"

She shook her head. "No, just this once. When the director of the orphanage learned where we were going, she offered to pay my fare if I agreed to take some children to their new homes. Poppa wasn't thrilled with the idea of traveling with ten children, but not having to pay my fare won him over."

Cade had learned what he needed to know—that she really did work for the Orphan Train. She may not be happy about finding a home for Annie, but she would. Miss Ruskin had a good heart, and he felt certain she would find a nice home for Annie.

"Would you like some more stew?" Miss Ruskin stood, and Cade shot to his feet, nearly knocking over his chair. He steadied it and pushed it back in place.

"No thank you. It was very tasty though. I do need to talk to you"—he glanced at Lizzie and then her guardian—"in private, if possible."

"Oh, of course. Lizzie, please finish your meal and listen for Annie while I talk to Mr. Maddox on the porch."

The girl nodded and waved at Cade. She wasn't making his leaving any easier. How was it no one had wanted the little charmer? If he were married, he'd adopt her faster than a hammer could hit an anvil. He returned her wave and smiled then sobered as he walked through the parlor.

Miss Ruskin crossed her arms. "It's gotten cooler out since this morning, don't you think?"

He glanced up at the trees, noticing the way they swayed in the breeze. He'd been so lost in his deliberation that he hadn't noticed. "The wind's out of the north. Usually cools down when that happens."

She stared in the direction of the trees. "Do you think we'll get more rain?"

Cade looked up at the blue sky. Was she worried she wouldn't be able to leave soon? "Doubtful."

"That's good. So, what did you need to talk about?" She gazed up with curious blue eyes.

He hated ruining her day, but he was sure to. He rubbed his neck, trying to find the words to express what he felt. It was important to him that she not think he was a yellow belly snake for giving up his daughter. But there was no easy way to say what he had to. "I. . .uh. . .when you leave, I want you to take Annie with you."

Chapter 5

Beth stared at Mr. Maddox, unable to comprehend what he just said. "What do you mean?"

He turned away and leaned on the porch railing. "As much as I want to, I can't keep Annie. Her recent accident proves she isn't safe with me. If she got hurt again. . ." His voice cracked, and he shook his head.

Full of compassion, Beth walked over and stood beside the big man, noticing the horse tied to the railing. Was Mr. Maddox going somewhere? Surely he hadn't meant what he'd said about her taking Annie. She could see he was hurting, and somehow she had to find a way to show him that his feelings were normal. How many times had she comforted upset parents while her father tended their children?

She reached out and touched his arm, surprised at the hardened muscles even in his forearms. "Surely you realize that few children grow up without getting hurt or sick at some point. Why, my father is a doctor, and I fell once and hit my head, requiring sutures. See?" She lifted the hair off her temple, revealing the small scar she knew was there.

He stared at it then shook his head. "A blacksmith's shop is no place for a little girl. I can't take a chance on her getting burnt if she touched the forge when I'm not looking."

"Surely you could hire a woman in town to watch her. There has to be someone."

"There isn't. Believe me, I've looked." He turned and faced her, anguish etched in his expression. "Please, Miss Ruskin. Take Annie and find her a Christian home with a man and woman who'll love her and care for her as she deserves."

The pleading in his voice brought tears to her eyes. She'd already tried to place Lizzie, who was healthy—other than needing spectacles—but she had failed so far. How would she find someone willing to take in an injured child? Annie's arm would take weeks to heal, and by then Beth and her father would be in Arizona. She had no idea what to expect there. "I'm sorry, but I can't. There's no guarantee I can find a home for her."

He stepped back, blinking his eyes. "I'm not asking, Miss Ruskin. I'm a danger to Annie. She deserves better than me. Find her a new family." He spun on his heel, ran down the stairs, and mounted his horse.

Beth followed him, her heart pounding. "No! Wait!"

"I'm sorry." He stared down at her with sad eyes then reined the horse around and galloped away.

Beth stared after him, dumbfounded. The last thing she'd expected from the big, capable man was that he'd run away from a problem—not that Annie was a problem. She sympathized with his difficult situation and was sure there had to be another answer. Giving Annie away wasn't an option, not as far as she was concerned.

She walked up the steps to the porch then turned and looked in the direction Cade had ridden. All she could see was the dust stirred up from his horse's hooves. "Help him change his mind, Lord. Send him back."

Annie needed him. She needed him. She didn't get a chance to tell him that she had no authority to accept Annie. Her contract was to deliver the ten children in her care, and she'd done that—all except finding a home for Lizzie. Sadly, the couple who'd planned to take her changed their minds when they saw her glasses. Who would have guessed that the man's brother was blind and he wasn't willing to take on a child who might face a similar fate, as unreasonable as it had been?

Beth sighed. Poppa would not be happy about this unforeseen event.

For the next few days, they were stuck in Advent, but surely the railroad personnel would have the tracks cleared before long. She prayed that Cade came to his senses before that day arrived. His abandonment of his daughter and putting her in such a predicament angered her, yet she'd seen how the decision had devastated him. No matter how much it hurt him to give back his daughter, he'd done what he had for her safety, and Beth admired that.

She walked back in the house, her emotions swirling from anger to heartache for both father and child. Annie had gotten used to her and Lizzie, and Beth felt Annie would be all right for a few days without Cade, but she was bound to miss him.

And how did one explain to a three-year-old that her poppa could no longer keep her?

૭૦

Three days later, Cade walked around the house he grew up in, surveying the work he'd done and making a list of what still needed fixing. He had neglected the old house since Nellie's death, as he had worked hard to get over the pain of her loss, to take care of Annie, and to keep his business going in a town too small for an adequate influx of work. He ought to sell the small ranch, but he had wanted to have it to fall back on in case he didn't make enough as a smithy to support him and his daughter.

He blinked and stared at the yellow winter grass in the distance. He had to remember that he no longer had a daughter.

Miss Ruskin had been surprised by his insistence that she find Annie a new set of parents, maybe even a bit angered at the inconvenience, but he had no doubt she would do the right thing. It was her job to find families for orphans.

Loneliness chased him like a coyote trailing a rabbit. He knew he'd miss Annie, but he hadn't expected to feel such a sense of loss—of failure. It pained him to think of Annie calling for him and him not being there to comfort her. Had he made a mistake? Was he merely chickenhearted?

No. He'd done what had to be done—to keep her safe.

Then why was it all so hard? Why didn't God comfort him for the sacrifice he'd made?

Ed Duffy trotted his bay up the road to the house. Cade waved and walked toward the neighbor who rented the ranch land for his cattle.

The man reined to a stop and nodded. "Been a long time since you was out this way, Cade."

"Yep. Been busy."

"You thinkin' on sellin' the place?"

Cade shrugged. "I can't decide. Part of me thinks I should unload it and be done with it, and another part thinks I should keep it in case things in Advent don't work out."

"How's business up there?"

"Pretty good. I stay busy for the most part."

Ed dismounted and ground-tied his horse. "I'm still interested in the ranch if you do decide to part with it. I know it's gotta be hard since you was raised here."

"Yeah." Cade lifted his gaze to the tree on the hill and the rickety fence that surrounded the graves of his parents and his two little sisters who drowned the day when they tried to swim in the pond alone. His heart clenched. His ma never recovered and followed them in death a month later. Then it was just him and his pa for years.

"Where's that little charmer of yours? She takin' a nap?"

Cade felt as if the butt end of a rifle had rammed him in the chest. He hadn't considered that he'd have to explain what he'd done over and over. "She uh. . .got hurt. . .and is stayin' in town with the doctor's daughter."

Ed jerked his head toward Cade. "There's a doctor in Advent now?"

"Just temporarily. Did you hear the bridge got washed out in last week's storm?"

Nodding, Ed swatted at a fly. "Yep. Myrtle's brother came to visit and mentioned it. Heard tell there was a bunch of train passengers that got stranded."

"Yep." Especially one very pretty Orphan Train agent.

"Guess they got the tracks fixed, 'cause I heard the whistle as it went over Boyd's Gulch this morning."

Cade stared at the man. "You heard the train?"

"Saw the smoke, too. It was going away from town, so I imagine them stranded folk are happy to get on the move again."

Cade turned away and closed his eyes. So that was it. Annie was gone. Miss Ruskin was gone. Lizzie. Why did the thought of them leaving hurt so bad?

"Well, guess I'll getta move on. Saw your smoke this morning and wanted to be sure it was you here and not squatters."

"I appreciate that." Cade held out his hand, and Ed shook it.

"You remember if you decide to sell the ranch that I asked about it first."

"I will. I need to make up my mind one way or the other."

Cade watched his longtime neighbor mount and walk his horse down the road, but his thoughts were on Beth Ruskin and her two wards. Did she hate him for what he'd done?

She couldn't abhor him any more than he despised himself. God had given him a precious blessing, and he'd thrown her away.

He climbed the ladder that leaned against the house. Now that the train was gone, he no longer had to hide out here. He'd finish repairs on the roof then ride back to town to begin the rest of his lonely life. Cade climbed onto the roof, laid down his hammer, then reached for a shake he'd made yesterday. His foot hit the hammer, sending it sliding. Cade pivoted, hoping to catch it before it slid off. His knee buckled, and he found himself sailing through the air. The ground rushed up to meet him. He collided hard, and everything went black.

Beth sat on the porch of the boardinghouse with Annie and Lizzie on the swing beside her. She'd taken up this spot partly because the girls loved the porch swing and partly because it gave her a clear view of Main Street. If Cade returned—and she was certain he would since he had a business to run and a home waiting for him—she wanted to be the first one to greet him and to give him a piece of her mind.

She had no doubt that he loved Annie, and she didn't truly believe he was a coward. He was scared. She'd seen the fear in his eyes when he'd whispered the comment about Annie getting burned. He was making a sacrifice that cost him something very precious—and rather than despise him, she admired him, even though she disagreed with his choice.

A pair of horses rushed around the far end of Main Street, pulling a wagon with a saddled horse trotting behind it, stirring up a cloud of dust. The driver looked right and left then hauled back on the reins. "Where's the doctor?" he yelled.

She jumped up, steadied the swing, then rushed to the railing. She waved her hands in the air. "Here! The doctor's here!"

She wasn't certain if the man had heard her, but another man on the sidewalk pointed toward the boardinghouse. Beth picked up Annie and helped Lizzie off the swing. "Come along. We have to let Poppa know he's needed."

Beth rushed inside to the first-floor suite her father had rented after the train passengers left town. He'd been away, delivering a baby at the time, so they hadn't been able to leave. Her father had been so busy with patients that he hadn't fussed about missing the train. She knocked on his bedroom door, hating to disturb him since he'd only been in bed a few hours. "Poppa. Someone's asking for you."

"All right. I'll be out in a moment."

"Lizzie, stay here for a minute. I'll be right back." The girl nodded, and Beth hurried back outside, carrying Annie on her hip. The man in the wagon pulled to a stop, his horses panting and lathered. He must have driven hard and fast for a long ways. Beth noticed another man lying in the back. Her heart lurched at the size of the patient and the dark hair that hung over the bandage surrounding his head. *No! Please, Lord. Not Cade.*

The driver untied the saddled horse and slapped its reins around the hitching post in front of the boardinghouse. He jogged back to the wagon, lowered the gate, and yanked off a blanket that had partially covered the man's face. Beth's heart dropped. It *was* Cade. Trembling, she turned so that Annie couldn't see her father. The girl had just stopped asking for him. What could have happened? Had he been attacked? His head wound was the only injury she could see other than some scratches on his knuckles.

Several men ran across the street and offered to help carry Cade inside. Beth pushed the door open, slid the iron pig-shaped stop in front of it with her foot, then opened the door to the suite. They'd have to put Cade on her father's bed because the room she and the girls shared would be too small for her father to work on a patient. Poppa pulled open his door and strode out.

"They're bringing him in now. It's Mr. Maddox," she whispered. She peered at Annie. "I need to get her out of here before she sees him."

"Go—and take that other child with you."

She took Lizzie's hand. "Come along, sweetie. Let's go see if Mrs. Reinhardt has any treats."

"Cake!" Annie bounced in Beth's arm and smacked her lips.

"Perhaps." Beth smiled at her, glad that each day she was more active and her arm hurt less. Annie didn't care for the sling Poppa had fashioned to keep her arm immobile, but once they'd stuck her doll in it, too, Annie had accepted it.

Beth quickened her steps to get the girls past the front door and into the other side of the boardinghouse, which included the parlor, dining room, and kitchen. Mrs. Reinhardt walked out of the kitchen, drying her hands on a towel.

"Miss Ruskin, what is that commotion? Do we have new guests?"

"Some men are bringing a patient in to Poppa."

Mrs. Reinhardt lifted her hands to her lips. "I did not expect he would attend patients here. I hope the person isn't sick with something contagious."

"No, ma'am. He has a head wound."

Lizzie pulled out a chair at the table and crawled into it.

"Me sit." Annie pointed at the table.

Beth's cheeks heated. "I was wondering if you might be able to watch the girls and perhaps give them a treat while I assist Poppa."

The older woman smiled. "You know I love these two cherubs. I'd be happy to, as long as it doesn't take too much time. I've already started preparations for supper."

"I don't think it should."

"Good. Just let me fix a quick treat." She spun around and, in less than a minute, returned with two plates, each containing a cookie almost as big as the dish.

Beth set Annie in the high chair and pushed it up to the table. "You two be good and obey Mrs. Reinhardt."

"We will," Lizzie said.

Beth rushed back to their quarters. All the men except for the wagon driver were gone.

"Thank you, Mr. Duffy. I'll take good care of Mr. Maddox," her father said.

"I'm obliged. His folks were good neighbors." Mr. Duffy nodded. "I'll see to Cade's horse."

Beth rushed past the two men and into her father's room. She gasped at the sight of Cade, limp and pale.

"Don't just stand there staring, Beth."

She spun into motion, emptying out the instruments her poppa would need. "What happened?"

"Mr. Duffy said he fell off a roof."

Beth blinked, confused. "But where was he when the accident happened? Not at his house."

"He also owns a ranch next to Mr. Duffy's." He cut the bandage off and examined the gash on Cade's head. "This doesn't look too bad. I'm concerned that he hasn't come to though. Mr. Duffy said he fell several hours ago."

Beth clutched her hands to her chest, suddenly realizing she cared for Cade. When had that happened? What if he never woke up? She knew that sometimes occurred with head injuries.

"I need some clean water."

Beth hurried to do the task, thankful to be able to help. She didn't have time to examine her feelings now, but examine them she would. How was it Cade Maddox had slipped into her heart so quickly?

"Please, Lord, let Cade wake up and be all right."

Chapter 6

Beth felt herself falling and jumped. She reached out and grabbed hold of the bedside table to keep from tumbling out of the chair. She blinked the sleepiness from her eyes and focused her gaze on her patient. Had he moved? Or did she just imagine it as she was jerked from her sleep?

She rose and carried the lamp across the room, casting flickers of light all around, to check the time on the mantel clock. Four o'clock. After she returned the lamp to its table, she stretched the kinks out of her back then took a drink from the glass she'd left on the table. Since she was awake, this was a good time to check on the girls. Beth reached for the door handle, and a groan emanated behind her.

Beth rushed back to the bed and set the lamp down. "Cade?"

His head slowly turned toward her. He lifted his arm and covered his eyes. Beth quickly turned down the lamp, leaving only a small flame.

"Where am I?" His voice sounded deeper—huskier—than ever.

"You're in our rooms at the boardinghouse in Advent."

"Who—who are you?"

Beth gasped. "You don't know? I'm Beth, Dr. Ruskin's daughter."

"Water, please."

Beth quickly poured a glass from the pitcher then lifted Cade's head and helped him drink. "Not too much."

After several swigs, he lay back, squinting. "How did I get here?"

"A neighbor, Mr. Duffy, brought you."

Beth pulled her chair close to the bed, hoping—praying—he hadn't forgotten her. "Do you remember what happened?"

"I remember flying through the air."

"Mr. Duffy said you fell off of your ranch house roof."

Cade lifted his hand to his head. Beth stood and tugged it away. "Don't. Poppa had to suture your forehead. Does it hurt? I can give you some more of the pain powder."

"It hurts some, but I don't want any medicine." His eyes suddenly widened, and he started to sit up but grimaced and fell back. "Annie—is she all right?"

"She's fine. She's sleep—" Beth gasped. "You remember Annie?"

Cade slid his gaze toward her. "Of course. You might think I'm a hardhearted curmudgeon for giving her up, but did you really think I could forget her?"

Beth dropped into her chair, smiling. If he remembered Annie, then he couldn't have forgotten about *her*. "No, it's not that. When you asked my name, I thought you had amnesia."

He turned his head toward the wall and mumbled, "I couldn't forget you any more than Annie."

Warmness flooded Beth's heart, but she forced herself not to get her hopes up. Just because he hadn't forgotten her didn't mean he cared for her. "Ease your mind. Annie is doing well, although she has asked for you probably a hundred times."

"You know how to make a man feel guilty."

Beth reached over and laid her hand on his arm. "That wasn't my intention, Cade. I just thought you'd like to know she missed you."

He rolled onto his back again, looking at her. His expression made her ache for him. "Did I do the wrong thing?"

She shrugged. "Only you can answer that."

Cade rubbed his hand across his bristly jaw. "I can't come up with any other option. I don't want to give her up—I love her—but I won't endanger her."

A solution rushed into Beth's mind. A solution that would solve more than one problem. What if—dare she even think it?—she and Cade were to marry? They could keep both girls, and Cade wouldn't have to worry about Annie anymore. And Beth wouldn't have to go to the uncivilized Arizona Territory. The idea stunned her to silence.

Could she marry him?

Would he even want her?

One thing was for certain, before she opened her mouth, she needed to pray.

⁂

Cade sat on the side of the bed while Dr. Ruskin checked his stitches. His head still hurt, but not as much as it had two days ago when he'd awakened with Beth at his side. If her father hadn't been sitting two feet away just then, Cade might have smiled. Her ministrations had been gentle and kind, and he'd enjoyed listening to her as they talked.

He enjoyed everything about her, from her pretty hair and sparkling eyes to her gentle voice and soft touch.

"I think you're going to live."

Cade did smile at the doctor's deadpan declaration. "That's good."

The man sat back in his chair and narrowed his eyes. "I hope you'll be ready soon to take that young'un off my daughter's hands. She's already got that other child she can't find a home for."

He didn't care for the man's tone, but his curiosity was stirred. "She can't find a home for Lizzie?"

Dr. Ruskin shook his head. "I was wrong to let her bring all those noisy children with us. I should have just paid her way, and then we could have endured our trip in silence."

It didn't sound like a journey Beth would have taken delight in. She loved children, and it must pain her greatly not to be able to place Lizzie. Who wouldn't want the charming girl? He thought back to how she'd called him Mr. Max. How had Beth managed to keep the two curious children away from him?

He longed to see Annie—to make sure she was doing as well as Beth had said. But unless he changed his mind and made the decision to keep her, he couldn't do that. It would only upset her more when they parted.

"I want you to stay here until tomorrow. Then you can return home if you feel you're up to it, but no blacksmithing for at least two weeks."

Cade thought of the work he'd already neglected at his shop. "Doc—"

The man held up a hand. "Two weeks. You have a concussion and must exercise caution. If you're still having headaches then, wait until they are gone to go back to work. Swinging those big hammers and listening to them bang the anvil will only make the pain in your head worse."

Cade nodded. The headaches still plagued him, but he hoped they would lessen soon. People counted on him to repair their wagons and tools and to make hinges and other things they needed. With the bridge out, they'd have to ride more than two days to find another smithy.

"You can get up and walk around, but if you start feeling dizzy, sit down or head back in here."

"Yes, sir." Cade longed to see Beth again, but if he went into the parlor of the suite, the girls would see him. "Do you have a book I could read?"

The taciturn man actually chuckled. "Not unless you like medical journals. I'll ask Beth to see if Mrs. Reinhardt has one you can borrow, but let me warn you, focusing on small letters for any length of time might worsen your head pain." Dr. Ruskin rose. "I'll have Beth bring your lunch in soon."

Great. What was he supposed to do all day, cooped up in a tiny room? Listening to the girls muffled chatter and giggles yesterday had just about driven him loco. Spending just a few days with Beth and Lizzie had already helped Annie to talk better. It pained him to think he hadn't spoken to her enough.

Once again wrestling with his decision to give up Annie, he stared at a picture on the wall of Jesus holding a lamb. "Did I make the wrong choice, Lord?"

The door slid open. Evidently the doctor didn't get it closed well. He started to rise when he heard Annie squeal with laughter, and listened, enjoying her delight. Suddenly the door flew back and she ran into the room. She skidded to a halt, blinked several times, and then smiled. "Pa!"

Annie rushed to him, and Cade lifted her up and hugged her, being careful not to hurt her arm.

"You got a owie." She lifted her hand and touched the bandage.

"Yes, I do." He reached for her little hand and kissed her fingers.

"Me got owie." She lifted her injured arm, which rested in a sling, and beamed proudly. She pushed up and kissed his chin then resettled in his lap and gazed up at him. "Why you hiding?"

Because he was a coward? She would never understand his reasoning—that he only wanted to protect her. "Pa got hurt like you did and has been resting here."

Content with his response, she cuddled up against him, increasing his guilt but filling his heart with delicious warmth. He needed her as much as she needed him. There had to be some other answer than relinquishing her.

A sudden thought tramped across his mind. What if he *were* to marry again? Not for love, but for Annie—and to help a woman in need like a widow with a child. Mail-order brides were not uncommon in Texas. Since he couldn't work for the next few weeks, he could care for Annie and search ads until he found just the right woman. He needed to pray about it, but the thought wasn't as appalling as he might have expected it to be. An image of Beth rushed across his mind, but he dismissed it. She had plans, and a refined city woman would never want to settle for a gruff blacksmith. Carl Peterson, a local farmer, had written back East to a woman who later came out and married him. They seemed happy and now had a passel of young'uns. He could do the same. He'd find a way to make it work. He lifted Annie up and snuggled his cheek against her head, relieved now that the decision had been made.

Lizzie ran into the room and halted. Her mouth dropped open, and then she grinned. "Mr. Max!" She jogged up to him and leaned against his knee. "You hurt your head?"

Beth followed, holding a hand to her lips. "Oh dear. The secret's out."

He flashed a wry smile and shrugged. "Yep."

She leaned against the doorjamb, looking relieved. "Maybe it's for the better."

"Maybe so."

Hope flared in Beth's eyes. "Does this mean—"

"It doesn't mean anything. It just happened, and I need time to rethink things."

She nodded. "Do you feel up to joining us for lunch in the dining room? Mrs. Reinhardt just let us know the meal is ready."

He thought about it for a moment. He still felt weak, but if he were going home tomorrow, he had to get up, and he was desperate to get out of this room. "I believe so."

Beth's warm smile was all the encouragement he needed. Cade kissed Annie. "You ready to eat?"

"You comin', too?" Annie gazed up, her expression puckered.

She was worried—afraid to leave him. Afraid he'd disappear again. That was his fault.

"I don't think you should carry her. You might be a bit unstable after being in bed for several days."

Cade nodded and set Annie on the floor. "You walk with Lizzie, sweetie, and I'll follow right behind you."

She looked like she didn't believe him, so Cade stood. The room shifted, and he reached for the table to steady himself. Beth hurried to his side and wrapped her arm around his waist. "Are you all right?"

"Just a bit dizzy. I didn't expect that." He cautiously opened his eyes, glad the room had stopped swirling.

"Do you need to sit?"

Both girls stared up at him with wide blue eyes. They looked enough alike that they could be sisters. He straightened, not wanting to frighten them. "I'm all right."

"Why don't we walk you into our sitting room? Then you can rest a moment before venturing to the dining room."

His head buzzed—but not so much from pain or his unsteadiness as from Beth's closeness. He glanced down, and she looked up, arching a brow. He held her gaze, and his heart pounded. When had he become infatuated with her? And he must be, because that was the only explanation for the way he felt with her at his side.

He saw her swallow and look away. "Do you feel up to walking into the other room?"

Cade wanted to say he'd walk around the world if she'd only stay at his side, but those weren't words a blacksmith uttered. He settled for a nod.

By the time they reached the parlor sofa, Cade was ready for a rest. Sweat beaded his brow, and his headache intensified, but it was bearable.

Annie walked over and touched his knee. "C'mon, Pa. I hungry."

"Just a minute, sweet thang. Pa's resting."

"Girls, come with me, and I'll get you settled at the table. Then I'll come back and help Mr. Maddox."

"I'll help him." Beth's father walked out of the bedroom, pulling on his jacket.

Disappointed, Cade flicked a glance at Beth and thought he saw the same expression on her pretty face. He sucked in a sharp breath. Dare he hope she might have feelings for him?

Chapter 7

B eth stared out the parlor windows. She ought to be happy that Cade was well enough to return home, but she missed him, even though he left only a few hours ago. She'd enjoyed talking with him over the past few days and watching him play with the girls once they'd discovered him in the bedroom. Lizzie had cried for the first time since they left New York when Cade and Annie returned home. Only the revelation that Cade had arranged to take meals with Mrs. Reinhardt and that they would see Lizzie at breakfast had gotten the tears to stop. The two girls got along as famously as if they'd known each other their whole lives. As if they were sisters. The thought brought tears to Beth's eyes, and she searched for a distraction.

A wagon slowly made its way down Main Street, and two men stood outside the mercantile, chatting. Advent was a minuscule town compared to New York City, but there was a quiet charm to it. If she lived here, could she be happy? She'd miss the concerts, lectures, and parties she'd often attended, but not the constant flow and chatter of people. And there weren't many women around.

When she left this town, she would miss Cade and Annie deeply—she already missed them. Both had sneaked in and wound around her heart like a vigorous vine, and she didn't want to sever her link to them. She was delighted that Cade had changed his mind about keeping Annie, but his problem of who would watch her when he returned to work remained unsolved. Too bad the boardinghouse kept Mrs. Reinhardt so busy. She'd be a wonderful caretaker, and Annie loved the older woman and her constant supply of treats.

"I see you finally got that child to sleep."

Beth spun around, startled by her poppa's voice. "I thought you'd retired." She crossed her arms. "Why do you insist on referring to Lizzie as 'that child'? She has feelings, you know, and can sense you don't like her. It's sad, Poppa."

He hung his head for a moment and looked up. "I distance myself from children because losing one is so hard."

Beth deflated. "I'm sorry, but hearing you say that does help me to understand."

He blew out a breath. "I also got a bit fed up with those hooligan boys you brought with us."

"That quartet was a handful." She thought about the four boys—two sets of brothers—who'd constantly pestered the six girls on the train. She was thankful she found two couples, each willing to take in a pair.

"What's going to happen if you don't find a home for"—he cleared his throat—"Lizzie."

Beth grinned at his use of the girl's name then sobered. "I don't know. I keep praying and asking around, but God hasn't provided the right family yet."

"Well, I'm certain He will."

The picture of the family she imagined for Lizzie was that of her and Cade as parents and Annie for a sister. She swallowed the lump in her throat and turned her thoughts away. "Christmas will be here before long, and I don't have any idea of a present for you. Is there anything you need, Poppa?"

He dropped down into a side chair. "I need to restock some of the medicines I've used while here and bandages. This town has a lot of sick and wounded people."

"I don't think it's just the town. I heard people for several counties over have been coming to Advent because they heard a doctor was here." Beth glanced at her father, who'd picked up a newspaper that Mrs. Reinhardt had received in the mail. Her heart increased its speed. "Maybe we should settle here and not go all the way to Arizona."

"We should do as we planned."

"But why? What's in Arizona?"

He sighed and lowered the paper. "For one, I paid Everett Jones to find a house for us to rent with rooms below for my office. I thought you wanted to go there."

Beth shrugged. "I didn't mind so much. It rather sounded like an adventure at first, but things have changed—and you're so needed here."

"Once I've doctored everyone, business will slow."

"But that's true of anyplace."

He blew out another breath and collapsed the paper into his lap. "What's this all about, Elizabeth?"

Beth swallowed. He never used her full name unless he was upset or angry. She walked over and sat on the chair opposite him. How did she explain how she felt when she didn't understand it herself? "Well, Poppa, you know how you've wanted me to marry now for several years?"

He nodded.

Heat suddenly warmed her cheeks. Was she actually going to tell him about her strong attraction to Cade? "Well, I think I have finally found the man for me."

Poppa's eyes widened. "When did that happen? Why didn't you tell me? If I'd known you'd met someone, I'd never have insisted you leave New York."

"I didn't meet him there."

Her father frowned. "Where, then?"

She stared at her lap, knowing he wasn't going to like her response. He'd always talked about her marrying a well-educated man. A college professor or businessman who could support her well. "I met him here."

He sat up. "In Advent?"

"Yes." From his expression, Beth knew his mind was racing.

He sobered then narrowed his eyes. "Surely you don't mean that blacksmith."

Beth nodded. "Yes, Poppa. It's Cade. I've developed feelings for him—and for Annie."

He jumped from his seat like a man years younger. "That's preposterous! He's not at all the kind of man you need. I warned you about becoming attached to your patients."

"It's not that." Beth stood so he wouldn't tower over her. "I was already attracted to Cade *before* he got injured." From the first time she met him when he strode into their temporary housing carrying the man who'd gotten injured when the bridge washed out, she'd had trouble keeping her eyes off the handsome, brawny man. Then she saw how much he loved Annie and how gentle he was with Lizzie, and she started caring for him on a deeper level. A man that strong and caring would deeply love and protect his family. He loved his daughter so much he was willing to let her go. That was a powerful love—the kind she longed for.

Her father took off his spectacles and polished them with his shirttail. "I think it's time for us to leave. Tomorrow I'll look into when the train will depart again." He returned his spectacles to his face. "I'm going to bed. Good night, Beth."

Stunned, she watched him make a beeline for his bedroom door. "What about Cade?"

He paused in the entrance and turned. "That man isn't good enough for you."

∽

The next morning, Cade glanced down the length of Mrs. Reinhardt's table at Beth. Gone were the happy smiles and sparkling eyes. She kept her head tucked and had barely acknowledged him when he came in. He'd been so anxious to see her again and to talk with her, but she practically ignored him. What had happened in the hours since he and Annie had left the boardinghouse?

Lizzie had parked next to Annie and had barely stopped jabbering long enough to take a bite. Dr. Ruskin, sitting at the far end of the big table, seemed so focused on his food that Cade wondered if he had a patient waiting. Beth glanced up and their gazes met. His pulse sped up. Her lips turned up in a sad smile.

What? he mouthed.

She shook her head and glanced at her father then stared at her plate as if she spied something profoundly interesting.

Cade sat back. What did that mean?

When the meal was over, Dr. Ruskin rose, mumbled something to Beth, then strode past Cade without looking at him. The man had never been friendly, but neither had he been rude. Baffled, Cade turned around from watching the man don his hat and leave to find Beth stooping down next to Annie's chair and tickling the girl's belly. Annie giggled and rubbed her stomach. Beth placed a kiss on his daughter's blond hair then lifted her eyes to him. His heart bucked. He didn't know how it had happened, but he'd come to care for her.

She moved closer. "I need to talk to you. Mrs. Reinhardt agreed to let the girls help her clear the table to give us a few moments alone. Let's go into the parlor."

Cade nodded his thanks to Mrs. Reinhardt—both for the fine breakfast and the time with Beth—then followed Beth from the room.

Instead of sitting on the sofa, she stopped in front of the wide window that looked onto Main Street and stared out with her arms crossed.

He waited a minute then stepped closer. "Tell me what's wrong."

She slowly turned and looked up with tears in her eyes. "Poppa is on his way to exchange our tickets so we can continue on our journey."

Cade felt as if icy cold water had rushed off a roof and slid down his back. Beth was leaving? "When did he decide that?"

"Last night. Right after I asked him if we could stay here."

Cade jerked his head up to look at her. Why would she want to stay in Advent. . .unless. . .

"Aren't you going to say anything?" Beth rubbed her hands up and down her upper arms as if she were cold.

He cared for Beth, but did he love her? "I'm sorry."

"That's it? You're sorry? But I thought—never mind." She turned toward the window again.

"Do you have to go just because your father does? I mean, you're a grown woman. You should be able to make your own decisions."

She slid a glance his way but didn't turn. "That's easy for you to say. You're a man with a way to support yourself."

"Advent is small, but there must be something you could do to make a living."

She swung toward him with hurt in her eyes. "I was hoping for something different. I'd better go get Lizzie. Mrs. Reinhardt is probably tiring of her and Annie's help." She spun and walked toward the door but paused in the entry. "I just wanted you to know that we're leaving."

Then she was gone.

Cade stared at the empty doorway. She was upset with him, but he didn't know why. What had she wanted him to say? He'd suggested she stay. Had she wanted more?

He remembered her in his house with the aroma of beef filling each room, Lizzie at the table. He wanted to encounter that homey scene again, but he barely knew Beth. And still, she wouldn't leave his mind day or night. The thought of her leaving town and him never seeing her again pained him, but did he love her?

Until he was positive of the answer to that, he couldn't say the words she wanted to hear.

⁂

Heart breaking, Beth walked to the kitchen to get Lizzie. She found Mrs. Reinhardt seated in a chair with the girls on the floor, a large bowl of dried cranberries between them. Lizzie handed one up to the woman, who took it, stuck a needle in it, and pulled it down a long piece of thread.

Mrs. Reinhardt looked up and smiled. "The girls are so kind as to help me string some cranberries for the tree Mr. Maddox is getting for me. I just love Christmas. I hope your family will still be here to help me celebrate. Christmas is more fun with little ones in the house."

"My turn." Annie waved a cranberry in the air.

Beth didn't want to be the one to disappoint their kind landlady by telling her they were leaving soon, so she would allow Poppa to break the news. With Christmas less than a week away, Beth assumed they'd be traveling that day. Still, she could buy several small presents to make the day special. "Lizzie, we need to go to the mercantile."

"Aww. . . Can't I stay and help?"

Beth shook her head as heavy footsteps approached from behind. She tensed. Why couldn't Cade read the affection in her gaze? She knew he had feelings for her because she'd caught his longing stares several times while he'd been recovering. But what she didn't know was if his feelings ran as deep as hers. She reached out her hand to Lizzie, and the girl took it. "Thank you for watching the girls while we talked."

Mrs. Reinhardt looked from her to Cade, her curiosity obvious.

"Yes, I'm obliged to you, ma'am. Annie, we need to go."

The little girl stuck out her lower lip. "Me help."

Cade squatted down. "You've been a good helper and that makes me proud, but now it's time to go."

"You can come back and help me another time."

"Can I?" Lizzie bounced on her toes.

"Of course. In fact, why don't you two help me decorate my tree once Mr. Maddox finds a good one?"

"Yay!" Both girls clapped and bounced on their toes.

Cade lifted Annie up and tipped his hat then turned and strode back through the dining room, rattling the cups and saucers on the sideboard, and marched out the front door. Beth sighed.

Mrs. Reinhart looked over the top of her spectacles. "I'm guessing things didn't go as planned, huh?"

"Unfortunately, no." Beth laid her hand on Lizzie's shoulder, and the girl leaned against her as if sensing her dejection.

"Men can be denser than mules sometimes."

In spite of her melancholy, Beth couldn't help smiling.

"You have to state things plainly to a man. Don't make him guess." Mrs. Reinhardt pointed her needle at Beth and jabbed it in the air, the string of cranberries bouncing. "If you care for that man, tell him."

Beth gasped, and Lizzie gazed up at her. "I couldn't do that. A woman is not supposed to express her feelings until the man does."

"Pish-posh. Most men would never get married if they had to do the asking."

As Beth guided Lizzie across the street to the mercantile, she considered what Mrs. Reinhart had said. Dare she tell Cade that she had feelings for him? What if he didn't reciprocate?

Chapter 8

Beth walked into the store, holding Lizzie's hand. The little girl looked up and gasped. Since the last time they were here, the store owners had run some pine branches along the top of the cabinets behind the counter. Red ribbon had been laced through the boughs and tied in several bows with long streamers hanging down. Beautiful glass ornaments hung in between the bows on the boughs.

"So pretty." Lizzie gazed up with her mouth open.

"Yes. They're Christmas decorations. Do you remember the Christmas tree at the orphanage last year?"

"Oh yes! It was beaut'ful." Lizzie's smile dimmed. "Will I get a present this year?"

Beth stooped down and took hold of the girl's arms. "Of course you will."

"I have a small stock of those glass balls if you're interested. They came all the way from Germany." The female clerk waved her hand toward a glass case at the far end of the counter. "I'm Mrs. Peavey. My husband and I own this store."

"Nice to meet you. I'm Beth Ruskin, and this is Lizzie."

"Oh, you're the doctor's daughter."

She nodded. "I'm looking for a Christmas gift for my father." Beth looked around the store but then spun back to face Mrs. Peavey. "On second thought, I would like to look at those ornaments."

They followed the clerk to the counter, and Lizzie gasped at the lovely decorations.

"I was thinking one of those might make a nice gift for Mrs. Reinhardt. She's been so good about watching you and Annie. What do you think, Lizzie?"

She bounced up and down. "Can I pick it out?"

"Which one do you think she'd like?"

The girl perused the ornaments then pointed at a bright purple one with silver trim. "What about that one?"

Beth smiled. "I think it would be perfect. Now let's find something for Poppa." And for Cade—something that would reveal her heart to him. After perusing the aisles, she settled for a lightweight suit for her father. With the warmer temperatures down South, he was certain to roast in the wool suits he'd brought with him. For Cade, she bought a shiny gold pocket watch, although she didn't tell the clerk whom it was for.

"My Arnold can engrave that if you'd like to leave it for a few days."

"I need to find out when we're leaving town first."

"If you're going by train," Mrs. Peavy said, "I can assure you that it won't be until the day after Christmas."

Excitement filled Beth to think she might be stuck in town another week. "You're certain?"

The woman nodded. "The train only comes through Advent once a week on Friday, and since this is Saturday, it won't return until next week—the day after Christmas."

"In that case, I *would* like it engraved." Beth scribbled down the short message and then penned another one to Mrs. Peavey, explaining she'd like to purchase two blond-haired dolls for Lizzie and Annie, and some blue and red hair ribbons. She paid for her items and walked out of the store, feeling better than she had in a long while.

"Beth!"

She pivoted at the sound of her father's voice.

He stalked toward her, frowning. "There won't be another train until next Friday."

Beth tried hard to hold back her smile. "That's not necessarily a bad thing. Now we can celebrate Christmas with Mrs. Reinhardt."

Poppa's expression softened. "I do like that woman's cooking."

Quirking a brow, she stared at her poppa. Was he sweet on Mrs. Reinhardt? Had that been one of the reasons he was so eager to leave town? Was he afraid he'd grow attached to her if they stayed?

"I imagine she will cook up a fine Christmas meal."

"Yes, that's true. I suppose it's not so bad to stay here another week."

Beth turned back toward the boardinghouse, this time letting her smile break free. It could be a wonderful week, if only Cade loved her as she did him.

⁂

Cade tied the sash on the pretty dress he'd bought Annie to wear for the Christmas dinner at Mrs. Reinhardt's. Then he brushed her fine hair, leaving it hanging free instead of confined in its normal braid. He'd even opted to let her go without her sling today since her arm didn't seem to be bothering her.

"We go now?" Annie spun around, blue eyes twinkling. After helping decorate the tree yesterday, she'd asked him over and over, last night and all morning, when their party was.

He smiled and nodded. "Yes, sweet thang, it's time to go."

She squealed her delight and raced for the door. Cade glanced in the mirror as he passed it. The last time he wore his suit coat during the week had been at Nellie's funeral. He missed his wife, and he suspected he always would to some extent, but he was finally ready to move on. As he'd recovered this week, he'd spent more time praying than he had in the past year, and he felt peaceful in the choice he'd made. He just hoped Beth felt the same.

He slung the bag of presents over one arm then opened the door and allowed Annie to scurry out. At Mrs. Reinhardt's, he paused on the porch while Annie knocked softly. He'd wrestled all week with whether he was doing the right thing or not, but in the end, he knew he couldn't let Beth go without her knowing how he felt. He added his firm knock to his daughter's.

Beth pulled open the door and greeted him with a shy smile. "Annie, are you excited?"

"Yes! Go see Lizzie." And she was off in search of her friend.

Cade chuckled. "She's been driving me loco, asking all morning if it was time to go yet."

"Lizzie has done the same. Please, come in."

His stomach rumbled at the wonderful aromas wafting from the kitchen. "I'm glad we're eating first thing. It's not nice to torture people on Christmas Day."

Beth's eyes glistened as she closed the door. "You won't have long to wait—we're about ready to put the meal on the table. But I do need to get back to the kitchen and help."

He watched her go, disappointed that she couldn't stay and talk, but there'd be time for that after dinner. He moseyed into the parlor where he found Dr. Ruskin sitting near the front window. Annie and Lizzie had plopped down in front of the tree that he'd cut yesterday morning and that they had decorated.

Dr. Ruskin stared out the window, ignoring Cade.

Cade sat near the girls so he could grab them if one got it in her mind to touch the pretty decorations. He hadn't had a Christmas tree since Nellie died, but he was glad they had played a part in preparing this one.

Dr. Ruskin cleared his throat and stared at Cade. Cade couldn't read the man's expression, though he thought the man seemed upset. "I suppose you're the reason my Beth wants to become a Texan."

Cade straightened, not sure he heard right. Was the man actually considering staying? That was great news, but he wasn't sure how to respond to Beth's father. "Uh. . .I don't know, sir, but I would like to think I am the reason she wants to stay."

"Why do you say that?"

The old man was direct, if anything. Cade tried to sit still and not squirm. "Because I have feelings for her, sir."

"What kind of feelings?"

Heat surrounded Cade's face. He glanced at the girls, who chattered happily, unaware of the tension in the room. "I'd prefer to tell her first, if you don't mind."

The doctor lifted his chin. "Where I come from, a man asks a girl's father for permission to marry before he does her."

Cade's eyes widened. "Marry?"

Dr. Ruskin narrowed his gaze. "Isn't that what this is about?"

Cade jiggled his leg. "Uh. . .yes, but it might be nice to court the lady first."

"In order for you to court the lady in question, I must make the decision to stay here and not continue to Arizona as I'd planned. I'm not sure I want to do that if you're merely toying with my daughter."

Cade surged to his feet, drawing Annie's gaze. "I resent that sir. I would never toy with Beth's affections."

The doctor blew out a loud sigh. "All right. Sit down and relax."

He eased back on the sofa, afraid he'd break it if he plopped down like he wanted. "I care for your daughter, sir, but I'm not sure she feels the same."

"She does."

Cade's head whipped up. "You're sure?"

"Do you mind if I speak for myself, Poppa?"

Both men lurched to their feet, the doctor looking dully chastised. Confused, Cade looked from Beth to her father.

"Aw. . .can't an old man have a little fun?"

"Not like that. Would you please take the girls and see to it they wash their hands, Poppa?"

"If I have to."

"Consider it punishment." Beth's lips twitched, and she smiled. "Girls, it's time to eat. Please go with Poppa and get cleaned up."

The girls hopped up and hurried to Beth's father, each taking one of his hands. As the older man left the room, he glanced back and winked at Cade, leaving him more confused than ever. When he looked down at Beth's pretty face, her cheeks were a bright pink. Hope surged in him. "You had something you wanted to say?"

Her eyes widened. Then she walked over to the tree and picked up a small gift. "Open this."

"Now?"

She nodded. "It says everything."

Cade took the pretty wrapped gift, untied the ribbon, and let the paper fall away. Inside was a box. He removed the lid and discovered a pocket watch. The case was engraved with the head of a spirited horse with a flowing mane. "Beth, this is too much."

"No, it isn't. Please, look inside."

He lifted the shiny gold watch from the box and admired it. He'd never owned a pocket watch before. Cade popped it open, revealing the fancy script inside. *All my love, Beth.*

His gaze jerked to Beth's, and the pink on her cheeks turned to a dark rose. "Beth, it's wonderful." He ducked his head, wishing he were more eloquent. "I'm not good with fancy words or those poems women like to hear."

She stepped forward. "All I need to know is if you feel something for me. Tell me I haven't imagined it."

"You haven't. It just took me awhile to pray about it and realize God's will for the last half of my life."

"And have you decided what you want?"

A smile tugged at his lips. He put the watch in his vest pocket and reached out, gently holding Beth's shoulders. "All I want is you—for you and me and Annie and Lizzie to become a family."

"You want me? And Lizzie, too?"

He nodded.

Beth's lashes fluttered as she fought the tears making her eyes glisten. "Oh, Cade. That's what I want so much."

His gaze roved over the face of the woman he loved, and then he bent and kissed her, expressing the affection he had trouble voicing. Beth responded, warming his heart and stirring his senses. Reluctantly, he stepped back, grinning. "Guess I'm going to have to ask your pa's permission to marry you."

Beth shyly ducked her head but gazed up at him. "I think that's a wonderful idea, Mr. Maddox."

"Oh, I forgot something." Cade reached into his coat pocket and retrieved the gift he'd made for her. Then he stared at her. It was nothing compared to what she'd given him.

"I see that look." Beth lifted her chin.

"What look?"

"The one that says you're unsure of something. What do you have?"

He opened his hand, and Beth gasped. "Oh, Cade, it's beautiful! Did you make this?"

He nodded again. "It's a rose—made of iron."

She smacked him on the arm. "I can tell what it is, you goose. It's exquisite. However did you make it?"

"I'll show you one day."

As she caressed the petals he'd so carefully fashioned, he stared down at the woman he loved. And to think he almost lost her because of his stubbornness.

"Did you know that my middle name is Rose?"

Cade sucked in a breath. "No, I didn't."

She smiled. "It is. Elizabeth Rose Ruskin."

"Not for long, if I have my way."

Beth grinned, the tint returning to her cheeks.

"You look charming when you blush." Determined to make her blush again, he bent and stole a delicious kiss—and then another.

Beth soon stepped back, somewhat breathless. "The food will be cold if we keep this up."

"I'll chance it." Cade flashed a teasing grin and held his arm out to her. As they stepped into the dining room, he leaned down and whispered, "Merry Christmas, my love."

Snow Song

by Olivia Newport

Chapter 1

1871

The violin's exquisite vibration captured Belinda's breath. She raised her eyes to watch the bow dance across the strings and could hardly keep from singing along to "Joy to the World."

"I didn't know there would be music." Belinda's smile broadened. "It's a perfect night!"

"It's lovely." Edith Michaels nodded approval at her daughter's glee. "And we have the best table in the restaurant. It will be a memorable occasion, to be sure."

"One only has a single opportunity to make an engagement official." Belinda grasped her mother's hand beside her and her father's arm on the other side. The sparkling white tablecloths, the glittering candles, the thrilling music—Belinda could not have imagined a more flawless engagement dinner. "Thank you both for giving this wonderful night to Hayden and me. We shall always remember it."

William Michaels cleared his throat. "Where is your Mr. Fairbanks? Did we misunderstand the time?"

"I'm sure he's coming." Belinda patted her father's arm. Why did Hayden's tardiness always seem to strike when an evening included her parents? Belinda had become accustomed to building in time for Hayden to be fashionably late, but he knew she hated it when he kept her parents waiting.

The waiter circled again and discreetly topped off their water goblets.

"Perhaps we should order hors d'oeuvres," Edith said. "I understand they have a mushroom pâté that is quite good."

William nodded. "No doubt they would bring some bread as well."

"We may even start on the soup," Edith said.

"Oh no!" Belinda sucked in alarm. "Let's not go so far as soup. Hayden will be here soon enough, and we'll all order together."

"We've been here thirty minutes already." Edith straightened a fork that was not askew.

"But we were early," Belinda countered.

"Nevertheless, I do feel we ought to order something. And I had no lunch today."

"The pâté, then." Belinda laid her hands in her lap and laced her fingers together to still them.

"He will get the restaurant right, won't he?" her father asked. "He knows to come to Larimer Street?"

"Yes, Papa. He knows." Ever since Belinda and Hayden knew they wanted to be engaged someday, they had planned to celebrate at this establishment.

The string quartet transitioned to the more subdued "Lo, How a Rose E'er Blooming," and the Michaels family awaited the beginning of their meal. Belinda

247

glanced up at every man with Hayden's build who moved through the spaces between the tables, but none of them was him.

⁓

Hayden Fairbanks was more than a little dissatisfied with the look of his tie, but he had no time to fret further. As it was, Belinda was likely to greet him with a cold glare. Her father's raised eyebrow would make clear his displeasure at Hayden's late arrival. The expense of this evening was an indulgence for all of them. While William Michaels was financially secure by Denver standards, he wasn't a wealthy railroad investor. He ran his simple shop catering to travelers and made prudent decisions about the use of his profits. Hayden suspected William didn't quite approve of Belinda's choice to marry a journalist whose deadlines sometimes made it challenging to keep to social time frames, but he had given his agreement, if not his blessing, when Hayden asked him for his twenty-three-year-old daughter's hand.

He sighed and brushed both sides of his mustache, determined that his lateness should not cast a pall on the evening meant to be a glistening memory for Belinda. Getting engaged just before Christmas was her dream. She also had her heart set on a winter wedding, so they would not wait more than a few weeks. Hayden picked a spot of lint off his best suit, which now struck him as insufficient for the evening's occasion. He would order a new one before the wedding even if he had to scrub the tailor's floor on his knees to pay for it.

The knock came just as Hayden was ready to buff the tops of his shoes with several quick strokes. He laid the shoe brush on the top of his chest of drawers and took the few short steps across his small apartment above a butcher shop to open the door.

"Mr. Hayden Fairbanks?" A boy not more than twelve years old stood in the hall with his hat in his hand.

"Yes, that's me," Hayden said.

"I've got a note for you. The man said I should be certain it got to you directly on account of how urgent it is."

"Urgent?"

"That's what he said." The boy held out an envelope.

Hayden took the note and then fished in his pocket for a coin to give the boy. He listened to the fading footsteps of the messenger's departure as he tore the end off the envelope and shook the message out.

> *Hayden, my good friend, I must ask a tremendous favor of you. Please go to my abode as soon as you receive this message. My daughter will be there waiting for you. I'm sorry I didn't have time to properly pack her things, but they are few. She is capable for a child of six, but I don't want to leave her alone a moment longer than necessary. In the sugar jar on the counter you will find enough bills for the journey and my sister's address. I will meet you there, and I will explain everything.*
>
> *Gerald*

⁓

Belinda nudged away the cherry pie without even picking up the dessert fork, and she shook her head when the waiter inquired whether she wanted coffee.

Her parents had the grace not to say much of anything, at least nothing that had to do with Hayden. Edith prattled intermittently about the party neighbors had invited them to for the following evening—a party where Belinda had fully expected to accept congratulations on her engagement—but her chatter focused on what she already knew the buffet table would hold and who was planning to attend. The lump in Belinda's throat seemed to thicken by the minute. She wished her mother would just stop talking.

Eventually, Edith did fall silent, alternating between sipping her coffee and dabbing her lips with her napkin.

William laid his fork down on his empty pie plate. "I'll settle the bill, then, and we should be going."

"You go," Belinda said. "I think I would like to wait a little longer."

"My dear daughter," her mother said, "we waited as long as we could to begin. Now we've had an entire dinner. Do you really believe he will turn up this late?"

"I'm not ready to go home," Belinda said evenly. "Perhaps I'll have some coffee after all."

"I'll be happy to make some for you at home. Anything you like. You hardly ate a bite."

The cheery Christmas music grated on Belinda's nerves now. She blocked it out. "Please. I won't stay long, I promise."

"But who will see you home?"

Hayden, of course. "I'll look for a cab," she said.

"They'll be hard to come by once the theater lets out."

"I won't stay that long. Or I'll find an omnibus." *Or Hayden will be here.*

Belinda met her mother's eyes. Even as a child she had matched Edith's stubborn streak, and tonight she meant to win.

"We'll go," her father said, "but if you are not home in one hour, I shall come fetch you myself."

"Thank you."

While the table was being cleared, Belinda indicated she wanted to keep her pie. She needed something to pick at. "May I have coffee, please?" she said.

✍

Surely Gerald hadn't left his motherless six-year-old child alone in their small house.

Hayden hustled through the streets uncertain he would recognize Gerald's home once he found the right lane. He had only been there one time, and that was more than two years ago when Gerald's wife fell ill and died far more quickly than anyone had anticipated. No one expected her to die at all, but she did. Hayden hadn't seen the girl on that visit. He had never seen her. Was she dark like Gerald or fair like his wife? When her mother died, the child was whisked away and sheltered from the funeral. After everything was over, Gerald soldiered on with the help of a woman who kept the girl while Gerald worked, but he took new employment at a monthly publication rather than a daily newspaper, so his hours would be more predictable. Hayden had not seen Gerald in the last two years either. If she was six, the child was old enough to begin her education, an endeavor Hayden doubted Gerald was prepared to undertake unless he had become more attentive to details than Hayden recalled.

Gerald must have lost his mind. If he did leave the girl, he was even more negligent than Hayden imagined. If he sent the note to Hayden as some kind of hoax—Hayden hated to think his old friend was capable of that.

Hayden found the street, or he thought he had. He stopped at the end of the lane to take his bearings. Gas lamps glowed in narrow windows, and chimneys released smoke in shadowy plumes against the night sky. The temperature had dropped, and after receiving Gerald's note, Hayden had dashed out of his building without thinking to snatch his overcoat off the hook. He shivered now with the cold and the uncertainty of what he would find—but also with the realization that he had dreadfully disappointed the one person he loved more than any other.

But a child.

How could he have set aside Gerald's note until a more convenient time?

The slush covered Hayden's shoes and wicked up through the fabric of his trousers. He pushed his feet forward, aiming for the tiny house at the end of the lane with a feeble light flickering from deep inside it. If he was to believe the note, a child sat vigil with that candle waiting for someone to come, someone to care.

This was not just another story to write before the deadline. He would explain to Belinda as soon as he could, and she would understand.

༼ঙ

Belinda took a handkerchief from her handbag and dabbed the wet blotches below her eyes.

"Will there be anything else?" the waiter asked.

"No, thank you." Belinda produced a wan smile. "I appreciate your patience."

She retrieved her coat on the rack near the door and buttoned it tight before tying her hat on her head. The doorman performed his task on her behalf. Crisp air bit into her cheeks as soon as she stepped outside. Her mother had been right. No cabs lined Larimer Street. Belinda would have to walk at least far enough to seek better odds of finding transportation. She looked both directions before choosing one. Lights from the train station at Twenty-First and Wazee caught her eye.

The train station.

Belinda blew out her breath and watched it curl in the night air. For more than a year, her cousin Vanessa had been writing from San Francisco, begging Belinda to visit. Just a month ago, Vanessa had written a cogent argument for why it wasn't too late for Belinda to come for Christmas even if her parents didn't want to travel. She fingered the soft bottom of her bag, feeling the thickness of the bills. She saved a few dollars at a time. Her income was limited to the weeks her father was of a mind to pay her for the time she spent working in his shop. Because she wanted for nothing at home, he saw little need to be generous, but she could count on something from time to time and had saved nearly all of it for three years.

How much would it cost to ride the train to San Francisco? Belinda hadn't considered Vanessa's proposition seriously, so she had never made the needed inquiry. Since she was going to become engaged at Christmas, it had hardly seemed like the time to plan a trip.

If she wasn't going to become engaged—which the evening seemed to prove—

what was holding her back?

∽

Hayden pushed gently on the door. It gave.

"Hello?" He wished he could remember the child's name. The house was small, just four rooms, and he could see straight through it. The candlelight he had seen from the street emanated from the kitchen at the back of the house. A plain wooden table, positioned against one wall just the way Hayden remembered it, reassured him he was in the right house.

"Hello?" he said again as he closed the door behind him. There was no fire in the grate. The only warmth in the house, as well as the only light, came from that candle on the kitchen table.

"I'm in here."

The tiny voice, on the brink of a tremble, guided Hayden's steps. He found the girl sitting in a straight-back chair tucked under the table with a closeness and security he doubted the child could have achieved on her own. Her feet dangled well above the floor. Brown eyes framed by dark curls under a red wool hat looked up in expectation.

"I'm Hayden," he said, "a friend of your father's."

"Yes, sir. Papa said you would come. I only had to wait."

Hayden swallowed. How could Gerald know any such thing? How could he be sure Hayden would get the note? If Hayden had left on time for dinner, he would not have been home to open the door to the messenger boy.

"You look like you have been very patient." Hayden sat across from the girl and stretched a hand out to warm it over the feeble flame. "What's your name?"

"Eloise."

"It's a lovely name." Hayden took a breath. "Eloise, do you know where your father is?"

She shook her head. "We're to meet him at Aunty's house."

"I thought we might try to catch him before we leave, but I can't think where to look."

"Papa said I will be safe with you and we'll be together again at Aunty's house." Eloise managed to slide sideways out of her chair, dropped to the floor, and crossed to the small length of counter. She returned to the table with the sugar canister.

"Have you eaten, Eloise?"

"I had lunch."

Hayden knew his first step would be to feed this poor child. He opened the canister and found an envelope matching the one he had received earlier. Inside were folded bills and a card with an address and the words, *Thank you. I promise to explain.*

Chapter 2

"Have you considered that you might be carrying this a tad far?" A few minutes after midnight, in her nightclothes and robe, Edith Michaels stood in her daughter's bedroom door frame.

Belinda had exchanged her own evening wear for a comfortable calico dress that allowed her to move freely and easily. "I only know I can't bear to be here over the holidays. How can I put on a cheery face for my friends when so many of them are expecting an announcement?"

"You might still make an announcement—perhaps New Year's instead of Christmas."

Belinda tugged open the lid of her largest trunk. "I can't think about that now. Everything has gone wrong."

"But you love Hayden Fairbanks. Anyone can see that when you are together."

A pair of shoes thudded into the bottom of the trunk. "Love hasn't always proven the best basis for a matrimonial match."

"Belinda Carol, I insist you stop this nonsense right this minute." Edith marched into the room and slammed down the lid to the trunk.

Belinda calmly moved to the wide mahogany wardrobe. "The sensible thing would be to first think about what I will need on the train and find a small bag to keep with me. Everything else can go in the trunk in the baggage car." She took a traveling skirt and matching jacket off a hook. The items were in good condition but not so new that she would be devastated if harm befell them on the journey.

Edith pointed to the clock. "Christmas Eve is in three days. You can't seriously be thinking of leaving now—and traveling unescorted. You are going to give your father a heart attack."

Belinda opened the trunk once more. "I already bought the ticket, Mama. If I wait for an escort or traveling companion, I'll never go."

"Would that be so bad?"

"I'm not going into the wilderness. There are trains and towns all along the way, and when I get there I will stay with Vanessa and her husband."

"For how long?"

Belinda folded a dress. "I'm not sure. That's why I'm taking the large trunk."

"Are you even going to tell Hayden?"

Belinda pulled open a drawer and chose her words with care. "I can write to him from the train tomorrow. By the time I get to Cheyenne, the letter will be on a mail train back to Denver." And it would be too late for Hayden to come after her.

"And if he shows up here first?"

Belinda shrugged. "Tell him whatever you like."

"You're being ridiculous, Belinda. Stay here. You and Hayden will sort this out."

"Perhaps." Or perhaps not. Maybe her father's hesitations about Hayden were well founded after all. "I only know I need to go somewhere I can step back and think clearly."

∽

The clock on Hayden's dresser announced two o'clock in the morning. He sat in an armchair with a soft gaslight burning low on the side table. Next to the door sat Eloise's tattered carpetbag. His wasn't in much better condition. If he had known he would be traveling, he might have gone into William Michael's dry goods store to inquire whether he had any suitable bags within a newspaper man's budget.

In his lap, with a book to provide a writing surface, Hayden held a sheet of stationery and a fountain pen. As soon as daylight broke, he would go down to the street and find a boy to take the letter. It was too late tonight either to find a messenger or to have a messenger pull the bell at the Michaels residence, but Belinda's day should begin with assurance of his love and a rudimentary explanation of his absence from his own official engagement. He read through his note one last time, finding nothing satisfactory in it but knowing he could do no better. In the morning, he would go to the last place he was sure Gerald had worked, return his daughter to his care, and then go directly to Belinda with a full account of events. And if he couldn't find Gerald—Hayden toyed with how to finish the thought.

Though she had at first been insatiably curious about everything in his rooms, the child now slept easily, perhaps from exhaustion at the late hour when Hayden brought her back to his home or perhaps in security that she was in no danger. She seemed to have no fear that her father had abandoned her. He had, after all, made arrangements for her and given her over to someone he trusted. The ultimate destination was clear, and Gerald had given a father's promise that he would be there at the end of her journey.

From Hayden's perspective, however, it was absurd. He knew nothing about taking care of a child, and in addition to an almost-fiancée, he had an editor who would want an explanation for an indefinite absence. Hayden decided to write a second note for the morning and hoped he still had a job when he returned.

He didn't particularly enjoy traveling. Gerald knew that.

He and Gerald had known each other well. But they had not seen each other since Gerald left the newspaper where Hayden still worked. Hayden refused to speculate about what was in Gerald's mind. He was a newsman who concerned himself with reporting facts, not wild guesses. Hayden watched the girl's chest rise and fall. Somehow Gerald had kept her secure and happy on his own for the last two years. If Gerald felt he must make this outrageous request, then Hayden was certain he had a good reason. In the end, he would do what Gerald asked, and if he missed the train to Cheyenne in the morning, he would lose an entire day tracking Gerald.

Now if only Belinda would find trust a convincing motivation for what Hayden was about to do.

∽

This would be the first time Belinda had traveled west on the railroads. She had been east through Kansas to St. Louis and up to Chicago the previous year with her parents; and when she was a child growing up in St. Louis, her family had traveled to several eastern destinations by rail. Comporting herself on a train didn't cause anxiety. Even the multiple train changes required between Denver and San Francisco didn't concern her. In fact, standing beside the network of tracks at Twenty-First and Wazee early the next morning, she felt oddly free of any anxiety. The last few months had a single trajectory—to become engaged to Hayden Fairbanks. The events of last evening had given her pause for the first time.

Perhaps she would work things out with Hayden—eventually. Her mother was right. She did love him.

But for now she sought to escape impending humiliation.

She needed to watch the countryside roll out before her eyes.

She wanted to feel the engines strain with the promise of a brighter day for every passenger on the train.

She craved Vanessa's arms around her and the knowledge that it was safe to speak the truth, no matter what it was.

She dreamed of a clear spot in her mind and in her heart.

Belinda was grateful for the warm wrap her grandmother in St. Louis had sent for Christmas just a year ago, and she now fastened the top button under her chin. Long strings of railroad cars filled two tracks, one a passenger train and the other freight. The third track stood open. This was where Belinda's train would pull in from the south. She had arrived long before it was scheduled to leave again to head north into Wyoming, but she had to leave her father's predawn silence and her mother's agitation. One last time before she crossed them, Belinda savored the view of the mountains stretching north and south as far as she could see. Every peak was snowcapped and shimmered in winter morning sun. Belinda inhaled the crisp air she wished could also clean her restless heart.

A train thundered on the northbound track from Colorado Springs.

⁂

Hayden never imagined traveling with a child would be so slow. In his family, he had been the little brother, and he wondered why everyone was in such a hurry all the time.

Eloise wasn't a difficult child, at least not yet. She woke easily when he touched her shoulder in the morning—after being awake all night himself—and she accepted his suggestion of oatmeal for breakfast without dispute. But Hayden was beginning to discern that her patience with the strange events of the night before was an extension of her general temperament. She was patient about everything. Too patient. Dressing. Eating. The arduous process of his figuring out what to do with a little girl's unruly dark tresses.

"I'm going to go down to the street to find a messenger," Hayden said. "You stay right here."

Hayden already understood her well enough to know she would, but he locked the door behind him and took the stairs down in a rapid staccato rhythm. He found a newsboy out with his early papers and persuaded him to run with the notes Hayden had written the night before. A telegraph in a couple of hours would further assure Belinda.

When he returned, Eloise was right where he left her. Hayden thought she would never get her stockings on and her shoes buttoned, as content as she was to sit on the side of the bed and hum snatches of various children's rhymes punctuated with random remarks about what she observed around his rooms.

"I'm afraid we must hurry, Eloise," he said with a gentle touch to her knee. He took a shoe in one hand and slipped it on her foot.

"Papa says I am not very good at hurrying." Eloise fumbled with fastening the flap.

Gerald had that much right, and perhaps it explained the choice he made to send Hayden a note rather than take his daughter wherever he had gone in such a hurry himself. Finally, Eloise was bundled up and walked with a hand in Hayden's overcoat pocket while he carried both their bags.

At the bottom of the stairs, the newsboy hurtled in from the cold. "I couldn't deliver your second note, sir."

"Which one?"

"To the lady."

"Why not? The address was clear."

"The lady is gone," the boy said. "Madam wouldn't say where she went. Said to tell you it was between the two of you."

Hayden rolled his head back and sighed at the ceiling. First Gerald, now Belinda. He pulled out his pocket watch, though he knew what it would say. He didn't have time to guess where Belinda might have gone.

✐

For a fleeting moment, Belinda thought about doing the math. How many cars on the train multiplied by how many passenger seats? The cars to Cheyenne would all be day cars. Going west on the Union Pacific from there, some of the cars would have sleeping berths—she had one reserved—while in others passengers would sleep as well as they could manage in upright seats. The line of cars snaked far enough that Belinda lost interest in the calculation. It was enough to imagine that even with transfers and meal stops, and subtracting out mail cars and baggage cars, one could journey a great distance and see only a small portion of the fellow travelers aboard.

Belinda had given her trunk to a porter when she first arrived at the station that morning and trusted that it would be securely stowed in one of the baggage cars and safely transferred to the second train. The bag she carried held a change of blouse, a nightdress, a towel, a book, and a few personal items. Once the passengers leaving the train in Denver had disembarked, railroad employees began indicating that new passengers could board.

As she settled into her seat, the first of the snowflakes drifted by the window. Belinda was rather fond of snow. Its appearance was so unpredictable in Denver that she enjoyed the surprise whenever the ground began to whiten. The railroads boasted that their engines could pull trains through even the severest weather. Belinda supposed that schedules might be delayed occasionally, but it was hard to see how the kind of snowfalls she had observed in the last several years in Denver would hamper the powerful engines that rolled on the tracks laid through Colorado.

Just for a moment, Belinda removed her hat and pressed her forehead against the glass to watch the dance of snowflakes swirling on the rising wind. If all she did between Denver and San Francisco was watch the snow, she would be content. She would arrive at Vanessa's with a clear mind and a quieted soul.

Hayden glanced down at Eloise's feet. In his effort not to seem as impatient as he felt, he had not been particular about the way she buttoned the flaps onto her shoes. With each step, they made a sound he found increasingly disconcerting. As little as he knew about little girls' footwear, though, he wasn't sure he could have done better himself even if he had taken twice as long.

"Are your feet warm enough?" he asked.

Eloise nodded, the brim of her brown wool hat bobbing with the motion. "Yes, sir."

"Do your feet get wet when it snows?"

"No, sir."

Hayden was glad to hear that, though he hoped they wouldn't be out in the snow long enough for it to matter. He raised his hand for a passing cab, but the driver shook his head, indicating he already had a fare. Hayden glanced around and decided he would have better luck at the next corner.

"Are we going to Aunty's house, sir?"

Hayden wished he had a better plan, but he could hardly try to place the child with someone else—someone he didn't know—when Gerald had trusted him.

"We will not get there today," he said, "but we will start an adventure. How does that sound?"

"Thank you, sir."

Hayden realized her feet were spinning quickly trying to match his pace while keeping her hand tucked in his pocket. He slowed down.

"Since we're going to be on a journey together," he said, "why don't you call me Uncle Hayden instead of sir?"

"Yes, sir."

They would have to work on that.

A horse trotted past them, and the wheels of the carriage it pulled threw slush at them.

"My coat!" Eloise removed her hand from Hayden's pocket.

He turned to see her struggling not to give in to tears. Reaching under his overcoat, he extracted a handkerchief before setting down the bags and stooping in front of her to dab at the moisture. Horses' hooves and wheels in the street did not take long to soil fresh snow, and the splotch that had landed on her chest was half mud.

"We'll clean it up. I promise."

"Yes, sir." Her bottom lip trembled.

"You're being very brave. I'll tell you what. I'll carry the bags in one arm and you in the other. If any more carriages come by, I'll be sure to turn away so your coat won't be soiled. How does that sound?"

She nodded but didn't meet his eyes.

He would have carried her anyway. It was their only chance of being on time.

Chapter 3

At the sound of the whistle, Belinda sank back in her seat. Around her the car had filled up while the snow mesmerized her, but the whistle meant that anyone intending to depart with the train should be aboard.

Belinda smiled at the middle-aged couple sitting across from her. The woman rested a hand in the crook of the man's arm and laid her head on his shoulder. He turned his head and glanced down at her. Envy shot through Belinda. She had always imagined she and Hayden would be like that twenty or thirty years from now. Comfortable, tender, content. Now she didn't know what to think.

"It's a lovely day to travel." The woman caught Belinda's eye. "The sun and the snow are so beautiful."

"I've been admiring the day for quite some time," Belinda answered pleasantly. "The sky does seem to be clouding over though."

"The snow may continue in Denver," the man said, "but we'll be long gone."

"We are the Barrows," the woman said. "Amanda and Ellsworth."

"It's lovely to meet you. I am Belinda Michaels."

"Are you traveling alone?" Ellsworth raised an eyebrow.

"Yes." Belinda infused her tone with brightness. "I'm going to spend Christmas with my cousin in San Francisco. And you?"

"We are only going to Ogden to our daughter's," Amanda said. "We have a new grandchild."

"After we change trains, that still gives us the whole of Wyoming to share the journey."

The train lurched in response to the brakeman's pull on the release. The whistle spurted its last warning and the train began to move, gradually gaining speed and finding the rhythm of moving parts collaborating to produce steady motion. A few more minutes of chatting with the Barrows yielded to companionable silence. When Amanda opened a magazine, Belinda reached for her book. The train stopped intermittently along the northbound route, and Belinda watched the exchange of passengers at the series of stations. The car took on additional riders who arranged themselves, as she had, to be as comfortable as possible. Eventually, though, she had to admit that a cramp was creeping up her calf and only a walk would work it out. Leaving her warm wrap but taking a shawl, she walked forward in the train through one car and then another. A porter held the doors as she stepped from one platform to the next.

Now that she was up and about, Belinda craved a cup of tea and wondered how long it would be before the train stopped to take on water or coal and whether there would be time to sit down and enjoy some refreshment. Newspaper accounts of rail travel lauded the dining cars—but only east of Omaha. Westward travelers had to plan their own menus. Belinda had a small tin of sandwiches and a bag of apples but planned to rely for most of her meals on the restaurants that served travelers in the small towns along the rail routes.

Belinda made her way up the aisle of a car. The little girl caught her attention because of the bright red-and-white plaid dress she wore. Black velvet cording trimmed the panels, and Belinda found the effect quite festive, particularly for train travel just before Christmas.

The girl sat alone across the aisle from a woman who could well be her great-grandmother. They glanced at each other a few times but didn't speak. Belinda wasn't persuaded they truly were traveling together—but surely the girl was not alone. Even the orphan trains carried chaperones for the children.

♁

Hayden was at a loss to know what to feed the girl. In the morning rush, he had stopped for a half dozen rolls to take on the train. The elderly woman across the aisle seemed to be far better prepared, but no doubt she had been planning her journey for more than just the last twelve hours. Eloise already had accepted two cookies from Mrs. Stromberg, who seemed quite eager to play the role of doting grandparent. Once she discovered the delightful little girl sitting nearby, Mrs. Stromberg introduced herself, produced her stash of cookies, and suggested that the young woman traveling with her—a paid companion, it seemed to Hayden—might like to move about the train while the opportunity presented itself. Leaving Eloise in Mrs. Stromberg's casual supervision, Hayden got up to seek information he had not had time to assemble before boarding the train.

The conductor in the car forward of Hayden's seats punched tickets gruffly, but Hayden was undaunted by his demeanor.

"I wonder if you can answer my questions about meal stops," he said.

"First one is Cheyenne," came the reply. "Plenty of time there."

"I'm escorting a little girl on this journey. Are the restaurants along the railroads going west suitable for a child?"

The conductor shrugged. "I suppose that depends on how hungry the child is."

"Thank you." Hayden was being polite, which was more than he could say about the conductor. He was going to offer Eloise a roll soon and perhaps insist that she eat it before consuming any more sweets. He suspected sugar cookies were not the extent of Mrs. Stromberg's selections.

He turned to go back to his seat.

♁

"My goodness, what a pretty dress." Belinda grinned at the girl as she approached. On the one hand, it was none of her business who was looking after the child. On the other hand, whoever it was had not made a convincing effort with the girl's hair—another reason Belinda did not think the older woman was ultimately in charge of the child. The woman was too tidy herself to suggest she would have left the girl's hair in such a state.

The child beamed and swung her feet in the empty space between the bench and the floor. "My papa had it made for me. I have three other dresses, but I am nearly too tall for them."

Belinda saw the cookie in the child's fingers now. "And you have a treat as well. What a lucky little girl you are."

"The lady gave it to me." The girl glanced across the aisle. "I can't remember her name."

Belinda followed the gaze. *The lady*. She was right. They weren't actually traveling together.

"Mrs. Stromberg," the woman supplied. "I've just met Eloise this morning, but I am sure we shall get along famously."

"I'm quite certain." What little girl wouldn't get along with an older woman with a tin of cookies? But who was escorting the child? Belinda offered a gloved hand, and Mrs. Stromberg took it. "I am Belinda Michaels."

"Are you sitting in our car, too?" Eloise hummed several random notes while she looked around.

"No, I'm not, though if I had known such a pretty little girl would be here, I might have asked for a ticket in this car." The child was enchanting, and Belinda imagined Eloise could be just the diversion she needed.

"Uncle's going to take me to Aunty's house." Eloise pulled on a curl.

"Where does your aunt live?"

Eloise sucked in her lips. "I forget."

"I believe your uncle mentioned it was San Francisco," Mrs. Stromberg said.

"Yes, San Francisco. That's it. My papa is going to be there."

"Then it seems we shall be traveling all the way together," Belinda said. "What is your destination, Mrs. Stromberg?"

"San Francisco also. My home is there. I've been visiting dear friends in Denver."

"I'm going to visit my cousin in San Francisco," Belinda said.

"I don't have any cousins. I don't have a mama either." The girl was matter of fact and took another bite of her cookie. "I wanted to ride in a car with a sleeping berth, but Uncle says he already bought tickets for regular seats. Have you got a sleeping berth, Miss Michaels?"

"I will after we transfer to the Union Pacific in Cheyenne."

Eloise's eyes widened. "Can I see it?"

"I'll tell you what. We'll ask your uncle about that when he gets back. First we have to change trains, but we can make sure to find one another. And we can't see the berth until the porter makes up the beds when it's time to go to sleep."

"Oh! There's Uncle now."

Eloise pointed over Belinda's shoulder, and Belinda turned.

Hayden Fairbanks moved quickly toward her.

✍∽

"Belinda! How did you know I would be on the train?" A glance at Eloise and Mrs. Stromberg provided Hayden the restraint required to keep from embracing Belinda in public. "I was told you didn't receive my note."

Belinda straightened and held her hands stiffly folded together in front of her. "No, I did not receive a note."

"But you're here. I don't understand."

"I am on my way to spend Christmas with Vanessa." Belinda balled her fists and moved her hands to her sides. "That you are here is merely a matter of coincidence."

"Or God's good blessing that we found each other." Hayden wanted to kiss her right there in the train aisle. "We might have traveled all the way to San Francisco and never realized we were on the same train."

"It will be a long train out of Cheyenne. I'm sure we need not run into each other again."

Her tone stung.

"But you said you would show me your berth," Eloise said. "You said we would be sure to find one another."

Hayden recognized the fluster that crossed Belinda's face. "We'll have to talk about that, Eloise."

"Oh my," Mrs. Stromberg said, "it seems the lady and the gentleman have a previous acquaintance."

"Uncle," Eloise said, "is Miss Michaels your friend?"

Hayden met the girl's large brown eyes and then turned to Belinda's steely blue eyes. "Yes, she is. My best friend."

Was it his imagination, or did Belinda's eyes soften?

"There's room for her to sit with us, isn't there?" Eloise reached into the aisle for Belinda's hand. "Please, Miss Michaels? Sit with us."

"Please do, Belinda," Hayden echoed.

"I'm afraid I can't do that." Belinda tugged on the hem of her traveling suit jacket.

Hayden lowered his voice. "But it would give me a chance to explain what happened last night."

Her terse reply matched the drop in volume. "This child calls you 'Uncle,' but your only brother died of the flu when he was fourteen. You can't manage to get to our engagement dinner, but you are taking a train across the country."

"That's what I want to explain." He took a step toward her.

Belinda pressed her lips together and looked away. "I'm not interested. I only want a peaceful journey and a pleasant visit with my cousin."

Hayden bit back his words. Mrs. Stromberg had an amused expression on her face that perturbed him, and Eloise furrowed her brow in confusion. Others seated nearby had begun to turn their heads. Hayden didn't want to make a scene.

"Perhaps later," he said.

"Ah, here is my companion," Mrs. Stromberg said.

A young woman, not more than nineteen, pushed past Hayden and sat beside Mrs. Stromberg.

"This is Virginia," Mrs. Stromberg said.

"I am pleased to meet you. I hope the journey finds you well." Belinda shook the young woman's hand and then pivoted and flounced down the aisle. A porter opened the door for her at the rear of the car.

"Miss Michaels is going to have a berth," Eloise informed Hayden. "I'm supposed to ask you if she can show it to me later. If she is your friend, why can't I see it?"

∽

Belinda's heart pounded.

Hayden. On the train. With a child. All the way to San Francisco.

Her imagination ran wild. Was this the first of a string of secrets he had kept from her? How much of his chronic tardiness could be explained by a part of his life he had chosen not to share with her, even though they had promised to have no secrets between them? Caught red-handed, he could hardly say that he didn't wish to explain, but under the circumstances why should she believe any explanation he offered? There was no telling what he would have conjured had she taken the seat next to Eloise.

Eloise what? Was her surname also Fairbanks?

Belinda forced herself to slow her breathing and regain her composure by the time she reached her seat. Ellsworth and Amanda Barrow looked as content as they had when Belinda left them.

Amanda raised her eyes from her magazine. "I imagine it is difficult to take much of a stroll on a moving train."

"I felt the need to stretch my legs for a few minutes." Belinda settled back into her seat. "I feel much better for having done so."

Except that she did not. The cramp in her calf had released, but a vice squeezed her stomach, and every thought turned the bar tighter.

She had behaved abominably. Hayden looked genuinely relieved to see her. Astonished but relieved. He didn't look much like a man who was trying to dodge an awkward encounter. And he said something about a note she didn't receive.

Still. He promised to be at the restaurant last night, and he hadn't come. He was well aware that she dreamed of that faultless intimate dinner with her parents before the holiday parties. He knew she wanted a perfect memory of that night, how eager she was to tell her friends about their coming nuptials, how badly she wanted to show him off, how much she wanted joy to overflow.

Whatever his excuse was, it could never undo all that disappointment.

"Are you well?"

Belinda looked up to see Amanda leaning forward and peering at her.

"You've lost your color," Amanda said.

Belinda's heart still thudded. Her pulse hammered in her neck.

"If you need something to eat, we have plenty." Amanda gestured toward a covered basket at her feet. "Or some water, perhaps?"

Belinda shook her head. "I'm fine. Thank you for your kind concern." They would be in Cheyenne soon enough, and she could buy some simple food to bring back to the train.

She would not walk the aisles of the train again no matter how hard her leg cramped.

༆

Hayden had watched for Belinda when he exited the train in Cheyenne. Railroad employees shifted baggage around, but Hayden had only the two small bags to keep track of—and Eloise. He murmured thanksgiving that she was a child content to stay where she belonged.

"Will the lady sit with us again on the new train?" Eloise asked.

"I didn't ask what sort of ticket she had, but perhaps we'll see her. It's a long way across Wyoming." Hayden reached for the girl's hand. They barely had time to eat. The food establishment was efficient enough, but the sheer number of people determined to have a meal slowed service, and he feared the confusion of passengers changing lines from the Denver Pacific to the Union Pacific would make it easy to misplace a small child at the station.

"Are we going to sleep on the train?"

Hayden certainly hoped so. The climb through the mountains west of Cheyenne would be long and slow given what he knew of the grades, the heights of the peaks, and the length of the train. Then would come the descent into Ogden, Utah, where they would change tracks to the Central Pacific Railroad.

"You can put your head in my lap," Hayden said, "and use your coat for a blanket."

Eloise rubbed her eyes. "I'm tired already."

The announcement didn't surprise him. Though she seemed to sleep well the night before, the hours between going to bed and rising had been few for a child. Hayden stooped to pick her up, carrying the girl and two bags for the second time in one day. This time she gladly laid her head on his shoulder and pressed herself into his chest. While he walked, he again watched for Belinda. From Cheyenne, there was only one rail route to San Francisco. She would have to be on the next train, and he would find her.

Chapter 4

Belinda woke in her berth, stiff. Falling asleep had taken a long time, and the unfamiliar bed confined her in strange ways. Curtains provided privacy but didn't shield her from the sound of people shifting in the aisles. While a lower berth was easier to get in and out of, an upper one would have provided more separation from motion beyond her private space. The berths themselves sometimes creaked in response to the sway and jolt of the train's lumbering journey toward a mountain pass or the controlled descent on the other side.

But most of Belinda's nocturnal restlessness was because she knew Hayden Fairbanks was on this train, and she couldn't do anything about it.

Every time the train stopped for a meal, Hayden would be in the crowd pressing toward the restaurant.

If Belinda got up to stretch her legs, she risked running into him. She resolved again not to.

When she closed her eyes, she saw him standing there in the aisle with little Eloise looking up at both of them. She should never have promised the girl they would talk to her uncle about seeing a sleeping berth.

Except he wasn't her uncle. At least Belinda didn't think so.

Eventually, she slept.

When she woke on the morning two days before Christmas, Belinda expected to hear the porter moving around the car or an announcement that the train would stop soon for breakfast. Belinda wondered if the line for the washroom at the end of the sleeper was long. Perhaps the silence meant she woke before most of the other passengers. She might be able to wash up, dress quickly and be clear of the rush that was sure to happen before the train pulled into a town for breakfast. Belinda couldn't remember which town was the scheduled stop. While she did not deny their rustic charm, the towns all looked alike to her. Laramee. Percy. Rawlings. Bitter Creek. What did it matter? The towns sprang up along the tracks with a few hundred people whose livelihoods depended on the railroads. Some had a decent hotel to accommodate travelers who preferred to break up their journey. All of them had perfected the process of feeding large groups of people rapidly while the train took on water and coal.

Belinda savored the morning quiet as she lay in her berth.

And then she sat bolt upright. Why was the train itself quiet? She heard no moving wheels, no whiz of iron bulk along smooth rails, no chug of the rods and pistons and cylinders that kept the train in motion.

She reached for the curtain over the window in her berth and pulled it aside.

Belinda saw a drifting wall of white where she should have seen the sun.

Hayden lifted the still-drowsy girl into his lap. With his head against the window and her head in his lap, they had slept reasonably well, but Hayden was not eager to spend too many nights upright on a moving train.

And Belinda. Her choice—knowing he was on the train—to keep herself wholly apart sliced through him with particular pain.

Especially now.

Through the night, as Hayden woke intermittently, he saw the snow begin and then thicken in the air and deepen on the ground. Straining against the growing storm, the train slowed gradually until it came to a stop.

And it was a storm. Hayden could see it was not simply a spectacular winter snow. As daylight broke, the heavy gray sky promised that crystalline moisture would continue to descend and obstruct the path of the locomotives, behind which crawled more than fifty passenger, mail, baggage, and supply cars. Whipped by the wind, ridges of white clung to the shape of the coach, unpredictably drifting against some windows while leaving others clear.

Passengers stood in the aisle perturbed, some of them looking at their watches. Behind Hayden, a baby cried. Under his hand on her shoulder, Eloise stirred.

"Look, Uncle, the snow!" She scrambled to turn around in his lap and press her face against the window. "I can't see the ground at all."

Hayden marveled at the wonder in her eyes. Eloise saw the novelty of mounding white without understanding how its presence would impede their travels. Even as he glanced at the distraught passengers rousing around them, Hayden envied Eloise.

"Isn't it beautiful!" Eloise had both hands pressed against the glass now on either side of her face. "I can't wait to tell Papa."

Eloise hummed, a habit Hayden had already come to expect from her. He stroked her back, resisting the impulse to explain that the snow meant he couldn't estimate when they would reach her aunt's house—and he had no assurance Gerald would be there when they arrived.

A door at the front end of the coach opened, and a conductor came through, his hat and shoulders dusted with snow. The rear door opened almost simultaneously, sending a blast of cold air up the aisle.

"How long are we going to be stuck?" A man's voice boomed out the question on everyone's mind.

Hayden turned to see the man who'd entered at the rear standing rigid.

"Please remain calm." The conductor looked around the coach. "We made reasonable progress through the night by using the snow plow attached to the front engine. However, the storm's intensity increased rapidly in the last two hours."

"How long?" the man repeated. "I have an important meeting in Ogden for business I must conclude before Christmas."

"We have telegraphed for help," the conductor said. "We need additional crews to help dig out around the engine and try to clear enough track to pick up momentum."

"How long will it take them to get here?"

"That is difficult to estimate, sir. The storm seems to be abating, but travel remains challenging. The snow is heavy and damp."

"And you expect us to calmly sit here in the meantime?" Belligerence burgeoned in the man's tone.

The conductor cleared this throat. "Yes, sir, that is exactly what we ask you all to do. Now, we do have some extra shovels. If any of the men would like to help move snow, that will make the job all the more expedient when the crews arrive."

Eloise turned around. "Uncle, are you going to help move snow?"

Belinda's stomach grumbled. She had not yet touched her sandwiches or apples, but under the circumstances she hesitated to satisfy her hunger too generously. The conductor had just come through with what Belinda thought was an honest assessment of circumstances—the truth being that no one knew how long the train would be stuck on the tracks or when the next opportunity to buy food would come.

She missed her morning cup of tea.

The porter had stowed the upper berths and converted the lower berths to day seats once again. From her position near the rear of the coach, Belinda returned a polite wave from Amanda Barrow, who was sitting several rows forward but facing the rear. Amanda's basket of food was likely to prove more fortuitous than she'd imagined when she'd packed it in Denver.

Icy air gushed into the car when the door at the front opened. Belinda expected to see another railroad employee—perhaps there was more news already—but instead the familiar form of Hayden Fairbanks stood in the aisle. He grasped Eloise's hand. Eloise, whose last name Belinda still didn't know. The girl spotted Belinda and broke away from Hayden.

"We were looking for the lady." Eloise climbed into the seat next to Belinda. "But you're Uncle's friend, aren't you?"

Belinda swallowed. Whatever she felt about Hayden's failure to appear at their engagement dinner, it would be harsh to deny she was his friend. "Yes, I know Mr. Fairbanks."

Hayden caught up with Eloise. "Good morning."

"Good morning." Belinda heard the flatness in her own tone and was glad she had achieved it. "Eloise tells me you were looking for Mrs. Stromberg."

Hayden nodded. "I wondered if she had a berth, but of course I don't know which car she might be in."

"I haven't seen her in this coach."

"Can't I stay with your friend, Uncle?" Eloise looked up with her wide brown eyes.

"Stay?" Belinda echoed.

"I thought I would go see if I can help dig out," Hayden said. "They are recruiting volunteers."

"I see. So you thought Mrs. Stromberg might watch Eloise?"

"I don't feel I should leave her entirely on her own."

"No, of course not." Belinda met Hayden's eyes. His willingness to help did not surprise her, and the child had charmed Belinda the day before. "I'm sure they would appreciate the assistance. Eloise can stay with me."

The blue wool scarf wrapped around the lower half of Hayden's face dampened quickly once he was outside. His gray overcoat was buttoned up to his neck, and he had been grateful to discover a black pair of gloves in the pockets that he didn't remember putting there. The wind had made him give up trying to keep his hat on his head though.

Hayden had first shoveled snow off the steps leading from the platform at the end of the coach to the ground. Few of the male passengers who volunteered were prepared for the task. Their clothing, while appropriate for traveling, was not constructed for warmth and dryness while standing underneath clouds dumping icy crystals into unrelenting wind. Hayden wore the only trousers and shoes he had for the journey. It seemed to Hayden that the conductor's assessment that the storm had begun to abate was overly hopeful. Fresh snow fell and filled in each place where shovels driven by fierce determination reached hard surface. If there was progress, it was only in the perception that the depth of snow did not accumulate immediately in the places they cleared, but Hayden had no doubt that it was only a matter of time. If they let up, they would lose their hard-fought ground.

They slammed shovels at drifts frozen against the side of the train and scraped snow from the undercarriage and wheels and rails. Hayden put his shoulder into one heft of the shovel after another to heave the weight of snow away from the tracks, all the while fairly certain that as much as half of the snow caught in the wind. He couldn't know where it landed. Male passengers, porters, brakemen, and firemen formed the squadron that would keep the train from disappearing into a cave of ice.

Hayden leaned on his shovel to catch his breath. He could barely see the three stairs he had descended when he left the train. Wondering what had happened to Gerald and looking after Eloise had consumed his attention so fully that Hayden hadn't noticed how many coal tenders were among the snake of cars the engines pulled, nor how much coal they might have taken on the night before. For the first time, he wondered how well equipped the train was to keep the passengers warm during an extended stay in this isolated location. Hayden didn't even know where they were.

Food was sure to run out quickly, a reality that would fuel tempers.

Someone thumped Hayden on the back and called above the wind. "We can't stop now, mate."

∽

"Is Uncle going to dig us out?" Eloise pushed loose hair out of her eyes.

"He's going to try," Belinda said. "He has lots of help and more is on the way."

"I hope it doesn't take too long. I want to see my papa."

Belinda eyed her bag, which was stowed on the rack above the seat. "Why don't I get my brush out and we'll see what we can do with your hair."

Eloise giggled. "Uncle doesn't know how to brush hair. I guess my papa never told him."

"Does your papa arrange your hair?"

"After my mama died, Papa had to learn to make braids."

Belinda's stomach burned as she fished her brush from the bag. This was the second time the child had mentioned she had no mother. "When did you and your uncle decide to take a trip together?"

"It was Papa's idea. He told me to wait very patiently at the kitchen table. Then he sent Uncle a note to come and find me and take me to San Francisco."

"Why didn't your father take you?" Belinda released the haphazard curls of the girl's hair.

"No one told me that part."

"Why did your papa ask your uncle to take you?"

Eloise shrugged. "I did what Papa said, and Uncle came to get me. Papa said he would keep me safe, and he did."

Belinda pulled the brush through Eloise's hair. The girl didn't object, so she pulled harder to reach the deep layers.

"I called him sir, but he told me to call him Uncle. I think Uncle is nicer, don't you?"

"Yes. Very much. Is he not your real uncle, then?"

"I don't think so." Eloise pursed her lips in thought. "I have Uncle Paul, but he lives in Chicago."

"So Uncle Hayden must be your father's friend."

"Papa said he could always trust Uncle in an emergency, and so I was to trust him, too."

Belinda parted Eloise's thick hair in the back and took half of it in her hands to braid. "Then I guess your father thought this was an emergency."

"Yes, but he didn't want me to be afraid. He knew Uncle would come as soon he got the note."

"And he did come."

"Yes. I slept at his apartment above the shops, and in the morning we got on the train."

Belinda swiftly plaited one braid and held the end together while she found a ribbon in her bag to secure it. "I don't think I have two matching ribbons for your hair."

Eloise giggled again. "Papa says not matching is more fun, but I think it's because he loses the ribbons."

As Eloise began to hum, Belinda started the other braid. Her mind spun with questions, but she suspected Hayden didn't know the answers any more than Eloise did. Hayden's quandary was becoming clear. How could he leave a six-year-old child waiting obediently and patiently at the kitchen table while he enjoyed a leisurely, celebratory dinner?

Of course he couldn't. He had done the right thing.

The train was not overly warm, but its temperature was a comparative blast of heat to Hayden when he rotated inside. He hustled, dripping, through the aisles to the place where he had left Eloise.

Belinda spotted him, stood, and rushed toward him. When she embraced him, she knocked snow loose from the woolen fibers of his coat, eliciting protests from a few passengers caught in the ensuing shower.

"I've been such a child," she said. "I have no excuse, and I won't try to make one up."

Hayden laid a hand over the one she put against his cheek and looked into the blue of her eyes. "I wanted to tell you the whole story. When I found you on the train from Denver—"

She put a finger over his lips. "I should have listened. I was rude and self-centered.

You were right. It is a blessing that we are on the train together."

"I wish I could kiss you right now," he whispered.

An achy breath escaped her lips as their eyes locked.

"We'll have our moment," she said.

Hayden shivered.

"We need to get you warm and dry." Belinda took his wet coat by the lapels and began to ease it off his shoulders. "Come to the heater at the back of the coach. Do you have dry stockings in your bag?"

"Yes, but it's in the other coach, four cars forward."

"Eloise can show me where it is."

She led him to the heater, set his shoes in front of it, hung his socks nearby and his coat on a hook to drip-dry. Then she took Eloise by the hand and let the girl lead her to their belongings.

Hayden watched her go, seeing in her everything he knew her to be despite her behavior in the last twenty-four hours. Compassionate. Tender. Organized. Resourceful. Though he was determined to await her return, when he let his head drop back against the seat, exhaustion washed over him.

Chapter 5

As long as no single coach became overcrowded, Belinda observed, the conductors seemed to overlook whether people remained in their assigned cars. She was less certain about travelers who'd paid for passage in the more comfortable sleeper cars, but she chose to ignore murmurings she overheard on the subject. She had taken in Eloise, an innocent child who should not be made to suffer for circumstances beyond her control. And who would dare suggest that Hayden, who spent hours at a time battling a blizzard, was not deserving of the creature comforts the sleeper coaches offered? Belinda was fully prepared with her best glare for anyone who would voice such an opinion.

The three of them shared a bench, with Eloise snuggled in the middle. Hayden thawed out and dried out. Belinda wished he didn't have to go outside again, but she knew he would. Hayden Fairbanks wasn't afraid of hard work, and he wasn't temperamentally akin to the haughty travelers who seemed to believe it was the responsibility of those of lesser means to keep them comfortable, including removing snow from in front of the train that carried them.

Eloise tugged Belinda's sleeve. "I'm hungry."

Belinda looked over the girl's head at Hayden. "Then let's see what we can do about that. I have scrumptious red apples. How does that sound?"

Eloise pointed to the space where her front tooth had fallen out. "I can't bite apples."

Hayden reached into his pocket. "I have a knife. I'll cut it up for you."

Belinda put a hand deep into her travel bag and extracted two apples. "We should all eat something."

"Only apples?" Eloise said. "That's a silly lunch."

"Of course not only apples." Hayden pointed at the sack Belinda had carried back with their bags from the day car. "Remember that ham sandwich you were too full to finish last night?"

"I'm hungry for it now." Eloise leaned forward and took up the sack. She removed the partially eaten sandwich and handed the bag to Belinda.

Belinda ran a mental inventory. She still had four apples and her tin of sandwiches. Hayden's bag contained three rolls, some beef jerky wrapped in paper, and two boiled eggs.

"You must be hungry after working so hard." Belinda took out an egg and a piece of jerky.

Eloise abruptly sat up straight. "What's that noise? Is the train starting?"

Belinda glanced at Hayden.

"The tracks can't be anywhere near clear," he said softly.

269

The train pitched forward. A cheer rippled through the passengers.

Belinda watched out the window as the train lumbered ahead, shedding itself of the cave-like walls of snow.

"We're going!" Eloise popped a slice of apple in her mouth.

Belinda handed the egg and jerky to Hayden. He cracked the egg on the window and began to peel it.

The train stopped.

⌇

Darkness cycled around. Hayden offered food to Eloise whenever she expressed hunger and once when she did not. He wondered where Mrs. Stromberg was with her tin of cookies. It was a rather large tin, but the passengers around her might have already taken advantage of her generosity.

"It's time for me to go out again," Hayden said.

"But it's dark," Belinda protested. "And there's no telling what the temperature will be overnight."

"I'd better find out what they've decided."

"Uncle," Eloise said, "I want you to be safe. You kept me safe."

Hayden surprised himself when he bent to plant a kiss on the top of Eloise's head. "We'll all keep each other safe. How does that sound?"

Eloise nodded. Belinda's eyes filled with protective worry.

"I'll come back and tell you what I learn before I go out." Hayden stood. "I'll make sure to say good night to you both."

Belinda raised her cheek and he kissed it, wishing he could put a finger on the side of her jaw and turn her lips toward his.

Bundled in his coat, scarf, gloves, and hat, Hayden walked forward several cars until he found a group of men huddled at the back of a car.

"We've lost a whole day of travel already," one of them said.

"But how much can we do in the dark?" another countered. "We can start again at first light."

"We have lanterns," came a response, "and enough fuel to keep them burning. We might even keep a fire going."

Hayden turned to look at one man after another as the conversation ricocheted among opinions.

"People are anxious about Christmas."

"It's too late for anyone to arrive for Christmas. The sooner we help people understand that, the better."

"Christmas is neither here nor there. What is important is that we stay ahead of the snowfall. We can't be certain when help will arrive, and if we've done nothing, it will only take longer for a crew to clear the tracks even with equipment."

"No one is coming tonight. That much is sure."

"Wyoming has already seen deeper snowfalls this winter than anyone remembers. Thousands of head of cattle are gone. Have you all forgotten the storm only three weeks ago?"

"The weather has to break at some point. I say we wait it out."

"People are already getting hungry."

"We'll share what we have."

"It won't be enough. Jesus isn't here to bless the loaves and the fishes."

"Jesus is here." Hayden broke in. "Jesus is always here. Blessing is always possible."

"Save it for church." A brakeman fastened his coat. "I'm going out."

"We'll split the night," a fireman said. "No man stays out more than two hours at a time, and no one goes out alone."

Heads nodded around the huddle.

Belinda walked Hayden to the end of the sleeper. "I wish you would wear your extra sweater."

"I need to have something dry when I come back in." He carried his bag. "The conductor promises to keep the stove going in the first car behind the engines. Any man who wants to can come in to warm up."

"Promise me you will." The temperatures were sure to plummet overnight. Belinda hated to think of Hayden—or any of the men—exposed. "Are you sure this is necessary? That it is the best choice?"

Hayden nodded. "We must do everything we can for a work train to reach us without putting themselves in danger."

Belinda swallowed her anxiety and braced herself for the blast of cold air that would come when he opened the door.

Back at her seat, she smiled at Eloise. "Did Uncle remember to pack a brush for cleaning your teeth?"

Two dark braids swung from side to side.

"A nightdress?"

"I slept in my clothes last night."

"Come on." Belinda picked up her own small bag. "It looks like you'll get your wish to sleep in a berth, but first let's see about washing your face. You can sleep in my extra shirtwaist."

Later, when the benches had been converted to a berth and the young couple with the berth above hers had settled in, Belinda lay beside Eloise and welcomed the child's desire to snuggle against her for warmth. It seemed to Belinda that the heat inside the car had dropped a few degrees. She spread her wrap across the top of the bedding, wishing she could so easily do something to keep Hayden warm as well.

Hayden woke to cold feet.

Overnight he had been outside twice. After the second two-hour shift, he hung both pairs of stockings to dry from a makeshift clothesline stretched across the car where work crews came and went. Now, as daylight filtered through thin curtains pulled across the windows, the towel he had wrapped his chilled feet in was askew. He sat up and rubbed his eyes. Three nights ago he slept a few fitful hours wondering what he was supposed to do with Eloise. The next night, he slept upright in a railroad coach afraid to move lest he wake the girl. Now a third night had passed with insufficient sleep.

Hayden tested his socks and found them dry enough to put on. It was a harder task to get the insides of his shoes dry, and he fastened them on in their slightly damp state. Once he began moving through the cars, he saw morning activities through the length of the train, ensuring he would alarm no one if he sought out Belinda in the sleeper coach. An agitated conversation jolted him though.

"What do they expect us to eat? If we don't starve, we'll freeze to death."

Hayden recognized the voice. Thomas something. Lewis. Yes, Thomas Lewis, the man who had protested the delay in his travel to Ogden and turned up his nose at the suggestion that a man of his standing should leave the train in a blizzard to perform manual labor. Lewis was entangled with Amanda and Ellsworth Barrow over the empty state of his stomach.

"It's true we can't have a hot, filling breakfast." Amanda spoke with commendable calm, given Lewis's tone. "But I'm happy to share a bit of our food."

Hayden could see into her open basket. They may have started out with an ample supply to supplement scheduled meal stops, but the basket looked nearly bare. How many people had she already fed? Lewis reached in, rummaged for a moment, and removed the last two slices of bread and an orange. Hayden saw one more orange rolling between a few slices of coffeecake.

Hayden started to object to Lewis's movements, but Ellsworth shook his head, and the three of them watched as Thomas Lewis retreated to his own compartment.

"He took nearly all the food you had." Hayden spoke through clenched teeth.

Ellsworth cleared his throat. "It seemed a better choice than the stir he was about to cause."

"Everyone is hungry," Hayden said, "and he has done none of the work."

"Pay him no mind," Amanda said. She closed her basket. "Help will come."

Hayden hoped so, but he resolved to keep an eye on Thomas Lewis and make sure he didn't repeat the scene. He moved down the aisle toward where Belinda sat with an arm around Eloise.

"Is what that man said true?" Eloise asked. "Are we going to run out of food and freeze to death?"

"He shouldn't have said that." Hayden lifted Eloise into his lap and kissed Belinda's cheek.

"I don't have to eat breakfast," Eloise said. "I'm not even hungry."

Hayden decided to wait a few minutes before insisting Eloise eat at least part of one of the rolls they still had.

"It looks like the snow stopped." Belinda gazed out the window.

Hayden nodded. The snow had stopped a few hours ago, and the early morning crew was making visible progress in clearing the tracks. But unquestionably they were still stranded.

⟡

"Someone found a kettle." Belinda ran a hand over her untidy hair. She reminded herself that she and Hayden intended to marry, so he might as well see what she looked like in the morning. "The woodstove outside the washroom was hot enough to boil water. I'll get you some tea."

When she started to rise, Hayden took her hand. "Not just yet. I only want to sit with the two of you for a few minutes."

He was rather tousled himself, she decided. She moved two fingers across the stubble casting a distinct shadow over his cheeks and wondered if he ever considered growing a beard.

"I'll shave in a few minutes."

"No. Rest. Eat."

Eloise slid off Hayden's lap. At least Belinda had tidied the girl's braids.

"Eloise, are you ready to eat?" Hayden asked.

"I'm ready to hop." Eloise demonstrated.

Belinda laughed. "Hop? On a train?"

Eloise shifted her weight back and forth between her feet. "Truly I want to run, but I'm old enough to know I mustn't run on a train. I won't hurt anyone if I only hop."

Belinda looked at Hayden, who shrugged.

"All right," Belinda said, "but be careful. If someone wants past you in the aisle, hop aside."

"I promise. Watch me. I'm a bunny." Eloise hopped forward.

"She's a delightful child," Belinda said. "I don't remember much from being a six-year-old girl, but she makes it look like a great deal of fun."

"A train trip should be an adventure for a child." Hayden's eyes followed Eloise's hopping path. "I wish I could shield her from the adults who are not responding to the circumstances as they ought."

Belinda looked into Hayden's pale green eyes and squeezed his hand. "What I wouldn't give for a moment truly alone with you right now."

His mouth broke into a half grin.

They looked up when they heard Eloise's feet falling in soft, rapid thuds against the carpet.

"The man is stealing!" the girl said. "I don't know where Mr. and Mrs. Barrow went, but the man ought not to look in their basket when they aren't there."

Eloise tugged at Hayden's hand, but Belinda pulled her back and let Hayden go on his own.

∽

Hayden stomped down the aisle, stood behind Thomas Lewis, and cleared his throat loudly.

Lewis spun around.

"Surely you aren't further prevailing on the generosity of the Barrows," Hayden said.

"If they are so sure everyone will have enough to eat, they won't mind." Lewis began to peel the last orange.

"You've had your breakfast." Hayden took the orange from Lewis's hands and dropped it back in the basket. "There are women and children aboard the train who have had far less to eat than you have."

"What are you insinuating, Mr.—?"

"Fairbanks," Hayden supplied. "I am insinuating nothing. I am stating facts. You've eaten by the generosity of others. This is hardly the way to express your gratitude."

Hayden turned when another passenger tapped him on the shoulder.

"The food doesn't belong to you either," the man said, "so I don't see how it is your concern what becomes of it."

"The food is not my concern." Hayden maintained his calm. "The people to whom it does belong are my concern. My guess is they have forgone their own breakfast in order to offer some to Mr. Lewis."

"They shouldn't have left the basket unattended."

"That is hardly an argument for Mr. Lewis's choice," Hayden said. "Even the child in my charge knows better."

"You have no right to stand there and insult me." Thomas Lewis's face reddened.

"And what right have you for your actions?" Hayden spun to face the second passenger. "Or you? Do you stand on conviction that the noble choice is to turn your head from wrongdoing? When one of us is wounded, do we not all feel the pain?"

Behind Hayden, someone began to applaud, and then another.

"Don't you dare preach at me," Lewis protested, but he began to back away—without his orange.

Hayden felt the blood drain from his face.

Chapter 6

I miss my papa." Eloise twirled the end of a braid and pushed out her lower lip. "Does he know I am stuck in a snowstorm?"

Belinda's heart sank. She wouldn't lie to a child. "I'm not sure. But I'm sure he knows Uncle Hayden is keeping you safe, because he knew Uncle would come for you when you were so brave to wait for him."

"I don't want to go to Aunty's house anymore. I only want to go home. When I see Papa, I am going to tell him I want to go home right away."

"He will be so glad to see you." The child needed her father. Short of that, she needed a hot, hearty meal, a clean dress, and some fresh air. Belinda could give her none of those things. She took Eloise's hand and pulled her to her feet. "Let's take a walk."

Eloise shrugged but complied. "Can we find the lady with the cookies?"

"Mrs. Stromberg? We can at least look for her. She might not have any cookies left."

"That's all right. She has a pretty smile, too. And she smells like flowers. I liked that."

"Bring your coat," Belinda said. "It's cold between the cars."

"You shouldn't take that child out," an eavesdropper said. "She'll catch her death." Eloise gasped.

"A child needs to move." Belinda tightened her grip on Eloise's hand. "We're not going to tromp through the snow."

She led Eloise down the aisle. The girl wasn't the only one showing distress. Though the sleeper was reasonably warm for the circumstances, people huddled under coats and blankets keeping a grip on their personal belongings. Assurances from conductors that help was on the way wore thin as a missed breakfast turned into a missed lunch. The pitch of conversation rose as travelers exchanged stories of people freezing to death in a Wyoming blizzard or claimed to have seen the countryside dotted with rotting cattle after a storm. Why was it, Belinda wondered, that in unusual circumstances every person felt compelled to tell a story more dramatic than the last?

They pushed out of one car and into the next, walked through, and stepped across another platform. Belinda would walk the train all day if that was what it took to wear out Eloise and prepare her for a deep sleep. If only people would stop telling the most frightening stories that came to mind.

"Let's go back," Eloise said as they entered the fourth car without a glimpse of the old woman. "Uncle won't know where we are when he comes in to warm up. We shouldn't make him worry."

Belinda bent and kissed Eloise's smooth cheek. "I believe you are the most thoughtful child I've ever met."

Her action didn't elicit the smile Belinda had hoped for. With drooping shoulders, Eloise turned and led the way back through the cars.

⚬⚬⚬

Hayden dropped his shovel. He saw movement over the hard-packed snow, a murky, ragged shape moving toward the train.

"The shift is not over." A brakeman grabbed Hayden's elbow. "We all agreed."

"I'm not quitting." Hayden shielded his eyes and then scrambled up a pile of snow discarded from the tracks. He drew in a frigid breath at the sight.

The brakeman was beside him now. "It's a stagecoach!"

"They must be lost." Hayden waved both his arms above his head. A stagecoach wasn't much shelter against the elements of the last two days—and none at all for the driver.

The coach, pulled by a team of four horses, made steady progress toward them until it was close enough that Hayden grabbed the harness of one of the front animals. The driver slid out of his seat, his boots stirring up puffs of snow as his feet hit the ground.

"You are a long way from the road," the brakeman observed.

"What road?" The driver clapped his gloved hands three times and rubbed them together. "I lost my landmarks a long time ago."

"Do you have passengers?" Hayden asked. "Or just mail?"

"The mail should have been on the train two days back. The passengers are four. A doctor and his wife with their two young daughters. They were determined to spend Christmas in Rock Springs with his ailing parents. We only set out earlier today when it seemed the snow had stopped. Then it started again, and it didn't take much to lose our way."

"Have you no conductor to help you?"

The driver shook his head. "The lad refused to continue after the last stop to change horses. He was young and new and a nervous wreck about whether the snow-pack would support the weight of the horses with a coach when we couldn't be certain what terrain lay underneath."

"I'm not sure what we can do for the horses, but we should take the passengers inside where it's warmer."

"The team will be snug enough next to the train," the brakeman said. "Do you have any food?"

The driver half grinned. "The missus asked me to be careful with her fruitcake tin when I loaded the luggage."

Hayden winced. Five more mouths to feed. He hoped the doctor's children liked fruitcake more than he did.

The stagecoach door opened and a man stuck his head out. "I'm Dr. Truman. I suppose this is as close to Rock Springs as we're going to get."

⚬⚬⚬

Belinda handed Eloise a magazine that Amanda Barrow had cast off, and the doctor's young daughters huddled around it with her. The three girls were soon giggling together as they turned pages and inspected the illustrations of fashion. Both of the new girls were older than Eloise and easily read captions and descriptions. Eloise delighted in picking out individual words she recognized and hummed freely in between.

"Thank you for taking us into your fold," Mrs. Truman said. "I suppose we were foolish to start out this morning, but it is difficult to think of not spending Christmas with our family."

Belinda wanted to say there was still time, but she knew she should make no such promise.

A young woman hurtled into the sleeper coach with eyes darting around.

Eloise pointed. "Look, it's Mrs. Stromberg's friend."

Belinda stood up and moved toward Mrs. Stromberg's traveling companion. "What's wrong, Virginia?"

"I need a doctor." Virginia's eyes flashed from side to side. "My employer has taken ill."

Belinda pivoted and returned to where she had left the Trumans. "Dr. Truman, come quickly. A woman is ill."

He stood and picked up his bag. "God certainly has His timing."

"I want to go with you." Eloise's brown eyes pleaded.

Not wanting to waste time, Belinda took the girl's hand. When they found Mrs. Stromberg, Belinda could decide whether to let Eloise see her.

Mrs. Stromberg's sleeper was five cars back. Belinda and Eloise had stopped only one car too soon on their earlier search. The elderly woman lay in a lower berth. The porter, who must have rapidly converted the day seats, was tucking in the corner of a gray blanket. Several passengers clustered around stepped back now for Dr. Truman, who extracted a stethoscope from his bag and listened to various spots on the woman's chest. He asked a series of questions about the symptoms and when they had begun. Mrs. Stromberg's color—or lack of it—alarmed Belinda, but despite her efforts to keep Eloise out of the way, the girl tugged her hand out of Belinda's grip and wormed her way next to the berth.

Eloise lifted the pale hand that lay above the blanket and held it between both of hers. "Your cookies were the best cookies I ever had. I can sing to cheer you up if you like."

Mrs. Stromberg gave a weak smile. "Perhaps later."

Belinda caught the doctor's eye. He stepped away from the berth and spoke in a low tone.

"I suspect she knew she was ill before she got on the train, though she might not have realized it was certain to worsen. She has a respiratory malady of some sort. I'm afraid I don't have any medicines with me."

"Is it serious?"

He pressed his lips in thought. "In a younger person, no. But I don't think this is the worst of it. We'll need to watch her through the night and try to get the fever to break."

∽

"You were smart to trade your berth for one in this car." Keeping his voice low, Hayden sat beside Belinda across the aisle from Mrs. Stromberg, where they both could hear her raspy effort to breathe.

"She needs someone to look after her," Belinda murmured.

"Where did her companion go?"

"She's is too rattled to be much good. I told her to find somewhere to go to bed." Belinda sighed. "Besides, Eloise doesn't want to leave Mrs. Stromberg. I finally got her to agree to go to sleep by promising we would be right here all night."

"She should be sleeping. She's a little girl, and it is the middle of the night." Hayden glanced across to the day bench where Eloise dozed. The porter had made up all the other berths, but they had asked him to leave the benches across the aisle from Mrs. Stromberg. Eloise could sleep on one, and Hayden and Belinda could sit up on the other.

The old woman coughed sharply. Belinda was on her feet in an instant and laid a hand on Mrs. Stromberg's forehead. "The fever has gone up."

"Shall I find Dr. Truman?" Hayden's query came in a hoarse whisper.

Belinda shook her head. "He would just tell us we need to cool her off. My mother used to drench a cloth in cold water when I had a fever."

Hayden stood and lifted his coat off its hook. "I imagine a bucket of snow would give us all the cool water we need."

"I have a towel." Belinda reached for her small bag on the shelf above the seats.

Mrs. Stromberg coughed again. This time it took hold, her chest rattling for half a minute or more.

"Uncle, what's going on?" Eloise threw off her blanket and sat up.

"We're just trying to take care of Mrs. Stromberg." Hayden laid a calming hand on Eloise's shoulder.

Eloise wrapped her blanket around her shoulders and stepped into the aisle. She climbed onto the berth beside the old woman and took the wrinkled skin and gnarled joints of Mrs. Stromberg's hand between her own smooth, soft, perfect ones. "I'm going to pray for you," she whispered.

Hayden and Belinda looked at each other.

"Dear Lord Jesus," Eloise began, her eyes squeezed closed. "My papa says I can talk to You about anything. I'm going to talk to You about Mrs. Stromberg. Being sick on a train stuck in the snow is frightening. I would like You to help Mrs. Stromberg not be frightened. Thank You that she smells like flowers. Thank You for sending the doctor to us today. Amen."

Hayden let out a slow breath. "I know where I can find a bucket. I'll be right back."

⁓

The sweetness of Eloise's prayer made tears well in Belinda's eyes. She reached into her skirt pocket for a handkerchief to wipe her nose. Eloise had plenty of reason to be frightened herself—she didn't know where her father was, she didn't understand how far away her aunt lived, she was stranded on a train in a blizzard and running out of food, people around her were irritable and argumentative. Yet the girl's prayer overflowed with peace and gratitude.

The coughing took siege again. Eloise calmly spread her small fingers on the woman's chest. When the spasm passed, she leaned forward to kiss a wrinkled cheek.

Awake now, Mrs. Stromberg turned her head toward Eloise. "I remember you. You would've eaten all my cookies if your uncle had not intervened." Her chest rose with the labor of taking in enough air to support speech.

"They were delicious cookies." Eloise grinned.

"The secret is lots of butter." Mrs. Stromberg winked one eye. "I still have some."

Belinda nudged Eloise. "We should let Mrs. Stromberg rest."

"I am resting," the old woman said. "I'm in bed, aren't I? The child is good medicine."

Belinda straightened the blanket around Eloise's shoulders, and then pulled Mrs. Stromberg's blanket snug before laying the backs of her fingers against the woman's forehead again.

"Burning up, no doubt," Mrs. Stromberg said.

"I'm afraid so. We're going to try to cool you off with some wet cloths."

"Sounds ghastly."

"Hayden went for snow."

"Ghastlier still."

"We want to help you get well."

"I am glad you two worked things out." Mrs. Stromberg coughed, air clattering out of her lungs with a fury.

Belinda moistened her lips. "Someday I will learn to get all the information before I draw conclusions." Being in love with a journalist should have taught her that much by now.

"Are you hungry?" Eloise asked. "When I am sick, Papa always tells me I must eat good food."

Belinda winced. Though she agreed with Eloise's father, at the moment the food options were few.

Hayden returned. Snow brimmed the bucket.

Eloise tightened her grasp on Mrs. Stromberg's hand. "It's all right. I'll stay with you while they put the snow on you." The little girl hummed a few notes.

⁂

Hayden handed the bucket to Belinda, who encased the top of the snow pile in her towel and transferred the ensuing dampness to Mrs. Stromberg's forehead.

"There's been a telegraph," Hayden said. "They expect the rescue crews will reach us by morning. A work train is coming from the west."

Belinda's eyes shone with anticipation. Her mouth, open slightly, asked unspoken questions. All Hayden could think was how much he wanted to kiss her.

"It will still take some time to dig out," Hayden said, "but we'll have better equipment and men with proper attire for the elements."

"Tomorrow is Christmas Eve," Belinda said. "Perhaps there is hope after all, at least for some passengers."

"Christmas is hope for all people," Mrs. Stromberg whispered. " 'Risen with healing in His wings.' "

Belinda moved the cold cloth to Mrs. Stromberg's neck. "That's a lovely reminder."

Hayden lowered himself into the seat across the aisle from where Belinda nursed Mrs. Stromberg and Eloise remained perched on the berth. Contentment washed over him. Two days ago the question most on his mind was what in the world he was supposed to do with a six-year-old girl. Now, with the prospect of rescue and finishing the journey, he wondered what he would do without Eloise.

The snow in the bucket melted. Seeing her eyes begin to droop, Hayden lifted Eloise off Mrs. Stromberg's berth and put her back in her own makeshift bed. He and Belinda took turns dipping the towel in the icy water and laying it afresh on Mrs. Stromberg's face, neck, and arms. The old woman dozed on and off. Hayden and Belinda murmured intermittent conversation in the dimly lit car as the yawning hours of the night passed.

Hayden roused when he felt the touch on his shoulder and looked up to see Amanda Barrow and Dr. Truman. Daylight was breaking. Belinda lifted her head from where she leaned against the window in a half sleep.

"The doctor wanted to check on your friend," Amanda said. "I came along in case you wanted respite yourselves."

Hayden glanced at Eloise, who slept soundly.

"I'll stay with her," Amanda said.

Hayden took Belinda's hand. "Yes, I do think we would like some respite. Thank you."

They left Dr. Truman with his stethoscope and thermometer. Amanda slid into the bench they vacated.

"Where are we going?" Belinda asked.

Hayden pulled her through the rear door of the car, and they stood on the platform above the joining of the cars. "I can't wait any longer."

He enfolded her in his arms, and as she tilted her face up, he lightly traced the line of her jaw with one finger and then drifted over the curve of her chin to the fullness of her lips. Around them the wintry morning brightened, but Hayden felt none of its chill, only the warmth of Belinda in his arms. When he finally bent his head to meet her waiting mouth, the heat of her sigh blew across his face. She had yearned for this moment as much as he had.

While not unwilling to shovel snow again, Hayden was relieved to hear the news that passengers were no longer needed in the effort. As the day progressed, the work train chugged closer every hour with its well-equipped crew throwing snow off the tracks. Hayden sat warm and dry in the sleeper beside Belinda for much of the day. Eloise moved back and forth, sitting snugly between them at times and climbing into Mrs. Stromberg's berth at others. Amanda and Ellsworth joined them for the day as well, leaving the Truman family their space. Dr. Truman came by every few hours and nodded in satisfaction at the patient's progress. Even Virginia stayed close. The day passed in rounds of chatter punctuated by reminders to keep their voices down so Mrs. Stromberg could rest, though she persistently announced that she felt much better and saw no reason to stay in bed. Around them other travelers were equally buoyed by the expectation of rescue at any moment. When suppertime came, they passed around Mrs. Stromberg's cookie tin, the last of the food that remained among their band of travelers.

Darkness fell. At the last sliver of sun sliding below the horizon, Hayden let his eyes rest on each of the people in their little cluster, all of whom he hadn't known three days earlier except Belinda. Stillness eased across them, the earlier cheer fading.

Amanda's hushed, silky voice broke the silence. "It's Christmas Eve. If you were home, where would you be tonight?"

Hayden and Belinda looked at each other.

"I suppose we would have gone to church," Belinda said. "My mother loves the music of Christmas."

"A late service?" Amanda asked.

Belinda nodded. "I love coming out of church at midnight and it's Christmas!"

"We would have spent the whole evening with Belinda's parents," Hayden said, "celebrating our engagement."

"Engagement!" Amanda smiled broadly. "My dears, how lovely for you!"

"I knew it," Mrs. Stromberg said. "As soon as I saw how miffed Belinda was with Hayden on that first day, I knew it! A woman only fumes that hot toward a man she loves."

"Uncle," Eloise said, "do you love Miss Michaels back?"

He grinned. "I do."

"Can I sing for you now?" She crossed the aisle to his lap.

"Yes. I wish you would."

"I'll sing the song Papa was teaching me." She cleared her throat. "Hark! The herald angels sing, 'Glory to the newborn King!' "

The clarity of the child's voice stunned Hayden, and he saw equal surprise on the faces of his companions. Her pitch was as perfect as any he had ever heard. By the time she finished the first stanza, he was breathless.

Eloise took a deep breath and began the second stanza. "Christ, by highest heav'n adored, Christ, the everlasting Lord."

Hayden couldn't hold back his own voice now. "Late in time behold Him come, offspring of the virgin's womb."

One by one the others began to sing. Belinda's glossy alto, Mrs. Stromberg's warbling soprano, Virginia's timid contribution, the Barrows' heartfelt harmonies.

At the beginning of the third stanza, the sound of a violin soared above them. "Hail the heav'n-born Prince of Peace! Hail the Sun of Righteousness. Light and life to all He brings, ris'n with healing in His wings."

Hayden dropped out to listen to the exquisiteness of it all.

~

"Hark! The herald angels sing, 'Glory to the newborn King.' "

While the strains cascaded from their soaring spirits, Belinda made up her mind. This Christmas was very different from anything she had imagined. Instead of celebrating in her childhood home by a roaring fire, she sat in a drafty train carriage stuck in snow. Instead of parties with friends, she found warmth in a huddle of strangers. Instead of the new dresses she had saved for the joyous announcements of her engagement, she wore the same traveling suit for the fourth day in a row. Instead of a bounty of holiday recipes, she had feasted on bread and jam for breakfast and shortbread cookies for supper.

And she wouldn't change a moment or detail.

"Hayden," she said, "would you hand me my bag, please?"

Eloise slid off his lap. Hayden stood, took the bag from the shelf, and handed it down. Belinda unfastened the latch and reached in.

"Eloise, this is for you."

Wide brown orbs stared back at Belinda as she put the bundle of tissue paper in the girl's hands.

"A present!" Eloise said. She looked at Hayden. "Uncle, should I open it now?"

"I think that would please Miss Michaels very much," he said.

"Yes, it would." Belinda looked up to catch Hayden's eye.

Eloise laid the package carefully in her lap and began unwrapping it. Belinda watched as the small glass bottle emerged.

The child sucked in her breath. "Is it perfume?"

"Take the stopper out," Belinda said.

Eloise's motion released the sweet fragrance of roses into the air.

Belinda dampened a finger with the mixture and rubbed it onto Eloise's neck. "What do you smell?"

"Flowers!"

"Is that rose water?" Mrs. Stromberg asked.

Eloise crossed the aisle and put the vial under the old woman's nose. "It smells just like you do."

Mrs. Stromberg nodded. "I got my first bottle of rose water when I wasn't much older than you are. Do you know why my mother gave me rose water?"

"Why?"

"Because my name is Rose." Mrs. Stromberg pushed herself up at the elbows.

"That's a pretty name." Eloise climbed up onto the berth. "I wish I had a present for you."

"My grandchildren call me Granny Rose. If you would call me Granny Rose, that would make me happier than any present."

Eloise beamed.

◦⁄◦

Hayden took Belinda's hand. "That was very sweet."

"Your gift is on the dresser in my bedroom at home," she said. "I would have given it to you tonight."

"I have one for you, too."

"Would you like to know what yours is?"

He shook his head. "Let's wait."

"If you're sure."

He glanced out the window. "The moon is out. It's nearly full. Let's go look at it."

She nodded and reached for her wrap.

They stood close together on the platform, brisk air rushing toward them.

"The sky is so clear," Belinda said. "I haven't seen the sky since Cheyenne."

The moon hung like a giant imperfect sugar cookie, not quite round but tantalizing nevertheless.

Hayden gripped the edge of the car with one hand and leaned out over the steps. "The tracks ahead are clear. I can see the lights of the work train. They'll be here soon now."

Belinda was quiet and only stared at the moon.

"Doesn't that make you happy?" Hayden pulled himself in again.

"It should," she said. "But this has been such a beautiful day. Such a wondrous time."

"It's like we've been in a cocoon, and we've only just found how we fit in it. And now that it is about to end, it's hard to imagine letting it all go."

She turned to him, her eyes brimming. "We must though. The train is going to start up again, and we'll be on our way to San Francisco."

"Your cousin will be there, and Eloise's aunt. And I hope Gerald."

Belinda chuckled under her breath. "I don't know whether to throttle Gerald for spoiling our engagement or embrace him with gratitude for the chance to know his enchanting daughter."

Hayden raised his eyes to the moon again. "Denver. San Francisco. It all feels as far away as the moon."

Belinda sighed and leaned against him. They stood, unspeaking, absorbing this moment they knew would never come again. Hayden kissed her cheek.

Belinda pointed at a shadow moving down the tracks.

"A hand truck, in advance of the work train," Hayden said. "It's probably food."

"We're rescued," she whispered. "We're rescued."

Chapter 7

Belinda woke first. She lifted her head off of Hayden's shoulder. Christmas morning. At her feet was the crumbly evidence of last night's feast of potted meats, dried fruit, and crackers. No one in the sleeper coach had complained about the menu as they passed food from one compartment to another.

Belinda rubbed her eyes and ran a hand over her haphazard hair, feeling the floppy bun at her neck. Hayden still dozed with his head against the window. Eloise's bench was abandoned. Belinda glanced to the berth across the aisle, expecting to see the girl sitting cross-legged and watching Mrs. Stromberg sleep.

Neither of them was there. The berth's curtains were wide open, and the bed was empty.

She jiggled Hayden's shoulder. "Wake up!"

He startled. "What is it?"

She pointed to the empty bench and then the empty berth. "They're both gone."

Hayden jolted alert. "Together?"

"I hope so." Belinda calmed herself with the thought. A small child and an elderly woman recovering from an illness—she hoped they were together. She stood up, straightened her skirt, and tried to think where to look.

"Good morning."

The voice came from behind her, and Belinda spun to meet it. "Mrs. Stromberg!"

For two days Mrs. Stromberg had not been out of bed to do more than hobble with great assistance in her nightdress to the washroom. Though still stooped, and with Eloise supporting her under one arm, she was dressed with her hair thoroughly combed and pinned up.

"Granny Rose is well." Eloise grinned up at Mrs. Stromberg.

"We may want Dr. Truman to tell us what he thinks." Belinda looked closely to discern whether the color she saw in Mrs. Stromberg's cheeks was artificial.

"You look wonderful." Hayden stepped into the aisle to take Mrs. Stromberg by the elbow. "But perhaps you should sit down. Take my seat."

"Get the porter," Mrs. Stromberg said. "Ask him to convert the berth immediately. I am not spending another day playing the invalid."

Eloise gasped. "I hear the engine. I hear the engine!"

Around them the shuffling and morning resituating paused briefly. Passengers froze their steps down the aisle. Women quieted the rustling of skirts. Feet stilled beneath the benches. Belinda held her breath, listened, and looked at Hayden. He nodded slowly and turned up one half of his mouth.

The train lurched and then began a steady chug. A cheer went up. Already the train was picking up speed.

Hayden settled Mrs. Stromberg into his seat and cautioned Eloise not to crowd Granny Rose. Virginia, who had wakened with the start of the train's motion, dashed to the washroom and came back in a presentable state. Eloise held Mrs. Stromberg's hand and with her other hand pointed out the window at the expanse of glistening white.

"It looks like mountains," Eloise said. "They just keep going and going."

She was right, Hayden thought. Along the tracks mounds of snow shoveled and pushed aside rose in rugged peaks and fell in craggy valleys. Every slope was different. Beyond the piles were wide, untrampled fields of pristine snow.

"The sunlight is dancing," Eloise said.

She was right again. Light reflected with such brilliance that Hayden had to squint.

He reached for Belinda's hand, lying on the seat between them and half hidden under her skirt. They would have children of their own someday, he hoped, but none of them would be Eloise.

"I want to talk to you," he said softly. "Can we go for a walk?"

She nodded.

Hayden leaned across the opening between the benches and tapped Eloise's knee. "Miss Michaels and I will be back soon. Can you sit quietly with Granny Rose?"

He stood up and stepped aside to allow Belinda to lead the way up the aisle. When they got to the platform between cars, she turned to him smiling.

"Are we going to sneak another kiss?"

He shook his head. "This time I really did want to talk."

She sobered. "You sound serious."

"I feel serious. I feel full and satisfied and grateful. But I'm also starting to feel lonely for Eloise."

"I know what you mean," she said.

"It's ridiculous for a grown man to feel this way about another man's daughter, but I hate the thought of leaving her."

"Do you?"

He nodded. "I wondered what you might think of living in San Francisco."

Her eyes widened and her lips parted. "You don't even know for certain that Gerald intends to settle in San Francisco."

"In my head, I know you make a perfectly logical point. In my heart, I feel this is what he has in mind."

"But we don't have any idea why Gerald left you that note. He did something outrageous, leaving his daughter with you with no explanation."

"Very true. Do you know what? I don't care anymore what his reasons were. Eloise is a secure little girl who trusts her father without a shred of doubt. I knew him well enough when we worked together to know he only has her best interests at heart."

"Mmm. San Francisco."

"Mrs. Stromberg will be there, too," Hayden pointed out.

"My parents will take some convincing. San Francisco is a long way from Denver."

"Granted," Hayden said, "this trip turned out to be full of unplanned adventure, but most of the time the trains run on schedule. George Pullman will bring his luxury sleepers to the line, and traveling will only get more comfortable. Visiting won't be so hard."

Belinda moistened her lips and nodded. "You're right. We should consider San Francisco."

The door opened behind them and a porter stepped out. "Mr. Fairbanks?"

"Yes?"

"A telegram has come for you. Your friends said you had walked this way." The porter handed an envelope to Hayden.

"Thank you." Hayden ripped open the envelope. "It's from Gerald."

"What does he say?" Belinda tried to read over his shoulder.

"Stranded train in news reports. Are you aboard? Please confirm E is safe. Awaiting you in SF." There was another line, but it was for Eloise.

"Shall I send a reply, sir?" the porter asked.

"Yes, please. Tell him 'All safe. Train moving. E sends love.' "

They scrambled back up the aisle. Belinda's mind churned. She was surprised at Hayden's suggestion of moving to San Francisco but relieved at the same time. How could one little girl cause them to make such a drastic change? Belinda took a deep breath. New track was laid every day in dozens of lines. Once two major lines had connected in Promontory Point, Utah, two years ago, railroads were building with frenzy, every line looking for the fastest way to connect to the transcontinental route. Sleeper cars got more luxurious every year.

And every city had newspapers, Belinda told herself. Hayden was a dedicated reporter and a talented writer. He would find work easily enough.

Hayden and Belinda slid back into their seats across from Virginia, Eloise, and Mrs. Stromberg.

"We got a telegram from your father," Hayden said.

"Papa?" Eloise sat up straight.

"He's in San Francisco," Belinda said. "He's just waiting for you to get there."

"He has a special message for you." Hayden held up the telegram. "Come over here and see."

"I don't know how to read very many words."

"We'll help you," Belinda said.

Eloise nestled between Hayden and Belinda. Hayden unfolded the telegram, and Belinda glanced at the final line, the one Hayden hadn't read aloud earlier.

She put her finger under the first word. "Do you know what sound *T* makes?"

"*Tuh.*"

"*Tell.*" Belinda moved her finger.

"I know this word. *My.*"

"The next word is a big one. It says *sweetie.*"

"That's me!" Eloise strung the words together. " 'Tell my sweetie.' "

"Do you know this word?" Belinda moved her finger.

"*Her!* And that word is *papa.* 'Tell my sweetie her papa.' "

Belinda couldn't wait any longer. " 'Tell my sweetie her papa loves her'! That's what it says."

Eloise sighed dramatically in satisfaction. "I can't wait to see Papa."

"I hope I shall get to meet him," Mrs. Stromberg said.

"Of course you will," Eloise answered. "You're my Granny Rose now."

Belinda swallowed the knot of joy in her throat.

"My papa taught me another song," Eloise said. "Let's sing it."

"All right," Hayden said. "You start us out."

Eloise took a deep breath. "Joy to the world, the Lord is come!"

Christmas, Maybe

by Janet Spaeth

Thy mercy, O LORD, is in the heavens;
and thy faithfulness reacheth unto the clouds.

PSALM 36:5 KJV

Chapter 1

Put the lily in the center, Suzette. Remember, the tallest goes in the middle, or else the arrangement will be out of balance. Keep the direction of the eyes in mind. Draw them upward, to God."

Suzette Longmont sighed and tried again, but the lily drooped to the right. The poor thing had been repositioned so many times that the stem was nearly broken.

Why couldn't people just let the flowers live in the garden, enjoying the sunlit days of summer until winter claimed them? The lily had done nothing to warrant the torture that she'd put it through.

"Watch me," Mother said. "We'll make this a suitable arrangement for tonight's dinner. Remember that we have guests. The planner for the new public garden will be here, and he will appreciate the glory of the blossoms."

Her mother's elegant fingers took the nearly wilted white flower from Suzette and, with an easy movement, righted it so it stood in the vase. "See?" she said.

She picked up three of the cut blossoms from the table beside her.

"Now we'll add other flowers and greenery to give it some strength so it will stand. Flowers are like people. The lily has suffered, but the other blooms will hold it up."

She added delicate pink roses and a cluster of fluffy blue hydrangeas, and tucked baby's breath and ferns throughout. A dramatic drape of bleeding hearts finished the arrangement.

It took only moments, but it was stunning. And, for Suzette, impossible.

"I couldn't even get the first flower to go in straight," she said.

Mother smiled. "It helps to really want to be able to do it."

"I don't have any talent for it." Suzette leaned her head against her mother's shoulder.

Mother's hand smoothed Suzette's hair. "Honey, you have to decide what it is you want to do. Flower arranging isn't, in the Lord's eyes, the most important activity. He already arranges flowers according to His will."

Suzette frowned. That was it exactly. Even her mother's beloved gardens, even her newly designed solarium where plants could be fooled into blooming year round, even the discussions of landscaped parks in the midst of the city's bustle—none of them could compare to the glory of wildflowers blooming as they were planted by the Maker's hand.

"Look at what you have to work with," Mother said, reaching out to the arrangement, her slender forefinger lifting one of the bleeding hearts and repositioning it. "Think of what's in front of you, and, using the gifts of each flower, put them together. They're not that different from people. We all have our strengths, our talents, which the Lord has given us. We need to gather together in beauty."

Suzette sighed. "And that's why you do the flowers, and I don't."

Her mother laughed. "You'll learn, my darling. You'll learn. Now, let's go into the kitchen and see how the evening's bread is going."

Suzette trailed after her. It seemed as if her mother was on a mission lately to make sure Suzette had all the housewifely duties well in hand. And she knew why.

Sure enough, as they entered the kitchen, Mama said, "You should wear your navy silk tonight."

"My navy silk?" Suzette took a deep breath. "It's heavy and hot."

"I know, but it makes your eyes even brighter. It's a good color on you, and the gloss of the silk adds a nice color to your cheeks."

"That's because I perspire so much in it."

Mama laughed lightly. "It's the price we pay for being ladies. At least we're not dressed like the men, in starched shirts, and vests and jackets and ties."

"I'd really rather wear one of the calicos. They're light and much more comfortable."

"Tonight, though, I'd rather you wore your navy silk. It goes so well with your dark brown eyes and dark hair, and you want to look good. Harrison is going to be there, after all."

Suzette resisted the urge to roll her eyes.

Harrison Farrington.

Their parents had, since Suzette and Harrison were children, plotted the young people's destiny. One day—one day soon, they clearly hoped—the two would be married.

Suzette couldn't imagine a worse fate. It wasn't that there was anything wrong with Harrison. He was kind and attentive, well-mannered, polite, with a solid future as an accountant in his father's department store—all in all, everything a woman should desire in a man.

If only he weren't so. . .boring.

That was it. He was boring. After eleven years of knowing him, she still only knew him by the adjectives that described him. She didn't know *him*.

He seemed to have no interests. Did he enjoy novels? She had no idea. Poetry? Possibly. Art? How would she know? Whenever she'd broached any of these topics, he had tossed it back to her and asked for her opinion.

He was nice. But he was boring.

Her musings were cut short when her mother stopped suddenly at the table in the kitchen.

"Suzette, did you remember to put yeast in the bread dough?"

There were two bowls on the table, both covered with red-and-white checked cloths. One bowl was mounded on the top, obviously with risen dough under it. Obviously, too, the one her mother had made.

The second bowl had no such mound. In fact, the cloth had collapsed into the bowl.

Next to it, in mute and guilty testimony, was the packet of yeast.

Mama's silence spoke volumes.

"I'm so sorry," Suzette cried, rushing to take the cloth off the bowl. The dough sat at the bottom, crusting a bit on the top, exactly the same as she'd left it earlier in the afternoon. She picked up the yeast package. "It's too late to put this in, isn't it?"

Her mother nodded. "We can rescue this. Waste not, want not."

In a quick series of steps, the bread board was floured, the wayward dough was plunked onto it, and Mama's hands patted the dough into a flat rectangle. She carefully draped the cloth back over it and turned to her daughter with a smile.

"Before our guests arrive, we'll butter the top, sprinkle on rosemary and salt, and bake it. We can serve it with the soup. The men will like that. They can dip it into the broth. The two savories—the herb on the bread and those in the chicken soup—will complement each other nicely. Actually, dear Suzette, you may have invented something brilliant here."

"I did it?" Suzette shook her head. "Not at all. You did it, and I know you too well. You'll give me the credit."

Her mother shrugged. "Some of the best inventions were creations born of seeming failure. Why don't you do this instead?" She motioned toward a bowl of strawberries. "Slice them for the topping on the cheesecake."

That she could do, and it was something she loved. The summery scent of strawberries rose as she cut into them. She popped one into her mouth whole, not worrying about the fact that a bit of the juice was now trailing onto her chin. Some things in life were perfect. Strawberries were one of them.

Too soon the fruit was sliced into ruby circles, and her mother sprinkled a light dusting of sugar over them. "That will make the strawberries juice up, which we need for the topping."

Everything her mother did was magic. She knew exactly what to do and how to do it. And she was patient, endlessly patient with her daughter.

Mama put the strawberries aside. "I'll finish the bread and prepare the chickens."

Suzette grinned at her. "Need my help?"

Her mother laughed.

"It might be faster if I don't help," Suzette said.

"You're doing fine. You're only eighteen, and you're old enough to learn, and that's what you're doing. Now, go on upstairs and decide what you're going to wear, dear. Our guests will be here in less than two hours."

Once in her room, Suzette sank onto her bed. Her room, with the thick draperies blocking out the sun, was cool but closed. Summer in St. Paul could be extremely warm, and now, with the still-heavy heat of September upon them, the thought of being encased in weighty silk was nearly unbearable.

She reached for her nightstand and opened the drawer. Inside, under the usual assortment of handkerchiefs and lotions, was a piece of paper.

Carefully she removed it and smoothed it over the brocade coverlet. It was a page torn from a magazine, an advertisement for a product, but she'd cut away the words so only the picture remained.

A girl was seated on a bucking horse, its pinto-spotted back saddleless. Her legs were covered with a deep coffee-colored leather fringed skirt, and on her feet were light brown riding boots. Her shirt was plaid with small pearl buttons along the front.

Her hair was unbound, trailing behind her in a glorious cloud of reddish-gold. The painter had caught her midwave, her cowboy hat held aloft.

She looked free and exactly opposite of how Suzette felt.

What would it be like to be her? To be riding across the prairie, the wind lifting her hair so that it trailed behind in a stream? What would it feel like?

She touched the braided bun at the back of her neck. A grown woman couldn't let her hair down, and she certainly couldn't let it be free in the wind, especially not while riding a galloping steed across the open prairie.

No, she had to wear an oppressive silk dress when the air was so hot it almost baked her like one of the chickens in the oven.

Her life was one of blessing. Her mother had taught her well on that part. Her family was well-off, and daily she benefited from that. There was always enough food, and it was deliciously prepared. In the winter she was warm, and in the summer she was cool. Her clothing was beautiful. She had a family who loved her. She closed every day with the same three words: "I am blessed."

She lacked for nothing.

It wasn't that she was ungrateful. In fact, it was just the opposite. God had given her so much. But should she live the life she'd been blessed with and accept it without question?

She'd been given the opportunity to do as her mother did. Mama supported charities—she was sure that tonight her mother would take the opportunity to promote one of her favorite causes, providing fresh produce to the needy, especially the elderly and the children of the community. She'd never seen her mother take advantage of the wealth they had except to find a way to use it for the good of others.

It wasn't that Suzette didn't want to do that. She'd offered as much as she could, guided by the skillful hand of her mother, but the fact was that in the midst of this, she had no vision of who she was. Her soul cried out to explore the world, to feel the wind in her hair, both metaphorically and physically.

Sometimes, although her mother had never shown the least amount of impatience or despair with Suzette's lack of abilities, she had those emotions about herself. She *was* impatient. The role she'd been given simply didn't fit her. It was like wearing someone else's shoes.

She looked at the picture one more time, feeling the longing in her heart, and with sadness she put it in back in the drawer.

Some things were just not meant to be. This was one.

She sighed and stood up and crossed to the armoire. It was elegantly carved teak, something her grandfather had brought back from one of his many trips overseas. It had made the voyage across the ocean, coming from some far-off land with an exotic name and interesting smells and unusual foods.

This armoire had seen more and done more than she had.

She resisted the childish urge to kick it, and instead opened the brass latch and took out the blue silk dress. Until something in the universe presented itself, the fact was that she was a rich girl in St. Paul, Minnesota, and that was her lot in life.

She could live with that. Maybe.

A thousand tiny buttons later, she was dressed for dinner. The aroma of roast chicken and freshly baked bread tickled her nose, and her stomach growled in anticipation.

Voices rose from the bottom of the staircase as she began her descent to join them. Some were familiar. She recognized the baritone of their minister, Reverend Williams, and the soft cadence of her mother's pleasant chatter. One voice she couldn't identify, and she guessed it was their guest.

As she joined the gathering in the parlor, her mother nodded at her. "Suzette, I'd like you to meet Eugene Caldwell. He's very active in the community garden project."

Mr. Caldwell rose and bowed. He was short, with closely cropped gray hair. "Miss Longmont, my pleasure indeed."

She curtsied slightly, feeling as if she were in an old-fashioned play with their courtly visitor and, behind their guest, saw her mother's eyes twinkle. "The pleasure is mine, sir."

Reverend Williams greeted her heartily, and by the side chair, she saw Harrison standing. "Suzette," he said.

"Harrison," she responded, summoning a smile she didn't really feel.

Every strand of his straight blond hair was in place. For a fleeing moment, she wondered if he'd ever dreamed of it disarrayed by the wind, but just as quickly as it came, she dismissed the thought. Harrison's life was as tightly ordered as his suit. Every bit of it was in order.

"Is Papa here?" she asked, turning back to her mother.

"He's delayed at his office, but he'll join us shortly," Mama answered. "Would you like some tea while we wait?"

The next half hour was filled with the sound of idle chatter, an art Suzette had never completely mastered. Harrison, she noticed, spoke only when spoken to—like a good child, she thought a bit nastily.

She had to quit that. He was a child of God. He had the right to her respect for that alone. He had never done anything to hurt her or anyone else, as far as she knew. She mentally rearranged her approach. Kind. She could be kind. She could.

Finally, Molly, their elderly housekeeper, made a brief appearance at the door to the room and motioned Mama over.

"Let's go on into dinner," her mother said. "I'm sure Joseph will be with us soon."

Suzette found herself sitting next to Harrison. Did he feel as uneasy as she did?

Mr. Caldwell spoke. "Your mother has told me that you prepared the lovely floral arrangement I see. It's as lovely as you are."

"Thank you," she began, "but—"

Her mother shook her head ever so slightly and interrupted her. "You may be interested to know that the flowers are from our solarium, Mr. Caldwell, and Suzette has shown a nascent talent in arranging."

Nascent? Suzette coughed into her napkin. Surely her mother meant *nonexistent.*

"You have a solarium here?" their guest inquired with interest. "Might I have a tour of it after our repast? The ability to grow blooms without regard to the external weather elements is fascinating to me."

"Of course you may," Mama answered. "It's very clever. Joseph saw one in Chicago, and he had one built in our house. We have only had it in operation for a few months, but so far it's quite charming. It's windowed, and cast-iron pipes will bring in steam in the winter to heat the room."

Reverend Williams added, "It's a lovely room, and we do quite enjoy the blossoms that the Longmonts share with us each Sunday. Why, as matter of—"

"I'm so sorry," Papa's voice boomed from the door of the dining room. "I was delayed by a courier, but I made the best time I could. I hope I'm not too late." He nodded at each of their visitors. "I'm glad to see you started without me."

"We have just begun," Mama said. "Now, let's try the soup. By the way, the cunning bread triangles are tinged with rosemary. I hope you like them. Again, we have Suzette to thank for them."

Suzette stifled a laugh. Her mother would never lie, and this was certainly not a falsehood. Only she neglected to mention that Suzette forgot to add the yeast, which resulted in having to invent a new culinary creation.

Dinner began in earnest, with many compliments from their guests and a lively discussion of the new community park and garden that were being planned. As Suzette had expected, her mother interjected her idea of a vegetable garden that would benefit those who weren't able to provide for fresh produce on their own.

She noticed that her father was unusually quiet. Occasionally he touched the breast pocket of his jacket, from which a slight piece of paper stuck out. What could it be?

Harrison didn't speak much as the others discussed the weather, the upcoming gardening project, the advantages of a strong railway system, and the growth of the city. Mama kept the conversation flowing, filling in adeptly for her husband's prolonged silence.

At last, Reverend Williams and Mr. Caldwell pronounced the dinner excellent, and after wiping their mouths on thick linen napkins, they adjourned to the parlor, where Mama served tea from china cups that had been in the Longmont family for years. They were so delicate that Suzette dreaded using them. She was sure eventually one would just shatter in her fingers.

After a tour of the solarium, which their guests pronounced splendid, Reverend Williams and Mr. Caldwell thanked the Longmonts for an excellent evening and left.

Harrison was reaching for his hat when Papa spoke abruptly as he withdrew the white rectangle from his pocket. "This is why I was late. I have a letter from Richard's Tom out in the Dakota Territory."

Suzette froze. Richard was her uncle, her father's brother. Her cousin, Tom, had married a lively woman named Winnie, and they'd moved to the Dakota Territory to try a new life. After they'd settled there, the announcement that a baby was on the way had been of some concern to Mama. Tom and Winnie were quite removed from them in Dakota, and they'd been adamant that they weren't returning to St. Paul so Winnie could have the baby in the new birthing hospital. What if something were to go wrong?

Compounding that had been the news that baby Annylee had been born in the midst of a tornado in early July. If the details of the event had gotten to Mama's ears, she hadn't shared them with Suzette. All she knew was that the baby was healthy and thriving.

Mama tilted her head and smiled. "Did he speak of their daughter? Annylee is such a lovely name."

"Winnie has broken both her arm and her leg in a bad fall, and Tom needs help," Suzette's father said bluntly. "She can't take care of the baby at all."

Everyone froze. Her mother's expression spoke volumes, as she was clearly trying to determine what to do to help.

Her father held the letter in his hand. His face was stony.

Beside her, Harrison stood, his hat partway to his head.

"I will go," her mother said, breaking the suspended moment. "I'll talk to the women at church to see if one of them is able to fill in for me and host the mission dinner. Oh, and the rally for the expansion to the sanctuary—that's next week—and, let's see, what else? Molly can certainly take care of the house and meals here. I can leave tomorrow afternoon, the day after tomorrow at the latest, and—"

Suzette heard herself speaking. "I'll go."

The three turned to her. "You?" they said in unison.

"I have no commitments. I can go."

"But it's the Dakota Territory," her father said. "It's wild. Untamed. Not at all predictable."

Her heart leapt as her mind began to unfold the plan. Wild? Untamed? Not predictable? It sounded like paradise.

She'd known Winnie since they'd been children. Winnie had lived next door to her for a while.

She remembered the early days with Winnie, when they both would play in the yard at Winnie's house, as they rode sawhorses left there by construction workers. It was a long-forgotten memory, buried under the day-to-day exercises of learning to become a woman of means.

Winnie's childhood had been the cause of much subdued discussion between Mama and Papa, conversations Suzette was sure they didn't know she was aware of. Winnie's mother had died when she was quite young, and she'd been raised by her father, a well-meaning man who was ill-prepared for single fatherhood.

When Winnie and Tom had met at the Longmont home, it had been truly love at first sight. Winnie had been invited to Suzette's fourteenth birthday party, which meant Winnie would have been nearly sixteen.

Tom had been there, a dashing young man of seventeen misspent years. His early life had also been the subject of consternation within the Longmont family. It wasn't that he had been bad. He simply hadn't had much of an interest in a career.

Marriage seemed to have settled them both—or so the families had hoped. And then, one day, they'd announced they were headed for the Dakota Territory to find their fortune in the free land being offered by the government.

As soon as they'd left, Tom's parents had gone on an extended European trip—probably, Suzette thought, to rest after the effort of raising Tom.

Letters had come from Winnie and Tom, letters of hope and promise, telling the Longmonts of the beauty of the territory. Crops, they'd claimed, fairly grew on their own. All one had to do was fling seeds onto the lush land and wheat grew. Corn grew. Vegetables of all kinds sprang up and prospered.

Or so the family had been told. Now they needed help.

Suzette looked at her parents hopefully. "How hard can it be?"

"But you can't—"

"You don't know—"

"It's not—"

The three spoke at once.

She laughed. "I know I can't arrange flowers, but is that going to be necessary out there? All I have to do is help with the baby. I'm only an extra arm and leg. That's all."

"It shouldn't be long," her mother said to her father. "And Winnie and Tom could use some assistance."

Her father's lips thinned as he pondered the situation. "I suppose, if it's not for too long."

"When will you come back?" They all turned as Harrison spoke. They'd forgotten he was there.

"I don't know," she said, laughing. "It's September now, so Christmas, maybe?"

Her father's glance shifted from Harrison to her mother. "It might be good for her, too."

Suzette seized upon the words. "It would be! I would learn to cook and garden and take care of the most beautiful baby in the world. Plus," she added, knowing that she was about to deliver the final point in her favor, "it's the godly thing to do."

For one very long minute, the world stopped moving. Suzette held her breath as her parents locked gazes, unspoken sentences winging between them.

She pleaded with God, begged Him, cajoled Him. *Please, God, let them say yes. Please. Please. Please.*

At last her father nodded. "All right. You may go. I'll arrange for a railway ticket for you tomorrow. But remember that we are here, waiting for you. I'll send enough money for a return trip home. Use it if you feel the need to."

Her mother hugged her then took her father's arm and left the room.

Harrison spoke again, this time softly. "Christmas, maybe. That's over three months away."

Three glorious months, she thought.

"You can come home sooner. Maybe you will," he continued. "You should, actually. The territory isn't safe for young women alone."

"I won't be alone. I'll be with Tom and Winnie and Annylee." She turned to him and stopped at the expression on his face.

For the first time, she saw emotion—clear, real, pure emotion.

He was sad.

⁂

Harrison sat alone in his room. He should go to sleep, he knew that, but the evening had taken a turn that he'd never expected.

So Suzette was leaving. Perhaps it was only for a brief period, but even the thought of that shook him more than he'd ever expected.

For as long as he could remember, their futures had been intertwined. Everyone, from the family to the community, assumed they'd eventually marry.

And so had he.

He stood up and paced the length of his room, his mind running through a litany of what he did wrong. He didn't ask her to go with him to any social events. He never tried to speak to her alone. He had not spoken his mind. He hadn't given her any indication that he felt anything more than an abstract friendship for her.

He simply wasn't interesting. He got up every morning, went to his father's railway transport business, opened the ledger, and wrote in small, neat, even letters. Then he came back to his family's home, ate dinner, and went to the living room where he sat with the dog and read the newspaper. Eventually, he retired to his room, picked up his Bible—he was determined to read it from Genesis to Revelation—and perused another chapter. Then he said his evening prayers and asked for God's grace on the poor, and went to bed.

Predictable. Boringly predictable.

What he wouldn't give for something to change. Anything.

At the base of it all, he knew, was that he had to change first. But what was he to do? He was an accountant. He was a good accountant, but did it matter? Perhaps there was nothing to do but accept what he was, and to realize that whatever he was, he'd have to be it without Suzette.

She was always on the move, energetic. Above all, she was funny. She could make him laugh, and that was a rare talent. He didn't laugh easily, but around Suzette he found himself smiling, mainly secretly, but smiling nevertheless.

She deserved someone like herself. A man who would live to his fullest, someone who could be everything she needed in life.

It wasn't him.

Tears pricked at his eyes, but he willed them away. Men didn't cry, even when their hearts were shattered.

He took his Bible from the nightstand and opened it to where he had left off. Ah, Jeremiah, the weeping prophet. He moved forward in the book to chapter 29 and read the words that he had memorized as a child: "For I know the thoughts that I think toward you, saith the Lord, thoughts of peace, and not of evil, to give you an expected end. Then shall ye call upon me, and ye shall go and pray unto me, and I will hearken unto you. And ye shall seek me, and find me, when ye shall search for me with all your heart."

It was the verse of promise. God had a plan for Harrison Farrington. But did that mean that he was to float through life, like a leaf on a stream? He looked at the last line of the familiar passage: "And ye shall seek me, and find me, when ye shall search for me with all your heart."

That was it. He needed to look for God—and Suzette, and love. God would never leave him, but Suzette would be gone tomorrow. It was almost too much to bear.

❦

The next afternoon, Suzette stood with her parents at the station, waiting for the train. Her hurriedly packed trunk was at her feet, and a sturdy valise rested against her side.

Papa told her to watch out for strangers, to guard her ticket, and to remember that a bank transfer was on its way to Fargo with enough money for a return trip home, as well as a liberal amount of money to contribute to Tom and Winnie's household.

Mama reminded her to mind her manners, even if it was the untamed Dakota Territory, to keep her hair tied neatly, and to always wear her bonnet to protect her face. She held on to Suzette's arm as if she could hold her back in St. Paul.

The sound of running footfalls echoed across the cavernous station. Suzette turned and saw Harrison. His usually neat clothing was disheveled, and his hair was no longer slicked into place. One strand fell over his forehead, and for a moment, she could imagine him on a horse, riding into the wild frontier.

"Suzette," he said, breathlessly. "I didn't want you to leave before I told you. . ."

His voice trailed off as he seemed to lack the words he needed.

"Yes?" she asked, her curiosity piqued.

"I wanted to tell you, that is, I thought I should. . .you understand. . ." His words plummeted over each other in an incoherent jumble.

His face was flushed—from running, or something else?

"It's just that—" He was interrupted by the blare of the train entering the station and drowning out the rest of his sentence.

The stationmaster motioned her rail-side, and she looked once more quizzically at Harrison. "What?"

He sighed. "I just wanted to say good-bye."

Her father hugged her and kissed her forehead, and her mother wrapped her in an embrace moistened with tears.

Impulsively, she opened her arms to Harrison. He reached for her, and as he held her to him, he murmured in her ear, "Suzette."

The time had come. She had to get on the train—and say farewell, for at least a while, to everything she'd known.

Her life was just beginning.

Hours later, Suzette sat next to the window, her nose pressed against the glass. A touch of early homesickness touched her, but she focused on the scene in front of her, pushing away the odd good-bye with Harrison.

She sat up straighter. He was nothing to her, she told herself. Instead, her future was ahead of her. The prairie flew past as the train chugged its way to the Dakota Territory, and the wheels on the tracks seemed to say one word, again and again.

Freedom. Freedom. Freedom.

Chapter 2

Suzette stood on the platform, her knees shaking from the long ride. All around her, people scurried, each one knowing his business. She, on the other hand, had no idea what to do.

None of them looked like Tom. The other passengers disembarking were greeted by family and friends, and soon she was left quite alone with her bags.

It would be all right, she assured herself. Tom would come and pick her up. Soon. He would be there soon.

She looked around at her first vision of Fargo. It was much bigger than she'd expected. There were substantial, squat brick buildings, and the station itself was really quite lovely. Planters bloomed with late flowers, and small trees surrounded the little depot.

She tugged her trunk closer to the bench that was provided, and she sank onto it.

What if Tom didn't come get her? What if she'd have to go into the station and right away buy a return trip ticket? Harrison would gladly come and get her. He always did the right thing, unlike her.

She couldn't do that. She just couldn't. If necessary, she'd find a nearby hotel and put herself up for the night, and the next day she'd find employment. Doing what, she had no idea, but at least it was a plan.

She shut her eyes for just a moment. She hadn't slept at all the night before she left, and she'd only napped for brief periods on the train. She was so tired, and the late afternoon sun was so warm.

"Suzette?"

She sprang to her feet, which was a mistake, as her legs had completely gone to sleep. She tumbled right onto the man standing in front of her.

Tom. She might not have recognized him if she hadn't known he was coming for her. It had only been a bit over a year since she'd seen him last, at his wedding, but he had aged a decade. A set of wrinkles creased his forehead, and what her mother called "worry lines" wreathed around his eyes.

"I'm sorry I'm late," he said, giving her a quick hug and reaching for her trunk and bag. "The baby was so fussy, and Winnie. . ."

His voice faded as he turned away. "Do you mind if we hurry on back? I don't like to leave them alone."

She trailed after him to the wagon he'd pulled up near the depot. He deposited the trunk and her bag in the back and helped her onto the bench beside him.

"How is Winnie doing?" she asked as he guided the wagon away from the station.

"She's doing fine." His mouth was set in a narrow line. After a pause, he added,

"Ah, who am I fooling? She's doing the best she can, but the baby takes a lot of care. We're both so glad you've come to help out."

Neither one of them spoke much, and they rode in uneasy silence out onto the prairie. The wind picked up, and she struggled to keep her bonnet on.

"It's always windy out here," he said. "There's nothing to stop it, and it gathers force as it heads across the open plains. It just blows and blows and blows, and the dust it carries seems to come right into the house."

As far as she could see, there was nothing except the occasional tree line. Tiny farmhouses dotted the landscape, most of them red. Small speckles moved across land, which was still green in the golden sunshine.

Overhead there was nothing but sky. No towering oaks. No lofty buildings. No smoke plumes from factories.

It was the clearest, purest blue sky she had ever laid eyes on. On the far horizon, three dollops of white hung suspended, distant clouds that held no threat of rain.

She'd never seen anything so beautiful.

"I should tell you," Tom said, keeping his eyes focused straight ahead, "that Winnie doesn't know I asked for help."

She spun around in the seat, losing the battle to keep her bonnet on. The ties cut into her neck, and impatiently she untied the hat and stuffed it into her lap.

"What do you mean? I thought—"

He looked miserable. "She is so set on us doing this on our own that every time I broached the idea, she shot it down. But there's Annylee. I'd do anything for her. And for Winnie. Maybe we could have managed on our own, but the way things are now. . ."

His voice trailed off.

"Does she know I'm coming?" Suzette's throat, suddenly dry with fear, contracted.

His face sagged. "She thinks you're coming to see Annylee." He paused. "Which you are, so that's not exactly a lie."

"Not exactly a lie?"

"I told her that you were coming for a visit and you wanted to see the baby." He looked at her, clearly begging for her understanding. "All that's true. You do want to see Annylee, don't you?"

"Of course I do. But I'm not comfortable at all with some kind of charade about why I'm here, Tom. She doesn't know that you contacted my father?"

"No."

Suzette chewed on her lip. There was no way she was going to go along with this pretense. "Tom, I can't. If you won't tell her, I will."

He nodded. "I'm no good at keeping secrets anyway. Not even at Christmas."

"Christmas is a long time away, but this is different. Promise me you'll tell her."

"I will."

"I'm going to hold you to that. Meanwhile, tell me about how things are going. How did Winnie get injured?"

"She fell." He took a deep breath. "The house isn't in the best of condition, to be honest. We're just starting out, you know, and it's sort of, well, ramshackle. I built it quickly, and it's very different from what you're used to. Not everything is done."

"I can understand that." For the first time since she'd volunteered to go, she thought about what awaited her. In her mind, Tom and Winnie and Annylee lived in a charming little house, with flowers around the perimeter and productive fields surrounding the homestead.

"We're almost there. You'll see."

She made some valiant—if unsatisfying—efforts at putting her hair to rights, but the wind that blew across the prairie undid it all. Her valise was at her feet, and she dug into it to find a clean handkerchief. She quickly scrubbed her face, trying to clear away the cinders from the train and the dust from the plains.

He laughed. "After a while, you get to realizing that it's useless. As long as the wind blows, which is daily, you'll be a bit grimy."

Within minutes, he pulled up in front of their home. Suzette tried not to be horrified at what she saw.

It was much smaller than she'd imagined. In fact, it wasn't much larger than her mother's new solarium. How could two people and a baby live in it? How could *three* people and a baby live in it, now that she was here?

The wooden exterior was unpainted, and in the windows she could see only pieces of cloth hung in lieu of real curtains. No flowers surrounded the home. Instead of a grassy lawn, there was only bare dirt with occasional scrubs of prairie grass.

An outbuilding stood to the side. It was no more than an obviously constructed hut, with a wide-open door hanging at a rakish angle. She could see inside it from the wagon and noted that there were some large machines in there and a makeshift stall. It must be what served as a barn.

The door to the house opened, and Winnie hobbled out and waved with her uninjured arm. Tom leapt from the wagon and ran to her side. "Winnie, honey, you shouldn't be up! Where's Annylee? Is she all right?"

"She's fine, and I'm fine," Winnie responded with the same laugh that Suzette remembered, and that cheered her immensely. Whatever was wrong here, her childhood friend had kept her sense of humor. "And look who's here! Suzette!"

Suzette ran to her side and hugged her. "Winnie, I'm so glad to see you again! It's been so long, and we have much catching up to do. And, of course, I must see that beautiful baby girl."

Winnie held Suzette tightly with her free arm. "I'm delighted you're here. As you can see, our accommodations aren't what you're used to, but you are so welcome. How long can you stay?"

Suzette looked at Tom over Winnie's shoulder, and said, "Christmas, maybe."

"Christmas! Why, that's months away! Three months!" Winnie grinned. "You were always such a prankster. Well, come on in. Annylee is asleep but, honestly, she looks like an angel when she's in dreamland."

Suzette's heart sank when she saw the interior of the house. The furnishings were minimal and quite worn. Tom and Winnie must have gotten them used, perhaps as cast-offs from other settlers.

There were two upholstered chairs, with the cloth so threadbare that the white stuffing shown through, and an unpainted rocking chair was placed in the far corner. A tiny table sat in the middle of the room, and she realized as she saw the stove next to it that the single room served as both the parlor and the kitchen.

A cloth hung over a doorway, hiding what must be the sleeping quarters.

But in the middle of the room was the centerpiece of the home—a bassinette draped with netting, and from inside it came little sounds, like a kitten mewing.

Tom walked over to it and pulled back the netting. He reached inside and gently lifted out the baby. Suzette's heart swelled when she saw the complete tenderness in his expression as he lifted Annylee to his face, kissed her gently, then held her against his cheek.

"The Bible says, 'For where your treasure is, there will your heart be also.' Suzette, meet our treasure, Miss Annylee Longmont."

He shifted his shoulder so the baby faced her. Her cheeks still rosy from her nap, she smiled faintly and looked at Suzette with eyes as blue as the Dakota sky.

Suzette felt herself being drawn toward the baby. She'd never had much to do with infants. They slept quite a bit, and when they were awake, they were either being cleaned or fed or getting ready to sleep. She much preferred toddlers, who had clear personalities and were mobile and could play.

However, with that single look, Annylee had changed Suzette's opinion.

"Can I hold her?" she asked softly.

Annylee snuggled against her father's jacket and blinked shyly at Suzette.

"Of course," he said, and cradling his daughter in his hands, he offered her to Suzette.

Annylee came to her easily. It was almost as if she knew what to do more than Suzette did, as the baby adjusted her length against Suzette's, curling her knees up against Suzette's chest until she found the softest part in the crook of Suzette's neck to nestle in.

And then Annylee sighed.

With that single exhalation, Suzette was won over. How could a single breath carry such comfort, such happiness, such peace? And yet it did.

The baby's head rested against her own skin. Suzette ran her fingers through Annylee's hair, as pale gold as an early morning sunbeam and as soft as a whispered promise. She was so tiny. Her delicate little fingers closed into tiny fists, and then her arms reached out and she yawned.

Suzette had never seen anything or anyone as simply and purely beautiful as Annylee.

Then Annylee's miniature face crumpled and she let out a cry.

"I think you'd better let me have her," Winnie said. "I imagine she's hungry."

Reluctantly, Suzette handed the baby back to her mother, who sank into the rocking chair by the window.

"Let's go outside, and I'll show you around the farm, such as it is," Tom said, and they left Winnie and Annylee to give them some privacy.

All Suzette knew about farming was what she'd seen in books and the occasional magazine, but this looked nothing like those pictures. The horse, which Tom had neglected to unhook from the wagon, grazed as well as it could in the same spot it had been left in.

A horse. A real prairie horse. It looked stockier and more muscular than the ones her parents had. And much, much bigger.

Carefully she reached out and tentatively patted its neck. "Good horse," she said weakly.

Tom laughed. "This is Whirlwind. He came prenamed. He used to belong to the neighbors, and their seven-year-old son named him that. He hasn't quite lived up to the moniker." He unhooked the horse from the wagon and led it to the shed.

She followed him, and as her eyes adjusted to the dark interior, she tried not to show her dismay.

"This is what passes as our barn," he said. "I'm not sure—I don't know what we'll do when the cold comes. It was touch and go last winter. We were blessed with a rather warm season, or so they tell me."

"How do you protect the horse when it's cold?" she asked.

"We put bales of straw up along the inside walls, and that worked fairly well. I also added bulwarks along the lower parts of the outside, and that helped, too. Of course, that also meant that we had visitors all winter long."

"Visitors?"

"Mice mainly, but the occasional skunk and raccoon came in, and the squirrels took advantage of it, too."

"Ah." She tried not to shudder. It was worse than she'd thought.

He looked at her squarely. "Suzette, this is the prairie. We don't live here alone."

She watched from the safe distance of the doorway as he made sure that Whirlwind had water and hay, and then the two of them walked out into the farmyard.

Again she was struck by how scruffy the land looked. Where were the orderly fields of grain? The neat green of the grassy expanses? Wagons filled with the wealth of the soil?

"We have a garden," he said, as if reading her mind. "Ever since the baby and Winnie's accident, we've let it go somewhat, but I have a great wife, and she got quite a bit put up for the winter."

"You have to prepare for winter in ways we don't," she said, mainly to herself, but he answered.

"Indeed. It's not easy. We were poorly prepared for our first winter here, and I can't say we're much better off for our second one. But we have time."

"And I'm here," she added with a false confidence.

"Exactly," he said. "I know how much your mother has taught you about cooking and gardening, and that will be of great help to all of us."

She chewed on her lip. There was no way she could lie. "She's *tried* to teach me, you mean. I haven't been the best student."

He laughed. "I'll believe it when I see it."

Uh-oh. This was not going well.

Fortunately, he redirected her attention to the garden, and they walked over to see it. It was at the side of the house, and from what she could see, they were growing a great crop of dried stalks and faded bushes. She leaned over a row of shriveled fern-like tops.

"Carrots, I presume?"

"That's what we hope."

She dug around the top of one and pulled out a rather withered orange root. "When were these last watered?"

He shook his head. "Last week, maybe?"

A droplet of perspiration dripped from the end of her nose. "I don't think that's enough. Where's the well?"

He pointed to the pump near the back of the house. "It's pretty good. There's an aquifer we've tapped into."

She sagged in relief. "Good. We'll get to that this afternoon then. And how about the farming itself? What are you growing?"

She was surprised at how knowledgeable she sounded. Maybe some of her mother's efforts had taken root. She grinned to herself at the pun.

"We're making an effort at wheat, but I haven't had much time to focus on it lately." He nodded toward the field, the husks rustling in the wind.

"We'll work on that, too." *If I have any idea what to do, that is,* she said to herself.

"Let's go back in and see if Winnie and Annylee are ready for us. This sun is a scorcher, isn't it? This is one time when the wind actually seems welcome."

Suzette took one last look at the pitiful garden and followed him into the house.

Winnie was singing softly to Annylee. Suzette recognized the melody. It was the hymn "Children of the Heavenly Father." They'd learned it in church school as children themselves.

"Would you like to hold her again?" Winnie asked, and Suzette took the adorable infant from her arms.

"She smells so good," she said.

"She doesn't always," Winnie retorted with a chortle.

"I imagine," Suzette said, burying her face in Annylee's hair.

"So," Winnie said, "tell me what's going on. How is your mother doing?"

Gladly on the safe topic of her family, Suzette told them of her mother's new interest, the solarium, and her father's solid dedication to his work.

"And others?" Winnie asked with a sly wink.

"Others?" Suzette asked blankly.

"Well, look at you, holding that baby and looking for all the world like a little mother yourself. When are you and Harrison going to marry and start your own family?"

Suzette froze in place. "Marry? I'm not—Harrison and I aren't—why would you say such a thing?"

Tom cleared his throat. "I think I'll make us some tea while you two chat. Suzette, how do you like it? With sugar? It's so warm, but a nice hot drink might cool us off."

Winnie waved him away. "Quit trying to change the subject, Tom. Suzette and I are talking about Harrison and when Suzette is going to marry him and have babies."

"We were not!" Suzette protested. "I'm not going to marry him!"

"Admit it. He has a place in your heart. You're going to have to acknowledge it."

"He doesn't." Suzette shook her head vigorously, but there was something catching at her, something that she dismissed. He was just a friend.

"You two are destined to be together. Your parents began planning it when you two were cradled in the same nursery at church. Everybody knows you're going to marry him."

"Everybody except me, apparently." Suzette smoothed the hair back from Annylee's forehead, marveling at the texture of her skin, and driving away the memory of the way his hair had fallen across his brow, the way he had held her, the way he spoke her name.

"Take my word on it," Winnie said. "You two will be married within a year."

"I don't think so. For one thing, he's not here, is he? And for another thing, I don't love him."

"Give it time. Things come in time. Or, the realization comes in time—the realization of what's been in your heart but you were too stubborn to see."

Suzette snorted. "There's nothing in my heart right now for Harrison. And I don't want to talk about him anyway."

"You'd rather talk about tea, wouldn't you?" Tom interjected smoothly. "It's all ready for you."

As the three of them sipped tea and Annylee gurgled happily in her bassinet, Tom and Winnie took turns telling her about living on the prairie, their words tumbling over each other in their still new excitement about the beauty around them.

"What about winter?" Suzette asked. "Is it as bad as I hear it is?"

Tom looked grim. "It's really cold, for sure. Of course, we've only been here for one winter, and we were told it wasn't bad, but nevertheless it was deadly cold. We spent most of the time in here, reading and rereading the books we have."

Winnie motioned toward the sparse shelf beside the rocking chair that held a few volumes. "Tom and I took to reading Shakespeare's plays out loud. I have to say, he makes a fantastic Richard II."

They smiled at each other, and the love telegraphed between them, still as bright and vivid as the day they were married.

"It's not all bad. Everything has something good in it if you'll just open your mind to it," Tom said philosophically. "Like spring here."

"The spring—oh, the spring, Suzette! It happens almost overnight!" Winnie's face glowed as she drew pictures in the air with her fingers. "The trees burst out with pale green buds, and here and there little flowers pop up, and you want to kiss each and every one because you're so glad to see them!"

"It does seem to occur that quickly," Tom added. "One day you're so frozen and you've despaired of winter ever ending, and then the earth turns green. It's wonderful."

"Tell me about the town," Suzette prompted.

"Hope?" Tom asked. "It's small. It has the usual businesses, like a post office and a bank."

"And the best church ever." Winnie leaned forward. "We haven't been there lately because it's dreadfully hard to go anywhere right now. It's simply called Hope Church, and it fits its name. We get so much encouragement from the services. The man who is our minister is also a farmer here, so he understands us."

"There is a store there, too, but unfortunately it's closing in a few weeks. The owners are going back to Wisconsin. I don't know what will happen if someone doesn't take it over before they leave."

"How far would you have to go for supplies then?" Suzette asked.

He frowned. "Probably all the way to Fargo. You know what that's like. In good weather, it's not bad, but what we'll do in winter, I have no idea. I know the present owners have advertised as far away as Minneapolis, so we do what we do best here in Hope—we hope."

"We'll be fine," Winnie said reassuringly, patting her husband on the arm. "You'll think of us this winter, sitting in your nice home, and be at ease knowing we're just fine here."

"About that," Tom began, and cleared his throat. "About that. Winnie, Suzette is here for as long as we need her. She's come to help us out for a while."

"Really?" Winnie looked from Tom to Suzette and back again. "Really?"

"I hope you don't mind," Suzette said. "I really do want to be here for as long as you need me. You know I've always wanted to live out in the Wild West, and the wild Dakota Territory is just the ticket. So it would be good for both of us. . .if you want."

Winnie beamed. "Are you teasing me? Please tell me you're not teasing me! Suzette, there's nothing I'd like more! It'll be just like old times—but with a baby and a husband."

Suzette exhaled in relief. This was going to be all right.

"How long can you stay?" Winnie continued.

"As long as you need me. If it gets too cramped here, I can move into town, too. But first, let's get things settled here," Suzette said with a confidence she didn't really feel.

"You're welcome for as long as you want." Winnie reached across the table and grasped Suzette's hand. "I'm so glad you're here."

❧

As Suzette laid across the makeshift bed that Tom had made for her in the tiny living room, she tossed and turned. This was not the same as her comfortable four-poster back in St. Paul, but she wouldn't change it for the world.

This was her adventure, and best of all, she knew she'd be able to help Tom and Winnie and Annylee. It was what she had prayed for.

Yet she had many things to do here. Was she up to the task? Why hadn't she paid more attention to the lessons her mother had tried to teach her? The garden was nearly dead. The house was in complete disrepair. Their furnishings were, at best, minimal.

They had so little—and yet they had so much.

She thought of Harrison—and her heart turned, just a bit. She missed him. It was an odd sensation, and she told herself she was just overtired.

And she hadn't said her prayers yet. She closed her eyes and phrased the simplest plea she knew: *Dearest God, I'm here, and I know You're here, too. Will You help me? Will You help them? Please?*

Outside she heard the low rumble of thunder and then the steady splat on the roof and the hard ground, as if a thousand tiny pebbles were falling.

She finally dozed off, listening to the blessed sound and knowing it was rain.

❧

Harrison sat in his parents' house and opened the newspaper.

The usual issues of crime, politics, and general mayhem filled the front page. He sighed. How could people take advantage of each other this way?

Christmas, Maybe

Aimlessly, he flipped through the pages, scanning the occasional humorous bit, looking at the advertisements for products he'd never use. There was an article about plans for the upcoming holiday festivities, if the funding could be found and if everything could be put into place. Christmas was so far away, and yet, as the mayor said, if they wanted to make it happen, the time was now to start.

It was a good point, but he couldn't get interested in Christmas. He'd heard what Suzette had said. "Christmas, maybe." It might be three months on the calendar, but it was an eternity in his heart.

Suddenly something caught his eye. Something—interesting. Something that had meaning. Something that could change his life.

He had to do this. He had one chance, and this was it. No matter how difficult it was going to be, he had to do it.

Resolutely, he stood up, tucking the newspaper under his arm. He climbed the stairs to his bedroom and sat in the chair in front of his desk. Taking the pen from the drawer of his desk, he leaned over a piece of paper from the stack beside him and began to write.

After a while, he took up his Bible again and reread the verse from Jeremiah. What he had to do, he had to do with all his heart. It was about time he started.

Chapter 3

The storm lashed against the tiny house, and the walls shook from its fury. The sky, even at midafternoon, was sunless and low with thick gray clouds. Bursts of lightning creased the iron-colored darkness, and thunder rumbled from one horizon to the other. Rain fell in heavy torrents, windblown to nearly horizontal sheets.

Annylee fretted constantly. She wanted to be held. She wanted to be put down. She wanted to be rocked. She wanted to be fed. She wanted to be sung to. She wanted to be played with. She wanted to be soothed.

"Basically," Winnie said, her patience worn to a frazzle, "she wants this rain to stop."

"I would, too," Suzette said, "except it's good for the garden—if it hasn't washed away every single withered carrot and dried-up cucumber."

She picked up Annylee and took her to the window. "Look, baby! God is watering the earth for us. Isn't that nice of Him? And listen to Him! He's saying, 'Watch this, Annylee!' Look at the pretty lights!"

Annylee was quiet, watching the lightning as Suzette rocked her back and forth, humming softly, until at last Annylee began to breathe evenly, and she knew that the baby had drifted off to sleep.

Gently, Suzette put Annylee in her cradle, and the three adults relaxed.

"I forgot to give you the gifts my parents sent!" she whispered, afraid to wake the slumbering Annylee. "They're in my trunk."

She knelt in front of her trunk and dug out a sewing kit and several yards of a pale yellow sprigged calico, a box of chocolates, a book of nursery rhymes, a bar of scented soap, and a packet of flower seeds. Winnie and Tom opened the candy immediately.

"This is such a treat," Tom said. "It's been ages since I've had a good piece of chocolate."

Winnie nodded in agreement and pointed at the trunk. "What's that?" she asked through a mouthful of dipped caramel.

"Promise you won't laugh?" Suzette asked.

"Not a chance. You know us." Winnie grinned. "Why? What is it?"

Suzette took out a carefully wrapped flat package and opened it.

"I don't believe it!" Winnie leaned forward. "It's the picture, isn't it?" She explained to Tom, "For as long as I've known Suzette, she's treasured this picture she cut out of a magazine. What was it, an advertisement for soap flakes?"

"I don't even remember." Suzette gazed at the image of the young woman on horseback. "I've had it for years."

Tom tilted his head and looked at it. "She looks happy."

"She looks free," Suzette said.

"When we were little," Winnie told Tom, "she'd pretend that she was this woman. She even got one of her father's coats and cut the sleeves, trying to make fringe."

Suzette chuckled. "I thought he'd go through the ceiling. He was so angry. I'd chosen his best jacket, and somehow, all I managed to do to it was ruin it."

"Women," was all Tom said, but he smiled as Winnie took the picture and put it on the bookcase.

The rain continued all day and into the next. Finally, there was a break, and the sun came back, and the land seemed to forget that there had ever been a storm. Instead, the grasses greened again, and even the garden seemed to perk up.

She waited for the earth to dry before venturing out into the garden. She'd been there almost two weeks, and so far she hadn't done much except sit in the house, helping Winnie cut the new fabric into a dress. They'd discovered there would be enough for a matching dress for Annylee, and the two women had spent hours figuring out how to put in the sleeves.

Grateful to be outside at last, Suzette tucked her skirts up and walked through the caked mud of the garden, pulling weeds that were clearly weeds, and leaving alone those which she didn't recognize. Time would tell if they were vegetables.

"It's really lovely out here," Winnie said, carrying Annylee with her good arm.

Suzette wiped her forehead with her hand, knowing that she was spreading dirt across her face but not caring.

She liked babies, as long as they were somebody else's, but Annylee, with her corn silk hair and bright blue eyes, was special. "Are you a pretty one?" she cooed to her. "Do you love your auntie Suzette? Oh, look at the birdie!"

Winnie's laugh behind her made her flush. "You're ready for a baby of your own."

"I think I might get married first," she retorted before she realized that she'd opened the conversation about Harrison again.

"It won't be long for you. I can feel it in my bones."

"Well, your bones are wrong."

Tom joined them. "I have to go into town this afternoon to get a machine part. Would you three ladies like to join me?"

Winnie shook her head. "As much as I'd like to, I think Annylee and I will stay here and enjoy the sunshine. You two go ahead."

Suzette almost skipped into the house to get her bonnet. Even though Hope was small, it was a town, and she couldn't wait to see what it held.

The road to Hope was rutted after the rain, and she felt as if every bone in her body was jarred as the wagon rattled its way into town.

"Do you suppose I could ride Whirlwind?" she asked, her eyes on the horse as it plodded its way along.

"Sure. Tomorrow would be good. The ground should be dry enough by then for a safe ride. I don't want him stepping in a soft spot and risk turning his leg."

She sat back and smiled. Whirlwind wasn't exactly a show pony, but he was a horse, and that was all that mattered.

The sun shone brightly and the air felt fresh and clean after the rain. She leaned back and let the warmth wash over her.

Soon he pointed ahead. "Look. There's Hope."

Ahead, a small knot of trees clustered together on the open plains—a prairie oasis. As they drew closer, she could make out the individual buildings.

Tom slowed down as they entered the town. "These are new," he said, indicating the houses that were around the perimeter. "We have a lot of hope for Hope." He chuckled at his own joke.

Most of the houses were recently painted, although a few were too new to have that amenity yet. They were neat and very small, and many of them displayed the pride the residents clearly felt about their community, with colorful curtains fluttering in open windows, and flowerpots along the entries, many of them with still-blooming plants.

"Here's the church. We'll get there this Sunday. We sure like it."

It was the largest building, and the white steeple pointed heavenward, adorned with a black cross. Really, she thought, it was simply a smaller version of the one she went to in St. Paul, and that made her happy.

He pulled the wagon to a stop next to the town square. "It's not much yet, but we're building a park here. We hope to have band concerts here next year. See the structure over there? That's the basis of what's going to be tiered seating."

It was charming. People walked along the street, and each one waved at them, some calling, "Hello!"

"Folks are sure friendly here," she said.

"Hope is a great little town. Now, if we can only get someone to buy the mercantile!"

He hopped off the wagon and came around to help her, but she was already on the planked sidewalk.

Already she liked Hope. It wasn't the Wild West at all, but it was lovely.

"The machine part should be at the store," Tom said.

She followed him inside. It was dark and cool and packed from one end to the other with all kinds of things from candy to brooms to horseshoes.

She went right to the ribbon reels as Tom inquired about his order. The thin white ribbon with tiny yellow flowers would be perfect for Annylee's new dress, and she could tie a little bow of it in her satiny hair to match. She trailed a length of it between her fingers, trying to determine how much she should buy.

They were the only customers in the store, and she heard a familiar voice.

She froze, the ribbon dangling from her fingertips, forgotten. That voice. She knew it well enough—she'd heard it nearly every day since she was a child.

She spun around. "Harrison?"

He stood behind the counter, in his suit as always, and smiling uncertainly at her. "Hello, Suzette."

She could barely breathe as a maelstrom of emotions overtook her. Anger won. "You followed me here."

"I did, and—" He cleared his throat. "I did, and I didn't."

Suzette sputtered. "This is terrible!"

Immediately she felt awful. His face fell, simply collapsed, and he looked down. "I'm sorry," he said.

Regret flooded her soul. Her mother had taught her better than this. She had no right to hurt him.

"I'm sorrier," she murmured.

"I'm sorriest."

She smiled at their old repartee. "Let's start over. Harrison, it's quite a surprise to see you here. What made you decide to come to Hope? Was it my parents? Did they put you up to this?"

"No!" he said with a surprising vehemence. "I came of my own volition."

"Really?" She tilted her head and studied him. She'd never known him to do anything that hadn't been squared away with either his parents or, in this case, hers. He grew in her estimation.

"I bought this store."

She laughed. He must be teasing her. "You did not."

"I did." He stood up straighter. "As of this morning, Carrifer's Mercantile is mine. The money exchanged hands and the paperwork was signed."

"Paperwork?" she asked.

"Of course there was paperwork. I'm a bookkeeper, remember?"

Tom reached across the counter and shook Harrison's hand. "Thank you. You have no idea what you've done for Hope. We were desperate, thinking that this store might be shuttered forever."

A man entered the store, and Tom said, "You have another customer. Why don't you come out to our place for dinner tonight, and you can tell us the whole story? I know Winnie would be glad to see you, and you can meet Annylee, the most beautiful baby in the territory."

Harrison looked at Suzette quizzically. "What do you think?"

Her world was still spinning from this recent turn of events, but she nodded. "Yes, come."

Tom drew him a quick map to their house, and as they left, he called over his shoulder, "If you find that part, bring it with you."

"I will. I'll see you later."

The words were spoken to Tom, but the message in his pale blue eyes was for Suzette.

⟡

In the apartment over the store, he knotted his tie yet again. How many times had he stood in front of a mirror and done this, yet now this action defeated him? It was sideways, it was uneven, it was crumpled.

Tonight could change the course of his life. He mused over the events of the afternoon, trying to gauge Suzette's reaction.

Of course she was surprised to see him. He had run scenarios in his head again and again on the train the day before, practicing what he'd say and do when he saw her, but when the moment came and she looked at him with those brown eyes that could, he was sure, see into his soul, he had floundered. Every single smooth response took wing and flew out the window, leaving him standing across the counter from her, blithering and blathering.

He frowned at his reflection. This tie was trouble. As he wrestled with it, he recalled the conversation with his parents the day before. They had been just as flabbergasted as she had been, and as much as his father had tried to poke holes in the plan, he hadn't been able to.

His mother, though, had taken a different approach. She'd asked him when she would see him again and he'd answered, "Christmas, maybe."

She hadn't spoken after that, allowing Harrison's father to bluster about the dangers of the Dakota Territory, the perils of investing in a business he hadn't seen and had no experience in, and the risk of leaving all that was comfortable. The more he spoke, the more Harrison's heart swelled with excitement.

After Mr. Farrington's speech had run its course, he'd departed to attend a meeting, leaving Harrison and his mother alone.

She didn't say anything for a moment. He had expected some tears from her, but instead an irrepressible smile flickered over her lips.

Slowly she poured a fresh cup of tea, offered one to Harrison, was refused, and painstakingly stirred in a partial teaspoon of sugar.

Still she didn't speak. She just sat down and let the smile out until her entire face was wreathed with amusement.

"Christmas, maybe?" she said at last. "How interesting."

He knew her too well. If he sat without saying a word, she would fill in the gaps. His father always said, " 'Nature abhors a vacuum,' and so does your mother."

Sure enough, she'd begun to talk. "You may fool your father, but you're not fooling me. I know you're going because Suzette is there, and that's a good thing. You need to speak your mind, my son. I've watched you two together, and I can feel something between you, but if you don't tell her what's in your heart, how is she to know? Is our Suzette a mind reader?"

She had a good point, but he sat stock-still, not responding.

She'd continued. "You know that we've always wanted you to find a good Christian woman, get married in a good Christian church, and raise good Christian babies. Of course, we'd hoped that the good Christian woman would be Suzette. And I think she is—she was raised well, and I'm sure her faith runs strong and true. The only thing more we could wish for you would be happiness and love. And I think you need to go and state your case."

Her eyes met his straight on. "Now, I do have a concern, and that's your idea that you'll stay out there, raising those good Christian babies, and I won't see you again. Promise me you'll come back for a visit."

He shook himself out of the memory and attended to his tie again. Every word his mother had spoken was true, and tonight was his first chance to make things right with Suzette.

And it all started with a tie that was knotted correctly.

He abandoned any pretense that the tie would lay flat. By the time he got there, he'd be disheveled anyway, thanks to the wind that rattled the window.

As he put on his coat, he remembered something else he'd heard his mother say often: *Never go empty-handed. Always bring a little something.*

He went down the stairs into the store and looked around. Pickles from the pickle barrel? A pair of new boots? A set of serving spoons?

He grinned at the idea of him walking into Tom and Winnie's house and offering any of those. Then he remembered that the store also sold fresh pies made by a woman in town.

He walked out of the store, a carefully wrapped apple pie in his hand, and stopped just as he was putting the key in the lock.

Ah.

A few minutes later, he had the apple pie—and the machine part Tom had ordered—tucked on the base of the wagon, and he headed out to meet his fate. To meet Suzette.

Suzette swept the living room so furiously that at last Winnie said, "If you don't stop, we won't have anything between us and the ground!"

She paused and leaned on the broom. "I just want it to be neat."

Winnie only smiled.

The goose that Tom had gotten earlier in the afternoon was cooking nicely in the small oven, and the aroma filled the little house. She'd found some carrots in the garden, and with the spinach that had taken heart from the rain and greened up, they had a good meal ahead of them. Under Winnie's tutelage, she'd made bread, too.

All in all, it was going to be a lovely dinner.

The creak of wagon wheels and the clop of a horse's hooves told her that he was arriving. With one hand, she smoothed the front of her dress and patted her hair to make sure nothing had escaped the low bun at the back of her neck, while trying to give the floor one last swipe with the broom she held in the other. None of her efforts were successful. Her dress would not lay flat, her hair would not stay put, and the floor was hopeless.

What did it matter? He was a friend. Only a friend.

He came to the front of the house, and before he could knock, Tom threw open the door. "Welcome!"

Harrison came into the house, and if he was surprised at the rather ramshackle surroundings, he didn't show it.

He smiled at them and shifted the packages he carried to shake Tom's hand and greet Winnie. He turned to Suzette and said simply, "Hello."

Why was her heart beating so loudly that he must surely hear it?

Annylee gurgled from the bassinette, and he crossed over to it. "Aren't you the most beautiful baby in the world? Yes, you are! You're so pretty, and, why, look at you! You're smart, too! Where did you get those big blue eyes? Did you know that your uncle Harry really loves babies? He does! What a sweetie you are!"

Winnie caught Suzette's attention and mouthed, "Harry?"

Suzette grinned at her and shrugged.

Harrison continued to coo at Annylee, the two of them making baby sounds in a conversation that only they understood.

Winnie said, "Sounds like somebody's ready for fatherhood."

She glared at her friend and turned her attention to Harrison, who had now tucked the package he still carried under his arms. He had withdrawn the ends of his tie from inside his vest and was dangling them in front of Annylee, who obligingly wiggled her hands in delight and babbled happily.

As she watched Harrison with the baby, she noticed the bottom of the package he held was wet and getting wetter. Something in it was spilling.

Tom must have noticed it, too, because he asked, "Could I take that from you? It looks as if the contents are leaking."

He flushed and held it out. "It's a pie. And," he added hastily, "the part you ordered, Tom."

Tom took the bundle and turned to hand it to Suzette, but stopped, laughing. "Suzette, dear cousin, it's probably time you let go of that."

She noticed with horror that she was still holding on to the broom, and she quickly popped into the bedroom to dispense with it. This was crazy, she told herself, to be acting like a little schoolgirl just because an old friend was visiting.

Visiting? It was more than that. Of course it was.

She lifted her head and returned to the living room. Harrison had seated himself in the rocking chair and was holding Annylee—and singing to her. Her downy head was cuddled in the nook of his arm, and her gaze was transfixed on him.

The song was the same one Winnie sang, "Children of the Heavenly Father."

Suzette leaned against the doorway and said softly, when he'd finished the last verse and was humming, "She's going to think that's the only song in the world."

Harrison shook his head slightly, so as not to disturb the moment with Annylee. "She'll have plenty of time to learn more. The world will introduce itself, song by song, and this bright little thing will know which is the best by what she hears from her mother."

"And from her uncle Harry," Winnie added.

"Yes, from her uncle Harry. I hope that's all right with you. I mean, she's not officially my niece."

"Yet." Winnie beamed triumphantly, as if she had just put the universe to rights.

He looked at Suzette and tilted his head. She swallowed hard to quell the funny thing going on in her stomach. He was—handsome. When did this happen?

Oh, this was not good. Not at all. Not at all.

Luckily, Winnie, who had hobbled over to check on the goose, pronounced it done, and they squeezed in together at the little table, which Winnie and Suzette had set with the best china—albeit somewhat pocked with chips and cracks. The bread, sliced and covered with a cloth, was tucked into a corner. The vegetables and the pie had been set beside the sink, and the goose, which Tom had taken out of the oven, was now on top of it.

Her mother would have put an artfully arranged bouquet in the middle of the table, but there was simply no room for it.

A ray of sunshine burst through the open curtain and bathed them in a golden glow.

"Grace." Tom spoke the word not as if it were a command, but as if it were a prayer of thankfulness itself.

They reached out and took each other's hands. With her left hand, she grasped Winnie's prairie-worn fingers, calloused and cut from the last bout of gardening they'd done in an attempt to retrieve the edibles from the spiny wild thistle.

Harrison held her right hand, his warm fingers twining into hers. Unlike Winnie's, his hands weren't coarsened with work but smooth and unlined.

"Harrison, would you lead us in the prayer?" Tom asked, and they all bowed their heads.

"Dearest Lord, our God, maker of all that we see and hear and breathe, we thank You for all the gifts You have given us. The food before us, we know You are the source. The friends and family around us, we know You are the source. The land outside us, the sky over us, the creatures that walk and fly and crawl beside us, we know You are the source. All are from You, and only You, and always You. We thank You. Amen."

Suzette lifted her eyes in amazement. "That was beautiful," she said to him. "I had no idea you could. . .you were. . .I mean, the words!"

"There is probably quite a bit you don't know about me, Suzette," he said, "and I about you."

The words she wanted to speak wandered in her mind, but before she could press them into sentences, Tom interrupted by passing the bread around the table.

"I'd rather hoped," Harrison said as he took a slice, "that you'd make that great flatbread you served in St. Paul."

"Flatbread? You mean *lefse*?" Winnie asked, referring to the Norwegian delicacy that many in the area ate.

"No, not lefse. I've had that. This was thicker, and herbs of some kind were sprinkled on the top. It was absolutely scrumptious," he answered.

"It was absolutely a mistake, you mean," Suzette said. "I'd left the yeast out of the dough and—"

Winnie threw her head back and laughed, startling Annylee who cried out in protest. Suzette fled the table to pick up the baby and bring her to join them.

"Mama showed me how to fix it, and that's what we served," she explained, hiding her face in Annylee's sunlit hair to hide her embarrassment.

"I don't know about yeast," Harrison said loyally, "and it may have been a mistake, but it was the tastiest mistake I've ever eaten. . .and I've eaten quite a few. If I had to live on my own bachelor cooking, I'd starve to death."

She smiled at him, grateful for his support.

The meal was excellent—probably, she thought, because she'd had little to do with it other than setting the table, and they soon were digging into the pie Harrison had brought.

After the meal, they pulled their chairs out into the yard, just past the front door, to enjoy the light breeze that had blown in. Tom put a blanket down for Annylee, and she occupied herself with watching a grasshopper that hopped lazily nearby.

"This is so pleasant, sitting out here like this. For once the wind isn't tearing my hair off," Winnie said.

Suzette closed her eyes. The early evening sun blazed over them like a blessing.

"Tell us about why you moved out here," Tom said to Harrison. "I'm rather surprised that you did. You never struck me as a frontier kind of fellow."

"I needed a change," Harrison responded simply. "Soon enough, life will contract around me, and I won't be able to explore my dreams. When Suzette announced her plans—and I have to say that she did so with undisguised glee—I had to reevaluate my own life."

Suzette sat up straight. "You weren't happy?"

He shrugged. "There's happy, and there's happy. I was comfortable, perhaps, but the thought of spending the rest of my life hunched over a ledger and never having seen the world beyond the small sphere of St. Paul, Minnesota, was a bit of an alarm. I knew that if I didn't seize the chance now, I would never do it."

Tom nodded. "I understand. That's basically what drew us out here. It's the land. It gives a man the opportunity to see how far he can stretch his talents and interests and gifts, and try his hand at making a life that he can be proud of. It's our chance at success."

"I wonder what 'success' is," Harrison mused. "I've been thinking about that for some time. Is it prosperity? Financial wealth? A nice house, good clothes, and costly outings? Or is it more than that?"

Suzette studied him as he spoke. She'd never heard him be so open.

"It's family, that's what I think it is," Winnie said, rescuing the grasshopper from Annylee's chubby fist. "I look at this little girl and at Tom, and it doesn't matter that our furniture is shabby and that the windows don't quite keep out the weather. I have everything that makes me happy."

Tom smiled at his wife, and Suzette felt a stab of envy. The love they had for each other was transparent and strong. She'd put that aside for so long.

Had she done that only because her family, and Harrison's, had presumed that they'd marry? She had to acknowledge that she was stubborn and, honestly, self-centered.

"So do you think that Hope is the place for you? Maybe being a shopkeeper—"

Tom's words were interrupted by a wail from Annylee. The sun had moved so it was directly in her eyes, and she blinked and swatted at her face as if she could bat it away.

"I think I'd better take Annylee and attend to her," Winnie said, as Tom picked up their daughter. "She may be my everything, but she's my hungry everything."

"I'd better help her," Tom said. "Why don't you show Harrison around the farm while we tend to Annylee?"

"I'd like that." Harrison turned to Suzette. "Would you mind?"

"Not at all. After that dinner, a walk sounds lovely."

She waited until Tom and Winnie were inside, and then she swooped her arm toward her surroundings. "There's the barn, and the garden, and the fields. Where should we go?"

"Let's head over there." He indicated a line of saplings. "I gather that'll be their tree line?"

"One day it'll be a shelterbelt, and as fast as cottonwoods grow, it shouldn't be long."

"Look at this," he said to her, indicating the span of sky and land. "It reminds me of the Psalm, 'Thy mercy, O Lord, is in the heavens; and thy faithfulness reacheth unto the clouds.'"

It did describe the land perfectly. God was everywhere here, from the clouds in the sky to the blades of grass beneath their feet.

As they strolled toward the neat line of trees, she said to him, "You didn't answer Tom's question."

"I didn't? Which one?"

"The one he didn't quite finish. You said you don't want to be a bookkeeper forever, but do you think keeping a store is better?"

"Better?" He frowned. "Maybe. I don't know that shopkeeping is better than bookkeeping, but I had to try. Here's what happened, Suzette. You announced you were coming out here, and I have to say that shook me out of my rut. I knew I had to do something like that. I saw the ad for the store in the St. Paul newspaper, and I answered it."

"You bought the store. You didn't rent it or lease it. You bought it. That's quite an investment for an adventure."

He chuckled. "I may have acted somewhat precipitously, indeed."

"I thought my parents had sent you out here to keep an eye on me, but they didn't, did they?"

"No, in fact they were diametrically opposed to it. They told me that if I came out here and settled in, you wouldn't leave either."

She stopped and took his arm. "Because they thought we would get married."

Crimson crept up his neck. "Suzette, let's be honest with each other. Our parents have conspired our marriage since we were in our cradles. It was one more thing that I felt I had no choice in, like working in my father's business. I like you, and I do love you as a friend. But marriage? Wouldn't it be better if we were in love, like Tom and Winnie? And we aren't. At least, I'm not."

He could have smacked her and she wouldn't have been more surprised. And, frankly, her ego was shattered. He didn't want to marry her?

"So if I went back to St. Paul tomorrow, you wouldn't care?"

He paused. That pause alone stole all the breath from her.

After a moment that seemed to stretch into eternity, he said, "We're friends. I think that there isn't a good marriage that isn't based in equally good friendship. I'd like to be your friend. Not just an acquaintance that you've grown up with, but more than that. I know you've rejected me. But would you—could you—consider letting our friendship grow?"

His eyes met hers. They were kind eyes, and she was astonished that she'd never really noticed it before.

"Yes," she whispered.

"And then," he continued, "if we both agree, I could begin courting you."

"Courting," she said softly.

"You deserve that. I deserve that." He swallowed. "We both need to go through that if we're to be married—and note that I said 'if.' "

"You don't want to marry me." The sentence came out brokenly.

"Suzette, it's not that I don't want to marry you. It's not that at all. I just don't believe that we're ready to even consider it. And," he added almost sadly, "I wonder if we hadn't been pushed so hard, we might have come to it on our own. It has to be our decision though."

"All right," she said. "All right."

The world spun around her. The tiny trees, their summer-sprouted leaves rustling in the breeze, seemed to be saying something to her that she couldn't understand.

He smiled. "And if the time comes when we decide that we are ready, we'll be prepared for it. Or maybe we'll determine that our families were wrong, that we're not meant to spend our lives as husband and wife. Whatever we learn, we'll know that it's the right thing."

"I've never heard you speak so clearly," she said. "I have to say that I like it."

"Then we've taken our first step together. We must agree to be forthright with each other. If the day comes when you realize I'm not the man for you, maybe because you've found someone else who fills your heart with joy, you must promise that you'll let me know."

She looked down at her hand, still on his sleeve. She'd never considered another man. How could she when they had been placed on the same road, based on an understanding a generation removed?

"I promise. But you must pledge the same promise to me." She fought back tears. Why was this so difficult, imagining the day that he might tell her that he had no love for her? Just two weeks ago, she had been glad to be away from him.

He took a deep breath. "I can smell winter in the air. Will you still be here?"

"I—I don't know." Freedom had never been so horrible.

"You told your parents that you might be back. 'Christmas, maybe,' was what you said."

That day seemed like a century ago. "I'm not sure what will become of me. I'm here to help Winnie and Tom, but at some point, her leg and her arm will be healed, and—Harrison, I just don't know."

The sun's glow dimmed. Dusk set in quickly on the prairie, and the bright afternoon gave way to twilight.

"You need to go back," she said reluctantly, "or else you'll be traveling to Hope in the dark."

"That's true."

They returned to the house, their footsteps slow, and neither of them spoke.

After he'd thanked them for the dinner, she followed him to the wagon.

"I'm riding Whirlwind tomorrow," she said, mainly because she had nothing else to say.

"Whirlwind?"

"Their horse."

"Do you mind if I come and watch?" he asked, a smile crinkling his face.

"I should warn you. I've never ridden a horse before."

"Then I'll definitely be here."

He climbed into the wagon, and she watched him go until he and the wagon became a tiny speck on the horizon that faded into the prairie.

⁓

He sat in his room above the store and ruminated over the events of the day. Where had this new, strong Harrison come from? Had he been buried all these years?

A full moon shown through the small window. It was the same moon that had shown over him in St. Paul. Why was it brighter here? It was almost white. Next month would be the harvest moon, when the orb would be larger and shine clearer than any other time during the year.

Maybe that was what it was. He'd heard that the full moon made people crazy. That would explain why he'd done what he'd done and why he'd said what he'd said to Suzette.

He leaned back. What a day this had been!

It was all Suzette. He'd known for a long time that he had special feelings for her. Was it love, though? Was she meant to be his wife?

He put his hands over his eyes. What did God want him to do? Now that he was free to follow His will, what should be his path?

Please guide me, he prayed. *Let me know if this is right.*

How would he know if this was right?

So many questions, and none of them had answers.

He opened his Bible, intending to continue his reading of the Word in a book by book, chapter by chapter method, but instead he turned to 1 Corinthians 15:10: *But by the grace of God I am what I am. . . .*

It tied in nicely with what he had read the night he had decided to leave. God had plans for him. And *I am what I am* meant that God's design for Harrison Farrington was based on how He had created him.

But Suzette. . . Did he know who she was?

He had promised her that if he decided that he couldn't love her, he'd tell her.

It would never happen.

It had already happened. Long ago it had happened.

He loved Suzette, and nothing could ever change that.

⌒∽⌒

She lay in the living room, willing sleep to come, but it was elusive.

What on earth had happened? She felt as if she were living someone else's life. This wasn't possible. How could she be so smitten with Harrison?

She considered the idea that their parents' scheme for them had backfired, and they'd ended up smothering whatever love there could be. Perhaps here, away from them, away from the closely built city of St. Paul, where their families were so intertwined that all individuality had been lost, they could start again.

Maybe she'd always loved him, but she had, to use his word, *rejected* him and the love. She was headstrong, that was true. One time her father had, in a pique of exasperation, told her that she'd argue her own name, given the chance.

But did she love him? For all these years, the answer had been no. Since she'd left her home, she'd missed him, his constancy, his presence.

The other aspect she had to consider was that she found him attractive only because she didn't have him. If he had come to her today swearing his love and begging her to marry him, she very well might have scoffed at him.

Moonlight crept around the edges of the curtain, and the stack of blankets she used as a bed was terribly uncomfortable.

She arose and went to the window and looked out at the moon-bathed prairie. Some folks said that there was nothing here, but there was much here, almost too much.

She laid her head against the window frame and sighed. If she weren't so tired, she would do her evening prayers, but her mind refused to settle down and phrase a coherent prayer.

Instead, the beloved Twenty-Third Psalm came to her. *He maketh me to lie down in green pastures: he leadeth me beside the still waters. He restoreth my soul. . . .*

That was it. This place, washed in moon glow, restored her soul. God was doing something in her heart. She could feel that.

One star twinkled in the silvery sky. When she was a child, she wished on the first star of the evening.

Tonight, though, she had deeper things to think about. If only she weren't so tired, she might be able to focus on the day and put her feelings in order.

She left the window and padded back to her pallet, and she finally fell asleep, praying wordlessly to the God who had created the prairie and the brilliant moon and the single glittering star.

He knew that she was struggling. It was enough. It was all.

Chapter 4

Suzette's mind wasn't on her work. When she flung a carrot over her shoulder while weeding the garden, she knew she had to stop before she pulled up the entire plot.

So she stood up, brushed the dirt from her hands and her knees, and went back inside to see what she could help Winnie with.

It was clear what her old friend had been up to. The table was covered with the still partially made mother and daughter dresses, and Winnie was scowling at a needle she was trying to thread. "Either the hole has to be bigger or the thread smaller."

Suzette took the offending needle from her and expertly threaded it. "The trick is to keep them very close together as you thread it. And not to shake." She grinned at Winnie. "And don't try to do this with a broken arm."

"Ah." Winnie smiled as she took the now-threaded needle from Suzette.

"I need something to do in here," Suzette declared. "I'm about ready to crawl out of my skin, I'm so excited."

"Suzette Longmont, cowgirl. Who'd have thought it? Do you have your cowgirl hat and your cowgirl chaps?"

"I have an old straw hat I found in the barn but no chaps."

"Well, don't expect much from Whirlwind. He's a secondhand horse to begin with, and he's rather ancient."

She needed something to occupy her while she waited for Tom to return, and she decided to tackle the window that didn't quite shut right.

After a quick trip to the barn where the tools were kept, she had the window taken apart. That was the easy part. Putting it back together again proved to be more of a challenge. "How can it be that things which fit in place once will never do it again?" she grumbled, trying to wedge the sash back into place.

"Maybe that's why it's like that," Winnie said. "Maybe it was the wrong size to begin with."

"Quit being so sensible." She sat back on her heels and examined the board. "I think it's too big. That's the problem. All I have to do is cut it down."

"Please shave outside. I just got Annylee down for a nap."

Suzette took the board to the yard. She needed a saw. Back to the barn she went, and the only saw she found was nearly half her size. It would have to do.

Finally, she gave up. There was no way she could manage the saw to cut something as small as this. Sweaty and covered with wood shavings, she wiped her forehead with her hand.

"You know what they say—the proper tool for the job." Harrison spoke behind her, and she jumped.

Painfully aware of the fact that she was wet with perspiration and covered with little pieces of wood, she stood up. "Harrison, I didn't hear you." She tried to blot her face as unobtrusively as she could, but she knew it was hopeless.

"You were busy sawing. What are you doing, by the way?"

"I'm trying to fix the window. The bottom sash never set right, so it doesn't seal."

A grin played across his face. "So you were fixing it. When did you learn that?"

"I didn't," she admitted sheepishly. "But it looked so easy."

"Let's go in and take a look." He helped her to her feet.

Inside, he said hello to Winnie and looked at the still-slumbering Annylee, and then he held the piece of wood to the frame. "About half an inch is all you need to remove, I'd say. Do you have a rasp?"

"A rasp. Maybe. What's a rasp?"

Winnie cleared her throat. "It's in the toolbox, there on the floor."

Within minutes, he had the board sized correctly. "When Annylee wakes up, I'll hammer it into place."

"Thank you," she said begrudgingly. She had wanted to do it herself. "How did you know that?"

He laughed. "I don't lay claim to being a handyman by any stretch of the imagination, but if there's more I can help with, I'd be glad to. What I don't know, I can find out. There's a book at the store that I found tucked behind the counter that tells how to do all kinds of things, from butchering a hog to making soap to putting a roof on a house."

"We don't have any hogs," Winnie contributed from the table, where she'd paused in her sewing, "and I buy soap, and the house came with a roof. But the door could use some balancing, and there's some uneven boards in the back room. I'm well acquainted with them, since that's how I fell. I tripped over them one night."

"Let me do what I can. I know that Tom is busy in the fields."

"What's this about Tom?" Her cousin spoke from the doorway as he came in and dropped a kiss on Winnie's forehead. "I can tell you this: Tom is tired. The wind is changing, and it feels like the temperature is about to drop. Summer is over."

Annylee stirred at the sound of her father's voice, and he picked her up and held her tightly.

"An older gentleman came into the store this morning and said his hip was telling him that a cold spell is coming in," Harrison said.

Suzette breathed in sharply. Cold? Already?

"Well, it is October. Sometimes the first snow comes this early," Winnie said.

"Let me help you, then," Harrison said. "I can do some repairs here, and if you need assistance in the harvest, I'd be glad to do what I can."

"There isn't much to bring in," Tom said, his voice filled with despair. "And thank you for your offer, but—"

"But we'd be glad to accept," Winnie interrupted. When Tom tried to disagree, she shook her head. "It's not just you and me anymore, Tom. We have Annylee, and she deserves a warm home. It was different when it was just us, bravely pioneering on, but now we have to think of her."

He sagged into a chair, still cradling his daughter. "You're right."

"There's nothing wrong with getting some help. I've never done any of this, but I'm always ready to learn." Harrison faced Suzette. "The two of us will pitch in and do what needs to be done. Right, Suzette?"

"Absolutely!"

"Before you get too caught up in this, I have a letter for you, Suzette. I suspect it's from your parents." Tom reached in his pocket and pulled out a white rectangle. "I forgot to give it to you yesterday."

"How can you forget a letter?" Winnie chided. "Honestly, Tom!"

"No worry," Suzette said, taking the envelope from him. She knew what it said. *Come home.* The longer she waited to read it, the more she could delay having to confront this.

"Take a moment, Tom," Harrison said, "and rest yourself. If it's okay, I'll unhitch both my horse and yours, and take Suzette for a ride."

"Oh, that's right!" Winnie exclaimed. "She's been so looking forward to this."

"Go ahead," Tom said, the two words wreathed in hopelessness.

Harrison took Suzette's hand and they left the house.

"Thank you for giving them some time alone," Suzette said. "I've never seen Tom so down."

"He probably bit off more than he could handle, and he's trying to do it alone. We'll help."

She thought of how inept she'd been in St. Paul. She couldn't make a flower arrangement, let alone a decent loaf of bread. Now she could do much, much more. But could she and Harrison fix this?

He freed the horses and turned to Suzette. "I don't know where the saddles are—if they even have any. Mine is back in town. We're going to have to do this bareback."

Despite the way the day had gone, she found herself smiling. Bareback!

"Wait a minute, please," she told him.

She went into the barn and took the old hat off the nail where it was hanging. With reverence, she put it on her head. It was too big, but that didn't matter.

She was going to ride a horse. Bareback. And she was going to wave her hat just like the woman in the picture.

Quickly she rejoined him, and he smiled broadly when he saw her. "A true Wild West girl, indeed. Are you ready?"

"Ready!"

He lifted her onto the back of Whirlwind, who looked over his shoulder curiously at his new burden. She gathered her skirts as modestly as she could, knowing that he was seeing more boot than was proper, but not caring. Her mother would have been aghast.

Then he got on the back of his own horse, clutched the mane, and with a click of his heels on the horse's side, he took off.

"Come on, Suzette!"

Whirlwind stood stock-still.

"You need to tell him what to do," Harrison called, coming back to get her. "He's a farm horse."

She copied him, holding on to Whirlwind's mane with one hand, and urged him with a tentative pat on his neck with the other. "Let's go," she said to him.

The horse didn't move.

Harrison moved close and slapped Whirlwind's flank.

"Don't hit—" she began, but the horse began to walk.

It wasn't like in the picture she'd treasured, but it was good enough. Whirlwind obligingly plodded across the farmyard while she waved her hat in the air. Her hair came undone, and the breeze wrapped it around her face and neck.

She'd never been so happy.

Together she and Harrison made their slow way down to the road. Whirlwind never varied his steady pace, the clopping of his hooves on the packed ground making a completely satisfying sound.

At the place where the road met the access path to the farm, Whirlwind stopped.

"I think he wants to go back," she yelled to Harrison. "How do I make him turn around?"

He grinned. "I suspect he'll do it on his own."

Sure enough, the horse turned around and headed back to the barn, not trotting along but simply walking, as if he knew that his rider was a novice.

At the door to the barn, Whirlwind stopped again, and Harrison pulled up next to her. He hopped off his horse and helped her down from hers, and took both horses over to the water tank.

"So how was it?" he asked.

She couldn't stop smiling. "Perfect. Just perfect."

He walked with her back to the door of the house. "Let me just pop in for a minute and talk to Tom."

Inside, Tom was asleep in the chair, and Annylee was on a blanket on the floor.

"He's so tired," Winnie said softly, "and I know it hurts his pride to even admit that he needs help."

Suzette remembered him saying the same thing about Winnie when he'd brought her here the first day. They cared so much for each other.

"I'm serious," Harrison said. "I'll be over as often as I can."

"Thank you," Winnie said. "It means more than you could ever know."

"I'll see you in church tomorrow?" he asked as he got his jacket.

Now that she was here, she could help Winnie and Tom get to church. "Yes."

Suzette walked him to his wagon and waited as he hitched the horse to it again. "You're a good man, Harrison," she said to him.

"And you, my dear Suzette, are a good woman. I'll see you tomorrow."

With those words, he got back into his wagon and left. Again, she watched him until he vanished into the sunset. The wind was indeed cooler, and she shivered as she felt the change of the seasons coming.

She walked back into the house, and Winnie asked her, "Did you forget to read the letter from your family?"

Suzette picked up the envelope from the table and held it, unopened. "I suppose I should."

She pulled the flap apart and pulled out the letter. It was written on creamy vellum in her mother's elegant script. The first part was about the changes in the solarium, the progress on the city park, and the events at the church, followed by assurances about her parents' health.

The second part, though, was the plea she knew was coming:

> *The Ladies' Guild is preparing the Christmas baskets for the needy. At this point, we're gathering the nonperishables, but there is much to be done. Your assistance would be much appreciated. You said you would be back by Christmas, and I do sincerely hope that Winnie's fractures are healing enough that she can manage without your help.*
>
> *We are aware that Harrison is nearby you. I am a bit concerned about the propriety of this. You know that we have never wanted anything more than for the two of you to find a home together, in marriage, but without that assurance, we must insist you return.*
>
> *Please prepare to come home. The weather will soon be unpredictable, so as soon as you can manage, you should make travel arrangements. If you need more funds to do so, let your father know. Know that our love goes with you.*

She sighed.

"Bad news?" Winnie asked.

"No," Suzette answered, pasting a false smile on her face. "It's just—a letter."

She couldn't return. But, at the same time, she couldn't stay forever in this little house. Tom and Winnie would need their home back, and, as for her. . .

But she couldn't leave Dakota. Not now, and possibly not ever.

∽

Harrison stood in the back of the church, scanning each worshiper who entered, watching for a set of familiar faces.

Just as the minister was about to begin, the door opened and Suzette, Winnie, Tom, and Annylee tumbled in.

"It's so hard to measure time out here," Tom said. "It took longer than we expected."

Annylee fussed as Suzette unwrapped her from her blankets. "It's really chilly this morning, and she was not happy to go outside."

"The clouds are rolling in across the horizon," Tom added. "I'm a bit worried. But we'll talk about that later. I think we need to get seated."

"It's been so long since we've been here," Winnie said as they entered the sanctuary, "what with my injuries. I hope I remember the hymns!"

The service began just as they slid into the back pew. Annylee snuggled against Suzette and fell asleep.

The message was one she needed. It was based on Genesis 8:22: *While the earth remaineth, seedtime and harvest, and cold and heat, and summer and winter, and day and night shall not cease.* Nothing could stop God's will, the minister said. They were the tenants of the land, keeping it for the Lord's good.

He asked them to think about the "seedtime and harvest." It meant more than wheat. They needed to consider what they were planting in their own souls—and what the harvest would be. Was it love? The danger, he warned, was ignoring the plight of their fellow men. Complacency in their own lives, and the resulting apathy, were what could bring the harvest down.

Exhorting them to plant the seeds of providing for others and thus reap the crop of caring, he led them into the hymn, "Come, Ye Thankful People, Come." She thought about the words as she sang along. Indeed, they were God's field.

The minister ended the service with the announcement that pie and coffee were being served in the anteroom, and Suzette smiled. Her church in St. Paul did the same thing, and her father had always said that there was nothing like a good rhubarb pie to confirm God's love.

As the congregation filed out, many stopped to greet them. They asked about Winnie's leg and arm, and cooed over Annylee, who had woken enough to smile charmingly at them all. They introduced themselves to Suzette and looked from her to Harrison and nodded approvingly.

"We can't stay," Tom said. "I have an uneasy feeling about what those clouds hold. I'm afraid I'm going to have to break my own rule about not working on Sundays. I need to get into the fields today. If I don't, I'm afraid I'll lose the entire crop."

"I'll help you," Harrison said as he buttoned his jacket. "Let me stop at the store and get some work clothes, and I'll meet you at your house."

As he walked quickly back to the store, he glanced overhead. The clouds were indeed menacing. He knew nothing, absolutely nothing, about bringing in wheat, but he would do what he could.

God would understand. It was His field, after all.

Chapter 5

The two men worked steadily as Suzette and Winnie sat nervously in the living room, playing with Annylee and trying desperately to pretend that everything was going to turn out well.

"It might be," Suzette burst out at last. "The harvest, I mean. It might be all right. Those are two of the godliest men I've ever met, and I—"

She stopped, afraid that if she said more, she might cry.

"I'm scared," Winnie said. "If we lose the crop, we lose it all. The house, everything. We'll have to go back and start over again. We owe money to the bank. If we can't pay it back. . ."

Suzette patted her friend's hand. "We have to trust. And pray."

They didn't speak, each of them talking privately to God about their concerns.

The sun began to set, and the air grew chillier. Still, they sat in the room, waiting and praying.

At last the two men came in, exhausted but happy. "We got most of it," Tom said, dropping into the threadbare chair by the door. "I've got it covered in the barn, and we'll take it in tomorrow. Right now Whirlwind is sharing his quarters with a load of wheat that should hold us through the winter."

"And none too soon," Harrison said. "It's raining. Actually, it's sleeting."

Winnie offered him a cup of tea, but he passed on it. "I need to get back to town while I can. The store will be busy tomorrow with people coming in to get extra provisions."

"We can't thank you enough," Winnie said.

He looked at Suzette. "Some things," he said, "are worth everything."

"And everything is worth something," Suzette responded.

He stopped. "Amen. Absolutely, amen."

∽

The first snow fell that night, early even for Dakota. From his position in his chair near the stove, Harrison could see the flakes, large and full, through the window, drifting downward in the faint moonlight. Summer was over. Fall would be short-lived, and then—and then, it would be winter.

He was huddled under a quilt and a knitted throw. He'd never get warm again, and if he did, he wouldn't be able to move. Today had nearly killed him. If he'd ever needed proof that he was city-bred, this day in the fields had done it, as the rain turned to sleet, and he learned that harvesting didn't mean that the wheat kernels leapt into the wagon, and that his horse really had no idea what to do in the crop rows and was waiting for him to issue commands, and that a bushel of wheat was very heavy indeed.

What little he could feel in his arms and legs ached.

Please, God, let this be enough for Tom.

He had to admit that this was a heavily self-centered prayer, as he would only care to do this once a year, and definitely not two days in a row—not unless there was a hospital nearby to take him in.

He wanted desperately to escape into the cocoon of sleep, but his brain wasn't ready to let go of him yet.

He'd meant to talk to Suzette today. During the service, while his soul was soaking in the message, his heart was composing what he was going to say. Inspired by the sermon, it had to do with planting and harvesting, and he'd come up with a poetic approach to telling her what she meant to him. It was time, he'd planned to say, to begin sowing the seeds of their life together and—

Not that he could remember where it went after that. At the time, it had seemed a fitting way to express his feelings, but now he couldn't put it back together again. In God's own time, he told himself, he'd find the perfect moment. It just hadn't been today.

Christmas, maybe?

He closed his eyes, intending to discuss it with his God, but instead blessed sleep overtook him and let him rest.

∞

October raced into November, and the snow fell and fell and fell. As often as possible, Harrison came to the house, his book of home management in hand, and they all worked together to make the house ready for the intense cold. They'd laid a hearth by the stove so the chance of fire was diminished. They'd built a surround over the well pump so it wouldn't freeze so easily. Windows had been secured and the door rebalanced. Even the furniture had been refinished as much as possible.

Through it all, Suzette found herself softening as she worked at Harrison's side. She couldn't imagine life without Harrison, and yet he still hadn't said anything. He hadn't asked her about courting, and he certainly hadn't said anything more about marriage.

The letters from her mother continued to come. *"You said you'd be home by now. 'Christmas, maybe'?"*

And each time, Suzette wrote back, "Not yet."

Christmas on the prairie. How could she even think of going back to St. Paul?

One evening, as they gathered in the little house, a gentle snow falling outside, they began to discuss Christmas. Winnie's casts were due to come off in mid-December, and she wanted to celebrate all the triumphs they'd had. Harrison had brought popping corn, and they were enjoying the treat.

"Let's make this a special year," Winnie proposed. "We will all make a gift for each other. Nothing store-bought. Everything should be from our hearts."

Harrison looked as if he'd been shot. "I have to *make* something? I have two left hands!"

Winnie laughed. "You'll think of something. And I have another idea. I want to have Annylee baptized on Christmas Eve."

"Now that's a lovely idea," he said. "But this notion of handmade presents?"

Suzette thought about it as the others talked. What could she make? She had no skills, and certainly no materials.

"I have a whole store filled with all kinds of things. Why can't I give you something from there?" he asked, his voice brimming with consternation.

"Because this year has been built by us. Let's make our gifts the same way, from the talents the Lord has given us," Winnie answered. "No fair telling each other what we're making either. It'll be fun!"

Suzette only half-listened to the conversation, trying to figure out what she could do. It was a good idea, but was it possible? She'd always shopped for her Christmas presents. It had been easy enough in a city the size of St. Paul. But here?

She also, it occurred to her, should do something about decorating the house for the holiday. Her mother always draped garlands over the mantels and ceremoniously placed the antique nativity set that had come with her grandmother from Norway when she was a child in the entryway so that all guests might see it.

Here there was nothing. Tomorrow she'd ask Tom to find them a tree, and at the very least they could make paper chains, and if Harrison would bring more popcorn, they could thread popcorn strings. Some families in St. Paul were already using electric lights to adorn their trees, but that was a fancy on the prairie.

Her spirit suddenly filled with the joy of the forthcoming Christmas. It was going to be good.

꧁

The house was filled with pre-Christmas secrets. Tom had been reluctant to chop down a tree for the simple sake of having it in the tiny house. "What if Annylee gets ahold of it? She's rolling over now, and we can't watch her every second," he'd pointed out sensibly, so she had abandoned that idea.

Instead, she and Winnie had cut apart the old magazines she'd been saving for fire starters, and they had draped chains of multicolored paper over the windows, out of Annylee's curious reach. It added a festive touch, and she found herself humming Christmas carols as she worked.

The gift projects were under way, and they were all taking them very seriously. Frequently, she'd come into the kitchen, only to see Winnie tuck something under her apron. Tom spent a lot of time in the barn, "tending to Whirlwind."

Even Annylee seemed to catch the spirit, smiling more than usual and drooling. Occasionally, though, she grew restless and finicky, nuzzling anxiously into her mother's shoulder.

"I think she's getting sick," Suzette said to Winnie one evening as Annylee simply would not be comforted. Back and forth they walked across the tiny room, so much that she was sure they were wearing a rut in the floor. Annylee gnawed furiously on her chubby fist and rubbed her nose against Suzette.

Winnie smiled. "I think she's working on a Christmas surprise of her own."

After some thought, Suzette decided what to do for Tom. She took apart an old sweater she'd found in the barn. It must have been Tom's, but it was snagged and torn. She unraveled it, wet the yarn, and wrapped it around a thin slat of board until it was straight.

Then, using Harrison's book, which he'd left there, she taught herself to knit. She undid more than she knit, and eventually a pair of socks took shape. The stitches were uneven, but they would keep his feet warm, and heaven knew the socks he wore were more holes than cotton.

For Winnie, she dug into her trunk and pulled out a pink silk blouse. Why on earth she'd brought it, she had no idea. She'd never had any use for it here. She took it apart and cut it into even pieces and resewed it. The hems weren't store quality, that was for sure, but she knew that Winnie would treasure the soft scarf, and the soft rosy color would brighten Winnie's pale cheeks.

Annylee was a challenge, but the baby was growing and becoming more aware of her environment. Suzette found a slender rod and some washers and nuts in the barn, and with the addition of pieces of ribbon taken from one of her slips and some shiny jewelry tied on, it became a bright mobile.

Harrison's gift was the most difficult of all. It had to be heartfelt but, at the same time, acceptable for a friend. She couldn't think of a single thing.

Winnie, though, told Suzette that she had the best gift of all: being able to celebrate without being burdened by her immobilized arm and leg. The casts had come off, and although she still limped, she was able to walk and do more in the house.

Suzette tried not to think about what that might mean. She couldn't stay with them much longer now that the reason for her being there was gone. She'd have to decide what to do, and soon.

Instead, she focused on what to give Harrison for Christmas. It was almost time, and she had nothing.

The last Sunday in Advent, as she sat next to him in Hope Church, she saw him flipping through his beloved Bible as he looked to find the day's Gospel reading. She saw that he was using an old note card to keep his place.

He looked over and noticed her staring at the piece of card stock, and shrugged. "I used what was near me."

She nodded, trying not to let her face give away what had just happened. She knew what she could do for him.

That evening, she took apart her own beloved picture of the Wild West girl and removed the velvet backing of the picture frame.

She cut it carefully and fringed it—this time more expertly than she'd done with her father's coat years earlier—and made him a bookmark for his Bible.

Yet it seemed unfinished. This was, she had to acknowledge, a gift for the man she loved. The revelation stunned her, but there it was.

She loved him.

The gift was supposed to have meaning. Through him, she'd come to love the land and had gotten closer to God. And, above all, she was giving a gift to the man she loved. It needed more than secondhand velvet.

That night she took a piece of kindling from the basket by the stove. It was left over from when he had fixed the front door, just the right size, and thin enough for her purposes. She sanded it until all the weathered stain had come off, and then, with a black pen, she carefully lettered on it: *Thy mercy, O Lord, is in the heavens; and thy faithfulness reacheth unto the clouds. Psalm 36:5.* It was the line he'd recited earlier, when they had stood near the cottonwoods and looked out over the prairie.

It was the perfect verse for the land, where all was heaven and clouds.

It was the perfect verse for him.

With a nail, she made a hole in the tag, and using some of the remaining yarn from Tom's gift, she tied it to the black velvet bookmark.

She smiled as she wrapped it. He would like it. She knew that.

Christmas Eve arrived. Winnie and Annylee were wearing their new Christmas dresses, and she put on her best skirt and blouse. She grinned to herself as she thought of the navy silk that her mother had had her wear to dinner when she'd decided to come to Hope. It seemed like that evening was years ago. Silk dresses, kid boots, little feathered hats—they were all a lifetime past.

"Let's bring our gifts with us," Winnie said at the last moment. "I have one for Harrison, and he's alone, so maybe we can make this more of a celebration if we open gifts with him."

Suzette gathered the socks, the scarf, the mobile, and the bookmark, and added them to the basket Winnie had placed in the wagon and covered with a red cloth.

They bundled under blankets and robes for the ride into Hope for the church service and Annylee's baptism. The sky was bright, even at night, and she'd never seen anything as beautiful as the prairie, white with snow, washed in moonlight. A low cloud hovered on the horizon, and as she watched, it moved toward them.

A night cloud! And on Christmas Eve!

She had no idea what it meant, but it was interesting to watch it grow and spread across the sky.

The church was warm when they arrived, and Harrison waited for them outside the sanctuary. "It's filling up. We should go in."

The minister motioned them to the front and whispered, "I'm putting you up here to make the baptism easier."

The sanctuary was illuminated only by candlelight. The message was the Gospel story of the birth of Christ, and Suzette followed it, mentally saying the words with the minister as he began: *And it came to pass in those days, that there went out a decree from Caesar Augustus that all the world should be taxed.*

Toward the end, the minister announced that Annylee was going to be baptized that night, and the congregation, in unison, sighed happily.

Annylee was transfixed by the candles around her, and her face shown. Suzette could barely breathe, it was so beautiful.

As the minister took little Annylee in his arms to start the baptism, Harrison reached out and took Suzette's hand. She looked at him and saw that his eyes were wet.

The minister began the familiar words, "Jesus said, 'Let the little children come unto me,' " and she couldn't restrain her tears.

God had been so good to her. He would, she knew, be good to Annylee, too. As the minister reminded the worshipers, they had a responsibility to her, too. When he asked if they accepted it, with a single voice, the answer came, "Yes!"

Too soon, it was over, and the people of Hope came up to coo over Annylee and to wish them all a merry Christmas. Annylee smiled at everyone, and Winnie gasped.

"Look! There's her present to us! She has her first tooth!"

Sure enough, a shiny ivory tooth was making its way out in Annylee's mouth, and Winnie and Tom proudly showed it off to everyone.

"That's why she was drooling and fussy," Winnie said. "I thought that might be it!"

As the church emptied, they went into the hall outside the sanctuary.

"I'm so glad you chose to do this," Harrison said, and Tom nodded.

"Sometimes Winnie has the best ideas, doesn't she?"

"Oh, speaking of my wonderful ideas, we have our gifts in the wagon. Let's go get them and we can—"

Winnie stopped as she opened the door of the church. Blizzard winds swirled outside, and icy crystals of snow blew into the church.

"We can't go in this weather," Suzette said. "Annylee can't be exposed to this!"

"My store is close by. Let's go there, and you four can stay in my lodgings upstairs. I can bunk down in the storeroom," Harrison declared.

"We can't impose—" Tom said, but Harrison shook off his objections.

"I won't hear of any other way."

Winnie wrapped Annylee tightly in two blankets, draping a light one over the baby's face to protect her delicate skin. Tom took her, put her inside his coat, and held her close.

Her muffler pulled over her head, Suzette followed Harrison outside.

After a stop at the wagon to retrieve the gifts and a few supplies for Annylee, they made their way to the store, covered as well as they could be against the frigid onslaught. The blizzard was fierce.

Inside the store at last, they clattered upstairs to Harrison's rooms, and he built a fire in the stove. Soon they were clustered around it, their hands stretched out to the blessed warmth.

"We can't thank you enough for this, and for all you've done," Tom said.

"Truly, it's my pleasure," Harrison assured him.

Suzette looked around her and smiled. Silvery streams of tinsel and bright green garlands draped the furniture, the windows, and the doorways. He caught her eye and grinned. "I found boxes of garland in the storeroom and thought I'd use it."

She was touched by this side of him. Every day she learned more about him. He was such a good man.

On the table by the window was a nativity set, not as grand as her parents', but just as beautiful. She crossed the room to examine it. Each piece was carved from wood and painted.

"Did you—?" she asked, and he nodded.

"Woodworking has been my hobby for years."

"I had no idea," she murmured. How could she have known him so long and yet not had any idea he had this talent? Because, she answered herself, she hadn't taken the time to find out.

"Gifts! Let's give our gifts!" Winnie cried.

They settled around the fire, warmed at last, and began the exchange.

Tom and Winnie and Annylee gave Harrison a picture of Jesus, taken from a book and framed by Tom himself, who said, "I'm not nearly at your level yet, Harrison, but I've developed some talents living here, and I'm now proud to say that I can nail strips of wood together."

Winnie gave Suzette a patchwork apron made from scraps of material. She nodded happily. It was bright and colorful, and above all, she needed an apron. The entire time she'd been in Hope, she'd used Winnie's.

Tom proclaimed his socks splendidly warm and put them on right away. Winnie wrapped the scarf around her neck and rubbed it against her cheek. "Do you know how long it's been since I've touched anything silk?" she asked.

Annylee reached for the scarf but was diverted by the mobile Tom dangled over her.

Suzette handed Harrison his gift and watched him as he opened it. He didn't say anything, but when he looked up, his face was soft in the crackling light of the fire. "You remembered," he said simply. "Our walk."

He didn't give her a gift in return, though, and she fought back the hurt. Awkwardly, he stood. "I'd better leave you alone to rest. Thank you for the presents, and above all, thank you for being my friends."

He left, and as Winnie and Tom played with Annylee, she sat to the side, nursing the pain in her heart. He couldn't have been any clearer.

She swallowed her pride and excused herself. If nothing else, she wanted to thank him personally for all he had done.

As she entered the store, she saw him. He was silhouetted against the window, and with the sound of the blizzard roaring outside, and in the diffused light from the moon's reflection on the wild snow, he stood there, holding the bookmark she'd made him against his heart.

He turned and wordlessly came to her. He wrapped his arms around her and pressed his lips against her hair in a cascade of kisses as he murmured to her, "I love you, I love you, I love you."

She knew she was crying, but she couldn't stop.

"I do have a gift for you, but it's not much. I hope you understand."

He reached under the counter and took something out. "Have you seen the picture on my mantel upstairs?"

She shook her head.

"Take a look when you go back. Then it'll all make sense, I hope."

He handed her the hat she'd worn when she rode Whirlwind. He had wound tinsel around it so it was nearly entirely silver and gold.

She held the hat in both hands, unable to speak.

He rushed to apologize for it. "I'm not artistic. I'm sorry, Suzette. I thought—"

"I know what it is," she said at last. "It's my Wild West hat, isn't it?"

"I wanted to give you as much of your dream as I could," he said. "That's all I ever want to do. Give you your dreams and make them our dreams."

In the magic of a Christmas snowstorm, between a pickle barrel and a bolt of calico, he dropped to his knees. "Suzette, will you marry me? I can't promise you a Wild West life, but I can assure you a life filled with adventure and love and God."

She nodded, unable to say more than, "Yes. Yes. Oh yes!"

Surrounded by tools and sugar and thread, they sealed their future with a kiss.

Together they walked back up the stairs and went into the living room.

Immediately she looked toward the mantel—and smiled when she saw what was there. It was a picture of a man on a rearing horse in a Wild West show. "I've had it for over ten years," he said to her in a low voice.

"Like mine," she said in wonder.

"What are you two chattering about?" Winnie asked.

"We have an announcement," Suzette said. "We're going to get married."

Tom and Winnie beamed happily. "It's about time!" Tom said. "When?"

Suzette and Harrison looked at each other and chorused, "Christmas, maybe."

Christmas, maybe? Or Christmas, definitely?

Or Valentine's Day?

The Christmas Bread

by Jennifer Rogers Spinola

Chapter 1

September 6, 1865

P ush! Push!" Juliet held Elizabeth's hair back from her sweaty forehead in the little corridor of patchwork quilts and smooth sheets hung from ropes between the wagons for privacy. "You can do it. She's almost here, Elizabeth—don't give up!"

"That's it. Take a breath." Posy squeezed Elizabeth's hand while two older women held her up. "She'll be born before you know it."

Elizabeth gasped and groaned, her cheeks rosy with effort. "I can't do it, Juliet—I just can't."

Juliet grabbed her satchel of medical supplies as she looked deep into Elizabeth's eyes. "Yes, you can."

Juliet quickly moved to check the baby's progress. "In less than an hour, I bet. Stay with me, and try again. Hear me? Push, Elizabeth, with all you've got."

One of the women poured a little more whisky for the pain into Elizabeth's panting mouth then put her hands on the laboring woman's back and shoulders, steadying her. Elizabeth scrunched her knees and bent forward with a groan, and this time Juliet saw a glimpse of pale baby hair on a healthy pink curve of scalp, like a tender peach.

"She's coming, Elizabeth—she's coming!" Juliet knew she shouldn't cry—a nurse was supposed to remain calm and impartial—but the sight of a downy baby head made the prairie grass blur like green stained glass. "Push again—one more time." She braced Elizabeth's knees with shaking hands. "One. Two. Three. Push!"

Elizabeth gripped Posy's hand and pressed forward, the muscles in her neck straining, mouth open in an anguished cry.

And the baby slipped forward, smeared with blood, almost into Juliet's hands.

"You did it," Juliet whispered as she reached for a damp cloth and wiped the baby clean. Posy helped dry the newborn with a towel, rubbing the fuzzy hair and round cheeks, and gently wiping out her eyes. The baby opened her mouth with a toothless whimper and then a wail.

And throughout the camp, a cheer went up. Hands clapped; pots rattled and banged.

"It's a girl!" Juliet called out, and they cheered again. She reached forward and squeezed Elizabeth's trembling hand. "You were right, Elizabeth. Congratulations. She's so beautiful." Juliet had to steady her emotions again. "What are you going to name her?"

"Carrie Ann," said Elizabeth between shaky breaths as tears streamed down her cheeks. Her face, still round with pregnancy fullness, glowed rosy and joyous and exhausted all at once. "If only Tom were here to see her."

And she slipped into sobs.

Juliet exchanged glances with Posy then looked down, occupying herself by cleaning her hands with a fresh cloth dipped in lye soap and running it underneath her nails. She tried to think of anything but Thomas Baker's pale, lifeless face and gashed crown, blood soaking through his hair. A wagon accident: an ox had dragged him, trampled him. The heavy wagon wheel had rolled over part of his shoulder, crushing his sternum instantly.

From all her years at her doctor father's side, Juliet knew enough about death to have recognized that Thomas wasn't going to make it. From the gray color that ringed his eyes when they brought him to her, Juliet had guessed five minutes.

He lasted three.

And it took every hour of the following four weeks to make sure his grieving young wife didn't give birth prematurely.

Juliet's hands worked, clamping and cutting the cord, so her mind could forget. She wrapped fine cloth around the stump of the umbilical cord and handed little Carrie Ann, warm and squirming, to Elizabeth.

"I'm so proud of you, Elizabeth," she whispered, as Elizabeth brought up the fragile, sweet baby, skin smooth as petals, to her own tear-streaked cheek. "And so is Tom. I'm sure of it."

Trying to keep her emotions in check, Juliet turned to her medicine kit and counted all the herbs and tinctures she'd administered, touching each cork top with her fingertip to make sure—then closed the lid.

"Come on, Posy. Let's give Elizabeth some space with her baby," she said softly. "The other women can help her until we get back."

Juliet, ready to stretch her numb legs, lifted one of the quilts and ducked through the space with Posy. They slipped between a cluster of women noisily shaking out laundry, past some children shouting as they played beneath a wagon. They steered far away from the Hendersons' temperamental dog and were careful not to step on any of the Wilsons' chickens. Which had, yes, accidentally hatched from some too-warm eggs.

The memory of Tom Baker's bloody hair and unblinking eyes made Juliet's head feel fuzzy and light, and she didn't stop until she reached the edge of the creek. As a group of boys fished on a lazy bank, she leaned against the smooth bark of a slender cottonwood, willing the images not to come.

"You're all pale, Juliet," said Posy, looking up at her. "You all right?"

Juliet breathed deeply, trying to focus on the smells of river stones and wet leaves and the rare tingle of moisture in the normally dry air. Then she wouldn't have to recall the screams—the moans—the last gasps of dying men dressed in Union blue, and the terrible stillness when they breathed their last. The gray tinge of skin like she'd seen on Tom Baker and the stink of infected flesh.

Good heavens. She must have been daft to sign up to work in a place like the military hospital, where grown men snorted opium just to blot out the horrible images.

And she, barely twenty, with hair hanging in perfect curls, had marched in with such naive high hopes. Juliet shook her head in wonder at her bravery—or rather, her youthful ignorance. Maybe a little of both.

But that's what Daddy would have done if he were alive—dear Dr. James, Daddy, who taught Juliet everything she knew until well in her teens.

The Christmas Bread

After they buried Daddy, Juliet and her younger brother, Silas, only had Mama. Until Mama met her gentle new husband, Walter—a graying widower with a bigger love than Juliet had imagined in his trembling, palpitating heart. Within a few months, Walter became dear "Papa," and Juliet couldn't imagine her life without him. Then Mama died of pneumonia, and there was only Papa.

In fact, it was Papa who'd brought Juliet and Silas to the West at his own expense—for the hope of new life with their relatives in Montana. Nobody could replace Daddy, but Papa was now the only close family she and Silas had left.

"Juliet?" Posy nibbled a nail, her brow wrinkled. She looked fresh and innocent at eighteen like Juliet had back then, before she knew. Before she'd seen.

"I'm fine, Posy." Juliet managed a smile. "As long as Carrie Ann and Elizabeth are okay, then my job is done."

"I'm not talking about your job. I'm talking about you."

"I'm all right." The dizziness came; everything spun and began to settle. Lines became trees and glistening stones, dazzling in brilliant Wyoming sunlight, and aspen leaves shook like sparkling golden-green hearts. "I just need a minute to catch my breath." Juliet closed her eyes and loosened her bonnet, letting it fall down her back. At least there in the dappled shade her scalp and ears wouldn't burn.

"Christmas, Posy—let's think about Christmas," she said. "My favorite time of year. When we get settled in with my uncle, I'm going to find the biggest spruce tree I can find and hang all my best ornaments. I brought as many as I could, you know— the glass and crystal ones. I packed my trunk full. I might not have anything to wear, but my tree will be beautiful."

"Ah." Posy giggled. "Clothes are overrated. I bet your uncle has something you can borrow."

"Probably one of those hats with a candle on the front. He's a miner, you know."

Posy held up a finger on the front of her bonnet like a light, and Juliet chuckled. "Whatever he has, it'll be better than these sweaty old dresses. I'm going to burn mine when we get to Helena. How about you?"

"Mine are so smelly they could probably light up on their own. And hey, at least that would kill the fleas!"

"Well, I packed a beautiful green velvet dress for Christmas. It's brand-new. No fleas." Juliet's eyes sparkled. "And then, Posy, I'll make Christmas bread."

"Christmas bread?"

"My Italian relatives call it *panettone*. It's a yeast bread made with butter and dried fruit." Her mouth watered as she imagined the buttery smell of the dough as servants kneaded and mixed, and the softness of warm bread on her tongue after so many hard beans and dry biscuits. "Raisins and orange peel and nuts. It's heavenly—you must have some Christmas bread when you come visit me in Billings. It's just not Christmas without panettone."

Billings. Juliet kept her voice cheerful, but the word stung, reminding her that she and Posy would eventually part ways at the end of the trail. Almost certainly never to meet again. Not with the vast expanses of prairie and jagged mountains with nothing but bumpy ruts between them.

Such was the pain of the trail, a pain that always ached, even after the end.

"Sure, I'll come visit," said Posy lightly, as if trying to keep her own spirits up. "As long as I can get one of those miner's hats."

"So you can work at a mining camp?"

"So I can see my way to the outhouse at night."

Juliet laughed.

"Well, I'm going to bake gingerbread and make molasses candy for Christmas—just piles of it." Posy dabbled the toe of her leather boot in the water, making sparkling rings. "And after that, I'll play in the snow."

"Snow." Juliet breathed in with a longing sound. "Can you imagine? A whole field full of snow after all this dust and heat?"

"People here on the trail would hock everything they have for a single snowball." Posy licked her lips. "Gracious, all this snow talk is making me thirsty."

She bent and cupped her hands to drink some water, and Juliet grabbed her wrist. "Don't do it! There might be cholera here."

"You think cholera comes from the water?" Posy wrinkled her nose. "That's crazy."

"I know, but I've ruled out so many other things. None of it makes sense. It can wipe out a whole camp, you know that?"

"But everybody drinks water from this creek—and it looks fine. Clearest water we've seen yet. What else are we supposed to drink?"

"I'm not sure." Juliet massaged her temples. "Maybe we need to try it farther upstream? Or maybe I'm just plain wrong. All I know is that cholera shows up out of the blue and spreads to everybody, and the one place everybody visits is the creek—for drinking, laundry, washing dishes, everything. Cleaning their gun parts and boots. Even soaking the wagon wheels so they'll stay on the axels in the heat. That can't be good."

She lifted her skirts and stepped over a couple of stones. "I heard some of the folks talking about diarrhea yesterday, and the party that came through last time got cholera here, too, and maybe typhus. It worries me, Posy. Cholera always starts with diarrhea."

"I'm worried about it, too, but I ain't gonna thirst to death trying to figure out where it comes from."

"Well, don't drink the water out of your hands like that, for goodness' sake—not here," Juliet scolded.

"Well, you're the nurse. You oughtta know." Posy shrugged. "I thought you got cholera from the air. Or maybe some kind of bedbug. Mrs. Henderson says you get it from eating overripe watermelon at the wrong phase of the moon."

"Mrs. Henderson says a woman can get with child by eating too many pickles. And I know from all my medical books that's completely impossible."

Posy blushed. "Heavens, Juliet—don't talk about such things! Shame on you."

"Well, you can't believe a word Mrs. Henderson says. She might make good corn cake, but she's been out here on the plains too long, if you get my drift." Juliet peeled off her apron, which was spattered with brownish drops of blood. And before she could dip it in the creek water, she saw him.

"Sakes alive," she whispered. "It's that Pike boy again." She stepped quickly behind a cluster of aspen trees and steadied herself on the sloped bank, hoping he hadn't seen her.

Posy ducked the long bonnet that hid her sunflower-orange hair to see better. "Yep, that's him heading this way. Looking for you, I reckon."

"Why? I've already told him I'm not interested in him, or anybody else. He's wasting his time."

"Seems like he doesn't think so." Posy snickered. "He's got flowers again, too."

Juliet peeked through the leaves, and sure enough, a bony figure with his arm in a sling was working his way through the field at the edge of camp toward her—carrying a pretty bouquet of lavender-purple blooms.

"Miss James?" he called out with that that wide, cheerful smile he always wore.

Out of the corner of her eye, Juliet saw Jacob shift the flowers to his wounded hand and tip his hat with his good one. An impressive feat—but she pretended not to notice him.

Jacob stepped through the thicket anyway. "How do you do, Miss Preston?" He nodded at Posy politely then turned to Juliet. "I know you're busy, Miss James, but could I give you something? It'll only take a minute."

That smile and that accent. That devilishly slow roll of words, the syllables pulled long and warm like Southern taffy. Poisoned taffy was more like it. The South that had torn their Union apart, that had fired on their valiant Maryland boys in blue. Juliet felt her cheeks heat with irritation, and she could hardly look into Jacob's thin, square face. She walked back to the water and knelt down, her back to him.

"I'm sorry, but I'm kind of busy right now." Juliet didn't look up as she scrubbed her dirty apron, dabbling it in a current of cold creek water. "And no offense, but you can save your flowers, Mr. Pike. We've been over this before."

"They're not flowers, exactly."

"What do you mean 'they're not flowers'?" She twisted around to peer up at him. "Are you ill, Mr. Pike?"

"I mean, they're *more* than just flowers." Jacob held them out again stubbornly. "They're prairie coneflowers. The locals chew the roots and leaves or boil 'em to make a tea that they swear cures just about everything—from snake and spider bites to just about every disease you can think of. You being so knowledgeable about medicine and all, I thought you might like some."

That drawl again. Slow and fluid, like the draining away of hope. Hope that died the day a messenger came to her front door, the letter in his gloved hands cinched with hateful black silk.

"If you wanted to give me roots for medicinal purposes, you could have just brought me the roots," said Juliet as she dropped her wet apron on a rock and rose to her feet. "Those are definitely flowers, Mr. Pike, and formed very nicely in the shape of a bouquet. With a bit of ribbon around them, if I'm not mistaken."

"You're correct, ma'am. But how else do you expect me to keep them together?"

"Twine?"

"Well"—Jacob shrugged and flashed a guilty smile—"you can't blame me for trying."

Juliet wiped her wet hands on her skirt and reluctantly took the bouquet then stepped awkwardly across a bumpy slope. "I've told you I'm not interested, Mr. Pike, but thank you just the same," she said coolly. "I must say I've never been given. . .um. . .specimens before in this form." She sniffed the daisy-like blooms. "You say it cures snake bites?"

"Yes, ma'am. Allergies, blood infections, everything."

"Allergies. I'll say." Juliet shook her head. "With all of the dust and grasses out here that we're not used to, it's a wonder any of us are alive."

The land flowed in a rippling wash of green, parted only by a few scrub plants and the furrow of wagon ruts leading into the distant hills along the lonely Bozeman Trail—all the way into Montana. A dismal ocean that stretched to a land Juliet had never seen. Didn't care to see. Nothing mattered anymore, really, anyway, after losing Robert first and then her home.

"Well, thank you, Mr. Pike, for the roots."

"The flowers," Jacob corrected. "You said so yourself. And you're sure welcome." The sunlight gleamed gold down Jacob's face, along the curves of his cheek. Glistening like his teeth when he smiled.

Juliet shook her head at Jacob's cocky rejoinder then held up the roots and studied them. Bits of dry soil still clung to the tiny taproots, and it crumbled in her fingers. "What are you, some kind of local herbalist?"

"No, ma'am. Just a boy who spent his youth sneezing his eyes out. And this works—I promise you that."

Juliet almost laughed. Just a bit. "Thank you, again." She studied him as he stood there, the late afternoon sun at his back illuminating the bits of wild red-brown hair under his hat. "And what happened to your arm? Did a horse throw you?"

Juliet had meant to be friendly—just for a moment—but all at once the colors of the sky and landscape seemed to change, to shift, to an awful tone. She shouldn't have asked. She knew she shouldn't have.

Everything, in one moment, slipped into sharp focus. *The broken arm. The Southern lisp.* She could almost see him in his gray-and-brown Confederate suit, shivering over a campfire.

"Got it nearly shot off in the war," said Jacob. Or something to that effect. Juliet didn't hear his exact words, because everything swirled into black—into screams. She sensed Posy pulling her away, shouting at her to remember her manners, for goodness' sake, and leave the poor fellow alone.

She swung again, trying with all her might to dislocate Jacob Pike's arm from its socket.

Chapter 2

J uliet was on her knees pounding him when Posy pulled her off. Her mousy light brown hair had spilled out from its braid, her bonnet on the ground. Across the field the Diamond twins peeked around the edge of their wagon, mouths open, darting their heads back only to whisper.

"For gracious' sake. What on earth got into you?" Posy snapped as she slapped Juliet on the shoulder. "Have you lost your mind?"

"Yes," whispered Juliet, feeling her face burn with shame. "I'm so sorry." Her hands shook, and she took a stumbling step backward. Reaching by instinct for the engagement ring that used to circle her finger. Instead, she touched the smooth, bare skin of her knuckle, slashed by blades of grass and the raw wood of the wagon, parched by prairie sun. Endless prairie, taking her farther and farther each day from the small white stone carved with Robert's name.

She could still see the messenger on her front step and the black-ribboned letter in his hand, with the words in fresh ink: *We regret to inform you. . .*

Juliet had thrown the letter down, unable to bear the words in that hateful script: *Robert McQuillin died May 23, 1864, of infection caused by gunshot wounds.*

Her Robert. The gentle jeweler's son from Baltimore, who had crafted an exquisite engagement set for her: a blue topaz brooch to match her eyes, woven with gold filigree in the delicate shape of a cross. An engagement ring with the same blue stone, the color of the Maryland seaside at dusk, the shell of a crab, the autumn sky through shivering white oak trees.

There she was, home on leave from the bloody medics' tents, and she'd still stumbled on death. The most painful one she'd encountered yet.

She'd worn the ring for a year after Robert's death and had watched their wedding date come and go in silence. The war ground on to a bitter halt, and when Papa's business faltered and word came of gold in Montana, Juliet followed numbly, right along with Silas. She had watched her polished cherry wood bedroom furniture sold at auction, her trunks and trinkets parceled up, and the slim remainder packed into a narrow little Conestoga wagon.

"Don't you worry, my dear," Papa had said as he wrapped his arm around her shoulder and planted a kiss on her cheek. "Your uncle says there's a fortune in Montana just ripe for the taking. You can have everything you've ever wanted."

But all Juliet wanted was Robert.

And now he was gone.

"That Pike fellow could have killed Robert," Juliet whispered hoarsely to Posy. "Maybe he's the one who shot him."

So now she knew—Jacob Pike, the Confederate war hero. She'd heard it murmured through the wagon train a week ago that a former Confederate soldier had joined them as they passed through Big Horn. A wounded man, they said, but Juliet had pictured someone quite different. Jacob seemed too young, too cheerful, to have sold his soul to Jefferson Davis and his horrible ranks of rebs.

Jacob groaned and lifted himself up on his good elbow.

"Hush, Juliet," scolded Posy. "You've no call to act like that. The man was just being friendly, is all."

"You're right. I'm sorry, Mr. Pike. Please forgive me. I was terribly out of line." Tears stung Juliet's eyes as she recalled patches of light and memory: the stiff leather of new high-buttoned boots, the smell of crabapple blossoms in spring. The tick of the walnut mantel clock echoing against the great, high walls of the James's house—if only it could have frozen that way, in time, leaving everything happy as it was. *I want my fiancé back. My house back. My life back, just as it was.*

Even Carrie Ann's soft cheeks and tiny hands only served as a reminder of the things she and Robert would never have. And Juliet hated herself for being so slow to forget.

She plodded to the creek and snatched up her dripping apron. "Excuse me. I've got to check on Elizabeth and Carrie Ann anyway."

Jacob was on his feet, dusting himself off. And instead of stalking off into the smoke-filled haze of the wagon camp, he took a step toward her. So close that his breath stirred the messy strands of fine hair that hung around her ear, and the rough homespun cotton of his jacket sleeve brushed her arm.

"Miss James," he said softly, looking down at her. "I'm sorry for your loss."

He said it so softly that Juliet almost didn't hear it. But she did. *"I'm sorry for your loss,"* he'd said.

She turned to look over her shoulder and exchanged a glance with him, just for a moment, before turning away. Blue meeting brown in a dimming ray of sun. Robert had brown eyes, too, that sparkled when they looked at her, just like Jacob's did.

"Please go away, Mr. Pike," Juliet whispered. "Please."

And she followed Posy through the milling crowds toward the wagon, leaving Jacob in the thin shadows of spindly aspens.

✑

Posy pulled Juliet, red-cheeked, through a tangle of women shaking out wet laundry. "My word," Posy snapped after she smoothed a curl of thick, red-gold hair back under her bonnet. "You look like you've gone and lost your senses, like that woman who tried to burn down her own wagon!"

Posy looked like a furious angel, so ruddy and disheveled. Her quiet vanity—her heavy waves of shiny hair, the exquisite shade of a ripe apricot—would be worth a fortune if she sold it, pound per pound. Juliet's skimpy braid, on the other hand, looked like she'd pulled a few thin strands together from the chin of the family billy goat—a fact that her late mother used to cluck about in distress.

"I just can't bear a Southerner like Jacob Pike—a man who fought against us and people we love. You're from Pennsylvania, Posy. Doesn't it bother you?"

Something about Robert must have registered with Posy, because her expression changed from irritation to one of pity. Her creased brow relaxed.

"Well, I understand, but it doesn't give you a reason to beat a man up. Especially when he's bringing you flowers."

"He's a Confederate." Juliet let out a shuddering breath. "They're all detestable."

"Hush. Let me fix your hair." Posy turned Juliet around and loosened her braid then smoothed her hair with her fingers before pulling it tight.

"Why are you so nice to him anyway?" Juliet craned her neck to try to see her. "Just think of what the Confederacy has done to the black race, to the Union, to everyone. They're criminals."

"Hold still. How am I supposed to make you look presentable with you wiggling around?" Posy forcefully turned her head. "And President Lincoln didn't treat 'em like criminals, even when they surrendered. We're all brothers."

"Nonsense."

"Fact is, they're not that different from us, Juliet." Posy finished the braid and handed Juliet her bonnet. "My cousins fought in North Carolina with the rebs. Are you gonna quit talking to me now?"

"Don't be silly." Juliet slapped the bonnet on her head and tied it under her chin. "And that's not a fair comparison! You don't agree with your Southern cousins. They're wrong. Plain and simple."

"Maybe yes, maybe no. From what I hear, they had some legitimate gripes about the way things were. It all depends on who you talk to."

"Posy. You can't justify slavery."

"Of course not! But we aren't as righteous as you think either. We're the ones who brought the slaves here in the first place, flying our flag, docking them horrible slave ships in our Northern ports. Just because the South made more profit from them doesn't mean we're any less guilty."

"I can't believe you'd say such a thing. And I'll never change my opinion about people like Jacob Pike."

"They're people just like us." Posy raised herself up on her toes to meet Juliet's eyes. "My family never owned slaves, and neither did my cousins. But there's good folks caught up on both sides, and they've got their own reasons that they think are worth dying for."

Juliet covered her face with her hands at the word *dying*. Remembering Robert's ivy-covered grave in the green Maryland glen, so lonely and far away. The rows of bloody stretchers and men moaning in pain. "I can't think about it any more right now, Posy—I just can't." She let out her breath. "I need to make sure Carrie Ann and Elizabeth are all right. Are you coming with me?"

"Sure." Posy took her arm and led her gently. "Just don't go whacking my arm off, okay? Last I checked, I still need them both."

⟡

When Juliet parted the quilts between the wagons, she found Elizabeth resting in a beautiful cane-backed rocker—an heirloom produced from somebody's wagon, where it had probably slept for weeks upside-down in a bed of dust, tightly packed linens, and sleeping children. Elizabeth had changed into a fresh dress, and from the looks of her long, damp curls, somebody had washed her hair and maybe even helped her bathe from a tub.

And wonder of wonders—little Carrie Ann lay sleeping in the crook of Elizabeth's arm, her butterfly-fragile eyelashes closed. Her tiny back rose and fell with gentle breaths, and Juliet's heart beat fast with joy.

"Oh, Elizabeth. You look wonderful." She touched Elizabeth's rosy cheek with the palm of her hand. "Just look at you."

Elizabeth took her eyes off Carrie Ann long enough to smile up at Juliet. "She's amazing, isn't she? I didn't know if I could make it, but. . ." Her eyes shimmered with tears.

Juliet knelt next to her. "I knew you could." She stroked Carrie Ann's tiny ear lightly with the tip of her finger.

She was about to ask some more nurse-like questions about bleeding and breast milk when, from inside the little corridor of fluttering quilts and sheets, Juliet sensed a lull in the normally bright conversation outside. The clatter of tin pans and cast-iron skillets paused, and even the Hendersons' dogs stopped barking.

"What is it?" Juliet pushed the quilt aside. "Is somebody hurt?"

Only the grasses stirred, rustling, over the low hum of whispering voices and stamps of tethered horses.

And then she saw it: a puff of hazy dust rolling out across the distant plain. The low thunder of hoofbeats echoed. The dust came from the ridge, the same direction the scouts had gone that morning when they rode ahead of the wagon party to check out the area to the west.

"Do you see that, Posy? Is that the scouting party?" Juliet stood on tiptoe to see over the wagons and lines of hanging laundry. In her long, narrow bonnet, it was hard to see anything at all—like peering through a tunnel. "I thought the scouts were back already."

"No, they went out again this afternoon. Shh." Posy motioned for silence. "I'm trying to hear what everybody's saying. Something about the fighting that was going on close to the Montana border."

Juliet fell silent, suddenly chilled, as the galloping grew louder. From a distance, over the waving grasses, the specks looked like Sam Crowley's small group of scouts led by Ned Blackfoot, the hired guide on his pinto mare. But they were thundering—pounding—rather than paced at the usual confident clip of horses returning to camp.

"What's going on?" The sweat trickling under Juliet's bonnet felt clammy, and she took a step backward. Out of the corner of her eye, she glimpsed Jacob Pike, who still stood there nursing his injured arm—wrapping and rewrapping the bandage. But his eyes, like everyone else's, were fixed on the horizon.

"It must be bad," he said to no one in particular.

Juliet turned around. "What must be bad?" She kept her tone frosty and aloof.

"The fighting. The Cheyenne and Arapaho have been attacking forts near the Montana border." Jacob ventured a tentative step closer, apparently careful to keep a good distance between Juliet and his sling.

"But I thought we were far enough away! Everybody said we were safe passing through here—that we had treaties in place."

"Ha." Jacob snorted. "Treaties. Whatever that's supposed to mean."

"Are you suggesting we don't keep our treaties? Of course we do. We're the great

United States of America." Juliet hoped he heard the pride in her voice. "No thanks to you Southerners, of course."

Juliet wasn't sure, but she thought she saw Jacob roll his eyes. She ignored him and turned back to Posy. "I don't understand. Papa said we'd be fine—that relations with the Indians are good in these parts. He said we'd given them everything they could possibly want, and then some. Isn't that true?"

Jacob chuckled, and she shot him a cold look. "What? What's so funny?"

"You really don't know what the world is like, do you, Miss James?" Jacob said it sort of sadly, shaking his head.

"And you do?" Juliet stuck her head around Posy to look at him. "What makes you think you know so much about Indian relations, anyway? I thought you were from Virginia."

"Yep. Plain old Irish settler stock from the Shenandoah Valley. But I've been through here twice on business, delivering goods. I'm no expert. I just listen to what goes on around me—and it isn't always pretty." He winked. "But that's all right. I'll leave the pretty part for you."

Jacob caught her gaze and held it a touch too long, and Juliet felt the sultry roll of his syllables like a breath of warm summer breeze over the prairie.

She whirled around to fire back a retort, but the scouts careened into the camp, and the press of the crowd interrupted her. Shoulders and arms brushed her as people elbowed past. All she could do was grab Posy's arm and lurch along beside her, feeling Jacob's jacket crush against her sleeve.

"What are they saying?" Juliet cried as she strained to hear over the snorting of the horses. They were lathered, foaming, and one of the riders had lost his hat. His sweaty hair was plastered back from his sunburned face, his eyes round and frightened.

Posy pointed with a squeal—to an arrow protruding from the bloody flank of the horse.

"It's a mess," Sam Crowley gasped as someone helped him off his horse. "They're everywhere! Cheyenne, if I'm not mistaken, and mad as hornets. We can't hold 'em off for much longer. Our cavalry guys were no match for them—not with the few we've got out there now. We barely got out of there alive."

"The US Cavalry post is in trouble?" Jacob murmured next to Juliet's ear. "The Cheyenne couldn't take over Fort Smith already, could they? I knew they were in a tough spot, but I didn't expect them to fall apart so quickly."

Juliet aimed a spiteful glare at Jacob. "Why not? After the war, there's practically nobody left, and no funds either. They're broke—thanks to you and your foolhardy rebels, sir."

"With all due respect, your power-hungry opportunists taxed us to death and then stirred up the first squabbles, if I remember correctly. And if the U.S. Cavalry in Montana had used their budget correctly instead of squandering it on ale and women, they'd be in fine shape."

"You're a liar!"

"On my honor."

"Rubbish! You don't know a thing about honor."

"Does this mean we're in trouble?" Posy interrupted, her blue eyes frightened under her bonnet.

"If it's the Cheyenne, yes, after we pushed them off their land again." Jacob stroked his stubbly chin. "I just hope they haven't teamed up with the Arapaho, or we're in for it."

The wounded stallion stumbled. Juliet's heart quavered as she remembered her beloved horses—rare and graceful Arabians, sleek Morgans—back in Maryland. The stables closed and boarded up, and the saddles and leather polished for a new owner.

"I need my medical bag. Excuse me." Juliet pushed her way through the crowd, hoping she had enough willow bark to ease the stallion's pain.

"Does that prairie coneflower really work?" she called over her shoulder to Jacob.

"Sure does." He met her eyes over the crowd. "But I don't know if I'm willing to give you that bouquet of it a second time."

"Please. I won't hit you. I promise."

A couple of lanky boys stepped between them, and Juliet couldn't see Jacob anymore. She found her medical kit and snapped it shut then hauled all her bottles and herbs back through the crowd. She pushed her way to the front and held out her hands for the reins, but Sam Crowley curled up his lip.

"Where's Doc Hadler?" he said, sponging his sweaty neck. "He didn't stay back in Sheridan, did he?"

"Gallstones." Juliet set down her sack of forceps and sutures. "So that leaves me."

Sam ignored her, squinting through the crowd. "Is that the only doctor we've got?" he fumed. "A girl?"

"I'm almost twenty-three," she said tartly then shifted her heavy satchel to the other side. "And I've helped perform surgery on a Union general, sir. I think I can handle your horse."

Sam mopped his forehead with his beefy arm, not answering. Juliet quietly set down her satchel and began tearing bandages from long strips of sheet, draping them over her arm. The stallion moaned, a low sound of agony.

Sam glared at Juliet then slowly handed her the reins.

Chapter 3

September 21

The Cheyenne were coming again—the scouts had seen their horses from the ridge.

"Huddle up! They're getting close!" the camp leaders shouted as they rode through the camp. "We're going to try and pick them off one by one. Take cover and keep your dogs quiet."

"Not again." Juliet put down the hot forceps she was sterilizing in the fire and poured water on the glowing coals. "Posy? I'm going to find Elizabeth."

Last time the raiders had ridden by in the foggy early morning they'd simply exchanged shouts and a few rifle shots. Now they came closer, emboldened—in the pure daylight of midmorning. The wagon party was stalemated in—wagons circled to protect the livestock and travelers and get a better aim at approaching raiders.

"Oh, Juliet—they're coming again?" Elizabeth quavered, pale, nestling tiny Carrie Ann to her shoulder and gently patting her back. "I'm beginning to wonder if we'll ever get out of here."

"Sure we will." Juliet put her arm around Elizabeth. "Come on. We'll stay together. Can I take Carrie Ann?"

And to her surprise, Elizabeth placed her gently in Juliet's arms.

"Thanks." Elizabeth coughed and tapped lightly on her chest. "I'm just not feeling so well. The other ladies told me it's normal after giving birth and nursing, but. . ." Her voice trailed off. "I just feel so weak. And thirsty."

Juliet felt her stomach lurch. "Thirsty?"

"I can't seem to get enough. I even dream about water."

Juliet touched Elizabeth's forehead, and it burned with heat. She sucked in her breath, willing her heartbeat to slow down. "Forgive me for asking, but you haven't had any diarrhea, have you?" She whispered, not sure how to phrase such an indelicate subject.

"Why, yes," whispered Elizabeth. She ducked her head in embarrassment. "Does that mean something's wrong?"

"Quiet everybody!" called Sam Crowley, who was riding through the now-quiet camp. "Keep your heads down and your children with you. We don't want to shoot anybody by mistake."

Juliet rocked Carrie Ann lightly and huddled next to Elizabeth and Posy on the grass, not realizing she'd just had her last conversation with Elizabeth Baker.

∽

Rifle shots cracked in the distance, echoing against the vast expanse of plains and fields. Juliet huddled next to her younger brother, Silas, as he peered through narrow gaps in the tightly circled wagons. She noticed his normally steady hands slip on the barrel twice as though they were sweaty. He wiped his palms on his pants before getting a better grip.

Out of the corner of her eye, Juliet saw Jacob kneel before a crack in between the wagons and feed his rifle carefully through the space. He kept his head low to the ground and shifted sideways, apparently to see better.

"I don't want to be scalped," Posy whispered. She twisted a handkerchief in her trembling hands like a rosary. "I hear the Indians scalp their victims, dead or alive."

A wave of nausea roiled in Juliet's stomach. "Hush, Posy," she whispered back. "Don't talk like that."

"Of course you're not worried. Nobody's going to scalp you. You don't have enough hair for anybody to scalp."

"Well, with all your pretty curls, somebody would want you for a bride, not a scalp. Think about that."

Posy moaned, and Juliet elbowed her in the side and broke the tension. "Shush. Sam Crowley said we're too big a wagon party for them to attack full-on. They're raiders. We can pick them off one by one."

"Or not." Posy's lips trembled. "They're not sure how many are headed this way. It could be ten; it could be a hundred."

"We won't know until they get here," whispered Jacob as he rose up on his knees, his rifle nestled against his good shoulder. "If it's horses they want, they might try to stampede the livestock and break up our circle. And they might be able to do it. There aren't but forty of us, and how many children? We're late in the season to be traveling through here, you know."

"Well, we wouldn't be, if it wasn't for the bad weather and the flooding," Juliet whispered back. "And then being stuck here for weeks. It's not our fault."

"Tell that to the Indians and the October snowstorms. I'm sure they'll let you off the hook."

"You're not making us feel any better about this, Mr. Pike, you know?" Juliet snapped as she shifted Carrie Ann gently in her arms. "Why don't you keep your thoughts to yourself?"

"I'd rather prepare for real life. You've been so protected in that rich world of yours, haven't you?"

Juliet whirled around. She felt her face heat. "You don't mean that."

"I certainly do."

"You should be happy Papa's hard of hearing, or he'd string you up from the nearest tree," she whispered fiercely.

"And spoiled, too, just a bit," Jacob went on, as if he hadn't heard her. "And there aren't many trees around here to string me from, in case you hadn't noticed. And besides—he agrees with me."

"I beg your pardon?"

"If I were you, Miss James, I'd be thinking through your best options at a time like this."

"Options?" Juliet hissed then scooted away from Elizabeth and Posy so they didn't overhear. "You mean like being shot or taken prisoner? Oh, that's a really pleasant toss-up. Or maybe running out of food and having to eat each other?"

"Well"—he shifted his position and squinted down the barrel of his rifle—"I hope not. You won't live long on me, that's for sure—but you're welcome to it."

Juliet fought the mounting urge to slug his arm again, and she scooted as far away from him as possible. "It's impossible talking to you, you know that, Mr. Pike?"

"Jacob. My name's Jacob."

"Whatever. You're infuriating."

"Thank you."

"Never mind." She cupped Carrie Ann's fuzzy head with her hand and stroked it gently. "We'll all die, then. That's it. I'm ready for it. There's not much to live for anyway."

Jacob glanced over at her, and his eyes glittered in the shadowy light, like a shimmer of wine in a glass. Not laughing this time. "There's plenty to live for, Juliet. Don't forget that."

"You can call me Miss James." Juliet turned away from him and felt for the slim pin of the gold brooch Robert had given her which she hid under the collar of her dress. She kept it there next to her engagement ring, stitched into the ruffles for safekeeping. Her own secret; her private pain.

Before she could reply, the sound of battle rose from behind them: shouts and gun blasts and the fierce cry of Indian warriors. She tore her eyes away from the skyline and listened, heart pounding, to the low roll of drums, like the beginning of an impending rainstorm.

"How many of them are there?" Silas whispered, and Juliet heard the sound of Posy's muffled tears. "They're all around us. We're hemmed in. We'll never make it."

"There's no other route?" Juliet demanded. She clutched Carrie Ann tighter. "This can't be the only way across the prairie, Papa. Tell me I'm mistaken."

"Seems like it is, on this side of the mountains," said Papa as he wiped his balding head with a handkerchief. "There's nothing out that way but prairie, and impassable travel the rest of it—no water and too many rocks." He shook his head. "This was supposed to be an easy stretch, my girl. Relations were peaceful. Nobody's had a lick of trouble with this part of the territories—not a lick."

"Well, it's a fine mess now." Juliet fumed.

Jacob glanced up. "It depends on how you look at it, Juliet," he drawled.

"What? There's nothing good about any of it."

"Oh yes there is. You're still alive."

⟡

"Elizabeth?" Posy reached out and grabbed her arm. "Elizabeth, are you okay?"

Juliet looked up just in time to see Elizabeth slide into a heap on the grass, her arms limp. "Oh, my goodness." She thrust squirming Carrie Ann at Posy and lifted Elizabeth's head into her lap. "Elizabeth?" She touched her face and neck to gauge her temperature. "What's wrong?"

Elizabeth's eyes fluttered, and she rolled to one side. "I'm sick," she murmured, and Juliet felt Elizabeth's body shake with tremors, like a chill after snow.

Chapter 4

October 16

J uliet." Somebody shook her. "Wake up."

Juliet forced her eyes open to a brilliant yellow lantern light. At first she thought she might have cholera like Elizabeth: her arms and legs felt stiff and cold, immobile under the heavy quilt, and her neck ached from sleeping in an awkward position, slumped up against Silas's shoulder, her head resting against the side of the Hubbards' wagon. She could feel deep lines from the wooden planks gouged in her cheeks, and her mouth felt as dry as biscuit flour.

When she shook out the folds in the quilt, fine bits of snow sprinkled out.

It had snowed like that the day they buried Elizabeth—just a few flakes, as if the sky itself was weeping lacy tears. Juliet had cried until her eyes swelled, shivering, barely able to eat. It was cholera that had taken Elizabeth—she was sure of it.

And nothing she had done could save Elizabeth. None of her tinctures, the quinine, nothing. Not even the prairie coneflowers. She'd saved Sam Crowley's horse, but she'd lost Elizabeth.

All that was left now was Carrie Ann, who nursed from Mrs. Diamond but would only sleep when Juliet held her.

Before she sat up, Juliet moved her hand across the warm spot where she'd been sleeping, feeling for Carrie Ann. There she was, a chubby ball of sweetness, wrapped in the softest blanket Juliet could find. Carrie Ann stirred in her sleep and stretched out a tiny hand as if to search for Juliet's warmth.

"I'm sorry to wake you." Posy knelt next to Juliet in a thick wool nightdress, her nose and cheeks cherry-pink with cold.

"Somebody else shot?" Juliet patted Carrie Ann's cheek and reached for her wool overcoat.

"Not since Mr. Diamond."

"Cholera?"

"Nope. Just the two they buried yesterday." Posy shivered under her quilt. "This time Mrs. Henderson thinks William has the croup. She's awfully worried."

In the distance a rifle sounded, like a crack of thunder, and Juliet jumped. "I can't believe we left a war back east just to come to another one." Juliet tried to rub the sleep out of her eyes as she buttoned her coat. "You sound awfully awake for this time of night."

"Can't sleep. Too hungry." Posy's eyes looked large and liquid in her thin face. She was bareheaded, with her pretty hair streaming over her shoulder. "We're gonna run out of food if this keeps up, you know—especially when the snows come. There's nothing to eat around here but some prairie chickens and a couple of field mice. One of the Carlson boys caught a rattler, and they ate it up before we could even divvy it up among everybody fair and square."

Juliet's stomach rumbled in response.

"The Hendersons split up their rations for our breakfast yesterday morning," Posy continued in a whisper. "But the Bagbys didn't. They held back some of their best flour and bacon. I saw it under the quilts when I helped Constance Bagby with her youngest baby."

Jacob was still gone. Juliet saw his quilt hastily tossed aside, and Silas's folded and hung over the wagon beam. "Jacob and Silas aren't back yet?" she asked as she picked up her medical satchel. "It's been three days."

"Nope. Out scouting for help," said Posy in a way that sounded to Juliet a little too quick—and too worried. "I know they were talking about trying to reach that French outpost on the other side of the mountain. If we can still cross."

"It'll take them ages to rescue us going that way."

"Right. And we'll probably all be dead of cholera by then, or something equally gruesome."

Juliet couldn't answer, remembering Elizabeth. She stroked a hand down Carrie Ann's rounded cheek and prayed against all hope for her to grow strong and healthy.

"How bad is William?" Juliet shook one of her little glass vials, hoping her tinctures weren't frozen.

"She said he's coughing up a storm. Whatever that means in doctor's lingo." Posy knelt down and stroked Carrie Ann's back. "I'll watch the baby for you."

Juliet patted her hair in place with her free hand as she lugged her satchel through the darkened camp, her lantern casting long shadows on wagon wheels and clotheslines. Dogs snoozed on their sides, and even the chickens slept, roosting underneath wagons. Mrs. Bagby must have been unable to sleep, too, because she looked up from rearranging their stacks of petticoats and corsets in the back of the wagon, meeting Juliet's eyes with a gaunt look. Juliet turned her face away in embarrassment, pretending not to see. With the wagons so tightly together, there was precious little privacy—either night or day.

Even using the bathroom in a wagon circle was an ordeal—in which, as in so many things in life, men again had a natural advantage.

"Hey, Juliet—slow down a second."

Juliet paused then turned her head toward the voice—and the brash use of her first name. Jacob Pike seemed to materialize out of the shadows and fell in step beside her.

"You're back already?" She held up the lantern to see him better.

"Snow over the south pass. We couldn't get through."

"So no word to the French outpost, then."

"Nope."

She leaned forward to see his arm, which looked strange straight down by its side, out of its sling. "You've taken your bandage off."

"It was about time, I guess. It's feeling better after that Army doc cleaned the last bit of infection for me back at the trading post." Jacob glanced over his shoulder like he was nervous. "Never mind my arm. We need to talk. Just give me five minutes at the horse pen, okay? Pretend I've got a sick horse."

"Pardon?" Juliet burst out.

And Jacob didn't answer. He disappeared toward the livestock pen, turning only once to look back over his shoulder before his face blurred with shadow.

Juliet seethed a moment, furious, then turned and followed Jacob. She squeezed between two wagons near the horse pen and stepped carefully, holding up her long skirts up from the soiled, straw-covered ground. There was Jacob with his back to her, kneeling on the ground by the spotted gelding.

Jacob looked up. "Oh, hey, Doc. Lucky needs you to take a look at his. . .um. . .spleen."

"You must be joking." She set down the lantern.

"Okay, his stomach. Whatever. And hand me that horseshoe over there, will you?"

"What, here?" She picked it up and held it out, but he ignored her. So she bent next to him, the long, cold grasses poking through her layers of petticoats and calico, and shoved the shoe at him. "Whatever it is, hurry up. I've got to go."

"We need to defect," he whispered, not looking up. "Don't react. People are watching. Just listen."

Juliet felt her heart beat in her throat. She ran her hands along the gelding's side and pretended to check his organs.

"We're not going to make it." Jacob spoke so quietly his lips barely seemed to move. "The Cheyenne are calling in reinforcements, if the scouts are right, and they want to lay claim to this whole area. But Sam Crowley doesn't believe it."

"Why not?" Her breath misted.

"He thinks the cavalry can hold them off if they get reinforcements from Fort Phil Kearny back near Buffalo. But I'm telling you—I've been there. They're wiped out from the war like everybody else. We all are. And if you'll forgive me for saying so, they've lost some of their best soldiers. Quite a lot of them."

Jacob's brown eyes settled on hers, and Juliet stiffened.

"And whose fault is that, Jacob?" she snapped.

"Do you want me to answer that?"

"No, because you can't tell the truth. It's the fault of the South, and you deserved to fall apart—but you didn't have a right to take us with you. At least we accomplished one thing: ending the horrible institution of slavery."

"You ended it in some ways. Yes."

"Of course we did! You know what the Emancipation Proclamation says. What do you mean 'in some ways'?"

"I mean exactly what I said—in some ways. I just don't think it's as cut-and-dried as you think. Reason with me here—if the righteous Union was so all-fired anxious about destroying slavery, why didn't you do it two hundred years ago?" Jacob tipped his head back to look up at her. "The truth is that your industries in the North profited just as much from slavery as anybody else's. Who buys our Southern cotton and our tobacco?" He tugged on her sleeve. "Why, you do, don't you? I might be mistaken, but I'm pretty sure cotton doesn't grow in Maryland. Please. Set me straight."

Juliet jerked her sleeve away—her pulse throbbing angrily in her throat—unable to form a reply fast enough.

"The same cotton and tobacco produced by the blood and sweat of slaves, with full knowledge on your part. That's where it gets a little less clear who's at fault, doesn't it? The truth is we're all guilty. The entire human race. We're sick, every single one of us, no matter which part of the country we're from."

He sat back on his heels. "Let me tell you something: A legal emancipation of slaves, as good as it is, will never make people view another human being as an equal, as a brother. And that's where the real slavery lies—in people's hearts and minds. And there's not a law on earth except the law of Christ that can change people to the core, where they really need it."

And with that, Jacob picked up the horseshoe and turned back to the gelding. "Anything else you'd like to discuss about the war?" His smiled showed straight white teeth, and Juliet hated him.

She started to stand up. "I don't know why I bothered to talk to you."

"Because you need to get ready to leave. Tonight. The snows are coming soon, and we're not going to make it if we stay here. I've got a map, and I'm pretty sure I can get us to the Crow camp—or at least into the general area."

"Pretty sure? What's that supposed to mean?"

Jacob ignored her. "I've talked to your stepfather and Silas, and they're in."

"What?" Juliet burst out. The gelding snorted and swung his head around, swishing his tail.

"Easy, boy," Jacob whispered as he motioned to Juliet to keep it down.

But Juliet didn't feel like shushing. "Leave, Jacob? Are you kidding? Papa's heart is bad—he can't take a journey anywhere. I'm surprised he made it this far."

Jacob put his finger to his lips again. "Shh!" he hissed, and shot her an indignant glare. "I told you to keep it quiet."

"And that's another thing. Why all the secrecy? It's shameful, slinking off at night—abandoning the others." A man looked up from cleaning a saddle to watch her. Juliet quickly leaned over the horse's head and made a pretense of checking his teeth.

Jacob tapped on the horseshoe again. "I've heard the other guys talking. They want to start shooting the horses and oxen for food, one by one—but Sam Crowley claims his cows have Texas fever and aren't fit to be eaten."

"What? No." Juliet jerked her head up. "They're as healthy a team as I've seen. I checked them myself."

"Don Bagby said the same thing. Suggested we draw lots for whose horses go first—and that he'd make up the lots."

"I don't trust that man a bit."

"That's just the beginning." Jacob leaned forward earnestly. "The others are hoarding food, too—and when it all comes down to push and shove, they'll let you starve. I'm sure of it."

Juliet twisted the strap of her medical satchel between her fingers, remembering what Posy had said about food hidden in the Bagby wagon.

"Where are we supposed to go? The moon?" She waved an arm. "There's nobody around here for miles, except the Cheyenne. You've already said the forts are struggling to fend off attacks—so what's your plan? We can't make it to Montana, and we can't turn back. There's no one left."

"There is somebody left." Jacob gave a few calculating blows on the horseshoe, groaned, then sucked his injured thumb. He put the hammer down.

"Who?"

"The Crow. Enemies of the Cheyenne."

"The who?"

"The Crow tribe—the Absaroka, in their language. If we can make it far enough north without getting shot. I've been through these parts enough to think I can get us there."

Juliet stared at him, her mouth partially open. "You've gone mad. You've been on the trail too long, and you've gone completely mad. What good is it to flee to another Indian tribe?" She threw up her hands. "They'll kill us and scalp us, too, just like the others."

"Not necessarily. We've had good relations with the Crow, and they've been known to treat white settlers with kindness." He scratched his head. "Although perhaps they shouldn't, with all the disease and thievery we've visited on them. But they're our only hope. If we can make it to their camp and bring them a gift—like some rifles or some gold—I believe they'll spare us."

"What in the world gives you that idea?"

"History. Don't you read the newspapers? I've seen stories like that enough times to think it just might work."

"And if it doesn't?"

"I think it will. But if it doesn't, at least we won't starve to death."

"Right. Because they'll shoot us."

"Well"—Jacob shrugged—"since you put it that way. But given the choice, which way would you rather go?"

"I can't believe this."

"Neither can I." Jacob shook his head, the dents in his hat shadowed in the beam of lantern light. "But it's the reality of things, and we don't have much time to make decisions. So we're making one. Stay if you want—but if you know what's good for you, you'll come with us."

Juliet scrambled to her feet then shook the dirt and grass from her apron and skirt. "You, Jacob Pike, have poisoned my brother and stepfather with your nonsense. You want us to surrender to savages? They're not our kind! They're violent, and I don't trust them."

Jacob scowled. "They're people, not cannibals. And they're not much different from the slaves you defend so wholeheartedly—except we don't keep them in physical chains. No, we just push them off their land, laugh at their customs, and shoot them down at the slightest provocation." He snorted. "Righteous Unionists that we are."

"Unionists? It's not about that. The tribes out there are uneducated. Pagan. Uncivilized."

Jacob put the hammer down and stood up tall, looking her in the eyes. "You've been deceived the same as anybody else. Same as my idiot cousin who thinks he's better than a slave because he's white." He pointed at her. "Admit it—pride is a hard thing to swallow. We're not as great as we think we are."

Juliet felt her face turn hot.

"You. Of all people," she stammered through clenched teeth. "A Southerner. A *Confederate*." She spat out the word. "Trying to teach me?"

Then she grabbed up her lantern and pushed her way through the gate, not looking back.

Chapter 5

J uliet. I've got terrible news." Posy gulped then covered a sob.
Juliet looked up from wiping William Henderson's little rosebud mouth after his last dosage of castor oil, glad to hear his tiny lungs breathe freer and clearer. He rested against her shoulder, cheeks flushed and light brown hair tousled like a tiny angel. Streaks of pink bloomed along the horizon under low-hanging stars.

"What's wrong?" Juliet froze. "How's Carrie Ann?"

"I don't know if it was cholera, too, or something else." Posy's voice cracked, and she wiped her eyes with her apron between gasps. "I'm sorry. I just can't seem to pull myself together."

Juliet couldn't speak. She stared at Posy, open-mouthed, then passed William back to Mrs. Henderson. She fled, leaving her medical bags and equipment behind—between women clattering pots and pans for an early breakfast, dogs stretching, roosters crowing—barely feeling the frost stinging her toes. Just in time to see a group huddled near her wagon, and the low, muffled sound of weeping.

Juliet pushed her way through. "Where is she?"

And then she saw the little bundle: skin nearly as white as the blanket, eyes stiffly closed. Motionless and still as a stone, barely parted lips that seemed to have frozen in midbreath.

Juliet couldn't speak, couldn't move. Her hand flew up to her mouth, barely covering the sob that choked itself out. She reached for Carrie Ann through her tears, for the silent bundle, and the woman holding it passed it to her.

She felt nothing—no wind, no cold. Nothing. Numb as ice. Just the slow crumpling of her knees and a light-headedness that swirled like clouds around her vision. "She was warm," Juliet whispered. Tears dripped off her cheeks. "Just a few hours ago. I felt her."

"Juliet." A male voice spoke to her.

She looked up with unseeing eyes.

"Give her to me." Jacob knelt beside her, reaching out his arms. A grim look shadowed his usually cheerful face.

Juliet didn't move.

"Give her to me, Juliet," said Jacob, his voice stronger this time. "It's time for her to go."

"Go?"

Juliet saw tears in his eyes. "Back to the earth from where she came."

She saw Jacob reach for the stiff bundle and started to resist, but her muscles seemed leaden, slow—and he lifted Carrie Ann easily. Her arms felt cold, empty, without the blanket, without Carrie Ann's weight.

"What are you going to do with her?" Juliet's mouth could barely form the words.

"You go get warm." Jacob spoke in the tone he used when ordering one of his horses. "I'll take care of her."

"Warm?" The words made no sense, even though her teeth rattled together in the cold. Not when Carrie Ann would never open her walnut-brown eyes, never raise her downy head.

"Now. Go. Or you'll freeze to death, Juliet. Posy, get her something warm to drink."

Posy took her arm and tried to lead her away, but Juliet held back, pulling the quilt tightly around her neck to keep from shivering.

"Where are you going to put her, Jacob?" she asked as she sponged her nose with a proffered handkerchief. "Put her on the hillside. Where she can see the sunrise."

He had turned his back to her so that she could no longer see Carrie Ann's face, but Juliet could smell the wood smoke from his jacket and the faint scent of leather and shave lather that she recognized as distinctly Jacob's.

"She won't see any of that." Jacob spoke tenderly. "You know that as well as I do. She's seeing heavenly light shine brighter and more beautiful than she ever could on this earth—right this minute."

"Put her there anyway. Outside of this horrible camp where we've been stuck for so long. At least she can be free."

"Can't do it." Jacob shook his head. "I don't want to upset you, but we can't even make a headstone. The Indians will dig her up for the cloth she's buried in. And then the wild animals might. . .well, trust me."

Juliet sniffled. "Where's she going to go, then?"

"Under the ruts of the wagon wheels. Nothing will find her there. Believe me—I'll lay her down as gently as I can."

"Come on, my friend, and have some tea," Posy whispered, pulling her away. "Standing around and watching won't do us any good. Just be thankful that the ground's not frozen yet."

∽

It was nightfall when Juliet finally looked up from the spot where she'd sat with Posy. She stayed there, stiff and spent, and watched the sunlight shift and fade along the wagon's slats. The light and shadows stilled as Silas came and sat next to her on the cold ground, not speaking for a long time.

"Jacob's right, you know," he finally said in low tones. "About leaving. We've got to get out of here. I don't want to say this the wrong way, but what if Carrie Ann had had access to better food? Don't you think she might have. . .well, hung on a little longer?"

Juliet didn't want to hear about Jacob again—not with the memory of him holding Carrie Ann in his arms.

"Don't talk about Jacob," she whispered. "Please."

Silas picked at a dried piece of grass, avoiding her eyes. "He found flowers for her," said Silas gently. "Some dried coneflowers and daisies, up on the hillside. I helped him pick them."

Juliet squeezed her fingers together and forced the tears down, willing herself not to cry.

"Come with us." Silas touched her arm. "I don't think Jacob will lead us wrong. And if he does, at least we tried."

"Fine." Juliet spat out the word. What else was there to say? Not when Papa had made up his mind as well—there would be no changing it. And besides, who else could help him if his heart went weak again?

"So you'll come?" Silas sounded hopeful.

"What choice do I have?"

"Well, get ready, then. Jacob says to bring anything valuable that we might be able to trade for our lives—any hair combs you brought, any beads or glass, like your Christmas ornaments. Your mirrors. Everything—even your jewelry from Robert."

Juliet felt angry heat rush to her face. "How does he know about the brooch and the ring?"

"I told him."

"You didn't!" Juliet turned to him. "Jacob's got precious little to give, while we sacrifice everything? Sorry, but he's not getting Robert's jewelry. I'd die first."

"You don't mean that."

"Oh, I do." She swallowed the lump in her throat. "Who else is coming with us?"

"Posy. But her aunt and uncle are staying. They don't think their health can take the trek. Mrs. Van Dame isn't well. But they want us to take Posy and bring back help—and the Diamonds told us to take the twins. The Parks said to take Elijah."

Juliet's hand flew to her mouth. "Is it really that bad, Silas?"

He looked at her with mournful eyes, and for a moment he appeared young and vulnerable again, the way he had as a child when he'd crawled next to her in bed at night, afraid of the dark. Afraid of the silence in the large James house and the shadows that sneaked across the polished bedroom floor from the curtains.

"The Cheyenne are building fortifications all over the area. Most people don't expect to make it out of here alive."

Chapter 6

Night wind blew sharp and cold across the plains as Juliet crept forward on her knees with the others. Her breath sounded loud in her ears, fast and frightened as she pressed her face to the grass, braced for a warning shout from the marooned wagon train behind them. Beaded necklaces, coins, and glass Christmas ornaments in her pockets clinked together, and the sharp point of a pendant poked her through all the layers of wool and muslin and calico.

Papa grunted behind them on his knees, his heavy frame making a low shuffling sound, and Juliet listened to the rhythm of his breath to make sure he was all right.

"Keep going," Silas whispered over his shoulder. "Up to the ridge, and we'll be free and clear."

"Come on, Elijah." Juliet held out her hand. "You can do it. Keep crawling."

Something squeaked—a mouse, a flicker of movement in the grass—where they'd startled it from its hiding place, and an owl swooped over the plain in a flicker of black against stars.

A rifle blast shattered the quiet darkness, and Juliet dropped flat on her stomach as she threw an arm over Elijah and Violet. The air reeked of black powder.

"It's the owl," whispered Papa. "They shot it."

Juliet craned her neck to see behind her and caught a faint flicker of moonlight from Papa's round glasses. Too embarrassed to admit that her mouth watered as he said it.

"Where'd that mouse go?" she whispered to Posy, trying to calm the rising rumble of her empty stomach.

"If I find it, I'm not sharing," Posy whispered back.

"Hush," Jacob snapped from up ahead—one of the first times she'd heard him speak since they'd crept away from camp. "You want them to hear us?"

"If they'll share the owl," Juliet whispered back. "Then yes, maybe."

Elijah snickered. Silas shushed her again with a hiss, and Juliet dropped her head back to the ground with a heavy, silent sigh.

"Come on." Jacob motioned with his head. "Let's go while they're distracted. And there's not much meat on an owl anyway, Juliet. Forget it."

Juliet pushed herself forward over lumps and hollows in the cold ground, over tangles of roots and hard soil. The rippling plain, which looked so smooth and sea-like from above, hid pieces of broken wagon wheels, discarded rabbit and pheasant bones tossed from the campsite, and even pieces of tin food cans and bumpy wheel ruts from previous travelers crossing the plains.

No wonder people died of disease along trails like these—stepping through trash in overcrowded campsites, oxen and horses polluting the water. No cover over their heads by night, and no protection from mosquitoes, insect bites, or the occasional bat that swooped down on unsuspecting children.

As the ridge loomed closer, the dry slopes grew rougher and arched upward. Clumps of hard clay dug into Juliet's hands and knees, and she found herself pulling on dry tree roots and rough boulders, carrying the younger children in her free arm. Smatters of stones trickled down the dry soil with a tinkling sound, and Juliet sank back on her heels, out of breath.

Her pack weighed her down—her herb bottles and medical kit, the last bits of burned biscuits and cheese she could find in the wagon. A jug of water shut tight with a stopper.

"Come on," came Jacob's whispered voice near her ear. "You can do it."

"Hmm?" Juliet lifted her head as she blinked bleary, sleep-swollen eyes. It seemed that she'd dozed a few moments as she'd rested her head on her arm.

Jacob held out his hand, while little Violet clung to his other shoulder. "We're almost to the top. Just a few more yards."

Juliet hesitated then reached up and reluctantly grasped his hand and let him pull her to her aching feet.

They trudged up the steep bank, with little rains of soil trickling down, breath by hard breath. Around a coil of pine roots and then up through a gap in the pines where the stars prickled through the bristly black of a few scraggly Ponderosa pines.

Jacob awkwardly released her hand, and she stood there at the top next to Victoria, looking back at the distant reddish fire glow of the campsite, pricked by a few dim lanterns. So lost and lonely in the vast expanse of the endless dark plain, like scattered rubies on the ocean floor.

Jacob ducked under a pine branch and stood next to her, fixing his battered hat. He ran his hand through his wild hair, making it stand up on end.

"It's hard to leave what you know behind, isn't it?" he said softly as he patted Violet's back. "It's always a risk."

Juliet couldn't answer, thinking of Carrie Ann. Of the flowers Jacob had plucked from the hillside. Even Maryland, so far away in her distant memory that it seemed like a dream, the fuzzy bits of a story she'd invented in another life.

Jacob's profile was shadowed in silver, speckled with moonlight that filtered through thick pine boughs. "But without risk, there's no adventure. And there's no miracle."

Juliet spun around, hugging Victoria to her waist. "There's no miracle, Jacob. We've left everything behind, and we might die between here and the Crow outpost. There's no miracle in any of it. No meaning."

"Oh yes there is. I'll wager there's a miracle or two in store if we wait long enough. There's always death before birth, you know."

"No. There's just death."

"You're wrong. The Israelites had to endure four hundred years of slavery before God parted the Red Sea and set them free. And Jesus lay in the tomb for three days before the angel announced He'd risen. Death before birth. Would Moses' staff that budded be a miracle if it was still attached to the tree? No. It had to die first."

Juliet didn't answer, thinking of Carrie Ann's quiet gravesite under the ruts of the wagons. She cleared her throat. "I don't know if I believe that the way I used to."

"You will." Jacob ran his knuckles lightly across her cheek.

Juliet stiffened at his unexpected tender touch, feeling her heart beat loud in her throat. She tried to keep her breathing still. A *Confederate*.

She ducked under a branch, moving away slightly.

"I know you'll believe again," said Jacob. "Ask God, and He'll show you it's possible."

Juliet studied the outlines of the children's tiny faces in the moonlight and swallowed the grief down, not ready to speak yet. Jacob stood quiet a minute as he rubbed the tender flesh of his wounded arm. He sucked air through his teeth while he flexed his fingers, grimacing in pain.

"Well, let's go, then," he said in that low Southern drawl, finally slapping his hat back on his head. "The moon won't be up all night, and we'd better get as far as we can by morning. Here. Gimme that pack you're carrying. You'll never make it with all that stuff. What are you, a turtle carrying your home on your back?"

"It's my medical kit. You'll break everything." Juliet held on tight.

"And what if I do? Who needs all that anyway?"

"You will, sir, if I have to amputate that arm."

"Well, if you don't mind me saying so, that sounds a whole lot better than having to carry you the whole way when your back gives out."

Juliet snorted her disgust and shoved the pack at him, too tired to argue. Let gangrene eat his arm off, then, if that's what he wanted.

She gave one last glance over her shoulder at the circled camp where she'd lived for so many weeks, at the place where Carrie Ann had taken her last breath.

"Good-bye, little one," she whispered, touching her fingers to her lips in a kiss.

Then she followed Jacob down the ridge, not trusting herself to look back.

Chapter 7

Jacob lit the lantern in the shadows of the other side of the ridge and coaxed the wobbly flame into a bright flicker. The glow reflected on his cupped hands and thinly bearded cheeks, and when he looked up at Juliet with little laugh crinkles in the corner of his eyes, those eyes gleamed with golden stars.

Juliet felt her cheeks heat and looked away, unnerved by his direct manner. Too direct, as if he thought he knew her somehow.

Foolishness. Juliet took a long drink of water from the jug and wondered what Robert would have thought of Jacob—brash, cheerful, and stubborn, as opposed to Robert's quiet gentleness. Not to mention the hateful gray uniform that he'd fought in, which tore the Union apart at the seams. His ragged clothes and rolling twang. Everything Juliet despised in a man, in one manner or another.

It didn't matter. Juliet put down the water jug, too tired and too heartsick to think about Jacob. Not when cold and exhaustion bit into her bones like a yapping coyote and all she wanted to do was sleep—and sleep—and forget.

"Up again," said Papa with a grunt. "We've only got a few more hours of moonlight left."

Juliet stood and followed Papa, lifting Violet onto her shoulder.

∽

Night melted into weary morning, with streaks of robin's egg blue and pink along the horizon, and Juliet walked as if in sleep—hardly seeing or comprehending. Just one aching foot in front of the other. She had no breath left, no sense. Her bones felt like jelly, water-like, feeble.

When Jacob found them a shrubby spot by a river at dawn, they dropped into it like felled ducks, limp and motionless. Juliet lay the children down on a blanket, tucked them in, then curled on her side next to Posy in the briery reeds—not caring that cold mud soaked through her skirts.

She awoke at the sound of rifle shots in the distance, blasting and echoing against the barren hills. Jacob's dirty face watched the sky, and he gestured for her to keep her head low.

"We're too close to the fighting," he whispered. "They must have fanned out toward the southwest. Stay quiet and keep the kids down. The Cheyenne will kill us, and I'm not taking my chances with the cavalry either. They're so nervous they'd shoot us by mistake." He moved a shrubby dried stalk ever so slightly, peering between the leaves. "In fact, if we rattle around too much in the bushes, somebody's bound to think we're food."

"You needn't worry about me moving around." Juliet ran her fingers over the children's windblown hair as they slept. "I could sleep for a week."

"Ha. Right." Jacob touched a finger to his lip, which had a bloody crack in the corner. "And what do you propose to do when it snows a couple of feet on top of us all, then, huh?"

"So what do we do?"

"We'll go around the bluff over there instead of through the pass, which would have been easier. But we'll make it."

Thirst clawed at her throat, and Juliet crawled forward through the reeds and cupped some river water in her hands. At least there was water—polluted and stagnant as it might be. Strands of light brown hair fell over her shoulder and tickled the skin of the water into shimmering rings. But not before she'd caught a faint reflection of her face: cheeks hollowed, eyes too large for her forehead.

"You said there was birth after death, Jacob," she said as she wiped her mouth with her fingertips.

He turned on his elbow, his brown eyes meeting hers. "Oh, there is. I promise you that."

"I don't believe you."

"You will."

"You're so sure of yourself."

"I'm sure of Him. There's a difference."

Juliet crawled to Papa, where he lay curled in a heap and breathed noisily. Long snores, open-mouthed, with his whiskers twitching. She pressed her head to his chest and listened to the low, steady tick of his heart.

You're still alive, Jacob had told her before as they huddled by the wagons, praying for one more moment, for salvation and rescue. Even now, Papa still slept with his chest rising and falling, and the sound of the children's quiet breathing whispered through the leaves.

Juliet let her eyelids fall closed and slipped into blessed quiet.

✐

When Juliet awoke at midday, briefly, Jacob sat nearby with the others, rummaging in his rucksack, his hair messy and disheveled. She watched through bleary eyes as he broke a hard loaf of bread in his hands and passed it around. As Juliet swallowed her bites, chewing them as long as possible to savor the sensation of fragrant wheat on her tongue, she felt—strangely—the way she had at the communion table back at her church in Maryland. The breaking of bread, the silent thanks.

Only this time there was a desperation to her prayers, to the quiet partaking. In Maryland she had eaten the bread from her plenty, following the lines and motions almost by rote. The lifting of the cup, the stifling of a yawn.

Holy bread, for the hundredth time.

Only now she tasted every crumb then searched her dirty apron—and even the muddy ground between the reeds—for any fallen fragments.

Had she ever needed anything like this?

Had she ever needed Him like this, when all else around her failed?

"You didn't eat," she said suddenly. She pointed to Jacob in accusation.

"Ah." Jacob smiled. "I'm watching my weight. It's a health regimen of mine."

"You shouldn't have done that." Juliet spoke forcefully.

"Why are you worried? I thought you didn't care a bit about what I do. You've made that quite clear."

"I *don't* care." Juliet crossed her arms stubbornly. "But you'll faint along the trail, and then how will we know where to go? Besides, you're too heavy to carry."

"I'm not going to faint." Jacob laughed. "Want to know my secret, Juliet, since you're dying to know?"

"Don't flatter yourself. I'm certainly not dying to know."

"Oh yes you are. And here's the secret."

Jacob leaned forward to speak, and suddenly—before he opened his mouth—Juliet knew what he was going to say. She felt it, in a strange wave of premonitory coolness that washed over her, both familiar and startling at the same time:

"'Man shall not live,'" whispered Jacob, "'by bread alone.'"

And Juliet heard herself finish it: "'But on every word that proceedeth out of the mouth of God.'"

"You got it." The smile lines at the corners of Jacob's eyes creased.

"I knew that already." Juliet tried to calm the trembling tingle that quivered in her stomach and feigned indifference instead. Scorn, even. "It's nothing new. But I certainly appreciate a Southerner trying to school me in the ways of the divine."

"You're welcome, ma'am." Jacob tipped his hat. "'Cause you sure need it."

She breathed faster, seething. "You're a horrible man, you know that?"

"Yep." Jacob plucked a dried leaf from one of the reeds, stuck it in his mouth like a piece of hay, and gnawed on the end. "Good thing God forgives."

And he flopped down on the cold ground with his arms under his head then dropped his hat over his face.

✍

November 1

More days had passed than Juliet could count; she'd lost track—they all blended into a dull blur of exhaustion and soaking rainfalls that later turned into sleet and then snow. With a shudder, she remembered how they had huddled under a sodden quilt for hours at the edge of a bluff, motionless, as a Cheyenne war party passed by, and hiked by lantern light when the rain let up—interrupting a pack of wolves snarling over a felled deer.

Then the stars had disappeared for two days, and Jacob had to navigate via landmarks from his much-marked map: the outline of a ridge, a portion of an overgrown trail once rutted deep by wagons.

Silas had shot a thin fox, the first fresh meat since Juliet could remember, and they roasted it over a makeshift spit in thin, sputtering snow. The air turned bitterly cold, with biting winds, and tiny pellets of ice had lashed their cheeks and fingers red. When Posy's feet had hurt too much to walk, they stopped to build a small fire and heat Juliet's last remaining jug of precious water for tea. So now they rested under barely sheltering trees, waiting for a chilling mist to lift.

Elijah and Violet and Victoria slept in an exhausted pile, open-mouthed—Victoria having cried herself to sleep from hunger and cold.

"The Crow scouts will probably kill us before we even reach camp, won't they?"

Juliet said, shivering under the damp quilt. "Maybe it's better that way—just to end it. I'm so tired."

Jacob smiled again as he watched her, the firelight catching a shaft of red-brown in his eye. The color of cherry wood, a gleam of polished chestnut.

"Trust in the Lord, Juliet."

The feeble fire hissed and sputtered, and a wisp of smoke curled upward. "Trust Him to do what? He's let more than one believer die gruesomely along the way, you know."

Jacob studied her there in the firelight, and his smile faded. "You cry out in your sleep," he whispered, and then he leaned close so that only she could hear. "Did you know that?"

"Me?" Juliet sat up straighter.

"Yes, you." He looked sad as he twiddled a stray twig in his fingers. "You talk about stopping the bleeding or removing a bullet. About infection and chloroform. Things a young woman should know nothing about."

Juliet didn't answer. She simply looked away. "Why do you care?" she finally asked. "And you snore, anyway."

Jacob ignored her comment. "You've seen too much. More than I realized." His eyes looked tender, pained. "I'm sorry if I've been harsh with you, Juliet. But don't harden your heart toward God. We made this mess—not Him."

Juliet swallowed and swallowed again. Her heart trembled.

"Papa's not well, Jacob," she finally stammered then scooted quickly away from the fire. "I don't know if he'll make it much longer, and I'm out of camphor. I used the last on William Henderson."

Jacob still watched her. Then he stared into the fire, snapping the twig between his fingers.

Suddenly Juliet raised a finger to her lips and listened. She'd heard something: a whisper, a rustling in the underbrush. And she whirled around in time to see a man leap forward, his rifle pointed straight at her head.

Chapter 8

H ands up," the man barked, and two other ghostly figures appeared from the mist, both with rifles bearing down on them. "Now, or I'll shoot."

Juliet gasped. Jacob put his hands up without a word, nodding for everyone else to do the same. She slowly lifted her hands.

"Who are you folks anyway?" The grizzled man with the rifle leaned forward, his face terrible and gaunt with a long, unkempt beard. A missing front tooth. The limp tail of a dirty coonskin cap hung over one shoulder.

"We're from the wagon train that's marooned south of here. We're trying to reach help." Jacob spoke boldly. "And who are you?"

"None of your concern." The man lowered his rifle slightly and began pawing through Juliet's bags. She started to protest, but Jacob reached over and squeezed her arm tight. She froze, hardly daring to breathe.

"Can you help us get to the Crow outpost, sir?" Jacob spoke again, and one of the other men produced a pistol, holding it against Jacob's head. "I guess not, then, huh?"

The man with the coonskin cap laughed. "That's a good one, son." He winked, but Juliet saw ice in his eyes. He swung the rifle around at them all, his voice harsh. "Give me everything you've got. All your money and food, and guns, too. All your jewelry. Ev'rything. Shoes. Now."

⚬⚬⚬

She was supposed to walk again, in bare stockings, and everything felt cloudy. "Are they gone yet?" Sleet stung her cheek, and she couldn't stop shivering. Her feet tingled with cold, and she watched the bright sky fade into gray and then black. She dreamed of someone calling out to her across the hills—in a voice that sounded like Robert's—and the sky exploding with a million tones of ruby. A carpet of light unfurling across the sky, rippling and sparkling like colorful ice.

"That's the northern lights," she heard Jacob whisper in her ear.

The world spun, black and red, dazzling with light—shivering, the chatter of teeth—movement shifting uphill and downhill under her frozen feet, sleet stinging her face. Until she felt the hard ground under her cheek and could not remember how to move.

This, thought Juliet in a spiral of ebbing thoughts, *must be what it's like to die.* Sparkling snowflakes rained over her field of vision like diamonds against gray.

Miracles. Jacob had spoken of miracles. And yet they had not come.

She felt herself lifted, carried. The sound of wind in her ears. A deafening weightlessness, a floating. And then nothing.

November 7

Brilliant light crept through Juliet's eyelashes like the crack under a door then spread brighter and brighter until she squinted and turned away. When she managed to squeeze one eye open, all Juliet saw was blue. Brilliant, pulsing blue through a hole over her head.

"Jacob?" She tried to sit up, groping for an arm, a piece of ground. "Papa? Where's Papa? Where are the children?"

She must have lurched too sharply, because the circle of sky spun like a cyclone, tilting dangerously to one side.

Gentle hands straightened her and smoothed her hair, and someone pressed a cup of something warm and bitter-smelling to her lips. She tried to push it away, but her fingers felt heavy, slow, and they slipped on the bowl.

"I need to find Papa. And that man took the children's shoes."

Someone put the cup to her mouth again, with urgent words, and this time Juliet let in a sip of something warm and savory, like broth. She tried to drink, and it sloshed down her chin and the front of her dress.

A woman's voice spoke softly as she mopped Juliet's chin and steadied the cup, but Juliet understood none of what she said. She closed her eyes and drank again, feeling a stinging, voracious warmth spread through her stomach, all the way to her toes.

From the corner of her eyes she watched hands lift a brittle cake of flat-baked bread and break it in half, splintering crumbs.

Man shall not live by bread alone. . . .

Juliet reached for the bread like a starving woman then crammed shaky handfuls of it into her mouth. She blinked again as she tried to make the blurry shapes and figures merge into one.

The hands that held the bread weren't Posy's. They were brown hands with short pink nails. Laced at the wrist with a leather bracelet studded with animal teeth.

The shapes began to merge, to straighten, and Juliet found herself looking up at a conical flap of leather hide stretched taut against poles. A single shaft of sunlight filtered across the darkened room so that warmth poured on the side of her face.

The skin lodge, or *tepee*, of the Crow.

"Juliet." Posy appeared so suddenly that Juliet startled before she looked up into her friend's pale and freckled face. "We're here. We're all here." She placed a hand on Juliet's arm, and the lodge poles began to ripple again. "Hush, Juliet. You're safe."

The woman who held the bread moved with a soft tinkling sound as her hair fell over her shoulder and brushed against beaded buckskin and rows of colorful necklaces. Thick, black, shiny hair, like the gleaming wing of a raven, and skin the color of maple sugar. Her belly rounded under her buckskin dress like a curved vase—heavy with child.

"Thank you," Juliet murmured with weak lips to the woman, to Posy. "Thank you. Thank you so much." She couldn't stop saying it; the sensation of a full, warm stomach and soft blankets beneath her made her want to weep.

"I don't understand. Did they take us prisoner?" Juliet tried to sit up, and Posy reached out to help. "Who is she?"

The woman said something to Posy in a low and guttural voice, with lilting words that rose and fell, then handed Posy the bread, patting it into her hand. She pushed it gently toward Juliet with a nod.

"Her name's Áxxaashe—'sun'—and she wants me to feed you." Posy thanked her and took the bread, breaking it into small pieces. "They've been taking care of you for three days now. If it wasn't for the Crow scouts, we'd have died in the snow."

Juliet let Posy place a chunk of still-warm bread in her mouth and chewed. She reached hungrily for more with shaking hands. "No, Posy—I remember. Those men took everything and left us there. We didn't eat for days."

"And the Crow scouts found us." Posy broke off another piece of bread. "They gave us blankets off their own shoulders. And food, Juliet—we ate from their own packs, right at their feet, like starving coyotes. Strips of dried buffalo, thick fried corn cakes." Her eyes fluttered closed. "I could have kissed their moccasins. In fact, I was so out of my mind I probably did."

Juliet's mouth felt dry. "But I thought the Crow were going to. . ."

"I know." Posy looked down. "We all did. But they not only brought us here to their camp, but they *carried* you. Did you know that? They carried you the rest of the way, through the early hours of the morning."

"The northern lights," Juliet whispered. "I remember."

"And they carried the children and me, too, when our legs gave out in the snow from cold and hunger. Jacob caught a fever and started talking nonsense, and Silas couldn't stop shivering."

Juliet chewed slowly. "I don't understand why they'd do that for us. We didn't even have anything to give them! Not a coin or a gun. Nothing."

"I don't understand it either." Posy shrugged and broke off another piece of bread. "They had pity on us, I guess—they're just kind folks. Jacob said relations between the Crow and most travelers through Montana had been generally friendly, and I guess he was right."

The tepee flap stirred in a cool breeze, and Juliet caught a glimpse of the camp outside: tall tepees painted with stripes and running horses, all bristling at the top with the tips of lodge poles. Cook fires smoked, and buckskin-clad boys played with a hoop, running and shouting—several dogs yapping at their feet.

Through the clearing, Juliet heard the sudden rise and fall of familiar children's voices in song, over the rhythmic pounding of what sounded like a mallet on hard grains, and her head turned. "The children. Violet and Victoria and Elijah. They can't have made it here alive, can they?"

"They're out playing with the kids," said Posy. Sunlight illuminated the side of her face. "Elijah has a cold and Violet's pretty weak, but after a few good meals they're up and around."

"I can't believe it." Juliet covered her face with her hands, feeling the tears come. "I just can't."

"God's miracle, I guess."

"Jacob said we'd see miracles, but I didn't think it was possible. Not after so much misery."

"Don't give up." Posy kissed the top of her head. "Sometimes all we have is the tiniest crumb of faith, and it's enough to last us through the famine until God shows up. Remember—Elijah lived for a year on nothing but bread."

"Bread again," Juliet whispered, remembering Jacob's hands splitting the hard loaves. "Huh?"

"Never mind." She wiped her wet cheeks. "Where's Papa?"

"Can't you hear him snoring? He's right over there. Sleeping like a bear."

Juliet shook off her blanket and crawled over to Papa's sleeping figure, nestled under woven blankets the colors of sun and rain, all yellows and blues. His thin gray-white hair spilled over his forehead, messy as stacks of scattered straw, and framed bushy eyebrows that wrinkled in what seemed to be a pleasant dream.

"Papa?" Juliet whispered. She listened to his steady breathing and smoothed his curly hair.

"See? I told you. He's fine. Rest." Posy spoke gently as she helped her back to her blanket. "He's sleeping. Don't wake him. And you need to get your strength back, too."

"What about Silas? Have you seen him?"

"Oh, Silas." Posy looked down, and her voice softened ever so slightly. "I reckon he's all right. He's been shivering a lot still, but he was eating a while ago like he hadn't seen his stomach in a week. Poor, sweet fellow." She sighed and covered her mouth with her hand.

Juliet thought for a second that Posy's freckled cheeks flushed ever so slightly. Or was her vision still giving her fits?

Wait a second. "Did you just call Silas sweet?" Juliet twisted around to see Posy.

"What?" Posy wrinkled her nose. "Me? 'Course not! Silas ain't sweet. He's rotten like the rest of 'em. You know how men are! And listen. There's some bad news, too, about Jacob." She changed subjects and spoke so quickly that it took Juliet a second to register her words. "He's still pretty sick. Worst of all of us, and. . .well, you'll just have to see for yourself. I reckon you'll know what to do."

"Jacob's still sick?" Juliet caught her breath.

"Juliet, do you think he'll be all right, so long as he keeps on eating?" Posy gripped her arm suddenly, her eyes bright as if with tears. "I mean, he's stopped shivering and all, but how are we to know if he's really all right inside?"

"Who, Jacob?"

Posy's gaze floundered back down to her hands. "Well, him, too, of course, but. . ."

Juliet's eyes fixed on her friend until it dawned on her slowly—the way Posy had folded Silas's blanket with extra neatness, her blue eyes bright as she looked at him over the rim of her tin cup.

"You're worried about Silas." Juliet meant to ask it as a question, but it came out as a statement.

Posy jerked her head up. "Me? Shucks, no—not like that, anyway. What's a matter with you, Juliet? You must still be sick—that's all. Hush and eat some more." She picked up the bowl and fed Juliet a few more mouthfuls of soup, effectively ending the conversation since Juliet couldn't talk with a full mouth.

"You didn't tell me if anybody here speaks English," Juliet interrupted after swallowing down the broth in a gulp for air.

"Not but a couple of words. They speak French though."

Juliet groaned. "I was terrible in French. My teacher laughed in my face."

"I know a little from one of our old farmhands," said Posy. "A Huguenot from France. Couldn't speak a lick of English, but sakes alive, the man knew how to make good cheese." She shoved the bowl at Juliet's mouth again. "Here. Have some more."

"Where's Jacob?" Juliet coughed down the last of the broth and grabbed the bowl. "Will you take me to him?"

Posy hesitated, biting her lip and looking like she might cry. "I don't know if it's a good idea. He's not in good shape, and I don't want to upset you."

"Upset me? Posy, I need to see him." Juliet started to get up.

"Well, can you walk?"

"You can help me."

"All right. I'll take you." Posy let out a shaky sigh. "But you might be sorry I did."

⁂

"Jacob?" Juliet knelt by his bed and turned to see his face.

When he didn't answer, she inched closer and put her hand on his forehead. Jacob stirred and his eyes twitched, shivering, but he didn't respond.

"Posy, he's feverish," she whispered. "Has he been vomiting? What's wrong with him?" She reached for his hand under the blankets and lifted it, bending his limp fingers. She checked his weak pulse, wishing to goodness she had her medical supplies.

"I don't know. I haven't heard him coughing, but he's stopped eating." Posy sat down next to him and looked as if she might cry. "Poor fellow. After getting us all here safely."

"How about water?" Juliet's mind spun through a list of possibilities. "Has he drunk anything? How long has he been like this?"

Posy straightened his blankets. "They called some people to look at him, but I don't know what they said. Honestly, I thought he'd be better by now, but he keeps getting worse."

Juliet opened Jacob's mouth and looked at his tongue then pulled his eyelids open and checked his pupils for dilation. He barely moved, and a shaky panic trembled in the pit of her stomach. She pulled the blankets back and lowered her ear to Jacob's chest to listen to his breathing, and then she ran her fingers along the tender glands at the side of his neck.

"It doesn't seem like cholera. Nor mountain fever either, or ague." She bit her thumbnail as she thought. "You said he hasn't been coughing?"

"Not that I've heard."

And then something awful occurred to her. Juliet pulled down the blanket and reached for Jacob's arm—the one he'd wounded in combat. She rolled up his sleeve and unwound a fresh bandage, carefully peeling back a strong-smelling herbal poultice—and she and Posy both gasped.

The arm the surgeon had sutured now was puffed, red and inflamed, and blotches of red streamed out in all direction across his skin in hateful, angry lines. Yellow pus boiled over at the site of the suture, and his whole arm felt hot and swollen with the stench of dead flesh.

"My word." Posy rocked back on her heels. "He's got infection again. That man who tried to clean it out didn't do a good job, I reckon."

"And the infection has probably gone into his bloodstream." Juliet clapped her hand over her mouth. "With so much exposure to the cold and so little to eat, his body just couldn't fight it. And what can I do? I don't have any of my medicines. This poultice might stave off gangrene for a while, but it won't cure him."

Juliet brushed Jacob's hair from his forehead as he tossed and groaned in his sleep. "There must be somebody close by who can help. Isn't there a fort nearby, wherever we are? An outpost, somewhere that might have a medical doctor?" She stroked her hand over his limp palm. "I hope they don't have to amputate his arm."

Posy spoke softly. "Seems like not long ago you were ready to knock that arm off yourself."

Juliet felt her face blaze with shame, and she couldn't look at Posy. Couldn't answer, thinking of Robert. Of the war, and all those soldiers in blue who'd bled to death right in the Union hospital. Their groaning and moans for help, and the nearly lifeless eyes that fluttered with pain.

So much like the thin face on the blanket in front of her, his lips moving as if in silent prayer. Chest lifting and falling, limbs trembling.

A man, flesh. Not so different from those who'd fought and died under the Union flag.

Only she wasn't about to lose another healthy man like Jacob to infection. Not again. Not when his face still bloomed with faint color and his heart still beat strong and sure beneath the blankets.

Not this time.

Juliet stood. A strange new strength surged through her shaky legs as she pushed back the tepee flap.

"I can't speak French, Posy. Can you help me find someone who can get a doctor?"

"I'll try." Posy stuck her tongue between her lips as she thought. "Let me see if I can find the fellows who were with him earlier."

"Hurry. There might not be much time."

Chapter 9

Juliet huddled under a woven Crow blanket and listened as Posy and a group of buckskinned men conversed in halting French. A slow fire burned in the center of the tepee, and Juliet inhaled pungent scents of smoke, sage, leather, and rawhide.

"The leader said they've applied the best poultice for infection," Posy whispered with a nod toward a wrinkled man with straight black hair parted into two long braids. Beads, bits of bone, and feathers twinkled at the ends of his hair, and the blankets around his shoulders glowed in rows of brilliant color. "Something about dried flower roots and tree bark. I didn't get the rest."

"Is he the chief?" Juliet whispered.

"No, one of the tribal leaders. The other two must be important people, too."

"I can't believe they'd even want to help us. Please thank them for me—they've saved our lives."

Posy did, in such emphatic terms that the men grunted and seemed almost embarrassed, bowing slightly as if to receive her thanks. The old man lifted his hand as if in blessing, his eyes milky with cataracts.

Juliet raised her head, suddenly ashamed. Ashamed of the broken promises and broken treaties Jacob had spoken of. "Savages"—she'd said it herself. And they'd poured broth down her throat when she was too weak to drink.

Posy translated. "He says he can ask the medicine man to do a prayer incantation, but he's not sure it'll work."

"Oh, no. Not that." Juliet remembered Jacob's hands breaking bread. "Tell Him the God of the Bible—Jesus—can heal him if He chooses. He hears our prayers."

"Goodness, you're pushing the limits of my French, Juliet." Posy scowled.

She talked a few more minutes, shaking her head and haltingly trying French and occasional English words, her arms motioning up to her shoulder and then her heart. They sketched what looked like a map on the earthen floor and argued back and forth as they pointed to different spots—drawing rectangles and lines. Finally, Posy threw her hands up and burst into tears.

"What's he saying?" Juliet tugged on Posy's sleeve.

"He says there's no doctor around here for miles, except for the French doctor the trappers use—and he's expensive. He won't come without gold in hand, up front—and the heavy snows are coming soon."

Juliet's breath quickened. "Is he good?"

"What does it matter? We don't have a thing to give him. No gold, no nothing. Not even our boots. We're lucky to be here alive."

"Ask him if he's good." Juliet said again.

Posy turned back to the group of men and repeated Juliet's request in French, and the older man nodded soberly.

"*Très bon*," the leader said with a sober nod. "Very good doctor. The best."

"How much does he cost?"

The old man held up a brown hand webbed with lines and counted on his fingers. He held up five, and then five more.

"That much?" Posy smacked her head.

"How fast can he get there?" Juliet interrupted.

"Juliet, you must be feverish. A couple of days, maybe, but what does it matter?"

"Trust me. Please ask him. See if they'll go get him."

Posy turned to face her. "Why do you care anyway? I thought you couldn't stand Jacob. You said so yourself—lots of times."

"Forget what I said. I need their fastest runners—please."

Snowflakes drifted past the tent's opening like thin bits of confetti, and the fire sputtered and smoked. Wind moaned past the tepee, a mournful sound like a man in agony.

And Juliet reached beneath her high ruffled collar with shaking fingers and withdrew her heavy golden brooch—its moody blue stone sparkling like sea waves at dusk. She held the cross-shaped brooch, still suspended from its gleaming silken gold chain, and coiled it into Posy's hand with a musical metallic clink.

"Take it." Her engagement ring dangled from the chain next to the brooch. "And give the ring to the Crow runners, if they'll agree. Please ask them to go as fast as they can."

The older man said something in Crow—a surprised exclamation—and reached for the brooch. Glistening dots of light reflected on his wizened face and glinted in his dark eyes.

"Whatever's left they can have. We owe it to them." Juliet handed him the ring. "They've given us our lives back—and besides, what good would it do around my finger anyway?"

Posy's eyes popped, but she dutifully translated into French. The others in the tepee huddled together around the brooch and the ring, passing them back and forth. The older man bit the tip of the brooch to test the gold and then made another exclamation—with an expression that Juliet thought was almost a smile. He nodded and held up the ring to the light, turning it so that the blue stone sparkled.

For a second, Juliet wanted to reach for it—for Robert—but she kept her hands folded tight under the blanket. She trembled, but not from cold.

"Juliet. That's Robert's engagement set," Posy whispered. "Are you sure you want to do this? I want to save Jacob, too, but bringing a doctor won't guarantee he'll live. We could do all of this, and Jacob could still die. You know that, right?"

"Of course I do." To cover her emotion, Juliet spoke more snappishly than she meant. "But we have to try, don't we?" She pointed. "Look. The leader is trying to talk to you again. What's he saying?"

Posy listened then tossed a few questions back in her uncertain French. "He says this is far more than the doctor needs, or his fastest runners," said Posy. "He says they could not accept such a high payment."

"Tell him it's a gift." Juliet's heart beat fast. "A thank-you gift for saving our lives."

The man's brow wrinkled, and he spoke, shaking his head.

Posy translated. "He says he does not need a gift for doing right."

"Please. Ask him if he'll help us as friends. Jacob desperately needs a doctor, and whatever's left, we share in the camp as partners."

The old man looked first at Posy, then at Juliet and down at the brooch—and then grinned and grasped Posy's pale hand in his wrinkled one.

Chapter 10

November 9

The doctor arrived two days later—his horse lathered with sweat from riding from dawn to dusk. A record, the Crow leaders told Posy.

He grunted a greeting in Crow and disappeared into Jacob's tepee with a lantern, shutting the flap behind him. And that was the last Juliet saw of him, except when he barged out for more whisky for the patient—and for himself. He was a foul man, a bearded, sweaty fellow who reeked of garlic and body odor and spat in the dust like a cantankerous mule. He didn't speak, he snarled—and Juliet kept a cold distance.

"If Jacob wakes up to that, he'll wish he were still unconscious," she mumbled as she stood nervously outside the tepee. She half wished she'd saved Robert's gold for a better candidate. "Are you sure he's a good doctor?"

"They said he's the best." Posy shrugged.

"He'd better be."

Silas, who had exchanged his tattered pants and dirty, ripped broadcloth shirt for a pair of buckskin trousers like the Crow, crossed his arms. "Jacob, the poor fellow. We wouldn't even be here if it wasn't for him, you know."

"No. We'd be like the others." Posy looked down at her hands. "You heard the news, didn't you, Juliet?"

"I did." Juliet winced and looked over at the children, who were playing nearby. "I just can't think about it. It's too awful."

"The whole wagon party killed or taken captive by the Cheyenne," Posy murmured as she wiped her eyes with shaking fingers. "Every last one of them. The horses and oxen divided up, and all their goods taken. It's just too terrible to be true. The children are grieving so much—they've lost their parents."

Juliet put her arm around Posy, the news still fresh in her mind like the garish kill of a wolf, spread gruesome and bloody.

"It broke my heart to tell them," said Juliet softly. "They're doing so well considering all they've been through."

"Poor little dears." Posy let out a shuddering breath. "At least my aunt and uncle stayed together until the end. So brave and so faithful. I don't think I could've taken a bullet in place of the Henderson children like they did. Both of them, one for one. It tears me up to think about it."

"You would have done it, Posy," said Silas softly as he gazed at her with tenderness. "You underestimate yourself."

"Oh no I don't." She wiped wet lashes. "I'm a chicken. A big, fat chicken." And she bawled into her apron.

"At least the poor Van Dames didn't suffer much, from what I hear," said Papa, his face lined with sorrow and exhaustion. "God rest their blessed souls. They'll get their reward from the Lord. I'm sure of it."

"I know they will. I just wish they could have made it here with us. And I hope that doctor will get word to the cavalry that we're here—so they can send help and find the children's relatives if they have any close by." She dried her face. "The Indians have been so kind to us, but I'm ready to go home."

Juliet heard the doctor's voice from inside the tepee, raspy and harsh—barking orders to his assistant—and she jerked her head up.

Papa, still weak but able to walk, rubbed his hands in the cold. "Is he going to have to take his arm, Juliet, my dear?"

"He said he'd try his best to save it."

Juliet heard Jacob moan from inside the tepee, a sound of agony, and she covered her ears. Her stomach reeled, lurched, and she backed away trembling. She'd seen the forceps and bone saws in the doctor's bag—horrible instruments—and in an instant it all came back: the wails of the dying. Blue Union wool spattered in blood.

Before she could flee, the tepee flap suddenly fluttered and the doctor stomped out, wiping bloody hands on his trousers. The doctor—Louis, they said his name was—cursed and spat on the ground, grinding it into the soil with his boot. "Well, that's about all I can do for the poor sot," he growled in heavily accented English as he pulled a cloth from his jacket pocket and wiped his hands and his forehead. Then he scrubbed behind his big ears. "God rest him."

Without warning, Louis draped a heavy arm around Juliet's shoulders and breathed his horrible breath into her ear. "And you, miss, probably just threw your money away. It's anybody's guess if he even survives." He squeezed her tighter and grinned, and a gold tooth gleamed in the gap of his mouth. "But as long as you're giving it to somebody, might as well be me."

"What do you think you're doing?" Silas hollered, and Papa swiped at the doctor with a beefy arm.

Juliet shoved Louis's arm off and stalked away, brushing her hair and pinafore back in place. She rubbed her cheek where his prickly beard had scratched it. "If you please, sir," she snapped as she pulled Posy a safe distance away, "I hired you to heal the man, and that's all. Have you done it?"

"I've done what I could." Louis stretched and popped his knuckles over his head. "On account of the painkillers, he's half out of his mind now."

"And so are you," retorted Juliet.

Louis roared, his ample belly shaking. He eyed Juliet with a leering grin, his hand stroking his long beard. "Oh, I see. You're a fiery one, aren't you?"

He moved toward her again, showing yellow teeth in a smile, and Juliet grabbed a heavy mallet the women used to pound dried meat, fat, and berries into pemmican. She raised it over her shoulder, ready to swing. "You come one step closer, sir, and you'll be sprawled next to Jacob, you hear? Now tell me what you gave him, and quick."

"Why does *madame* care what I gave him? Do you know medicine?" Louis stroked his beard again, his eyes bouncing back and forth from Juliet to Posy as if he couldn't believe his good luck. "Well, for starters, whiskey. Lots of it." He grinned.

"Did you take his arm?" Juliet tried to keep her voice steady and warned herself not to slap him.

"*Non.* I managed to leave most of it. And you should thank me, too, because, I usually get paid more for amputations than for cleaning out wounds. This kind of work doesn't pay as many of my debts, but I take what I can get."

"That's disgusting."

"It's the truth." Louis blew his nose on a handkerchief and stuffed it in his pocket. "This fellow, though, I doubt even God himself could save."

"Watch yourself, sir," Juliet snapped, "when you speak of the Lord."

Louis laughed. "Well, I'll put it this way. I've seen worse. Much worse."

"Did any of them live?"

"*Non.*" Louis spat again. "Can't remember any that did. But. . ." He leaned forward, and his giddy, bloodshot eyes suddenly sobered. Thick, bushy black brows pulled together like twin caterpillars. "But—there's always one that beats the odds." He held up a fat finger. "Mark my words."

"It's going to be Jacob." Juliet lowered the mallet slightly, but she didn't relax her grip.

"Well, for your sake, I hope so." Louis took a sidelong step toward her. "But if not?"

Juliet raised the mallet again. "Don't even think about it."

Chapter 11

December 24

J uliet—it's Christmas Eve." Posy poked her.

Juliet opened her eyes to white flakes drifting past the dark opening at the top of the tepee. Her back was warm where she'd huddled against Posy in the predusk cold, under thick blankets and buckskins. A fire sputtered in the center of the tepee, and her pinafore and faded calico dress hung next to Posy's on a rawhide line stretched across part of the ceiling.

"Christmas Eve? Are you sure?"

"I counted the marks. See for yourself." Posy scooted over to a row of marks she'd lightly scratched on the rawhide of the tepee.

Juliet leaned forward in the fading light, her long braid falling over her shoulder, and followed the ticks with the tip of her finger. "I can't believe it. Who would have thought our Christmas would be like this? Why, I don't even know if we're in Wyoming or Montana—or where we are at all."

"And I guess we'll be here awhile. Snow's cut everybody off since last month, so I reckon we'll be stuck till next summer."

"But it's not such a bad thing." Juliet looked down at her hands, which were rough from pounding berries and dried buffalo. "It's a pretty good life, if you think about it." She picked at a rough nail. "Better than I would have guessed."

"You look more at peace." Posy smiled over at her. "I think we all do."

Juliet didn't answer as she thought back to her days in Maryland—the polished walnut tables and clink of metal trays. Servants that bowed and disappeared through the open doors, shadow-like, rarely speaking. The date cakes and oranges of Christmas; horses and carriages that clipped down cobblestone streets.

Here she could braid her own cane baskets—albeit lopsided ones—and form clay into pots with timid hands. She watched as Crow braves brought home a slaughtered buffalo and skinned it and tanned the hide, and she helped smoke and dry strips of meat for the winter. She'd held Áxxaashe's newborn baby boy—rosy, with chubby cheeks of cinnamon cream—and helped the tribal leader recover from kidney stones and indigestion with her tinctures and dried herbs. She had stitched Wemilat's hand when he gashed it open with a flint knife, nursed and scolded Arapoosh back from an alcohol-induced stupor, and taught English words and Bible stories to smiling, dark-eyed children who liked to pop out from behind tepees to surprise her.

She'd studied the herbs, roots, teas, and poultices of the herbalists—their snakebite cure that worked on the spotted dog Kajika when all her American remedies failed—and tried her best to replicate the intricate beadwork on a leather dress collar.

Even her clothing had shifted from the thin calicos and petticoats of sheltered, seaside Maryland to the borrowed buckskin dress of the Crow woman, complete with beaded moccasins and leather leggings tied just above her knees. Otherwise she would have frozen to death right there in her black stockings, the way the frigid winter wind tore across the plains—frosting twigs with ice.

"Come on, Juliet—let's celebrate Christmas with the others." Posy reached out her hand. "We can sing a song or two. Just to remember."

To remember. Candied pears, fir trees, candles. Mistletoe and laughter and stolen kisses. Stars and good-byes, and carols sung with happy lips. All of it gone. Even her Christmas ornaments and green velvet dress, probably sold by bandits at some sleazy trading post.

Juliet let the pain come and sting and gently die. She followed Posy into the gray twilight, where snow whirled down like bits of goose down, lofty and floating. Posy held out a lantern but nearly ran into Silas.

"Sorry." She ducked her head as if in embarrassment. "You gonna celebrate Christmas with us?"

Silas stood taller and more rugged than Juliet remembered. He was wearing a long, thick Crow tunic banded in reds and blues at the neck, leather trousers, and moccasins. His sun-bleached hair was the color of a dry cornfield. Snowflakes caught in his eyelashes.

"Well, what do you know? Christmas. You're right." He lowered the split pine lodge poles from his shoulder and rubbed his stubbly jaw. "I'd almost forgotten."

"Not me." Posy shook her head. "I've been dreaming about gingerbread for days now. I can almost taste it."

"Well, I don't have any, so I won't be much help."

"No, but you can remember with us. It makes it almost seem real." Posy pushed Silas toward the tepee. "Come on. We're looking for your pa now."

"Papa's out picking pine boughs. I saw him."

"Pine boughs?" Posy clapped her hands in childlike joy. "Really? For Christmas?"

"He and Mama always loved Christmas." Juliet smiled wistfully. "Our house smelled like oranges and cinnamon all through December."

"Yeah, but the funny thing is, I think I almost like the smell of these outdoors better." Silas scuffed at a spot on the earth with his leather moccasin.

"What, wood smoke, buffalo chips, and our body odor?" Posy wrinkled her nose. "You're a funny one, Mr. James."

Silas gave a sudden laugh then looked down at Posy with an expression that made Juliet's heart skip a beat. The raw hunger of his gaze, like she'd seen in Robert's eyes when love began to stir. "Well, no, that's not all, Posy," he said in an almost tender tone. "Freedom. The outdoors. Sometimes I hope nobody ever comes to rescue us. It's almost like Eden, you know?"

Silas moved closer to Posy as if to say more. His breath misting in the snow.

And Juliet carefully backed away, shivering under her blanket. Her blood beating fast and joyous.

❧

Papa caught up with Juliet, his arms full of fragrant green boughs, and the sharp, sweet scent of pine filled Juliet's nostrils. "Merry Christmas, my dear." He grinned and kissed Juliet lightly on the cheek. Snow gathered on the top of his head, making his gray curls look white—like a stocky, red-faced Father Christmas in his woven red Crow robe and blanket.

"Merry Christmas, Papa." Juliet wrapped an arm around him and deftly steered him away from Silas and Posy. "You didn't forget."

"Of course not. How could we forget, of all days, the Lord's birth? I bet He felt a bit like we do now—cold, far from home, and a bit out of place."

"That's what it's all about, isn't it?" said Juliet softly. "The birth of our Savior on Christmas Day. The greatest day of all."

Christmas, and a Savior who called Himself the "bread of life." Juliet needed to think—to clear her head of its whirl of memories—and ponder what Papa said. Something so simple, so obvious, that she couldn't believe she'd overlooked it.

Christmas wasn't ever about parties, or gingerbread, or anything like that. It was about Him—and always had been.

And strangely enough, it was also about upheaval. Loss. Grief.

In fact, the first Christmas probably looked far more like this one, right here among buffalo rawhide tepees, than it ever did in Juliet's warm parlor, crowded with Christmas guests.

There was no fragrant cinnamon or hot cider for Mary and Joseph, and no festive violin. No doting aunts cooing over newborn rosy cheeks, and no proud grandmother to receive the little warm bundle with tears.

Instead, it had all been taken from them in an instant. In an unexpected whirl of events—a swollen belly, a blush of shamed red in the cheeks. Strange dreams and strange stories, and one by one the eyes turned cold and condemning.

Just Mary and Joseph now, alone, and the stench of livestock. Their numb fingers clumsily wrapping the rough swaddling cloths for the first time. And the raw, unspoken prayer of a broken heart: *Why, Lord? Why me? Why us? Why this child, and why now? Why not a year from now, when the circumstances would be different, better, more acceptable?*

This isn't what I expected.

Is this really the way it has to be?

A raw part of me still wants to go home, and to have everything just the way it was—before this strange, divine interruption.

The first Christmas, colored with confusion and sorrow.

But miracles, too.

Juliet pulled the blanket over her mouth to hold back a sob.

◌﹏◌

Firelight rippled in shadows against the taut sides of the tepee as Juliet lifted the door flap. Two things hit her at once: beautiful warmth and the mouthwatering, unmistakable fragrance of Christmas bread. Sweet, fragrant, and pungent—like fruits and sugar.

It had been so long since Juliet smelled panettone that her hands began to tremble. But of course not—not here at the Crow camp. That was impossible.

"Jacob?" Juliet brushed the snowflakes from her hair as she bent through the opening. "What's that smell? What are you making?" She jiggled the snow off her moccasins and shook out her blanket.

Jacob looked up from the fire, the amber-colored light playing on his auburn hair and the curves of his face and jaw. He grinned, and a puff of sparks showered behind him like golden fireworks.

"Christmas bread." He poked a pan over the fire with his good arm. Two large, pale, fat loaves nestled there in honey-colored light. "The best I can make it under these circumstances. Have you had it before?"

"Christmas bread?" Juliet froze in midshake.

"My German grandma used to make it every year at Christmas until she died." Jacob turned back to the fire with a pleasant wistfulness in his face. "It's called *stollen*. The smell of my childhood."

Juliet still stood there, not moving.

"What?" Jacob turned again. "You okay?"

"Yes." Juliet put the blanket down. "It's just. . . How did you know?"

"How did I know what? About stollen? I dunno. Watching her, I guess. It's supposed to be a fruit bread—with raisins and orange peel, and maybe some almonds."

Juliet could hardly swallow over her dry throat. "I can't believe it. It's just like our panettone from Italy. What could you possibly find here at camp to make Christmas bread?"

"I used the finest cornmeal and wheat flour they could give me here at the camp, and a little sugar—which is pretty impressive, because almost everything the Crow eat is meat. They must have bought it off a settler or at a trading post somewhere. I traded that knife I made for it." He stoked the fire, sending up another shower of sparks that popped and snapped. "And the fruit? A few handfuls of dried plums and chokecherries and honey. I guess buffalo tallow will have to do in place of butter. But it smells good to me."

Juliet's heart beat faster. "It's a yeast bread, Jacob—you can't fool my nose. The Crow don't even make much bread, except for that kind made with wild turnips. How'd you make yeast bread?"

"You're forgetting something."

"What?"

"I'm Irish." He winked. "And we know potatoes. Haven't you ever cooked before?"

She felt color rush into her cheeks. "Not really. We employed a cook."

"Well, yeast comes from potatoes. You feed it with sugar."

"Where did you get potatoes?"

Jacob held up two fingers. "I found two left on the ground that the bandits didn't take. Just two. They must have rolled out of my pack."

"What! And you didn't eat them?"

"I saved them for trade with the Crow, but they didn't take anything in trade."

Juliet looked down at her hands in embarrassment. "They're better than us, you know that? Our people would have taken them."

"Probably so." Jacob sighed. "But anyway, two potatoes were enough to make yeast for the bread."

"You know how to make yeast." Juliet tried to smother a smile.

"My grandma taught me. And anybody on the farm who wanted to eat. We all pitched in." Jacob poked at the coals. "When you're hungry and poor, nobody really cares who does it, so long as it gets done."

Juliet swallowed, thinking of her Maryland kitchen bursting with fresh chicken and parsley, crab and ripe plums. Imported lemons and cinnamon and tea. Until the war, and the wagon trek West, she'd never really known what it felt like to go hungry.

"Well, that's exactly the same reason Daddy taught me medicine," said Juliet softly. "He said it didn't matter who did the mending and the healing, so long as someone did. Silas can't stand the sight of blood, so that left me." She shrugged. "I guess you and I have more in common than I thought."

"Except I'm not as easy on the eyes." Jacob smiled.

Juliet laughed. "Well, Christmas cake is a beautiful end for your potatoes, anyway."

"The end? Don't you know how yeast works? It's made to multiply—to go out and breathe new life into something still and dead. All it takes is a pinch of starter, and if I feed it the right sugars, we can make bread for years."

"So we can feed a thousand people, technically, from two potatoes."

"That's what my Grandma always said. It's a divine arithmetic, Juliet—the way God intended it from the beginning. For the physical elements of our world to prove the eternal."

Juliet's mind whirled, and all the sermons she'd heard over the years came pouring back like a snowstorm, roaring bits and pieces into her ears. Things about miracles and faith and extraordinary multiplication.

"Like Jesus feeding the five thousand, Jacob." She spoke suddenly without meaning to. "The fish and the bread."

"Exactly. Because bread sustains life. And He is our bread."

The Bread of Life. Juliet suddenly felt like smacking herself. How could she have missed it? How could she have missed Him—the most important thing of all, her breath, her whole heart—in all of her pain, her yesterdays and tomorrows?

He was there among the bloody stretchers, the groans of the dying—working through Juliet's own fingers to suture and salve, to hold a shaking hand. And she had missed Him—refused to see Him. Let her heart harden with bitterness.

It was this same Jesus—the Bread of Life—that walked with her along the desolate plains of Wyoming, step by frozen step, holding her up in His arms. The same way He carried Carrie Ann and Elizabeth—and Robert, even—as they took their final journey to Him.

How could she not have believed He was there? And turned to Him, even for a moment?

For even the crumbs of His presence were enough to fill her deepest hunger.

Jesus, the Christ—Christmas Manna—Bread from heaven, scattered in the wilderness and lonely places for those who seek Him. Who hunger for Him. Who let Him lead them, even through the deserts and darkest paths.

" 'And he humbled thee, and suffered thee to hunger,' " Juliet whispered, " 'and fed thee with manna, which thou knewest not, neither did thy fathers know; that he might make thee know that man doth not live by bread only.' "

"You knew that." Jacob lifted his eyes.

"Of course. One of my teachers made me memorize a chapter of Deuteronomy for every foolish prank I played."

"How many chapters?"

Juliet spread her fingers, warming them by the flickering flames. "Don't ask."

"I'm asking."

"Twenty-seven."

"There are that many chapters in Deuteronomy?"

"Thirty-four."

Jacob chuckled and scratched his hair with his good hand. "I guess you paid him back by making him listen while you recited, didn't you?"

"There are lots of laws in Deuteronomy. Lots." Juliet raised an eyebrow. "I can tell you all about the Feast of Weeks, if you want."

"Well, right now the only feast I'm thinking about is our Christmas feast." Jacob poked the bread with a piece of deer antler. "They're done, except for rolling them in sugar. Granny would be proud, God rest her."

He tipped his head as though to study his loaves. "Or not. My concoction might taste pretty awful. I'm not a chef, you know."

"It'll be wonderful. You'll see."

"Ha. You have more faith in me than I do."

Juliet sat silently next to Jacob as he blew on his fingers from the chafing heat, and her eyes crept up to his wrinkled shirt sleeve and buckskin vest. "How's your arm, Jacob?" she asked quietly. "Does it hurt much?"

"Nah." Jacob looked away, and Juliet felt in the pit of her stomach that he wasn't being completely honest. "Not so much that I can't bear it, anyway."

"Can you move it?"

He kept his face turned away. "Not much. It'll probably be stiff like this most of my life. Doc had to cut some tendons, apparently."

Juliet looked down and traced the hem of her skirt with her finger. "You know we didn't expect you to live, right?"

"It might be awhile until I get my strength back, but I'm alive. Guess it wasn't my time to go yet."

Neither of them spoke for a moment, and a log popped, sending up a shiver of sparks.

Jacob cleared his throat as shadows flickered on the lines in his suddenly serious face. "I never got to properly thank you, Juliet, for what you did. For me." He swallowed. "Posy told me you gave away your engagement set."

"It wasn't doing me any good anyway, you know. Robert's. . .well, he's gone."

"I'm sorry."

Sure you are. Juliet picked at a loose bead.

"No, really. I'm sorry you lost him. And I'm sorry for the whole war—for the whole mess of it. And what it's done to you." He reached out with his good hand and gently stroked a strand of hair out of her eyes. "I'm so sorry."

Juliet nearly flinched at his touch but managed to stay still.

"Don't say it." Tears swam in her eyes.

"Don't say what?"

"All that ridiculous sap about what a wonderful fellow he must have been—and then change the subject. You can't, and you won't, understand. Ever. People just say that to shut me up so I won't cry or blabber on about him—but I loved him, Jacob. Do you hear me? I loved him. I still do."

"I know you do." His voice sounded soft, aching. "And he provided for you, up to the very last moment with his gift."

Juliet wiped her eyes with the palm of her hand. "No, he provided for *you*—so I could hire the doctor."

"You've got it backward." Jacob sat up straighter then moved his bandaged arm. "It was always for you. With that exquisite piece of jewelry you could have bought your life from anyone—from raiders, bandits, even from the Cheyenne bent on revenge. Did you ever think of that? I'd wager that Robert of yours thought of the possibility of just such a thing when he had it crafted."

"Nonsense. He didn't know I'd ever go west."

"He didn't have to. Men live to provide for the women they love ahead of time. And he knew the bigness of your heart, too, and what you might do with such a gift."

Jacob leaned forward suddenly, boldly, and reached for her hand, curling his warm fingers between hers. "I don't know if I can give you gold like that, Juliet, if you marry me," he said softly. "But I'll try my best to give you the family you wanted. A little girl like Carrie Ann all our own. Just marry me."

Juliet sat there speechless, her lips halfway open between something she was going to say—and forgot—and a startling numbness.

"If the children can't find their relatives or don't have any left, we'll take them," said Jacob. "You and me together. What do you think?"

His eyes shone bright, deep, with pupils so large and velvet black that their intensity made her almost forget how to breathe.

Juliet opened her mouth to answer, but voices outside startled her. Dogs barked, and Juliet heard movement, running feet. Shouts. Jacob slowly released her hand.

"What's going on?" Juliet stood up quickly, too embarrassed even to look at Jacob. "Are we being attacked?"

She felt weary of war—of running—sick to her stomach. She'd seen enough of cannonballs and bloodied limbs, of bandits and arrows and hiding. It felt so familiar and so terrible that she wanted to weep just standing there, not bearing to move.

And before she could lift the tepee flap, a man stuck his head through.

A man in a blue US Cavalry cap.

Chapter 12

"Are you Juliet James?" The man stepped inside the tepee. He looked around, sniffing, and Juliet saw his mustache twitch. "What's that I smell? Christmas bread? It can't be."

"Excuse me?" Juliet stepped forward. "Who are you, sir?"

"My apologies." The man doffed his cap. "I'm Captain Gregory Scott of Montana's Fort Smith with a detachment from Lame Deer." His brass buttons gleamed in the firelight. "The folks outside say you're Juliet James. Is that true, ma'am?"

"I am, sir. Why, are we in Montana?"

"Yes ma'am. We've been looking for you and your party a long time." Captain Scott took her hand and shook it, and Juliet thought his eyes held weariness. "Your uncle Frederico has been moving heaven and earth to try to find you."

"Uncle Frederico?" Juliet let out her breath.

"He's been searching for you ever since the wagon train was reported missing, and he's probably contacted every post in the entire territory. You and your stepfather weren't found with the others that perished—God rest them." The captain bowed his head briefly. "But we did track down some of the children the Cheyenne had taken captive, and now you."

The captain removed his cap and banged it against his knee to remove the snow. "We got turned around about thirty miles from here, and it took us six days to find our way out of the mountains with the snow coming." He slapped the cap back on his head. "Your uncle must really like you, Miss James—he's offered one heck of a reward and sent out more search parties than I can count. We almost lost one coming over the mountains."

Juliet's forehead crinkled as she tried to understand. "You're talking about my uncle Frederico. My mother's brother."

"That's the one. Frederico Dominico."

"The miner."

Captain Scott laughed. "Miner? No, miss—he's no miner. Not anymore, anyway. He's the richest man this side of Billings."

Juliet's eyebrows shot up. "My uncle? You must be mistaken."

"No, ma'am. He struck gold about two months ago in a silt vein everybody said was a waste of time, and he's the one laughing now. They call him 'Noah,' because he believed in a miracle against all odds. Well, he was right."

Juliet's legs turned wobbly, and she reached out for a lodge pole to steady herself.

"Well, Noah or not, he's awfully concerned about you and your group. Is there anyone else besides the folks outside? Who's this fellow?" The captain gestured with his head.

"Jacob Pike, sir," said Jacob in his Southern drawl as he stood.

And just like that, Juliet saw the captain's eyes darken. "Where are you from, young man?" he demanded. His voice turned hard.

"Virginia, sir."

"Virginia." The captain muttered something under his breath. He pointed with a gloved hand. "How'd you hurt that arm?"

Jacob seemed to hesitate, and Juliet turned to the captain, ready to sputter something, anything to change the subject.

"Captain." Juliet began. "I can explain."

"I injured it in the war, sir," said Jacob quietly as he stepped forward. "Fighting for the Confederacy."

Juliet saw a vein in the captain's neck bulge and the lines in his jaw tighten. "We lost a lot of good men in Virginia, Mr. Pike," he muttered through clenched teeth.

"With all due respect, sir, so did we."

A bristling silence filled the tepee for a moment, so cold that Juliet could hear the wind moaning around the rawhide sides. Furious color gathered in the captain's cheeks.

"Well, the Confederacy no longer exists," he snapped, his breath coming fast and angry. "Thank God for that."

"You're right," said Jacob simply. "It doesn't."

And then he spoke again: "It's Christmas, Captain Scott. Would you like some Christmas bread?"

Juliet heard the lodge poles groan in the wind, and the snaps and pops of the fire. The captain blinked twice, and his leather boots creaked faintly as he shifted his weight. And to Juliet's surprise, his hard expression faded, like the slightest slackening of a taut rope.

"Christmas bread?" repeated the captain as he rubbed his gloved hands together. "I thought that's what I smelled."

"You guessed correctly." Jacob's face was pleasant. "The way my grandma used to make it. It's awfully good. Or it was, when she laid it out on the table with the sweet potatoes and fresh black walnuts."

"I used to eat it as a boy." Captain Scott crossed his arms over his chest and seemed to drift away. "Every Christmas. Full of fat raisins and candied cherries. Best thing I ever put in my mouth. I still dream about it sometimes, all powdered with sugar."

"Me, too," said Juliet. "It was so beautiful to look at—like stained glass. We'd cut it into hot slices fresh from the oven and eat it with our bare hands."

"With coffee," said Jacob.

"With coffee," agreed the captain. "Strong coffee. Nothing better."

"Well, sir." Jacob gestured to the pans now cooling near the fire. "Would you join us? Call your men, and we'll all eat together."

Captain Scott rubbed his chin. His thick mustache twitching. "I suppose it wouldn't hurt anything."

"I'd be pleased."

"We've brought fresh provisions," said the captain slowly. "Coffee, too. Shall I prepare some?"

"Coffee?" Jacob cried. "You've brought fresh coffee?"

The captain studied him a moment. "You poor fellow," he said finally with a sigh. "You've had a rough go of it, haven't you?" His eyes bounced back and forth from Jacob to Juliet. "Both of you, I imagine. Well, it's all over now. You're among friends."

◊

The tepee was small, but that night, to Juliet, it seemed to swell larger and larger, making room for not only Posy and Silas and Papa, but the whole search crew as well: five in all. Jacob called the Crow elders and anyone who would listen, and invited them all in to celebrate.

Captain Scott crouched by the fire, grinding coffee beans in his small metal grinder, and one of the men produced a harmonica—puffing out a rollicking tune while Papa hung pine boughs around the tepee. A tiny pine sapling served as a Christmas tree, and Posy decorated it with beads, feathers, and pinecones then wrapped an Indian blanket around the base.

Popcorn emerged from the packs of provisions, and apples and nuts, and a single fresh orange—which they divided into sections and passed around, one by juicy one.

Snow fell, the fire burned, the harmonica trilled, and Jacob took the cake out of the pans. A bit of orange juice with fresh white sugar made a drippy glaze for the golden-brown cakes, fragrant with fruit.

Juliet hugged her knees, watching the happy scene with bright eyes. It was the Christmas she'd never wanted, never imagined. Christmas in the wilderness, barren and beautiful.

"So, are you going to answer me, Juliet?" She jumped at Jacob's voice so near her ear. "You never told me if you'd marry me or not."

Juliet turned to him, his happy face illuminated by dancing lantern light. "Yes, Jacob—yes." She traced his stubbly cheek with the tip of her finger.

"Everything starts small, Juliet—faith, even love. But it's enough to live on, even through the lean times until the miracle comes. Because it will." He wrapped his arms around her and drew her close, and she breathed in the smell of leather and furs, the smell of his skin—so foreign yet so familiar. "I saved the cuttings, you know," he whispered.

"What cuttings?"

"From those two precious potatoes." He held up two fingers. "We'll have a whole field full of potatoes from those little green shoots. We'll make bread for years, Juliet. Our daily bread—you for me, and me for you. Our Lord and His gifts, good or bad. Everything we need."

Juliet chewed on a nail a minute and thought. "I guess that's why Christ chose to multiply bread."

"Because when you're the most empty, the most hungry, you're ripe for a miracle. And He's really the miracle that you need."

The harmonica tune ended, and Juliet sat there in the half light, thinking of love, of life, and of bread. Part prayer, part pure thanks—just feeling the firelight and the snowfall, and the scent of wild plums and sugar.

Stollen (German Christmas Bread)

1½ cups milk
½ cup white sugar
¾ cup butter
½ teaspoon salt
2 eggs
2 egg yolks

5⅔ cups flour, divided
1 oz. active dry yeast
½ teaspoon ground cardamom
½ cup raisins
½ cup candied citrus peel
½ cup candied cherries

Scald milk. Add sugar, butter, and salt. Cool to lukewarm. Add 2 whole eggs and 2 yolks. Mix. Add 3 cups flour and yeast to butter/egg mixture and pour into a food processor. Process and let rise until double (about 1 to 2 hours). Add cardamom, raisins, citrus peel, cherries, and rest of flour. Place on floured board and knead. Let rise in greased bowl another 1 to 2 hours. When risen, punch down and cut into three to four pieces. Roll each into an oval, butter, and fold in half lengthwise. Place on greased baking sheet, cover, and let rise until double (about 50 minutes). Bake at 375 degrees for 25 minutes. Remove to rack. When cool, drizzle with Orange-Sugar Glaze and decorate with candied cherries.

Orange-Sugar Glaze

1 cup confectioner's sugar
¼ teaspoon grated orange zest
1 tablespoon freshly squeezed orange juice

Whisk sugar with orange zest and orange juice in a small bowl until smooth.

Christmas Bounty

by MaryLu Tyndall

Chapter 1

Santa Barbara, California
August 1855

What kind of God would allow children to go hungry?

Caroline Moreau jingled the few coins left in her purse and gazed over the colorful assortment of fruits and vegetables displayed across the vendor's cart.

"Mama." Her son, Philippe, called to her from the next stall, where he pointed to a hunk of raw beef—enough to feed them for a week. Shooing flies away from the display, the Mexican butcher cast her a toothless grin. "You buy, señora. Good for growing boy." She wondered whether the man ever got to enjoy the meat he sold, for he was no doubt just a farm worker employed by a rich ranchero. Regardless, her mouth watered at the sight. It had been months since she and the children had enjoyed meat for supper.

"Please, Mama." A stiff ocean breeze tossed her eight-year-old son's brown hair across his forehead while blue eyes alight with hope tugged on her heart.

What she wouldn't give to satisfy that hope, but she had only enough money for a few vegetables and a sack of beans.

"Not today, Philippe." Frowning, the boy dragged himself back to stand beside her while Abilene, her youngest, tugged on her skirts and pulled the thumb from her mouth. "I'm hungry, Mama."

"I know, *ma chère*." Caroline felt like weeping. Instead, she raised her chin and spoke to the vendor. "A red pepper, one onion, two tomatoes, and a bulb of garlic, please." At least that would give the beans a different flavor from last week. She glanced down at the despair tugging on her children's faces and added, "And twenty-five cents worth of cherries."

Abilene cheered, while a tiny smile wiped the frown from Philippe's lips. "For dessert," Caroline said, drawing them both close.

After gathering her purchases, Caroline scurried among the throng that mobbed the busy public square, still amazed—even after living in the California coastal town for nearly three years—at the vast diversity of people inhabiting Santa Barbara. Spanish dons, attired in black embroidered coats and high-crested hats, strolled the streets with ladies in multilayered skirts, colorful silk scarves, and long, braided hair. Beside them, servants held fringed parasols to protect them from the sun. Mexican vendors and shop owners abounded, dressed in plain trousers and colorful *sarapes* with wide *sombreros* on their heads. A cowboy tipped his hat at Caroline and smiled, while the chink of coins drew her gaze to a group of gold miners exiting the bank, where, no doubt, they'd converted their gold dust into money. Facing forward, she nearly bumped into a monk. He barely acknowledged her before proceeding with his brown cowl dragging in the dirt and a Chumash Indian following on his heels.

Turning left on Bath Street, Caroline headed toward the coast, where she'd left her buckboard. The crash of waves soon drowned out the clamor of the town as sand replaced dirt, and the glory of the sea spread out before them. Sparkling ribbons of silver-crested azure waves spanned to the horizon where a thick band of fog rose like the misty walls of a fortress. When the sun set, those walls would roll in and cover everything in town just like the many hoodlums who would roll down from their hide-outs in the hills to enjoy the nighttime pleasures of Santa Barbara.

The California coast was so different from New Orleans where she'd grown up. There the steamy tidewaters had been filled with all manner of shrimp, oysters, crawfish, and crabs. Here the water was icy and wild, like the city itself, and filled with kelp forests, sea lions, otters, and whales.

She drew in a deep breath of the salty breeze and allowed the wind to tear through her hair. With it came the sense of freedom she so craved but had not felt since her husband died six months ago. Shielding her eyes against the sun, she spotted a ship anchored offshore. Could it finally be the packet bringing mail to Santa Barbara? She'd sent a post home several months ago, informing her family of her dire situation, but still no response had come. But no, this ship was much smaller than the normal paddle-wheel steamship that brought the mail.

Regardless, she must get the children home before the sun sank into the sea. Santa Barbara was not a safe town at night, especially not for women and children. Though she'd heard the city hadn't always been like that. Before the Americans arrived, the Spanish had kept it orderly and civilized, built a mission, and introduced culture. But all that had crumbled when America won the territory in 1847 and cowboys, fortune hunters, and gold miners had flooded the city. Because the town employed so few law officers, mayhem ruled, not only the streets, but the countryside as well. Every week for the past two months, vigilantes had attacked her vineyard, stealing valuable farm equipment, burning grapevines, and even striking her foreman unconscious for several hours. Caroline had spent many a sleepless night worrying for her children's safety.

"Here ye! Here ye!" a man shouted first in English and then in Spanish from down shore. Caroline glanced up to see a crowd forming around a wooden scaffold. No doubt some poor criminal was being hanged. Most likely a horse thief or highwayman. At least they had caught one of them. Turning, she started toward her buckboard.

"Mama, can we go see?" Philippe asked, running beside her.

"No. We should not see such things."

"But it's a hanging, Mama!"

"Precisely why we are not going, Philippe."

"Don't you want to see who it is?" He scratched his head as if he couldn't make sense of her attitude.

"No."

Abilene plucked out her thumb. "Me neither," she said.

"There you have it." Caroline smiled. "Two against one."

"Ah, that doesn't count. You're girls. Boys like to see hangings."

"Not civilized boys, Philippe, of which you are one."

Lowering his chin, he slogged beside her, kicking sand as he went and slowly falling behind.

"Hurry along, children. I have dinner to make. You can help me, Philippe. Would you like that? I'll let you build the fire in the stove." Surely that would cheer the boy up.

When he didn't answer, she turned around to see him speeding down the sandy street heading straight for the scaffold.

"Oh, *bon sang!*" Growling, Caroline spun around and darted after him, dragging poor Abilene behind. But her son was quick. He got his speed from his father, along with his mulish disposition! The boy disappeared into the burgeoning crowd as the sheriff began listing the man's crimes.

"I, Samuel Portland, magistrate of Santa Barbara, do hereby charge you, Dante Vega, with the following crimes: thievery, drunkenness, licentiousness. . ."

Halting at the edge of the crowd, Caroline peered through the swaying bodies for a sign of her Philippe.

"Forgery, cheating at cards. . ."

Caroline pressed through the mob.

"Making a lewd suggestion to a lady," the man continued, causing some ladies to gasp. "And piracy."

"Hang him! Hang him!" someone shouted.

"Cuelgalo a el!" others repeated in Spanish, stirring the crowd into a frenzy. Even a few of the ladies joined in.

"What does 'hang' mean?" Abilene asked.

"Nothing." Caroline drew her daughter close, glad the little girl was too short to see what was happening.

Caroline, however, had a full view of the man who had committed all those horrid crimes as a masked executioner escorted him up the steps of the scaffold to a waiting noose. Dark hair jostled over the collar of his brown open shirt. A red velvet sash was tied about his waist, while baggy black trousers fed into thick boots that clacked up each wooden tread of his death march. He glanced toward the crowd. Her heart froze. She'd never forget a face like his. Nor his imposing figure. The only thing that was missing was the sword and pistols he had kept stuffed in a thick leather belt—now conspicuously absent from his chest. Yes, she'd know him anywhere. Particularly when his eyes now reached through the crowd and locked upon hers. Coffee-colored eyes, if she remembered. Eyes that—against her best efforts—had once made her insides melt.

Eyes that had assessed her with impunity above a devious grin, while he and his crew had plundered the ship that had brought her and her husband François to Santa Barbara.

"What have you to say regarding these crimes?" the magistrate asked him.

The villain pulled his gaze from her and faced the portly man. "I am innocent, of course!" His baritone voice bore a slight Spanish accent, while a boyish grin elicited chuckles from the crowd. "On what evidence do you charge me, señor?"

One man pointed toward the ship in the bay. "On the evidence of your ship, you vile pirate!"

"My ship? It has done nothing wrong. As for myself, I was coming ashore to purchase supplies."

The eloquence of his speech surprised Caroline. Certainly not what she expected from a pirate.

"Purchase? You mean steal!" another man yelled.

"And then murder us all in our beds," someone added.

The pirate snapped hair from his face. "I had no such intentions, I assure you."

One of the wealthy ranchers stepped forward, adjusted his embroidered vest, and nodded toward the pirate. "This bandito robbed me of my money and my wife of her jewels when we sailed from San Diego to Santa Barbara three years ago." He glanced over the crowd and huffed. "And he even propositioned my poor wife. She has never quite recovered from his lewd suggestions."

The pirate shrugged with a grin.

"I was there as well," another man shouted. "I can vouch for what Señor Lucero says. This man boarded our ship and looted all the passengers."

Caroline could very well add her testimony to the others, for she had been on that same ship. But her experience had been quite different. This pirate—this Dante Vega—had done her and her husband no harm. In fact, quite the opposite. He had hidden them away in their stateroom and forbidden his men entrance. Not only that, but he had not taken their money or any of their possessions. Nor had he frightened the children. In fact, he seemed quite intent on keeping the little ones safe. Caroline could make no sense of it, though at the time she had thanked God for giving them favor in the cullion's sight.

"Therefore," the magistrate shouted, bringing her back to the present, "as judge of the court of Santa Barbara, I deem that you shall be hanged by the neck until you are dead."

The executioner slipped the noose over Dante's head. Still, his eyes held no fear as he faced the magistrate. "Is there no mercy to be found in this hellish mockery of a court, sir?"

"No mercy for pirates," the potbellied magistrate spat back. "Unless "—he grinned and scanned the mob—"according to our law, one of these ladies agrees to marry you. Make a decent man out of you." His jovial tone spoke of the lunacy of the statement.

Laughter swept through the crowd. Caroline's heart thrashed like a storm at sea. This man had obviously not come here to pirate. In fact, for all she knew, he'd given up the trade and had become an honest man. And she needed a man. A strong man. A man who knew how to fight. Someone to protect her and her children from vigilantes and help her workers harvest the grapes. If not, they would lose everything, their wine, their grapes, and eventually their land.

And her husband's dream.

"Very well." The magistrate gave a nod to the executioner to pull the lever.

Hoisting Abilene in her arms, Caroline plowed through the crowd, ignoring the gasps and moans, and stood before the scaffold.

"I'll marry him!"

Chapter 2

Dante couldn't believe his luck. If there *was* a God, He must be looking out for Dante. Though why, he couldn't imagine. Dante had broken every one of His commandments—at least the ones his mom had pounded into him as a child. Yet, to not only save his neck but give him a beautiful wife. . . Well, perhaps Dante should rethink his rejection of religion as a guilt-ridden cult of greedy hypocrites. Still, the woman was an American. And Dante hated Americans. He'd spent the last seven years plundering American ships along the California coast—beautiful shores and golden rolling hills that had once belonged to Mexico. And would belong to her again, if Dante had his way. Perhaps it was for the best that the lady was his enemy. That way he wouldn't feel the least bit guilty when he took what he wanted from her, repaired his ship, and sailed away.

His new wife had not spoken a word to him after the ceremony except to say they'd discuss terms later. *Terms?* He smiled. The only terms he was interested in was sharing this lovely's bed for a night or two and then pilfering her goods.

She snapped the reins, urging the horse forward down Delavina Street. Wisps of hair the color of the sun trickled from beneath her straw hat, drawing his gaze to a neck as graceful as the lady herself. A blue gown, bordered in lace tightened around a tiny waist then flowed down to her mud-caked ankle boots. Though her hands were small and delicate, rosy cheeks and glowing skin revealed that she didn't shy away from the sun like so many American ladies. Eyes as green as sea kelp glanced his way. He swallowed. Why hadn't this beauty been snatched up by one of the wealthy ranchers in town?

The wagon dipped into a hole, creaking and groaning and nearly sending Dante over the side. The children giggled behind him. He could feel their little eyes boring into his back and glanced over his shoulder. Wide, innocent grins met his gaze. Handsome children. But then he always did like children. They were so honest and pure before the harsh realities of the world tainted them—taught them to lie and steal and cheat their way through life.

Because in the end, it was every man, *or woman*, for themselves.

A salty breeze stirred the sycamores and bay laurels lining the street as they jostled past several adobe homes and a few wooden ones, a warehouse, a string of shops, and a Baptist church, of all things. Not something he'd expected to see in this nefarious town. In the distance, final rays of the setting sun swept over the hills bordering the city on the east and then shimmered off the white mission with its stark belfries shooting into the sky.

Jerking the reins, the lady turned down Micheltorena Street, crossed over a bridge, and headed beneath an arched sign that read MOREAU WINERY. Row after row of vines, heavy with grapes, spanned out from the dirt road like spokes in a wheel. In the distance, an adobe home with a red-tiled roof nestled among the golden hills. Not only had he married a beautiful woman, but a rich one as well! Things were looking up, indeed.

"Are you a real pirate?" the little boy asked Dante as they stepped into the cool interior of the home. The lady ushered in the little girl and set a satchel atop a wooden table.

"That's not a polite question, Philippe." She removed her bonnet and turned to face her son.

"But Mama, that's what the other man said."

"Forgive my son, Señor Vega. If you would care to sit?" She gestured toward a stuffed sofa in the corner, but Dante had trouble taking his eyes off of her. Ringlets of gold framed a face that would stop a thousand ships. Yet there was something familiar about her. He would never forget a woman possessing such beauty.

She must have seen the desire in his eyes, for she drew a ragged breath and lifted her chin. "These are my children, Philippe and Abilene."

"Nice to meet you, señor." The young boy reached out his hand and gave Dante's a firm shake. The little girl, a mass of red curls surrounding a freckled nose and green eyes, peeked at him from within the folds of her mother's skirts.

Now he remembered them. The beautiful señora, her adorable children, and her spindly whiffet of a husband, who had been too cowardly to defend them from pirates. "Thank you for saving me from the noose, Señora. . .Señora. . ."

"Moreau. Señora Caroline Moreau. And you are welcome." She inched backward toward a rack of rifles hanging on the wall. "But your life comes at a cost."

"I have no doubt." Dante snorted as he glanced around the room. A rug covered most of the redbrick floor while white-washed adobe walls boasted tapestries, brass sconces, and oil paintings. A piano sat in one corner, an olive-green sofa in another, and next to the beautiful señora stood an oak dining table. Open french doors framed in yellow velvet curtains led to a veranda overlooking the vineyard, while arched openings on either side of the room led to additional chambers. Perhaps there were more valuable items elsewhere, for there certainly wasn't anything worth stealing here.

"They were going to hang you, señor." Philippe's eyes widened.

"Indeed, they were," Dante replied with a smile.

"What's 'hang,' Mama?" The little girl, still clinging to her mother's skirts, pulled the thumb from her mouth to ask.

"Never mind that now, ma chère. Philippe, please take your sister and go fetch some water from the creek. I wish to speak to Señor Vega alone."

"Ah, Mama," the boy complained, but one stern look from his mother made him grab his sister and slog out the door.

Turning, she plucked a rifle from the rack, spun back around, and aimed it at Dante's heart.

∽

Caroline judged the distance between her and the pirate. A good fifteen feet. Time enough to shoot him before he charged her. Oh, bon sang, what had she done? Why did she always rush into things before considering the consequences?

Before the pirate could do whatever evil deed his salacious gaze bespoke, Caroline cocked the rifle. "I know how to use this."

He chuckled and rubbed his dark bristled chin. "Yet it makes no sense why you would save me from the noose only to shoot me."

"Regardless, I *will* shoot you if you try anything untoward."

"Untoward?" He took a step in her direction, his dark eyes twinkling with mischief. "Now, why would you presume such a thing?"

"I know that look in a man's eyes."

He took another step toward her.

"Stay where you are." Her hand trembled, sending the barrel of the gun oscillating over his chest—a very muscular chest that peeked at her from within his open-necked shirt.

Stopping, he shook his head with a snort. "You marry a known pirate, bring him into your home, and you expect him to act like one of the monks from your mission?"

"I expect him to be grateful for his life."

"I *am* grateful." He stepped closer, his boots clacking on the brick floor. "Let me show you how much." He reached for her, his eyes flashing. Before she could react, he jerked the gun from her hands. "You've no need for this, señora." He unloaded it and set it down on the table. "I have no intention of hurting you or your children."

Heart crashing against her ribs, Caroline backed away from him. He towered at least a foot above her, all muscle and man, and she knew he could do whatever he wanted. But the look in those coffee-colored eyes made her almost believe what he said. Almost.

"Don't point a gun at me again, señora." A breeze brought his scent of sweat and the sea to her nose, a briny aroma not all too unpleasant. He gestured for her to move away from the rifles. She did. Over to the piano out of his reach. He raked back his slick dark hair and stared at her. "Why bring me here if you fear me?"

"Because you were kind to me once," she said.

He nodded.

"So, you remember?"

"You are a hard lady to forget, señora." One side of his lips quirked as his eyes roved over her yet again.

She hugged herself, trying to hide from his gaze. "Why did you help us? On the ship. Why did you protect us?"

He rubbed the back of his neck and stared out the open french doors where the sun stole the last of the light. "My men would have. . ." He hesitated and faced her. "Let's just say they would have sorely used you, and then. . .well, a white woman of your beauty would bring a great price down south."

A sour taste climbed up Caroline's throat. She had always longed for freedom. She had wanted to live life outside the strictures of her wealthy family back in New Orleans. And so, against their will, she had married François, a penniless Frenchman with a dream of producing the best wine in America. But she hadn't realized that freedom came with a price: hard work, uncertainty, scarcity, and worst of all danger—danger to herself and to her precious children and finally, death to her husband.

"And the little ones," the pirate added. "I could not tolerate their innocence stolen at so young an age."

So the man had some kindness in his heart, after all. Perhaps she hadn't been completely wrong about him. "That is why I chose you, Señor Pirate."

"Where is your husband?" he asked. "The man you were traveling with."

"Dead. Trampled by a horse." Only six months ago, but sometimes it felt like a lifetime.

"I'm sorry." There was genuine sympathy in his voice. He pulled a chair from the table and sat down, leaning forward on his knees. "What is it you want from me, Señora Moreau?"

"Protection."

His brows rose. "From what?"

Philippe's laughter drifted in from the window. "I'll explain later, señor, when the children are asleep. But for now, I want your promise that you won't steal from us or hurt us."

"I already told you I would do you no harm. Besides"—his sultry grin returned—"why would I hurt my own wife?"

There he went again, looking at her as if she were a sweet beignet served up on a platter. Though her insides trembled, she forced authority into her voice. "Wife in name only, Señor Pirate. There will be no marital relations between us."

༄

Though the woman held herself sturdy, Dante sensed the terror storming through her. No marital relations? That would be impossible with a woman like her. He'd intended to tell her just that when the children returned, sloshing water from a bucket they fought over between them. With her head held high, Señora Moreau grabbed the pail and left the room, dragging her children with her. Within moments, the sizzle of a stove sounded, followed by the scent of garlic, and Dante made himself comfortable on the sofa, looking forward to his first home-cooked meal in years. Whatever the reasons the lady had brought him here, it couldn't hurt to stay for a night of good food and a warm bed. Especially if he shared that bed with her. Plus, it would give him a chance to scour the place for any valuables he could use to redeem his ship from the city council.

Dinner consisted of a meager portion of beans and bread—hardly enough to satisfy the children, let alone a grown man—making Dante wonder at his first assessment of their wealth. Nevertheless, he was about to shove a forkful into his mouth when the lady shot him an accusing glance and asked Philippe to bless the food. The young boy gladly complied, lifting up a prayer of thanks so sincere it would make a priest rejoice.

It made Dante uncomfortable.

Still, the simple fare was delicious. And the company even more enjoyable as the children prattled on about their day helping some man named Sisquoc tend the grapes. The little girl, Abilene, never took her eyes off Dante, even as she partook of her meal. The adoring, curious way she looked at him made his insides feel funny. He gave her a playful wink, finally eliciting a grin in return. Philippe, on the other hand, boldly asked Dante question after question about how he got caught and how many ships he had plundered and whether he had killed anyone.

Señora Moreau, barely touching the small portion she'd served herself, chastised her son and apologized to Dante, but he shrugged it off. "Curiosity is a good thing in a lad."

"He is much too curious about the wrong things." She gave her son a look of reprimand, but embedded in her eyes was a love Dante had never seen before. His own mother had done quite a bit of chastising but had omitted the loving part.

After supper the children happily assisted their mother clearing the table and helping to clean the dishes. So much giggling poured from the kitchen that Dante wandered to the door and leaned on the post, watching the three of them smiling and laughing as they worked together. An unusual sadness swamped him. He harbored no such memories of his childhood. No laughter, no smiles, no warm embraces.

Dante should leave. Go back to the harsh, cruel world where he belonged. There was nothing for him here. He could join one of the many games of faro downtown and win enough to get his ship back in a matter of months. But curiosity kept him in place. That and the way the little girl now stared at him after the dishes had been done and they all sat together in the main room—as if he were her best gift at Christmas. She no longer clung to her mother's skirts but instead even dared to take a seat beside him on the sofa.

Señora Moreau brought out a small bowl of cherries for them to share and coffee for Dante. He'd prefer something stronger. Much stronger if he was to combat the odd sensations flowing through him. Especially when Abilene slid her tiny hand in his and looked up at him with those innocent green eyes and said, "Are you my new papa?"

Red blossomed on Señora Moreau's cheeks as she drew the little girl away from Dante and set her on her lap. "No, Abilene. Señor Vega is only staying a short while."

"Ah, Mama." Philippe plopped a cherry in his mouth. "Can't we keep him?"

⁂

"I saved your life, señor. In return I need protection. Only until the grapes are harvested in a few months." With the children finally abed, Señora Moreau had invited Dante out onto the veranda. She gripped the railing and stared over the shadowy fields where grapevines reached for the dark sky like multiclawed monsters.

Dante slipped beside her. "A few months, señora? I don't—"

"We've been attacked four times so far," she interrupted, desperation creeping into her voice. "Equipment stolen, grapes destroyed. I'm starting to fear for our lives."

Lantern light flickered across her back, sparkling over a loose tendril of hair, but her face was lost to him in the shadows. She smelled of sunshine and sweet cherries, and it took everything in him not to lower his nose to her silky hair for a deeper whiff.

"Who is attacking you?" he asked. "And for what purpose?"

She released a heavy sigh. "I have my suspicions, but I don't know for sure. Let's just say there are many men in town who don't believe a woman should be running a vineyard and who would love to possess it themselves."

Dante would agree with that. American women were spoiled, selfish, fickle, and manipulative. Despite her beauty, this particular woman before him was no exception. She had saved him for her own selfish purpose and was now manipulating him into doing her bidding. That she hailed from money was obvious by her manners and speech. That she stared down her haughty nose at others was evident. But that she stubbornly forced herself into a man's world would be her undoing.

"Why not sell the place and go back to wherever you came from?"

She spun to face him, indignant. "Because this vineyard is my husband's dream. For François's sake, I will not give up now."

Pig-headed woman! Dante huffed and glanced into the shadows.

"After the harvest, you are free to go, Señor Pirate, with no further obligation to me and the children. It is a good bargain. Your life for three months of work. During which time you'll have a roof over your head and food in your belly."

"Listen, señora. I know nothing about grapes or wine or farming. I am a sailor, a privateer."

"You don't need to know anything about a vineyard. I simply need your protection. Fighting is something you are skilled at I presume?" Her voice was sarcastic.

He cocked his head with a frown "You can hire fighters."

"In case you haven't noticed." Her luscious lips grew tight. "I have no money. Nor will I have any until last year's wine is ready to sell and this year's harvest comes in."

He rubbed the back of his neck. "I appreciate you saving me, I do. But I am not the marrying kind, señora. I have a ship to redeem. And when it is back in my possession, I intend to sail away and never return to this waste of a town again."

"Back to pirating?" she quipped.

"You call it pirating. I call it fighting for land stolen from my country."

"From *your* country? You aren't Mexican. Your accent and speech betray you."

"My father is Mexican, señora. And California was ours until the arrogance of America trampled my people." He tightened his grip on the railing as thoughts of his father filled his mind, igniting his ire.

"California was won in war. And if that wasn't enough, my country paid Mexico for the land as well."

Dante's blood simmered at the American's lies. He faced her.

"Fifteen million for the disputed territory," she added. A flicker of fear crossed her eyes when they met his. She backed away. "Or perhaps your government did not inform its people of that fact."

She bumped into the post.

He approached her. "All Americans lie."

Her chest rose and fell, but she lifted her chin and met his gaze. "All people lie, Señor Pirate. But I speak the truth."

Whether she spoke the truth or not, he wanted to kiss her. He wanted to drag her into the bedroom and take what was his right as a husband. Instead, he allowed his anger to grow. Jerking back, he leapt down the steps and stormed into the night.

Five hours later and well into his cups, Dante sat in a saloon that smelled of sweat and spirits. He'd seen several of his crew, including his friend and first mate, Berilo Diaz, who informed him the men were happy to enjoy their time ashore until Dante could redeem the ship. An endeavor he was well on his way to achieve. He'd already won ten dollars at faro and was about to win more from a group of goose-brained miners when whispered threats from a nearby table pricked his ears. As a captain, he'd honed his listening skills for any mention of mutiny or rebellion. This time he heard only snippets over the clamor of fiddle and laughter and cursing that filled the room: *fire*, *rifles*, *run off*, and the word that sent icicles down his spine, *Moreau*.

The men finished their drinks and rose from the table, scraping back chairs and grabbing guns as they made for the door, grins of anticipation on their faces. Six of them, from Dante's count. Six armed men attacking Señora Moreau's vineyard. She and the children wouldn't stand a chance.

Chapter 3

Caroline woke with a start, perspiration covering her body. A breeze stirred the gauze curtains of her open window, casting ghoulish shadows etched in moonlight onto her ceiling. Every creak of the house, every rustle of leaves outside her window, the distant howl of a coyote—all jerked her from her semiconscious state. Ever since that foul pirate, Dante Vega, had stormed off in a rage, her nerves had refused to unwind. She knew he didn't want to be here. She could tell he hated Americans. But she'd seen something in his eyes during dinner and later with the children—a deep yearning, some kindness, even. Or perhaps she was only deluding herself. A man like him felt no obligation to repay her for saving his life. A man like him thought only of himself. And Caroline's impetuousness had once again caused her to make a huge mistake.

A horse let out a frightened whinny. Gunshots cracked the air! Caroline leapt from bed, her heart spinning in her chest. Tossing a robe over her shoulders, she darted to the gun rack in the main parlor and grabbed two of the loaded ones as another gunshot thundered across the valley.

Philippe ran into the room, rubbing his eyes. "Mama, what is it?"

"Philippe, take Abilene and go to your hiding place. Stay there until I tell you." She didn't have time to ensure he obeyed as laughter and the pounding of horse hooves drew her outside. She crept onto the veranda, peering across the vineyard, rifle raised and ready. Torches—at least seven—bobbed up and down in the distance, heading her way.

Sisquoc, her foreman, appeared out of the shadows, fear in his eyes and a gun in his hands. She was surprised the aged Chumash stayed on with her in the face of so much danger. "They try to set barn on fire, señora. I shoot and scare them, but they keep coming."

"Did you wake the others?"

"Yes. And they got guns. Two guard barn, and here is Diego and Manuel." He gestured toward two men, one who positioned himself behind the watering trough and the other behind an old wagon.

All four of her workers. One Chumash and three Mexican. None of whom could hit a beached whale from two feet away. If the vigilantes succeeded in setting the barn on fire, she'd lose her horse, her milk cow, chickens, hay, and most of her farm equipment. And possibly even her wine stored in the cellar beneath. "Get the animals out of the barn, Sisquoc. I'll hold them off."

He cast her a worried look but ran off to do her bidding. She forced her trembling legs to descend the stairs, one by one, and walk onto the path to intercept the attackers. Cocking her rifle, she raised it to shoulder height, waiting until they materialized out of the shadows and she could hear their voices bragging about their impending victory.

"That's far enough!" she shouted. "Any closer and I'll blow your heads off!" Her muscles strained beneath the weight of the rifle.

The men laughed—course belly laughs as if she'd told a joke. Still, they came, their torchlight twisting their features into maniacal threads of light and dark. "Now looky here. If it ain't the mistress of the vineyard herself. Hello there, pretty!" They stopped some twenty feet before her, each one of them eyeing her up and down and licking his lips as if she were one of their trollops from the saloon.

Blood pounded in Caroline's ears. Her knees began to wobble. But she must remain strong. For her children. "You will leave my vineyard at once, or I swear I'll shoot!"

Again they laughed. A cow lowed, and out of the corner of her eye she saw Sisquoc leading the animals from the barn.

"Don't matter 'bout your animals, señora; we will still burn it down. And your grapes, too."

"But not before I shoot one of you dead," she replied, anger crowding out her fear. "You go back and tell your boss that he's never going to get my land."

"Mama!" Abilene's voice spun her around. A man dragged her precious girl out of the house with one hand while Philippe squirmed in the other. Caroline's breath abandoned her. Gasping, she pointed the rifle at the man, even as several of the men behind her cocked their guns in response. Philippe kicked the villain in the shin. He howled and bent over to rub his leg. "You ill-bred *mocoso!*" he shouted, while her brave son attempted to tug his sister from the man's grip. With a heavy hand, the man knocked the boy aside and sent him sprawling onto the dirt.

Terror gripped Caroline. *No, Lord, not my children. Please protect my children.* She gripped the rifle tighter as it swayed over the man's frame. Her finger hovered over the trigger, desperate to shoot, longing to save her children. But she feared to hit Abilene.

"Put down your gun, señora, and tell your men to do the same, or ol' Pedro will have to hurt *los niños.*"

Pinned within the man's harsh grip, Abilene's teary eyes reached out to Caroline. Blood rushed to her head. She grew faint. With one hand raised, she slowly lowered her rifle and called for her men to do the same.

The ominous crack of a gun thundered across the valley. The man holding Abilene let out an ear-piercing howl. Releasing the girl, he stumbled backward and gripped his shoulder. Caroline dove and scooped Abilene in her arms before searching for Philippe in the shadows. Shouts and curses rumbled behind her. More shots split the night sky. Grabbing both children, she spun around, intending to take them into the house when another shot struck one of the vigilantes. He slid from his horse to the ground with a thud. Two of the others began shooting into the darkness, while the rest scattered for cover. Gun smoke bit Caroline's nose and throat.

She scanned the darkness but could see none of her men. Could *they* be the ones shooting? Another shot exploded. Ducking, she hurried the children into the house and ordered them to crouch behind the table. Outside a *thwack* and a grunt sounded. She peered around the open door to see a man strike one of the vigilantes across the jaw with the butt of his rifle then shove the other one down with his boot. A third one already lay prostrate in the dirt. She couldn't make out her rescuer's face in the darkness. But moonlight gleamed off the knife in his hand. Caroline's breath stopped. He tossed the blade with precision. It met its mark, and another villain dropped to his knees before falling face-first to the ground.

A barrage of shots peppered the area. Grabbing a pistol and rifle from the dirt, the man darted behind the water trough and returned fire. A groan of agony rose in the distance. Movement to her right caught Caroline's gaze. The man who had held her children was starting to rise. Dashing into the kitchen, she grabbed a frying pan, and before she could consider the wisdom of her action, she rushed toward the man and slammed it over his head. The *thunk* of iron on a skull sent bile into her throat, but the man once again returned to the dirt. She glanced toward her rescuer, lit by a shaft of moonlight. It was Dante Vega, the pirate!

And he was smiling at her.

More shots sent her racing back into the house. But after she ensured her children were safe, curiosity kept her peering out the door. An eerie silence invaded the vile scene, made all the more spooky by smoke spiraling from torches abandoned to the dirt. A cold sweat snaked down Caroline's back. Crouched behind the water trough, the pirate remained so still, she feared he was dead. But then one of the villains fired, giving him a target, and he shot back. A howl spoke well for his aim.

"We can do this all night, amigos!" he yelled. "I've already shot five of you. Come on out, and let's finish this!"

Silence again. One of the men left his hiding place among the vines and sped toward the house. Gripping her throat, Caroline thought to warn Dante. But he'd already seen him. With precise aim, he followed him with the barrel of his pistol and fired. The man stumbled forward like a broken wheel on a wagon before tumbling to the dirt.

Cursing floated on the wind, soon joined by the sound of a horse galloping away.

Dante rose to his feet and rubbed the back of his neck as casually as if he'd just been working in the fields. Slowly, one by one Caroline's farm workers, including Sisquoc, came out from hiding, rifles in hand.

"You, you." Dante pointed at two of the closest men. "Go check the perimeter. Make sure no one else is coming."

Sisquoc quickly translated into Spanish, and the men sped off.

"And you two." Dante gestured toward the remaining men. "Tie up these injured men, set them on their horses, and send them on their way."

Sisquoc translated again, and Dante gripped the old man's shoulder. "Thank you, friend. Can you make sure the man who galloped away has indeed left?"

The old Chumash Indian nodded and without hesitation obeyed Dante's orders. On shaky legs, Caroline went to fetch her children. Abilene flew into her arms, but Philippe darted past her and out the door before she could stop him.

"Golly, Señor Vega!" The boy glanced at the injured men who were being hoisted up by the workers. "Did you knock out all of these men by yourself?"

Dante glanced toward Caroline. "I had a little help from your mother." The look in his eyes nearly stole her remaining breath. It was more than admiration. It was a knowing look, an intimate look that bespoke a long acquaintance. Or perhaps the moonlight played tricks on her. Abilene's sobs drew her attention, and she tightened her embrace on the little girl. "It's all right now, ma chère, we are safe."

"Because Señor Vega shot all the *bandidos*, Mama!" Philippe exclaimed. "*Parbleu!* Did you see?"

"Yes, Philippe. And we are very grateful to you, señor."

Kneeling by the trough, Dante scooped water and splashed it over his head then stood, raking back his dark hair. "I don't think they'll bother you for a while, Señora Moreau." He ascended the steps and stood beside her. The sting of gunpowder and danger hovered around him.

Abilene, still hiccupping with sobs, lifted her head from Caroline's shoulder and reached out for the man. Without hesitation, he took her in his arms. "You are safe, little one." Though Caroline had said the same thing just moments before, there was something assuring in his deep voice, a soothing confidence that caused Abilene to immediately stop crying, heave a deep sigh, stick her thumb in her mouth, and settle onto his shoulder.

If Caroline hadn't seen it with her own eyes, she never would have believed it possible that her shy, frightened little girl would allow anyone to hold her, especially a stranger. A pirate! Yet, as she watched him wrap his thick arms around Abilene and whisper assurances into her ear, Caroline suddenly longed to trade places with her daughter. Ever since François had died, she'd lived in a constant state of fear and uncertainty. How lovely it would be to feel protected and safe. If only for a moment.

⸎

Caroline woke before dawn with visions of Dante—the pirate—holding Abilene affectionately in his arms. For some reason, it caused an odd sensation within her—not at all an unpleasant one. After stirring the coals in the stove and putting on some water, she drew a cloak about her and made her way through the morning fog to François's grave beneath a large oak in the middle of the vineyard he had loved so much. Though François had adored his children, he'd rarely showed affection—to them or to her. He was a dreamer, a man with a thousand ideas buzzing through his head—so many, he rarely allowed real life to intrude. A brilliant, innovative man who would have made the best wine this side of the Mississippi just as he said he would.

If he hadn't died.

Fog enshrouded the scene with a ghostly white and sent a chill down her spine.

"Dear Lord, thank You for sending Señor Vega to save us last night. Thank You for all You provide. But please, please help us. I don't know what to do. I don't know how—"

A twig cracked. Gasping, Caroline spun around. Señor Vega materialized out of the mist, his dark eyes smiling at her. "I didn't mean to startle you."

She faced forward, embarrassed that he'd heard her praying.

"I saw you leave the house and worried."

"I'm quite all right, as you can see, Señor Pirate." She snapped her gaze to his. "I thought you'd gone back to town."

He ran a hand through his hair. "I slept in the barn just in case those men returned."

The sentiment sent her emotions whirling. "When you stormed off last night after supper, I assumed you were gone for good."

"Do you want me gone for good?" His eyes held a playful glint, yet his tone was serious.

"I've already told you what I want, señor." She returned her gaze to the grave.

⁂

"What was he like?" Dante knew he shouldn't ask, but he could not reconcile the man he remembered from the ship with a man who would have won the heart of such a woman. A woman who had stood her ground, rifle in hand, against seven well-armed men. He'd never seen the likes of it. Especially not from a proper lady who'd obviously benefited from an education only wealth could provide. When he'd heard the shots and seen her in such danger, a foreign sense of terror had screeched through him. He couldn't remember ever being so angry or so afraid—even on his crew's most dauntless raids.

Fingers of fog slithered over the wooden cross marking the grave.

"He was a good man," she finally said. "Wise. Creative. He had wonderful dreams for his life."

"Yet he seemed unwilling to stand up for you when we raided your ship."

"He was not a violent man like you, señor," she spat. "He was a gentle man. A man of peace."

"Peace or not, if I had a wife like you and children like your little ones, I'd fight to the death to keep you safe." Hanging his head, he silently cursed himself. Why had he said that? Why was he feeling this way toward an American?

She stared at him as if he'd told her he intended to become a monk.

"Why did you marry him?" He nodded toward the grave.

"You are too bold, Señor Pirate." She shifted away from him and hugged herself. Creamy mist swirled about her, coating her cheeks with glitter. "I loved him, of course." Her tone was curt. "Why else does a woman marry a man?"

Dante chuckled. "Apparently for protection."

Even through the fog, Dante saw her face redden. She shifted her shoes over the gravel and let out a sigh. "I mean a *real* marriage." She flattened her lips. "Besides, I wouldn't have risked defying my father's wishes and losing my family's favor if I hadn't loved François."

Then why did she sound like she was trying to convince herself of that fact? Dante rubbed his chin. "So, let me guess. Your father finally refused one of his precious daughter's requests? And you went and had your way regardless."

"You know nothing of me, Pirate!" Blazing eyes snapped his way. "You are an insolent brute, señor."

He grinned. "I agree. But I speak the truth, don't I? You hail from money—one of those long-standing families out east, I'm guessing. And from your accent, somewhere near New Orleans. My bet is you ran away with this François to escape the strict rule of your parents."

She pursed her lips and huffed. "You may think what you wish." Moments passed before she swung a suspicious gaze his way. "But what of you, Señor Pirate? You are obviously schooled here in America, not in Mexico."

"Harvard, in fact."

"A Harvard-educated pirate?" She laughed.

"Privateer, señora, if you please." He grinned.

"Whatever you call it." She waved a hand through the air, stirring the fog into a whirl. "You must have had an American mother, a wealthy one, since you seem to find success so disdainful."

Dante narrowed his eyes. The woman was not only beautiful but smart. "I abhor neither success nor wealth but rather what they both do to people."

She studied him with those green eyes of hers—the color of a tropical sea. The fire went out of them, replaced by understanding. "Your mother was cruel to you." It was both a statement and a question.

Dante tightened his jaw. He wanted neither understanding nor sympathy. Especially not from an American. All he wanted from this woman was the means to redeem his ship from the city. "If you wish to know, perhaps you should ask the God to whom you were praying a moment ago."

She jerked her gaze back to the grave. "How dare you spy on me!"

"I'm curious, señora, why an intelligent woman like yourself believes that God actually cares about our troubles."

"Of course He cares! How can you say such a thing?"

"If He cares so much for you, why are you speaking to a husband six feet under? Why do you barely have enough to eat? Why is your vineyard being attacked?"

Her chest began to heave like a sail catching the wind. "I insist you leave at once, Señor Pirate. I don't want an American-hating, atheist thief around my children."

He smiled, dipped his head, and turned to leave. "You should have thought of that before you married me."

Chapter 4

Philippe's laughter drew Caroline to the kitchen window where she brushed aside the gauze curtains and gaped at the sight before her. Dante and her son sat on a bench in the shade of a tree, their heads bent together over a long, coiled rope. On the ground lay several knots tied in other pieces of rope—unusual knots, the likes of which she'd never seen. The pirate's husky voice came to her on the wind, confident, kind, and patient as he taught her son how to tie what she assumed were ship knots.

"You try it now, Philippe," he said, handing the boy the rope.

Caroline stiffened, waiting to see if her son failed in his attempt. The poor boy had already suffered enough beneath his father's neglect. Caroline would not allow any man to wound her son's tender confidence with more rejections or rebukes.

Philippe finished and held up the rope, but then he shook his head. "It's not right, is it?"

"No." Dante took it. "But it's almost right. Here, let me show you again. These knots are not easy to learn." He slowly slid the rope through loops and circles, while Philippe watched with more focus than Caroline had ever seen from the boy.

This time Philippe tied the knot correctly, his blue eyes gazing up at Dante in expectation and pride.

"Well done!" the pirate exclaimed, tousling the boy's hair. "We'll make a sailor out of you yet."

Philippe beamed, and Caroline's heart filled to near bursting with joy for her son. Slipping from the window, she returned to clean the final dishes after breakfast, her mind awhirl with the events of the past few weeks. Despite her insisting that Dante leave, the stubborn man had stayed on. At first she'd been worried at his intentions and also that he'd get used to a roof over his head and cooked meals and then never leave. The last thing she needed was another mouth to feed. Yet, not only had the pirate behaved as a perfect gentleman, but he had actually assisted Sisquoc in tending the grapes, feeding the livestock, and irrigating the land. He'd even fixed a broken wheel on their wagon and replaced a few tiles on the roof.

He took his meals with her and the children and seemed to actually enjoy their time together. But every night after supper he headed downtown. Some nights when she couldn't sleep, she heard him stumble into the barn well after two in the morning. Oddly, even though she kept a pistol beneath her pillow as a defense against *him*, she felt safer when he returned.

They'd not spoken privately since that morning by François's grave, but that was for the best. Not that she was looking for a husband, but this particular one possessed all the wrong qualities: he hated Americans and America, he didn't believe in God, he was often rude and ill-mannered, he drank and gambled. And worst of all—lest she forget by his civilized behavior—he was a thief and a pirate! Bon sang, she shouldn't even be thinking of him this way at all. Tossing down her towel, she stormed from the kitchen. If she had a thimble of brains, she shouldn't even allow such a man around her children. He'd told her more than once that as soon as he redeemed his ship, he would leave.

And the way Philippe was starting to look up to the man, she knew her son would suffer. Not to mention Abilene, who also seemed to have developed an affection for the pirate. Ensuring the little girl still played contently on the sofa, Caroline marched onto the veranda. "Come, Philippe. We are going into town."

"Ah, Mama, but Señor Vega is teaching me to tie sailor knots."

"I need you to come with me, Philippe. Now." She kept her voice stern.

The boy scowled and handed the rope to the pirate. Dante stood and faced her. "Something has upset you, Señora Moreau?"

"Of course not. I simply need to purchase supplies."

"Then I will go with you."

"There is no need."

"Nevertheless, you married me for protection. And protect you I shall. Since I am not permitted any other privileges of the sacred union." He winked above a disarming grin.

"If you consider protecting us a privilege, I am happy for it, señor." Clutching her skirts, she spun around before he could see the red creeping up her face. Infuriating man! She wasn't a woman to blush easily, but this pirate seemed to know just what to say. And just how to look at her—as if she were a precious gem he longed to touch.

After a brief argument, she allowed him to take the reins and drive them into town, and within minutes, Dante parked the buckboard near the public square. After helping them down, he guided them through throngs of donkeys, carts, horses, and people to the vendor stalls and booths. The smell of human sweat and animal dung joined the briny scent of the sea and the sweet perfume of fresh flowers in a dichotomy of odors as they passed carts stuffed with all manner of dry goods, fruit, meat, fresh flowers, *objets d'art* from the East, furniture, and rugs.

"Mama!" Philippe called, luring her to where he stood before a leather shop, a whip in hand. "Can I have one?" His expectant gaze met hers, and she'd give anything to be able to see his smile grow larger, but the price read $2.50. And $2.50 would feed them for a month.

"Not this time, Philippe," she said, hoping to placate him with a smile, but the disappointment on his face broke her heart.

Dante gripped the braided leather rope and nodded his approval. "Every young boy needs a whip."

Caroline chastised the pirate with her eyes.

"But not every boy gets what he wants when there's food to buy," he instantly corrected. "A man needs to earn these things on his own." He placed the whip back in the cart, and Philippe's scowl faded as he nodded his understanding.

"Mama." Abilene tugged on Caroline's skirts and pointed to a booth filled with dolls of all kinds: some made of cornhusk, some wood, some wax, some cloth, and some porcelain—all dressed in lavish gowns. Before Caroline could divert her daughter's attention, the little girl darted to the cart and shyly brushed her fingers over a doll perched up front, a porcelain beauty with long ringlets of black hair, a satin ruffled gown, pearls around her neck, and a feathered bonnet.

"A beautiful doll for a beautiful señorita!" the vendor said as Caroline approached.

But another two-dollar price tag caused her heart to sink. She'd not been able to buy the children anything special in years. Not even for Christmas. To her rescue yet again, Dante swept the little girl in his arms and diverted her attention to a woman in the next booth who was weaving straw hats.

While the children watched the woman, Caroline slid beside Dante. "My children are not the type to ask for such expensive gifts, señor. I do not know what has come over them." Even as she said it, her eyes landed on a bonnet in the millinery behind the booth. It was fashioned of sheer gauze embroidered in gold thread and embellished with pink silk bows. She fingered her own plain bonnet with its frayed edges and torn ribbons and felt the pirate's intense gaze on her. Flustered, she turned away. "Come, children, we have shopping to do."

He smiled, handed her Abilene, and dipped his head. "I must go to the council to discover the redemption price for my ship, señora. I will meet you later." And off he went with that confident gait of his, drawing the eyes of more than one female in the plaza.

Caroline huffed. Some protector he was. But she didn't need protection in the daylight, not with all the people milling about and the vendors and cantinas and shops filling the square. Gathering her children close, she found the things she needed: soap, beans or *frijoles* as they were called here, oil for lanterns, and oranges. Now, to check on the price of fresh fish. The fish monger, however, spoke no English and insisted on arguing with her over the price. They bartered back and forth until Caroline's frustration was near bursting. Stealing herself for her final offer, she glanced down to ensure her children were still beside her.

But they were gone. She scanned the market square. They were nowhere in sight!

"Philippe! Abilene!" Caroline shoved her way through the crowd, her heart pinched tight. How could she have let them out of her sight? *Oh, Father in heaven, please help me find them.* Desperation dizzied her as she pressed through the throng shouting their names. Finally, she spotted her son's mop of brown hair and Abilene's red curls across the plaza. They sat in a café under the shade of an awning, eating as if they hadn't nearly put their mother in an early grave.

Furious, she marched toward them, intending to *first* take them in her embrace and *next* to give them a scolding they wouldn't soon forget. Before she could reach them, a man drew close and placed two cups next to their plates and then lifted his gaze to hers. A slick smile tugged on lips below a thin mustache. He straightened his gold-fringed black vest and shifted his boots over the ground. The chirping of his spurs grated her nerves. Gray streaked across the dark hair circling his handsome face. Deep-set eyes she had never trusted met hers. Domingo Casimiro de Iago.

"Señora Moreau." He bowed elegantly. "I am sorry to have alarmed you, but when I saw your children in the square, I couldn't help but offer them a *fardelejo*. I know how much they love the Spanish pastry."

"Mama, this is so good!" Abilene glanced up at Caroline, crumbs dancing on her lips.

"Thank you, Señor Casimiro!" Philippe beamed from ear to ear while he shoved another forkful of the almond-filled pastry into his mouth.

Trying to contain her fury, Caroline drew Señor Casimiro aside, noting as she did that several of his men lingered just outside the café, watching them from beneath sombreros.

"Señor Casimiro," she began.

"You may call me Domingo, *por favor*, señora."

"Señor Casimiro, while I appreciate you buying my children treats, I must protest you doing so without my permission. They are my children, and I should decide what and when they eat."

"Ah, but they are only los niños, señora, and you know how much I adore them." His smile was sickly sweet.

Did she? He had told her more than once, yet she'd never seen him actually speak to them except with trifling flatteries such as "what a good boy" and "what a beautiful girl."

He leaned toward her, smelling of Spanish cologne and spicy mustache oil. "I know you cannot afford such treats, señora. Why not allow the children to enjoy?"

She took a step back. "Again, I thank you for your generosity, but in the future, I would prefer you ask me. And my finances are none of your affair."

"But I would like to make them my affair, as you say, señora. I would like to wipe away all of your troubles. A beautiful woman like you shouldn't have to worry about such matters."

Acid welled in her belly. Ever since François had died, the wealthy don had not hid his interest in her, nor stopped pursuing her—even in light of her continual rebuffs. Certainly marrying the man would solve all her problems. She'd live on the largest ranchero outside the city, have a bevy of servants attending her every need and tutors for her children. But something in the man's eyes caused her insides to squirm. Something in his arrogant demeanor made her realize she'd lose the freedom she'd grown to love. Still, she *would* marry the pompous man for her children's sake, for them to have a better chance at life, if only she didn't catch the flickers of dismissal in his eyes when he looked their way.

"Perhaps you have not heard, señor, but I am newly married." She glanced at her children still enjoying their pastry then up at the don whose face had tightened into thin lines.

"A pirate, I am told, señora. What were you thinking?" Though his voice was still sweet, one side of his lips twitched.

"I saved a man from the noose."

"A villain who deserved such a death. Or perhaps it is his warmth at night that pleases you." He raked her with his gaze.

"How dare you, señor?" She raised her hand to slap him, but he caught it. The veneer of civility shattered from his face, replaced by a sinister glower. Clutching her arm—a bit too tightly—he led her off the porch to the side of the café. "Do you think such a villain will stay with you? *Estúpido!* He will take what he wants and leave."

"You're hurting me!" She raised her voice, hoping passersby would notice and come to her rescue, but even the few who glanced up didn't dare to confront the most powerful man in town.

"How could you marry a thief, a villain, a man of no consequence, no wealth, while you dare to shun me?"

"Let go of me!" Though she tried to hold them at bay, tears filled her eyes.

Señor Casimiro's men gathered close, forming a barricade around them.

"Mama!" Philippe's voice rose above the crowd.

Hot sun seared her skin. Perspiration beaded on her forehead and neck as the men's boots stirred dust in her face.

"Please let me go to my children," she sobbed, coughing.

"I will, señora, I will. But not until we come to an understanding. If you insist—"

She kicked him with all her strength. Howling, he leapt back. Her thrust hadn't landed where she'd hoped. Instead of incapacitating him, she'd only infuriated him. Raising his hand, he slapped her across the face.

The sting radiated from her cheek down her neck.

"Mama, where are you?" Abilene whimpered.

Caroline tugged against the man's grip.

"I have been kind to you, señora. But my patience will soon come to an end. When your pirate lover leaves you, and you have nothing to feed your little ones, you will come to me then. You give this pirate everything now, but you will soon be mine. *And* your precious vineyard."

Chapter 5

S he will never be yours, señor!" Dante gripped the man by his gold-embroidered collar and tossed him away from Caroline. *Señor Casimiro* stumbled backward, his expression brimming with shock and fury. He reached for his pistol. Dante kicked it from his hand then leveled his own weapon on the don's advancing men. One of them seemed familiar, his shock of light hair a beacon among so many brown-haired men. He walked with a limp as eyes bent on revenge pierced Dante. These were the men who had attacked Caroline's vineyard. And this popinjay was their boss.

Philippe, a weeping Abilene in hand, pushed through the growing crowd and ran to Dante. He nudged the children toward their mother and took a stance before them. Not that he could stop all these men by himself. But he would die trying. More than anything, he hated when the strong picked on the weak. As his mother had done to him his entire childhood.

"Call off your men, señor. I've already proven able to beat them. Or will you now attack women and children in the light of day?"

"I know not what you mean, *pirate*." The Spaniard spat as he rose to his feet and brushed dust from his clothes.

"I think you do."

"This was only a misunderstanding. One which you would do well to stay out of." He plucked his hat from the dirt and eyed Dante with disdain. "Señora Moreau and I were merely discussing her future. Nothing more."

"A future which required your hand striking her face?"

"Disrespect from women must be dealt with, or it will grow like a cancer. Surely you agree?"

"I do not." Dante scanned the men waiting for one word from their boss to pummel him. But a crowd formed around the altercation, and he doubted the don wanted his reputation soiled. Dante glared at him. "Stay away from Señora Moreau and her children."

"Of course. I mean them no harm." The Spaniard slipped on his hat and dipped a bow toward Caroline. "When this pirate is through with you, señora, you know where I am."

⚬℀℀

Caroline would like to tell the man that even if he lived in a golden palace, she'd never seek him out, but she didn't want to cause more trouble and upset Abilene, who still clung to her chest as tight as a barnacle to a ship, her thumb stuck in her mouth.

Philippe, however, spit after the men as they and Señor Casimiro sauntered away. "Hush, Philippe." She held him back, lest he try something else. Her son, where did he get such courage? Certainly not from his father. Trying to settle the pounding of her heart, Caroline drew a deep breath as Señor Vega turned to face them. Once again he had saved their lives. Once again he had stood up against overwhelming odds when he could have run. Why? The look she now saw in his eyes made her forget he was a rogue, a thief. And that he'd soon leave. It was a look of concern, protection, and even affection. But that couldn't be.

Steeling herself against the longing rising within her, she thanked him politely and started on her way, but Abilene reached toward the man. The pirate took her in his embrace, her red curls tumbling over his brown open shirt, her tiny hands reaching around his neck and gripping his collar as she nuzzled her head beneath his chin. He rubbed her back and glanced down at Philippe who stared at him with awe. "You were very brave, Philippe," he said, patting the lad on the back.

"I was?" The young boy's eyes flashed. "If I'd had a pistol, Señor Vega, I'd have taken care of them all!"

"No, you wouldn't have, Philippe," Caroline said sharply, still trying to recover from her daughter's complete trust in this pirate. "And you won't have a gun until you're fully grown."

The excitement fled from Philippe's face, but it couldn't be helped. She would not have this pirate influencing her son to become a fighter like he was.

After gathering the supplies she'd dropped, Caroline followed Dante back to the buckboard, ignoring the curious eyes of the townspeople staring at the enigma who was both a family man and a pirate. She couldn't agree more, for she was having just as much difficulty associating the two. At the moment, however, she was thankful for both. Her arm still throbbed from where Don Casimiro had clutched her, and a shiver ran through her at the thought of the horrid man. If Dante had not come when he did. . . Well, it was best not to think of it. For now, he sat beside her on the driver's perch—so close their legs almost touched. Yet she felt safe. Very safe.

He snapped the reins, and within moments the sea came into view. A sheen of dark blue spanned to the fog bank on the horizon as waves tumbled ashore in a foamy dance. The same ship she'd seen two weeks ago rocked in the choppy waters.

"Is that your ship, Señor Pirate?" A blast of wind nearly tore off her bonnet, and she held it in place.

He pulled the horse to a halt and gazed out to sea, the longing in his eyes confirming what Señor Casimiro had said. This man would leave. He would sail back out to sea where he belonged. But what did she care? As long as he stayed through the harvest as he'd promised.

"The *Bounty*," he finally answered.

"How much is the council charging to redeem her?"

"More than I have." He smiled, but his eyes remained on the ship.

"You miss being at sea," she stated rather than asked.

He said nothing.

"Can I come aboard your ship?" Philippe poked his head between them from behind.

"Now, Philippe, that's not polite to ask. And besides, when Señor Vega gets his ship back, he won't want children running about on deck."

"But I won't run, and I can tie knots now and help."

Dante smiled down at the boy. "You would make a great sailor, Philippe."

Abilene pulled out her thumb. "Me, too. I can learn knots. And I can clean floors. Mama lets me help at home."

"We can all become pirates!" Philippe shouted, beaming.

"We are not becoming pirates!" Caroline said with horror as Dante chuckled and snapped the reins.

༄

Dante dabbed a moist cloth on the edge of Caroline's lip, where a bruise had formed from *Señor Casimiro's* strike. Supper was over, and after several stories were told and prayers were said, the children had finally fallen asleep. Prayers, bah! Even after her harrowing day, the lady had still thanked God for His love and protection. Now, as they sat on the veranda under the light of a single lantern and a full moon, Dante finally did what he'd been longing to do all evening—tend to the lady's wound. He hadn't been sure she would allow his touch, but when he'd brought the bowl of water and a cloth onto the veranda, she hadn't flinched like she usually did when he drew near.

"I'm sorry he hurt you." Dante forced down an anger that, even now, threatened to send him over to this don's estate and teach the man chivalry. He'd been searching the plaza for Caroline and the children when he'd seen her kick the brute. Even with several armed men surrounding her. What bravery! What pluck! Then, when the man had slapped her, Dante's blood had boiled.

She closed her eyes to his touch and let out a sigh. A cool breeze stirred the loose curls at her neck. "Do you truly believe he's responsible for the attacks on my vineyard?"

"I recognized one of his men. *Si*, he's the one, all right."

"He is one of the wealthiest dons in the city. His family came here in 1815, hailing from royalty in Spain, they say. What does he want with me?"

Dante raised a brow at her naïveté.

Even in the dim light, he saw the lady blush. "But until today he's always been polite, even kind to me. Complimentary."

"Of course he's polite. Has it been so long since a man courted you?"

"In truth, yes." A little smile graced her lips. "Yet attacking my vineyard is hardly a path to my heart."

"I don't believe your heart is his goal, señora. Just a means to an end." He dipped the cloth in the water and dabbed her lips again. The blood was gone and the cut was small, but Dante didn't want to stop. She smelled of lilacs and fresh bread, and her closed eyes afforded him a chance to study her delicate features: the slight upturn of her nose, the curve of her chin, the sweep of thick lashes resting on her cheeks.

"I can hardly believe it of him," she said.

Leaning closer to get a whiff of her hair, he pressed the cloth to her mouth once again.

"Ouch." She opened her eyes.

"Apologies." Dante withdrew. "He won't give up. You need protection. A group of farm hands to defend you."

"Or just one pirate." She smiled, but then it slipped away. "But you will leave soon."

Dante could not deny it. He was not a man meant to be landlocked. The sea called to him day and night. He longed to be back aboard his ship, free again to travel where he wanted, to seek his fortune, make a difference for Mexico.

"Thank you." She scooted away from him. "I cannot afford to pay more men. But God will provide. He always has."

Dante flattened his lips. "You are safe now because of me and not this God of yours."

"But He sent you to us, did He not?" She smiled then gazed up at the starlit sky as if she were looking at the Almighty Himself. Faith settled like a peaceful stream in her green eyes, and Dante felt a stirring of envy. What would it be like to have a Father who was all-powerful and who truly loved you? One on whom you could depend, one who would never disappoint or leave you.

She must have read his thoughts, for she laid a hand on his. "Where is your father, Señor Vega?"

"In Mexico. Veracruz. He runs a merchant business."

"So, that is how he met your American mother? In his travels?"

He nodded, uncomfortable with the turn of the conversation. "Si, in Boston."

"Then why were you raised in America?"

Dante dropped the cloth in the bowl. "My mother's family had fallen on hard times, and her marriage to my father supplied much-needed wealth. An arranged marriage. After the wedding, she refused to move to Mexico. Then, when I was born, she used the excuse of wanting the best education for her son." He stared at the wooden porch beside his boots as anger smoldered in his heart. Dante had been a mistake, an unfortunate product of a loveless marriage.

"But your father didn't move to America?"

"No. His business, his life, was in Mexico. I hardly ever saw him. Once a year, perhaps. My mother's family was very powerful."

"I'm so sorry."

Dante rose and walked to the railing. "It was for the best. He didn't turn out to be much of a father. After I left Harvard, I traveled to Mexico to be with him, but he disapproved of my idea of privateering. Vehemently disapproved." He snorted. "Told me no son of his would ever be a pirate."

"Then, why become one, Dante?"

The sound of his Christian name on her lips brought him around. The look in her eyes made him continue his tale.

"America had taken everything from me, my childhood, my father, my national identity. And then they took my homeland. I couldn't understand why my father wouldn't do something about it. I was as disappointed in him as he was in me, I suppose. Yet suddenly I was a man without a home. Neither my father nor my mother wanted me. In the end, it was the sea that gave me a home, a life, a purpose."

"So, you truly believe in this cause of yours? Provoking American ships for Mexico?" Disapproval laced her tone.

"We all have our causes, señora. You have this vineyard, this dream of your husband's. I have my revenge."

"But yours will lead to death."

He chuckled. "Perhaps. But it seems yours might as well." Turning, he gripped the railing and gazed over the dark vineyard. "Is your husband's dream worth dying for, señora? Don't you have any dreams of your own?"

⁓

Dreams? Caroline had never asked herself that question. When she'd lived with her parents, their dreams had been hers. After she married François, his dream took their place. Now she supposed all she wanted was a good life for her children. A good home. Someday perhaps, a loving husband. And the freedom to make her own choices. Rising, she slid beside him. "My dream is for my children, *Señor* Vega."

A breeze blew his black hair behind him. "I liked it when you called me Dante."

She had liked it, too. Too much. It sounded right on her lips. Not the name of a pirate, but the name of a man who was kind and good, albeit a bit wounded by life.

"If you dream for a good life for your children, Caroline, you must keep them safe. I know men like Señor Casimiro. They strive for things they cannot have. He will not give up. Not even with me here."

She hadn't thought about that. The danger she was putting this man in. Before, it hadn't really mattered. He owed her for saving his life. But now the thought of him being killed caused her insides to clench. "I have put you in danger."

"I don't fear him. I fear for you." His eyes were lost to her in the shadows, but his sincerity thickened the air between them. "You must have protection, Caroline," he added.

"God will protect us."

"Blast it all!" He huffed and rubbed the back of his neck. "What has this God of yours done for you?"

Caroline lifted her chin. "He gave me a husband and two beautiful children, a vineyard, wine in the barrels, my freedom, hope for a future. And He brought us you. I'd say He's done quite a bit."

"You speak of Him as if you know Him."

"I do. You can, too, Dante."

"No, thanks." He leaned against the post. "My mother showed me what God was like. I had my share of punishments for not obeying Him."

Caroline's chest grew heavy at his statement. "Your mother was wrong. God is not a set of restrictions and rules. He's a father, He's a friend. He's a savior. And He wants to help you with your life."

She could feel his gaze pierce her. "You make me want to believe that," he said.

"Then do." She stepped toward him.

"This is what I believe." Lifting a finger, he ran the back of it over her cheek. "You are the most precious woman I've ever met. Brave, kind, caring, a good mother—so unlike my own." His touch sent a prickling feeling down to her toes. What was wrong with her? His gaze dropped to her lips, and he swallowed. Was he thinking of kissing her? Her breath came fast. Her world began to spin. His scent of leather and earth swirled beneath her nose like a heady perfume. Then his lips met hers in a soft caress so at odds with the rough pirate. She knew she should stop him, but when he wrapped his arms around her and drew her close, drinking her in like a desperate man, her knees reduced to mush, and she wilted against him.

A coyote howled in the distance, a cow lowed, and a breeze stirred the leaves on a nearby tree, but nothing seemed real to her except the man who held her so protectively. The kiss was sweet, deep, and went on far too long. Another second and she'd be lost to him forever.

She pushed away, stepped back, and turned her back to him. How could she have done such a thing? Was she some hussy to kiss a man she hardly knew? "Forgive me."

She could hear his heavy breathing, his deep groan as if someone had stolen his last meal. "No need to be ashamed, Caroline," he finally breathed out. "We are married, after all."

"You are married to the sea, Señor Vega, not to me. And I insist you never touch me again."

Chapter 6

With a hand to her aching back, Caroline stepped onto the veranda and drew in a deep breath. She'd spent the morning scrubbing floors and kneading bread and longed for a glimpse of her children. She knew they fared well. Their laughter had serenaded her during her chores, but now as she scanned the vineyard all she saw were clusters of nearly ripe grapes hanging from vines like plump plums from trees. From the taste and feel of the few grapes she'd sampled yesterday, it may only be another two weeks before Sisquoc and the crew could start harvesting the fruit—a late harvest this year due to their unusually cool summer. Of course, after they picked the grapes, the men would press them and then place the strained juice in jugs to ferment for days before transferring it to oak barrels in the cellar to cure for next year's batch of wine. Good thing she already had a buyer for the wine from last year's harvest. She'd been testing it and adding water to top it off just like her husband had instructed her, and hopefully, it would meet the standards of her buyer, a merchant who intended to sell it to another merchant in New York. Things were looking up, indeed.

To say this past month had been one of the happiest in her life seemed a betrayal to both herself and François. To her husband because, even though she'd kept her distance from Dante, just having the pirate around—hearing his confident voice, watching him with her children, and exchanging pleasantries over their meals together—had made her far happier than she'd ever been in the intimacies of her marriage to François. And it was a betrayal to her own sentiments because she allowed them to grow for a man who would soon be gone.

Taking her heart—and she feared her children's hearts—with him.

But how could she have held her heart at bay? How could she ask her children not to follow Dante around, not to speak with him, not to crawl into his lap and receive his embrace, when she'd give anything to be able to do that herself?

Dante stepped into view, carrying Abilene in one arm and an ax in the other hand. Philippe strutted by his side, chattering like a magpie. Caroline smiled. She couldn't help but smile. Though they'd not shared a private moment since their kiss—she'd made sure of that—Dante had never faltered in his care of her and her children. He'd worked side by side with Sisquoc and the other men tending the grapes, he'd repaired a hole in the barn and cared for the chickens and the cow, he'd periodically rode along the perimeter of the property to ensure all was well, and he'd even assisted in hauling water from the creek. The Chumash foreman liked him, as did the other workers, and they readily obeyed his orders. He was a leader of men. A hard worker. Kindhearted. A good man. And a gentleman. Despite his occasional suggestive teasing and the desire in his eyes, he had not once pressed her for marital privileges.

He set Abilene down on the bench, stuck the ax in a stump, and pulled his shirt over his head. Noon sun gleamed on his bronze skin and rippled like sunlit waves over the muscles in his back and forearms. Philippe removed his shirt, too, tossed it aside just like Dante had done, and beamed up at the pirate with pride.

As if sensing her eyes on him, Dante turned around, giving her a glimpse of the molded muscles of his chest and stomach. He smiled and waved. Heat expanded out from her belly until it flooded every inch of her. Still, she could not turn her eyes away. She returned his smile.

No doubt a man like him had been with many women—could have any woman he wanted. Why, then, did he stay with her? Surely it wasn't the roof over his head. He slept in the barn. Nor the scant meals she served when, instead of beans, he could purchase a steak downtown. What other reason could keep him here other than the one that made her heart soar—the one that made her want to run to him and beg him to stay.

She huffed. She'd become a dreamer like François. The pirate was just being kind. Perhaps he liked playing the hero to the damsel in distress. Perhaps he enjoyed the adoration of her children. That must be it, for night after night he continued his treks downtown, where she'd heard he'd drained the pockets of many of the drunken gamblers. He was only biding his time until he could redeem his ship and leave. Still, she would cherish the moments she had with him, for he had proven himself a good man. A worthy man.

"I'm teaching your son how to chop wood," he shouted.

Fear buzzed through her, and taking a step forward, she opened her mouth to tell him that it was far too dangerous, but he held up a hand and chuckled. "I know, señora. I'll be careful. He's using a smaller ax."

Philippe hefted the small blade and stood bare-chested beside Dante. "Please, Mama! I'm not a little baby anymore."

Abilene nodded her approval from the bench. Where was the thumb that was normally in her mouth—that had been in her mouth since her father had died?

Outnumbered, Caroline finally nodded her consent, but stood there for several more minutes watching the muscles roll across Dante's back and arms while he raised the ax and chopped wood. Periodically, he'd set aside smaller branches on another hewn stump for Philippe to hack. The boy picked up instruction well, and assured that he was in good hands, Caroline decided it was best if she got back to work before she made a fool of herself gawking at the man like an innocent maiden—imprinting his image on her mind so she'd never forget him. Not that she could ever forget a man like Dante Vega.

∽

Taking her children's hands in hers, Caroline gestured for them to bow their heads while she thanked God for the food. On one side of Dante, Abilene slipped her tiny hand into his, while across the table, Philippe stretched his arm to grab his other. Dante's eyes moistened, but he kept them open while Caroline prayed. She spoke with such honesty and sincerity and genuine thanks, as if she were speaking to someone sitting beside her, some generous benefactor who provided for all their needs. It baffled Dante. She was so grateful for so little, while his mother had been disappointed with so much. His mother's prayers had been rote, austere, recited. Empty. But this beautiful señora's prayers touched a place deep in his heart, a longing to believe in something more than himself.

The prayer ended, and they all enjoyed a supper of home-baked bread, frijoles with eggs, and squash from the garden. Though the food was slight—barely filling half of Dante's belly—the joy and satisfaction filling his heart more than made up for it. At their request, he entertained the children with fanciful tales of sea storms and mermaids as they oscillated between oohing and aahing and giggling until tears flowed down their cheeks. All the while, Caroline ate and watched, casting him an occasional smile, despite the sorrow he sensed lingering about her. She'd been aloof since their kiss. He'd chastised himself more than once for taking such liberties with a lady like Caroline. But she'd been so beautiful in the moonlight, so easy to talk to, he'd been unable to resist. She'd not mentioned it since, nor had she allowed them to be alone.

Which was for the best. The way Dante was feeling—like he could find no joy in life aside from seeing her smile—he doubted he could resist her. And he must. A lady like Caroline would never settle for a scoundrel—*should* never settle for a scoundrel like him. No, she deserved a gentleman, someone with education and fortune and culture, a godly man who shared her faith. Someone who would raise her children right, not prune them to be pirates and ne'er-do-wells. Based on her offish behavior, she'd no doubt come to the same conclusion and was looking forward to him leaving after the harvest.

Which is why he intended to enjoy his remaining time with the Moreaus. But with each passing day, it grew harder and harder. This was *true* family. The family he never had. The family he never thought existed. The affection, the care and unity between mother and children, never failed to put a lump in his throat. The gentle way she scolded her children, always in love and with purpose, caused anger to well at his own childhood. But the look of trust and adoration in the children's eyes, and sometimes in Caroline's, when they looked at him made him want to give up the sea and become a husband and a father. Almost.

Later that night, after playing a game of jackstraws with the children, Dante headed to the barn as was his custom, not trusting himself to be alone with the lady after she put Philippe and Abilene to bed. He grabbed his rifle and strolled among the grapevines, ensuring all was well. The sweet scent of grapes and rich earth joined the salty brine of a sea that called to him from the distance with each mighty crash of its waves. Fog rolled in, masking the moonlight and muffling each tread of his boots, making them sound hollow. Like his soul.

A scream pierced the night. A child's scream! Terror gripped every nerve as he dashed for the house, burst inside, and made for Abilene's bedchamber. A single candle cast flickering light over Caroline holding her sobbing daughter.

"What happened? Is she hurt?" Dante dashed to the other side of the bed.

Caroline rocked Abilene back and forth. "Just a nightmare." Concern moistened her eyes. "She's had them since François died." The little girl's body shook as she glanced up, her face hidden beneath a web of auburn curls, and reached for him. Emotion clogging his throat, Dante swallowed her up in his arms and kissed the top of her head. "Just a bad dream, pumpkin. All is well. You are safe." Her sobbing stopped, and she melted against him as if she trusted him to protect her forever.

Caroline, her golden hair tumbling to her waist, gazed at him with such appreciation, it brought moisture to his eyes. *Moisture!* He lowered his chin to sit atop Abilene's head and forced back his tears, ashamed.

Pirates didn't cry.

He sat there holding the precious girl until slowly Abilene's tight little body relaxed and she drifted to sleep. Setting her down on her pillow, he brushed curls from her face. She moaned in her sleep, peeked at him through slitted eyes, and said, "Thank you, Papa," before her breathing deepened and she drifted off again.

Overcome with emotion, Dante rose from the bed and backed into the shadows, lest Caroline see his weakness. She stood and approached him. Her night robe clung to curves not normally revealed by her gowns. Her lips were red and puffy, her eyes shimmering.

And worst of all, they were alone.

"I don't know how to thank you, Dante. You have such a way with the children." She smelled of lilacs and life and hope. Candlelight haloed her in shimmering gold, making her look like the angel she was—an angel sent to rescue the wayward pirate.

He wanted her. He wanted to make her happy. He wanted to love and protect her and be a father to her children.

Instead, he grabbed his rifle and dashed from the room.

Two hours later, Dante was on his fifth mug of ale and his third game of faro. The more he drank, the more he seemed to win. And the more his heart ached. He cursed himself for growing soft. Since he'd been a child, he'd prided himself on being able to control his emotions. When his mother had ignored him, belittled him, punished him unfairly, and finally sent him away to school, he'd kept it all inside, never allowing her to see his pain.

But this woman and her children. They had bewitched him. A plague on all women! For they truly possessed the power to destroy men—just like his mother had done to his father.

"*Capitán!*" A shout brought his attention from his cards to Berilo, his first mate, sitting down at a table beside his. "Do you win much?"

Tossing down his cards, Dante bowed out of the game, grabbed his mug of ale, and joined his friend. Two scantily dressed women sashayed up to the table. Berilo welcomed one onto his lap, but Dante waved the other away. Women were a curse. And besides, Caroline had ruined him forever to anyone but her.

Berilo showered kisses over the trollop's neck until she giggled and slapped him playfully. "When do you get the ship back, Capitán? The men grow restless."

"More than likely it is their pockets that are empty." Dante snorted.

"Si. That is true. But they are anxious for the fight."

Dante frowned and sipped his drink. Anxious to fight? Somewhere in the past few months, he'd lost that desire. But he would get it back. He *had* to get it back.

"Go get us drinks." Berilo flipped the woman two coins and slapped her behind as she sped off, smiling.

Dante leaned back in his chair. "If I continue to win, I'll have enough to redeem the ship in a month." And his obligation to help with the harvest would be completed by then as well. Then he would leave. Leave behind the only family he'd ever known. But it was for the best. For him *and* for them.

"Let us drink to redeeming the *Bounty*!" Berilo took one of the two mugs the woman plunked on the table and slid the other to Dante.

"To the *Bounty*!" Dante raised his mug. "And to leaving this paltry town!"

They continued to toast everything from Mexico, to freedom, to the sea, to whiskey, to loose women, to frijoles, until the world spun around him. Stumbling home, Dante intended to tell Caroline that she could no longer trap him with her feminine wiles or her children's adoring smiles.

He burst into her bedchamber, squinting against the darkness.

Shrieking, she tossed back her covers and leapt from her bed, grabbed her robe, and held it to her throat. "What are you doing, Dante? Get out of my chamber at once!"

Chapter 7

I have something to say to you." Dante's intimidating form stepped into a shaft of moonlight. Dark hair brushed his shoulders as he teetered where he stood.

"In the middle of the night?" Flinging on her robe, Caroline groped for a match on her bed stand, and after lighting the lamp, turned toward him. "Are you injured?"

Lantern light flickered over his handsome face as he studied her with an intensity that should have frightened her. But it didn't. Perhaps she was a fool, but she trusted Dante Vega. With her life.

"No," he replied, rubbing his stubbled jaw. He leaned one hand on the bed frame for support.

She inched closer and touched his arm. "Ill?" Surely that must be it from the way he seemed unable to stand straight.

"No," he replied.

The smell of alcohol stung her nose. "You've been drinking!" Releasing him, she backed away.

"I have, señora. It is what pirates do. Or hadn't you heard?" He huffed and crossed his arms over his thick chest as if proud of the fact. "And I've come to tell you. . .to tell you. . .that I'll not allow you and those. . .children of yours to weasel your way into my heart and trick me into"—he waved a hand through the air—"staying in this house with your good cooking and charming family and your. . ."

Caroline's face grew hot. "How dare you insinuate such a thing? We. . .I am not tricking you!"

He wobbled and took a step toward her, leveling a finger toward her face. "Then, stop being so kind and patient and gentle and"—withdrawing his finger, he rubbed his temple as if it ached—"absolutely wonderful. I'm not falling for it."

Her anger dissipated beneath his compliments, no matter their drunken delivery. "You're making a fool of yourself, Señor Pirate. I suggest you go back to the barn and sleep it off." She attempted to turn him around and shove him toward the door, but even in his besotted condition, she couldn't budge him.

He chuckled. "You call me Señor Pirate when you're cross with me."

"Then you have no doubt as to my current disposition." She managed to turn him to face the door. "Nor that my anger will only rise if you do not leave immediately."

"And one more thing." He spun back around. "Tell your children to stop calling me Papa. I am not their papa, and I will never be." Though his tone was harsh, the look in his eyes spoke otherwise. Was the moisture she saw there from emotion or alcohol? He stepped toward her and gently fingered a lock of her hair. "And stop being so beautiful." His voice softened. "With your gold spun hair and sea-green eyes and skin a man longs to touch." He ran the back of his fingers over her cheek.

Why, when he'd burst into her bedroom, shouting and accusing her of tricking him, did his touch feel so good? Stirring a longing in her she'd never felt before, not even with François. "I'll do my best Señor Vega to not be so appealing," she breathed out in a whisper.

"Impossible." He huffed, dropping his hand to his side.

"Let's get you to bed, Señor Pirate."

He grinned, his gaze shifting to her tousled covers.

"To the barn I meant." Shaking her head, she grabbed his hand and started for the door.

He pulled her to him, pressed her against his chest, and wrapped her in his thick arms. He smelled of leather and ale and the sea, and she settled her head against his shirt. Despite his drinking, despite his intrusion in her bedchamber, she felt safe in his arms.

For the first time in many years.

A shout and a crackling sound drew them apart. Dante darted to the window. In the distance, yellow flames reached for the sky.

"My grapes!" Caroline threw a hand to her mouth. "The vineyard is on fire!"

Dante instantly sobered. "Stay here. Protect the children," he shouted before storming off.

But she couldn't stay. Not when her livelihood, her very survival, was at stake. Instead, she got dressed as quickly as she could, roused the children, instructed Philippe to stay with Abilene on the veranda, and then sped into the darkness. But it wasn't dark anymore. Fires had sprung up in every direction. Red flames licked the sky, casting a hellish glow over the entire vineyard. Where had they come from? Smoke burned her nose. Men sped past, hoisting buckets of water from the creek. First Sisquoc then Manuel, Diego, and finally Dante, who ordered her back in the house. Clutching her skirts, she grabbed a bucket to assist them. She would not stand by and do nothing.

The sound of rifle shots exploded over the crackle of flames. *Pop! Pop! Pop!* Halting, she spun around. The men crouched to the ground as more shots thundered. One zipped past her ear. Fury started its own fire in her belly. *Señor Casimiro!* It had to be him and his men. He would not burn her out! She would not let him! Dropping her bucket, she started for the house to get a rifle. Dante hid behind a large grapevine and returned fire, gesturing for the other men to stay low. But what did it matter? Half her vineyard was aflame. Flames she could feel from where she stood as heat seared her in rolling waves, bringing with it the sting of smoke and the sour scent of burning grapes. Halting before her house, she stared benumbed at the sight of everything she'd worked so hard to achieve devoured in an instant.

"Get in the house!" Dante shouted, his voice muffled by the roar of the fire. But she couldn't seem to move. How would she support her children now? What would happen to them?

In the blur of heat and haze of smoke, she saw Dante running for her.

A shot fired. He clutched his shoulder, stumbled, and fell to the dirt.

❧

Blackness as thick as coal surrounded Dante. Someone was hammering. *Thunk! Thunk! Thunk!* The vibration sent piercing pain through his head. He tried to rub it away but couldn't move his arms. *Make the pain stop. Oh, God, make the pain stop.*

"Will he live, Doctor?" The words were distant and muddled yet distinctively Caroline's.

"Yes. He'll recover in time. A quarter inch to the right and I'd be saying something different, but with lots of rest, your husband will be back on his feet in a month, maybe less."

Light tried to penetrate the darkness. It failed. Dante was swept back into the night.

Sometime later—an eternity or only a moment, he didn't know—he heard Caroline praying by his bedside, pleading with her God for Dante's healing, thanking God that he lived. Oddly, it brought him comfort. Other moments came and went like scattered dreams. Children's laughter, sunlight, darkness, someone spooning broth into his mouth, a weight on his chest. Pain that sent him back into the darkness. Heat. . .fire. . .why was it so hot? His mouth felt full of cotton. His head spun. Someone held his hand, caressed his skin. A kiss on his cheek. He smiled and fell back asleep.

Thoughts came alive in his mind. Instead of drifting atop a nebulous mist, they landed on reason, where they stirred more thoughts to life. Sounds alighted on his ears. Children's voices, Caroline singing, birds chirping. The smell of smoke filled his nose. *The vineyard!*

He pried his eyes open and blinked to focus. The wooden ceiling beams of a bed-chamber came into view. He lowered his gaze to a pair of walnut Victorian chairs then to the matching wardrobe and over to the lacy covering atop the dresser, the glass candlesticks, bottles of perfume, jars of cream, and the brush and comb lying before a framed mirror. Definitely a lady's bedchamber. He pressed a hand against his chest and groaned.

"You're awake." Caroline entered the room, rubbing her hands on an apron, and dropped beside him, smiling.

"How long?" His voice came out scratchy.

"Four days. You had a fever." Taking a cool cloth, she mopped his brow. He tried to move. Pain rumbled through his shoulder.

"You're not going anywhere, Dante. You've been shot and you need your rest." She propped the pillows up behind him then took a glass from the table and held it to his lips. He hated being coddled, but the water tasted so good.

He wiped his mouth. Even that small effort pained his chest. "The vineyard?"

She sat back with a sigh and looked out the window. "Burnt to the ground."

"I'm sorry."

"It's not your fault."

"Yes it is. If I hadn't been drinking, maybe I would have seen the men coming, stopped them before they set fire to the grapes."

"You don't know that." She leaned forward and took his hand in hers. "Besides, you saved my life." Sunlight glittered on spirals of golden hair framing a face that looked drawn and tired.

"I got shot is what I did, and that does you no good."

"It certainly didn't." She arched an accusing brow. "I and the children have been worried to tears over you."

"You have?" No one had ever worried about him before. Not even his own mother. Emotion burned in his throat. "Thank you for caring for me."

She smiled. "My pleasure, Dante."

"What will you do?" he asked.

"What can I do? I'll sell the wine I have, start a new crop with the few vines that remain, and"—she sat back with a sigh—"pray."

"Why not just sell the land and go back home?"

She rose and made her way to the window. "I promised François on his deathbed that I'd keep the land, raise his grapes, and make the wine he dreamed of making his entire life."

"He was a fool to ask you that. To put you and his children in jeopardy."

She shrugged. "How could I deny a dying man his one request?"

Dante could not believe the selfishness of this man. "What of next year when you have no wine to sell?"

"I will learn a trade." She hugged herself. "We will trust God to take care of us."

Dante ground his teeth together. "You're a stubborn woman, Caroline. I don't know whether your faith in God is commendable or crazy."

"He has never let us down. There's a verse in the Bible that says, 'I have been young, and now am old; yet have I not seen the righteous forsaken, nor his seed begging bread.' "

Dante snorted. "I'd rather do things my way. As soon as I am well, this Señor Casimiro will pay for what he's done."

"No, please." She turned, worry lining her face. "You cannot fight a man like him. He is too powerful."

"Perhaps not alone, but you forget, I still have a crew in town. And by now they will be itching for a fight."

"Then it will never end. And more people will get hurt." She sat beside him and took his hand again, pleading. "Leave it to God, Dante."

He was about to respond that he didn't trust God to right wrongs when Philippe and Abilene skipped into the room. Their faces lit when they saw him, and making a mad dash, they both leapt onto the bed. Philippe perched beside him, while Abilene tossed her arms about Dante's neck. His shoulder throbbed beneath her weight, but it was worth the pain for the love these precious children lavished upon him.

⚭

Dante hated being bedridden. He'd always been a man of action, strong, capable, able to do anything he put his mind to with wit and vigor. But he'd never been shot so close to his heart, and the wound took its toll on his strength. It also took its toll on the way he looked at things. Facing one's eternity had a way of making a man think. And he had plenty of time to do that while he recovered.

Caroline and the kids entertained him well enough: they played card games, Philippe practiced his reading, Abilene regaled him with made-up stories, and Caroline spent countless hours talking with him. He cherished those moments the most, listening to her soothing voice, her pleasant laugh, watching the adorable way her nose scrunched when she disagreed with him, the sparkle in her green eyes when she teased him, the shy looks of affection that made his heart leap.

At night she'd read to him from the Bible, stories of adventure, romance, and war—exciting tales he never dreamed were to be found in such a holy book. With every inflection of her voice, with every tear of joy that slid from her eye, he knew she believed every word she read. Words from a God who loved His creation more than anything, who wanted the best for them and agonized when they chose a path that caused them pain. Words from a God who, when all else failed, sent His own Son to redeem people from the depths of hell.

Words that woke a deep hunger within Dante.

One night, after all had gone to sleep, he called out to this God of hers, expecting nothing but silence in response to a man like him. But instead, a glow ignited in his heart. It spread to his limbs in a tingle that brought a chuckle to his throat. Wind stirred the curtains, and though the night was foggy, silvery light spun ribbons of glitter through the room. And a voice sounded from deep within him. *"I love you, son. You are home now."*

Dante drifted to sleep, comforted by a Father he'd never known, but One who was here to stay. He'd also made up his mind on another important matter. If Caroline would have him, he would forsake the sea, stay with her and the children, and become the man she needed him to be.

Chapter 8

I t's only a week until Christmas, Mama." Abilene bounced up and down on the sofa as Caroline gathered her children close after supper.

"Yes it is." She smiled. "A very special time of year."

Philippe tugged from his mother's grip. "Will Santa bring us presents?"

Caroline's chest grew heavy. Children should have gifts at Christmas, but for two years now, hers would have none. "Christmas is not about gifts. It's about the birth of God's Son, Jesus. He is our greatest gift."

Abilene seemed to ponder this a moment. "I think He would want us to get other gifts, too. Don't you think so, Mama?"

Caroline *could* purchase gifts. She'd sold the wine to Mr. Norsen, the merchant who already had a buyer in New York. Heaven be praised, he'd been quite pleased with the quality of the merlot. But she must save the money to provide food and other necessities for the next year when they had no wine to sell. "I'm sure he would, ma chère, but sometimes"—she hesitated, asking God for the best answer—"God gives gifts to children who have more need of them. We have everything we need, don't we?"

Both Abilene and Philippe nodded, though she sensed their disappointment. A disappointment she shared, for she wished more than anything she could afford something this year. Still, she felt guilty for even thinking such a thing. God had more than blessed them. They had a home, food, and each other. And most of all, Dante was nearly recovered. Why, he'd even been eating supper at the table with them the past week. His color had returned, along with his sarcasm and wit. She smiled. And even better, he seemed different somehow. Not so restless—at peace, happier. She could not understand it, would not allow her heart to hope. For a man like Dante would never be happy landlocked and burdened with the responsibility of a family. No, she must steel herself to accept that once he was fully recovered and had enough money, he'd set sail and leave them behind.

"Can we get a tree to decorate, Mama?" Philippe asked.

"Of course. And we'll pop corn and make beautiful ornaments. Won't that be fun?"

Abilene's eyes sparkled. "And we can make fruitcake, too."

Caroline kissed her daughter's forehead. "Indeed."

"And your mother can read *A Christmas Carol* to us all." Dante's voice brought Caroline's gaze up to see him leaning against the frame of the open french door. He'd gone outside after supper to check the perimeter, and she hadn't heard him return. His brown shirt, open at the collar, flapped in the incoming breeze, revealing the bandage covering his wound. His black hair was pulled back in a tie. Leather boots led up to thick thighs that seemed not the slightest bit weakened by his illness.

And she thought him the handsomest man she'd ever seen. Would he really stay for Christmas? Part of her desperately wanted him to, part of her feared that if he did, her heart—and her children's hearts—would be forever lost to him.

After spending an enjoyable evening with her and the children, Dante, for the first time, helped her tuck them into bed, embracing each one, listening to their prayers, and kissing their foreheads. Once back in the parlor, he sat on the sofa and held out a hand for Caroline.

"Will you pray with me, Caroline?"

She blinked. "Did you say *pray?*"

"I did." He grinned.

"Do you mean that you want me to pray *for* you?"

"No." He took both her hands in his and pulled her down beside him. "Please allow me to pray for you and the children."

Shocked, elated, and ignoring the hope rising within her, she nodded and bowed her head. His prayer was awkward, cumbersome, and disjointed, but it was the most beautiful prayer she'd ever heard. He asked for God's protection over her and the children, for Him to provide for them during the lean years. He asked for good health, joy, and peace to flood their lives. By the end, tears trickled down her cheeks. "You believe in God now?" She squeezed his hands, his face blurry in her vision.

He brushed the moisture from her cheeks. "I do. Because of you. I gave my life to Jesus a week ago."

Joy bubbled up in her throat. "Oh, Dante, I'm so glad!"

"And He has already shown me so much." He smiled.

Unable to control herself, she flung her arms around his neck and hugged him tight. "This is wonderful!" She withdrew and kissed his cheek. An innocent kiss of joy that sparked something deeper in his eyes. He eased a curl behind her ear, drinking her in with his gaze. A gaze that finally settled on her lips. He swallowed, brushed fingers over her cheek, then leaned in and kissed her. This time there was no shout, no rifle shots, no fire to stop them. This time she didn't care. She wanted to give herself to this man. Her husband.

But then he would leave and break her heart.

He swept her in his arms, carried her to her bedchamber, and set her down on the bed. Against everything within her, she moved to the edge and stood. He drew her close and kissed her again.

"I can't," she whispered against his cheek.

He cupped her face and met her gaze. "Do you love me?"

"With all my heart."

"Then believe I love you, too. And I promise I'm not going anywhere. I will never leave you."

At that moment, with the adoring way he gazed at her, the gentleness of his touch, she *did* believe him. God help her, she did.

Later that night, Caroline snuggled beside Dante with her head on his chest and listened to the beat of his heart. Steady, strong, just like the man himself. He brushed fingers through her hair, drew her closer, and kissed her forehead. "I love you so much, Caroline. I never thought it possible I could be this happy."

"Are you truly happy?" She propped her chin on his chest to look at him.

He ran a finger over her bare shoulder and down her arm. "You are everything any man would ever want."

"But what of your ship, the sea? How could you be happy as a farmer? You'll be miserable." Fear battled her newfound joy—fear and sorrow. Yet love demanded the best for those in its embrace.

"With you, señora? Only a fool would be miserable."

"Are you still planning on redeeming your ship?"

"I believe the good Lord would frown on my career as a pirate." A chuckle rumbled through his chest.

"But there are legal vocations upon the sea."

Releasing a heavy sigh, he gazed into the dark room, and she knew he thought of his ship and the sea. But then his eyes snapped back to hers, and he smiled. "We need my winnings for the vineyard. To survive until we can produce more grapes."

"But—"

He pressed a finger on her lips "That's my final decision, wife. Doesn't the Good Book say you must obey your husband?"

"I suddenly regret reading you that section." She pouted.

He brushed a curl from her face then leaned forward and kissed her. Deeply. "Any more regrets?"

"Not when you kiss me like that."

"I can do so much better than that." He winked and swallowed her up in an embrace.

◦∕∘

The twitter of birds drew Caroline from her deep slumber. She pried one eye open to see shafts of sunlight swirling dust into glittering eddies as memories of the most wonderful night she'd ever experienced filled her heart and soul to near bursting. She stretched her hand across the mattress, anticipating the feel of hard muscle but found only air. Opening her other eye, she sat up, drawing the sheet to cover herself. Dante was gone.

A momentary prick of fear quickly dissolved when she realized he'd no doubt gotten up early to tend the animals or chop wood or start the fire in the stove or do any of the various chores he'd been so diligent to perform.

An hour later, storm clouds gobbled up the sun, while a fierce wind tore over the vineyard. And Dante was still nowhere to be found. He hadn't even come in for breakfast. Sisquoc hadn't seen him, nor had any of the other workers. No matter. If anyone could take care of himself, it was Dante. He was probably on some errand in town. In fact, she had an errand of her own to run—one she was most excited about.

A gust burst into the house, swirling in leaves and knocking over a candlestick on the table. With the children's help, she closed and latched all the doors and windows and waited until the wind settled. It finally did after lunch as the blaring sun resumed its reign, sweeping away clouds and sparkling over the moist grass.

Putting on her best gown, she gathered the children and headed to see Judge Albert Packard, whose vineyard bordered hers on the south. She'd made up her mind even before speaking with Dante last night what she would do, and even now as the horse plodded along on the muddy road, excitement made her as giddy as a child at Christmas.

"What are we doing, Mama?" Philippe asked from his spot beside her on the driver's perch.

"We are going to get Dante a Christmas present."

"We are?" Abilene's smile was as wide as the sea.

Caroline nodded. And he's going to love it. She expected her children to mention the gifts they wanted for themselves but was quite pleased when they seemed more excited at doing something nice for Dante.

"Is he going to be our papa?" Abilene asked.

Caroline smiled, wondering if she should tell them yet, but thought since it was nearly Christmas, it would make a nice gift. "Yes, he is."

"Yay!" Philippe shouted. "He's the best Christmas gift of all, Mama."

Wiping tears of joy from her face, she halted the buckboard before Judge Packard's home, and with her children in tow, knocked on the door.

The man was thrilled at her proposition, and within an hour he had summoned the city commissioner—a personal friend of his—along with the clerk of records to complete the transaction.

The deed of trust was exchanged for money the judge had in a safe on his property, and just like that, she had sold François's vineyard.

Though sorrow tugged at her heart at betraying him, she felt a great deal of satisfaction that Señor Casimiro would never get his hands on the property. Or on her. She also could hardly wait to see the look in Dante's eyes when she presented him with her gift.

The surprise, the twinkle of delight, the thankfulness. . .the love.

Yet, as she drove up the pathway to their home, she drew a shaky breath. In a few days, they'd have no place to live. She was relying completely on a man—a pirate—whom she'd only met four months ago. And that pirate still wasn't home. Nor did he come home that evening. Worry began to fester in her soul like a cancer, keeping her up all night. First thing in the morning, she hitched up the buckboard and took the children into town. There was something she had to do anyway, and it would give her a chance to ask whether anyone had seen Dante.

First stop was the City Council's office. She halted at the clerk's desk, Philippe and Abilene by her side. The spectacled man finally glanced up from his paperwork, his smile widening at the sight of her. "Ah, Mrs. Moreau. What may I do for you?"

Opening her reticule, she drew out a stack of bills then another and another and set them proudly on the desk. "I wish to redeem the *Bounty*, sir."

For a moment, he merely gaped at the bills, but then he slowly lifted his confused gaze to hers. "The pirate's ship?"

"That's the one."

"He's my papa now," Abilene announced proudly.

Offering the girl a look of concern, the man shook his head. "But he already redeemed it."

"Who?"

"Señor Vega. Yesterday morning, I believe." He stood, removed his spectacles, and walked to the window to look out. "Yes, and it appears he's already set sail."

Numb, Caroline could barely move her feet, let alone thank the man, grab her children, and leave. She managed to get outside, where the sea breeze could revive her before she fainted like some weak-hearted female.

"Why did Dante set sail, Mama?" Philippe asked. "I'm going to go see." Before she could stop him, he sped around the corner of the building.

"Bon sang," she muttered and hoisted Abilene in her arms to follow him.

"Mama, where is Papa?" Abilene asked, her voice teetering on the edge of tears.

"I don't know, but I'm sure he's safe." She forced strength into her own wobbling voice. That wobbling sped to her legs when she caught up with Philippe and followed his gaze offshore to the spot where the *Bounty* had been anchored. Setting Abilene down before she dropped her, Caroline knelt to gather her children close.

"Where did he go, Mama?" Philippe asked.

"I told you it was foolish to trust a rogue like Señor Vega." The familiar voice scraped down her spine. She stood and faced Señor Casimiro, fingering his pointed beard beneath a grin of victory.

"I'm sure there is an explanation for his departure," she returned. "Not that it is any of your affair."

He snorted. "I assure you. There *is* an explanation. My man overheard him down at the saloon telling his first mate that he got what he came for and he was itching to return to piracy." He grinned. "What did he finally get from you, señora? Shall I wager a guess?"

Chapter 9

Christmas Eve

Caroline stood on the shore, one hand holding Abilene's, the other Philippe's, while their trunks were stacked on sand beside them. All they had left in the world was stuffed in those portmanteaus. All except her heart, which was out on the sea being devoured by a man she'd never see again. Fog as thick as the heaviness in her soul crowded around them, muffling the sounds of crashing waves and embedding a chill in her bones. A chill she hadn't been able to get rid of the past two days. She'd spent them in a benumbed haze of conflicting emotions that threatened to bury her in the dirt beside François.

Where she no doubt belonged for her stupidity.

Still, she had done her best to remain strong for the children, to put on a happy face and spout hopeful words of their future. But every time either of them began to cry about Dante, she unavoidably joined them. Now they stood forlornly gazing at the steamer ship that would take them to the port of Los Angeles, where they'd catch a larger ship that would escort them around Cape Horn and up to New Orleans. Though she still hadn't heard from her family, Caroline held on to the hope that they would forgive her and take her and the children in.

If not, she didn't know what she'd do. The money she'd procured from the sale of the vineyard wouldn't last forever. And she couldn't very well marry another man when she was still legally joined to Dante.

Soon the small boat returned, her trunks were loaded, and a sailor carried the children through the crashing surf into the wobbly craft. Caroline turned to glance at Santa Barbara, her home for the past three years, but the gray shroud hid it from view. Just as well. She had very few pleasant memories of the place. A squab, round man who reeked of fish assisted her into the boat, and once she was seated, he shoved off from shore, leapt in, and along with two other men, plunged oars into the foamy wavelets.

Tears burned in her eyes as the sight of the steamer brought thoughts of another ship to mind. A two-masted pirate ship that had once sat majestically in these waters.

All of Dante's kindness, his hard work in the vineyard, his protection, his risking his life for them, his goodness to her kids, his compliments and charm, even his supposed encounter with God, all had been a ploy to get in her bed. She could come up with no other explanation. Yet why go to such trouble when he could have any of the many women who haunted the saloons downtown? Perhaps he'd grown bored with wayward women. Perhaps Caroline had presented a challenge for a man who possessed no scruples and needed to pass the time while he earned back his ship. Why else would he leave town the day after they'd consummated their marriage? The tears flowed freely now, and she pounded her fist on her knee. How could she have been so stupid? So utterly and completely gullible. When she knew better! He was a *pirate*!

And worst of all, she'd allowed her children to become attached to him, had stood by and watched as he broke their hearts and shoved another wedge of bitterness and mistrust into their innocent souls. Some mother she was.

As the ship loomed larger, Caroline quickly dried her eyes. It would do no good to have her children see her agony. Perhaps the excitement of the voyage would help them forget the man who said he'd be their papa. Perhaps it would help her forget the man who'd said he'd never leave her.

She doubted it.

Once their trunks had been hauled below to a cabin, Caroline gathered the children and stood at the railing, watching the other passengers come aboard, along with crates and barrels of goods to be sold down the coast. The fog bank had already begun to roll out to sea, allowing sunlight to christen certain sections of town. Like the mission that now gleamed white on the hill in the distance—a beacon of goodness in a city gone mad with debauchery.

Soon, all was brought aboard, and as passengers and crew milled about the deck, the captain shouted orders to weigh anchor.

Philippe tugged on her skirts. "Mama."

"Yes, Philippe." Her gaze remained on town, memorizing the streets and homes, the red tile and adobe of some, the wooden walls of others, the pastureland and cattle, the churches with steeples, and the many vineyards lining the hills.

"Mama!" His voice heightened in excitement.

No doubt a sea lion had surfaced to play among the waves.

Abilene plucked out her thumb—having returned to the bad habit after Dante left—and pointed. "It's Papa's ship!"

Caroline snapped her gaze to the sea where the *Bounty* sped toward them, all sails to the wind. She rubbed her eyes, expecting it to be gone when she opened them again. But the crew had seen it, too.

"Captain, a brig heading our way off the starboard side," one of them said.

"Blast it all! What could they want?" the captain replied, scope in hand. "I have a schedule to keep."

Within minutes, the *Bounty* lowered sails and halted expertly alongside the steamer, some twenty yards away. Dante Vega, looking more like a pirate than he ever had, hailed the ship through a speaking cone and requested an audience. Without awaiting a reply, he ordered a boat lowered, climbed down into it, along with a few of his men, and with white flag raised, began rowing toward them.

"Papa is coming for us!" Abilene squealed with glee.

"Told you he didn't leave us." Philippe crossed arms over his chest.

The captain, a young, barrel-chested man approached. "Do you know this man?"

Caroline could hardly find her voice. "He's my husband," she mumbled out.

"Your husband? Well, he's delaying me! What does he want?"

A very good question. As she watched him and two of his crew row toward them, a battalion of emotions raged within her: anger, hope, love.

"This is ludicrous," the captain said as he marched away. "I must be under way. Raise topsails, Mr. Blaney."

"Captain." Caroline swung about. "Please, just a moment more, I beg you."

Whether it was her pleading tone or the look in her eyes, the gruff man finally relented and belayed his last order. "You have one minute, lady."

The boat thudded against the hull, and Caroline leaned over the railing to see Dante gazing up at her, his hair flailing around him, and a look of shock on his face. "What are you doing, Caroline?"

"I'm taking the children home to New Orleans. What else would I be doing?"

"Why? What about the vineyard?"

"Where did you go?"

"Hi, Papa!" Abilene waved down at him.

"Hi, pumpkin. Hi, Philippe." He waved and smiled.

"Where did you go?" Caroline demanded.

"I went to Los Angeles. Did you get my note?"

"What note?"

"I left it on the table with a candlestick on top."

Caroline shook her head, only then remembering the storm that had come up suddenly the morning Dante had left. Was it possible the paper had blown out the window before she'd closed up the house? "I never saw it."

Crewman and passengers lined the railing with interest.

Dante raked a hand through his hair. "You must have thought"—his voice trailed off as he shook his head—"and then my ship was gone."

"What was I to think when the day after"—she hesitated, heat flooding her cheeks—"the day after you promised to stay, you redeem your ship and sail away?"

"I didn't redeem my ship," he shouted up. "I sold it."

"Do you take me for a fool? It is right there!" She pointed behind him.

"I sold it to my first mate on the condition he let me borrow it for a short trip to Los Angeles."

"You expect me to believe you sold the most precious thing in the world to you?"

"You are the most precious thing in the world to me."

One lady at the railing sighed with delight.

And though Caroline longed to join her, she couldn't. Not yet. "Why did you go to Los Angeles?"

His lips flattened. "A surprise. Please, Caroline, I love you. Come with me. Berilo will take us wherever we want."

"I don't believe you."

"I meant what I said that night. I won't ever leave you. I'm here, aren't I?"

"Ah, go with the poor fellow," one man beside her said.

A lady passenger brought a handkerchief to her eye.

"Mama." Abilene jerked on her skirts again. "I want to go with Papa."

"Lady," the captain said. "Your minute is up. I must be under way."

"At least come down here and talk about it," Dante pleaded.

But if she went down, she'd never get back up. Her heart said to go, but her heart had been wrong more often than not.

"Lady, I beg you, please relieve the man of his suffering," a man dressed in a posh suit said, looking at his watch.

Before she could stop him, Philippe swung both legs over the railing, grabbed ahold of a dangling rope, and made his way down to Dante's waiting arms.

"Philippe!" *Oh, that boy!* "Captain, do you have a rope ladder?"

"Aye." He snapped his fingers and a crewman grabbed one that was already tied to the bulwarks and tossed it over the railing.

"Abilene, hold on to my neck and don't let go." She hoisted the girl in her arms and slowly made her way down. The scratchy rope bit into her palms. The ship rocked. The ladder swayed. Abilene's harried breathing filled Caroline's ears as the girl's grip tightened on her neck. "It's all right, ma chère." But it wasn't all right. Caroline glanced down at the boat bouncing in choppy waters at least ten yards below them. And froze.

"Hold on," Dante shouted. "I'm coming to get you."

Hungry water lapped against the hull, reaching for Caroline. She could do this. She didn't need to be carried like some child. A wavelet struck. The ship careened, groaning, and the ladder slapped the hull. Pain throbbed through her fingers. Her sweaty palms slid on the rope. Her foot slipped, and she knew it was all over. She and Abilene would plunge into the icy water and drown before anyone could save them.

But instead of water, she fell against Dante's thick chest. He wrapped one arm around her and Abilene and inched down the ladder, his warm breath wafting over her neck. "I've got you. Now and forever."

⟡

Later that night as the *Bounty* rose and plunged through the ebony sea, Dante brought Caroline, Philippe, and Abilene on the foredeck where they could sit and watch the stars.

"There's so many of them!" Caroline exclaimed with delight as she tossed blankets over the children.

"And they all twinkle!" Abilene added, plopping to the deck.

"Look at that one." Caroline took a seat beside Dante on a crate and pointed to a particularly bright one in the eastern sky.

Philippe tightened the blanket around his neck. "Is that the star that led the wise man to baby Jesus?"

Dante threw a coat over Caroline's shoulders. "It must be. It's Christmas Eve, isn't it?"

"Will it lead *us* to Him, Mama?" Abilene asked.

"No need," Dante answered. "He already lives in our hearts, pumpkin. And He will never leave."

The ship careened over a wave, spraying them with a chilled mist. The children gripped the deck and laughed then settled to gaze back up at the stars.

Caroline's eyes met his, so full of love and admiration, he gulped down emotion before he made a fool of himself. "You sold your vineyard to redeem my ship." Dante still could not believe it. "That was all you had."

"It was to be your Christmas gift." She gave a lopsided smile and reached for his hand. "But you sold your ship. I can't believe you sold it. It was so important to you."

"How else could I provide for my family, save the vineyard, and"—he raised his voice so the children could hear—"buy Christmas gifts?"

"Christmas gifts!" Both squealed and turned around.

Grabbing the sack he'd brought on board, Dante untied the rope, feeling a bit like Santa Claus himself. "What have we here?" He pulled out a porcelain doll dressed in a lustrous silk gown and gave it to Abilene.

For a moment, she merely stared at it, her eyes wide and sparkling like the stars above. Then she took it in her arms and embraced it like it was her own child. "I love it, Papa!"

His heart near bursting, he peered into the sack again. "Now, what is this?" He pulled out a leather whip and handed it to Philippe.

"Wow," was all Philippe said as he grabbed the whip and began to unravel it. "Thanks! Mama, look at this!"

"But you must keep it coiled on the ship," Dante said. "I'll teach you how to use it when we reach land." Philippe nodded, and Dante gave Caroline a reassuring glance. "It will be okay."

"Merry Christmas, Papa!" Both children said as they began playing with their gifts.

"Merry Christmas," he replied.

"There's something else in your bag." Caroline's voice was teasing as she pointed to the sack.

"Is there?" He scratched his head and peeked inside. "I do believe you're right." Reaching in, he pulled out a box containing a bonnet, the latest fashion from Paris and quite popular among high society ladies—or so he'd been told by the woman at the millinery.

And apparently—if the look on Caroline's face was any indication—she'd been right.

"Oh, Dante." She opened the box and caressed the silk ribbon, seeming about to cry. "I can't believe you bought this for me. And here I thought you'd abandoned us." She dabbed the corner of her eye.

Placing a finger beneath her chin, he raised her eyes to his and placed a gentle kiss on her lips. "Never."

Their gazes held for several seconds, several magical seconds, during which Dante thanked God for such a precious woman and vowed to make her happy the rest of his days.

"Where are we going, Papa?" Philippe looked up from fingering his whip.

Dante shrugged. "I thought perhaps Veracruz to see my father. He has a merchant business he's been begging me to join. That is, Señora Vega, if you'll come with me?" He brought Caroline's hand to his lips for a kiss.

"Señor Pirate, I will follow you anywhere."

About the Authors

Award-winning, *New York Times* bestselling author, Wanda E. Brunstetter, enjoys writing historical as well as Amish-themed novels. Wanda and her husband, Richard, live in Washington State but take every opportunity to visit Amish settlements throughout the States, where they have many Amish friends. To learn more about Wanda's books, visit her website at www.wandabrunstetter.com and find her on Facebook at www.facebook.com/WandaBrunstetterFans.

Susan Page Davis is the author of more than forty novels in the romance, mystery, suspense, and historical romance genres. A Maine native, she now lives in western Kentucky with her husband, Jim, a retired news editor. They are the parents of six and the grandparents of nine fantastic kids. She is a past winner of the Carol Award, the Will Rogers Medallion for Western Fiction, and the Inspirational Readers' Choice Award. Susan was named Favorite Author of the Year in the 18th Annual Heartsong Awards. Visit her website at: www.susanpagedavis.com.

Two-time Carol Award winner and bestselling author, Melanie Dobson is the former corporate publicity manager at Focus on the Family and owner of Dobson Media Group. Because of her husband's work in the film industry, their family has lived in multiple states as well as Germany. Jon and Melanie have adopted two girls and help lead the orphan care ministry at their church in Portland, Oregon.

A former advertising copywriter, Cathy Liggett is a Carol Award winner for Women's Fiction and also received a nomination for Best Inspirational Novel of the Year from RT's Reviewer's Choice Awards. But as much as Cathy enjoys writing women's fiction, she can't resist writing romance, too. However, she didn't have to do any romantic plotting whatsoever at her ten-year high school reunion when she re-met and quickly wed a childhood sweetheart. Married over thirty years now, their two grown children are spread across the country, thankfully in cities that are wonderful to visit. Luckily, too, several years ago, she and her husband rescued a boxer-mix named Chaz. Now they have another creature to spoil and keep their house hopping.

Bestselling author Vickie McDonough grew up wanting to marry a rancher, but instead she married a computer geek who is scared of horses. She now lives out her dreams in her fictional stories about ranchers, cowboys, and lawmen in the West during the 1800s. Vickie is the award-winning author of more than thirty published books and novellas. Vickie is a wife of thirty-eight years, mother of four grown sons and one daughter-in-law, and grandma to a feisty eight-year-old girl. When she's not writing, Vickie enjoys reading, antiquing, watching movies, and traveling. To learn more about Vickie's books or to sign up for her newsletter, visit her website: www.vickiemcdonough.com

Olivia Newport's novels twist through time to find where faith and passions meet. Her husband and two twentysomething children provide welcome distraction from the people stomping through her head on their way into her books. She chases joy in stunning Colorado at the foot of the Rockies, where daylilies grow as tall as she is.

In first grade, Janet Spaeth was asked to write a summary of a story about a family making maple syrup. She wrote all during class, through morning recess, lunch, and afternoon recess, and asked to stay after school. When the teacher pointed out that a summary was supposed to be shorter than the original story, Janet explained that she didn't feel the readers knew the characters well enough, so she was expanding on what was in the first-grade reader. Thus a writer was born. She lives in the Midwest and loves to travel, but to her, the happiest word in the English language is *home*.

Jennifer Rogers Spinola, a Virginia/South Carolina native and graduate of Gardner-Webb University in North Carolina, just moved back to the States with her Brazilian husband, Athos, and two sons. Jennifer lived in Brazil for nearly eight years after meeting her husband in Sapporo, Japan, where she worked as a missionary. During college, she served as a National Park Service volunteer at Yellowstone and Grand Teton National Parks. In between home-schooling high-energy sons, Jennifer loves things like adoption, gardening, snow, hiking, and camping.

MaryLu Tyndall, a Christy Award finalist and bestselling author of the Legacy of the King's Pirates series, is known for her adventurous historical romances filled with deep spiritual themes. She holds a degree in math and worked as a software engineer for fifteen years before testing the waters as a writer. MaryLu currently writes full time and makes her home on the California coast with her husband, six kids, and four cats. Her passion is to write page-turning, romantic adventures that not only entertain but open people's eyes to their God-given potential. MaryLu is a member of American Christian Fiction Writers and Romance Writers of America.